D0871642

NOVELS BY JUDITH MICHAEL

Deceptions
Possessions
Private Affairs

JUDITH MICHAEL

Inheritance

POSEIDON PRESS
New York   London   Toronto   Sydney   Tokyo

This book is a work of fiction. Names, characters, places and
incidents are either the product of the author's imagination or are
used fictitiously. Any resemblance to actual events or locales or
persons, living or dead, is entirely coincidental.

Copyright © 1988 by JM Productions, Ltd.
All rights reserved
including the right of reproduction
in whole or in part in any form.

Published by Poseidon Press
A Division of Simon & Schuster, Inc.
Simon & Schuster Building
Rockefeller Center
1230 Avenue of the Americas
New York, NY 10020

POSEIDON PRESS is a registered trademark of Simon & Schuster, Inc.

Designed by Irving Perkins Associates
Manufactured in the United States of America

For
Ruth Barnard
with admiration and love

Part I

CHAPTER 1

L AURA and Paul made the bed together, laughing as they raced to see whose side would be finished first. "I'll never learn," Paul sighed in mock resignation when he lost. "Women were born to make beds; men were born to lie in them."

"They were born to lie *about* them," Laura retorted. "When we're married, you'll be amazed how fast you learn all kinds of things."

"I'm fast at the important ones," he said, "like falling in love with you."

She laughed, loving the way his smile and glance embraced her, the deepening of his voice when he spoke only to her, the memory of his hand on her breast when she had awakened that morning and they had moved into each other's arms, warm and half asleep, closer and closer until he was inside her and they had begun another day joined together, just as they planned to be joined as husband and wife for the rest of their lives.

But then her eyes grew somber. "How can we be so happy? It isn't right to be laughing and doing everything the way we always have, when Owen isn't here. And won't be, ever again. And he won't see us married, and he wanted to so much."

Paul knotted his tie and pulled on his suit jacket, glancing in the mirror as he ran a hand over his unruly black hair. "He knew we were getting married; that was what he cared about." He put his arms around

Laura and held her to him. "And you know he hated fancy parties and ceremonies."

"He wouldn't have hated our wedding," Laura said. "Oh, Paul, I can't bear it that he's gone!"

"I know." Paul lay his cheek on her hair, picturing the proud head and piercing eyes of Owen Salinger, his great-uncle and his very good friend. "And you're right, he would have loved our wedding, because he loved you and thought the smartest thing I ever did was agree with him." He held Laura away from him, searching her eyes for what she was feeling. Her slender face, with high cheekbones and wide, generous mouth, was somber in thought, as if frozen in time by a painter who had caught her arresting beauty but could only hint at the changing expressions that made her vivid face come alive with joy or sorrow, warmth or coldness, pleasure or dismissal. And no painter could capture the elusiveness that made everyone, even Paul, wonder if they really knew her or could keep her close, or her biting wit that contrasted so intriguingly with her innocence, making others remember her unpredictability long after they had forgotten the exact chestnut of her hair, glinting red in the sun, or the precise dark blue of her wide, clear eyes.

Paul brushed back the tendrils of hair that curled along her cheeks. "You're so pale, my love. Are you worried about this afternoon? Or is it just your suit? Do you have to wear black? We're not going to a funeral, after all; we're only going to Owen's house to listen to Parkinson read his will."

"It's what I feel like wearing," Laura said. "A will reading is like a second funeral, isn't it? We keep slamming shut the doors of Owen's life." She slipped out of his arms. "Shouldn't we go?"

"Yes." He locked the door of his apartment, and they walked down the two flights of stairs to the tiny lobby. Boston's August heat rose to meet them in shimmering waves that made trees and gardens ripple like reflections in a pond. Children danced on the grass, dreamlike in the white-hot sun, and sailboats on the Charles were like white birds, dipping and swooping above cool splashing waves.

"I'd forgotten how hot it gets," Paul murmured, pulling off his jacket. "Strange, isn't it, to be thinking about Owen here, in the city, when he'd never spend August anywhere but the Cape?" They reached his car and he turned on the air conditioning as they drove away. "My God, I miss him. Almost three weeks already, but I keep thinking I'll see him for dinner and hear him tell me again what I ought to be doing with my life."

Laura sat close to him and he held her hand as he drove beneath the arching trees along Commonwealth Avenue. "If I didn't have you," he said quietly, "I'd feel as if the center of my world was gone."

"And so would I." She twined her fingers in his, responding to the pressure of his thigh against hers, his shoulder against hers, the strength and desire that flowed between them whenever they touched. It was the same wherever they were, whatever they did: the rest of the world would disappear, leaving them alone with the love and passion that had grown steadily ever since the day, two years before, when he had finally noticed her.

"So would I," she said again. Because even though she had her brother Clay, and Paul's family, who had taken her in four years ago, when she was eighteen, and made her feel like one of them, it was Owen, the head of the family, who had adored her and who had been the adored center of her life, until she met Paul. Then she had clung to both of them. And now, when she still felt young and unsure of herself and hadn't yet begun the things Owen wanted her to do . . . now he was gone and there was only Paul to take care of her.

"Do you think we'll be there long?" she asked Paul. She didn't want to go at all. She didn't want to see everyone gathered in Owen's house where she had lived so happily—and still lived, though she had spent most of her time with Paul since Owen died—and hear the family lawyer read Owen's words when what she longed to hear was Owen's voice. She didn't want to hear Owen's sons Felix and Asa talk about finally being free to do what they wanted with the empire their father had built with love and pride, when their plans were so different from the ones Owen had been sharing with her for the past years, up to the time of his stroke.

"Not long," Paul said, turning up Beacon Hill and finding a parking place near Owen's enormous corner town house. "It's mostly a formality. Felix and Asa get the remaining stock in the company that Owen had held, the girls will get enough to make them happy, and I'll get a token because he loved me even though he knew I preferred a camera to a high-level job in his hotel empire. Half an hour, probably, for Parkinson to read the whole thing." Standing beside the car, he took Laura's hand again. "I'm sorry you have to go through it, but since Parkinson specifically asked for you—"

"It's all right," Laura said, but she was knotting up inside as they climbed the steps to the front door that had been hers for four years, to the rooms where she had lived as Owen's friend, nurse, protégée, and, finally, as close to a granddaughter as anyone could be.

When the butler opened the door she looked automatically across the marble foyer at the branching staircase, almost expecting to see Owen Salinger descending the stairs at his dignified pace—ruddy, healthy, his bushy eyebrows and drooping mustache like flying buttresses as he sent orders, opinions, and declarations to every corner of his house. Her eyes filled with tears. He had been so courtly, commanding, and overwhelming, she couldn't imagine a world without him. Where could she go without missing him?

You'll always miss him. But get today over with and get on with your life. That's what Owen would say. And he'd be right. He was always right.

She looked up at Paul. "Let's get away from here when this is over."

"Good idea," he said, and smiled at her, relieved that her somberness was lifting. It had seemed exaggerated from the beginning, making her appear worried, almost fearful, instead of mournful, as he would have expected. One of her moods, he thought, and reminded himself of how alone she'd been when Owen first paid attention to her and gave her the kind of enveloping love he bestowed on only a chosen few. "Relax," he said as they went in. "I'm here. We're together."

His hand held hers tightly and they went into the library where the Salinger family had already assembled, crowded together on leather couches and armchairs, the younger great-granddaughters perched on ottomans or sitting cross-legged on the Tabriz rugs Owen and Iris had collected in their travels. At the far end of the room, near the mahogany and marble fireplace, Laura saw Clay talking to Allison and Thad, and she smiled at him, thanking him silently for taking time from his job in Philadelphia to be near her for the will reading.

Behind the massive library table Elwin Parkinson, Owen's lawyer, sat with Felix and Asa Salinger, Owen's sons, the heirs to his empire and his fortune. Paul shook hands with them, paused to greet his parents, and then he and Laura went to a far corner, standing before a leaded glass window set in a book-lined wall. He put his arm around her; she was trembling, and he kissed the top of her head lightly as Parkinson began to speak.

"I have before me the last will and testament of Owen Salinger, dated three years ago this month. The non-family members are named first. Heading the list is a bequest of five hundred thousand dollars to Rosa Curren who, in Owen's words, 'kept my house and my family for fifty years and sustained me through the darkest years after my beloved Iris died.'

"There are smaller bequests," Parkinson went on, "to several of the longtime employees and concierges of the Salinger Hotels; various gardeners, barbers, and tailors; the captain of a sailboat in the Caribbean; a salesman at a boot shop in Cambridge; and sundry others I will not take the time to list. There are also sizable bequests to organizations which

Owen held dear, foremost among them the Boston Art Museum, the Boston Symphony, and the Isabella Stewart Gardner Museum, but also including the Foxy Theater Troupe of Cambridge, the Wellfleet Oysters, and the Cape Cod Mermaids."

A rustle of laughter whispered through the room at the reminder of Owen's eccentricities and whimsies when it came to spreading his wealth; the family had long since gotten used to them, sometimes even agreeing with them. Only Felix and Asa were flat-faced; they had never found their father amusing.

Parkinson pulled a separate document from his briefcase and read from it. "'Of my thirty percent holdings in Salinger Hotels Incorporated, I leave twenty-eight percent, divided equally, to my sons Felix and Asa—'"

"*Twenty-eight percent?*" Asa sprang to his feet, peering over Parkinson's shoulder. "He owned thirty p-p-percent. We share thirty percent. There was never any question of that." He peered more closely. "What the hell is that you're reading? That's n-n-n-not the will."

Felix sat in silence, staring at his locked hands as Parkinson cleared his throat and said, "This is a codicil Owen added to his will in July."

"Last m-m-m-month?" Asa demanded. "After his stroke?"

Parkinson nodded. "If you will allow me, I should read it in its entirety."

"If we allow you!" Asa repeated grimly. "Read it!"

Once again Parkinson cleared his throat. "'I, Owen Salinger, in full possession of my faculties, dictate this codicil to the will I made three years ago. Of my thirty percent holdings in Salinger Hotels Incorporated, I leave twenty-eight percent, divided equally, to my sons Felix and Asa Salinger. And to my most beloved Laura Fairchild, who has brought joy and love to the last years of my life, I leave the remaining two percent of my shares in Salinger Hotels Incorporated, plus one hundred percent of the Owen Salinger Corporation, a separate entity, which owns the four hotels with which I began the Salinger chain sixty years ago, in New York, Chicago, Philadelphia and Washington, and also my house and furnishings on Beacon Hill, where she has been living and should continue to live. She will know exactly what to do with her inheritance; she has shared my ideas and helped me make new plans, and I trust her to keep our dream alive and make it flourish.'"

In the brief, heavy silence that enveloped the room, Laura's eyes were closed, warm salt tears flowing down her cheeks. *Dearest Laura, I've left you a little something in my will.* That was all he had said, and she'd thought of money, perhaps enough to buy a small lodge and have something of her own, even when she was married to Paul, where she could put to use everything Owen had taught her about hotels.

Across the room, she saw Clay's look of excitement; his eyes danced and his lips mouthed, "Wow! You pulled it off!" Shocked and angry, she turned away.

Paul had followed her look and was watching Clay with a puzzled frown. In the rest of the room voices had risen to a cacophony while Parkinson banged a brass letter opener against an inkwell, trying to regain control.

"I w-w-won't have it!" Asa fumed. "Enough is enough! We've g-g-given her a home for years—"

"Owen gave her a home," Leni said quietly, but no one paid attention.

"I think it's lovely," Allison exclaimed. "Laura took care of Grandfather; why shouldn't he give her something if that was what he wanted?"

"He didn't know what he wanted." Felix's hard-edged words rode over all the voices in the room. He stood, putting a restraining hand on Parkinson's shoulder to keep him silent, and waited for the family to quiet down and give him their attention. They did; they knew it was he, and not Asa, who was the real head of the Salingers now.

"He didn't know what he wanted," Felix repeated in measured words. "He was a sick old man who was manipulated and terrorized by a greedy, conniving witch and for the entire month after his stroke—"

"Felix!" Paul's deep voice cut across his uncle's raspy one. "What the hell are you talking about?"

"You fucking bastard!" Clay bellowed, riding over Paul's words. "Who the fuck do you—"

"Keep your mouth shut," Felix snapped and went on, never breaking stride. "—entire month after his stroke was a helpless invalid who could neither move nor speak—"

"Felix!" Paul said again.

"He could speak!" Laura said. "He talked to me—we talked—"

"—neither move nor speak intelligibly, and it was obvious to everyone that he had lost his ability to think clearly. And that obvious fact was taken advantage of by this *girl*, who was only one of his whims until she wormed her way into his life, and then, when he was dying, kept the nurses out of his room so she could be alone with him and manipulate him into changing his will—"

"That's enough," Paul said furiously. "God damn it, Felix, you're mad; what the hell has gotten into you? This is a goddam pack of lies—"

"Owen didn't want the nurses!" Laura cried. She had barely heard Paul. "He told me to keep them out!" She shivered with cold; her tears had dried in cold streaks on her cheeks. "He didn't want strangers; he wanted me!"

"He didn't know what he wanted—" Felix began for the third time.

"Shut up!" Paul roared. "Let Elwin finish reading! and by God you'll explain this to me later; you'll apologize to Laura and to the whole family—"

Ignoring Paul, Felix put his head back, looked down his thin nose, and flung his voice at Laura. *"He didn't know anything, did he?* He didn't know that you're a criminal with a record, that you have a criminal for a brother, and that you lied to him—you lied to all of us—for four years while we took you in and gave you everything."

Laura's gasp was like a cloth ripping across the dead silence of the room.

"Four years," Felix said, his words like hammer blows. "And we all know that four years ago, the summer you and your brother appeared at our door, our house was robbed of an irreplaceable collection of jewelry and—"

"We didn't have anything to do with that!" Clay shouted.

Everyone was talking at once, turning to each other in alarm, calling out to Felix to explain what he meant. But Felix spoke directly to Laura. "You don't think we'd believe that! From the evidence I now possess, I have concluded that you came here for one purpose only—to rob us— and then decided to stay when you saw you could wrap you tentacles around my father, *just as you'd done once before with another old man who left you a fortune before he died,* and then!"—he shouted above his family's rising clamor, with a glance at Paul—"then you wrapped yourself around a *young* man of wealth, because professional fortune hunters never miss a chance, do they, Miss Fairchild?"

"I'm not! I loved Owen!" But the words lacked force; she felt crushed beneath too many accusations. "I love Paul. You have no right to lie—"

"Don't you talk to me of *right!* You came to us with lies; you came to entrap, to ensnare; you wormed your way into our household... *and you robbed us of my wife's jewels and almost killed my father!"*

"It's a goddam lie!" Clay shouted. "We didn't do that job; we changed our—"

He stopped, his face deathly pale. Laura, her tears gone, almost numb with cold, felt Paul's arm drop from her shoulder, saw Leni's look of disbelief, and saw Allison—dear Allison who had been so good to her—stare at her in shock and growing anger.

"You changed nothing," Felix said with contempt. His eyes had gleamed when Clay blurted his fatal words, but then he masked his triumph and now stood at the table with the look of a remote god. "You're a couple of common criminals, you've never been anything else, and I'm going to see to it that everyone knows it. I'm going to break

that codicil in court; I'm going to see to it that you don't get a penny of my father's fortune. You'll leave the way you came, with nothing; you'll leave now, and you'll never have anything to do with any of us again!"

Laura put a hand against the windowpane to steady herself. The glass was warm in the sunlight, but nothing could warm the coldness within her. She felt a movement beside her and looked up. Paul had moved away from her; he was looking at her as if he were meeting her for the first time.

It was all over. The nightmare she had lived with for four years had become real.

CHAPTER 2

"IT looks awfully tough," Clay mumbled as he eyed the clustered rooftops of the gray shingled Cape Cod mansions that were their target. "Guardhouse, fence, and I saw a dog..." He was trying to sound like a cool professional instead of a seventeen-year-old in unfamiliar territory, but his hand was cold as it clasped Laura's. Hers was cold, too, but she looked calm to him; she always seemed more daring and determined than he, but then she was a year older and had already graduated from high school. Moving closer to her in the back seat of the rented car Ben was driving past the Salingers' summer compound, he said, "I'll bet they have lots of dogs."

"Probably," Ben agreed. He slowed to catch a glimpse of the ocean and the sailboats and motorboats moored at private docks. "But once you get me inside, I won't have any trouble getting away."

"They can follow a boat as well as a car," Clay argued. "Why'd you pick this place, anyway? It's a goddam fortress."

"Cut it out," Laura said, her voice low. "We'll get it over with and then quit. I told Ben this was the last time I'd help him; you can, too. I wouldn't do this one, except I promised. But you know"—her voice wavered as she thought back to the pine forests and stretches of stark sand dunes and wild grass they'd driven past in their circuit of the Cape before coming to Osterville—"it is kinda scary to be this far from home, and everything so . . . different . . ."

Ben caught her last words and grinned at them in the rearview mirror. "I thought I taught you to have more confidence in yourself. Is there any house in the world my clever brother and sister can't break into? You've helped me crack some very tight places."

"In New York," Clay said. "We know New York. It's got alleys and subways and crowds of people you can disappear in, not a million acres you have to be a cross-country runner to beat the dogs across—"

"Five acres," Ben said softly. "The Salingers' summer home. Six houses on five acres surrounded by a fence with one guardhouse. That's all we know so far. We'll know more after you and Laura start working there. Listen, Clay, I'm counting on you. Both of you. I trust you."

Laura felt the rush of pride Ben's praise always gave her. He was much older than she; the child of her mother's first marriage. Her mother had remarried when Ben was almost nine, and a year later Laura was born, and then Clay. They'd always adored Ben, trailing after him around their small rented house in Queens, trying to peek into his private attic room, following him outside until he sent them home. Then, when Laura was fourteen, her parents were killed in a car accident; and Ben Gardner, twenty-three years old, handsome, grown-up, with lots of girlfriends, suddenly became Laura's and Clay's guardian. From then on he was more like a mother and father than a stepbrother to them: he stayed home most nights to be with them, he took them for rides in his car, he helped them with their schoolwork.

He also taught them to steal.

Of all the jobs Ben ever had, stealing was the only one that kept him interested. He didn't make a lot of money at it and kept apologizing for not being professional enough, but he wouldn't join a gang and never found a way to become part of the tight-knit group of fences who controlled prices and outlets in New York. Still, he stayed with it, and filled in by working as a waiter. They'd moved to a tiny, dark apartment way up on West End Avenue, but still they had lots of expenses, and stealing was what Ben had always done so he kept on doing it—better than ever, he said, because now he had assistants.

Clay and Laura were good. Their bodies were agile, their fingers quick, their minds alert as they climbed drainpipes or tangled branches of ancient ivy, slipping silently through narrow windows into darkened rooms, opening the windows wider for Ben, afterward climbing swiftly down and disappearing in the shadows of the graffiti-coated, anonymous subway.

They learned fast and trained themselves to remember everything. They could distinguish between a policeman's footsteps and those of a casual passerby; after one tour of a room they knew indelibly the location of stereo equipment, paintings and objets d'art; they could hear an elevator start up in a lobby twenty floors below; they had a feather touch and were almost invisible when they shoplifted or picked pockets on the subway or among the after-work crowd jostling for cabs on Wall Street.

It was always exciting and dangerous and, best of all, it was something the three of them could share: planning the jobs, carrying them out, reliving them later. So when Laura suddenly found herself wanting to stop, she kept it to herself. She couldn't tell Ben she'd begun to hate what they did; it would be like saying she hated *him*, when he was the only one who loved her and Clay and took care of them.

But then things got harder. She was lonely. It was her senior year in high school and all the other girls had friends to bring home after school, or have sleep over, or stand around in the schoolyard with, giggling about dates and new clothes, Saturday night parties and boys feeling them up, monthly cramps, and their awful parents. But Laura couldn't get close to anyone and so she had no girlfriends or boyfriends; she didn't go to Saturday night parties; and she couldn't have a girlfriend sleep over, because Ben slept in one room and she and Clay in the other, with a pair of drapes that they'd found in a dumpster on Orchard Street hanging between them. She could talk casually to classmates in school corridors about their studies or a show on television, but never about how she felt inside or what she really thought and dreamed about. She was always alone.

But even worse than being lonely, she was afraid. Ever since she and Clay were caught, when she was fifteen, she'd been afraid. Everything about it was still fresh; she'd never forget it: the pounding footsteps chasing them down the street, the gray smell of the police station, the way a policeman pinched her fingertips when he rolled them on the grimy ink pad, the flat face of the policeman who took her picture, growling, "Turn left, turn right, look straight at the camera, you little cunt . . ." and then grabbed her ass and squeezed so hard she cried out.

Ben came down to the station with a lawyer he knew, who got them out on bond, and then nothing happened for almost a year until their case came up. They were found guilty, and put on probation for another year, and released in the custody of Melody Chase. She was just one of Ben's girlfriends, but he'd been sure the social workers in court wouldn't release two kids in the custody of a single guy, and also he didn't want the law to connect him with them, so he brought Melody to court with him and she said she was Laura's and Clay's aunt, and the four of them walked out together. Nobody cared, really; all the court wanted was to pass them on to somebody else.

So they were free. But the police had their pictures and fingerprints, and Laura dreamt about it for weeks: she had a record.

That was one of the reasons she finally told Ben she didn't want to help him anymore. She didn't want to be a thief; she wanted to go to college and make friends. She'd had some parts in school plays, and she thought she might like to be an actress—or anything, really, as long as she could be proud of herself.

They quarreled about it. Ben knew she felt bad about picking pockets; she always mailed wallets back to people after taking out the money because she hated thinking about them losing all the things inside: poems and recipes, scribbled addresses and phone numbers, membership cards, insurance cards, credit cards that were no use to her, and especially pictures of people they probably loved. When she told Ben she didn't want to steal anymore, he thought she was being sentimental, the way she was about wallets. But she'd figure out a way to make him understand that there was more to it, that she was really serious. She had to; she'd promised herself the Salinger job would be the last one she'd do. Ever.

"I know you trust us," said Clay, still clinging to Laura's hand in the back seat of the car, "but we've never done a job in a place like this. What the hell do they want with all this *space* and *light?*"

Ben stopped the car a block from the guardhouse. "You're due there in five minutes. Keep your cool; just remember how we rehearsed it. And don't worry; you'll get hired. Rich people in summer houses are always desperate for help. I'll be right here, waiting for you."

"*He* isn't the one who has to go work for them," Clay muttered as the guard passed them through the gate and they followed his pointing finger to a nearby cottage. "He just sits around while we plan everything and then he waltzes in and lifts what's-her-name's jewels and waltzes out. And we're still here."

"That's not true," Laura said hotly. "Ben won't do anything till we work out an alibi." She turned her back on Clay's scowl, and then kept turning, around and around, as she walked, straining to see as much as she could through the thickly wooded grounds. She caught glimpses of velvety lawns, the windowed bay of a house, splashes of color from flower gardens, a pond with a fountain, a greenhouse roof. The estate of six houses clustered along the ocean was bigger than it had seemed from the road, and much grander. Like a picture postcard, Laura thought: everything beautiful, with no torn-up streets, no graffiti, and no litter. "Anyway," she said to Clay, "we're not hanging around very long after he's done it; just a little while, so nobody thinks we're connected to the robbery."

"We're still *here*," Clay repeated glumly.

They reached the small stone cottage with flowered curtains at the window and slatted furniture on the front porch, and Laura swallowed hard. "Damn it, we've been through this a hundred times. I'm already jumpy, and you're making it worse. Ben knows what he's doing. And he's the one who's really taking chances: he could get hurt, or caught, and what could we do to help him?"

Clay was silent. Laura knew he wasn't really angry; he worshiped Ben. It had been all she could do to keep him in school after he turned sixteen and wanted to drop out and do whatever Ben did. She didn't know what would happen now that she'd graduated. If she could get enough money for college, she wanted to move out; she dreamed of a room of her own, with shelves of books and posters on the wall, and pretty furniture, and her favorite music on the radio. But then what would happen to Clay?

"See you later," Clay said as a tall woman approached them. "She's yours. I'm for the head maintenance guy at the greenhouse." He was gone as the woman reached Laura.

"Laura Fairchild? I'm Leni Salinger; let's sit on the porch and talk, shall we? The cottage belongs to Jonas—the guard, you know—and I don't like to take over his living room unless it's raining. But it's pleasant today, isn't it? June is often a little confused here, not quite spring and not quite summer, but today is perfect. And, of course, we do love the quiet; it all changes in July, when the tourists descend. You said on the telephone you had references from your previous jobs."

"Oh." Lulled by Leni's serene voice, Laura had almost forgotten why she was there. "I have them . . ." She fumbled in her black patent purse. She'd known the purse was wrong for June the minute she saw Leni Salinger's white straw hat; she knew everything else was wrong, too, when she pictured herself beside this tall, angular woman in perfectly pressed slacks and a cotton shirt with ivory buttons, her fingernails long and polished, her face and voice perfectly calm because she had nothing to worry about: she knew that whatever happened to her would always be wonderful.

I could never look like that because I'm never sure of anything.

"Laura?" Leni was studying her. "You mustn't be nervous; I don't bite, you know, I don't even growl, and we do try to make our staff comfortable, but I really must find out something about you, mustn't I, before I bring you into our household."

"I'm sorry; I was thinking how beautiful you are, and how you don't have nothing to worry about. I mean, you don't have *anything* to . . ." Laura's voice trailed away and she bit her lip. How could she be such a baby? She blurted things out and made the same stupid mistakes her grammar teacher always had marked her down for. What would this elegant lady, who never would blurt anything, or talk wrong, think of her? Trying to look confident, she handed Leni the three reference letters Ben had typed out and signed with made-up names, then held her breath as Leni read them.

"Very impressive," Leni said. "To have done so much at eighteen. I'm not familiar with the people who wrote these, and I must say they've been very careless—all of them, how surprising—in not including their telephone numbers. O'Hara, Stone, Phillips; goodness, even with a first initial, how difficult to find the right ones in the directory. Do you recall their telephone numbers?"

"No." Laura paused, just as she and Ben had rehearsed it. "But I can find them. I mean, if you want, I'll call everybody who has those initials until I get the right one and then you can talk to them. I really need this job; I'll do anything . . ."

"Well," Leni said thoughtfully, "it's only a temporary position, of course . . . and it's hard enough to find anyone, much less someone truly anxious and agreeable . . . I'll have to mull this over a bit." She gazed at Laura. "Tell me about yourself. Where do you live?"

"New York." Ben had warned her it might get personal; she sat very straight and spoke carefully but quickly to get past this part as fast as she could. "My parents are dead, and my brother and I lived with some relatives, but they didn't really want us there, so a year ago we got our own place. I graduated high school last week."

After a moment, Leni said, "And what else? Are you going to college?"

"Oh, I'd love to. If I could get the money . . ."

Leni nodded. "So you need a job. But why not in New York? Why did you come to the Cape?"

Laura hesitated an instant; they hadn't rehearsed this part. "Just to get away, you know. We have a tiny apartment, and it gets awfully hot in the summer and sort of closed in . . . And somebody at school said it was nice here." She looked beyond the porch at the sparkle of the ocean through the trees. "It is. More beautiful than I ever thought."

Leni was watching her closely. "And how did you get here? Do you have a car?"

Laura felt a surge of impatience. Why did she keep asking questions? "A friend drove us," she said briefly.

"And how will you get back?"

"I hope we don't have to." She looked at her hands. "I mean, I was hoping you'd hire us and then we could just . . . stay."

"Stay where?" Leni asked gently.

"Oh, we'd find a place. We bought a newspaper and there are some rooms for rent in Osterville and Centerville... If you'd give us a chance I know we could manage everything. You wouldn't have to worry about us; we can take care of ourselves, you know."

"Yes, I think you can," Leni murmured. She looked around. "Yes, Allison, is there something you need?"

"A tennis partner." The young woman who stood at the foot of the porch steps was about Laura's age and looked like a young Leni, as tall and angular, though her long blond hair was straight, while Leni's was short and curled, and she had a touch of arrogance that Leni lacked. "Patricia doesn't feel like playing. Would you like a game?"

"My daughter, Allison," Leni said to Laura. "This is Laura Fairchild, Allison. She's applying for the job of Rosa's assistant."

"Rosa's a sweetie," said Allison. "She's also an absolute tyrant in her kitchen; she'll wear you out in a week. Or maybe she'll take you under her wing and then you'll gain fifty pounds." She turned to her mother. "Can't you just hear her telling Laura she's too thin?"

"Am I?" Laura asked anxiously. She was ashamed of her cotton dress and black patent shoes, bought at a resale shop, and the way her hair hung lankly around her face in the salt air of the Cape, and she knew her face had a city pallor beside these two tanned women, but she hadn't thought about being thin. *I won't get the job if I'm skinny and ugly; they only want pretty people working for them.* Ben and Clay always told her she was pretty, but they were her brothers. Nervously she pushed her hair behind her ears, tried to look taller on the chair's slippery cushion, and kept her legs close together, her feet flat on the porch.

But it wasn't just her looks that bothered her; she was envious of the warmth between Allison and her mother. She had never known anything like that, even when her mother was alive, and she envied them and liked them at the same time. *It's too bad we have to rob them,* she thought.

Another one of Ben's warnings came back to her. *It's better not to know the mark at all. But if it's unavoidable, don't get close; keep your distance.* Laura felt a pang of regret. It might be nice to be close to Leni and Allison.

"There's nothing wrong with your figure; you mustn't worry," Leni said. "Well, perhaps a few pounds, a little rounding out... young girls do seem gaunt these days. They want to be willowy or sway like a reed or some such thing—it always seems to involve some damp and probably unhealthy plant. Yes, I do believe you could use a few pounds... Perhaps you don't eat properly. Do you have a hot breakfast every day?"

Laura and Allison looked at each other and burst out laughing. "Oh, well," Leni sighed. "I suppose you do hear that a great deal." But she wasn't really thinking of her words; she was hearing Allison's laughter and watching it banish the supercilious amusement that usually curved her daughter's perfect lips without allowing laughter to escape. Leni often worried about Allison's cool, amused silence; and at that moment, as her daughter and this strange girl continued to smile together, and even though she was sure those reference letters were faked, she decided to hire Laura Fairchild as a kitchen helper for the Salingers' summer stay on Cape Cod.

* * *

Clay worked in the greenhouses and flower gardens shared by the whole family while Laura was at Rosa's side in the kitchen of Felix and Leni's house. It was the biggest in the compound, and Ben had instructed her to explore and sketch it for him. But by the end of their second week at the Cape she still had not done it, nor had she looked for Leni's jewels so Ben could go straight to them when he broke in. She knew what they looked like because Leni was frequently photographed wearing them at dinner parties and balls—she even took them to the Cape for the big parties in July and August—but Laura had to find out where she kept them.

"What are you waiting for?" Clay demanded, looking up from his own drawing of the layout of the compound. They were sitting in the tiny two-room apartment Ben had rented for them over a garage in downtown Centerville before he went back to New York, and Clay had been trying to figure out the exact distance from the guardhouse to Leni's bedroom window. "How are we going to get out of here if you don't do your part?"

"I'm *trying*," Laura said. "But Rosa expects me to be with her all the time."

"Rosa's a dictator," Clay said.

"Rosa's a sweetie." Laura remembered Allison saying that and wondered why she hadn't seen her once since she started working in her parents' house.

In fact she saw hardly anyone but Rosa and the house staff from the time she and Clay rode up in the mornings on the bicycles Ben had bought them to the time they rode away in the late afternoon. Leni was the only one of the Salingers to come to the kitchen; she came every afternoon, to plan the next day's menus with Rosa. They sat in the sun that stretched the length of the great room, from the panes of the wide breakfast bay that faced the rose garden, swimming pool and tennis courts, all the way to the brick fireplace at the other end. On the long maple table recipes were fanned out, and books of menus from past summers, and with them the two women, like generals planning a campaign, put together the schedule for the next day: usually a luncheon for a small group and then a dinner party for fifteen or more. But none of the other family members came to the kitchen, and after two weeks Laura was not even sure who was at the compound and who was away.

"In Maine," Rosa said when Laura finally worked up the courage to ask where Allison was. "You'll find this family is very big on travel. Somebody's always somewhere and just when you think you know where everybody is, somebody comes back and somebody else goes."

"They just leave their houses empty?" Laura asked casually. In her white kitchen uniform, her hair in a neat ponytail, she felt almost like a cook, almost Rosa's equal, and that made it easier to ask questions about the family. Still, as she stacked breakfast dishes in the double dishwasher, she was careful not to sound too curious.

"Some of them are empty," Rosa replied. "Some with the staff, some stuffed to the ceiling with houseguests. You'll find this family is very big on houseguests, probably because they're in the hotel business and they think something's wrong if all the bedrooms aren't full."

She chuckled and Laura smiled with her. It was easy to be comfortable with Rosa. At sixty-seven, with unflagging energy, she was short and round with small hands that were always moving, nimbly flicking pastry from marble board to pie plate, or cutting vegetables and stirring soup almost at the same time, or knitting a vest for her nephew while she waited for bread to rise or a roast to be done. She had promised to make Laura a sweater when the vest was finished. And no matter what she was doing, she talked steadily and shrewdly about the Salingers and the other families from New York and Boston who, generations before, had come to the towns of Osterville, Centerville, and Hyannis Port on Nantucket Sound, on the south coast of Cape Cod, to build the sprawling summer estates now being used by their children and grandchildren.

"Mr. Owen built this one," Rosa said as she and Laura took salad ingredients from the wall of refrigerators and spread them on the long maple work table. It was the first time Laura realized that Rosa casually called all the Salingers, except Owen, by their first names. "In 1920 he brought Mrs. Owen here—Iris, her name was, she was a lovely lady— and a year later Felix was born. That's when I came; there were only the three of them, and I cooked and cleaned and took care of the baby, and Asa, too, when he was born a year after Felix, and had time to get married myself and not too long later be a widow, and some time after that, I nursed Mrs. Owen when she got sick and died, and all that in the space of ten years. Which I suppose is why I never married again; I was so busy being a mother to Felix and Asa, and Mr. Owen, too, at least for those first few years when he was mourning, I just never had time."

"But who are all the others?" Laura asked. "I don't even know all their names."

Rosa reeled them off in a rhythm that matched her busy hands, chopping and slicing vegetables for the salads she was making for lunch. Owen Salinger, founder of the Salinger hotel chain, had two sons, Felix and Asa; Felix had one daughter, Allison; Asa had a daughter, Patricia, by his first marriage. So Owen had only granddaughters. "Not one grandson he can count on to keep his empire going," Rosa said. "No nephews, either. This family is very big on women, and not one of them shows the slightest twinge of interest in running hotels. Mr. Owen's great-nephew could do it—that's Paul Janssen, the son of Leni's sister, Barbara, and her husband, Thomas—but he's something of a playboy, Paul is, and even if he does settle down, which I may not live long enough to see, it's photography that makes his eyes light up, not hotels. Who'll take over the company after Felix and Asa retire I can't imagine."

As Laura asked questions, Rosa described them all, with their foibles and eccentricities and triumphs. "Allison broke her finger on the slide when she was seven and never went near a swing set again, even though Felix offered her a hundred dollars because he wanted his daughter to have courage and said he'd buy it if he had to." She told Laura about the house Felix built for his father. "It's attached to this one; the door is at the end of the long gallery. After Mr. Owen gave this house to Felix and Leni, Leni wanted him to live with them in the summers—he has a mansion all to himself in Boston—but he said he liked being on his own and planned to build a small house for himself. Well, they argued and argued, and finally Mr. Owen said all right if he could draw the plans himself and also have a door he could lock. So everything worked out. When a man is seventy-eight, he should have people nearby, but he has a right to privacy, too."

She told Laura which houses belonged to the other family members, and where they lived the rest of the year—mostly New York, California, and Boston. And she told her who was in grammar school, high school, and college, who was working and where, and who spent most of the year in Europe.

Gradually Laura put together a picture of the whole family, even though she hadn't yet met most of them. Owen was in Canada, visiting friends; Asa and his family would not arrive from Boston for another week; Leni's sister, Barbara Janssen, her husband, Thomas, and their son, Paul, were returning from Europe in two weeks; others had arrived at the Cape but were always sailing or taking flying lessons or shopping, and when they came to Felix and Leni's for dinner Laura had either left for the day or was working in the kitchen while the maids served.

"You could serve," Rosa said, studying her. "You're not bad looking, you're quick and neat, you have a nice smile which you don't use often enough and if someone asked you to do something, you'd remember it. What a memory you have! I told Leni you'd memorized everything in the kitchen in one day; never have I seen such a memory, I told her."

Laura flushed and turned away, striking her elbow against the table. "Shit," she muttered, nursing it.

"But you're not ready," Rosa went on. "You need to be smoothed out. A real lady doesn't use vulgarity, my young miss. A real lady doesn't have a temper, either, and I've seen signs of one in you. And you have a lot to learn. You'll find this family is very big on form, and you don't know which side to serve or take a plate from, or how to bring somebody a clean knife, or when to refill a water glass. It's a wonder to me those people wrote those fabulous letters about you, unless of course they just liked your smile."

Laura flushed again and concentrated on slicing red peppers. "I didn't serve; I worked in kitchens."

"My eye," Rosa said pleasantly. "You never worked in a kitchen, my little Laura, not a decent one, anyway, unless it was to wash dishes and scrub the floor." She watched Laura's face. "You needn't worry, I'm not about to tell anyone, or ask questions, either. I've been there myself, you know, a long time ago: poor and hungry and willing to do any job people would give me. I'm sure you worked hard for those people; I'm sure they liked you and that's why they wrote those letters. You'll find I'm very big on instincts, and my instinct says I trust you."

Laura's hand slipped and the blade slashed her finger. "Damn it!" she cried, slamming the knife on the counter. Tears filled her eyes. She wanted to curl up inside the circle of Rosa's plump arms; she wanted to tell her how wonderful it was to be in her warm kitchen with her warm voice and her trust. But she had to hold it all back, just as she had to keep her distance from Leni and Allison. She couldn't return Rosa's trust, she couldn't let herself like anyone in this family, she couldn't let down her guard.

She was there to rob them. And she couldn't ever let herself forget it.

*　*　*

The hallway was silent and cool and her feet slid silently on the hardwood floor as she opened doors for a quick survey, then closed them to go on to the next room. She had already sketched the first floor:

Owen's house, at one end, was a blank, since she'd never been inside, but she had drawn the kitchen at the other end, and the full width of the house stretching between them, with a long porch in front and the wide glassed-in gallery along the back, opening onto the living room, den and dining room.

Now, for the first time, she was on the second floor. *Guest rooms across the back of the house, each with its own bath; Allison's suite along the whole east side—bigger than our apartment in New York—then Felix's office, bedroom, dressing room and bath, then Leni's sitting room, dressing room and bath, and her bedroom on the west side.*

That was the one she wanted. Silently she opened the bedroom door and slipped inside, taking in with a swift glance the seafoam and ivory colors, ivory shag rugs on gleaming hardwood floors, the bed in the next room draped in seafoam silk and ivory lace. The rooms were cool and serene, like Leni. Laura thought of what it would be like to come to a mother in rooms like these, and curl up and talk about the things she worried about.

Well, I never will, that's all. And it doesn't matter; I've outgrown that.

She had to hurry. She surveyed the spacious rooms with a more calculating eye. Sitting room desk, coffee table and armoire—all of them with drawers. In the bedroom and adjoining dressing room, four bureaus and a dressing table, nightstands flanking the bed, a wall of closets. Swiftly and silently, Laura opened them all, her slender fingers slipping among silk and cotton and lace without disturbing one perfect fold; she looked beneath the furniture without moving it; she tilted pictures from the walls without changing one angle.

Nothing, nothing... where would she keep them... there's no safe...
Then she came to the last closet, and found it locked. *Finally...* She knelt before it. She could get it open; she'd done it so many times. She reached in her pocket for the small set of steel picks Ben had bought her for her birthday, and it was at that moment that the sitting room door opened.

"What the hell—!" Allison's voice exclaimed. She stood in the doorway, her eyes changing as she recognized Laura. "A burglar!" she cried in mock alarm. "How terrifying! But I know you! Rosa's new assistant ... yes?"

Laura nodded. She had leaped to her feet but she was dizzy and her legs were weak, and she leaned against the closet. Her throat was dry, her heart was pounding; she thrust her clenched fists deep inside the pockets of her uniform to hide the picks in her shaking hands. Rosa had said Allison wasn't due back from Maine until tomorrow, and everyone else was spending the day on Felix's yacht. *It was supposed to be empty up here all afternoon.*

"But what are you doing in my mother's room... Laura, isn't it? Have we started cooking dinner up here? Or were you looking for my great-grandmother's sterling that she brought over from Austria? It isn't here; Rosa could have told you it's in the dining room commode."

Laura shook her head. "I wasn't looking—" She cleared her dry throat. "I wasn't looking for sterling." She took a step forward. "I ought to be downstairs..."

"Indeed you should. But first let's have a talk." Allison strode across the room, grasped Laura's arm, and forced her to walk beside her out of the room, down the full length of the hall, and into another suite at the opposite corner from Leni's. "This is mine. Perfectly private. Sit down." Laura stood indecisively. "I *said*, sit *down*."

Laura sat down. Her white cotton uniform seemed plain and harsh in the delicate white wicker chair with its chintz cushion. The room was bright and airy, in gold and white with lamps and throw pillows of sea green and indigo blue. It seemed that all the colors of the Cape were there, shimmering in the sunlight that streamed across the ocean and the beach and the smooth lawns of the estate for the sole purpose of brightening Allison Salinger's rooms.

Finally Laura's eyes rested on the stack of suitcases in the corner of the room. "I came back early," Allison said. "I was exceedingly bored." She had watched Laura survey the sitting room and the bedroom, visible through its open door, and now she gave her a keen look. "Maybe this isn't the first time you've been here." Laura, frozen in her chair, said nothing. "Have you already been here?"

Laura shook her head.

"My God, have I petrified you into silence? What are you afraid of? It isn't a crime to look at people's rooms; I poke around to see how my friends fix up theirs; why shouldn't you do the same? I won't turn you in, if that's what you're worried about. I don't care what you do; you work for Rosa, not me. It would be different if you'd been going through Mother's closets; if the alarm had gone off there'd be hell to pay."

Laura's heart began to pound again, the blood hammering in her ears. *I should have thought... I should have known... What's happened to me that I don't do things right in this house?* "Alarm?" she asked, making it sound as casual as she could.

"A siren that wakes the dead. It's because of Mother's jewelry, you know, all the incredible stuff my great-grandmother brought from Austria with the sterling. My father keeps telling Mother to keep it in the safe in Boston, but she says what good is jewelry if you can't wear it. If something is really important to you, you ought to do whatever you want with it, right? She loves all those things because they came from her grandmother to her mother and then to her and someday they'll be mine, so if she wants to wear them anywhere in the world, why shouldn't she? What do you do besides explore bedrooms?"

Laura flushed deeply. For the first time she was angry. Allison was playing with her like a cat trying to trip up a mouse. "I work," she said shortly and began to stand up.

"Not yet," Allison snapped. Her voice made it clear that she knew exactly where the power lay between the two of them. "I said I wanted to talk. You work for Rosa. What do you like best? Do you like to cook?"

Her tone had become warm and curious, catching Laura off guard. "I guess so. I haven't done it very long."

"You haven't? Mother said you'd done it forever. Lots of good references, she said."

"Oh, sure," Laura said swiftly. "I've worked in kitchens for years. I thought you meant cooking here, for your family."

"Well," Allison said when she stopped, "do you like cooking for my family?"

"Yes."

"What else do you like?"

"Oh, reading and listening to music. And I'm getting to like the beaches around here."

"And boys?"

"No."

"Oh, come on. How old are you?"

"Eighteen."

"Same as me. And no boys? Not even one little date? Everybody dates, for heaven's sake."

"Why do you care?" Laura burst out. "I'm just a cook—not even that, really; I'm just Rosa's assistant. What do you care whether I date or not?"

"I don't know," Allison said frankly. She contemplated Laura. "There's something about you—something about your eyes—like you're thinking of two things at once and I don't have all your attention. It's like a game, getting to know what you're thinking, getting you to . . . see me. Do you know what I mean?"

"No," said Laura flatly.

"I'll bet you do. You're not from around here, are you, like most of the summer help?"

"I've lived in New York."

"You still live in New York?"

"Yes."

"So what do you do in New York?"

Laura tossed her head. "I go out with five university guys. A couple of them are just friends but the other ones I see a lot, and on weekends I pick one or the other of them and we go to their apartment and screw. Sometimes I'm with two of them at once. Is there anything else you want to know?"

Allison tried to stare her down but Laura stared back. *Prying bitch. Who says everybody dates? What do you know about it?* "Do you have a good time?" Allison asked curiously. Her voice had changed again—not quite believing Laura, but not quite sure.

Confused, Laura was silent.

"I don't," Allison said. "I've been with three, no four, guys, one at a time, I'm not gutsy enough for two at once, and I don't much like it. I tell myself I should because everybody else does—or at least they say they do—but, I don't know, all the boys seem so damn young. If you have college guys, you're lucky. They're probably better. The ones I know can't *talk.* All they want to do is get in your pants, and as soon as they get a finger in they think they've got it made and they start to babble and slobber and it's all so stupid. I mean, I have a brain, and feelings, but every boy I know treats me like some kind of doll they can play with but don't have to pay much attention to. I think they ought to carry a cantaloupe with a hole in it and whenever they get the urge just stick their cock in and jack off, and then they'd never have to make conversation at all."

Laura broke into nervous giggles and Allison giggled, too, and then they were laughing as they had when they met. "They're probably scared to talk," Laura said. "They can feel like big men when they screw, but they sound pretty silly when you want them to talk about something serious, and I guess they know that."

"That's it; you've got it." Allison sighed. "You know that bit about the cantaloupe? I've been thinking that for a long time but I never said it to anybody before. I haven't got anybody to talk to, that's the problem. I mean, everybody from Boston and around here thinks I'm so fucking grown-up and cool, and they all know each other, and with people like that, if you show them you're worried or not happy about something, in an hour everybody knows it and . . . oh, what the hell. It's just that I feel alone a lot of the time. Do you know what I mean?"

"I know what it's like not to have anybody to talk to."

"Well, we're talking. Do you have a good time in bed with your college guys?"

"Sure." *She's not a friend; I can't confide in her; I'll never see her again after a few more weeks.* "I always have a good time. You just have to know what you're doing." She hesitated. She hadn't the slightest notion of what it felt like to be in bed with a man. All she had had were quick couplings in the back seats of cars that had made her feel, for a few minutes, like she was special to the boy she was with, and then, afterward, more lonely than ever. "You have to care about him," she said, letting her fantasies fly. "And keep the lights on so you can see each other, 'cause it's more sexy that way and you feel like you're with somebody you know. And do it slow and easy so you have time to feel good. And make him know what you want. Don't let nobody take you"—she cleared her throat—"don't let *anybody* take you without your being ready. You just tell them: *God damn it, I'm a real person! Listen to what I want!* That's all there is to it. I've got to get back; Rosa said three o'clock sharp—"

"Sit down; it's only quarter to." Allison was frowning again. "I tell myself that, that I shouldn't do anything I don't want to, but they're all over me and it's just easier to go along and get it over and then get out of there. I don't want to be *raped*, after all . . ."

"You're raped every time you do it and don't want to," Laura said in a clear voice. And as she said it she realized she was right; it was the first time she'd known it. *I'll never do it again, never, unless I really, truly want to and really care about somebody. And then he'll have to care about me, too.*

"You're smart," Allison said. "God, that is a smart thing to say. Do you want to come up here a lot, and talk? It's a pretty room, isn't it? I used to hate it because it's so different from my rooms in Boston— they're all velvet and satin, sort of like a warm bed—but now I like this, too. It's different, but it's just as comforting, and God knows I need that."

"You've got your mother's room, and your mother," Laura blurted.

"Well, of course, but . . . Well, you know Mother. She's wonderful and I love her, but she's perfect. And how do I go to somebody who's perfect and say, 'Listen, I fucked up'?"

"If she's perfect she'll understand," Laura said, and they burst out laughing.

"Right," Allison agreed. "She's not quite perfect. But close."

Their smiles held and Laura felt warmth flow through her. Maybe they could be friends after all; only a little bit, because she had to be careful, but closer than any friendship she'd had until now. After all, here she was, sitting in a girl's room for the first time ever, talking about private things the way girls were supposed to. Even if she'd lied a lot, she'd told some truths, too, and having to lie didn't change anything: it was still the kind of afternoon she'd always dreamed of. Why shouldn't it go on? Why shouldn't she have a real friend, just for these few weeks?

Allison was studying Laura's face. "I really would like to talk to you again and get to know you. I like you. Did I get it right about what you were doing in Mother's room? Or were you doing something else?"

The spell was broken. Laura's warmth was gone; she was tense and calculating. *This is how it always has to be.* She lowered her eyes and made her voice a little higher than usual, sounding young, very earnest, very innocent. "No, you were right; I just wanted to see what it was like. Rosa mentioned that everyone was gone—she doesn't know I came up here so *please* don't blame her—and I thought I'd just take a little peek because I've never ever been in a house like this—it's like a fairy-tale castle, isn't it?—and I thought just once I could see how it felt to walk around in it and even pretend I lived here or might live somewhere like it, someday..."

She raised her eyes and looked at Allison with a little quiver on her lips. "I didn't mean any harm."

Allison's frown was deep and angry. "You're very complicated, aren't you? And maybe a good actress, too. I think I *will* get to know you better."

Laura jumped up. "I'm sure it's after three. I have to go—" She was at the door, pulling it open, almost running into the hall and toward the stairs.

Allison was close behind. "I'm interested in you. And I intend to get to know you *very* well. In fact," she added, leaning forward a little as Laura stood on the top stair, frozen, "I'm going to find out everything about you."

CHAPTER 3

C LAY slipped the manila envelope into the mailbox at the Centerville post office, then pushed off on his bicycle to catch up with Laura. "That gives Ben the layout of the grounds and houses," he said as they rode toward Osterville. "I wrote him everything you told me about the alarm on the closet, and I said we'd find out what kind of a security system they've got. Oh, and what's-his-name, the guard's, schedule—"

"Jonas," said Laura. "And Billy and Al on the night shifts."

"Right. You know them all. All that shit that doesn't matter. But then you find an alarm and you don't even have the smarts to ask Allison or Rosa what kind of system it is and how it hooks up to Leni's closet!"

"Mrs. Salinger to you," Laura snapped. "And I wish you'd leave me alone. I couldn't ask, right then. When I have a chance, I'll find out. I've never let Ben down and I won't this time."

She sped ahead, rounded a corner and turned down a private drive she knew Clay had not discovered, to come out on the beach. It was early and no one was about; it was as if she had a private ocean, all to herself. She walked her bicycle in the soft sand, listening to the gulls and the wash of the waves, tasting the salt air on her tongue. Two weeks earlier, she would have preferred Main Street in Centerville, or even downtown Osterville, crowded with gift shops, fudge shops, bayberry candle shops, restaurants, and boutiques, because even though they were small they were more like New York than were the silent stretches of beach. And in some ways she still felt peculiar on the beach, alone in all that space and stillness.

She felt even more peculiar about the forests of pine, beech, oak, sassafras and fifty-foot holly trees that shared this part of the Cape with drifting sand and clumps of wild grass bending in the wind. The idea of forests terrified her. How would she find her way out without street signs, and familiar sidewalks beneath her feet, shadowed by buildings crammed together so that wherever you looked there was a place to get shelter from the rain or to hide if somebody had felt you pick his pocket?

There were no hiding places on the beach, either, but this morning Laura found its quiet and emptiness comforting. For the first time she felt its serenity, and she was annoyed when she saw someone up ahead and realized she didn't have the ocean to herself after all. It was an old man, she saw as she drew closer, very tall and thin, with a white, drooping mustache and white hair that reached his shoulders. As she approached, she was struck by the contrast of his heavy eyebrows and wide, sensual mouth in a face so thin it was almost gaunt.

"Have you ever noticed the way this shell swirls?" he asked conversationally as she passed within a few feet of him. They might have been old friends sharing an early morning stroll. "It's peculiar to this part of the country, you know; I've never found another like it."

Laura stopped and took the shell he was holding out to her. Pink and white and rose, it curled in on itself like a whirlpool reflecting the sunset. She traced its whorls with her fingertip: silken smooth except for a tiny raised ridge in the center of each curve. "I've never seen one like it either," she said, not telling him that she had never seen any shell at all.

"Like people," the old man said. "Like fingerprints. Each has its own character. No, keep it," he added as she handed it back. "I like to give them away to people who appreciate them. Just as I like to share the morning solitude with someone who appreciates it." He bent closer to peer at her. "But I've intruded on your solitude, haven't I? You thought you had all this to yourself and then I pop up and obstruct the view."

Instinctively Laura looked at the wide expanse of empty beach all around them and a small smile curved the corners of her mouth. The old man saw it and smiled broadly. "You think there might be room for both of us? Of course we can go our separate ways, but we might also share our pleasure." His speech had an old-fashioned cadence that reminded Laura of books she had read, and his smile was warm and private, drawing her toward him.

But she held back. He had known she didn't want anyone else on the beach, and no thief can afford to hang around a mind reader. She put her hands on the handlebars, ready to walk off. "I don't own it. It's somebody's private beach; we shouldn't even be here."

"But now that we are, we can enjoy it," he said gravely, and she looked up, and met his eyes, slate gray, serious, intent on her own. "Are there a great many things that you do own and wish to protect from intruders?"

"No," Laura said sharply—why did people have to pry?—and she turned again to leave. "I don't own anything," she said over her shoulder.

"Yourself," he responded quietly. "And I hope you're the only one who does." Laura frowned. "Aren't you valuable enough to own?" the old man asked.

She looked back at him. "I never thought about it."

"I think about it," he said. "About myself, that is. How much I value myself, how much pride I take in myself." He studied her gravely as she stood some distance away, like a wary bird poised to fly. "Perhaps you don't take enough pride in yourself. I'm sure you care about yourself, but perhaps not enough, or for the wrong reasons. You might give some thought to that. Having faith in yourself."

Laura nodded, fascinated but also afraid, because once again the old man had seen inside her. How could he know about the things she'd been wanting for over a year, almost more than anything else?

He was still studying her: about eighteen, he thought, and still gangly; not yet a woman. Long, well-formed legs, though, with good muscles, probably from riding her bicycle. Her hair was tied back with a ribbon, and she wore a cotton shift and sandals. She should wear silk, the old man thought suddenly, and then wondered why he would think that about a rather ordinary, pretty girl with poor posture and an uncomfortable wariness in her stance. Perhaps it was her eyes: dark blue, almost too big for her slender, delicate face, showing in their depths a strong will that did not yet know its own strength or direction.

"Of course," he went on, "usually it takes a long time to have faith in ourselves. I've had seventy-eight years to work at it. But I think you'll do it; one of these days you'll truly believe you are the most valuable possession you have." He smiled at her again. "And you'll protect yourself from intruders."

Laura stared at him. Without realizing it, she had moved closer and now stood beside him. "I have thought about it," she confided. "I'm going to change my whole life. I have to figure out how to do it, but someday I'm going to change everything; I won't even look the way I look now—"

"I like the way you look," the old man said gently.

She shook her head. It was nice of him to say it and it was nice to hear, but he was old; what did he know? "I'm not beautiful or glamorous; I don't know how to dress right or even walk the right way."

"One foot in front of the other," he suggested.

"You wouldn't joke about it if you knew how serious it is," she said angrily. "Rich people have a way of walking that's different: they come into a room as if they own everything and can just reach out and take whatever they want. They're not unhappy and they're not afraid they'll do something wrong; they just do what they want."

"You mean they have confidence."

"I guess," Laura said doubtfully, thinking that was a poor word to describe the way rich people made the world their own.

"But their confidence rests on their money," he said. "What about inside themselves? Don't you think rich people ever worry about love and friendship and health, and doing things well, and being whatever they most want to be, deep inside?"

Laura shook her head again. "Not like the rest of us."

"And how many people have you known like that?"

"I haven't—a few."

There was a silence. So young, the old man thought, contemplating her small frown. And yet she is close to being a woman. "Tell me what you like about the beach," he said.

"The way it goes on forever." She turned to take in the shining sand, pale and sparkling in the sunlight, darker where the waves slid up and then retreated. "There's so much space, like a huge house, and I can go from room to room and it's all mine."

His eyes brightened. "I've called it my castle ever since I was a small boy. Even when I was unhappy, if my father had scolded me or I was worried about something, when I came out here I was king of everything I could see. And I was always very selective about which friends I'd bring with me."

"I wouldn't bring anybody," Laura said decisively.

"No one? Not even your closest friend?"

"I don't have no—I don't have very many friends. I don't need them." He was watching her and she shrugged. "They're all right for people who need them, but if you're strong you don't." She looked at him as if daring him to contradict her. "You just need yourself. That's what you said a few minutes ago. You should believe in yourself."

"That wasn't exactly what I meant," he responded quietly. "Poor child, isn't there anyone you want to share your happiness with?"

"Don't feel sorry for me!" Laura said furiously. "I don't want anybody to feel sorry for me! I don't give a shit—" She bit her lip. "I don't care about sharing, and I wouldn't bring anybody here; it would be my secret."

Casually, as if she had said nothing unusual, the old man gave a bow. "May I visit you in your house? I'd like very much to sit down." He pointed to a hillock of sand covered with tufts of wild grass. "Lately I've begun to tire easily, and I would appreciate the use of your sofa."

Laura felt a sudden rush of warmth; he was trying to make her feel better. For the first time she laughed. "Please do. I'm sorry I can't serve tea."

He laughed with her but inwardly he was stunned at the change in her face. She wasn't ordinary, he thought. She could be a beautiful woman, with a smile that would break men's hearts. She lay her bicycle on the sand and they sat down, contemplating the ocean's long gray swells and furling white caps that broke along the shore in rhythmic whispers. "I've never told my family about my castle on the beach," he mused. "They think I'm often tyrannical and occasionally wise, mainly because I've reached an advanced age, and I don't want them to think I fantasize empty rooms around every sand dune. And I certainly can't tell them that what I like best is the silence. In my family everyone has a vocal opinion on everything. The silence here is wonderful. I never get enough of it."

"It makes me feel odd, though," Laura said. "As if it's going to swallow me up."

"Ah." He nodded. "That's what an empty beach does. Swallows you up. A lot of people find the silence too much and they bring those terrible radios . . . they have a name . . ."

"Ghetto blasters."

"Blasters," he echoed. "I gather they're called that because they blast ghettos."

She laughed. "They blast everybody's ears. They make little people feel big because you can't ignore them. And it's even better if you hate the noise, because then they've really made you notice them and they feel important. More real."

He looked at her sharply. "You're very perceptive."

She shrugged. "You have to be on top of what's happening around you or you don't make it."

A child of the streets, he thought. No wonder the beach makes her feel odd. "Where do you live?" he asked.

"In Centerville."

"And when the summer ends?"

She hesitated. "New York."

"New York is your home?"

She nodded and in the silence she drew a circle in the sand with her finger, and another circle inside that. Could she talk about herself? She never had, except with Cal, and now he was dead and his bookstore was closed. But why not? she thought. The old man was a stranger; she loved his smile and the way he paid attention to her; and she was longing to talk to someone. "I've always lived there; I never went nowhere— anywhere—until we came here. For the summer. I like the crowds, and the buildings, all piled against each other, and everything has a beginning and an ending so you always know where you are, and you can find your way where you're going." She paused. "It seems awfully far away."

"And do you feel lost when you're here?" the old man asked.

"I never feel lost," she said strongly. "Just not always sure how I'll get where I want to go. But I'll get there, and I won't let nobody—anybody —stop me."

The old man stared into the distance, smiling faintly. "I said that, too, when I was young. And I was lucky; nobody stopped me." They looked at the waves. "What else do you like about New York?"

"The noise," Laura replied promptly. "It never stops, you know, even if you close all the windows. Even then the noise comes in, and it's nice because you're always part of it."

"You mean the noise there swallows you up as much as the silence here," he said, watching the changing expressions on her face.

It had never occurred to her. She narrowed her eyes as she thought about the city and the beach in a new way, and then she laughed. "I like that. I love new ideas. I had a friend once, named Cal—you remind me of him—and he did that: told me new ways of looking at things. He owned a bookstore in the East Village, in New York—used books—and he'd let me sit near his desk in the back and read dusty old books full of wonderful new ideas. I loved him a lot."

He noted the wistfulness in her voice. "I once spent a lot of time in used bookstores," he said reflectively. "Then I got too busy earning a living. Lately I've rediscovered them. Old books and new ideas. That's nicely put. Are you in school in New York? Where do you live?"

"I'm starting at the university in the fall," Laura lied swiftly. "And living in the dormitory."

He gazed at her. *He knows I've lied. It's not definite; I can't go unless Ben helps me. And even if I do go, I'll still live with him and Clay; I can't afford a dormitory. He knows I'm lying and now he won't like me anymore.*

"I went to a university for two years," the old man said. "Then I left and started my own company. I made a great deal of money but I always disliked it when people asked me about college, because I didn't have a success to talk about. Perhaps when you graduate and have a success to talk about you won't mind questions."

"Thank you," Laura said in a low voice. Reluctantly, she stood up. "I'll be late for work if I don't go."

He nodded and stood with her. "If you come this way tomorrow, we can talk some more. I'll be right here, swallowed up in my thoughts."

"If I can," Laura said, though she knew she wouldn't. Ben wouldn't like her talking about herself so much and she knew it really wasn't smart. *But it isn't fair that I can't make friends with Allison or this nice old man, or anybody else around here who's nice.* She picked up her bicycle. "Good-bye," she said, and wondered if it sounded like she meant it for good.

He held out his hand. "I hope you come back."

Awkwardly, Laura touched his hand, not shaking it but brushing his palm with hers. Then, as she put her hands on her handlebars, he kissed her forehead. "I hope I haven't made you late."

He was smiling at her in that personal way and Laura became angry. Why did he have to be so nice? "Good-bye," she said loudly and pushed off, struggling to keep the bicycle straight in the shifting sand. She wished she were smoother about getting along with people. It was like collecting shells: something she'd never had a chance to practice. To make up for her abruptness, she turned to wave good-bye. He was watching her, holding up his hand. It was a farewell wave but it was also like a benediction.

All day, working in the kitchen, she carried the memory of the old man's private smile and the way he had raised his hand, palm toward her, as she walked away. She wished she could see him again but she couldn't; one of these days she and Clay and Ben would do the job and then they'd be back in the city, together again. Her two brothers, her family.

"Laura, stop dreaming," Rosa said. "I'm asking you to work tonight. Is it yes or no?"

"Yes," Laura said.

"We might be here late."

She shrugged. It was better to work in Rosa's bright, warm kitchen than sit in a tiny room over a garage and watch Clay make endless schedules of guards and watchdogs to impress Ben.

"A real lady doesn't shrug her shoulders, my young miss."

Laura started to shrug, then she caught herself and put her head back, standing straight. She'd never heard that ladies didn't shrug. But Rosa would know. Rosa knew all about ladies.

"—home from Europe," Rosa was saying. "And Mr. Owen is back

from Canada, and Allison from Maine. The whole family will be together for the first time this summer. Twenty-four, at last count."

"Who's home from Europe?" Laura said, thinking that all the houses
would be full now and maybe Ben had lost his best chance. She should
have told him about the empty houses. But she hadn't told him or Clay
most of the things Rosa told her about the Salingers. After she'd told
them about the jewels in the closet and the alarm, she'd felt so awful she
stopped telling them things. It wasn't important, anyway; they didn't
have to know Rosa's little stories about— "What?" she asked. "I'm sorry,
Rosa; I didn't hear you."

"I said for the third time, my dreaming miss, that Paul and his parents
are back from Europe. You really ought to show a little more interest in
this family, Laura. You'll never be a success at any job unless you're
interested in everything about it."

"You're right," Laura murmured and went on rolling pastry and wondering what it would be like to be part of a family of twenty-four people.
It isn't size that counts, she told herself. It's being loved and cared for
and having a place to go when you're afraid of being alone.

But still, that evening, listening to the rising tide of conversation as
the Salingers came into the dining room from the ocean-facing front
porch where they'd had drinks, she wished again she belonged to so
many people. From the many voices she made out Leni's and Felix's—
"he sounds like a fingernail on a blackboard," Clay had said after meeting him—and she heard Allison's cool laugh. Finally, when the cold
soup had been served, and Rosa sent her to the pantry for extra platters
for the roasted game hens, she couldn't resist stopping on the way to
inch open the swinging door and take a quick look into the dining room.

Her stomach contracted. The old man from the beach was sitting at
the head of the table, his head bent courteously as he listened to Felix,
on his left. She felt faint with fear. *Owen Salinger.* Who else could it be?
The head of the family at the head of the table. *Mr. Owen is back from
Canada.* Rosa had said that this morning. And Laura Fairchild, her
tongue running like water from an open faucet, had talked to him about
herself as if he were a friend, not part of a family they were planning to
rob. Frantically thinking back, she didn't think she'd given anything
away, but that wasn't the point. Ben's first rule had been that no one in
the Salinger family could know anything about them, and not only had
she violated that rule, she'd picked the head of the family to do it with,
the one all the others would listen to if he had suspicions about her.
Stupid. Unprofessional. What was it about these people that caused her
to let down her guard? What would Ben say when he found out?

"Laura?" Rosa called. "The platters?"

Rapidly, Laura's gaze swept the table and she filed each face in her memory. Her swift glance stopped when she found herself looking directly into the eyes of a young man seated next to Allison. His eyes were almost black beneath straight brows; his face was thin with a long, narrow nose above a wide mouth and quick smile, and he brushed his thick dark hair back from his forehead with an impatient hand. He was young and handsome, with the piercing gaze of Leni and the barely disguised arrogance of Allison, and he was looking at Laura with amusement and a faint curiosity that infuriated her. Backing away, she let the door swing shut, grabbed three platters from the shelf, and marched into the kitchen.

"What's got into you?" Rosa asked.

"Nothing." Laura concentrated on arranging the platters on the counter. "I had trouble finding the platters."

"My eye," Rosa said amiably. "You put them away two days ago after we used them for lunch. All these moods you've got . . . But it's not my business; you'll find I'm very big on letting people work out their own demons. But you'll have to forget yours for a while; we have work to do."

She looked up sharply. "Mr. Owen! Do you need something? Is something wrong?"

"Look on the happy side, Rosa," Owen Salinger said with a grin, more lighthearted than Laura remembered him. "Maybe I came to tell you everything is perfect."

"Well, I should hope—" She saw Owen looking at Laura. "This is my assistant. Laura Fairchild, Mr. Owen Salinger."

Owen held out his hand. "Welcome, Miss Fairchild." Meeting his eyes, Laura saw that he was inviting her to play a game, and she felt the same rush of gratitude she had felt earlier when he'd tried to put her at her ease. "Have you met our family?" he asked as she put her hand in his. "Or has our strict Rosa kept you too busy? Perhaps she'll spare you one of these days so you can be introduced to everyone."

Laura flushed deeply. He had seen her spying on them and was making fun of her. She worked her hand free of his. "I'd rather stay with Rosa."

"Laura!" Rosa frowned in disapproval. She couldn't understand what Owen was thinking of—when had he ever introduced temporary help to the family?—but no one in her kitchen was going to be rude to Mr. Owen Salinger if she had anything to say about it. "You owe Mr. Salinger an apology for your rude behavior. You should be grateful."

"I'm sorry," Laura said to Owen. "But I've seen your family." She heard her voice waver.

"But you haven't been properly introduced. Rosa, can you spare Laura for a few hours one of these days?"

He and Rosa discussed days and times while Laura silently repeated Owen's words. *Properly introduced.* Maybe he hadn't been making fun of her; maybe he knew she'd felt like an outsider when she peered at his family and he wanted to make her feel better about herself.

"Next week?" Owen was asking her courteously.

I'll do it for Ben, she thought. To learn more about the family. "Thank you," she said. "I'd like to meet everyone. Properly."

"Very good." He turned to go. "Oh, by the way," he said casually to Rosa, "I'm reorganizing my library and I could use some help. Do you know anyone who wants to work eight to ten hours a week, shelving and cataloguing? Someone who loves old books and new ideas." Laura looked sharply at him. What was he up to? "Hard work, good pay," he went on, smiling at Laura.

Rosa pursed her lips. "There's always people looking for work. But . . . books? I'll have to give it some thought."

"I'd like to do it," Laura said in a rush. "I'd like to try, anyway. I know about books."

Owen's smile broadened. "A good idea. A very good idea. We'll start tomorrow, shall we? Two to four every afternoon."

"Mr. Owen . . ." Rosa began. She was distinctly uncomfortable. "Are you sure—? I mean to say, Laura learns fast and remembers everything you tell her, and she's nimble as a cat, but she sometimes—I don't mean to criticize her; I'm fond of her—but she is very big into saying she's done a thing when I'm not at all sure she's really . . . done it."

"I do know books," Laura said quickly. "I've been in bookstores a lot—in one bookstore, anyway—and sometimes I helped catalogue. I really do know books!"

"I believe you," Owen said, smiling again at the fierce determination that reminded him of his own when he was about her age and starting to make his own way. He had seen it on the beach that morning; together with her wariness it was what had most attracted him. But this evening, she had touched his heart, as well, when he looked up from his talk with Felix and saw her looking at the family. He had had only a glimpse of her slender face and enormous, longing eyes as the pantry door swung shut, but it was enough: as wild as she seemed, she was hungrier for love than anyone he had ever known and it was that vulnerability that sent him looking for her.

Someone new, he thought. We don't see new people often enough. The same faces at parties, the same circle of friends, whether we're in

Boston or the Cape or New York. Even the same conversations. I can use something new to think about, someone to help. And why not help someone who reminds me of myself, so long ago?

"We'll try it," he said firmly to Rosa. "I'm sure you can spare Laura from two to four every afternoon; if she has to stay later at night, I'll pay her overtime." He gave neither Rosa nor Laura time to respond. "We'll start tomorrow. And," he added to Laura, "I'm uncomfortable with uniforms. Can you bring something casual to wear in my dusty library?"

Laura avoided Rosa's eyes. Rosa loved uniforms and had told her to wear hers whenever she was on the Salinger grounds. "Yes," she said. And the next day, promptly at two, when she knocked on the door leading from Felix and Leni's long gallery to Owen's house, she wore blue jeans and a pink cotton shirt, scuffed loafers, and a pink ribbon tying her hair in a ponytail.

"Ah," said Owen, admiring the color in her cheeks and the depth of her deep blue eyes, less wary, more eager than the day before. "Come in, look around, then we'll begin work."

It was a man's house, with oak floors, Persian rugs, and oversize couches and chairs upholstered in dark suede. On the walls were oil paintings of the Cape and its wildlife in different seasons; the lamps were pewter, the windows bare. Beyond the living room was the library, its walls lined floor to ceiling with books, precarious towers of books stacked on the floor, books on reading stands, books strewn on long tables, window seats, and the arms of chairs. "It needs order," Owen said thoughtfully.

Laura gazed at the chaos. "I thought you said re-organize."

"I did. What you see is my first organization. You and I will accomplish the second. Perhaps it will be more successful."

Laura looked at him and they laughed together. "I guess it can't be any worse," she said, and rolled up her sleeves.

Every day they worked side by side, alphabetizing, cataloguing, labeling shelves, wading through the new piles they made as they sorted old ones. And they talked. Owen told Laura about his parents and grandparents, the first four hotels he bought—still his favorites though his company owned over fifty in America and Europe—and about Iris, the woman he had loved since he was fifteen, his wife and the mother of his children, whom he still longed for every day, though it had been almost forty years since she died.

And Laura talked, too, carefully choosing the memories she would share. She told Owen the same story she had told Leni: how she and Clay had lived with relatives after their parents were killed in an automobile accident, and recently moved out because they didn't like it there. She told him, truthfully, what she remembered about her mother and father, a few anecdotes about her brother Clay—*but nothing about Ben; don't slip and say anything about Ben*—and the classes she had liked best in high school. For the first time she talked about her dreams of being an actress. "I've had three parts in school plays and everybody says I'm really good. And I love being on the stage, all that make-believe..." She talked about studying acting in college, if she ever found a way to go. "I mean," she fumbled when she remembered she'd lied about college the day they met, "I was going to start this fall, but I don't know, it may not work out..."

"There's nothing wrong with pretending," Owen said gently.

"I wasn't pretending!" she said hotly. "I thought I'd go! I will go!"

"I'm sure you will," he said, still gentle.

She bit her lip. "I'm sorry. I don't know exactly what I'll do about college. I'll figure something out."

"Well," he said offhandedly, leafing through a leather-bound book, "I could loan you the money for tuition. And board and room, too, if you need it." He heard Laura's sharp breath and nodded slowly. "I could certainly do that. A loan, of course, though I wouldn't expect you to pay it back until you had graduated and were earning your living, acting or perhaps something else. However, there would be one condition." He looked up and met her quick frown. "I'd expect you to write to me, and visit me, too. I wouldn't want to lose track of you."

Laura's face was radiant, her mind racing. "It's so wonderful..." *I never have to steal again. I can go to college and learn to be somebody. And I have a friend.* She put out her hand, then drew it back. She wanted to touch Owen, she wanted to kiss him, but she thought he might be angry. All he'd done was offer to loan her money. He probably loaned money to lots of people, and he wouldn't want them to start slobbering over him. She kept her hand in her lap. "*You're* wonderful. Thank you, thank you so much... I'll make you proud of me, I'll work so hard..." She turned her head away to hide the tears that stung her eyes. "I'll write to you every day," she said briskly and picked up a book, staring at it blindly until her tears dried.

"Once a week will be sufficient," Owen said with a calm smile, and they went back to work.

From that day, Laura found it easier to talk about her life in New York, her favorite books, the hours she had spent in Cal Hendy's book-shop. She was still careful, she still had to stop herself sometimes in mid-sentence, but by the end of their first week together the best time of her day was with Owen. It was a time when she could almost relax and forget everything outside his quiet rooms.

The only thing she couldn't forget, as hard as she tried, was Clay's admiring voice when she had told him about her part-time job. "God, you're clever, Laura. Who else could have wormed her way into the family and made the old guy trust you in less than two months?"

* * *

Owen met her in the kitchen just after lunch and took her to meet the family. They went from house to house along paths lined with old-fashioned gas lamps and rhododendron bushes, and Laura was reminded of books she had read about an earlier century, when people made calls in the afternoon, leaving calling cards if no one was home. But for Owen, everyone was home. And though they were puzzled, and Laura was almost mute from shyness, everyone was kind. Only Felix and Asa made clear how peculiar they found the situation, even allowing for their father's famous whims, and Asa's wife, Carol, didn't know whether to echo her husband's chilly greeting or Leni's pleasant one.

As they were leaving Asa's house, Allison arrived with her cousin Patricia. "Oh, we've met," Allison said casually when Owen began his introduction. Laura held her breath, but Allison breezed on. "When mother hired you, remember? I was so glad she did. When Rosa does the hiring she always finds elderly ladies with thin lips who play bridge and only cook lamb chops and Jell-O. She did hire a terrific college girl last summer who mixed up oregano and marijuana. Fortunately Rosa discovered it before we ate the lasagna. Grandpa said we would have been known as the Stoned Salingers, which annoyed my father, but his sense of humor is rather dim."

"Allison," Owen said, "that is no way to talk of your father."

"You talk about him that way." Allison's voice deepened and she drew her brows together like Owen. "'Felix, you'd live longer and make the rest of us much happier if you learned to laugh occasionally.'"

Owen smiled, but Laura thought there was a sharpness in the way Allison talked about everyone, from elderly ladies to her own father.

"I assume," Allison was saying to her, "you can distinguish between oregano and marijuana and you excel at something besides lamb chops and Jell-O."

"I don't excel at anything yet," said Laura, *but I can make it in a tough neighborhood better than you ever could.* Standing beside Owen, staring at the porcelain beauty of Allison and her silent cousin, she felt a surge of anger. Why was it that people who had lots of money also had perfect figures and beautiful faces and respectability, too? Why weren't those things parceled out so everybody could at least have something? "But I will. I'm going to college and be an actress, or maybe"—she cast about, trying to sound as self-assured as the Salingers—"I'll own some-thing, a business or a bookshop, or maybe a restaurant, and hire people to work for me."

"Why not a hotel or two?" Allison asked with amusement.

"I might," said Laura. She raised her chin. "I'd like that."

"Would you? From what I can see, it's hard work."

So is being sent to Cape Cod to help my brother rob your house. "I don't mind work. There are so many things I want and there's no other way..." Her voice trailed off. How would someone like Allison ever understand what that meant? All she and Laura had in common was that they were both eighteen.

"I think you'll do and be whatever you want," said Owen. "But one thing you may not do: when you open your first hotel you may not steal Rosa from us to run your kitchen."

Laura smiled, grateful for his intervention when she was feeling infe-rior, and in a few minutes they left for the Janssens' house down the road.

"Come back another time," Allison said, keeping pace with them. "We can talk and get to know each other. I'll teach you to play tennis, if you like. When could you do it? Rosa gave you time off today; she'll do it again."

Laura was silent, ignoring Owen's curious glance.

Allison's eyes gleamed. "I'll invite you for dinner; you won't have an excuse."

"I work for Rosa at night."

"Which nights?"

"As often as she needs me."

"I'll invite you on your day off."

"I like to spend time with my brother."

"All day?"

"Allison," Owen said as they reached the Janssens' front porch, "why do you press someone who seems reluctant to accept?"

There was a pause. "You really are, aren't you?" Allison said to Laura. "Reluctant to be with me. Most people think it's a big deal to socialize with the Salingers. And here's Grandpa wanting us to be friends and you absolutely refuse. Because you don't like me, right?"

I'm afraid of liking you. I'm afraid of talking to you. "I'm just so busy," she started to say, but she stopped. It would be socially right to say that, but not personally right, because Allison would know it wasn't true. Laura Fairchild had never thought about the difference between socially and personally right. I'm learning, she thought. I could live the way they do. And what's wrong with learning? As long as I have to be here for Ben, I might as well get something out of it. And if Owen really wants us to be friends . . .

"Maybe I could get away for dinner some time," she said to Allison. "And I'd like very much to learn tennis."

"Then it's set," Allison said with satisfaction. "I'll tell Rosa and we'll do it in a couple of days. Tennis in the afternoon and then a swim."

"I don't swim," Laura said, ashamed that there were so many basic skills she had never learned.

"Well, you'll learn that, too. We have all summer. What fun; I love being a teacher. Maybe we could tackle some other things, too. Have you thought about a haircut?"

"Allison," said Owen.

"I'll let you know which day," Allison said hastily to Laura. "Wear tennis shoes and bring a swimsuit—do you have a swimsuit?"

Laura shook her head.

"I'll loan you one; I have dozens. Talk to you soon." Without waiting for a reply, she ran back to join Patricia.

Laura looked at the ground and then raised her head and met Owen's eyes. "I feel like I'm her newest project."

He looked at her thoughtfully. "You're very wise. Allison needs projects; she needs to feel needed. You could make her very happy." He paused. "And I think she could help you be happy."

"I am," Laura said swiftly. "I am happy." And then Thomas Janssen opened the door and Laura was led into another large house with bright, spacious rooms facing the ocean, a volleyball court and horseshoe strip on the beach, and a long oval swimming pool like a bright blue gem in the center of the smooth lawn. The rooms were furnished in pale blue wicker with blue and white cushions and straw-colored raffia rugs strewn at angles on bleached wood floors. Barbara Janssen was arranging roses, and she turned as Laura and Owen came in with Thomas.

"How nice of Owen to bring you to us, Laura; I hardly know the people in my own kitchen, much less my sister's. Rosa is a dear, isn't she? A trifle opinionated, but very clever. Would you like iced tea? Do come and sit for a while. I'm hoping Paul will get back soon; he took Emily shopping and they've been gone some time. Do you take lemon?"

Laura started. "No. Thank you." She took the glass and sat next to Owen, sinking back into Barbara's steadily flowing words that sounded so like Leni's. The two sisters looked alike, as well: tall, blond and angular, with long necks and imperious heads, their voices like murmuring rivers in a cool forest. "I was always hoping for blue roses to match my furniture," Barbara was saying to Owen. "But a blue rose would be quite unnatural, and one shouldn't try to circumvent nature unless one is incredibly arrogant or incredibly clever. I've never been either, so I don't try." Laura listened, now and then looking up to find Owen watching her, or Thomas, his quizzical eyes moving from Owen to her and then back again. He was small and dark, with a short black beard and rimless glasses, and he almost never spoke. Laura tried to imagine him and Barbara in bed together, or even happily married, when they were so different, but she couldn't.

Barbara stopped talking. The silence was as palpable as if a cloud had covered the sun. It was broken when Thomas said quietly, "Come in, Paul, we were hoping you'd be here."

Paul Janssen stood in the doorway, a camera slung over one shoulder. His eyebrows went up when he saw Laura, then he smiled broadly and went to her, holding out his hand. "I see my uncle had the good sense to bring you out from behind that kitchen door. I hope you feel more friendly toward us now."

Laura took the hand he offered, shivering slightly as his long, thin fingers enclosed hers. His distant amusement at the dinner table was gone; his smile was warm and open and his body curved above hers as she sat in the deep wicker chair, looking up at him. Suddenly she felt heavy, and hot inside, as if she were melting and everything was going to run out, all over the floor. She tightened her muscles, trying to hold herself in; then, her face burning, she let out her breath in a sigh as Paul shook her hand, like a business associate or a casual friend. He kissed his mother on her cheek and sat on the arm of his father's chair. "Have you met everyone else?" he asked Laura.

She nodded. There was a small silence. Then Owen began talking about their other visits.

"And did Allison take you in hand?" Paul asked.

Laura nodded again. She felt like a fool, clumsy and tongue-tied, not clever. That was Barbara Janssen's favorite word, and it was probably her son's, too. Paul would expect cleverness. He probably couldn't wait to get out of there and find someone clever. And beautiful.

Owen stood up. "I promised to return Laura to Rosa in good time." He turned to Barbara. "I had a thought on the way over here. Would you talk to Leni about that caretaker's cottage in the south corner? It's been empty for some time, and I thought we might offer it to Laura and her brother. They're living over a garage in Centerville, and I'm sure they'd be much more comfortable here. And of course that way they can work longer hours if we need them." He put his hand on Laura's shoulder, giving a brief smile to her stunned look. "Of course she may prefer living apart from us, or she may want to pay rent instead of having free lodging, but we might ask Leni if she has other plans for it, don't you think?"

"A lovely idea," said Barbara serenely. "Leni and I have talked about doing something with that cottage. We could let Rosa's assistant have it every summer, whoever she is. I see no reason why Laura and her brother—Clay, isn't it?—I've seen him in the orchard and he has a wonderful way with the orchids in the greenhouse, have you noticed?— yes, it would be far more comfortable for the two of them if they lived here. Laura, I'm so pleased we met; do consider the cottage. I know how much young people treasure their independence, but you might enjoy it here as much as we do."

She walked with them to the door as Thomas nodded a farewell. Laura heard him say to Paul, "What about Emily?"

"I'm driving her to New York," Paul answered and then the door closed and Laura heard no more. *Emily. New York. I'll bet she's beautiful and rich and very clever.* But it was a fleeting thought as she and Owen walked back across the compound; she was still dazed by Owen's offer.

"Did you mean it?" she asked when they reached the kitchen door.

"I never make an offer I don't mean," he replied. "I told you, I like your spirit. When a family lives behind high fences it needs new people, my dear, and it pleases me to make sure we find them. Call it an old man's whim; a strong desire to shake up my family at frequent intervals. And I think you could use some shaking up, too. You might even let Allison talk to you about cutting your hair."

Laura felt herself grow hot again. "You don't like it."

"Not especially," he said frankly. "I could be wrong—I'm getting old, after all—but I once was considered an expert on women's beauty, and when Allison mentioned it, I knew I still had my eye. But don't worry about it; you don't have to do anything you don't want to do. Take what you want from us; we'll have a good summer and perhaps the beginning of a real friendship. Can we agree on that?"

This time Laura didn't hesitate; she flung her arms around his shoulders and kissed his cheek, soft and lined beneath her firm lips. "Thank you for making me feel like a nice person." He held her, and then she ran into the kitchen. "I'm sorry, Rosa, everyone talked and the time passed—"

"That is the story of this family," Rosa said. "Lots of talk, not enough time. By the way, your brother was here; he asked if you'd stop by the greenhouse as soon as you can. Better do it now, before we start stuffing the ducks."

Clay had never done that before. Something was wrong. Laura dashed across the flagstone path to the other end of the estate and found Clay in one of the greenhouses. They could see the head gardener through the doorway. "Listen to this," Clay said as Laura came close to him. "Ben called at noon: he says he can't wait any longer. We've got to set up our alibi; he's set the job for Sunday. A week after that we can wave good-bye to this place and take ourselves off. And we'll be through with the Salingers for good."

CHAPTER 4

BEN picked them up a few blocks from the Salinger compound, and they drove to Falmouth for dinner, blending into the crowds of tourists along the waterfront as they made their way to a table at the edge of the dock outside the Clam Shack. Ben turned the chairs to face the fishing boats in the harbor, their backs to the restaurant. "I like to watch the people," Laura protested. "No one knows us here; nobody even cares who we are."

"We can't be sure of that." Ben sat down and waited until she did the same. "How many times have I told you never to take anything for granted? Maybe next week, after we've pulled this off and the police are looking around, someone will remember the three of us. These are small towns; people who work in them know each other."

"Then why are we here?" Clay demanded. "I told you we should stay on the beach or somewhere private."

"I wanted to buy you a dinner." Sitting between them, Ben put his arms around their shoulders. "It's been almost two months that I haven't been able to take care of you. You're here and I'm in New York and there's nothing I can do for you." He sat back as a waiter approached. "I've missed you. Too damned quiet around the apartment."

Laura swallowed hard against the love and guilt that welled up inside her, and she looked away while Ben ordered for the three of them. He'd been missing her, but the truth was, she'd hardly missed him at all, after her first week with the Salingers. She'd been too busy envying the way they lived and thinking about college and how to make a life for herself even farther from Ben than she was that summer.

She heard him ordering the dishes she and Clay liked best, and she loved him with a kind of helplessness that made her want to cry. He was so good to them and she'd always been able to count on him; how could she turn her back on him and walk away?

"I've worked out the rest of the plan," Clay said to Ben as soon as the waiter left. His voice was low but Laura heard his excitement; he'd done what Ben wanted and now Ben would be proud of him. "It's simple and it's neat. The kind you like."

Ben looked at Laura. "Do you like it?"

"It's Clay's plan," Laura said evasively. "I couldn't do much; Rosa's very strict."

"But a sweetie," Clay said pointedly. "You spend an awful lot of time with her."

"I work for her," Laura retorted. "And I don't have the run of the place the way you do."

"You have the run of Owen's little pad," Clay said blandly.

"Owen?" Ben asked. "Owen Salinger?"

"I've done some work for him. That's all. Why are we talking about things that aren't important?"

Ben gave her a long look. The waiter returned with oversize paper cups filled with steaming clam chowder; overhead, a gull swooped past; at the tables behind them people laughed and chattered, isolating them in a small island of silence.

"All right," Ben said at last. "We'll talk about that later. Let's hear your plan, Clay. Laura did find out about the jewels, and you've been the best partner I could want; I have you to thank for these." He took two keys from his pocket and put them on the table.

"You got them made," Clay said, flushing with pleasure. "I wasn't sure I did the wax impressions right; I was in a hurry. Leni was on the yacht but I didn't know for how long, and it took me a while to find the keys in her dresser drawer." He picked up one of them. "I think this turns off the alarm and the other one unlocks the closet."

Ben glanced at Laura, but she was gazing at the fishing boats, her chin in her hand. He sighed. "Let's go through it," he said to Clay.

They bent over a small diagram, and Laura turned to look at their blond heads, so close they were almost touching. They looked so much alike and yet they were so different: Ben handsome and sophisticated at twenty-six, the cleverest man she knew; Clay, nine years younger, still unsure of himself, almost as handsome but without Ben's smoothness.

From their mother both of them got blond hair, a rounded chin, and heavy-lidded blue eyes, but Ben inherited from Judd Gardner, his father, a devil-may-care look, while Clay inherited from Alan Fairchild the cautious look of someone worried about all the obstacles life could throw in his way. Laura admired Ben; she felt protective toward Clay; she loved them both and knew she wasn't like either of them.

"We'll be on Felix's yacht," Clay was saying. "There's a big deal with some politicians he wants to impress, so he and Leni are giving a dinner on the boat on Sunday night. The whole family will be there, and a few of us volunteered to help out."

"So you're safe," Ben said. "Nobody can accuse you of robbing a house if you're on a boat in the middle of Nantucket Sound."

Clay nodded. "But before we go out, I'll fix the alarm. I did what you told me and bought a timer, and I found the alarm system in the basement, and I'll hook up the timer the way you said, so it goes off at one in the morning. You break in at midnight when the party is going strong; you've got my diagram of where you climb the fence, and the path to the house, and then the drainpipe to the second-floor hall window. Leni's room is to the right, at the end of the hall. You jimmy the window open, turn off the alarm with that key, and break the lock on the closet door, or use the key and break it afterwards to make it look like an outside job, whatever's fastest. Take the jewels and anything else you find, open all the other closets and dresser drawers so it'll look like you had to search around, and use a rope to rappel down the outside of the house."

Ben was smiling. "And leave the rope behind."

"Right. And tire tracks too, if you can, on the road outside the fence. Then, at one o'clock, the alarm goes off, the guard calls the police and they find all the evidence of a break-in, while Laura and I are with the hired help on the yacht."

"What about the timer on the alarm?"

"I'll get to it as soon as we come in. I figure the guard will call the police first, and then the yacht, and we'll get back in about an hour, while the police are still checking the house and the grounds. They won't have any reason to check the alarm; as far as they know, it worked fine. I can have the timer off in less than a minute."

"Without anyone seeing you?"

"Everybody'll be busy with the police, and nobody uses the back stairs until Rosa comes in to start breakfast around six."

Ben nodded again. "I like it. Good job, Clay."

Clay beamed. "I thought you'd like it. It's foolproof."

"No plan is foolproof! I've told you that. The minute you think it is, you've begun to make it fail."

"Sorry," Clay mumbled.

"But it's good," Ben said. "Damned good. I'm proud of you. Laura? Don't you think Clay deserves some praise?"

"Sure." Laura drew on the table with the moisture that had beaded on her glass of iced tea. "Clay's very creative. He worked hard and he wanted you to be pleased."

"But," Ben said flatly. "What's the rest of it, Laura?"

"I don't want to do it," she said in a rush. "Please, Ben, can't we change our plans and not do it?"

"Not do it?" Clay echoed incredulously. "After we went to all the trouble of getting jobs with them, and I worked out this neat plan? *Not do it?*"

Ben was watching Laura closely. "Pretty sudden change of heart."

She shook her head. "I've thought about it a lot."

"It's Owen," Clay said abruptly. "Ever since you started mooning around after him you've been different about all of them. Like you're choosing them over us. Like you like them better than us."

Vehemently, Laura shook her head. "I'm not choosing them. I'm not choosing nobody—anybody."

"Not your brothers?" Ben said softly. "You're not choosing your brothers?"

"I didn't mean . . . oh, damn it, Ben, you know what I mean. I don't want a contest; I just want to skip this one job. We've done so many and we can do another one—somewhere—I'll keep my promise; it's just that I don't . . ."

"Want to rob the Salingers," Ben finished when her voice trailed off. "Why not?"

"Because they trust us and they've been nice to us, and—"

"That's a stupid reason," Clay cut in, but Laura rushed on.

"—and we *know* them. It's not like other times when we'd break into a place and never meet anyone or even know their names . . . I mean, if I saw pictures on a desk or dresser, I'd wonder what they were like and how they'd feel when they came home and found their things missing, but I never *knew* them, and I do know Allison and Leni and Owen . . ."

"So we know them," said Clay. "So what? What have they ever done for us? We work our asses off to earn a few lousy bucks a week, and we're always working overtime—"

"You wanted overtime," Laura flung at him, "so you could check the guards' schedules."

Clay shrugged. Ben looked at her through narrowed eyes. "They can afford to lose a few jewels; their insurance will pay for them anyway. So maybe the real problem is you're afraid they'll suspect something after you leave and not like you anymore. Right? But you'll be gone, so what's the difference? Anyway, why should you care whether they like you or not? You're better off if they don't; they're a rotten bunch of crooks. They take care of themselves and fuck everybody else and wouldn't let anybody who's not a royal Salinger have even a little piece of what they've got—"

"That's a lie!" Laura cried, striking the table with her fist. "They're not like that! They're just the opposite—they've been good to me, and Clay, too—they're going to let us live in one of their cottages, and Owen is loaning me money for college and—"

"What?" Clay shouted. "Live where?"

"Wait a minute." Ben's face was frozen. "Keep your voice down, Clay. Felix Salinger offered to let you live in the compound and send you to college?"

"Not really," Laura conceded. "Owen thought of the cottage, and everybody goes along with him, and he was the one who talked about college—"

"Felix won't agree," Ben said.

"Why not?" Laura asked hotly. "I mean, he's not as friendly as the others—well, Asa isn't either, I guess—but if the others want to help us, why wouldn't Felix go along? Is there some reason he wouldn't?" She stared at him. "You know something about him that you're not telling!"

Ben looked at his hands as they gripped his mug of beer; the knuckles were white. "Amazing," he murmured. "The Salingers, of all people."

"Why not the Salingers?" Laura demanded.

"It's a wonderful chance for you," he said slowly, as if she had not spoken. "I couldn't have swung college for you, at least not this year. And you'd have a place to live for the whole summer, and save your money..." He stared at his hands, then shook his head heavily. "I can't do it, Laura; I can't give up this job. Maybe someday I'll tell you why, but right now you'll just have to trust me. You could stay with them after I do it, but I think they'd find you out. Damn it, Laura, I'm the one who cares about you, not them, and I'm asking you to help me. I've been thinking about this job a long time, and I can't throw away the chance now that I'm so close."

"How long? How long have you been thinking about it?"

"Longer than you can imagine. Years. Why can't you just go along and not ask questions? I'd do the same for you. If you told me you had to do something and I had it in my power to help you, I'd do it, no questions asked."

"I have to like myself," Laura said coldly. "I want to go to college and be respectable, and not sit with my back to a restaurant because I'm afraid somebody will notice me."

Ben winced. Clay scowled at Laura. "You never mentioned living with them or getting money for college."

"You were too excited about robbing them. I wanted to see what Ben said."

"You wanted to pull this out from under me." Clay's voice rose. "My whole plan. You wanted to talk Ben into killing it, and you didn't even tell me."

"What would you have said if I did tell you?"

"What Ben said. We have to do it."

"So what difference does it make that I didn't tell you?"

"I had a right to know what you were going to do! We're in this together!"

"You're in it alone! I told you, I don't want to do it!"

"Stop squabbling," Ben ordered, "and keep your voices down. Laura, I'll do everything I can to help you, *but I've got to do this, first.* Can't you understand? It's like getting something off my chest. Once I've done it, I can concentrate on other things, like getting you to college."

Slowly, Laura shook her head. "I don't want you to keep stealing to give me money for college. That's what you'd do, isn't it? You've always stolen and you like the excitement, so you wouldn't even try something else."

"What, for instance?"

"Like a better job, for instance! Aren't you ever going to think about that? Or about what happens to Clay?"

"What about me?" Clay demanded.

"He thinks you're wonderful," she said to Ben. "But what's so wonderful about a guy who spends his whole life being a waiter part of the time and breaking into places the other part? And feeling scared every time there's a policeman around? Why don't you quit all that and get a better job? You'd probably have to work harder; so big deal! Don't you give a shit—don't you care what happens to us? You think we like the way we live?"

"I like it fine!" said Clay hoarsely. Everything was happening too fast; the conversation was getting out of hand. "It's fine; why don't you just shut up!"

"I can't get a better job," Ben said to Laura. "I never went to college; I haven't any skills—"

"How do you know? You're the smartest person I ever met; how do you know what you could do if you tried? You could be an executive! Or something like that. But you won't even try! Well, the hell with it. I don't care what you do; I'm talking about me, and *I don't want to steal anymore!* It's not exciting or fun like it used to be . . . and I'd go to jail if I got caught again—it would be a second offense—and I won't take the chance. I don't want to live on your stealing, either; that's almost as bad as doing it myself. And I don't want to rob the Salingers! I'm asking you, Ben, please, *please*, don't rob them. I like them; they make me feel nice, and I want to stay with them as long as I can."

She saw the hurt and anger in Ben's eyes and she felt she was being torn apart. "Don't be unhappy, Ben, please, I love you and you've been wonderful to us, but I've got a chance to change things, to change *me*, and maybe I'll never have it again! Owen asked me to write to him and visit him when I'm in college—he's my friend!—and I don't want to risk losing him, losing all of them . . . *I don't want them hurt!*"

They were silent, looking away from each other, and the talk and laughter behind them seemed louder and happier than before. The waiter brought coffee and Ben drank his black, hot and steaming. Laura, who had decided she should drink it because Allison did, poured in cream and sugar and then sipped it, telling herself it tasted good. Clay, watching Ben, drank his black, making faces as it scalded his tongue.

"I'll think about it," Ben said at last.

"No, Ben, tell us now," Laura pleaded. "Say you won't do it. Say you'll think up another job, and we'll come to New York and help you do it—we can come on a weekend and then come back—"

"I didn't say I was staying!" Clay exclaimed.

"I want you to stay with me. That way you'll finish high school and maybe think about college instead of—" She bit back her words.

"Instead of being like me," Ben said flatly.

"I want to be like Ben!" Clay stormed. "There's nothing wrong with that. You wanted it, too, once. And if you'd shut up about Owen and his rich bitch family, we could get going on my plan and then get out of here and go back to New York where we belong!"

Laura bit her lip. "I don't want to go back to New York; I want to move into the cottage. Ben, we'll visit you, we'll still be a family, and I'm sorry if you'll be lonely but I want this so much . . ." She took his hand. "Ben, *please*."

He shoved back his chair, pulling his hand away. "I told you I'd think about it. That's the best I can do. It's more than I want to do." He stood and took out his wallet. "I'll drive you to Centerville, then I'm going back to New York. I'll call in a few days." His lips were tight. "Listen to me, Laura. I'm still your guardian; when I decide, you'll do what you're told."

"Damn right," Clay muttered. He and Laura walked to the car while Ben paid the waiter. "Ben wanted a reunion and a nice time, and you ruined it."

"You don't care about Ben. You just don't want to give up your plan."

"What's wrong with that? What good's a plan you can't *do?*"

Ben joined them and they drove to Centerville in silence. All around them were cars filled with people on vacation; the sidewalks were kaleidoscopes of people all looking happy. Laura watched them and wanted to cry.

She kept wanting to cry all week, waiting for Ben to call, but she couldn't cry in front of Rosa, and she refused to cry in front of Clay, so she held it in. It was easier because they were so busy; Felix and Leni had houseguests, which meant fifteen or more people at every meal, and Rosa had already begun preparations for the Sunday night dinner dance on the yacht. As the weekend approached, she grew more frenzied, her fingers a blur as they flew from mixers to mandolins, whisks to rolling pins, terrines to casseroles. Laura was mostly on her own, preparing breakfast and lunch for the large groups that seemed to materialize in the dining room or on the porch for another meal before she had even finished cleaning up from the last one. As she cooked, Rosa would appear beside her now and then with a sharp criticism or brief suggestion or, best of all, a touch on the arm and word of praise that made Laura feel she loved Rosa and all the world.

But then she would see Rosa putting covered dishes in the two wall freezers, for the party on the yacht, and she would remember she could lose it all in a few days. She began to avoid everyone, talking to Rosa only about food, never anything personal; telling Allison she couldn't take tennis or swimming lessons; telling Owen she couldn't work in his library that week: there was too much to do in the kitchen.

Then, on Friday, two days before the party, Ben called. "I talked to Clay yesterday; he says you're not very friendly to him."

"I'm busy and tired," Laura said shortly. "And he keeps telling me I'm crazy to pass up a golden opportunity, and he won't listen to anything I say. I guess I don't feel very friendly."

"Well, I've been thinking about what you said." Ben let out a long breath. "We'll call it off, Laura."

"Ben—!"

"I still have to deal with Clay, but I can handle him. I guess what I can't handle is the chance that you'd hate me."

"Oh, Ben, I love you—thank you—I love you. Are you coming here soon? We'll have another dinner, we'll have a good time, better than last week, I promise. When can you come? I can get off early; we could even spend a day together. We haven't done that in so long . . ."

"How about Saturday? I have to be in Boston that night; I could come to the Cape in the morning and we'd have all day. Don't you have Saturday off anyway?"

"Oh. Yes, usually, but . . ." She debated thinking up a lie to tell Rosa, then decided she couldn't. "Not this week. There's so much still to do for the party on the boat Sunday, and the Janssens are having a hundred people for dinner Saturday night; they're putting a tent on the lawn. Any other Saturday . . ."

"We'll find a time." Laura heard the smile in his voice and thought how nice it was when Ben was happy and loving. "I'll call soon," he said cheerfully. "Maybe that busy family will let you go next Saturday."

After they hung up, Laura repeated his words to herself, wondering how much disappointment and anger he might have been hiding. She didn't have to wonder about Clay: his frustration and fury burst out and then he stopped talking to her completely. And late that night he went out and didn't come home.

Laura found him Saturday morning in the orchid greenhouse. "We still live together," she said angrily. "We have to get along. Clay, I was worried about you!" *And I hated being alone; the garage underneath me creaked and our apartment creaked and I thought of how I'd never once been alone all night and I was scared to death.* "Where did you spend the night?" she asked.

"With a couple of guys passing through. They let me sleep in their car."

"Which guys? Who?"

"I didn't ask. We fooled around for a while and had dinner at that place in Bass River."

"Which place?"

This time he looked sheepish. "I don't remember. I think I had a little too much to drink."

Laura gazed at him. "How much money did you lose?"

"Lose?"

" 'Fooling around.' When Ben says that, it means poker."

"Shit, Laura, I don't do everything Ben—"

"How much did you lose?"

He shrugged. "Not too much."

"How much?"

"A bill."

"You lost a hundred dollars?"

"You want me to lie?"

He needed taking care of. She knew that. She admired Ben, but she wanted to protect Clay. "Well, it's done; we won't think about it. We can't get it back. But from now on things are going to be different around here; we're going to have a real home and a chance to be somebody, and I won't have you ruining it by getting drunk and gambling and sleeping in cars—"

"You can't make me stay!" Clay shouted. "I'm going back to New York!"

"You're going to live with me!" Laura tried to sound stern and grown up but she was beginning to feel frightened. She needed Clay. Because as wonderful as the Salingers were, she didn't want to be all alone in the midst of their big family; she wanted somebody of her own to cling to. Then she saw the confusion in Clay's face. "How come you're still here? Ben isn't going to do the robbery, so why haven't you taken off for New York?"

"I'm going to," Clay mumbled. "Soon as I get around to it."

"When? What are you waiting for?"

He shrugged. "There's a lot of work to do for the party."

"And you love the Salingers so much you want to do it all." When Clay was silent, she turned away. "Well, then, don't tell me. I don't care. You can leave any time; it doesn't matter to me."

"I didn't want to run out on you," he said quickly.

Laura turned, her face bright. "Really? Oh, Clay, thank you. I was hoping you'd want to stay with me." She watched his face redden. "What is it?"

"Well, there was something else."

"What else was there?"

He mumbled something.

"What?"

"Allison asked me to do the table flowers; she's got these complicated ideas . . ."

"Allison?" In an instant Laura recalled a host of small incidents: Clay talking about Allison's favorite orchids, Clay mentioning that Leni and Allison had been in the greenhouse, Clay saying that Allison liked the cutting garden . . . She started to say something about Allison being a year older than Clay and looking for older men, but she held her tongue as Clay's face grew even redder. She felt like putting her arms around him and telling him everything would be fine. "Well, that's fine," she said, and added casually, "How long do you think you'll stay here?"

Clay gave her a grateful look. "I thought I might stay for the summer, but if you move into that cottage I don't know what I'll do."

"Move in with me," Laura said quickly. "There are two bedrooms."

"You think I'll change my mind and stay with you for good."

"Maybe." She grinned at him, feeling good again. Clay couldn't resist a real home once she'd made one, and then she'd be able to take care of him. And she wouldn't be alone.

"If I stay for the summer, you won't tell Allison what I said?"

"What do you think I am? Of course not. It's our secret."

It was the first nice secret she could remember between the two of them. Nothing would come of it because Allison was going to college in the fall and Clay still had a year of high school, but it kept him at the Cape and it made them friends. And when she saw him that afternoon in the garden with Allison, she thought he was even handsomer than she'd realized.

He and Allison were cutting flowers for the Janssens' party that night, and Laura caught glimpses of them while she worked in the kitchen with Rosa. Rosa was grumbling as she sifted flour into a huge bowl. "Why I always end up cooking for the Janssens when they're having a catered dinner is more than I can understand. There's the yacht party tomorrow night, which I have slaved over for two weeks; there's regular meals for all the houseguests—I might as well be cooking in a hotel—and I predict there will be a great demand for a substantial brunch on Monday, when everybody recovers from being on the yacht all night—"

"You love it," Laura said, "having Barbara Janssen ask for your special cake instead of trusting her own cook or the caterers."

Rosa chuckled. "You're getting cheeky, my young miss. A month ago you wouldn't have talked to fierce Rosa that way."

"You weren't ever fierce. I was just scared."

"And now you're not. For which we have Mr. Owen to thank."

"And you. I have you to thank, too."

They worked all day, talking quietly or not at all but comfortable with each other as they followed the timetable Rosa had made that morning. *I'm part of Rosa's kitchen, and that means I'm part of the household. I belong here.*

She belonged with all of them, she thought that night at the Janssens'. She was helping Rosa in a corner away from the caterer's staff, and through the open door she could see Clay and Allison, in a huge white tent across the lawn, arranging centerpieces on round tables draped in creamy linen. Clay wore dark pants and a white shirt and tie, Allison a long silk dress that was like a pastel flower garden, and the two of them talked companionably as they moved among the tables placing white lilies and ruby red ginger flowers in crystal bowls. The setting sun turned the sky to copper and pink, the air was cool and still, and everything seemed so perfect that Laura had to give someone a kiss, and Rosa was the closest, so she did. "My oh my," said Rosa, beaming. "We seem to be very big on affection tonight."

"Yes," Laura said simply, and when Owen stopped in briefly to say hello before everyone gathered for drinks, he saw a new look on her face. Calmer, he thought; no longer that skittish child on the beach. And something else; she looked more open, as if she finally believed she didn't have to hide her feelings after all.

He wondered who had done it for her: Allison through her offer of friendship, Rosa through her mothering—and perhaps I had something to do with it, he thought as he joined the party, by making her feel needed and letting her know I need her, too. He let his thoughts drift as the members of his family moved from one group of guests to another, meeting the political and entertainment celebrities Felix always brought to the Cape to enliven his summer. Ambitious, aggressive Felix, Owen reflected. He takes after me.

But in fact he knew Felix did not take after him at all. For the past few years, as he grew older and more detached from his family, he gradually had admitted to himself that his eldest son was pompous and humorless, a rigid man who thought he could impose his idea of order on the world around him. I wasn't like that, Owen thought; Iris would have let me know if I ever was as insufferable as Felix. Everyone would have let me know. And I still have many friends, so I must be a fairly pleasant fellow. I don't suppose Felix will ever be pleasant. What a shame; he's got such a lovely wife, too.

Once the thought would have made him smile at the tricks life played on people, but tonight he felt only sadness for Leni and regret that neither of his two sons was as attractive or likeable as his great-nephew Paul, who was standing nearby, looking politely bored as a senator expounded something at great length.

I don't feel well, Owen thought; that's probably why everything seems sad. I feel tired. In fact I feel rotten; I wonder if I'm coming down with something. Why the devil am I spending a whole evening with a bunch of people I don't care anything about? He made his way to Leni and said quietly, "My dear, do you think Barbara would mind if I leave as soon as we've had coffee?"

A look of worry shadowed her calm eyes. "Aren't you feeling well?"

"Just tired," he said. "And, I confess, a trifle sick of celebrities."

She smiled faintly. "Felix does collect them, doesn't he?"

"Well," Owen sighed, "I suppose he could have worse hobbies; it's expensive but not dangerous. And he worries too much about running the hotels; he does need something to help him relax."

"Wouldn't it be nice," Leni murmured, "if he came to his wife for that."

Owen turned his shrewd eyes on her. "Have you suggested it?"

"When was the last time Felix listened to something you suggested?"

"When he was five. But if you told him you're unhappy?"

"I'm not unhappy, dear Owen. Don't worry about me."

"You are unhappy. I can always tell."

"If I am, I'll take care of it. You have yourself to take care of. Shall I walk home with you? Or I can ask Clay; he's helping in the pantry and I'm sure they can spare him. I don't think you should be alone."

He shook his head. "If I can't make it across the compound I shouldn't be out without a wheelchair."

They smiled at each other, and when the guests had finished coffee and crepes and the waiters were serving cognac, Owen quietly left his chair and made his way from the tent. Through the open doorway of the house he caught a glimpse of Laura in the kitchen, and Rosa nearby, and the staff in the pantry, and then he walked slowly home.

There was no moon but he knew the way from memory and the feel of the flagstones beneath his feet. To the right here, to the left there, just past Leni's rose garden to the door of his house. He slipped inside, breathless and a little dizzy—probably ate too much, he thought; damn stupid thing to do when I already felt sick—and he was reaching for his armchair when he heard a door softly close somewhere in the main house.

One of the staff, he thought, and then remembered there was no one there; they were off for the evening or working at the party. The wind, then. But there was no wind; the night was still. Odd, he thought; Felix or Leni must have come back, too. Better see if everything's all right.

His door was ajar and he slipped through it into the gallery, where he stood motionless, listening. Nothing. Imagination, he told himself. A tired old man with not enough to think about. But then he heard the whisper of careful, stealthy footsteps in the upper hall. They came from the direction of Leni's room. A moment later Owen heard them on the stairway directly in front of him.

"Ho, there!" he called and flicked on the light switch. As he closed his eyes against the chandelier's sudden blaze, he heard a curse and a rush of footsteps, and felt rather than saw the dark form that flung itself upon him. "Damn!" he cried. "Get off me—!" But it came out as a strangled croak; he was face down on the floor, struggling to push himself up beneath the weight on his back. Then a terrible pain burned through his chest, like stabbing flames. *I'm going to die*, he thought and, in the midst of a dizzying terror, fell headlong into darkness.

CHAPTER 5

"HOW could you?" Laura cried. The telephone was wet with her tears and it kept slipping in her hand as she sat hunched over in the cramped booth, wiping her nose with a wadded tissue. Through the glass door she saw lunchtime customers filling the restaurant and she turned her back on them, leaning her elbow on the small shelf beneath the telephone. "You promised you wouldn't! You told me—you told Clay—*you said you wouldn't do it!*"

"I didn't do anything! Laura, goddam it, if you'd listen for a fucking minute—"

"I listened once and you lied to me!"

"I didn't lie! I told you I wouldn't rob them—"

"And I believed you! I trusted you! And you went ahead and did it anyway! It didn't matter what I wanted, you didn't *care* what I wanted, all you cared about was your damned robbery, and Owen had a heart attack and he's in the hospital, and everybody's crazy with worry—"

"*Shut up and listen!* I didn't rob the fucking Salingers. I've been in New York since I was with you at the Cape; I was with a friend last night—"

"It wasn't last night; it was three nights ago."

"I was with a friend three nights ago, too. Why didn't you call when it happened?"

"I did; I've been calling you for three days! You haven't been there—

where have you been?—never mind, I know where. You've been selling the jewels you stole . . . after you promised—!"

"I kept my promise! Look, damn it, I don't work that way; I wouldn't jump a guy just because he turned on the light—"

"How do you know he turned on the light?"

There was a pause. "You told me."

"I did not. I just said he had a heart attack and he's in the hospital. I never said anything about a light."

"Well, so I figured it out. There wouldn't be any other reason to jump him, would there? But that's not my style, and you know it. I stay away from people and get out, clean; I don't get into wrestling matches that make a mess of—"

"That's what you did. You made a terrible mess of everything and the police are everywhere and I'm scared to death. It feels like everything I've got in the whole world is falling apart."

"You've got me. I'm not falling apart."

"I haven't got you! I don't trust you; I'll never trust you again!"

"I didn't do it! Damn it, I told you—"

"All right, then, if you didn't, who did? How come somebody just happened to rob the house the same way you and Clay planned it, practically on the same night you planned it?"

"I don't know who did it. Have you asked Clay?"

The blood rushed to Laura's head. "He was with me all night! Anyway, he doesn't do jobs alone and he doesn't lie! Don't you ever, ever say anything against Clay again—how could you—"

"All right, all right, I'm sorry. All I meant was you should talk to him."

"You were accusing him! Throwing blame on a . . . *kid* . . . because you don't have any excuses!"

"I don't need excuses! Listen, I've taken care of you for three years; you can't believe I'd—"

"You won't take care of me anymore! I won't let you!"

"You haven't got any choice; I'm your guardian and you'll do what I tell you. And I'm telling you to come back to New York. That's an order, Laura! You're coming back to me, where you belong!"

"I'm never coming back to you!" Laura felt once again that she was being torn in half. She hunched lower, holding herself tight to keep her voice from shaking. "I'm staying here. I'm going to make up to them—somehow—for what you did."

"*I didn't do a goddam*—!"

"And Clay's staying with me. I'm not letting him go back to a thief . . . and a . . . liar . . ." Tears choked her and she wiped her nose on the back of her hand. "We're not coming back to you, and that's all."

"I'm coming up to get you. I'll be there this afternoon. I expect you to be packed and ready."

"I'll be at work. I have a job. *And a family*," she added cuttingly.

"What the hell is that supposed to mean?"

"I have the Salingers."

"You're crazy. You really think you 'have' the Salingers? You're out of your mind. The Salingers don't give a shit about you or Clay; you aren't their kind of people. You *work* for them, for Christ's sake, and if you think they care about servants, or play fair with them, you're more stupid than I thought."

"Then I'm stupid, and you wouldn't want a stupid person in your family, would you, Ben? So you don't care whether I stay here or not."

There was a small pause, the space of a heartbeat. "I do care. I'm sorry I said that. I know you're not stupid; you're wonderful and I miss you. You're my family, Laura."

"Not anymore," she said defiantly.

"God damn son of a bitch!" Laura heard his fist strike the table. She knew where he was; she could picture him sitting in the kitchen, on a chair she had painted red to make the room more cheerful, making marks with his thumbnail in the linoleum that covered the table. "One last time," he said. "I didn't do it and I expect you to come back. We'll forget we said all these—"

"You're lying. You told me you'd be in Boston on Saturday; you wanted to spend the day with us. And I told you we'd be working at the Janssens' party, so you knew the house would be empty." She shook her head. "I never should have told you. If I hadn't, you wouldn't have robbed them. I'm going, Ben; I told Rosa I'd only be gone half an hour for lunch."

"You stay right there and listen! I'll be at the Cape this afternoon, and if you and Clay aren't packed you'll leave everything behind, because I'm taking you out of there! We'll go to Europe. You'd like that, wouldn't you, Laura? We've talked about doing it for a long time and I've already got tickets—"

"*You've got the tickets?* You knew you were going to rob them—you were all ready to get out of the country—you only pretended to be thinking it over!"

"I bought them when I thought I'd do the job; I just didn't get around to returning them. Listen to me, Laura: we've got all these tickets and reservations; everything's settled. We'll take a month, before school starts, and travel all over. . . . Are you listening?" She was silent. "You're coming home with me!" Ben roared. "I've had enough of your—"

Laura slammed down the telephone, cutting off his furious voice. Her hand was shaking. Ben always had been able to dominate her, and now she felt herself wanting to call him back to beg his forgiveness so he would be loving toward her again. Instead, she ran from the booth, snatching a handful of paper napkins from an empty table and ignoring the curious looks from the lunchtime crowd as she wiped the tears from her face.

Clay was waiting in a small park nearby. "Ben's going away," she said.

He sprang to his feet. "Where's he going? Why did he do the robbery? After he promised . . ."

"He didn't say." Laura wheeled her bicycle onto the path. "He even tried to deny he did it."

Clay waited for more. "And?"

"He expected us to go back to New York with him."

"Well, we are, aren't we? Everything's changed. Where's he going?"

"Europe. He says."

"And we're meeting him? When? Where?" He waited. "Laura, when are we going to Europe?"

"We're staying here." She got on her bicycle. "I haven't figured it out yet, but that's what we're doing."

Clay let out a yell and caught up with her on his bicycle, and they argued all the way to the Salingers'. At the shed where they kept their bikes, Laura put her hand on his arm. "It's just the two of us now; we'll take care of each other and we'll be just fine."

Clay ignored her hand. "Where *exactly* is Ben going?"

She shrugged. "All he said was Europe."

"I'm going with him."

"No you're not." She thought of telling him Ben had tried to blame him for the theft, but she couldn't. Let him think some good things about the stepbrother he'd idolized for so long. "You're going to stay with me and finish high school and learn something useful. After that you can go anywhere you please. Clay, I need you," she said, her assurance crumbling. "I can't count on anybody else; please stay and help me. Just for . . . for a year, that's all, one year, till I get used to being on my own, and then if you really want to go away I won't say anything. I'll even help you."

Clay studied his shoes, his blond eyebrows drawn together. "What did you mean about staying here? You mean on the Cape?"

"With the Salingers. I hope, anyway. We still work for them, we're earning money, and most of them like us. And if we work hard enough we can make up a little bit for what Ben did."

"It's not our fault he robbed them."

"Yes it is. You figured out the way to do it and I found out where the jewels were and about the alarm, and I told him we'd all be somewhere else that night. It's because of us that Owen may die. Clay, we *owe* them something."

Still staring at his shoes, Clay said, "What happens in September, when they go back to Boston?"

"I don't know. Maybe we can keep working for them."

"In *Boston?*"

"Maybe."

"We don't know the first thing about Boston."

"We could learn. There are plenty of high schools there, and colleges."

Clay gave her a long look. "You really like them."

"Well, you like Allison," she said defensively.

"Yeh, but I'm not changing my whole life because of it. Anyway, she thinks I'm just a gardener." He hoisted their bicycles and hung them on hooks in the shed. "If you really want me to, I guess I'll stick around for a while. It might not be so great living with Ben without you around. And maybe I'll do school for another year. I won't promise I'll finish, but I guess I could try. Shit, I thought I was through with that crap, those fucking little desks and being ordered around by people who don't know shit about real life . . . I'll just try, that's all. I'll probably flunk."

"You won't. You're too smart." Laura put her arms around him and kissed him. "I love you, and I'm so glad you're staying. Everything's going to be fine." She kissed him again. "I have to go; I'm awfully late. I'll see you after work."

But late that afternoon Owen began asking for Laura, and Leni sent her to the hospital in one of the family limousines. Laura had not seen him since his heart attack, and as she tiptoed into his room behind the nurse, she expected to see a dying man. Instead, he looked no different from before, except that he was lying flat in the narrow bed and his eyes were closed.

"Mr. Salinger," the nurse said softly, "Laura is here."

His eyes opened. "Ah. My dear." He motioned slightly to the nurse. "You can go."

"I'll be right outside," she said and kept the door open when she left.

Owen winked at Laura and gave a small grin. "She's an ogre. Now you can kiss me."

She bent down and kissed his forehead. It was cool, almost cold. "Does anything hurt?"

"My pride. Old man jumped by a burglar. No respect for age. Rotten coward."

"He wouldn't have done it if he'd known— I mean, I can't believe anyone would hurt you if . . . if he knew you were a lot older than he is."

Owen squinted slightly as he studied her. "Maybe he's eighty. Thought I was a youngster."

Laura gave a small laugh. She was knotted up inside, angry at Ben but defending him, loving Owen but angry at his calling Ben a coward. *But Ben was a coward—I shouldn't defend him—and it's wonderful that Owen is making jokes because that means he's going to get well; he won't die because of us.* "You're going to get well," she said.

"I expect to. Sit down; I can't see you this way."

She pulled a chair close to him and leaned over, her elbow on the bed, her chin on her hand. "The nurse said I could only stay a few minutes."

He shook his head. "I want you to stay." He opened his palm and waited until Laura put her hand in his. "I have plans."

He had no strength to grip her hand, but Laura felt the warmth of his palm against hers and she twined her strong fingers through his. "What kind of plans?"

"For you. I want you to come to Boston and live at my house and help me. Would you mind?"

A wave of excitement surged through Laura, and then just as quickly began to fade. *The Salingers don't give a shit about you or Clay; you aren't their kind of people.* "I'm not a nurse. I don't know anything about—"

Owen was shaking his head. "Not a nurse, a companion. A job. Talk to me, read to me, help with my library. It's even bigger than here. And messier." He squinted again, watching her. "And you could go to college."

Her breath came out in a long sigh.

"I thought you'd like that," Owen fretted.

"I do. It's everything I want. I'd love it. But . . . I have Clay with me."

"Clay." He paused, his breathing quick and shallow. "Leni likes Clay; she'll find something for him. But you're what I want. Tough and hurting. Like I was once." A small chuckle came through his lips. "Like I still am sometimes. You'll do it?"

"Yes. Oh, yes. Thank you, I can't tell you . . . thank you."

His breathing slowed, barely stirring his mustache. He smiled at Laura, too weak for the grin he had given earlier. "Read to me now." He tilted his head slightly toward the windowsill, where Laura saw, amid a small jungle of flowers and green plants, his favorite collection of short stories. She brought it to the bedside. "What would you like?"

"Something funny. With a happy ending."

She leaned over him and kissed him, holding her lips against his bristly cheek for a long moment. "I'll take care of you and you'll get well and strong. I promise. I love you."

Slowly, Owen raised his hand and rested it on her head. "Dear Laura. Lay here thinking—can't die yet; too many things to do. And Laura will help me." His eyes closed and his hand slipped back to the bed. "Read. I might sleep. You don't mind?"

Laura smiled, blinking back hot tears. "I don't mind."

"You'll be here, though. When I wake up."

"I'll always be here, as long as you want me." She bent her head and a tear splashed on the book in her lap. Carefully she wiped it away with her fingertip. "Thank you for caring about me," she whispered. And then she leafed through the book, looking for a happy ending.

Part II

CHAPTER 6

A T eight in the morning the other courts were empty and the only sound in the huge, high-ceilinged room was the hollow bounce of the tennis ball in the long, steady volleys Laura and Allison played before one or the other scored a point. "Damn!" Allison exclaimed as her shot landed outside the baseline. "What was I thinking of when I taught to play this game?"

"You were thinking you'd improve me," said Laura. "And you did."

They played in concentrated silence, well matched, both of them hard, fast players; but it was Allison who finally scored the winning point by making a cross-court drop shot beyond Laura's reach. "Haven't lost it all," she said breathlessly, touching Laura's arm affectionately as they changed sides. "But I will if I don't watch it. I can't believe you never played until three years ago; are you sure that wasn't a put-on?"

"You know it wasn't; I never held a racket until you taught me. It's because I love it. Don't you always learn faster when you love something?"

"Probably. But you're a natural athlete, you know. I never saw anyone move the way you do, like a cat."

A shadow seemed to touch Laura's face, then it was gone. "I learned it all from you," she said smoothly. "One more game?"

Allison nodded and served, and from above, in the glass-walled restaurant overlooking the courts, Paul Janssen watched the fast play, admiring his cousin Allison but drawn again and again to watch Laura Fairchild, whom he hadn't seen in almost a year. That had been the summer before, when he'd come home for a week after traveling through the West with friends. It had been obvious then that she'd become a part of his family, but he had given her no more than passing attention. He remembered noticing that she was growing up: no longer the brusque, uncomfortable girl he'd met at the Cape, or the elusive one who kept to herself when she arrived in Boston, spending her time with Owen, or at Rosa's side in the kitchen, or at the university. But she was still rough-edged then; pretty, but self-conscious and withdrawn, with none of the beauty and confidence Paul Janssen required before he was attracted to a woman.

He was twenty-eight years old, and experts had told him he had a brilliant eye and a future as a great photographer if he concentrated on it. But he'd never stayed in any one place long enough to concentrate on anything or anyone. "You're young," his mother said. "You'll settle down when you're ready." "You'll regret these years," his great-uncle Owen said. "They could be your most creative ones, and you're frittering them away." But his aunt Leni told him not to hurry: "It's better to go slowly and make no mistakes." His father said only, "You'll find your own way," frustrating Paul, who occasionally still looked to him for advice. And his uncle Felix snorted contemptuously, "He's spoiled"; and Paul, though he had no fondness for his cold, rigid uncle, in this case had to admit that Felix was probably right: he was spoiled by wealth. Earning money wasn't urgent, and so it was easier to drift, dabbling in photography and other agreeable pastimes and avoiding commitments, whether to a job or a woman or even to a particular country, as he wandered from one playground for the wealthy to another.

The trouble with that, and the reason he had come back to Boston, was that he was finding it harder to get absorbed in anything: after a while, casinos and clubs and chic restaurants all began to look alike. He was bored; he needed to figure out what to do next. Now, watching Laura, he felt his interest stir. He wondered at the change that had occurred in her, giving her poise and grace and a distinctive quality for which beautiful was too weak a word. Striking, he thought, and not easy to categorize. His artist's eye studied her slender face: her broad forehead and enormous long-lashed eyes, her high cheekbones with delicate shadows beneath, and her wide, expressive mouth, free of makeup, lips parted in the excitement of the game. Her thick chestnut hair was no longer tied back, though she had restrained it, for tennis, with a band around her forehead; still, the loose waves fell below her shoulders, and damp tendrils escaped the band, framing her flushed face, making it seem smaller and somehow vulnerable.

Yet there was toughness in the determined lift of her head, her powerful serve, and the muscles of her strong, lithe body uncoiling with explosive energy as she sprang across the court. Tough but delicate, Paul thought. Sultry but innocent—or, rather, untested; there was experience in that lovely face, though it was impossible to tell what kind without knowing her. His family told him she was cool but loving, private but grateful for affection, hot-tempered but quick to laugh. And watching her race across the court to scoop up and return a low-bouncing ball, he saw she was graceful but fiercely bent on winning. Of all the beautiful women waiting to hear from him in Europe and America, none, at the moment, intrigued him with so many contradictions.

He watched as Allison gained the advantage. Laura was pressing to tie the score when she returned a serve into the net. "Fuck it," she said, then swiftly looked on all sides to see if anyone was close enough to hear. Paul, reading her lips, laughed aloud. A gamine, he thought, and also very much a woman. He opened a nearby door and stepped out onto a balcony just above the court.

"Paul!" Allison called as the movement caught her eye. "When did you get here? Doesn't Laura play wonderfully? Would you like a game?"

He shook his head, trying to catch Laura's eye, but she had turned away and was putting a towel over her shoulders.

"Then come to a party," Allison said. "Tonight. Laura, do you mind if I invite Paul to your party?"

Laura said something Paul could not hear.

"Well, I know it's my party," Allison said, "but you're giving it." She looked up at Paul. "Laura's throwing a gala in honor of my engagement to the most eminent Thad Wolcott the Third. I didn't know you'd be in town, so I didn't invite you. But you will come, won't you?"

Paul looked at Laura until, as if forced by his steady gaze, she raised her eyes and met his. They looked at each other across the space between them. "Yes," Paul said to Laura. "I'd like very much to be there."

* * *

The guests arrived at seven, taking the small mahogany-paneled elevator to Laura's fourth-floor apartment in Owen's Beacon Hill town house. The windows were open to the soft June night, and the sounds of the party reached the quiet orderliness of Mount Vernon Street as old and new acquaintances mingled in small shifting clusters like jeweled fragments in a turning kaleidoscope. Piano music came from the stereo;

Rosa's nephew Albert tended bar; her other nephew, Ferdy, took silver trays of hors d'oeuvres from the dumbwaiter on which Rosa sent them up from the kitchen, and carried them around to the guests. "The place looks terrific," Thad Wolcott said to Laura, his arm carelessly around her shoulder as he surveyed the living room. "You've transformed it."

"With Allison's help," Laura said, but her eyes were bright with pleasure in what she had done. For months she had worked on the three-room apartment to make it as softly glowing as a garden at sunrise. Oil and watercolor paintings by Nantucket artists hung on the walls; antique fire irons, restored with hours of rubbing, stood by the fireplace; and silk shantung drapes framed the high windows. Once she had longed for a room of her own; now she had three, more beautiful than any she had ever dreamed of, and she had made them truly hers.

"I made a few suggestions," Allison said. "The rest Laura did by herself. Who'd ever guess my father and his brother grew up here? It was as dark as a bat's cave, with the walls covered with cork so they'd never run out of bulletin board. I love it now; don't you think she has an artist's eye?"

"She has something special," said Thad appraisingly. "She's kept you friendly for three years, and you usually get bored with people long before that."

As Allison's color rose, Laura said coolly, "Maybe we like each other. And Allison is much more than friendly; she's generous. You didn't admire my dress, Thad."

He stepped back and gazed at her. "By Carolina Herrera, from Martha at Trump Tower, worn, to great applause, by Miss Allison Salinger at last year's Thanksgiving Ball."

"Thad never forgets a dress," Allison commented drily.

"And Laura Fairchild looks fabulous in midnight blue satin." He kissed Laura's hand. "It's your color; you should wear nothing else. Though"—he was still holding her hand—"as I recall, you also look terrific in red. And emerald. And of course white. And—"

"He never misses a chance to hold a lady's hand, either," Allison said.

Laura pulled away, trying to think of a simple, sophisticated quip. As hard as she worked at it, she still wasn't as quick as Allison and her friends, who always seemed to have a sharp comment on the tips of their tongues. "Is everyone here?" she asked, looking around the room. "I should tell Rosa what time we'll want dinner." *Why isn't he here? He said he'd be here. He said he'd like very much to be here.*

"Everyone but Paul," Allison said. "But he's frequently late; he's known for it. And Rosa knows nobody expects dinner before nine. I'm going to take Thad away and introduce him to your college friends; do you mind?"

"No, of course not," Laura said automatically, wondering why someone would be late so often he would be known for it. "I should be circulating, too; I'm not acting like a hostess."

It was the first time she had ever been a hostess. It was the first time she'd worn midnight blue satin, the first time she'd decorated an apartment, the first time she was waiting for a man who had looked at her with admiring eyes.

For a long time everything had been new, beginning with the moment three years before when she entered Owen's Beacon Hill house, walking beside his wheelchair as the chauffeur pushed it into the foyer. Owen held up a restraining hand and the chauffeur stopped halfway to the elevator that was tucked into the wall beside the branching stairway. "I thought I might never see this place again," Owen murmured, almost to himself. He looked up at Laura and a joyous smile lit his face. "But here I am, and I've brought you with me."

He reached his hand toward her and she held it in hers. "How I love this house," he mused. "There was a time when I thought I hated it, when I even planned to sell it." He shook his head, his gaze moving past the marble statue in the center of the foyer to the French drum tables with huge arrangements of gladioli and roses. "So much laughter here, so long ago... And now I can share it. Have you noticed how we appreciate all the more what we have when we can give its pleasures to someone new? There's a selfishness in appreciating what we almost lost; there's a different kind of happiness in sharing it. I hope you are very happy here, Laura, and I bid you welcome."

"I will be," Laura said. "Happy, I mean." She bit her lip. Why couldn't she speak elegantly, as he did? "Thank you," she burst out. He might think she was clumsy, but at least he'd know she was grateful.

Owen smiled and folded his hands in his lap. "Let Rosa take you around; she'll help you figure out the maze Iris and I created. Make yourself at home while I take a nap; then come to my room when I ring for you. My dear," he added as the chauffeur turned the wheelchair, "I am so very pleased to have you here." And then the elevator doors opened and closed behind him.

Rosa appeared in a doorway on the other side of the foyer. "Come on, my young miss, we'll have a fast tour and then you can unpack. I'll take care of Clay when he gets here, after he finishes at Felix and Leni's." Rosa had never asked how it happened that Laura Fairchild, a summer kitchen assistant who had appeared from nowhere to apply for a job in mid-June was, in mid-September, moving into the Beacon Hill house as Owen Salinger's companion, and bringing her brother with her. Owen always did as he pleased, and his family had long since stopped telling him he was arbitrary, whimsical, foolish, or, far worse, vulnerable to clever people who could take advantage of him. Rosa knew they all thought it, but, because they were smart, they kept their mouths shut.

And so did she. But it was easy for Rosa; she had no stake in Owen's fortune. Besides, she was fond of Laura. "Don't put your hands all over the furniture," she said as they walked through the main salon on the second floor. "Fingerprints, you know."

"I never leave fingerprints," Laura said hotly. "I was trained better than that."

"My, my," Rosa said mildly, wondering why the girl suddenly looked frightened. "I wasn't criticizing the way you were raised—I'm not big on criticizing people—but how would you know that too much polish ruins fine woods and so we try to keep fingerprints off the furniture?"

"Sorry," Laura muttered.

"No harm done. I should remember how people like to touch something they're seeing for the first time. Go ahead; I won't say a word."

Laura forced herself to smile, afraid to say anything. *Be careful; be careful. Even now, even in Boston, be careful.* She found herself holding her breath and walking on tiptoe as they passed through rooms leading to more rooms; down long hallways lined with portraits of staid men and satin-gowned women; past nooks, closets, cupboards, unexpected stairways, and window seats. And then she began to relax beneath the spell of enfolding luxury, and soon she was reaching out and touching the silkiness of polished woods, the nap of gleaming velvets, the tightly-woven wool of the French tapestries on the walls.

Something stirred within her and came awake: a longing for luxury and beauty she had kept locked away because the chance of having them was so remote. Her fingertips felt alive; she seemed to merge with everything she touched, as far away as she could be from the linoleum-covered kitchen table where Ben would sit, making marks with his thumbnail, while she cooked dinner and told him about her day at school.

"Mr. Owen bought the house as a wedding present the month he and Mrs. Iris were married," Rosa was saying. "All twenty-two rooms of it. They'd always dreamed of living on Beacon Hill and having a family and giving big parties in a ballroom. And that's what they did. Here it is, the ballroom, closed up now; it has been since she died."

The ballroom, surrounded by dormer windows, took up the top floor. Below, on the fourth floor, was the apartment Felix and Asa had shared, as well as two extra rooms and baths for friends. Owen and Iris had a suite on the third floor with a guest suite across the hall; on the second floor a spacious salon stretched the width of the house, with the dining room and library behind it; and on the ground floor were the kitchen and pantry, Rosa's apartment, a receiving room, and the entrance foyer and an elevator leading to the upper floors. In the basement were a laundry room, a pantry lined with Rosa's jams and preserves, and a paneled room with a billiard table, fireplace, leather furniture, and a full bar.

"Mr. Owen always said those were the ten happiest years of his life, when he lived here with Mrs. Iris. He was building his company in those years, going like a house afire, buying hotels and building new ones right and left—there must have been two a year, sometimes three. The company got so big they finally took up half the top floor of the Boston Salinger. You haven't seen it yet; it's on Arlington Street, just off the Public Gardens. And he and Mrs. Iris were at all the parties, their pictures in the paper, their closets full of new clothes. . . . Then they started giving dinners, one a week, very intimate, just twelve people. Nobody else was doing it and pretty soon everybody was hinting for invitations. They had style, Mr. Owen and Mrs. Iris, and if I could have bottled and sold it I could have gotten rich. But style isn't something you can buy; either you have it or you don't."

I'll have it, Laura vowed silently. Whatever it is, whatever it looks like, I'll figure out how to get it. And people will admire me and love me and beg to be invited to my parties.

"But then Mrs. Iris died," Rosa said as they took the elevator from the basement billiard room to the fourth floor. "Mr. Owen shut the door on their suite and never went in it again. He talked about selling the house but he couldn't bring himself to do it; he said the thought of someone else living in the rooms Mrs. Iris had made drove him crazy. So he stayed. He moved into the guest suite, and a couple of years later the housekeeper and I made the old master suite into guest rooms, even though there aren't any guests in this house and haven't been since Mrs. Iris died. Until you, that is."

"I'm not a guest, I work here," Laura said.

"Well, yes, that's true. It's just that we never had a companion in this house before."

But now you do. I'm here, I'm part of this. I don't have to climb out a window and leave it all behind. I belong.

On the fourth floor Rosa opened the door to the three rooms where Felix and Asa had grown up. "This is yours."

Laura looked at her uncomprehendingly. "What is?"

"The apartment. Not beautiful, by a long shot, but Mr. Owen said it's to be yours."

The walls were covered in dark cork, the furniture was scarred walnut, everything was brown. "Felix and Asa did the decorating, if you can call it that," Rosa said. "It's the only part of the house Mrs. Iris didn't touch. It was theirs, it was private, and we didn't go in until they'd both moved away." She gazed at it. "My oh my, it is definitely a dark and dreary place."

"Change it," Owen said to Laura the next day after Rosa told him it was a grim place for a young girl. "Tear it apart, paint it, furnish it, and have the bills sent to me. Felix and Asa aren't interested in it anymore and I approve of progress. Make it yours."

"I think I should wait, if you don't mind," Laura replied. She was sitting beside his bed, a book in her lap, thinking about the word *dark*. Felix and Asa's dark apartment was harsh; Owen's dark rooms were a sumptuous haven of paisley velvets, Oriental rugs, heavy silk drapes in green and gold, and gleaming brass floor lamps. "It isn't as beautiful as yours," she went on, "but just having three whole rooms to myself is so wonderful—I have to get used to being alone, without Clay and Ben—" Her nails dug into her palms. "One of—one of Clay's friends, you know; all his friends would come over and it would be so crowded and noisy"—*just change the subject*—"and I want to learn about Boston; it's so different from New York, so old and beautiful . . ." She took a deep breath. "I'll decorate the rooms later, if that's all right with you."

"They're yours to do with as you please, Laura," Owen said gently. "They're your home." Watching the play of alarm and confusion on her face, he longed to banish her fears, but he would not pry into what was bothering her. She would tell him when she was ready, or not at all. But as so many times before, he was amazed at how strongly he wanted to help her, to make her happy. Something about her brings that out in me, he thought, and he wondered how many other men would feel the same and go out of their way to bring back her smile.

He closed his eyes as she picked up the book and returned to her reading. He loved the sound of her voice, low and vibrant, slipping occasionally into a roughness that hinted at a harsh background, but then becoming smooth again, with a slight lilt, almost as if she were learning English as a new language. When she read aloud, whether from his favorite books on Cape Cod, or collections of short stories or poetry, her voice found a rhythm that sounded to Owen almost as if she were singing, and he dozed and woke and dozed again to that musical cadence that made him regret that he was past the age of courtship.

Laura knew none of this, though she knew he liked the sound of her voice and rang for her frequently. He had at his bedside an array of buttons with which he could call one of the around-the-clock nurses who had taken over a guest room across the hall, or Rosa or any of the maids, or the housekeeping couple in the carriage house. But it was Laura he called most often, and even after she began classes at Boston University, she sat beside his bed when she was not at school, reading to him, talking, even doing her homework when he fell asleep.

Owen had arranged for her to start college. He had instructed his secretary at the Salinger executive offices to call a few key people at the university, and since none of them had to be reminded of his generosity as a benefactor, Laura was accepted as a special student within a week.

From the first she loved it. Everyone else seemed to take college for granted, but to Laura it was always a dream. The robbery at the Cape faded away; so did the police who were still working on it. And so did Ben. She was in a new life. Now and then she reminded herself how fragile it was—it all depended on Owen and she walked a thin line of possible discovery with him and his family—but then another month would go by, filled with the excitement of new ideas, new friends who accepted her without question, even a small part in the freshman class play, and she would forget there was any danger at all.

And with each month she knew she was becoming less like the Laura she had been. She explored the little side streets and enclosed neighborhoods of Boston, not because she was looking for homes to rob or escape routes or crowded shopping malls for picking pockets, but because she wanted to learn about her new home. She loved the narrow cobblestone streets of Beacon Hill, each like an old English town frozen in time, with gas lamps burning day and night, solid rows of narrow, five-story houses of worn, mellowed brick with high, narrow windows, most of them fronted with wrought-iron balconies just deep enough to hold window boxes of geraniums, and tiny front yards with even tinier flower gardens. It was all snug and private and privileged, and often Laura found herself breaking into a small skipping step as she walked along Mount Vernon Street from Owen's huge corner house, because everything was settled and secure—and hers.

In New York, even though many buildings had been preserved from earlier times, everything seemed to be rushing toward tomorrow and the day after, but Boston always seemed to make room for yesterday, its history and memories, its small-town feel. Laura stood on street corners, craning her neck to see glass and steel skyscrapers towering above small brick buildings with white steeples, or stone churches so old the walls had taken on the color of the earth. In small byways, tiny houses crowded the narrow streets, and she could almost hear the clip-clop of horses and the crunch of wooden wagon wheels as they negotiated the tight corners. Time-worn cemeteries and brass plaques were everywhere, marking the nation's oldest church, its first bookshop, Paul Revere's house—and at every plaque Laura stopped and tried to imagine the city as it had been.

She had never understood what history meant until she seemed to walk within it in Boston. And when she did, she discovered another meaning for family: a private history, the story of where each of us came from, just as Boston was the story of the nation's birth and growth.

Ben's smile came to her, and his serious frown as he helped her and Clay with their homework or planned their next break-in. *Ben is my history, part of what I am now. And I've lost him. But maybe someday* . . . She tucked the thought away. Someday, maybe, she would have a history she didn't have to hide.

Each week she discovered a different part of Boston, a different kind of city. She spent hours in its museums and wandered through the Fens and sat in the Public Gardens. She would glance at the Boston Salinger, which faced the Gardens, with Felix's office at the corner of the top floor, and then look back to the lush landscape where she sat, watching the ducks, squinting at the statue of George Washington, and wondering who had planned the perfect symmetry of the flower beds. She window-shopped along Boylston and Newbury streets, and once, by herself, bought a ticket for the symphony and discovered the soaring joy of a full orchestra. And wherever she went, she eavesdropped, listening to the broad Boston *a* and clipped syllables and watching the people as they talked: they had a careful way of holding their mouths that kept the corners almost motionless while the lips softly opened and closed, making murmured pronouncements.

"Prim," Owen said, laughter rolling from him as Laura mimicked the speech at dinner. "Perfect."

"You're not like that," she said.

"No, I escaped. Felix does it for the family. He thinks he should sound like Beacon Hill. I'd rather look like it: old, a little prudish, proud of my heritage, protective of my privacy."

"But that's what Boston is like," Laura said.

"Much of it, not all; it's a modern city with race riots and crime and poverty and the rest. A lot like New York."

Laura shook her head. "New York is like somebody running, dashing across the streets, always in a hurry. Boston is . . . Boston is like people walking and crossing at the corners and waiting for the lights to change."

Owen laughed again. "You've figured us out." But he noted that once more she had avoided telling him about her life in New York.

Most of the time in those first months in Boston no one asked any questions, and Laura was content to listen, making friends at school, reading to Owen or letting him reminisce about his life with Iris, and listening to Clay, who, for once, was not complaining. He lived in one of the rooms on the fourth floor, across the hall from Laura's apartment, and after school and on weekends he worked at Felix and Leni's sprawling home in the leafy North Shore suburb of Beverly. He and Laura had dinner together twice a week; on the other nights, when she ate with Owen in his rooms, Clay ate in the kitchen with Rosa or out with friends Laura did not know. But she didn't try to find out who they were: he was happy, he was busy, he was away from Ben. And that left her free to make her own life.

She was always learning something new, and everything she learned she remembered. Some of the family had ideas about how she should look and behave, and she stored in her memory all their suggestions. She also was discovering in herself a flair for doing things in a way that was uniquely hers.

It began with gentle lessons from Leni on buying clothes, and more peremptory ones from Allison when she came home from college for Thanksgiving. "Winter colors," declared Leni, appraising Laura's skin and hair as they stood before a three-way mirror at Jana's on Newton Street. So Jana brought out dresses in midnight blue, wine, rose, hunter green, white, ivory, and black, and Laura tried them on.

"Makeup would help," observed Jana.

"Yes," Leni agreed. "But that is for Laura to decide. I think she will, when she has proper clothes."

Laura contemplated herself in the mirror. Even beneath the rose-colored lights in the small, jewel-like salon, she was pale, with faint freckles from the summer sun at the Cape. Her hair was a mass of long, loose chestnut curls with stray curls on her forehead; her eyes were a darkly anxious blue. "I wouldn't know what to buy or how to put it on," she said.

"You need a few lessons," Jana told her. "My services are available; I have taught the most photographed ladies on the eastern seaboard. It is very simple, believe me. You would have no difficulty; you have excellent bones. It is like an artist, working with the finest canvas; even the most basic materials make such a difference you would not believe—"

"Yes," Leni repeated. "Laura will decide."

Jana fell into practiced silence, handing Laura the dresses to try on. Their vivid colors brought a glow to her pale skin. Soon, without realizing it, she was standing straighter, her head higher, and the worry was fading from her eyes. She saw hints of the kind of sophistication that seemed so natural in Allison: straight shoulders, the confidence of a level gaze, the smooth line from neck to back, with no slouch. That could be learned. It was much easier to learn it in an expensive dress. With Leni's approval, she bought two, all she could afford until next month's paycheck from Owen.

Then Allison cleaned out her closets and gave eight dresses and skirts to Laura, who added her own touches to them: in the flea markets around Salem and Marblehead, she bought Afghan belts, an ivory choker and stickpin, a fringed stole, sodalite beads which she twined with a strand of faux pearls, and a lace collar and cuffs from France.

Allison took her to buy sports clothes. "You're tall enough for long lines and bulky tops. No frills and curlicues—you can't ever be cute; you're definitely the elegant type—so stick with long sweaters, long skirts and jackets, wide belts, high boots. Then if you'd remember to stand straight you'd look like a dancer." Laura concentrated on standing straight. And in the next weeks, on her own, she added long fringed scarves that made her look almost like a gypsy, her delicate face like a cameo above the vivid folds at her long throat.

"Wear hats," said Barbara Janssen. "It's such a shame women have forgotten how much they do for one. They frame the face with refinement and distinction, and who doesn't benefit from that?" Tilting her head, she gazed at Laura. "Wide brims, small crowns. You have a wonderful head if you'd only hold it high." Laura concentrated on holding it high, and added feathers and silk bands, scraps of lace and antique buttons, and, in summer, fresh flowers to the hats Barbara gave her from her closets, saying she had new ones and didn't know what to do with last year's.

"Why is everyone doing so much for me?" Laura asked Rosa.

"Well, they like you," Rosa said. "But I think mainly it's because you take care of Mr. Owen. They love him and they visit often enough, but they're very big on their own busy lives, and this way they know he's not counting the minutes until they come again." She glanced at Laura's downcast face. "Of course they do like you. I'm convinced that's the main reason."

"Thank you," Laura said and kissed her.

On their first Christmas together, she and Owen exchanged gifts. They sat on the sofa in his study, flames softly burning in the fireplace, their breakfast on trays on the coffee table before them, and she gave him a scrimshaw letter opener, not rare, but of singular beauty. "For when you go back to work," she said, and he grinned with pleasure because he was strong again and because Laura had chosen his gift with love and care.

"And for you," he said, handing her a leather briefcase. "For college. I thought of jewelry, but perhaps this is more useful right now."

"It's perfect," said Laura. She ran her palm over the soft suede and smelled the pungent odor of fresh leather when she opened the case to see the compartments inside. She rested her head on Owen's shoulder. "But I don't need a gift; just being here is like getting a gift every day. I don't need any others."

"You need dozens. Hundreds. Everyone does; don't ever believe we don't need expressions of love and admiration. I mean," he added when Laura looked puzzled, "all of us need to be told how wonderful we are, and how much we're loved and needed, but it's just as important for us to know that someone was thinking of us at a time when we were apart. If I suddenly wandered off to climb the Himalayas, wouldn't it please you if I brought you a gift when I returned so you would know I thought of you even in the midst of overwhelming new experiences? Isn't that another way of telling you I love you, to think of you and bring you something that allows you to share at least part of my exciting adventures?"

A smile curved Laura's lips. "You could take me with you, and then I could share all of them."

Owen burst into laughter. "By God, so I could. So I shall. Would you like to go to the Himalayas?"

"I'd love to go to the Himalayas."

"Then we shall, someday. But I also intend to buy you gifts, because there aren't enough ways to tell you how happy you make me or to thank you for making this house a happy place again."

Rosa knocked at the door and came to take away the trays. "Laura, this is for you," she said, handing her an envelope. "It came yesterday but it got buried in all the Christmas cards. Is there anything else you need, Mr. Owen?"

"Coffee and brandy," he growled.

"You know perfectly well—" Rosa began amiably.

"Then find me a doctor who says it's all right."

"You keep following orders and one of these days your own doctor will say it's all right." Rosa picked up the trays and as she straightened up, she glanced at Laura. "Good heavens, child, what is it? What's wrong?"

Owen, too, had seen Laura's stricken look. "She's probably shocked by the idea of brandy for breakfast. We don't need anything else, Rosa. What time are you leaving for Felix and Leni's?"

"As soon as I clean up. We're forty for dinner, so I'd like Laura, too, if I can have her."

"Later," Owen said. "I'll send her over about two." When Rosa left, he asked gently, "Would you like to talk about it?"

Laura shook her head. "I was just . . . surprised . . . for a minute. I'm fine now. Would you mind if—"

"Of course not. Go off by yourself and read your letter."

"Just a few minutes . . ." Her words trailing away, Laura left the room so she could read Ben's letter by herself.

Dear Laura,

   I haven't written in all this time because I was afraid you'd still be angry and not want to hear from me. I didn't like leaving the way I did but after what happened I had to get out, as far and as fast as I could. I miss you. I think of you a lot and remember what it was like when we were all together. I wonder what you're doing and how you and Clay are getting along with the Salingers and whether they've ever suspected you of anything. I wish you'd write to me at this address; I'm working as a busboy and a bellhop in a hotel. Not great jobs, but they give me time to think and to decide what I'll do next. I keep remembering what you said about being an executive. Maybe I'll get back to the States one of these days and see you. Write to me, Laura. I feel awfully far away and I miss you and I've got to know what's happened since the Salingers were robbed.

"'Since the Salingers were robbed,'" Clay scoffed when Laura read him the letter. "Why doesn't he say since he robbed the Salingers? He makes it sound as if it just sort of happened. All by itself."

"He sounds lonely," Laura said.

"I guess." Clay stretched out his legs and stared at his feet. "But we can't help that, can we? He did it, we didn't. I mean, I'm sorry for him, but things are really good here and what are we supposed to do?"

"I think we should write to him."

"Not me!" he said vehemently. "And I don't think you should either. Aren't you having a good time here? I mean, why risk it? I'd rather not even know where he is."

"In London, at a hotel called Blake's. And I think he really wants to hear from us."

"Damn it, it's too dangerous! I'm sorry, Laura, but—"

"You think Ben is dangerous? Or it's dangerous for us to write to him?"

"I don't know. Maybe both. Anyway, he only wants us to write because he's afraid we might give him away."

"That's ridiculous; he knows we wouldn't."

Clay shrugged. "I just think we've got something pretty good going here; why should we risk it?"

Laura gazed at the letter in her hand. As long as Clay liked it with her, he wouldn't leave. As long as he thought Ben was dangerous, he wouldn't go to him. "Will you go to college?" she asked.

"Oh, shit." Clay made a face. "Listen, I'm a lousy student and I know it. I'll learn on the job; I'm good at that."

"What job?"

"I don't know yet. Maybe in a Salinger hotel. Felix was saying there might be a chance."

"Felix?"

"He probably only said it because Leni told him to. But I didn't ask; he brought it up and I said I might be interested."

"What about high school?"

He shrugged. "Shit, I've gone this far; I might as well finish and wear that cute little cardboard hat and get that cute little rolled-up diploma and then tell 'em all to fuck off. By then I'll be smart enough to do anything I feel like, right?"

Laura smiled. She felt good about Clay and even about Ben. She hadn't forgiven him, but he missed her, and whether she liked it or not she missed him, too—she couldn't help it—and now that she'd decided to write to him she felt better. It wouldn't hurt to keep in touch with him and maybe she could even find a way to get Leni's jewelry back—if he hadn't sold it all. "Are you helping with Christmas dinner?" she asked Clay. Ben wouldn't have a family dinner, she thought; it would be the first Christmas he didn't.

"Allison and I are hanging holly and greens all the hell over the house."

"Is that all you two do? Handle plants?"

"Very funny. I'd rather handle her, but she's hung up on"—he put his nose in the air—"mature cocksuckers."

"Clay! She never said anything like that!"

He shrugged. "You should know; you're always yacking, the two of you. I'm just the baby brother, right? What do I know? I'm not big enough for mature screwing or any other fucking thing."

Laura bit back a question about how much screwing he'd done. He would be eighteen in a couple of months and she'd be nineteen; they were old enough to have their own affairs and they were entitled to privacy. "Find someone your own age," she said lightly. "It's a lot simpler and probably a lot more fun." She kissed him on the top of his head. "I'll send Ben your love and tell him you miss him."

"Bullshit." Suddenly his truculence vanished; his voice was young and almost wistful. "You can tell him I'm fine and I don't even remember what it was like to live with him."

"I don't think I'll say that," she said quietly, and that night, on the walnut desk that had been Felix's, she wrote to him.

Dear Ben,

    I miss you, too, and I want us to write and be friends again, but please don't come here or call us. No one knows about you and it has to stay that way. You've got to understand that. Everything is wonderful here, we're happy, and we don't want to leave. We don't want to be forced to leave. I'm doing so many new things. . . .

It was three months before Ben replied: a very short letter about London and a new job he had in a different hotel. He sent his love to both of them, as if they were just good friends. After that, he and Laura wrote every few months and sent cards on their birthdays. Laura would have liked more, but she wasn't sure what. She was still angry at Ben, but the robbery seemed so distant that her anger had lost much of its force. And she missed him and wanted back the strong brother she remembered, but she didn't know how they could do that. So she went along with the sporadic correspondence he had started. At least she knew she hadn't cut all her ties with him.

Clay refused to read any of Ben's letters, though Laura always offered them to him, but he listened when she told him about Ben's new job in London, and another one after that, and then about his moving to Monte Carlo, where he worked in two hotels in eight months, and finally about his moving again, this time to Amsterdam, where he had a job at yet another hotel, on the security staff.

"What a good place for a thief," Clay said.

Laura did not reply. By then it was Christmas again; she was in her second year of college and she didn't get as emotional about Ben as she had. In fact, it was hard to remember what it had been like to depend on him and be part of his life. It was Owen she depended on now.

They had breakfast on Christmas morning, sitting in his study as they had a year ago. This time Owen's present to Laura was an envelope, and inside it she found a blank check.

"To redecorate your apartment," Owen said. "Stop living in Felix and Asa's shadow. Make those rooms your own. I can't imagine why you've waited so long."

"I thought I should make sure you liked having me here. What if you'd sent me away?"

He smiled in that quiet, intimate way she had loved from the first time she saw him. "You didn't really worry about that."

She returned his smile, shaking her head, but it wasn't true. The worries were always there, even when she thought she'd forgotten them for a while. Even at this late date the police could find something about Ben and tell Owen, or the Salingers might learn from the New York police that she had a record as a thief, or Clay might let something slip and give them away. She felt safer with the passage of time, but the worries were never really gone, only held down beneath the surface of her new life; and in the early dawn hours when a garbage truck rumbled by or a car door slammed, she would awaken with a start and lie curled up in bed, fighting off her fears.

But she kept them to herself, and after another year she found she could turn over when she woke at night and go back to sleep. It had been three years. The police had a thousand new crimes to solve; no jewelry was worth fretting over for such a long time. Besides, Owen was fully recovered, playing golf in the summer and tennis in the winter, and spending a few hours a week in the Salinger executive offices, semiretired but still insistent on knowing what was going on in his hotels. And Laura was no longer the girl she had been. If anyone came looking for her, it would be evident immediately that she had become someone else, that the girl who had been a thief was gone.

Clay was different, too, handsomer than ever and beginning to achieve a smoothness like Ben's. He had graduated from high school and was working in Philadelphia; surprisingly, Felix had kept his word and had found him a job as assistant desk clerk at the Philadelphia Salinger. He visited Boston on weekends to see friends he'd made in high school, and when he came to Laura's engagement party for Allison he brought a pretty blond girl whom he introduced as Bunny Kirk. "Bunny waitresses at Fotheringill's," he told Laura. "And Laura studies business at Boston University. Two ambitious ladies."

Laura and Bunny talked briefly, but Clay was surveying the room, and when he found Allison he focused on her with a brooding look. He can't still believe he wants her, Laura thought, but she realized she hardly knew Clay anymore. Once, before he moved to Philadelphia, she had asked him where he got the money to date as much as he did. "I only spend what I earn at Felix and Leni's," he replied.

"Clay, you aren't stealing, are you? You told me you weren't."

"Shit, Laura, you know I'm not. Who do you think I am? Ben?"

"He's not stealing anymore."

"How do you know?"

"He told me in his letters."

"Sure."

Laura didn't pursue it. When Clay didn't want to talk, it was impossible to get past his stubborn silence. She knew he wouldn't talk about

Bunny Kirk either. If she asked, he would only say that she was a good friend.

And why shouldn't he? That's exactly what I tell him about the men I meet at college. The trouble is, it's always true: they're just good friends.

A toss in the hay to keep the doctor away. As Ben used to say.

Owen had asked her, a year ago, if there were no young man she loved. They had been dining at his favorite restaurant, celebrating his recovery. "You've spent enough time on a cardiac patient over eighty," he said. "You need men your own age, and other kinds of love."

"I'm happy with the way I am," she said. But she'd known he was right.

She remembered that as the sounds of her party rose and fell rhythmically around her and she thought of Paul Janssen. *He's not here. He isn't coming. Not on time, not late, not at all.*

"Champagne for the hostess." Thad Wolcott was beside her, replacing her empty glass with a full one. "A dreaming hostess, I see."

"I was remembering when Owen got well," Laura said. "We had a private celebration at Loch Ober's and he gave me a lesson in how to know good wines."

"One of his many talents."

Laura looked at him. "Why do you always talk about people as if you're making fun of them or don't like them?"

"I like all the Salingers."

"You didn't answer my question."

"I complimented you on your dress. Was I making fun of you?"

Laura shrugged, then caught herself. *Ladies don't shrug their shoulders, my young miss.* That was the hardest habit to break. "I'm never sure how you feel about anyone," she said. "I suppose I'd have to know you as well as Allison does."

He smiled obscurely. "Allison doesn't care how well she knows me; she only wants to reform me."

"I didn't know you needed reforming."

"If I didn't, Allison wouldn't want me. Even if I were perfect—which I must admit I am not—I would pretend to have faults so Allison would want to make me her project."

Laura knew he was making fun of Allison and she looked around, wondering where she was.

"One thing you might remember," Thad said. "I can make her happy. She'll take me in hand and I'll turn out very well. She'll be proud of me and so will you; I promise you that."

"You should be making promises to Allison, not to me."

"That's too easy; she expects them."

"Sometimes the easy things are the hardest to do."

He looked at her with an alert eye. "What does that mean?"

"It's easy to love," Laura said coolly. "But to do it well, you have to think of someone besides yourself. And that's something you haven't learned how to do, isn't it? Now if you'll excuse me, I should be taking care of my guests."

She glimpsed his startled look as she made her way through the crowded room. For a brief moment she was proud of herself for thinking of a sharp, clever remark at the right time, just like Allison and her friends. But then she thought about Allison. *I have to find out if she knows how Thad talks about her.* She moved among her guests, smiling as they praised her apartment and her party and Rosa's hors d'oeuvres, but not pausing to talk until she reached Allison.

"Laura, did you hear?" Allison asked. "One of Mother's bracelets showed up—from the robbery, you know? Just this afternoon, in a pawnshop in New York. Isn't that incredible? After all this time . . . Oh, let me introduce my friend from school; his father's a lawyer in New York, and he knows a private investigator who's been hanging on to our robbery for years . . ."

Laura did not hear his name. *Ben is in Amsterdam. How could he pawn a bracelet in New York?*

". . . and they're looking for other pieces. Of course, it could be months or years before they show up—"

I just got a letter; he didn't say he was coming to New York.

"—but they think now they have a chance to find the thief. Wouldn't that be something? They might even find him before he sells Mother's necklace, which would be the most wonderful—"

Ben, if you ruin everything I have, I'll never forgive you; I'll never have anything to do with you again.

"I'm sorry I'm late," a voice said just behind Laura. "I really wanted to be on time but something came up."

She turned. Paul Janssen had come to her party.

CHAPTER 7

EVERYONE stayed and stayed. "Great party!" they exclaimed to Laura. "So different!" Clay and his girl left early, but the others lingered, eating and drinking, shifting from one group to another until the noise level rose so high no one could hear the music, and Ferdy, stacking dessert dishes in the dumbwaiter, paused to turn up the volume.

Laura had to escape the noise. Allison's words echoed in her mind—*pawnshop... bracelet... a chance to find the thief*—and she fled to her bedroom to catch her breath and try to think. But when she turned to close the door, she found Paul standing there. "If you want to be alone I'll leave," he said before she could speak, "but if you only came in for some quiet, I'd like to share it."

He was taller than she, and Laura looked up to meet his eyes, dark, probing, quizzical. She had thought about him so often over the past three years that now it was as if her thoughts had somehow come to life, dimming the fears that had seemed so terribly important just a moment before. I'll think about all that tomorrow, she thought, stepping aside, and when Paul walked into her room she closed the door behind them.

"Much better," he said, grinning at her in the sudden silence. "That's a noisy group; you've done something they're not used to."

"What have I done?" she asked defensively.

"Mixed up completely different kinds of people, given them a chance to have conversations they don't usually have. It's like a tossed salad out there. Those students never mix, you know."

"You mean my classmates don't mix with Allison's."

"Not in the normal course of things. And they never socialize with the others you invited—Owen's landscaper, who's out there talking to a very high-toned poet, and my mother's favorite cabinetmaker, who's drinking scotch and exchanging profound ideas with one of Harvard's top law students, or the fascinating greengrocer from the corner whom I talked to—"

"You're making fun of them. Those are my friends."

His eyebrows rose. "On the contrary. I'm admiring your courage. You invited the people you wanted instead of taking the easy way and having only Allison's friends, who know all about each other since they're together at every party all year long."

"Courage," Laura repeated. A mischievous smile touched the corners of her mouth. "More like fear, probably. I was afraid I wouldn't have anyone to talk to."

He chuckled, admiring her swift change from prickly defensiveness to sophisticated self-mockery. Another contradiction, he thought. "Tell me how you've gathered such a wide circle of friends."

"You mean peculiar," she said coldly. "You wouldn't ask that if my friends all lived on Beacon Hill."

"It wouldn't be a wide circle if they did." He stood relaxed in front of her, his hands in his pockets. "Are you always armed for battle, even when someone asks you an innocent question?"

"That wasn't innocent. You were saying I must be different if I have such different friends."

"You are different; that's why I'm here." He reached out to take her hand. "Could you invite me to sit down for a few minutes? It's difficult to get a friendship going standing up."

Involuntarily Laura glanced sideways at her bed. It seemed to be oozing in all directions, looming huge and inescapable, filling her room. And Paul seemed to be bigger, too, taking up more of the private space she'd never shared with a man. She shivered slightly with anticipation and apprehension; all she could think of was Paul and her bed, a few feet apart.

"I said friendship."

She looked up and saw his amused smile. Stung, she turned without replying and led the way to the wing chairs flanking the fireplace. They weren't really close to the bed; they were fifteen feet away, and their high backs blocked Laura's and Paul's side vision like blinders on a horse. The two of them sat facing each other in a circle of amber light, a small table between them, the shadowed room like a retreat as sounds of the party drifted through the closed door.

"I've been hearing about you for three years," Paul said conversationally. He sat relaxed in his chair, an ankle resting on one knee, watching her almost lazily. "And I should have spent some time with you last summer; I'm sorry I didn't. You've become a real member of the family. I assume that means you like us."

"I love you," Laura said. She flushed. "I mean, I love Owen and Allison and Leni and Barbara—they've all been wonderful to me."

"I don't hear my uncles Felix and Asa on that list."

She shrugged, then caught herself. "I don't see much of them."

"A careful answer. They're not easy men to get along with, although Asa can be pleasant when he gets out of Felix's orbit. Don't you miss your own family?"

"No. I mean, Clay is here and . . . he's all I've got."

"No one else? I didn't realize that. It must have been hard, then, to leave your friends in New York."

"It's always hard to leave friends." Laura's face was smooth. "But I like meeting new people; it gets dull having friends who know all about each other since they're together at every party all year long. Rosa says you've been traveling for the past few years."

Something wrong there, Paul thought. She'd used his own words and they'd rung false. He wondered what was forbidden territory: her friends, or New York, or leaving New York. "Europe, Africa, India," he said. "It keeps me out of trouble."

"And what else do you do?"

"I take pictures."

"And sell them?"

"No, why should I? I do it for pleasure."

"Some people might need the money," Laura said dryly.

He nodded. "I'm luckier than most. My great-uncle Owen set up a trust for me when I was still crawling around his study and charming him with my baby wit. I probably looked as restless and unambitious then as I am now and he took pity on me and ensured my future. I did go to college; does that make me sound a little less frivolous? And now and then I do think about taking photography seriously. I'm told you're in college. What will you do when you finish?"

"Something in hotel management; that's what I'm studying. And maybe some acting in my spare time." At his look of surprise, she said defensively, "Why shouldn't I? Other people have hobbies. I've had parts in four plays and everyone says I'm very good."

"And you like it?"

"It's wonderful. To be somebody else and have all your lines written so you never have to worry about what you might say—because playwrights use words more beautifully than the rest of us."

He pretended he had not noticed her abrupt shift in mid-sentence. "I thought your hobby might be making friends. You were going to tell me how you met all those people out there."

"Oh. It's nothing special; I don't know why you think it is." She was frustrated because instead of talking about himself the way most men did, he kept trying to find out about her. But she realized she wasn't angry, as she usually was when people asked prying questions; she was more concerned with saying the right things and keeping that warmth and interest in his eyes. And she knew why. Because he was the most attractive man she'd ever met; because he had an aura of excitement about him, something she might share if she could be clever and quick enough; because he was like a magnet, pulling her closer, making her want to talk instead of running away.

It's dangerous to get close to anyone who makes me want to talk.

"You were saying?" Paul prompted.

I'll be careful. I won't say too much. "I like to listen. People love to talk about themselves; all they need is somebody who's interested and they'll go on for hours. And I guess I'm interested in just about everybody."

He smiled. "You'd be good in the hotel business."

"That's what Owen says."

"Does he? He doesn't say it to many people. Has he offered you a job at the Boston Salinger?"

"Yes," she said, adding almost defiantly, "and I'm going to take it."

He looked at her thoughtfully. "Doing what?"

"Assistant to Jules LeClair. The concierge." When he made no response, she said, "You don't know him?"

"I don't pay much attention to the hotels. When do you start?"

"On Monday. Full-time for the summer and then part-time when I go back to school."

"To study hotel management. Why don't you major in theater since you like acting so much?"

"Owen wants me to learn the hotel business."

"In case you don't make it as an actress?"

"He calls acting a hobby." She smiled, almost to herself. "And he says anyone who manages his hotels has to be good at acting and have dozens of other skills."

Paul's eyebrows rose. "His hotels?"

"I could do it," Laura declared.

"I'm sure you could. But Felix and Asa handle the management of the chain."

"Yes, but Owen was talking about his own hotels—the four oldest ones that aren't part of the family corporation. He has some plans for them. He says Felix and Asa aren't interested in them."

"Don't fool yourself; they're interested in every dust ball in every Salinger hotel. And Owen knows it. What kind of plans?"

"I don't know much about them; they aren't put together yet. What do you photograph when you travel?"

Skittish and secretive, Paul thought. What the hell did she have to hide? And what were she and his uncle up to? "Animals and people and sunsets. Have you convinced Owen to start a new hotel chain?"

"I haven't convinced him of anything! I'm learning from him, not telling him what to do!"

"Hold on," he said softly. "I wasn't accusing you of anything. I just thought an active, discerning man might think up a new project with an attractive young woman as a clever ploy to keep her close to him for a long time."

Laura's anger disappeared; her eyes danced. "You mean you think Owen behaves the way you would."

Paul laughed aloud. In some ways she was like a child, he thought, feeling her way around a strange house, pretending she knew what she was doing, quick to anger when she thought she was being suspected of something. But in other ways she was a woman of beauty and spirit, and a cache of secrets. A challenge, Paul reflected; it had been a long time since anyone had seemed so interesting to him.

"What do you do besides photograph when you travel to all those countries?" she asked.

"Read a lot, hike, ski, bicycle cross-country, and wonder what's over the next border."

"Don't you ever want to stay where you are?"

"No. Do you want to stay where you are?"

"Yes." *Safe with Owen, forever.* "If I could, I'd stay here and do all the things I want..."

"You can't want many things if you can do them all in one place."

"I do! I want so many things! And I suppose I can't do them all here... everything I need to do to be special and secure—" She bit off her words. "I'm sure that sounds foolish to you but I never had a trust fund—I never even had a bank account when I was younger—and I have to make my own safe place. It's what I most want in the world." She stood up. "I'd better get back to my party."

"Stay a little longer," he said. "Your party can roll along for hours on its own steam." He stood up with her. He was surprised at the feelings of tenderness she had aroused in him. She had sounded so ingenuous about being special and secure—whatever that meant—that he wanted to comfort and reassure her. "Listen to me," he said and put his arm around her shoulders, pulling her to him like a child. "You're already special. You're a lovely young woman with nothing to stop you from doing whatever you want or being anything you want." He felt the slender bones of her shoulders beneath the satin dress, her silken chestnut hair brushed his cheek, and desire surged through him. He tightened his arm and turned her toward him. "I'll help you; we all will. There's nothing to stop you. It's not as if you're alone, or have some dark past to live down, or— What is it?"

She had pulled away, her eyes wide, her face pale. "I have to get back," she stammered. "I'm supposed to—"

"What the hell are you afraid of? Me? Because I held you? For God's sake, Laura—"

"No, no, it's not that; it's not you; it wouldn't ever be—I'm sorry, I really am. I'm not being very smart about this—"

"What does being smart have to do with it? Come here, sit down, just for a minute. I'd like to understand. . . ." He looked about for some way to change the subject. "Tell me about your room. I like what you've done with it."

Giving her time to calm down from whatever was bothering her, he studied the country French furniture he remembered from Iris's rooms, newly reupholstered in ivory and apricot silk, and the ceiling moldings and carved fireplace surround, all painted in soft ivory against the palest of mint green walls. "Dawn," he murmured, almost to himself. "Clear, cool, and warm, all at once. Depth and intimacy. My God, what wonderful light." He smiled at Laura. "You've given this place life. It's been in the doldrums ever since I can remember. Perfect colors—you have a good eye."

"Thank you." She was looking at him in surprise, seeing a different Paul Janssen. No longer the careless playboy with no ambition or direction, he was absorbed, intense, an artist who cared deeply about color and light, whose praise was generous, whose smile was warm and intimate. And at that moment Laura knew she would be with him as much as he wanted her to. It might be risky to be close to him, but she was drawn to his intensity, and she wanted more of his praise—and his smile.

He was standing before a shelf of books near the fireplace, running his fingers along the spines. "Where did you get these?"

"A friend named Cal Hendy gave them to me. Left them to me,

really: he owned a bookstore and when he died he left me the ones he knew I loved the most."

"A good friend." He took one down and leafed through it. "Do you have any idea what they're worth?"

"No, why should I? I'm not going to sell them."

"You might want to someday, and this one could be worth a good bit: there can't be many first editions around of Washington Irving's *Legend of Sleepy Hollow*. Would you mind if I had it appraised?"

"If you'd like. It's really not important, though; they were a gift from Cal and I loved him and I'd never sell them, no matter what."

"'Never' is a long time. Anyway, you ought to know what you have. I'll bring it back in a week or so." He put the book on the coffee table, then moved a few steps to gaze at a large framed black-and-white photograph Laura had hung over the mantel. "Where did you find this?"

"In Owen's library. I was admiring it one day and he said I could hang it here. You don't mind?"

"Photographers never mind seeing their work displayed." He studied the three children in the photograph as if he had not spent hours watching them one day on the beach at Wellfleet, photographing them again and again. And then he had spent a week in his darkroom to get a set of prints that satisfied him. That had been five years ago, when he was twenty-three, and it was because of those prints that he had decided that if he ever took anything seriously, it would be photography.

Owen had bought four of the prints after Paul gave him the first as a Christmas present. The one Laura had chosen showed the little girl and her two brothers quarreling over a sand castle they had just built: the girl had made a flag from her hair ribbon and wanted to fly it from the highest tower; her brothers had insisted on flying their own skull and crossbones. Paul had printed the photograph with high contrast to intensify the emotions; the children's eyes flashed, in the background dark waves broke in a stark white froth onto the sand, a white gull was brilliantly outlined against a deep, cloudless sky, the sand castle was scored with long, angular shadows.

"Why did you choose this one?" he asked Laura. "Most people prefer softer prints. More fantasy, more like a dream."

"This is the dream," she said without hesitation.

He looked at her curiously. "Why?"

"Because the castle is finished."

His eyes moved back to the picture. No one else had ever said that about it. "And you have a castle somewhere, waiting to be finished?"

"Everybody does, don't you think? Or do you have everything you want?"

There was a small silence. "I have everything I want," he said reflectively. "But sometimes I wish I wanted more."

She shook her head. "I don't understand that."

"Well, neither do I," he said carelessly. "At least not most of the time." He moved to Laura's side and took her hand. "But I do want to see more of you. Will you have dinner with me tomorrow night? Better yet, we'll start early, with one of Rosa's lavish teas, and then go out for a late dinner. Can you arrange that?"

"Yes," she said. She did not hesitate or wonder about it after she agreed. He might be dangerous, but he was someone she could love.

* * *

The bracelet found in a New York pawnshop had been bought in Austria by Leni Salinger's grandmother as a gift for her thirteen-year-old daughter, to ease her sadness at leaving home to make a new life in America. It was solid gold, with a monogrammed locket that sprang open to reveal a picture of Leni's grandfather. When the police returned it, and Leni held it in her hand, looking at the tiny picture of her smiling, curly-haired grandfather, she began to cry. "I know it's silly; so many terrible things could have happened, far worse than losing a bracelet, but it seems so important to have it back and not in some stranger's hands..."

"It is important," Felix said. He fastened his cummerbund and reached for the cuff links he wore only with his tuxedo. "But mainly because it will help us find the son of a bitch who took it."

Leni was sitting at her dressing table in a long satin slip, waiting for her maid to arrive and help her into the intricately draped gown she had chosen for the opera ball, the last of the season before everyone left town for the summer. "I'm not sure anymore," she said. "I did want to punish him, whoever he is, but now...do you know, Felix, the only thing I really care about is getting everything back so it can all go to Allison and then, someday, to her daughter. That's why I want the necklace most of all; my father got it from his grandparents in Denmark and gave it to my mother, and she gave it to me...and Allison knew it would be hers one of these days. That's what means something to me. I don't like jewelry that's just stones and gold or silver; I want it to have meaning and a history so we don't lose touch with our past, and how else can that happen except by being passed down from one generation to the next?"

"Yes, that is a pleasant romantic view," Felix said, struggling with his cuff links. "Can you help me with these? But romance is irrelevant in this case; I would hardly indulge in it when it comes to punishing a criminal—"

"You never indulge in romance," Leni murmured.

"—and when he's found I'll see to it that he suffers. The bastard invaded my home and took my property, and no one does that to me and goes unpunished."

"He did it to all of us," Leni said quietly. "And after all, he is unpunished, isn't he? It's been three years and this is the first clue we've had."

"There will be more; I guarantee it. That's fine, thank you. I don't know why I still have trouble with cuff links after all these years. Will you be ready soon? We'll be late."

"We're never late. You are the only man in the world who times arrivals to the second." She slipped the stem of a diamond earring through the neat hole in her ear and fastened it. "I hear Clay Fairchild is doing very well in Philadelphia."

Felix glanced at her, then reached for his jacket.

"Isn't it odd," she said, "how I think of Clay and Laura every time we talk about the robbery? It's very wrong of me—poor things, it's not their fault they started working for us that awful summer. Thank heavens they didn't get scared off and leave. Owen adores Laura, and she's so good for him; I've never seen him happier. He got her a job, Rosa says, as one of Jules's assistants, and in their spare time he teaches her about running hotels—"

"Why?" Felix's eyebrows had drawn together. "He's using her as his secretary—I can't imagine why, when there are a dozen at the office he could have any time he wants—and I knew she was working with Jules, and she's at the university. What more does she need?"

"She wants to be more. All young women today want to be more than whatever it is they are, don't you think?" Leni's voice murmured through the bedroom like a quiet stream and Felix leaned down to hear her. "And she gives as much as she gets from us. She gave that lovely party last night for Allison; she even insisted on paying Rosa for the food. Owen stopped by and said it was very lively. Paul was there, too, he said, and very attentive to Laura. That won't go anywhere, of course —their backgrounds are impossibly different—but it does seem a good thing for her to take an interest in the hotels. She'll have to earn her living and it's good for Owen to be able to help someone . . . to nurture, in a way. He hasn't had anyone, you know, for such a long time. You and Asa weren't exactly cuddly and loving, Rosa says; you kept Owen at arm's length. So he lost Iris and then he lost you, and I think it's wonderful that after all these years he's found someone like Laura who's smart enough and loving enough to let him help her. And Clay, too. I'm so glad you got him that job in Philadelphia when Owen asked you to; he'd never have gotten it without help. And maybe he'll think of some

ways to make the hotel better. Poor old thing, it's gotten quite shabby—
you said so yourself—and you won't put money into it. Owen says you
want to sell it, but of course he never would do that. I could have told
you he wouldn't: it's his, and he loves it—that one and the other three
he started with—and if Clay can bring some new ideas to it and learn
the business at the same time, isn't that a fine thing?"

She fastened her other earring and picked up a matching necklace.
"Felix, would you do this for me?" She closed her eyes, fighting the
shock of desire that ran through her at the touch of his fingertips on the
nape of her neck. It has nothing to do with Felix, she thought. It's
because I don't have anyone to hold me. No lust, no love . . . and I've
got to have one or the other. I'll have to find someone; it's been so long
since I sent Ned away . . . "What?" she asked.

"I said, when is your maid coming? I don't like being nervous about
the time."

"She'll be here any minute; we have plenty of time. There's no reason
for you to be nervous." She watched him pace. "You're not nervous,
you're excited."

"Nonsense."

"No, I can tell . . . It's my bracelet, isn't it? You've been this way ever
since they brought it back. You think they'll find the thief, even after all
these years." She shook her head. "I don't. It seems impossible."

"Not anymore. Not when there's a new development. They know
what they're doing. They're relentless—when they're dedicated, that is.
They don't give up; they don't forget. And they'll track the scum down,
and his accomplices, too. Whoever they are, they don't have the brains
to understand that people like us don't allow anyone to invade our lives
and upset the order we've made. Sometime, sooner or later, they'll be
cornered, however many there are, and if I have anything to say about it
they'll be kicked into a hole, like the filth they are, and kept there until
they're old or dead. Pity we have to waste money and feed them; they
ought to be shot. The only good they'll do is be an object lesson for
anyone who thinks there's something glamorous about burglaries; they
might change their mind when they know we'll have them rotting in
jail."

The room was very quiet. Seated at her dressing table, her tall, lean
body slanting away from her husband, Leni watched him straighten his
jacket, tuck a silk handkerchief in the front pocket, and stand at the pier
glass to examine himself for imperfections. When he let out a long
breath of approval, Leni knew he had found everything in place, everything correct. Hidden behind the impeccable Almaviva white-tie tuxedo
was a caldron of hatred and rage and implacable vindictiveness—but

the world would not see it. The world would see only perfection.

Leni stood as her maid arrived with the freshly pressed gown. How amazing, she thought, that my hands are as cold as ice. I don't know why I still have trouble accepting Felix for what he is, after all these years. It's not as if I don't understand him or remember why I stay with him.

She raised her arms and let her maid slip the silken dress over her head. There's no reason to be upset, she told herself. Whatever Felix does about the thief or thieves who robbed us, it won't have anything to do with me. I just want my jewels back; after that, if he wants some kind of revenge, he can do what he likes. It won't touch me or the rest of us; we're too far from it. We won't even know when it happens.

* * *

Clay had been calling Laura for three hours before she answered. "I even called Rosa," he fumed. "She said you were out."

"I went to dinner with a friend. Why are you so angry? I didn't get mad when you weren't there this morning when I called. And I left a message at the hotel, but you're just now calling back and I'm not—"

"I got your message. What friend?"

"Just a friend. We had tea here and then went to a place called Julien's. You'd love it, Clay, it's very elegant—"

"Which friend? You sound different. *Happy,*" he added accusingly.

"What's wrong with that? Clay, what's the matter with you? Don't you want me to be happy?"

"Sure I do, it's just that—oh, fuck it, Laura, you know I hate it when things happen and I don't know about them . . . when I'm *outside* . . ."

"But you can't be in the center of everything," Laura said gently. "Even if you still lived here, I wouldn't tell you everything I do."

"You'd tell me more. What did you call to tell me?"

"They found some of the stolen jewelry."

"*They what?*"

"In a pawnshop in New York. What do you think we should do?"

"Shit, I don't— What did they find?"

"One of the bracelets."

"Just one?"

"That's all they told us about. They—"

"What else did they say?"

"Nothing much. They don't know who pawned it but—"

"But the guy who owns the pawnshop! He must have said something!"

"Clay, if you'd let me talk . . . He said it was a young man with blond hair and dark glasses; nothing unusual—"

"But the receipt! They always sign a receipt! The police must have seen it!"

"It was signed Ben Franklin. With a fake address."

"And that's all they have? Nothing else?"

"Aren't you even surprised at the name?"

"Yeah. Real cute of Ben. Is that really all they have? No other clues? Not even where to look next?"

"They say they don't, but I don't suppose they'd tell me if they did. Clay, I can't think of—"

"You're sure they didn't say anything else? Some little thing you might have missed? Damn it, think about it! Are you sure the owner didn't spot something? How come he called the police?"

"He recognized the bracelet from the description the police sent out. Clay, I can't think of anything to do. Can you?"

"No. Stay out of it. We're not involved; nobody thinks we are. How come Ben's in New York, anyway? I thought he was in Europe. You're the one he writes to; did he tell you he was going to New York?"

"No, I didn't know anything about it. You'd think he'd call if he was this close."

"You told him not to."

"Well, I know, but if he really wanted to see us . . . Sometimes I think it would be so nice to see him."

There was a silence. "Yeah, it would," Clay said finally. "He was really great . . . most of the time. Like, remember the time we did that job in Brooklyn, and the people came home early and we had to get out through the attic and across the roof? We were so scared, and Ben kept telling us jokes and he took us to a movie and afterwards we had hot dogs and ice cream. Shit, I have ice cream all the time now, but it tasted better when Ben bought it. Except—Christ, if he gets us in trouble . . ."

There was another silence. "I'd better go," Laura said. "Owen expects me in a few minutes. I'll talk to you in a couple of days. But call me first if you think of anything we should do."

"Just keep cool and quiet. And call me if anything else happens. Take care, now."

"I will. I love you, Clay."

"Me, too." Clay was scowling as he hung up. Fuck it, he thought. Things were going pretty good; he was starting to make plans; now this had to happen. Three years, for Christ's sake; you'd think any decent pawnshop would throw away police descriptions of stolen goods when they hadn't been heard of in three years. What was wrong with those idiots; didn't they ever throw anything away? You couldn't count on anything these days. You thought you were all set and then—

"Clay! You playing with yourself in there?" He shot up as the manager's voice bellowed from the front office. The son of a bitch could still scare him, even though he wasn't making any noises about firing him. Clay knew they didn't like him but, what the hell, why should they? He was a kid of twenty who'd never worked in a hotel in his life, and he'd been foisted on them by Felix Salinger, telling them this was their new assistant desk clerk, whether they liked it or not. What were they supposed to do? Cheer?

They didn't cheer, but they didn't make too much noise, either. They were old and shabby, like the hotel; they'd been around forever, like the hotel, and they knew Felix wanted Owen to sell the hotel and build a fancy new one on a bigger lot, which would mean the end of their jobs. They didn't know why Owen hadn't done it, but they didn't ask: they kept their mouths shut and hoped nobody would pay attention to the Philadelphia Salinger. It may have been fading and shabby, but to the old-timers it was home.

None of which, Clay reflected, prevented them from treating him like shit, scheduling him for night shifts and talking around him when he was in the room. But lately he'd begun to win them over. Owen Salinger liked this old hotel for some reason, and Clay figured if he played his cards right he could someday replace Willard Payne as manager and run it himself. Laura kept saying there was a future for them with the Salingers, so why shouldn't he be a hotshot executive? After all, if Ben could be a security expert, for Christ's sake, in a hotel in Europe, why couldn't Clay do better than that with the Salingers in America?

"Sorry," he said as he walked into the manager's office. "I was talking to my sister in Boston. She sends you her love and says thanks for keeping an eye on me."

Willard Payne adjusted his steel-rimmed glasses. "Bullshit."

Clay grinned, man to man, and sat on the corner of the desk, leaning close to the old man's hearing aid. "What she said was, I should listen to you. I was telling her you worked the hell out of me and she said it was good for me because I need settling down, and I could learn a lot from somebody who's been in the business as long as you. And I guess she's right."

Willard nodded several times, his loose jowls flapping softly. "A smart young lady, your sister; you could learn from her. Age is wisdom, young man; age is wisdom. You're young, you're impatient, you learn that age is wisdom and you'll be getting smart." He pushed back his chair. "You take over. I'll see you tomorrow."

"It's awful late for you to be here," Clay observed. "Almost midnight."

"I'm checking something," Payne said vaguely. "See you in the morning."

Alone, Clay reclined in Payne's chair, his feet on the desk. "Checking up on *me*," he mumbled. "Treating me like a goddam high school kid." He knew he was young; it drove him crazy that he wasn't silver-haired and smooth, like a politician or a Mafia don. He wished Laura were there; she'd have said Payne was jealous because Felix had done Clay a favor, and that would have made him feel better. She always could make him feel better; that was one great thing about her. But here he was alone in Philadelphia in a run-down hotel and he hadn't found a girl yet and nobody gave a damn about him. Ben was gone, and Laura had Owen and some guy, whoever he was—took her to *Julien's*, for Christ's sake; it probably cost a pile—and who else was there? Nobody.

Shit, nobody in the whole goddam world was as alone as he was.

I need a drink, he decided. The office can take care of itself for half an hour.

He waved at Terry Levonio as he walked into the crowded Brass Ring Saloon, just off the lobby. Terry grinned back beneath the handlebar mustache that had become part of Philadelphia lore. The Brass Ring was a hangout for newspaper and television people, it was listed in Philadelphia tour guides, and it was the only part of the Philadelphia Salinger that consistently made money.

"Midnight, the hour of melancholy," Terry observed as Clay took the last empty stool at the bar. "And you are in need of a small friend." With dextrous fingers he mixed Clay's favorite scotch and soda. "A companion to cheer night's darkest depths."

"Cheers." Clay drank it off and held it out for a refill. "Was Payne asking about me?"

"The usual. How much time do you spend in here, how much do you drink, do you ever talk about the Salingers, why are you here? Same old stuff. Take this one slowly; I expect customers to let my perfect drinks slither down like a caress, not a fucking Niagara."

"Why not." Clay sipped the drink. "Nice cuff links," he said, eyeing the jet and diamond rectangles on Terry's starched cuffs.

"A gift."

"Who from?"

"Me to me." He left to serve two women standing at the curved end of the bar; Clay recognized one as a news anchorwoman, the other as the host of a noon talk show. Where did Terry get the money for jet and diamond cuff links? he wondered idly. And the Porsche he drove. And Brioni ties and a Loewe wallet. Taken singly, they were expensive but not impossible; Clay had some Brioni ties, too. But taken together,

Terry's lifestyle was a hell of a lot flashier than Clay's. And Clay knew his salary and could guess at his tips.

Only one way, he thought, finishing his drink. He's stealing it. He brooded over the idea. Shit, the guy's probably been stealing the whole time I've been here; something going on practically under my nose that I didn't know about. He can't do that to me; I'm assistant desk clerk; he can't play me for a fool. Another idea struck him. Shit, if there's money missing from anywhere in the hotel, who'd get blamed? Me, who else? Christ, just when I'm straight and making something of myself, this son of a bitch comes up playing tricks.

He did not look up when Terry returned and refilled his glass; he was thinking about how somebody could rip off a bar. The easiest way would be to pocket the money for every third or fourth drink and not ring it up on the cash register. That's what he's doing, Clay decided. He's too cheerful to be honest; he never stops smiling.

He began to watch. The hours passed; he kept his eyes on Terry's whirlwind fingers, pouring, mixing, serving, playing the keys of the cash register, collecting money and dropping it into the register's compartments without missing a beat. "Who's minding the store?" Terry asked a little after two in the morning.

"They'll call me if they need me," Clay said.

"Some wise fella said the mice play when the cat's not looking," Terry observed cheerfully.

Clay nodded. "I was thinking the same thing."

But he'd been watching for over two hours and whatever Terry was doing, it wasn't pocketing money or failing to ring the charges; he'd swear to that. So it was something else. I should have known, he thought; Ben told me plenty of times that smart thieves make their tricks look legal. He slid off the stool. "Put it on my bill," he said to Terry. "I'll see you tomorrow. What time do you get here?"

"Three o'clock, as you well know since you check my time cards for my inhuman hours."

"You don't work them every day."

"Tomorrow I do. Shall I call you an hour from now to make sure you haven't fallen asleep at your desk?"

"I won't fall asleep. I know how to keep my eyes open." He waved as he left, and the next morning, when the bar was dark and the maids were all upstairs, he slipped quietly into the employees' room in the basement of the hotel and picked the lock on Terry's locker.

He felt like a detective solving a crime. But he felt a different thrill, too. Just like old times, he thought, reveling in the coolness of the metal pick in his hand, the feeling of power when the door swung open. Wait'll I tell Laura I can still do it. No, can't tell Laura; she wouldn't appreciate it. It's my own secret. Except for Terry, of course. Because if I find something, I'm going to stop him dead in his tracks.

* * *

Paul reached the top of the seawall and turned to help Laura. But she was already there, taking a smooth, high step to stand beside him, and together they looked out at the silver-blue ocean. This part of the shore of Cape Ann, a knob of land thrusting into the Atlantic north of Boston, was lined with enormous rocks dredged up by reclamation teams and wedged together in a wall that stretched as far as the eye could see. On the rocks gulls perched in small congregations; farther out, belted king-fishers wheeled above the ocean's waves, diving to snatch unwary fish from just below the surface, then, their wings beating strongly, climbing straight up to vanish into the bright afternoon mist. Waves pounded the rocks below Paul and Laura, and when the wind shifted a fine spray blew across them, leaving tiny droplets in Laura's hair that shimmered like jewels in the afternoon sun. Paul touched one and then another, and they clung to his finger when he put his arm around her.

"You took those rocks as if they were a stairway," he said. "I never had a chance to be gallant. You didn't tell me you're a climber."

"I haven't been for a long time." She put her head back, feeling strong and free in the fresh salt air. "I used to climb on the rocks up the Hudson with my brothers."

"Your brothers?"

"My brother's friends." She moved away and sat on a rock, tightening her shoelace with shaking fingers. She felt angry and a little sick. She didn't want to lie. She never wanted to lie to Paul or any of the family again. She'd done so much lying she couldn't remember which lie she'd told to whom, and that scared her, but it was more than that. She and Paul had gone out five nights in the two weeks since her party, to dinners and concerts and piano bars where they sat and talked for hours, and she knew she wanted it to go on forever, just as she wanted everything with the Salingers to go on forever. And that meant being honest with them. It was as simple as that. But, still, if she kept making stupid mistakes... *How do I get out of a lie that's gotten so big and gone on so long?* She stood up but she stayed a little distance from Paul. "Can we walk along the rocks for a while?"

"Good idea. I haven't done it since I was a kid and my father brought me here."

"Your *father?*" She was taking a long step to another rock; when her feet were securely planted, she looked back at him. "You and *Thomas* jumped around here?"

He laughed. "My very quiet father was a champion rower and mountain climber until he did something to his back and had to quit." He took the step and joined her. "And who taught you to do this? Not Clay, I'll bet; from what I've seen, he isn't nearly as surefooted as you are."

"No, it was . . . someone in New York."

"A friend of yours?"

"For a long time he was the best friend we had."

She left him behind, jumping lightly from rock to rock, remembering how it had been to climb brick and graystone walls, clinging with callused fingertips to windowsills and drainpipes and ivy. She speeded up, exulting in her strength. Tennis and swimming, long walks to and from the university, and exploring Boston had kept her muscles taut and responsive. *I could do it again if I had to. But I never will.*

Paul watched her slender body flowing in long, smooth lines. She reminded him of a dancer whose movements are so liquid there seems no break between them. Or a gazelle, he thought: elusive, wary, quick to flee when startled, beautiful to watch. He followed her, thinking that he knew more about her than he had known two weeks earlier, but still far less than he had expected. After two weeks with any other woman, he would have known about her past, her friends, her likes and dislikes, and the feel of her beneath him. He would have been able to categorize her. He hadn't realized, until now, how predictable his affairs had grown, or how absorbed he could become in a woman who was so different: frustrating, annoying, fascinating, and enthralling. And fitting into no category that he could think of.

Some distance ahead, Laura had stopped and had bent down to pick something up. "It's a tiny ring made of stone," she called, the lilt of her voice carrying over the crash of the waves below them. "Or maybe it's bone. Isn't this amazing?"

He caught up to her and looked at the tiny ring in her palm. "Crinoid. Distant cousin of the starfish and the sea urchin." He took it from her palm. "It's a fossil, probably about three hundred fifty million years old."

Laura stared at him. "*Three hundred fifty million?*" He handed the fossil back and she touched it with her finger. "It's so hard to comprehend; it's like touching infinity." She smiled. "You'd think, if something can survive this long and this perfectly, love affairs and reputations could, too."

He laughed. "Well put. It makes us sound fickle and hopelessly short-lived."

She was still rolling the small ring in her palm. "What did it look like?"

"It probably had arms, like plumes on top of a stalk. A paleontologist would know for sure."

"Starfish... sea urchin," she whispered as if the words conjured magic images. "Incredible... so many marvelous things waiting to be discovered." She tucked the fossil into the pocket of her jeans. "Wouldn't it be wonderful to have a collection of things like this? Then when something bad happened we could take them out and remember that some things are perfect and don't disappear and if we keep try-ing..." She flushed, then gave Paul a quick smile. "Of course, lots of people wouldn't need that."

He put his hand under her chin. "You have the strangest notion that the world is full of people who have no problems. I don't know where you got it. Even this crinoid isn't perfect; after all, it died."

Laura broke into laughter. "You're right. I'd better find something else to envy."

"No." He held her face between his hands. "There's nothing and no one you should envy. My sweet girl, you outshine everyone; if you'd just learn to trust yourself as much as everyone trusts you—"

"Thank you," Laura said quickly. She felt dizzy, as if all of her were being drawn to the warmth of Paul's hands and she could scarcely feel her feet balancing on the rocky ledge. "Don't you think we should turn back? Isn't it getting late?"

He shrugged, feeling purposely misunderstood, and followed her as she made her way along the rocks. She was moving quickly, almost flying, and as he kept up with her, Paul began to lose his annoyance and respond to the beauty around them and the exhilarating harmony of his body. The ocean had quieted, its waves lapping at the dark rocks that seemed to change color from moment to moment beneath lengthening shadows and a copper sun low in the sky. The air was warm, but a breeze brought a hint of evening coolness. When he saw the parking lot, he was regretful; it was almost like leaving childhood.

"I'm glad you suggested that," he said to Laura as they sat in the car. "You brought back my youth and made it better than it ever was, even in my memory." He backed out of the parking lot. "I don't know when I've had a better day."

"When you photographed the beautiful women in the marketplace at Avignon," Laura said mockingly.

"Did I say that was wonderful?"

"One of the best days you ever had."

He smiled. "It was, in its way. But I wasn't with you, so it can't have been as wonderful as I thought. In fact, the memory is fading fast; I can barely remember it."

She laughed. "Can you remember where we're eating dinner?"

"The King's Tavern at six-thirty. Are you hungry?"

"Famished."

"So am I. We'll be there in ten minutes. Maybe less."

The King's Tavern was built on a small rise overlooking the main street of Gloucester and, beyond it, the crowded wharves where salt-encrusted fishing boats swayed and creaked in the light breeze. At the back of each boat, rope as thick as a man's wrist and heavy nets stiff with ocean salt were wound on huge drums or coiled on the deck; gulls swooped in to strut on them and perch on the prows where names generations old were boldly lettered. Beside the harbor, the shops and restaurants on the main street were of wood darkened by the sea, making the small town seem rooted in earth and ocean and sky, tolerating the modern cars of tourists but unchanged by them.

Laura savored it all, especially the sense of timelessness that reminded her of her favorite neighborhoods of Boston, and then Paul had parked at the King's Tavern and they were being shown to a small room at the back. Somehow he had arranged with the owners for a place where they could wash up and dress for dinner: a spare room at the back of the restaurant with two chairs and a tiny bathroom. Laura went first, carrying the overnight bag Allison had given her. "Dress simply," Paul had said, but she had agonized over what to take. In the tiny room at the King's Tavern she pulled off the jeans and khaki shirt that smelled of the sea, washed as well as she could in the small basin, and dressed in white polished cotton, full-skirted with long sleeves and a deep V neck. Around her throat she fastened a turquoise necklace she had found in a small shop in Provincetown, on the Cape. There was nothing she could do about her hair: the damp air turned the loose waves into long chestnut ringlets that would not comb straight, and so she left them, even the tendrils that curved onto her cheeks and forehead. Not sleek and sophisticated, she reflected, but there wasn't time to worry about it; she had to let Paul have his turn in the room. But she did pause when she took a final look in the small mirror and saw her glowing face. I look too happy, she thought, too excited. He likes cool, clever women. He'll think I look like a Girl Scout. But she didn't know what to do about it, and after a moment, since no one was watching, she shrugged. *This is me. He'll like me or he won't.*

He was waiting for her in the bar, looking out over the town and the wharf, where crews were unloading the square, white lobster pots they had just brought in. Laura watched him for a moment. His face was somber, almost severe, and for the first time she wondered about his secrets instead of worrying about her own.

He turned and saw her and smiled, his eyes glad and admiring. "You're lovely and you put me to shame; I feel like a grubby rock climber. I ordered wine for you; I won't be long."

She sat at the table where his half-finished drink still stood and gazed, as he had, at the purposeful activity of the sturdy men on the wharf. Gloucester. Cape Ann. A coast less than fifty miles north of Boston where one could climb on rocks and dine on fresh-caught lobster and still get back home before midnight. If one wanted to get back home. She pictured in her mind her overnight bag and felt again Paul's fingers touching the droplets of water in her hair, and his arm around her shoulders. If one wanted to get back.

Happiness surged through her and she put her hand to her cheek: she thought she must be blushing, she felt so hot. This is silly, she thought; I'm acting like a virgin. But in a way she felt like one. The quick, furtive couplings in the back seats of cars when she was in high school and the brief affairs at the university had left her untouched; her body had moved in all the expected ways, but she hadn't ever been able to care about what she was doing or even feel it had anything to do with her. It had been as if she stood apart, watching. She helped the panting, insistent boys who mounted her because that was what she was supposed to do. But each time she'd gone home to Beacon Hill feeling cheated and bewildered. Why did people go to so much trouble to do this?

Now, sitting in the King's Tavern, filled with a happiness as heady as noon wine, more rare than sex, more difficult to find than passion, she began to understand. *My sweet girl, you outshine everyone.* Her body seemed to lift out of itself, toward whatever they would find together.

The scene on the dock had changed. Fishermen and their families were arriving with floats they were finishing for St. Peter's Fiesta, when the fishing boats would be blessed. It was a tradition that went back hundreds of years. I'd like to be here for the parade, Laura thought. But then I'd like to be everywhere: Europe, Africa, India, finding crinoids at Cape Ann, marching with the Portuguese fishermen of Gloucester, shopping with the women at the market in Avignon. I wasted so much time stealing and dreaming, and now I'm twenty-one and how will I ever have time to do everything I want to do?

She felt Paul's hand on her shoulder and looked up, meeting his dark eyes. I have time for Paul, she thought.

The words settled inside her as they sat at dinner in the soft light of ship's lanterns. Around them was the murmur of voices and the soft clatter of dishes on polished wood tables, while they spoke in low voices, their hands brushing as they turned to each other to share a smile, letting desire build. Only once was the spell broken, halfway through dinner. "You're the only woman I know," Paul said, "who can crack open a lobster without turning her plate into a disaster area. You'd make a good magician. Or a pickpocket. Would you like more wine? I'll order another bottle."

"No. This is fine." She sat still, looking at the bright red tail and neatly split claws on the plate before her, the white lobster meat lying beside them in long smooth pieces. She hadn't even thought about it; her fingers, trained and sensitive, had done the job while she had talked to Paul and thought her thoughts.

Paul, the joke already forgotten, was talking about visits to Cape Ann when he was a boy, staying for weekends with a school friend whose family had a home in Marblehead Neck. "The backyard sloped to the bay, and we'd have races to see who could roll fastest down the grass and into the water. After a while his parents got the idea it wasn't the safest playground for kids, and they put up a fence. It was one of my first experiences of someone telling me what was best for me."

Laura laughed softly. Her happiness had returned, and she felt light-hearted and at ease. "Is that why you travel all the time—because you hate fences?"

Surprised, he said, "I don't know. I'll have to think about it. You're right about my hating them; I always want to jump over instead of using the gate. Do you? You must be good at it, the way you climb rocks. Are you good at jumping fences?"

"Yes," she said boldly, wanting to share it with him, "but I haven't done it for a long time."

"Neither have I. We'll do it some day, shall we? Pretend we're kids and leap a fence?"

"And convince ourselves we can't be kept out?"

"And convince ourselves there's nothing we can't do."

Laura smiled. "I like that."

"Better yet, do you believe it?"

"Yes," she said simply, and they smiled together, and then sat quietly, listening to the music that drifted up to them from the wharves where people were dancing, and gazing through the huge windows that encircled the room. The moon had risen, turning the fishing boats to ghostly shapes gently swaying in the harbor. Paul took her hand in his. "I'll take you back to Boston, if that's what you'd like. Unless you'd rather stay up here."

"I'd rather stay."

He lifted her hand and kissed the palm. "My friend's house is empty. He only uses it on weekends."

She nodded, not asking how often he had used it when it was empty, not caring. Each of them had a past they would never share with the other.

The house was at the end of Marblehead Neck—a cluster of gray shingled mansions strung on a narrow curve of land jutting into Marblehead Bay. Across the water Laura could see the lights of the town of Marblehead, but in front of them everything was dark as Paul turned into the driveway. "I didn't call ahead; there won't be anyone here to pamper you and fix breakfast."

Laura smiled in the darkness. "I was counting on you for that."

"Trusting woman. How do you know I can cook?"

"It doesn't matter if you know how to pamper."

He chuckled and slid out of the car, reaching into the back seat for their bags. "Hold on while I find the key. It's here somewhere... on top of the lamp post as I recall..."

He hasn't been here in a while, Laura thought, then remembered she didn't care when he'd been here last.

The house smelled faintly musty when the door swung open and Paul walked through the living room, switching on lights and opening windows. "The kitchen is through that door. What would you like? Something to eat? Or drink?" Laura tried to think of something to say. She was nervous, trying to retrieve the pulsing happiness that had glowed within her at the restaurant. *I want you to love me. I want you to tell me what to do. I want everything to be simple and wonderful.*

"We'll go upstairs," he said. His arm was around her waist and they walked up the curved stairway with matching steps, into a long room that was white with moonlight. When Paul turned her to face him, it was as natural to put her arms around him as it had been to walk into the house at his side, as if they belonged together. "Two weeks," he murmured, his lips brushing hers. "An eternity."

"Not for me—" she started to say, but his mouth was on hers, opening it, and she tasted the sharpness of cognac on his tongue. It was a long kiss; he held her mouth with his and her body in the tight clasp of his arms until she felt there was nothing but the two of them in a small enclosed place that roared with a pounding that was like the surf. It came from her own heart but it shook her with a force like the ocean's.

Paul lifted his head and she took a tremulous breath. "I'd better sit down."

He laughed softly. "There's a bed." Holding her hand he led her the length of the room, along a silver ribbon of moonlight, to a high four-poster bed hung with white curtains and covered with a worn patchwork quilt. A small mahogany step stool was beside it, and Paul kept Laura's hand in his as she climbed the three steps and he followed, bending over her as she lay back, his mouth covering hers again, his hands holding her face. "My lovely girl, my darling Laura . . ."

Laura was burning. She had never wanted anything the way she wanted Paul's mouth, his hands, his body joined to hers. When he pulled off his sport coat, her urgent fingers were unbuttoning his shirt, and then he was opening her dress, slipping it off her shoulders and lifting her to pull it down and toss it aside, and all the time her hands were touching him, curving, stroking, learning the feel of the hard muscles in his arms, the dark hairs on his chest, the yielding at his waist, until he drew back and tore off all his clothes and came back to lie on her.

Moonlight flooded the room. The bed canopy and curtains glowed like sheltering moonbeams, lightening his dark skin, turning Laura's pure white. "My God, you are so beautiful," he said, the words like a long flame against her breasts. Laura's body moved of its own accord; she couldn't lie still. "I'm sorry," she whispered, ashamed of her eagerness. "Don't!" he responded sharply, then said quickly, "I didn't mean to snap at you. But don't apologize. Ever. My darling girl, we do what we want because we want each other, because we have joy in each other. . ." "Yes," she said; it was no more than a long breath. "Yes, we do. Yes." With her hands in Paul's hair, she brought his mouth to hers, drinking him in, and felt his hardness between her legs. Yes, she thought, the word chiming within her. We have joy in each other. And she let herself become part of the joy; she let herself want everything: to do everything, feel everything, taste everything.

Paul raised himself and slipped his hands beneath her underclothes, pulling them off, and as the cool air and his warm hands embraced her she gave a small cry that pierced the quiet room.

He took her breast in his mouth; her nipple tightened beneath his lips and tongue, and a long sigh that was his name broke from her at the pleasure radiating through her. As his mouth held her breast, his caressing hand slid along the curve of her waist and down her thighs, opening her flesh with his fingers, sliding into the wet darkness within, and even as she cried out with longing her hands were following the harder curves of his body until she raised them and again took his head between her hands, fiercely kissing him, taking his lower lip between her teeth, then, still hungry, still moving, sucking and biting the smooth skin of his neck, tasting the fragrance of the soap they had used when they changed before dinner.

Abruptly, Paul stopped caressing her and raised himself on his elbow, holding her still with one hand as he looked down at her. Until that moment, he had accepted her desire without questioning it. He was accustomed to having women desire him, and he had let his hands follow the skillful patterns he had used with so many of them for so many years. But Laura was not like any of them; she was sexual but almost clumsy, demanding but unsure, not a virgin but oddly inexperienced. An urgent woman and an unschooled girl. The fleeting thought came to him that he wasn't sure it was just a man she wanted, or him.

"What is it?" Laura asked. Her breath trembled and she tried to see his eyes, but they were shadowed in the moonlight; his face was almost a mask. "Paul, I want you, I thought you wanted me, I thought you felt this, too—I never knew I could feel it—this wonderful wanting... I never knew what it was like..."

"My God," he said roughly and lay on his side, pulling her against him. He kissed her long, tangled curls, her smooth forehead, the delicate eyelids that hid her large clear eyes. His hands explored the curves of her body as if she were the first woman he had ever known, and he felt himself aroused and absorbed by her in a way that startled him. "So much a child, so much a woman..." he said, and then he was as urgent as she, almost savage in his need to be part of her. He turned, and turned her with him so she was spread beneath him. Laura's hunger flared again and again, flames fed by the flint of his body; she opened her legs wide and pulled him inside her, deep, thrusting, filling her. He raised himself on his hands and they watched his shaft, hard and glistening in the moonlight, disappear deep inside her, then slide up and thrust down again, while her hands moved over his chest and down his hard stomach, and held him when he pulled out of her before thrusting down once more. Then his weight was upon her again, his hands raising her hips, his tongue meeting hers, and Laura felt an overwhelming sense of wonder—that need and desire and joy could merge and become one, in one instant, with one man. And the wonder buoyed her up as Paul's closeness buoyed her, his lips murmuring her name against her mouth, their bodies moving together, and within her the rhythmic thought that everything was perfect, and would be forever.

CHAPTER 8

IT took Clay a month to figure out what to do with the television remote control he'd found in Terry Levonio's locker, and then he waited another month to make sure he was right. It was so simple he was filled with admiration. Who'd have thought Terry the grinning bartender would have the brains to think it up?

He finally tried it out one night in the quiet hour before dawn while the night staff sat staring fixedly at magazines or television in a desperate effort to stay awake. The lobby was empty, the restaurant closed, the bar dark and shuttered.

"Going to the bathroom," Clay told the back of the night manager's head nodding in front of a John Wayne movie. Around the corner from the lobby, he unlocked a back entrance to the bar and slipped inside. The bottles were put away, the glasses washed, the bar wiped clean. Thorough, careful Terry. Clay stood behind the bar, holding the remote control he'd taken from Terry's locker a few minutes earlier. Pointing it at the cash register, he pressed buttons at random until he heard, in the silent room, a distinct click.

How about that, Clay marveled. If somebody planned to skim a nice living from a bar, he'd fix up a little electronic thingamajig that would temporarily disable his cash register when he wanted it to. He'd push his little button—out of sight, under the counter—and when he rang up the price of a drink, so that anybody watching could see him do it, *it wouldn't register.* Something like typing without a ribbon. And he pockets the money. And when he goes home, he'd have—how much? How much would he have in his pocket?

He left the bar, locking the door behind him, and went downstairs to the employees' room where he replaced the volume control exactly as he'd found it in Terry's locker.

At the end of his long hours he'd have skimmed maybe ten percent of the night's booze. We do sixteen, seventeen hundred bucks a night in that joint. At least that's what the cash register says. Which means we're probably doing closer to two thousand and friend Terry takes home a couple hundred each and every night. No wonder he drives a Porsche.

"Everything quiet?" he asked the night manager when he returned.

In response he heard a gentle snoring. Shit, Clay thought, this place needs a good shaking up.

He sat on his high stool behind the reception desk, and thought. He could tell Terry what he'd found, and that would end it—no more danger that Clay Fairchild would be blamed if somebody else found out. But he ought to be able to do better than that. He ought to get a medal for saving thousands of dollars for the hotel. For the Salingers. He ought to get a promotion.

Why not? he thought. Laura had gotten close to them, and look where she was. If he made a big thing of this so they'd think he was God's gift to the Philadelphia Salinger, he'd be in as solid with the Salingers as she was. Then wouldn't she be proud of him for really getting ahead!

Goddam, he thought, sitting straight on his stool. That's where the future is. It's a pain in the ass that it has to be a job, but if it's a big job . . . And the Salingers are as big as they come: they could find a neat place for me if they wanted to.

Shit, he told himself with a grin, if we're smart and take our time, there's no reason why Laura and Clay Fairchild can't end up right in the middle of the Salinger empire. And then let anybody try to take anything away from us.

The next morning, as soon as Willard Payne walked into his office, Clay knocked on his door and said he wanted to talk to him about a serious problem in the hotel.

* * *

Laura's desk was dark gray steel, crammed in a windowless room with gray steel filing cabinets and typewriter tables and three other assistants at their own steel desks. Sitting beneath the unsparing glare of fluorescent lights, it was hard to believe that just beyond the closed door was the elegant lobby of a grand hotel. "Someday we will make this place beautiful," Jules LeClair said vaguely once or twice a month, but he never got around to it; he was very busy.

"The concierge of a great hotel must do everything—exquisitely," he had instructed Laura when she first arrived. "He is the eyes and ears and the mother and father of the hotel. A guest also once called me the mayor of the lobby. He was, of course, exactly right."

Jules LeClair, wearing a perfectly cut black suit and red brocade vest, his mustache clipped, his silver hair precisely waved, ruled from his carved walnut desk set at an angle in the most prominent corner of the lobby. Fresh flowers bloomed in his Waterford vase every day, his pencils were sharpened before he arrived, the heavy glass protecting the desktop was polished until he could see his reflection—a satisfying sight he permitted himself before plunging into the day's work.

"The hours are 7:00 A.M. to 5:00 P.M., four days a week," he told Laura. "You may, of course, work longer; it is the only way to learn, to become a true concierge. There is, naturally, someone always at this desk, around the clock, but the truly crucial times, when we are absolutely indispensable and everything would crumble without us, are seven to seven. Therefore, I, Jules LeClair, work those hours. Anyone who dreams of being as superb as I will work those hours at my side. We allow ourselves exactly one hour for lunch. The remainder of the time it is our delight to please our guests so that they return and also tell their friends how well it is here. Each day we hand them their room keys, of course greeting them by name. If they have been here before, we arrange for their favorite drinks and flowers to be in their rooms when they arrive; we remember whether they will want tickets for the theater or the symphony or the basketball. And they think we are wonderful. And they are exactly right. Are you always so quiet, like a little mouse? This is excellent; this means you will learn."

Each day Jules gave her a different job to do, and soon Laura had her own private file of information about the city, the hotel, and returning guests. "There are always times to rely on other people," Owen told her, "but not on their information. You must have your own. If you don't, you'll always be an assistant, never an authority. You'll always have to rely on others."

"I won't," Laura said. "Not on Jules, not on anyone."

Owen smiled. "Very good," he said, and did not point out to her that she had already taken the first step away from his tutelage. She'll do just fine on her own, he thought, and he was pleased.

Mornings began for Laura before Owen left his room. Rosa had breakfast waiting for her at six-thirty and she was at the hotel twenty-five minutes later, while Arlington Street still seemed to sleep and the lobby of the Salinger Hotel was hushed and waiting for the day to begin. "Good morning, my good staff," Jules said amiably and perched on the corner of Laura's desk. "Here is the first work of today." He handed out folders with assignments. "Laura, for you I have a special task: you will arrange for a yacht for the Countess Irinia, for two weeks from today, for a period of five days. Use our check to reserve it; the countess's secretary will naturally reimburse us when they arrive. Insist that the company assign chef Louis; the countess commended his *crème brûlée* last year. When this is done, you will write to that effect to the countess; I of course will sign the letter. Also, Madame d'Allessio wishes to visit the Dior showroom when she is in Paris next week; this I will take care of myself because it is very sensitive, keeping my good friend in Paris happy so he does us these favors, but you will please write to madame and tell her we are delighted to arrange this for her. That letter also I will sign. Now, a few other matters..." He went over them rapidly while Laura nodded and said nothing, annoyed because Jules, possessive of his status and the enormous tips he received, always refused to let her deal directly with the wealthiest guests.

The door from the lobby opened and Jules looked up. "Yes, yes?"

"May I see you," Felix said. It was not a question.

"But of course," said Jules, his small careful mouth clearly showing that he would allow no one but someone of Felix's importance to take him from his work. "Laura, you will sit at my desk. Make no decisions; simply hand out keys, write down requests, and smile often. I will not be long. So," he said cheerfully to Felix, "shall we sit on the couch beside the window? From there I keep an eye on my desk and my very pretty assistant."

Laura watched them sit together. She had smiled at Felix when he came in, but he had barely acknowledged her presence and she wondered, as she always did when she saw him in the hotel, what he thought of the fact that Owen had bypassed him to get her the job with Jules. She looked up as the first of the morning joggers stood before her, asking for his key. Drops of sweat dripped on Jules's immaculately polished glass. "Good morning, Mr. Starrett," Laura said, smiling as she took his key from the board in the top desk drawer and handed it to him. "Would you like me to have pecan rolls and coffee sent to your room?"

"Right." He peered through the cascade of sweat that blurred his vision. "You're new here. I'd remember you."

"I usually work in another office."

"Smarter to have you out here. You're a hell of a lot prettier to look at than that Frenchified little dandy they usually have. You knew my name, too."

Laura smiled again, thinking that even if her memory were terrible, the loud Dallas twang and the many demands of Wylie Starrett would be impossible to forget. "We remember our favorite guests," she said and picked up her telephone. "I'll order your breakfast. And let me know if you need a driver for your appointments today."

She had made the call to the kitchen, and greeted six other joggers, when a small, pale man, fussily folding a handkerchief in his hand, appeared before her. She tried to think of his name and failed. She couldn't even recall seeing him before. "If I may help you?" she asked warmly to make up for her failure.

"Security Systems Incorporated," he said. "I have an eight o'clock appointment with—"

Laura missed the next few words in the pounding of her heart. But as swiftly as the fear had gripped her, it was gone. What was wrong with her that she still jumped when she heard someone say 'security' and even when she saw a policeman walking in her direction? Nobody was after her; there was nothing to be afraid of. And then she smiled to herself. *Except not being able to tell a security man from one of the Salinger's wealthy guests.* "I'm sorry," she said, "who is it you want to see?"

"Mr. Asa Salinger."

Laura called upstairs to confirm the appointment, gave him directions to Asa's office, and had only a moment to wonder what security problems Asa was worried about before she was caught up in a rush of early-morning guests who needed information or wanted tickets for events that evening. As she responded to each of them she jotted down their names and their requests, and when Jules and Felix returned she handed Jules the list. "Ah, excellent. You see?" he said to Felix. "My little Laura is as efficient as she is pretty. I have written to Mr. Owen Salinger to thank him for sending her to me. But, Laura, I have returned. My chair?"

She relinquished it, hiding her reluctance beneath a cool smile. "I'll be in my office."

"Laura," Felix said, "I'd like you to have a cup of coffee with me."

Masking her surprise, she looked at Jules. He was less successful; his curiosity clearly showed as his gaze flicked rapidly from Felix to her and back again. When he could learn nothing from their faces, he sighed and nodded. "For a brief time. We are, of course, extremely busy."

Laura was smiling as they walked away.

"Is there a joke?" Felix asked.

"I was thinking about Jules. With his red vest and the way he moves his head, he reminds me of the ruby-throated hummingbirds at the Cape."

He gave a small smile. "I hadn't thought of that." Clever, he thought; I hadn't given her credit for being clever. And damned attractive. He gave her a sidelong glance, approving her pearl gray suit, her white blouse buttoned to the throat, and the dark blue silk scarf, worn like a man's tie, with an ivory stickpin in the center. Vaguely recalling the ordinary, gawky teenager who had come to work for them three years earlier, he wondered who had taught her. Allison, he supposed. She was always taking somebody in tow: stray animals, stray people, even friends and family members who she thought needed her help. Damnedest thing how she always had to help people. Like her mother, he thought. She gets it from her mother. Not from me; I leave people alone. If they need something badly enough, they'll ask. "We can sit here," he said, coming to a stop. "They'll bring coffee to us."

Laura sat on the striped sofa. *The president of Salinger Hotels Incorporated can have coffee brought to him in the lobby. Why can't everyone? If I had my own hotel . . .*

"—understand you're learning everything about hotel management," Felix was saying.

"Everything Owen and Jules can teach me. I suppose between them they know just about all there is to know."

"And you're studying it in college?"

"Yes."

"And what will you do with all this knowledge?"

"Use it." Laura watched the waiter from the hotel's Bostonian restaurant arrange cups, a pot of coffee, napkins, and a basket of croissants on the table before them. *He should have brought fruit; I'll remember that.* As he filled the cups, she said, "Owen wants to help me find a job when I graduate."

"You have a job. With Jules."

"I want more than that. Someday I want to manage a hotel."

"Only one?"

She smiled. "One at a time."

"But you've thought of others."

"I've thought of possibilities," she said carefully. She studied him, wondering why he had changed toward her. His face was expressionless, but his voice was warmer than at any time in the three years she had been with his family. "Was there something special you wanted to ask me?"

"Not special, no. I simply thought it would be good for us to talk. Jules is pleased with you; Owen says you're a quick student; my daughter Allison calls you her best friend. And I hardly know you. Leni tells me all young women want more these days; she was speaking of you and it seems she was right. Which hotel do you expect to manage?"

"I don't expect anything. We haven't talked very much about it. I'm sure it will be a small one, but it's up to Owen to decide."

"An older one, I assume."

"The older ones are the small ones." They were sparring now and Laura was tense. Whatever he claimed, he did want something from her, and she didn't know what; and she was afraid she wasn't quick enough to keep up with him. At that moment she saw Owen crossing the lobby, and instinctively she stood.

"What the hell—" Felix began, not used to having people interrupt a conversation before he was ready; then he followed her gaze and saw Owen, who was smiling broadly as he joined them.

"Laura, my dear"—he took her hand, holding it for a moment—"and Felix, and breakfast. An irresistible combination." He sat in an armchair beside Laura's, but he spoke to Felix. "This is fortuitous; I came in early to find you before your busy day began."

"Is something wrong?"

"Not to my knowledge." He took the cup of coffee Laura had poured for him. "Thank you, my dear. I try to keep up, Felix; you know how interested I am, and retirement has not changed that."

"We send you weekly reports."

"So you do. Can you tell me a little more about the new hotel we are building in St. Kitts?"

"What about it?"

"The rooms are small."

A tight defensiveness pinched Felix's face and he bent forward, explaining in clipped words why they had chosen to put money into the conference rooms and golf course instead of larger bedrooms. Laura watched him: the small but urgent gestures he made with his hands, the ramrod back inclined toward Owen, his anxious eyes, and suddenly she felt she was seeing him for the first time. He's desperate for Owen's approval, she thought, astonished at the humanity of a man she had always thought of as unfeeling. For a moment she pitied him. But then, as Owen made a comment about gracious surroundings, impatience flashed over Felix's face and his grating voice became even harsher. "Just because you like nineteenth-century bedrooms it doesn't mean our customers do. They don't. They want frills: swimming pools, exercise rooms, golf courses, marble lobbies, French chefs. And we give them all that, but it costs money. It makes money, too. What other reason is there to do anything, unless you're stuck in a swamp of sentiment? The way you're hanging on to those old hotels of yours—being romantic about bricks and mortar—when any fool could tell you we should be tearing them down and building new ones..."

Owen slowly shook his head. "Romance is the only magic we have left, and I have plans for those hotels." His somber look settled on Laura. "One of these days you and I will see what we can do with them. I've always wanted to, you know, but we were busy building up the chain and the years passed, and so did much of my energy. But now, with someone young to stimulate me... well, we'll see what we can do. Otherwise, Felix will wait until I'm dead and then tear them down and build fancy high rises with swimming pools and tiny rooms."

"And profits," Felix said shortly.

"Those four hotels break even; they've never lost money." Owen contemplated his son. "Why does this bother you so much? Four hotels, Felix, out of fifty-eight Salinger Hotels in this country and Europe."

"Four of the top markets in the country—New York, Chicago, Philadelphia, Washington—where we don't have modern hotels because I can't go into competition with you by building new ones. Four cities where the Salinger name means shabby and second-rate."

Owen nodded. "A good point. Our name should indicate excellence. And something will be done about it."

"How? You won't let us touch those hotels; you keep them locked in your own damned private corporation, separate from the rest of the hotels. It makes no sense! It's not good business!"

"But it might be good romance." Owen smiled at Laura. "And maybe I'm not too old to try to mix a little romance with business. It's worth a try, wouldn't you say, Felix?"

Felix shrugged. "Whims," he muttered. "If you'll excuse me, I have a busy day. Someone from Security Systems is supposed to be here and I want to see him."

"He's here," said Laura. "He asked for Asa and I sent him upstairs."

"Problems with security?" Owen asked.

"Not a big problem yet, but it might be. Two guests in the past month have had their pockets picked in front of the hotel. We hired a detective and he stood around for two weeks, but the second incident occurred five feet from him and I've got to find a way to prevent any more from happening."

"Yes. Good God, people will see us as unsafe; it has to be stopped. You're hiring more detectives?"

"I'll hire a dozen if I have to. I want to get some suggestions from an expert first."

"Why don't you have your detective sit down?" Laura asked.

Owen and Felix frowned at her.

"I mean," she said nervously, "standing up is no good; his eyes are at the wrong level. If he's sitting down he's looking at pants pockets and he can see better."

"By God!" Owen roared, causing nearby guests to turn in disapproval. "Wonderful! Who would have thought of that? Eh? Felix, get a chair for your man!"

"He'd attract considerable attention," said Felix dryly.

"What about that?" Owen asked Laura.

Warmed by his praise, Laura ignored Felix. "Put him in a wheel-chair."

"With a tin cup!" Owen exclaimed. "And a monkey!"

"Let's not overdo it," Felix murmured, but for the first time his interest was caught. "It might work."

"It's worth a try," Owen said. He grinned at Laura. "It takes a creative mind to think like a pickpocket. Thank you, my dear—"

A woman screamed.

It cut like a sword through the morning crowd. For an instant the lobby froze. Then it came to life. Everyone was milling and talking at once, as if a film had speeded up and might soon be out of control.

Felix had shot out of his chair and was gone. "I must go," Laura said to Owen. "Jules will want me."

"Yes, yes, go." His bushy eyebrows were drawn together. "We've never had violence here. Never..."

Laura kissed the top of his head and quickly made her way through the milling confusion toward her desk. But before she got there she saw Felix bending over a woman sprawled on a love seat; he looked helpless and enraged. "Can I help?" she asked.

His mouth was tight. "She won't say what happened. She doesn't want a doctor; she doesn't want the police."

The woman's hands were clasped tightly beneath her chin and her eyes were closed. Late fifties, Laura thought, too much makeup, bleached hair, expensive suit, fine pearls. Her nails were manicured and she was crying. Jules arrived but held back as he saw Laura bend over and gently push the woman's hair from her eyes. "I've ordered tea for you," she said quietly. "Can you sit up?"

Her eyes still closed, the woman shook her head. Laura gestured to Felix, who struggled briefly with his desire to ask her who the hell she was to be giving orders, then decided a peaceful lobby was more important. "Jules," he said, "get tea. And something to eat."

Jules went through the same struggle, then turned furiously on his heel and marched away without a word. "I'm going to help you sit up," Laura said, her voice low. "If you can't manage it, we'll have to carry you to the lounge until we know how badly hurt you are."

"Not hurt." The woman struggled to sit up. She opened her eyes and looked at Laura. "Knocked around, but I should be used to..." She closed her eyes, then opened them again. "Do you work here?" Laura nodded. "Well. Sorry I made a noise in your lobby." The nonchalant pose failed and she closed her eyes again. "My God, my God, what will people say?"

"That doesn't matter."

"It does, it does, you don't understand, you're too young." She sat up with Laura's arm around her, once more opening her eyes, and her tears returned, spilling over and leaving wavering tracks in the thick powder on her face. "I'm sorry, I'm so sorry. I knew I shouldn't come. I told myself a hundred times I was better off in Dallas not knowing what he was up to, but then I just found myself here, and of course he had her in his room after he promised he wouldn't see her again, ever..."

"I don't think you want to talk about this here," Laura said firmly.

"She was in bed—nude, the little slut—waiting for him to come back from running." The woman laughed harshly. "Good healthy activity, first thing in the morning. Nobody ever said Wylie Starrett doesn't take care of himself. He's in top form, they say.... Oh, God, what got into me that I had it out with him here, in the lobby, when I knew he'd use his fist; he always uses his—" She bent over in a fit of coughing as Jules and a bellhop arrived with a tray.

Laura smiled absently, as if it were perfectly natural for Jules to wait on her. "Thank you... if you'll just put it here... Oh, good, you brought something to eat." She filled a cup. "I want you to stop talking, Mrs. Starrett, and drink this and eat some biscuits. And then we're going to put you in a room upstairs. I assume you have luggage."

She nodded, her eyes startled. The puffy half-moons below them were streaked with mascara, and Laura wiped them gently with her handkerchief. "Drink your tea, Mrs. Starrett," she said softly.

"It's Virginia. Ginny. I want you to call me Ginny."

Laura smiled. "I'm Laura Fairchild. Will you wait here while I get you a room? We can talk later, if you like, when you've had a chance to clean up and rest."

"I want to talk. You'll take me to my room." The authoritative voice contrasted oddly with her red eyes and tear-streaked face, but it was obvious that she was used to giving orders.

"Of course," Laura said, standing up.

She saw Jules make a quick gesture. His staff went only where he directed. Laura looked at the woman on the couch and spread her hands slightly so Jules could see she had no choice. "I'll take care of your room," she said to Virginia Starrett, and crossed the lobby to the reservations desk.

"Very efficient," Felix said to Jules. "You're lucky she was here."

Behind him, Owen had been watching. As he saw Jules's face darken, he put a friendly hand on his shoulder. "You've trained her well, Jules. She does you credit."

"Ah." Jules let out his breath and reorganized his thoughts. "It is, of course, difficult, the responsibility for shaping a good and trusted staff. But your protégée, Mr. Salinger, is a fine young woman. She learns well from Jules. I am proud of what she has learned."

And all three men, each pleased in his own way, stood guard over Virginia Starrett as she drank her tea in the midst of a discreetly murmuring lobby that had returned to normal.

* * *

After dinner in the kitchen bay of Owen's house, Laura told Paul about her day and finished with a performance of Jules LeClair in action. "I am proud of what she has learned," she finished with a small precise bow, her French accent perfectly mimicking Jules's, her voice just deep enough to sound like his.

"Exactly," Paul said as they laughed together. "It's exactly Jules. You're wonderful."

"How do you know? You told me you don't pay attention to the hotels."

"I'm paying more attention now. I've stopped by a few times, just to make sure your working conditions are acceptable."

Laura smiled but her eyes were serious. "What would you have done if they weren't?"

"Taken Jules by the scruff of the neck, dropped him into the bay, and fed him to the lobsters."

"And been lynched by the lobstermen for changing the taste of Boston lobsters. Paul, you wouldn't have done anything."

He shook his head. "I just wanted to be able to picture you in your job when I think about you during the day. I do that quite a bit, you know. Go ahead, finish your story. How did you hear Jules congratulating himself for your skills if you'd gone off to get a room for the lady in distress?"

"I walked very slowly; I wanted to hear what they said."

"Wise woman. Always know what's going on behind your back." He poured coffee for her. "You had a good time, didn't you?"

"I loved it. Jules doesn't let me work with people very often; I got to Ginny Starrett just before he did. If I could do that kind of thing all day it would be wonderful."

"You wouldn't want a steady stream of crises," he said, amused.

"Why not? Solving them is what makes heroines."

He laughed. "You're already a heroine to me." He looked more closely at her. "You don't really want to be a heroine to Jules LeClair."

"No, to myself. To know I'm perfect at a job."

"In this job?" he asked. "What happened to being an actress?"

"That was only an idea I had. Acting is a hobby."

"Wasn't Owen the one who said that?"

"I'm saying it. I can mimic people, and it's fun, but it's different to try to make it a whole life, and I haven't got time to find out if I really could or not. I can be successful much faster this way, and I do love it; it's something I can talk about and not hide—" She stopped. "It's something I can be proud of."

"Hide," Paul said musingly. "Why would you have anything to hide?"

"I hope I don't," she said, tossing it off. "But what if I tried to be a famous actress and failed and then turned to a life of crime?"

He smiled and shook his head. "You couldn't do it. You won't even pick up something in a department store to look at it, much less make off with it." He wondered what she really had meant. He wouldn't force her to tell him—she had a right to her own secrets—but it was a curious thing for her to say. "Anyway, let me help you become a heroine. Shall I register at the hotel and demand some exotic service and say you're the only one who can provide it?"

"We don't provide that kind of service," she said with a straight face. "The international concierge association forbids it."

He burst out laughing. "Good for them. Well, then, you'll have to make it on your own; it's foreign territory to me."

"You mean a job is foreign," she said. "Any job."

"Probably. I've never had one, but I suspect I'd feel like a foreigner if I had to satisfy someone else's fantasies instead of my own."

"But you can satisfy your own fantasies; you have your photography. Why don't you do something with it?"

"I don't need to."

"I didn't mean money. I meant doing something with your life, giving it a direction."

"Laura, my life is fine. Nothing is missing."

"You said—that night at my party—that you have everything you want but you'd like to want more."

"And you said you didn't understand what I meant."

"But now I think I do. You have all the things you want but there's no center, nothing that makes all the rest mean something. You don't have anything important in your life—"

"You're important."

"Can't you take me seriously?"

"I am taking you seriously."

"No, you're not. I'm talking about the Paul Janssen who does nothing all day but sports or sailing with friends or reading or taking pictures when he feels like it but usually not even developing the negatives, or . . . whatever else you do before you pick me up at work. You don't do anything that has a beginning and a middle and an end; nothing has a shape or a meaning; you can't look back at night and say, 'I did something good today that I'm proud of, something that will last.'"

There was silence in the kitchen. "You're a passionate and wise lady," Paul said at last. "But you're talking about something I don't need. I find my shape, as you call it, in my own ways, and I'm perfectly satisfied. But what does that matter to us? If we don't agree about work we'll talk about other things. Would you like more coffee?"

She hesitated as if about to say something more, then changed her mind. "Yes. Thank you."

Paul filled their cups, then turned away, looking beyond Laura at the fading streaks of a russet sunset, and at Owen's garden, dark in the shadow of its brick wall. He didn't want to argue. He'd learned long ago, from his father, that if one could avoid controversy and tension, almost everything eventually came out all right. It was quarrels that confirmed people in their ways, making them cling more tightly to ideas they might have shed or modified if they'd been left alone, turning them inward to protect the beliefs others were challenging. Nothing is worth a quarrel, Thomas Janssen had taught his son, and while Paul thought that probably was going too far, he wasn't sure what really might be worth the fervor and involvement of controversy.

"Let's leave it alone," he said to Laura. "And maybe we'll end up agreeing with each other."

She smiled and began to clear the dinner dishes. She didn't think it was that easy, but she didn't want to quarrel. Everything was so wonderful between them; why think about disagreements? She moved back and forth between the table and the sink. Around them the house was quiet, the rooms dark and empty. Owen and Rosa were at the Cape; the housekeepers were on vacation. All the Salingers had finally left that morning, later in the season than usual. Laura would join them on the weekends; the rest of the week she would live in Owen's town house. This was the first night she would be there alone, and she was feeling uncomfortable. It was too big; it was too much. She felt like a fraud. What am I doing here? she thought; how can I have this whole house to myself when just three years ago I was living in a New York tenement and dreaming of a room of my own? Five floors, twenty-two rooms on Beacon Hill. I don't belong here.

"You're bustling," Paul said as she stacked and rinsed dishes and put them in the dishwasher. "You don't have to do that; the maid will do them in the morning."

"I can't leave dishes overnight," Laura said.

"Why not?"

Because of cockroaches and other things that crawl in the dark. "It's just not right."

"Is that what your mother taught you?"

"Of course. Don't all mothers teach that?"

"Did you do the dishes together?"

"Yes," she said. That was true; she could remember standing at the sink with her mother. But she couldn't remember what they'd talked about. It was all gone, drowned in the torrent of tears she had shed when suddenly she had no parents and there was only Ben, saying he'd take care of them forever.

"Then I'll do the same," Paul said and carried the coffee cups to the granite counter with its stainless steel sink. He kissed the top of Laura's head, enjoying the silence around them. There was a charming domesticity to the scene, he reflected; in Owen's home and Rosa's kitchen they were like two children playing house. But they weren't children, and as Paul watched the play of light on Laura's long chestnut hair he wanted her as if it were the first time, in that empty house in Marblehead Neck. That was new for him—usually his interest began to wane as the weeks of an affair passed—but the novelty wasn't important enough to distract him from his desire. "Laura," he said, his voice low, and she came to him and moved into his embrace.

"I was thinking"—her lips were beside his ear, her words as soft as a sigh of wind—"how strange it feels to be here alone. . . ."

His mouth covered hers and then, together, they left the dishes and went upstairs to her apartment.

That was the pattern of that golden summer. When Laura left work, Paul was waiting for her in his car outside the hotel, and they ate dinner at a restaurant or at the round mahogany table in the kitchen bay, where tall beeswax candles cast a warm circle around them. After dinner they went to a concert or a play, or walked through Harvard Square, browsing in the shops, watching the people, holding hands as they strolled, until desire sent them back to Laura's rooms, where they made love and slept and woke to make love again until morning, when they made breakfast in the kitchen, bright this time with sunlight. And then Paul drove Laura to work before going to his studio and darkroom because, as he told her casually one morning, he'd gotten interested in photography again and had begun to make a series of portraits of her.

On the weekends they went to the Cape, where Laura stayed in the cottage Owen had offered her just before the robbery and Paul stayed with his parents. "I can't spend the night with you with your whole family around us," she said when he objected. "It's like flaunting us in their face, and your father doesn't approve of me—"

"He approves of you. He likes you."

"He calls me your diversion and wonders how long you'll keep it up."

"How the hell do you know that?"

"Allison told me."

"Allison should keep her mouth shut."

"Shouldn't I know what your family thinks?"

"If it matters. It doesn't."

"You love your father. You care what he thinks."

"Unless I know he's wrong. Laura, they know I stay with you in Boston."

"I don't care. I just can't walk out of the door in the morning as if I'm saying to all of them, 'Look, we just got out of bed.'"

"It would be honest."

"Sometimes it's better not to be honest."

He shrugged. "Whatever you want." But he had seen the sudden flash of worry in her eyes, and with a quick grin he put his arm around her. "Do you know how remarkable you are? For the first time in my life I find Boston in July so attractive I stay there five days a week."

They laughed together, and by the end of the summer Paul had come to believe she was right: why force the issue with his family when there was nothing to gain? He had Laura's passion, whether all night in Boston or for the early part of the night at the Cape; he had his own fascination with her, growing deeper each day; and he had her love. Even if he hadn't been sure of that, Allison confirmed it.

She and Thad were traveling in Canada but she telephoned almost every day, talking to her family more often than when she lived with them. When she called others in the family she talked about scenery and weather; she and Paul talked about each other. "She adores you,"

Allison said when she called one morning from Lake Louise. "You must know that. She doesn't exactly hide it. You do know it."

"Yes," he said. "But I like hearing it from you. Are you having a wonderful time?"

"Didn't I send you a postcard saying I was?"

"You did; Laura and Owen got them, too. But you also told us you wished we were there and we got the impression that you meant it."

Allison gave a short laugh. "I did. Why didn't you come dashing up to Canada and join us?"

"Dear Allison, if you can't enjoy a vacation with Thad how can you marry him?"

"A good question. Are you going to marry Laura?"

"I haven't thought about it."

"Bullshit."

"I've thought about it but there doesn't seem to be any rush. Did Laura say something when you talked to her last week?"

"No, but according to everybody else it's been a hot and heavy summer. I'm sorry I'm missing it."

"According to everybody?"

"Well, Mother said you're very attentive and more settled down than you've been in a long time. Daddy said he sees you in front of the hotel every day, picking Laura up—does he spend most of his time peering out of his office windows? And a few of the cousins mentioned long walks on the beach, and boat trips to Nantucket and the Vineyard, and nuzzling on the veranda of the cottage. You two aren't invisible, you know. Do you love her?"

"Do you love Thad? As I recall, you're marrying him in October."

"Well, I don't think I will. Or I'm not really sure. Anyway, I won't have a wedding that looks like a coronation. If I decide to marry Thad it's going to be very quiet and maybe at the last minute."

"Will I hear about it beforehand?"

"Of course you will; I want you there. And Laura too. I wish you'd talk about her. Are you angry because I asked if you love her?"

"Dear Allison, I couldn't be angry with you." His voice was oddly gentle. "If I can help with your dilemma, will you call me? And when I want to talk about Laura, I'll call you."

"She's good for you. You're a lot nicer these days. Not as impatient. And it's such a novelty having you with us for more than a week or two at a time. Paul, I love Laura and I love you; I don't want you to hurt each other. And I don't want to have to take sides. So be nice to each other, will you?"

"That's one of the things we do best." He was smiling as he hung up.

Nearly everyone in the family tried to talk to Paul about Laura to find out how serious he was. But Owen said nothing until September, when everyone was preparing to return to the city, and then he talked to Laura.

They were packing the books he wanted for his library in Boston, and he leafed through each one before putting it in a carton. "What an interesting summer this has been," he murmured casually while studying an engraving in a history of Rome.

Sitting cross-legged on the floor beside him, Laura smiled. "Yes, it has been. I've learned so much from Jules; I can't thank you enough for getting me that job."

"I didn't mean Jules," Owen said, peering at her. "But if you want to talk about him I won't argue."

"I'm sorry," she said, ashamed. "I knew you meant Paul. But you've never asked me about him, so I thought you approved of us."

"Of your sleeping together or being in love?"

At Laura's quick look of surprise and embarrassment, he rested his hand on her head. "Did you really think I didn't know? I may be in my declining years, my dear, but my powers of perception are intact. Also, Leni told me."

Involuntarily, Laura smiled. "Does everyone talk about us?"

"Of course they do; can anyone resist talking about young lovers who walk around oblivious to everyone else? I did think you might come to me and tell me about your feelings."

"I'm sorry," Laura said again. "I wanted to, but I thought you'd disapprove."

"Of your sleeping together, you mean." She nodded. "Well, I confess it is not a form of courtship I can speak about from experience. Leni says all young people do it these days; I find that surprising, but I don't pass judgment. Customs change, and it takes time to know whether for better or worse. But I have some nostalgia for the time when I was young, when a decent man wouldn't even try to kiss a young woman until they were engaged. Even then he asked her permission. He didn't always get it, either."

"Did you ask Iris's permission?"

Owen smiled. "As I recall, we both had the idea at the same time. There wasn't a great deal of discussion."

Laura's smile met his. "And then you asked her to marry you?"

He gazed across the room at a photograph of Iris standing beside a gnarled tree at the Cape. Her hair blew straight behind her; she was shading her eyes with her hand and laughing. "You know, I don't recall asking. One night we were sitting in her living room—we could see her father through the open door to his study; he was reading and I remember he held his newspaper in front of his face so we could kiss—and we just found ourselves talking about where we would live."

Laura's face grew wistful. "Did you always have ideas together?"

"A goodly amount of the time." Once again Owen put his hand on her head, this time stroking her shining hair in long slow movements that matched his recollections. "More and more, the longer we were together. I was a little wild at first, not yet a man, and Iris was a woman who knew what she wanted. She didn't try to change me—at least not that I could see—but she was determined to shape her own life in a way she thought was good and important, and after a while I had the same ideas. I never knew what magic she worked, but suddenly I was a family man, coming straight home from work, raising children, building up my hotels for my wife and sons instead of just for myself, and buttoning myself into tuxedos two or three times a week because my beautiful wife liked fancy balls."

He looked down at Laura. "She once told me," he said softly, "that she liked me best with nothing on, and next best in blue jeans and a lumberjack shirt, and then in a tux. I thought it was wonderfully daring of her to say that."

"It was. You must have had such fun together."

"You know, we never called it that. But you're right; we had fun. Oh, my dear, what we had was so joyful and good; it was as if a lantern lit our way through the years and it was always bright. When she died the darkness came. I stood beside her coffin and I couldn't see her because the light was gone. I could only see her in my memory, smiling at me when she lay beneath me, laughing as she danced through the house on Beacon Hill for the first time, nursing our baby in a rocking chair in our bedroom while I lay on the bed beside her, sharing the peace and beauty of that moment. Ah, my dear child, if I could make you feel what we had . . . A man can sow his seed, he can build an empire, and none of it is worth a damn if he can't bring it to a woman he cherishes and say, 'Take this from me; I did it because of you and now it is yours.' Iris was my life, the center and also the boundary, all I ever wanted."

He stopped and cleared his throat. "And then she was sick. Such a short time, we barely had a chance to say good-bye. And she died . . ." His voice fell into a long sigh and he closed his eyes. His hand still on Laura's head, he cleared his throat again and again, but still he was hoarse when he went on. "I wandered through that house and I reached out for her but my hands were empty, as empty as my life. I got angry and I shouted at her clothes hanging in her closet. '*Damn you to hell for leaving me when you know I love you and need you!*' For a while I was so angry I didn't mourn. And then the anger left and I had nothing. That was when I stopped paying attention to anything. For two years I didn't go out; Rosa took care of Felix and Asa—she took care of everything—and I sat in the house reliving the years with Iris, because those were the only years I cared about. Rosa would stand in the doorway with her hands on her hips and tell me it was time I found someone to give me companionship and perhaps love, but I couldn't do it. I ached, I hurt, and I wanted the darkness because Iris was in the dark."

The room was silent. Laura took his hand as it rested on her hair, and when she kissed it Owen felt the tears on her cheek. "She had a way of smiling," he said, "as if everything was new. As if everywhere she turned she made wonderful, exciting discoveries. You smile the same way; your eyes light up the same way. I almost see Iris when you smile. And her hair was the color of yours; a bit darker, but not much. And it was long, though she wore it pinned up in some complicated way. And sometimes she had a faraway look in her eyes, as if she could see something the rest of us couldn't see . . . no, it was more; as if she had a secret, something that was hers alone. You have the same kind of look."

Startled, Laura looked up at him. "As if I have a secret?"

He nodded. "It was the first thing I saw about you that day on the beach, and you still have it. Mystery. It made me want to know what lay behind that faraway look. Iris was the same. She had mystery and she had beauty. And you always had beauty, in your eyes and smile, before the rest of you caught up." He paused, but Laura was silent. "Well, for those two years I sat in my chair reliving my life with Iris, and then one day for some reason I started thinking about the hotels. And even though I tried not to care, because it was more important to think about Iris, I did care and I couldn't stop caring. And that was when I started paying attention again. And went back to work." He paused again. "So you see, dear Laura, I care a great deal about love and sex, and also marriage. And I care about you. So when you have an affair and I have some concerns about it, I must speak up."

Surprised, Laura said, "Concerns? About Paul?"

"About you and Paul. I love that boy, but I see him clearly and I know he has the wandering urge of a hungry coyote."

She gave a small smile. "Couldn't you find a nicer comparison?"

"There is nothing wrong with coyotes. They've gotten a bad name, but the fact is they're strong and handsome, sharp, creative, good to their families, and superb survivors. They also move around a great deal, and they've been known to forget what they leave behind."

Laura turned away and reached for a new stack of books.

"My own great-nephew," Owen said. "I've loved him since he was a baby. He used to totter around my study, and nothing was safe from him; he had an insatiable curiosity and stubbornness. It was one of my greatest pleasures to introduce Paul to the wonders of the world; he cared about learning, he responded to beauty, and he wasn't stingy. He knew how to take life in his hands and enjoy every bit of it. I'm afraid I spent more time with him than I spent with my own sons; with Paul I was having fun. But then he grew up and started wandering around the world, picking up projects and dropping them and then moving on. I'm told he does that with women, too. I would not like to think he would do it to you." Silent, Laura looked through the window at leaves tinged with gold and red. "I don't want you hurt, you see. Of course, I don't want you angry at me, either."

Laura kept her eyes on the trees. "I'm not angry. But I don't think you should criticize people in your own family."

"Horsefeathers. I see people clear and straight, whether I want to or not. After I hit seventy, I couldn't fool myself anymore, couldn't pretend people were kind or good-hearted or fascinating when I knew damn well they weren't. I can't even pretend I love my own sons, and that hurts, but I don't ignore it. So why shouldn't I be honest about my greatnephew when I love you as much as I love him and worry about you more? Damn it, girl, I don't want you hurt!"

Laura looked at him over her shoulder. "What if someone had warned you about Iris?"

"I wouldn't have listened. In fact, I'd probably have run him out of town for saying anything against her."

She turned, kneeling before him. "Were you smarter than I am now?"

"I knew more about the world."

"But you said you were wild. Not yet a man, you said."

"Damn it, young woman, who gave you permission to use an old man's words against him?" But he was grinning, and he leaned forward to kiss Laura on her forehead. "Well, perhaps I should stop. I may be wrong, though I haven't been very often. But I'm getting old, and maybe Felix is right; maybe I should stay out of people's lives."

"I don't want you to stay out of my life; I want you to share it. I'm so happy. I've never been so happy."

He looked at her shining eyes and felt, oddly, like weeping. "I do know something about happiness. And maybe you'll be good for Paul, settle him down. If you work the same kind of magic Iris worked on me—"

Laura shook her head. "You and Iris were married. Paul and I aren't, and we're not talking about it." *He hasn't even said he loves me.* "I have another year of college, and then I'm going to work—you said you'd help me find a job in a hotel—"

"I'll do that whether you and Paul are friends or roommates or husband and wife. As long as you want to work, I'll help you. But"—his voice grew wistful—"you will stay with me until you finish college?"

"Yes, of course; I couldn't leave. I want to stay with you as long as you'll have me. And you said I could help you with your plans for your hotels . . ."

"To revive them and make them grand again." He smiled. "And we'll do it together. Well, it sounds like a fine year. Now bring the sherry and we'll have a drink together before dinner. Or are you going out with your young man?"

Laura rose and went to the tall wine cabinet wedged between overflowing bookshelves. She took out a bottle of amontillado and two glasses and put them on the table beside Owen's chair. "We planned to; do you mind?"

"If I did I'd keep it to myself. I can't dictate your schedule or keep my eye on you, out of bed or in."

"You wouldn't want that," Laura said, her eyes dancing.

"Ah, but I might. Think what I might learn: Paul's more a man of the world than I ever was." He peered at her. "Now I've made you blush. I beg your pardon." He sighed. "You've become so lovely, my child, and you have a quick mind and a good imagination. If you trust yourself and give yourself time, you'll be a strong woman and a fine executive. And if you ever needed to, you could have your pick of half the men on the eastern seaboard."

"What about the other half?" she demanded.

He grinned. "They're after Allison, or they would be if she'd get rid of that solipsistic, preening peacock she's decided to marry, God knows why." He sighed again. "Well, you'll all do whatever you want. I might as well keep my wisdom to myself. I spent a lifetime accumulating it, and who's interested?"

Laura laughed and kissed him. "I am, and you don't feel half as sorry for yourself as you pretend."

"True." He took her hand between his. "I feel privileged because you do listen, and proud because I've helped you change from a scared little girl to a happy woman, and I feel loved, which is the most profound feeling of all. As if you brought back the lantern I lost when Iris died."

That was what he thought about later, after Laura was gone. She reminded him of Iris and she had made his world bright, but she was also distinctly herself: warm, loving, enchanting, unique. He'd hoped she would someday trust him enough to tell him her secrets, but she'd given no sign that she even wanted to, and there was no way he could tell her how unimportant they were. Of course she had a right to guard her secrets for as long as she wished, but he knew they were burdensome, and he would have liked to make the load easier by sharing it.

Maybe someday, he thought. He refilled his glass and then sat quietly, watching the light fade over the water and letting memories fill his thoughts, less painful than before, but no less vivid. *Iris, I wish you could be here; Laura is the daughter we never had.*

CHAPTER 9

I N the unusually hot May sun, the black robe clung like a blanket, and Laura tried to think cool thoughts as the commencement speaker droned on. Pay attention, she told herself. Enjoy the ceremony. You'll only graduate from college once, and it took a lot of work to get here. But she was too hot to concentrate; her thoughts kept drifting to Paul, who was sitting with Allison and Owen in the first row of the Nickerson Field stands. Clay had called from Philadelphia at the last minute to say he couldn't be there. "Willard's got the flu, and ever since I became a hero and assistant manager after they fired Terry, I'm stuck if he's not around. I'm sorry; I really wanted to be there."

"It's all right." A year ago she would have been upset, but by now Paul and Owen and Allison were her family, too, and she wouldn't feel alone. "I'll tell you all about it."

"And I suppose your handsome *beau* will take lots of pictures."

"I hope he will," Laura replied calmly, refusing to be drawn into an argument about Paul. It was foolish of Clay to worry about her loving one of the Salingers, saying things like, "Sex makes women drop their guard," and after a while she got tired of telling him that neither passion nor anything else would lull her into giving them away because she'd shut the door on the past.

It had been four years since the robbery. None of Leni's jewelry had been found after the bracelet in the pawnshop, and except for increased security in their houses, the Salingers behaved as if it had never happened. And that was almost the way Laura felt about the first eighteen years of her life: they were like a dream. She was twenty-two now, and a different person. *As if I were born the night of the robbery,* she thought. It was fanciful, but most of the time it seemed almost true, because she had been with the Salingers long enough to see changes in them, and only when we share change are we truly connected to someone or something else.

In the past year, Leni had begun to spend increasingly more time in New York. She was on the boards of hospitals and museums there as well as in Boston, and Felix frequently remarked, with a tight smile, that he'd given his wife to charity. But Laura saw that as long as Leni was at his side for major galas and business functions, he never suggested she spend more time at home, or with him.

Allison had left college and married Thad, but after a four-month honeymoon, and three more months to settle into a condominium on the harbor, they had an erratic schedule that reminded Laura of an employment agency: Thad tried one occupation after another while Allison, anticipating his boredom, would already be looking for another. They socialized every night, usually with new acquaintances; their old friends were uncomfortable with the silences between them, like heavy gray fog.

Laura didn't pay attention to most of the family gossip; she knew whom she loved and she knew what she believed about them. She looked at them as she stood on the commencement platform, meeting their smiles, and she raised her hand in a quiet greeting as the speaker ended his peroration with a long quotation in Greek that almost no one understood. The applause swelled hugely from universal relief that he was done, and then the graduates received their diplomas, and a few moments later Laura stood on the artificial turf of the field with her family. "Just a minute," she said as Allison and Paul reached out to embrace her, "I have to get out of this robe."

"I thought you must be melting," Allison said.

"I am." Laura dropped the robe and, with Paul's arm around her, took Owen's hands as he held them out to her. "I'm so glad you were here."

"How could I miss it? You were my pupil at home before you ever came to the university. Do you know Jules wanted to come today? I had to tell him you could only get three tickets."

"He really wanted to come?"

"He wanted to take credit for you; he thinks he's taught you more than your professors have."

"He's right. But you've taught me more than anyone."

Owen chuckled. "I won't tell Jules you said that." He reached into his pocket and took out a small velvet drawstring bag. "Your graduation gift, my dear. With my love."

Laura pulled the tiny cord to open the bag. Her fingers felt the cool metal and the sharp point of a pin before she took out a piece of jewelry and held it in the palm of her hand. It was a single iris of blue-violet opal with a gold center. She gazed at it for a long moment, then looked up at Owen, her face glowing. "Was it Iris's?"

He nodded. "I had it made for her on our first anniversary. It was very special to her."

Laura put her arms around him and kissed him. "Thank you, thank you . . . it's very special to *me* . . . how can I tell you—?"

"You don't have to. I saw it in your face." He held her away from him. "And you looked so much like her, excited and full of wonder . . . Well, now. Time for you to go. Allison is driving me home; you and Paul go off on your honeymoon." At her startled look, he struck his fist against his forehead. "Vacation. I meant to say vacation. Go on, now; you've worked hard; you deserve some play." He held her close. "I'm very proud of you, my dear."

Laura kissed him again. His drooping mustache was feathery against her cheek, and it struck her that Owen had aged. She'd been so preoccupied in the past weeks with final papers and exams and keeping up with her job that she hadn't really looked at him; now she thought he looked almost ethereal. His cheeks were more sunken than she remembered, and his face was crinkled with webs of fine lines, like ancient parchment. His eyes were as bright as ever, but they seemed more deepset, his thick eyebrows overhanging them like wild grass on bluffs on the Cape. *He's eighty-three, but he's never seemed old; he isn't old, not really; he has so much vitality.* "Are you all right?" she asked him.

"I'm fine; why shouldn't I be?" He put on a scowl. "I mixed up a couple of words; that doesn't mean I'm falling apart. It's hot, that's the problem, and you're keeping me here in the sun when Allison and I could be eating lunch. I thought you were in a hurry."

"Good-bye," Laura said softly. "Don't try to be fierce with me; I'm not fooled." She took Paul's arm. "We've been dismissed."

"About time," he said with a grin, and they left Owen and Allison standing together as they walked through the tunnel beneath the stands and out onto the street. "I want to make love to you," Paul said conversationally as they reached his car in the next block.

"Here?" she asked. "Or shall we stop at a more private gas station along the way?"

He laughed and they kissed in the front seat. "If those are the only choices, I prefer your cottage at the Cape. Would you be willing to wait a couple of hours?"

"I would always wait for you," Laura said, her voice low, and he glanced at her quickly before turning onto Commonwealth Avenue and driving toward the turnpike.

They had learned to be leisurely in their lovemaking. After the storms of their first weeks together, when it seemed they could never satisfy their hunger, they began to come together more slowly. And when they could stay together for the whole night, they took even longer, talking as they caressed and laughing together, even as their passion grew. When they finally fell asleep, their hands were clasped between them, and in the first moments of waking, before opening their eyes, they turned to each other and lay full length together, encircled tightly in each other's arms. Their legs were twined, her lips against his chest, his on her forehead, as they slowly came awake to the light in the room and the small, fluttering movements of their bodies. Each morning they held each other for a long quiet time, drifting in warm silent closeness until desire flickered and then grew, like a small ripple far out in the ocean that gathers force and becomes, at last, a thundering wave. And as desire built they moved even more slowly, learning to hold back, to find new forms of pleasure, to draw arousal out like the long ripple moving to shore until passion overtook them, and together, one voice, one heart, they rode it to its crest, and together drifted back to the somnolent embrace in which they had begun.

In Osterville, they had the summer compound to themselves; they almost had Cape Cod to themselves, since few visitors came in May. They spent the days out of doors, sailing on the sun-sparkled water, picnicking in cool pine forests, climbing barefoot in the sand dunes, leaving footprints that overlapped as they walked closely, hand in hand. And they walked by moonlight along the beach, laughing at the clownish gait of sandpipers hopping just ahead of them, and speculating about the long-ago women who had paced the widow's walks atop gray shingled houses overlooking the sea, waiting for their husbands, the whaling captains who had gone to seek the ocean's riches and instead were taken by the ocean to invisible graves.

"Two weeks," Paul said on their last day. "Not enough. Let's extend it; we need at least another month to ourselves."

Laura buttoned her shirt. "I wish we could. But what excuse do I give Jules for not being there first thing tomorrow morning?"

"I'll call and tell him his chief assistant concierge has been kidnapped." He swept her long hair to the side and kissed the back of her neck. "I'll say I need her to help me clear the dinner dishes because it's not right to leave them until morning."

Laura laughed and reached for her hiking shoes. "Jules would say you're mad. He doesn't clear the table at his house."

"And if I tell him I dry while you wash?"

"He'd say that isn't man's work."

"Well, it shouldn't be yours, either, while you're working full-time. We'll need at least two maids to run our house."

Laura's fingers stilled, then, slowly, she resumed tying her shoes. "I couldn't tell a maid what to do," she said lightly. "I've never had one."

"I have. I'll lay down the law and all you have to do is give praise when it's due. A perfect partnership."

She gave a small smile. "It sounds like it."

"Of course, it depends on where we're living." Paul was bent over, tying his boots. "If we stay in Boston, Mother or Leni will find us the perfect maids who already know everything, and we won't have to worry. Or Rosa will send over one of her dozen or so nieces to take charge of our household. If we're not in Boston, then we're on our own. Do you think we should stay in Boston?"

"But Owen—" Laura's heart was racing and the words caught in her throat. "Don't you remember I told you Owen may want me in Chicago?"

"Is that definite? When?"

"Not for a while, I think. I'll stay with Jules until . . . until something is settled."

"Well, it doesn't matter; we can live very well in Chicago. I have friends there; you'll like them. I'll be one of those husbands who happily follows his wife from job to job and greets her at the door every night with a martini. But you don't drink martinis."

"No." Laura's throat was choked. "But if you could find a nice red wine . . ." Tears stopped her and she turned away, blindly reaching for a tissue.

"My God, what have I said?" Paul got to the box before she did and wiped her eyes. "You don't want me in Chicago? You don't want me at all? For God's sake, why would this make you cry? It all seems so natural—"

"Oh, hush," she said. "Please stop talking. Of course I want you in Chicago. I want you anywhere. I don't know why I'm crying—"

Paul kissed her, and then they held each other for a long time, while her heart slowed. And she felt his slow, too. "This was all serious," she said, drawing back to look at him.

"Did you doubt it? Of course it's serious; it's the most serious thing I've ever done. I should have done it long ago; I've loved you for so long I can't remember what it's like not loving you. But why would I want to remember? I'll never have to live that way again."

"No. We'll always be together." She put her head on his shoulder, feeling the sinewy muscles of his arms beneath her hands. It was all right now. Everything was all right.

She was safe.

They stood quietly until Paul tilted up her face. "Laura, my love, what are you thinking about?"

"Owen," she said with a small smile. "I asked him once how he proposed to Iris, and he said he didn't, really; one night they just found themselves talking about where they would live."

"Did he? I never heard that. But Rosa always said they were perfect together. Now she'll have us to talk about. And she can make our wedding cake; ever since I finished college she's told me she's been waiting to make one, whenever I decide to settle down. Is next week all right—here at the Cape? There's a wonderful old church in East Dennis; I always thought I'd like to be married there. And I'd like the family to be with us. You would, too, wouldn't you? It will make it seem more official."

Laura's words were soft. "Of course I would. And next week would be wonderful."

But Leni declared it impossible. She needed time to make a proper wedding; it would have to be in August. In private, she told Owen she had serious doubts about the whole affair. "They're so very different, their backgrounds are different, Laura has no money at all and Paul doesn't even know what it is to work, and whatever she earns will always seem like pin money next to his fortune—"

"It's the best thing that could happen," Owen said firmly, omitting all mention of his warnings to Laura the year before. "Leni, this girl has made the past years a joy for me, and she's going to make her mark in the hotels; you just wait and see what she and I are cooking up. And look at Paul; have you ever seen him stay with one woman or in one place for so long and so happily? And Allison says she feels as if they're sisters. My God, if Laura weren't marrying into the family we'd have to adopt her!"

Leni smiled. "She's delightful, I don't deny it, and I'm very fond of her; I just don't know what to predict with the two of them."

"How were your predictions when you married Felix?"

"Wrong," she said briefly. "And that reminds me. Felix is extremely angry; he says Laura is a fortune hunter. That's why I'm giving them a splendid wedding."

Owen chuckled, but when she had left, his eyes grew somber. I'm eighty-three, he thought, and, no question about it, a little more shaky than I used to be. I have one of the world's great hotel chains and two sons. But—

What does a man do with the work of a lifetime when he doesn't like what his sons have become?

There was no one he could talk to; the only confidante he was comfortable with was Laura, and he couldn't bring her into this. Nor anyone else. He had to work it out alone.

He sat in his library through the early part of June while the family prepared to leave for the Cape. Often he saw the sunrise; he slept badly and would leave his bed to sit in the high-backed leather chair in his library and watch the stars or the setting of the crescent moon. In the afternoons, he would doze in the same chair and waken when he heard Laura come in from work. But mostly those days he wrote, filling page after page with his bold, sloping handwriting, summarizing the plans for his hotels he and Laura were working on. He had thought about them for years without any sense of urgency; now he knew the project had become a way of saying he wasn't really old, wasn't anywhere near death. How could anyone be close to death when he was making such grand, far-reaching plans?

"Nearly done," he said on a Friday evening when Laura sat across from him at his desk. It was a massive two-sided piece of furniture made by Chippendale the Younger in 1804. Leni had bought it for Owen years before, envisioning Felix and his father sitting cozily across from one another, working together. But it was Laura who sat there; Felix had taken advantage of the double width only a few times and not at all after Owen retired. Owen had thought of giving the desk to Thomas, who admired it, especially after he discovered a flaw in it: there was a crack in the wood behind one of the drawers where papers got stuck and seemed to disappear forever when the drawer was too full. But he didn't want to hurt Leni and the crack wasn't serious; he just used other drawers. Later he was glad he had kept the desk. Some of his happiest times came when he and Laura faced each other across its gleaming mahogany, each having what amounted to a full desk with drawers and cabinet doors flanking the kneehole opening that went through from one side to the other.

"Nearly done," he repeated with satisfaction, handing four manila folders across the desk. "New York, Chicago, Philadelphia, Washington. We'll keep them separate for now, for accounting purposes, so we know what each of them costs to renovate and furnish, but we'll buy for all four when we purchase supplies."

Laura nodded, feeling little jolts of pleasure every time Owen said "we," making her part of every step in the plans for restoring his hotels.

"Of course we'll begin with Chicago," he said, "since that's the one you'll manage."

"If I'm ready."

"You will be. My dear, you learn more quickly than anyone I've ever known, and you have at least another year to prepare. You'll be far more ready than most managers; my God, Willard Payne was a bellhop straight out of high school when I bought the Philadelphia hotel fifty-odd years ago, and he got to be manager just by outliving everybody else. Of course the hotel was fading by then; we were so busy buying new ones, building new ones, expanding to other countries . . . I let those old ones slip badly, I fear. And then none of the young hotshot managers wanted them; they wanted the glamorous modern ones." He paused. "You see, Felix is right in a way. Everyone does want only the most up-to-date of the important things. We'll find guests who like my kind of antique charm, but every one of them will demand modern plumbing and television and this new beeper system I understand they're putting in some of the Hyatts. So we have to give them both. Yesterday and today."

He gestured toward the folders. "Well, it's all there; we've talked about most of it. I've added a few more ideas; Felix won't like them—too expensive and risky—but he won't like the whole project, which is why I've always kept my small corporation separate from the family one: he has nothing to say about what I do or don't do with those four hotels. Now, what else? Ah, Clay. I'd like him to be assistant to a professional manager for a few years; then if we both decide he's ready, we'll find a hotel for him to manage. Is that satisfactory?"

"You know it is. You're wonderful to both of us." Laura walked around the desk and kissed his forehead. "I'll read through these later. You're having dinner with us, did you remember?"

"I never forget invitations from people I love. Is it just the three of us? Or do I need a tie?"

"You don't need a tie; it's just us; I'm cooking at Paul's apartment. And he's doing the dishes. We'll see you at seven."

"Laura." She turned at the different note in Owen's voice. "You haven't told Paul about these plans, have you?"

"No; you asked me not to until we were ready to start."

He nodded. "There's a chance it might get to Felix; it will all be so much easier if he isn't trying to create obstacles. Does that bother you, to keep it secret?"

"I'd rather tell him, but if it will please you I can wait."

"Thank you. And my dear—" He paused and pulled his sweater more tightly around him. He always felt chilled these days, even in June; he didn't know why. "I've written you a letter with all our plans—financing, renovation, everything—in one document, instead of four folders: a summary of them, really, and an explanation of some things that I've done, so everyone will understand. I want you to have it in case you have to handle the project yourself."

"But why would I? You can manage everything far better than—" Her eyes widened and quickly she returned to his chair. "Is something wrong? Are you ill?"

"No. But neither am I young. A wise man thinks ahead, and if I am not wise at eighty-three, when will I be?" He held out to her a long envelope with her name on it. "Take it; put it away somewhere for safekeeping. You may not need it but I want you to have it."

"Keep it in your desk," Laura said. "Do you mind? I'll always know where it is but I'd rather you kept it." *I don't want to think about your dying; I don't want to have anything that reminds me I'm going to lose you.* "It's yours until . . . until I need it."

"If it makes you feel better." He dropped the envelope into the top drawer of his desk. "Now I'm going to take a nap so I can be scintillating at dinner. Go on, my dear; I'll see you at seven."

Laura left the house slowly and walked down Beacon Hill, crossing the Arthur Fiedler footbridge to the promenade that ran alongside the Charles River. It was one of her favorite walks. On one side of the grassy, tree-shaded strip of land was the wide river dotted with sailboats; on the other was a narrow finger of the river; and just beyond glowed the soft red brick of old Back Bay houses. Their blunt shadows enfolded her in that special aura of sedate age and fixedness that was what she loved best about Boston. Nowhere else, she thought, would she have been able to feel so secure, with the past wiped out so completely. And nowhere else would she have felt protected enough to write to Ben about her engagement. He was still in Amsterdam— that job seemed to be lasting—and she had written to him about her graduation and her plans for marriage and a job in Chicago. She had told him most of it—but she had not told him Paul's name. There was plenty of time, she thought; once we're married, he'll keep his feelings about the Salingers to himself. Maybe he'll even change the way he feels. There's time for all of that.

Paul's apartment took up the third floor of one of the old four-story apartments in the Back Bay, a block from the river. He had taken the basement for his studio, and Laura found him there, reorganizing photographs; old ones, she saw; he hadn't made any new ones, except pictures of her, in months. He turned and kissed her. "I set the table this afternoon, but I regret to tell you that dinner is not ready."

She laughed. "I wasn't expecting miracles. Anyway, it's going to be simple: fish chowder and salad." She leaned against him within the circle of his arms. "I'm so grateful for you. For finding you and loving you, and knowing you love me."

"And whom do you thank?" he asked with a smile.

"The fates," she said gravely. "The three daughters of Zeus. They spin the web of life, and measure it, and cut it out."

"And brought you to our family four years ago?" She was oddly silent and he said, "Well, whoever did it has my deepest thanks. He or she or they changed my life. All our lives, when you think about it. We'd all be different in some ways if you weren't here."

"Shall we take a walk before dinner?" Laura asked.

"If you're up to it after a full day with Jules." Something had caused that sudden silence, he thought; something from her past. He wondered why she didn't understand that nothing mattered but the present and the future they would make together. He took her hand as they walked along Fairfield to the corner, coming upon the crowds of students from the colleges housed in the old buildings along Commonwealth. "Was it a good day?"

"It was a wonderful day; we pleased the Countess Irinia. I told you about her last year—the Romanian exile who wanted a yacht for a week, and we got the yacht and her favorite chef. This year she wanted ideas for a different kind of party, and I thought of a resort Jules had checked out about six months ago and raved about. It's called Darnton's and it's on its own island in Lake Champlain, and I called the owner—Kelly Darnton; she and her husband run it together—and arranged a week for the Countess and her party, with entertainment, and then Jules leased a private train to take them there. She was so pleased, like a little girl who gets to show off for her friends; she kept telling me how wonderful I am."

"She's right." Paul put his arm around her shoulders. "Shall we go to Darnton's for our honeymoon? Or would you prefer Africa?"

She smiled. "Are those the only choices?"

"I thought of London and Paris and Rome but everyone goes there—"

"I don't."

He stopped walking. "I'm sorry; you've never been to Europe; of course that's where we should go."

"No, you choose a place you want. I really don't care, but I would like to see Europe someday."

"You'll see everything, my love. I'll make everything yours." They walked on, silent in the hazy sun that made their shadows long, thin figures trailing lazily behind them. Clusters of students and young executives coming home from work filled the sidewalks, but they barely noticed; they walked in a circle of silence, golden and dreamlike, until they were once more at Paul's building. But as they climbed the stairs to his apartment, the telephone was ringing, and when Paul answered it Laura could hear Rosa's voice, crying, saying over and over, "Mr. Owen... Mr. Owen..." and she knew he must be dead.

*   *   *

"No," Leni said as soon as they arrived at the hospital. "Not dead. But he had a massive stroke, and Dr. Bergman thinks he might not last the—" She bit off her words, as if saying them might make them true.

"Can we see him?" Paul asked. "We'll just look in the door..."

Leni was shaking her head. "They're not letting anyone in. Anyway, he's unconscious; he has been since Rosa found him..."

The waiting room was crowded with family members who arrived as they heard the news and then, as the hours passed, came and went, bringing food and coffee, trying to read magazines, murmuring about Owen and how frail he'd looked lately and how they should have taken him to the Cape early this year. Every hour, Dr. Bergman stopped by and said he had nothing new to tell them. But at midnight, he said Owen was stable. "We don't know the extent of the damage; we'll know better in a day or two. I think you should all go home and get some sleep. We may be in for a long stretch."

"I want to see him," Felix said flatly.

Leni put her hand on his arm. "We'll be back early in the morning. I'm sure we can see him then."

"Perhaps," the doctor said, and the next morning he did let Leni and Felix spend a few minutes beside Owen's bed. He seemed to be strung up with wires and tubes, and Felix kept repeating, "Terrible, terrible"; he could not believe this was his dominating father, this frail-looking figure lying like a puppet with strings hanging lax all around him. But part of Felix's shock was a dizzying wave of anticipation so powerful he felt he could barely stand up. He had been expecting his father's death for a long time—any son would, he told himself, with a father over eighty— but the years had passed and Owen had begun to seem eternal. Everyone still saw him as the head of the Salinger family and the head of

Salinger hotels, though for years Felix had been president and fully in charge, even when his father appeared at the office and asked questions or participated in executive meetings. But now Owen was dying. Felix knew it; this time he was certain, and the certainty unleashed all his expectations with a force so overwhelming it was almost more than he could bear.

He could not show it; he had to share the others' fears and grief with a calm dignity befitting the head of a family. But inside him expectancy flowered and spread, dominating his thoughts. He was fifty-five years old and for the first time in his life there would be no shadow over him. Asa would do what he said; there was no one else to gainsay his decisions. Salinger Hotels Incorporated would at last bear his mark, and his alone. In every sense of the word, it would finally be his.

"Felix," Leni said. Her hand was on his arm and she was leading him out of the room, thinking he was frightened or crushed by the inescapable fact of his father's mortality.

"I'm going to the office," he said. "I'll come back later." He left, almost scurrying, before she could respond. He had to get out of those long corridors lined with grotesque equipment, patients in wheelchairs, carts loaded with medicines, television screens with green lines peaking and undulating to show heartbeat, brainwaves, whatever they measured in that antiseptic hell. Felix was always healthy; he prided himself on his strength and energy and the force of his will that kept him calm, never losing his temper or feeling fear or panic. But he was almost running as he reached his car, and that afternoon he called Leni at the hospital and told her there was no way he could return that day; too much depended on him at the office.

Asa knew Owen's illness changed nothing in the daily business of the hotels, but he also stayed in the office: someone had to keep an eye on Felix.

So the women kept vigil: Leni; Asa's wife, Carol, and their daughter, Patricia; Barbara Janssen, Allison, Laura, and, frequently, Rosa. Thomas Janssen was on an inspection tour of Salinger hotels in the Midwest and flew in to Boston on the weekend, but the rest of the time Paul was the only man who sat with the women in the waiting room, bringing coffee, snatching meals with them in the cafeteria, and finally, after a week, walking beside the gurney as Owen was wheeled to a private room. His uncle could not speak or move his left arm or leg, but he was conscious and not about to die.

Two weeks later they brought him home. "As long as you have twenty-four-hour nursing, he might as well be there," Dr. Bergman told

Leni. "There's nothing we can do that all of you can't do, and he's probably better off in his own home. Make sure Laura spends a lot of time with him; he responds best to her."

Laura would have been with Owen anyway: she didn't want to be anywhere else. She took an unpaid leave from her job and spent her days beside Owen's bed, reading to him, talking to him even when he made no response, describing the sunrise and the sunset, the humming-birds in the garden, nannies who pushed baby carriages and strollers along Mount Vernon Street, boys on skateboards, young girls on bicy-cles, their hair flying behind them, couples with clasped hands and rhythmic footsteps on the cobblestone walk.

And one day, in the middle of July, Owen smiled. And a few days later he began to talk.

At first only Laura could understand the slurred and misspoken words. Then, as he grew angry at his clumsy tongue, Owen tried to form each word separately, and others were able to decipher much of what he said. Still, it was easier for Owen and the rest of the family to let Laura repeat his words in her low, clear voice, as if she were translating a foreign language. And so when he suddenly asked for a lawyer, it was Laura who called Elwin Parkinson and greeted him when he was shown to Owen's room.

She stood up from her chair beside Owen's bed. "Do you want me to leave?"

"If you don't mind," Parkinson said.

"I'll be glad to stay and help you understand—"

"No, no. We'll get along just fine." He closed the door behind Laura and then sat in her chair and put his head near Owen's.

"Will," Owen said. He went on, one wrenching word at a time. "Meant to change it. Didn't. Do it now."

Showing no surprise, the lawyer took out a pencil and a pad of paper. "We can write a codicil; is that what you want? You're adding a new bequest?"

Owen told him what he wanted. Parkinson frowned deeply, but he wrote it down; then he moved his head so he was directly in Owen's line of sight. "This is a radical decision to make on short notice. It would perhaps be prudent to give it more thought; wait until you're better, more yourself—"

A harsh sound came from Owen's mouth and it took a minute for Parkinson to realize it was a laugh. "Don't have time. You fool. I'm dying. Last chance . . ." Suddenly his words burst out, clear and firm. "*Do it!*"

"Yes, of course, if you insist. I can have it for you to sign—can you sign it?" Owen nodded. "I can have it in a week—"

"God—!" His face contorted with rage, Owen tried to raise himself in the bed, and Parkinson, terrified that he would die and everyone would blame the lawyer who was with him, said quickly, "Tomorrow. Is that all right? I can have it for you tomorrow."

Owen's face grew calm. Closing his eyes, he gestured toward the door.

"Until tomorrow," Parkinson said, and scurried out. He saw Laura come down the stairs and slip into Owen's room as he left, and wondered where she had been while they talked, and whether she had overheard them. But he was in a hurry and did not pause in his rush down the stairs and past the library where he glimpsed members of the family having tea. Damned odd, he thought, as he drove back to his office through the afternoon traffic. He's had years to think about changing his will. If he really wanted to do it, why didn't he take care of it sooner? That had always been his way, of course—take a long time to make up his mind and then rush ahead to accomplish whatever he'd decided— but he was a top-notch businessman, and he knew that important decisions should never be made in the midst of a crisis. He could barely talk, barely move, barely think straight—but still he insisted on this radical bequest to a person none of them really, even now, knew anything about. It was damned odd. One could even say it made no sense.

For Owen Salinger's own good, Parkinson told himself solemnly, it behooves me to learn more about this young woman, before it is too late.

* * *

The family was again at tea when Parkinson returned the next afternoon and went directly to Owen's room. Once again Laura left the two men alone, and as soon as the door closed behind her, the lawyer began speaking in an urgent whisper. "Owen, I have information about that young woman—it will change your mind—it will change everything— I've found out she has a—"

"Will," Owen said, the word almost strangled in his throat.

"Yes, yes, I have it; it was finished before I got the call from New York, but you mustn't sign it—you won't want to when you know who she is—"

"*Shut up.*" Owen's eyes were glaring at Parkinson, his mouth was twisted as he tried to speak through his fury. "Will. Read it."

"Why? I'm telling you, you won't want to sign—"

"*Read!*"

Angrily, Parkinson pulled a single sheet of paper from his briefcase and read it. The instant he finished, Owen said, "Pen. *Pen!*"

"Wait. *Listen to me.* This woman is a thief, a convicted thief; she preys on old men—"

Owen's lips worked. "No."

"It's true, I have the information, I spoke to a police officer in New York—"

"No! No . . . it! No . . . difference. Fool." A ragged sigh broke from him. "Witness. Get Laura."

"I didn't understand what you said."

"*Get Laura.*"

"I want to know what you—" Parkinson saw Owen's face twist and he sucked in his breath, thinking once again that the old man was about to die. He will die, he thought, but not with me in the room. I've done my best; the hell with the rest of it. "We need someone else," he said. "A beneficiary in a will cannot be a witness to its signing. But the nurses will do. If you'll wait just a minute . . ." He crossed the hall and brought them back.

"I've asked you to listen to me," he said rapidly to Owen. "I've done my best to make you listen. No one can blame me—" He saw Owen's eyes and clutching fingers. "Yes, yes, yes." He placed a pen in Owen's fingers.

"Help . . ." Owen gasped, and the nurses lifted him to a sitting position high enough to see the document Parkinson held on a book on the mattress. Owen wrote, his sloping handwriting barely recognizable in the shaky scrawl he left on the bottom line. Then he gave a long sigh that was almost a moan. "Nearly missed," he said with a shadow of a grin at Parkinson as the nurses signed as witnesses. "Last victory." He closed his eyes. "Laura," he whispered.

"I did warn you," Parkinson said through tight lips. He slipped the document into an envelope and returned it to his briefcase. "I hope someone believes that."

"Laura," Owen whispered again. One of the nurses was arranging the blankets and the other was unrolling the cuff to take his blood pressure as Parkinson left the room.

He found Laura on the landing, near the door. "He wants you," he said shortly. At the cold anger in his voice, she looked at him with startled eyes. "He's a sick man," he snapped, but as he said it he saw Laura's eyes change; there was a sadness in them so deep he almost felt sorry for her. But he caught himself. More likely she was just waiting for him to leave.

"Good-bye," Laura said and went into Owen's room, closing the door behind her. The nurse was rolling up the blood pressure cuff; both of them left as Laura sat beside the bed. "He's a peculiar little man," she said to Owen's closed eyes. "He seems to be angry about something. Did you shout at him?"

Without opening his eyes, Owen made the sound that Laura knew was a laugh and held out his hand. She clasped it between hers and he gave a slight nod.

"Do you want to take a nap?"

He nodded again. She rose and pulled the heavy velvet drapes across the windows overlooking the walled rose garden. The room was dark and somber. "Do you want me to stay?"

"Here."

She sat beside the bed. "What would you like?"

"Tell you." His eyes were still closed, his face ashen. "Dearest Laura. Left you a . . . little something . . . in . . . my will."

Laura's eyes filled with tears. "Don't talk about it. You're getting better. I saw you move your other hand this morning—"

"No." He opened his eyes and it was as if he were looking at her from deep within himself. "Love you, my child. Gave me such joy." Laughter trembled in his throat. "Sometimes . . . wished I was Paul. Paul's age. So much love."

Laura was crying. "Don't go. I love you, Owen. I'll take care of you, I'll make you well, I promise. I love you. Don't leave me, there are things I want to tell you . . . please, please don't go . . ."

Her head was bent over him, and Owen raised his hand and touched her tears. His fingers rested on her wet cheek. "Dearest Laura. Finish . . . our plans. Yours now. I wish . . . I could see . . . them . . ." His eyes closed. " . . . finished." His fingers slipped down her cheek. Laura grasped his hand before it could fall and took it between hers. She kissed it and held it against the tears that streamed unchecked down her face.

"You gave me my life," she said through her sobs. Her head drooped until her lips brushed Owen's still face and felt the irregular, frail breaths that barely stirred his mustache. "Everything I am. You made me proud of myself. I didn't thank you enough; I didn't even tell you the truth about myself so you'd know how much you did for me. I wanted to tell you; I want to tell you now . . . can you hear me? You gave me my life; you're part of it; part of me . . . Please say you can hear me; I haven't thanked you enough, I haven't made you understand how much you did and what it means to me . . ."

The room was hushed and dark. Laura wept, her tears falling onto

Owen's cheeks so that he seemed to be crying, too. "I love you," Laura whispered at last. "I know you can hear me, because we can always hear when someone gives us love. Can't we? Dearest Owen, I love you."

The next day, without awakening, Owen Salinger died.

CHAPTER 10

FELIX was in his office when Parkinson called. "I've been trying to speak to you for three days—even today, in the cemetery—but I felt uncomfortable about discussing business there."

"My secretary says you told her it's something about my father's will," Felix said impatiently.

"More accurately, it's about Laura Fairchild."

Felix sat straighter. "What about her?"

"I'd rather tell you in person. I can be there in half an hour."

"Just give it to me now."

Parkinson felt a flash of longing for Owen's old-world courtesy. Briefly he considered telling Felix what he thought of him. But he knew that would be unwise: the Salinger account was vastly bigger than Elwin Parkinson's pride. "Well, then. She has a record, in New York, for theft. She and her brother Clay."

"Theft," Felix repeated tonelessly. "When?"

"Seven years ago. She was fifteen; her brother was fourteen."

"And the parents?"

"According to the police report they were killed in an auto-truck accident the year before. It isn't clear who was their guardian; most likely their aunt. They were released in her custody after the arrest. Melody Chase."

"What?"

"I know it sounds improbable, but that was the name I was given."

"Probably a fake. What else?"

"Two years later, when she was seventeen, she was named in a will filed for probate—a bookseller named Hendy. He left her ten books."

"Anything else?"

"I wouldn't treat that lightly; it may be significant, especially if the books had value."

"Why?"

"Because the day before he died your father changed his will; he added—"

"He what?"

"He added a codicil leaving two percent of Salinger Hotels Incorporated and one hundred percent of the Owen Salinger Corporation to Laura Fairchild."

"Two percent? To that woman? You knew he was going to do this and you didn't tell me?"

"A lawyer doesn't talk about his client's decisions to others."

"Not others, you damned fool! His son! What the fuck were you thinking about, letting him do this? Are you out of your mind? His corporation, too? With those four hotels?"

"And his house on Beacon Hill."

"Goddam son of a bitch! He broke up his estate? And you didn't try to stop him?"

"I did try—"

"Not very hard! Not hard enough!" Felix felt as if his insides were twisted into knots; his stomach was taut, his teeth clenched. "He was mad."

"I don't think so; he knew he wanted to sign it; he even argued with me about it. And he knew it had to be witnessed; he forced me to bring in the nurses. His mind was very clear." Parkinson paused; it was time to make himself indispensable to Felix. "However, I did have a feeling—"

"What?"

"That he was very tired. And perhaps—of course one can't be sure—" He stopped.

"Fuck it, Parkinson, stop dancing around. Sure of what?"

"I did have the feeling he might have been under some kind of pressure."

The words reverberated in the air. Felix let them settle slowly into a new idea, and his muscles began to relax. "You mean someone was influencing him."

"Someone might have been."

"Someone who had a habit of getting old men to change their wills."

"I didn't say that."

"No," said Felix thoughtfully. "But if you were asked for your opinion . . ."

"I would have to say I had the distinct impression that Owen Salinger was highly agitated and acting under some kind of coercion or persuasion. I might add that I was alone with him in his room on two consecutive days, having asked Miss Fairchild to leave before we talked, and on both occasions, when I left I found her hovering outside the door."

"Thank you, Elwin," Felix said softly. He sat for a moment, hearing the slight whine of Parkinson's breathing on the other end of the line. "We've set the reading of the will for next week; you'll probably hear from me before then." He hung up and walked to his corner windows to look across the Public Gardens toward Beacon Hill. And his thoughts began to churn again. *Left the house to that woman. And his hotels. And part of the company. My company. Insane. Vindictive. Making me look like a fool. At the last minute, when we couldn't stop him . . .*

But I will stop him. He's dead and I'm alive, and I'll tear that woman apart; I'll tear his fucking codicil apart. We'll make the old will stick. It was good enough for him when he made it; it's good enough now. Everything else gets destroyed.

Looking at the Gardens, he felt a sudden alarm. Maybe there was more than the will. What else did the old man dictate or write? What other secrets did he have? What else needed destroying?

He had to find out. He couldn't wait; he had to know.

At seven he telephoned Paul. "I thought we might have dinner together, just the two of us. It's late, I know, but I've been tied up."

"How about lunch tomorrow?" Paul asked. "Laura's here and she's so upset, after the funeral this morning, I don't want to leave her."

"Fine. My secretary will call you in the morning."

And having made sure they were both away, he went to Owen's house.

"Good evening, Rosa," he said, walking past her and starting up the stairs. "I'll be in my father's study. You can go to bed; I'll let myself out."

Rosa bristled. Never in fifty years had Mr. Owen sent her off to bed. "Would you like coffee? Something to eat?" She sent her voice up the stairs after him. "Or I might help you find something? I've been doing a bit of cleaning—" She turned away to swallow the sudden tears that were always near the surface these days.

But Felix was already crossing the upstairs foyer to the third-floor stairway. "I can help myself," he said over his shoulder, and as he took the stairs two at a time he repeated the words to himself. I can help myself.

Owen's study was lovingly dusted, the books that had been scattered on tables and the floor made into unnaturally neat stacks, the papers on his desk aligned in perfect piles. Felix switched on the lamp on the Chippendale desk and began to go through the papers on top and then in the drawers. It took only a few minutes to find the envelope with Laura's name, and to read the letter inside.

Beloved Laura,
It is a fine day outside, as fine as I feel. But at my age a prudent man contemplates his mortality, and the things he may never have a chance to finish, and so today, while my mind is clear and my hand still strong, and my heart perhaps steadier than ever, I am writing to put in concise form the plans you and I have made together, for my hotels, because you know better than anyone what they mean to me. But first I want you to know that I am planning to change my will, leaving to you a small part of the family company, and this house, and all of my own corporation. This means the hotels will be yours when I die, and therefore you will be the one to oversee their rebirth if I cannot.

Felix stopped reading. There were ten pages, closely covered with his father's bold, sloping handwriting, but now that he knew what they were, he could not read them: he couldn't stand hearing his father's voice, through his written words, saying he preferred Laura to his own son. His hands were shaking and he realized he was holding his breath. Bastard, he thought, letting it out in an explosive burst. To do that to me. Telling the whole world you didn't care about me; you cared about *her*; you were giving her what I wanted. Only a sick man would do that to a son.

Sick. Under pressure. Coercion.

With a surge of energy he went through the papers on top of the desk and pulled everything out of the drawers, searching them for phrases, sentences, odd words that would show a mind unhinged. And then, in the midst of his frantic reading, both hands full of papers and envelopes, he heard the front door open, and voices from below: Rosa, loud and pleased, then Laura, then Paul. He couldn't make out their words; they were two floors below. What the hell were they doing here? Why weren't they fucking in bed?

He shoved the papers into the top drawer, stuffing them to the back so he could close it. No, damn it, some of them had been on top. Neat piles. He remembered. Pulling out papers at random, he put them squarely on the desktop and forced the drawer shut. Something was jammed at the back, and he gave a final push as Rosa's voice reached the other side of the closed door. "—got here about an hour ago; he said he'd be in his father's study."

There was a knock at the door. "Felix," Paul said, but Felix was moving silently into his father's adjoining bedroom. He heard the door from the hall open. "Sorry to bother you, but Laura needs—" There was a pause, and Felix heard him say, "He's not here."

"My goodness," Rosa said. "And I never heard him leave. I must be getting old. Though Felix always was very big on creeping about and surprising people. Well, we won't be bothering him, that's clear. Can I help you find something, Laura?"

"No thank you," Laura said, her voice almost inaudible. "We just came for a few of my things; I'm going to stay at Paul's for a few days."

Felix crept into the hallway from the bedroom and then down the carpeted stairs. *Creeping about.* That stupid woman would be fired as soon as he could manage it. He eased open the front door and closed it quietly behind him. Staying at Paul's, she said. There would be plenty of time tomorrow to come back for the letter and anything else he could find.

Unless that was what she'd come back for.

He cursed himself. He could have taken it instead of shoving it back into the drawer; what in God's name had gotten into him? He stood beside his car, torn between getting away before they saw him or waiting until the house was dark and then going back to find out for sure. He had his own key; he'd never used it but this was the time.

He waited. He had to know.

Half an hour later, he saw Laura and Paul leave. It took another two hours for Rosa's light to go out. And then he waited another hour before returning to the house and using the key he had had made after Owen's heart attack four years earlier.

He felt his way in the darkness up the two flights of stairs and into the study, closing the door quietly behind him before turning on the same lamp he had used hours earlier. And then he opened the drawer and rummaged through it, looking for the letter.

Which wasn't there.

He yanked the drawer out of the desk and turned it upside down, but only a single invoice was still in it, caught in a crack on the side. He went through the papers on top of the desk. Not here, not here, not here. She took it. The bitch took it. Conned a sick old man, then stole papers from his desk.

She didn't con him. The letter proves it.

Rage flooded him; his throat was filled with bile. He stood beside the desk, breathing in ragged gasps, trying to think.

He had to get it back. She'd use it to prove the old man wasn't sick and coerced, to show he knew what he was doing and did it on his own. Have to get it back, he thought; have to find it. Not let that bitch and that old man make a fool of me in front of my family and the whole world.

Have to think of something. And I will. I'm not the kind who panics and makes mistakes. I'll think of something; I'll figure this out the way I always do.

I can take care of myself.

* * *

At the will reading, he attacked. He had thought of nothing new, and so he charged forward, as if the letter did not exist. Everyone in the family was talking at once and he stood up, to take charge. He stood behind the heavy library table with his hand on Parkinson's shoulder to keep him silent. When he had his family's attention, he spoke to Laura, who was standing in front of a window with Paul's arm around her. His voice was flat.

"He didn't know what he wanted. He was a sick old man who was manipulated and terrorized by a greedy, conniving witch, and for the entire month after his stroke—"

"Felix!" Paul's deep voice cut across his uncle's raspy one. "What the hell are you talking about?"

"You fucking bastard!" Clay bellowed, riding over Paul's words. "Who the fuck do you—"

"Keep your mouth shut," Felix snapped and went on, never breaking stride. "—entire month after his stroke was a helpless invalid who could neither move nor speak—"

"Felix!" Paul said again.

"He could speak!" Laura said. "He talked to me—we talked—"

"—neither move nor speak intelligibly, and it was obvious to everyone that he had lost his ability to think clearly. And that obvious fact was taken advantage of by this *girl*, who was only one of his whims until she wormed her way into his life and then, when he was dying, kept the nurses out of his room so she could be alone with him and manipulate him into changing his will—"

"That's enough," Paul said furiously. "God damn it, Felix, you're mad; what the hell has gotten into you? This is a goddam pack of lies—"

"Owen didn't want the nurses!" Laura cried. "He told me to keep them out!" Her tears had dried in streaks on her cheeks. "He didn't want strangers; he wanted me!"

"He didn't know what he wanted—" Felix began for the third time.

"Shut up!" Paul roared. "Let Elwin finish reading! And by God you'll explain this to me later; you'll apologize to Laura and to the whole family—"

Ignoring Paul, Felix put his head back, looked down his thin nose, and flung his voice at Laura. *"He didn't know anything, did he?* He didn't know that you're a criminal with a record, that you have a criminal for a brother, and that you lied to him—you lied to all of us—for four years while we took you in and gave you everything."

Her gasp ripped across the room and he knew she would lose.

"Four years," he repeated, hammering at her. "And we all know that four years ago, the summer you and your brother appeared at our door, our house was robbed of an irreplaceable collection of jewelry and—"

"We didn't have anything to do with that!" Clay shouted.

Everyone was talking at once, turning to each other in alarm, calling out to Felix to explain what he meant. But Felix spoke directly to Laura. "You don't think we'd believe that! From the evidence I now possess, I have concluded that you came here for one purpose only—to rob us— and then decided to stay when you saw you could wrap your tentacles around my father, *just as you'd done once before with another old man who left you a fortune before he died,* and then!"—he shouted above his family's rising clamor, with a glance at Paul—"then you wrapped yourself around a *young* man of wealth, because professional fortune hunters never miss a chance, do they Miss Fairchild?"

"I'm not! I loved Owen!" Laura flared, but she sounded breathless. "I love Paul. You have no right to lie—"

"Don't you talk to me of *right!* You came to us with lies; you came to entrap, to ensnare; you wormed your way into our household . . . *and you robbed us of my wife's jewels and almost killed my father!"*

"It's a goddam lie!" Clay shouted. "We didn't do that job; we changed our—"

Triumph flashed through Felix. He saw Paul's arm drop from Laura's shoulder, saw Leni's look of disbelief, and saw Allison's shocked, angry stare. Good. Let her try to bring up her letter now; it was too late. He had her.

He looked at Laura with contempt. *"You changed nothing.* You're a couple of common criminals; you've never been anything else; and I'm going to see to it that everyone knows it. I'm going to break that codicil in court; I'm going to see to it that you don't get a penny of my father's fortune. You'll leave the way you came, with nothing; you'll leave now, and you'll never have anything to do with any of us again!"

In the cacophony of the room he saw Laura put a hand against the windowpane; he watched her look up as Paul moved away, putting distance between them. And then he saw her eyes change, as if she remembered—

"Wait! Wait a minute!" she cried. "Owen wrote a letter... before his stroke... before he was sick! He told me about it—about what it said. I didn't force him to do anything—I can prove it—!" She turned and almost ran to the door.

"I'll come with you," Paul said. His eyes were dark with doubt, but he followed her and slammed the door behind them. "Will you tell me what the hell is going on?"

"I can't talk about it," Laura said. *He isn't sure; he thinks Felix might be telling the truth. How can he think that if he loves me?* "I just want to prove that I didn't force Owen to love me. He really did love me, God damn it, and I can prove it! And then I'll get out of here so no one—"

"Why?" He was keeping up with her as she sped up the stairs to the third floor. "If everything Felix says is a lie—"

Laura yanked open the door of Owen's study and ran to the desk.

"Is it all a lie?" Paul demanded.

She pulled the drawer toward her and sucked in her breath at the disorder within. "It never looked like this... I'll have to look through everything..." Sitting down, she pulled out all the papers and put them in her lap. The room was quiet. And when she finally looked up, Paul saw in her eyes bewilderment and then despair. "It's not here."

He looked at her, wanting to go to her but holding back, remembering.

Laura mimicking Jules. A superb actress.

Laura climbing, like a cat. "I used to climb on the rocks up the Hudson."

Her job as assistant concierge. "It's something I can talk about and not hide."

Her refusal to handle merchandise in department stores. As if someone might accuse her of trying to steal.

Her collection of ten perfect first editions worth forty-five thousand dollars. Left her by an old man in his will.

"I asked him to keep it; I didn't want it," Laura was saying, almost to herself. "I didn't want to be reminded that he'd die, so I asked him to keep it and he said he would, and he put it in this drawer. I saw him."

"What did it say?"

"I didn't read it. He said it was an outline of all the plans we'd been making—plans for his hotels, the ones he owns separate from all the others."

"The hotels he left you."

"Yes but I didn't know he was going to leave them to me."

"You had a letter from Owen and you didn't read it."

"I didn't need to. Don't you understand? It was only in case he... died...."

"Was Felix lying about the rest?"

"Damn you!" Laura leaped to her feet. "Damn you, damn you, how can you ask me that? You saw me with Owen—you know how I was with you—*I loved you and I loved him!* Everything I did—everything you saw for a whole year—I did with love. And you know it! You're not a fool—you know what you saw, what you heard, what you felt... You know what you felt! It wasn't a lie! Was it? Were we lying—a whole year together—*were we lying?*"

"I wasn't." He was frowning as he looked at her, and Laura knew that for the first time he was listening to her as if there might be a double meaning in her words.

She held her head high and looked straight at him. "Owen believed in me. I gave him my love and my trust and he was proud to have them and he gave me... he gave me the same... so much I could never thank..." She swallowed hard. But her voice was husky. "He loved me, he believed in me, and damn you—*damn you*—for making me believe in your love as much as I believed in his and then not trusting me when Felix—"

She turned away. She was cold inside, and numb, and her eyes were dry. *I won't cry. I'll never let anyone make me cry again, not through love, not through pain.* Her back to Paul, she said, "Every day the world seemed new and wonderful because of you... and I thought you felt the same. But you pulled away from me, you cut us apart as soon as he started talking. You didn't believe in me enough to wait until we could talk... until we could sort it out. You didn't believe in our love... or in anything. Not even in your own feelings. Or yourself."

They stood without moving in the heavy silence. Laura's hands lifted slightly, then fell. Her back straight, her head high, she walked to the door.

"Was he telling the truth?" Paul asked.

"Yes," she said and left the room.

The family's voices stopped abruptly as she opened the library door. She saw Felix look at her hands and wondered why his eyebrows shot up. Why did he still pretend? He knew she wouldn't find the letter; he'd taken it the night Rosa said he was here. She looked around the room, her eyes moving impassively over Allison's bewildered, angry face, Leni's bleak sadness, Barbara Janssen's puzzled eyes, the confusion among all the others in the Salinger family. Her look reached Clay's scowl. "We're leaving," she said.

Rosa would send her clothes; she'd stay in Philadelphia, with Clay, until they decided what to do next. She had to find a lawyer, to see if they had any chance against Felix. But there's probably not a hope in hell, she thought. What judge would believe Laura Fairchild, who had a police record in New York, against Felix Salinger, president of Salinger Hotels Incorporated and a prominent member of Boston society? She had to try, but it wasn't something to count on.

No one had spoken. She looked at Felix, and their eyes held for a long moment. *I'm going to do everything I can to ruin you. However long it takes, whatever I have to do, I'll make you pay for lying about Owen, and about me, and for taking those hotels and this house away from me when he wanted me to have them—and died thinking I would.*

Without looking back she and Clay walked out of the library, and out of the house, into the heavy heat of the August sun. Laura turned to look once more at the house, gazing at the red brick, the dark green shutters, Owen's windows on the third floor. *Dearest Owen . . . dearest friend. Godspeed. God bless you. I love you.*

Part III

CHAPTER 11

THE lawyer's name was Ansel Rollins. Rail-thin, with pale eyes, long jowls, and a few strands of hair across his smooth brow, he was the father of one of Laura's classmates at the university, and as firmly a part of Old Boston society as Felix's lawyer, Carver Cheyne. "I know Carver and I understand him," Rollins told Laura and Clay as they sat at a round table in his air conditioned office. "A fine attorney. We don't know, of course, what kind of a case they think they have, but we do have a chance. Of course, they would not even start this fight if you could find the letter you say Mr. Salinger wrote: it would prove he knew what he wanted long before he had his stroke; it would establish irrefutably that you are entitled to this inheritance. . . ."

"I can't get back in the house," Laura said.

"Well." He pursed his lips. "Everyone knew how close the two of you were . . . we certainly have a chance."

Otherwise, Laura thought, you wouldn't have taken the case on contingency; working for nothing in the expectation of getting a third of what we win.

Rollins squared his yellow legal pad in front of him. "We have several decisions to make. First, we will of course request a jury trial."

"We're *entitled* to a jury," Clay said heatedly.

"Indeed. But you could waive it if you wished, in favor of a hearing by a judge. It would probably occur sooner and take less time than a jury trial but"—he surveyed Laura's face—"a jury would be more responsive to a beautiful young woman in distress than a judge sitting alone in his courtroom."

"How long must we wait?" Laura asked.

"Six months to a year—"

"What?" Clay was on his feet. "Laura gets cheated out of her inheritance and nobody does anything for a fucking *year?*"

"We will be doing a great deal," said Rollins. "Do please sit down, young man. I cannot speed the wheels of justice, try as I might."

Clay sat, and for the rest of the afternoon they went over and over the past five years. Laura and Clay told Rollins everything—but left out Ben. They had decided that together. Clay had been vehement about it. "He'd ruin us; he'd ruin our chances. We're okay now; nobody can prove we robbed them—"

"We didn't rob them!" Laura had exclaimed.

"Ben might say we did, to cover his ass. And they already think it. I just don't want him here! Keep him out of it!"

Laura, more quietly, had agreed. Telling about Ben would be admitting to another five-year lie, making them seem even more untrustworthy. So they kept Ben out of it while revealing everything else.

Rollins pursed his lips as they talked. "I see a number of dangers," he murmured, making notes. "But if we're prepared for them . . . All right," he concluded. "I'll call you soon and we'll plan the next step. I can reach you at this number, in Philadelphia?"

"No." Laura wrote on his legal pad. "We'll be here after tomorrow."

"Darnton's," he read. "Jay's Landing, New York. Darnton's?"

"A resort. We'll be there for a while, anyway. But we'll come to Boston whenever you need us; we'll do whatever has to be done. And we'll wait as long as we have to, but I hope you'll try to speed it up; it's very important to me."

"Money always is," he said dryly.

"I'm not talking about money." *I'm talking about revenge. And getting back what Owen gave me. And fighting, to help me forget I've lost a family, and what I thought was love.*

"What's our chances?" Clay asked bluntly as they shook hands.

"Fair to good," Rollins replied. "Assuming of course, that everyone manages to keep calm."

"Cold son of a bitch," Clay muttered as they left the office. He repeated it in the restaurant where they had lunch before leaving the city. "Cold son of a bitch. *He* doesn't have anything at stake."

"A lot of money," Laura said absently. Her thoughts were racing, from fury at Felix, to a hollow sense of loss over Owen and Paul, to uncertainty about the future. She knew, whatever Rollins said, that the trial was a long shot and that she had to make plans for afterwards.

Looking out the window beside their booth, she saw her ghostly image in the glass. I forgot makeup, she thought, and I need a haircut. And Rosa would tell me to sit straight. But Rosa was gone.

Her breath came faster, as if she'd been running; she was knotted up inside with anger and hurt. There was too much to think about all at once, too much to sort out, and no time to do it. They had to be on the move; they had to earn a living. I wish I had a quiet minute, she thought; I wish I could wipe everything out and start fresh and know what's ahead of me.

I wish I was somebody else.

Abruptly, she stood up. "I'll be right back," she told Clay and went to the powder room at the back of the restaurant.

For a moment she stood before the mirror, looking at herself. Then she took a small scissors from the manicure kit in her purse and started cutting her hair. She chopped and hacked, a few strands at a time. The ends were uneven, and the more she tried to even it the more ragged it became. But as it grew shorter it became more curly until finally she was left with a cap of springy hair with small ends protruding like tiny antennae. Her face looked smaller, her cheekbones higher, her eyes enormous.

Clay was paying the waiter when she rejoined him, and his mouth fell open. "What the hell did you do to yourself? Christ, I hardly recognized you."

"Good. I don't want to look the same."

"You were prettier before."

She shrugged.

As they drove away and headed north out of the city, he said, trying to sound casual, "Rollins said you'd need to be beautiful and pathetic on the witness stand."

"I'll be whatever I am. They'll believe me or they won't."

"Laura." Worriedly, he peered at her. "You're not giving up, are you?"

"No."

He was silent as he negotiated a traffic circle. "You'll be fine," he said, as much to himself as to her. "You'll be great."

She did not answer. How stupid, she thought, to try to change anything by cutting my hair. I have to change the way I think and feel and remember. Looking different doesn't mean anything; being different does.

She pushed her thoughts ahead, and tried to picture Kelly and John

Darnton. She had never met them except over the telephone, but they had offered her a place to stay when she had called the week before, in desperation.

"You always have a place with us," Kelly had said without hesitation. "You didn't think I'd say no, did you? My God, lady, you sent us the Countess Irinia and a trainload of rich friends for a whole week—you practically saved our summer—and you think I'd say no? I wouldn't turn you down for anything you asked! I'd probably *give* you the place, if you asked for it!"

So they were still having trouble, Laura thought as she and Clay drove across the Massachusetts state line into New Hampshire and she began to look at the scenery. Until now, she had been careful not to look too closely at the forests and meadows, the marshes, the ponds with flocks of birds darting above them, because everything reminded her of long rides with Paul through just such countryside, but when the highway began to follow the Merrimack River, she looked up and let herself enjoy it. There were no memories in New Hampshire, nor in Vermont, and by the time they were driving through Montpelier, past its vast granite quarry, she and Clay were talking about the landscape, the neat houses and white New England churches behind long low walls of tightly fitted rocks that early settlers had cleared from the stubborn New England soil, and about Darnton's. "I'm not sure how successful they are," Laura said. "The countess told me she was very pleased, so it's far from shabby, but I have a feeling they really stretched themselves to impress her. I hope we can help them."

"Fuck it, we could have been millionaires, and instead we're on our way to rescue some people on the brink of bankruptcy."

She broke into laughter. "They're not on the brink, and they're the ones rescuing us, not the other way around."

"And we still have a chance to be millionaires. Right?"

"I don't know." She looked away from him, amused but a little troubled by his casual assumption that her inheritance would be his, too. She was glad it was his turn to drive; she could look at the Green Mountains that had suddenly risen up to surround them, as lush and bright as their name. They were her first mountains and she stared at their massive beauty, mesmerized by the way they enfolded the road and the car, making the rest of the world seem distant and unreal. A person could forget everything here, she thought, but Clay brought her back by pulling over beside a small lake in Waterbury.

"Your turn," he said. "I'm going to take a nap."

So she found Darnton's by herself, turning south at Burlington to follow the shore of Lake Champlain until she came to the small town of

Jay's Landing, and the causeway Kelly had described, leading to the island. No guest cars were allowed on the island—"But you can drive over," Kelly had said. "Unload your luggage and let us make you welcome."

That was what greeted Laura when she drove up: Kelly's welcome. She rushed from the lodge and gave Laura a hug that made her breathless, then stood back, grinning, her red cheeks crinkling in her fair face.

Laura smiled back. Everyone, she would discover, smiled at Kelly Darnton, unable to resist the warmth of her black eyes, the halo of her long black hair that defied comb and brush to fly out in all directions, and her vigorous carrying voice that announced her arrival before she herself appeared. She was taller than Laura, and broader, and twice her age, but her exuberance made her seem younger, especially beside Laura's reticence.

"Hi," she said to Clay, who had emerged from the car. "Did your sister do all the driving?"

"Why should she? I drove my share."

"Good. We need a chauffeur. We don't allow guests to drive on the island, so we have a bunch of very classy vintage cars and we drive everybody to our golf course on the mainland and wherever else they want to go. Sound interesting?"

"God, it sounds terrific."

"I thought it might. Come on."

She had taken charge, and Laura watched with gratitude as she led Clay to the double row of garages behind the main lodge and introduced him to the head chauffeur. Clay was so young in so many ways; even working in Philadelphia hadn't seemed to make him grow up. Perhaps Kelly and John would find a way to help him get past his boyishness, as charming as it often was.

Alone, she walked up a small incline to get her bearings. Darnton's main lodge, a sprawling two-story white building with red shutters and a red roof, straddled a gentle rise at the far end of its own island, outlined against the deep blue of Lake Champlain and the pine-covered slopes of the Adirondacks in the distance. A pine forest covered much of the island itself, crisscrossed by horseback and walking trails, the trees giving way to a sweeping lawn in front of the lodge, tennis courts at the side, an outdoor pool to match the indoor one used mostly in winter, croquet and badminton fields, and a long flagstone walk leading to the marina and docks.

In the midst of one of the busiest resort areas in the country, Darnton's island was serene, wooded and beautiful. And the forests and beaches reminded Laura vividly of Osterville, on Cape Cod.

"Give a boy a bunch of cars and he's happy for a day," Kelly said, joining her. She gave Laura a sharp look. "What's wrong? Memories? I never asked why you wanted to come up here. Somebody died? Or betrayed you? Or kicked you out?"

All of the above. "Kelly, do you mind if I don't talk about it yet?"

"You don't ever have to talk about it. Come on and get settled. I fixed up a couple of spare rooms for the two of you; you even have your own sitting room. Dinner's in an hour. And by the way," she added casually, "I've done a fair bit of haircutting in my time."

Laura's hand went to her short, ragged hair. "It looks terrible, doesn't it?"

"Mostly amateurish." Kelly ran her blunt fingers through it. "It's not beyond repair. Maybe after dinner we'll give it some loving care."

"Thank you," Laura said. "Loving care would be wonderful."

That night Kelly trimmed her hair, helped her make the beds in the two tiny rooms, joined by a small sitting room, at the back of the lodge, and hung clothes in the closet as Laura unpacked. "Nice," she said, fingering the cashmere sweaters, silk blouses, and challis skirts Owen had insisted she buy. "I still have some of these left over from the days when I bought clothes instead of spending everything my parents left me on this lodge."

"But you're doing well here," Laura said, somewhere between a statement and a question.

"Surviving. Do you want some brandy? John was in such a hurry to get to the mainland we didn't offer you an after-dinner drink."

Laura shook her head. "It would knock me out. I haven't been sleeping too well."

"Tea? Darjeeling. Dark, soothing, good for a soul in turmoil."

A laugh escaped Laura's composed lips. "That sounds perfect."

They sat in armchairs in a lamplit corner of the great hall, drinking tea and talking late into the night. The room had a soaring pitched ceiling, walls of knotless pine paneling framing two massive stone fireplaces at each end of the room, a dark plank floor strewn with animal skins, and groupings of buffalo plaid couches and armchairs. Fur throw pillows, willow-twig rocking chairs, pewter lamps, and ceramic vases with arrangements of leafless branches of mountain ash still holding their red-orange berries, gave color and warmth to the rustic comfort of the room. It was, after all, completely different from the airy wicker and chintz of the Salinger homes at the Cape, and the velvets and brocades of Owen's house on Beacon Hill. It was a place where one could forget the past.

"We didn't do all the furnishing," Kelly said, taking one of the amaretto cookies the chef had served with their tea. "Most of it was left here by the oil baron who built it and then sold it in the middle of an acrimonious divorce. Trouble was, he and his wife hadn't been speaking for a long time, so they'd let the place deteriorate and there was an awful lot for us to do. Are you going to miss working at the Salinger?"

"I'll miss the job. I liked it."

"I have a couple you could handle whenever you're ready to work again."

"Do you really? I was hoping you might have something. I'll do anything, Kelly, any job you have."

Kelly smiled. "Whatever they are?"

"I need work. So does Clay. We have to start somewhere."

"How about assistant manager of Darnton's?"

"Assistant manager?" Laura repeated. "But you must have one. You couldn't run the place without one."

"True. But you see, you have arrived in the midst of a crisis." Kelly held her cup with both hands and rested her feet on the edge of the glass-topped coffee table supported on four pine logs. "Last week my short-fused husband fired the assistant manager and two maintenance men for soliciting tips from guests—which, of course, isn't a hell of a long way from blackmail, so I agree with his decision, it's the timing that bothers me. End of August, almost Labor Day, just about the busiest time of the year, and we have close to a full house. We're desperate for help. You'd be doing us a favor."

"I can't believe it; it's so perfect... And you want Clay to be a chauffeur? He could do other things; he was a desk clerk at a hotel in Philadelphia and he'll learn anything you tell him."

"First we need a chauffeur. If he passes John's driving test, he's got the job. After that we'll find other things for him to do. Why not? My friend, you are manna from heaven. First you send us the countess and now you bring us yourself. Except, you know we only have a hundred rooms, Laura, a third of what you had at the Salinger. You might be bored."

"I won't be bored." Laura hesitated. "There is one other thing. We'll have to be in Boston now and then for... business... some things we didn't get to finish. If that makes too much trouble for you, maybe I ought to take a job that isn't so important."

"How long will you be away?"

"I don't know. We'd make it as short as possible."

"Well, we'll work it out. Is this business going to go on very long?"

"It may take a year."

Kelly gave a small grunt. "Sounds like lawyers; nobody else drags things out that long. Let me know ahead of time when you'll be going."

"Thank you, Kelly."

It was almost three months before they went back for pretrial depositions, just before Thanksgiving. They drove the opposite direction, through the Green Mountains, white and pristine this time beneath drifts of snow that had not yet turned to ice, then through the meadows and forests of New Hampshire and into Massachusetts. With each mile the scenes grew more familiar, and by the time they arrived in Boston and parked near the glass and steel building in the financial district where Carver Cheyne had his office, Laura was tense with holding herself in, trying to ignore the waves of memory and desire that swept through her.

Once in Cheyne's office it was easier: his window blinds were drawn, fluorescent lights glared, the furniture was dull brown. With Ansel Rollins and a court stenographer sitting beside her, and Clay waiting his turn in the reception room, she answered Cheyne's questions in a level voice, her face betraying no emotion, going over the same story she had told Rollins, in exactly the same way. But Cheyne was not Rollins: not sympathetic, not gently leading her step by step through her story. He was cold and deliberate, returning again and again to her relationship with Owen, asking how she began working in his library, how often they went for walks, how many meals they ate together, how often they were alone instead of with other members of the family, how many times she wrote personal letters for him that no one else knew about, how many of his business affairs she handled alone so that he had to turn to her and no one else when he wanted to refer to them.

"He didn't *have to* turn to me," said Laura angrily. "He wanted to. We worked together and he trusted me."

"Of course," Cheyne said smoothly. "Tell me again, would you, why he fired his secretary."

"He didn't fire her. I told you, she worked for the executive offices in the Boston Salinger, and now that I was with him he didn't need to take her from her other work anymore."

"Now that you were with him. Was it your suggestion that he fire his secretary and use you instead?"

"He didn't fire his secretary!"

It went on and on, but Laura and Rollins knew it could have been worse: Cheyne could have brought up her arrest and conviction in New York. "It's a good sign that they didn't," Rollins said as they left Cheyne's office after Clay had gone through the same procedure as Laura. "It's obvious they're convinced it would do no good to bring it up in court; I'd be ready for them, and I'm sure the judge would not allow it; it has no bearing on this case."

"How sure?" Clay demanded.

"Sure enough," Rollins said shortly. "What happened today showed us what they have. You may have thought the questions were difficult, but they were what I expected. The whole purpose of depositions is to get information. And of course to make sure no one springs any surprises at the trial."

"Then why bother to have a trial?" Clay asked, recalling dramatic trial scenes in films and on television.

"So a jury can decide who is telling the truth," Rollins said dryly. "You were the one who told me that was your right."

Clay mumbled something and Laura asked, "We'll know everything everyone is going to say before the trial begins?"

"Unless something is discovered at the last minute, or witnesses change their stories."

A flash of fear went through her. "Why would they?"

"They might remember something they'd forgotten or be asked a question one of the lawyers didn't ask at the deposition. It doesn't happen often." He led them to the door. "I'll call you soon."

He called in December. Laura was in Kelly's office, and she went into her small one adjoining it and closed the door to talk to him. He had conducted his depositions in his office, questioning the Salingers, the doctor and nurses, and Parkinson. "Nothing startling," he concluded when he had related them to her. "But that gives me concern. At the moment they have a weak case, and I would expect Carver to have more than we've seen. He's very confident."

"You mean we should be worried."

"I mean we should be alert. You and I should meet several more times before the trial. We'll begin in two weeks; can you get here?"

"Of course."

"Good. Make sure your story is clear."

"It is clear, since it's the truth," Laura said coldly. "Didn't the doctor and nurses say everything was normal?"

"As I told you, they said as far as they could tell Mr. Salinger was weak, and frustrated by his limitations, but not unduly agitated. That was the most definitive they would get. Our best hope is Parkinson: he's a fine lawyer and he was absolutely straightforward in answering my questions. He wouldn't have prepared that codicil or allowed Mr. Salinger to sign it if he thought something was amiss; no reputable lawyer would. As long as he says Mr. Salinger knew what he wanted, I think we're in excellent shape."

"Is that all?" Laura asked after a moment. "Didn't . . . anyone else give a deposition?"

"You're thinking of Paul Janssen. No. I understand from Carver that he doesn't want to testify. No one wants a reluctant witness—you never know what you'll get—so at least for now he won't be called."

Laura was silent. She didn't know what Paul was thinking. I could write to him, she thought; but she didn't know what she could say. Are you reluctant because you still love me? But if you do, why not tell the jury I would never rob the family or take anything from Owen or try to make him act against his will? Or is it that you still believe I'm guilty of those things and you don't want to have anything to do with me, for good or ill?

She didn't want to think about it. Whether they won or lost in court, Paul was gone; he was making a new life, as she was. No court case would change that.

She concentrated on work, learning the business of running a resort. She had written to Ben, telling him where they were. "Things didn't work out at the Salingers'," she wrote. She couldn't tell him about Owen's will and how they'd been forced out; it would only prove to him that he'd been right about the Salingers from the first, when he told her they didn't care about her and never would. So she sent him her new address, and a short note, and that was all. And then, with all the others, she pushed Ben out of her thoughts and buried herself in the large problems and small details of the resort.

She and Kelly had divided the domestic and business affairs, while John handled transportation, sports, and the physical plant. They all worked in harmony, especially as Laura took on more responsibilities. From her first tentative days at the job she had, over the months, grown more sure of herself. Everything she had learned with Jules LeClair about the whims and demands of guests, she used at Darnton's. She used everything she had learned from Owen about the organization of hotels and priorities of management; she used the case studies she had done at the university; she used everything Kelly taught her about the peculiarities of a resort. She worked all day and late into every night, studying the way Darnton's functioned, and how it might function better; and when Kelly or John urged her to relax, she thanked them but went back to work. If she won at the trial, she could relax. If she didn't, she had to earn a living while she tried to figure out a way to get back some of what was rightfully hers.

After Christmas the lodge suddenly was quiet, and the island seemed deserted. "We ought to close down and go to Florida," John said.

"Too much work to do," Kelly responded.

It was an old argument, and it flared and faded as the weeks passed and they made plans for the summer. The three of them coordinated the different staffs that worked on the island, made lists of equipment, and wrote schedules for tennis, horseback riding, swimming and aerobic classes, speed- and sailboat cruises on the lake, golf on their eighteen-hole course in Jay's Landing, card games, and first-run movies shown at night. And, since people judge a place largely on food, they spent extra time on the dining room and bar menus for more than two hundred guests, depending on how many families were at the resort at any one time.

"It's expensive so we don't get too many kids," John said as he and Laura walked back from inspecting the marina one morning in January. "I don't want them—too much trouble, and the doc on the mainland on call more often—but Kelly thinks we might fill more rooms as a family resort. Do you have an opinion on that?"

Laura frowned slightly. "I don't understand why it can't be a family resort and very expensive, too. Don't wealthy people take vacations with their children?"

He stopped walking and looked at her, a giant of a man with a ruddy face, high forehead, and a heavy black beard. "Possibly."

"Maybe you ought to make Darnton's so expensive wealthy parents will think it's too good to pass up. Then they could stop feeling guilty about leaving their children with a nanny while they go off to play."

"You think they feel guilty?"

"I have no idea. I would. I'd love to have a place to bring my children and know we could do separate things and still share a good time."

He smiled. "You should have children; you'd be a good mother."

Laura flushed. "We're talking about Darnton's."

"Okay," he said. "Darnton's with rich little boys and girls romping in the fields. I like it. You impress me, Laura; I like a woman who thinks we can have it all." They began walking again and he shot a glance at her. "What about you? When are you going to have it all, instead of working every night?"

"I'm doing what I want to do," she said. "I might ask you the same question. When was the last time you and Kelly had a night out on the mainland?"

"She doesn't want it. All she thinks about is this damn resort, making it pay, making it bigger . . . anyway, I was talking about you. What's the problem that you don't go anywhere or—"

"I said I'm doing what I want!"

"Hey," he said, stepping back and putting up his hands in mock fear. "Don't bite, Miss Fairchild, you've got a scared fella here—"

"Oh, fuck it, John, grow up." Abruptly she heard Rosa's voice: *Ladies don't swear, my young miss. Or lose their temper, as I've told you many a time.* "I'm sorry," she murmured, to Rosa or John, she wasn't sure which.

Clay liked John; the two of them spent hours with Darnton's fleet of vintage cars after John had Clay drive him around the island and pronounced him an excellent driver. From then on, when he wasn't on call to fill in as a desk clerk, Clay's passion was cars, second only to the young women who staffed the resort, especially a tennis instructor named Myrna, long-legged and experienced, the way he liked them.

His favorite car, just ahead of a 1920 LaSalle and a 1925 Packard, was a 1927 Silver Shadow Rolls-Royce that he polished and cosseted more than any woman he'd ever known. He knew absolutely—and was reminded each time he ran sensuous palms over its gold and mahogany fittings, leather-bound steering wheel, and soft upholstered seats—that he was definitely made for the finest things in life.

The trouble was, most of the finest things had eluded him lately. He no longer even had his own apartment, as he had in Philadelphia. "It would be okay for somebody who didn't know any better," he grumbled, pacing around the small sitting room that linked his bedroom and Laura's, and eyeing the sturdy furniture and cotton throw rugs. "But, shit, if it wasn't for that bastard, we'd be on Beacon Hill with everything we have coming to us. You know what we're doing? We're going backward, for Christ's sake! Living in a little place, the two of us, just like five years ago, above that garage in Centerville. We were doing better, and now all we have is this fucking little—"

"It's home and we're lucky to have it," Laura snapped. Then she put her arm around him. "I know you're disappointed, Clay, but I wish you'd just learn as much as you can while we're here and let me take care of the future. I'm thinking about it; I intend to take care of Felix one way or another. And you could help; a little cheerfulness would go a long way around here."

He dropped into a chair and stretched out his legs. He hated criticism.

Laura looked at the room. "Do you suppose the fireplace works?"

"I don't know; the housekeeper always took care of them at Owen's. How can you tell?"

"Make a fire."

"The place might fill up with smoke."

"Then we'll know it doesn't work."

Clay laughed and jumped to kiss her. "You're okay, you know? I really like being with you. I don't want you to think I don't appreciate what you do—making a home and—well, what the hell, you know what I mean. I'll get some firewood, okay? Be right back." He went outside, wishing he could tell Laura how great he thought she was without getting embarrassed. She really was clever, and nice, and she really cared about him. She'd been miserable the whole time they were in Philadelphia, after that fucking will reading, and he'd been so furious at the family he hadn't done much to help her. He didn't even have a job; he quit the hotel before Felix could fire him. So there they'd been, the two of them, with their own problems, and he'd kept sounding off but Laura hadn't said much. She hadn't cried, either; her face had been like stone, and she'd spent a lot of time alone, just walking around the city.

She was miserable, and Clay knew it. But he didn't know what would be the right thing to say, so he left her alone. He knew she'd work everything out; she always did. She didn't seem to need other people very much.

She said she needed him, though, which was why he was here. He'd followed her from the Cape to Boston and from Boston to this goddamned island—an *island* in the middle of some *mountains* when what he craved was New York!—because she said she needed him; he was her family. Well, what the hell. He'd stick around for now. There was Myrna, and the spectacular cars, and John Darnton, who liked him and said he'd give him a raise if they had a good season. And besides, they weren't all that far from New York; he might be able to get there for a weekend now and then.

Anyway, where else would he be but here? He wouldn't go to Ben; he didn't trust him. Of course he could go anywhere—he was twenty-one, strong, healthy and free, with the whole world to choose from—but he'd decided to hang in there with Laura for a while more. It wasn't so bad, having a family of your own.

* * *

"You want to tell me about those trips to Boston?" Kelly asked Laura one fragrant morning in March as they sat on the front porch. "And why you jump every time the phone rings in your office, like you're expecting something?"

"I'd like to, Kelly. And I will. But not yet."

"Quite a shell you've built around you," Kelly observed casually. "I'm here, you know, willing and able to listen."

"I know it. Thank you."

Kelly poured coffee from the thermos jug they had brought from the kitchen. "One thing, you do look a lot less peaked than when you got here. I hope we have something to do with that."

"You do," said Laura with a smile. "More than anyone or anything." She turned to a clean page on the clipboard in her lap. "We haven't gone over the wine list yet."

"Don't you ever quit? We could take a break; the management allows it."

"No, I'm fine; there's still so much to do."

"All work and no play," Kelly sighed, but she, too, picked up her clipboard. "Oh, what about linens? Did we finish with them yesterday? We did bed linens and restaurant stuff, but how about the health club?"

"It's on my list: fourteen towels and two dozen sheets for the massage rooms that should be replaced. I'm going into town this afternoon; I thought I'd stop at the laundry and tell them they have to be more careful."

"Good. I hate doing those things; I end up listening to their family problems and telling them not to worry about a few torn sheets. You're tougher than I am, my friend."

Laura thought of her sleepless nights. *Not as tough as I'd like to be.* "They tell me their problems, too," she replied. "But I know people can live with their problems and still do a good job."

Kelly made the small humming sound that meant she was thinking and didn't want her thoughts interrupted by someone changing the subject.

"Kelly's humming," John Darnton said, coming onto the porch from the great hall of the lodge. "What did I miss?"

"A fascinating discussion of the laundry," Laura said.

He chuckled and kissed the top of Kelly's head. "Girl talk." He leaned over his wife's shoulder and read the top page in her lap. "Wine. I forgot to tell you, I found a new supplier yesterday. He specializes in boutique American wines instead of French and Italian. I'll bring you his price list and then we'll decide." He took the clipboard from her hand and riffled through the papers. "Better add some new bar glasses; breakage was up last season. Season. Lousy word, isn't it? We thought this place would be year-round."

"It will be," Kelly said. "It takes a while."

"'A while' seems to be going on longer than I expected." He was trying to sound playful, and as if the effort was too much, he returned the clipboard to her and straightened up, rubbing the back of his neck. "I'd call four years a meaningful amount of time."

"You've said that before," Kelly noted flatly.

"About three thousand times, probably. And it's still dead around here from December to May, except for Christmas week—thank God for Christmas week—and what have we done about it?"

"We're working on it."

"How are we working on it?"

"What is this, a quiz?" Kelly demanded. "You know perfectly well what we're doing, we work together. Or did you *again* forget that?"

"Hoo-ee, the lady is on her crusade again." He clasped his hands behind his head and looked down at Kelly. "One time. One fucking time I play around with somebody and you absolutely will not let go of—"

"Who'd believe that? If there was once there was twice or a hundred. Young chicks come here to work and you follow them to the mainland like a dog with his tongue hanging—"

"Did I ever expect my loving wife to call me a dog?" John asked the cloudless sky. "Was I warned?"

"Don't talk about me as if I'm not here."

"I'll talk about you any way I goddam please."

Laura walked deliberately to the front door of the lodge. "I'll be in the kitchen," she said.

"Shit!" John exploded. He dropped his arms, his palms slapping loudly against his thighs. "I'm going; I interrupted a conference. Sorry we put you through this, Laura; can you forgive us?"

Without waiting for an answer, he turned to leave. As he passed Kelly's chair, he reached out to touch her shoulder, then jerked his hand back and kept going, down the steps and across the lawn.

"Damn, damn, *damn*." Kelly's fist pounded the arm of her chair. "Why can't I be cooler about things, like you? Because I can't; I start boiling when I think of him tangled in the sheets with some cute unattached chick who hasn't been married to him for ten years and doesn't have to worry about a resort sucking up an inheritance and every penny of savings like a vacuum cleaner and still needing more." She took a long breath. "Sorry, Laura, you've heard this before. First John apologizes, then I do; we keep making you our audience. It's just that there isn't anybody else around here who listens and doesn't gossip, and sometimes things pile up and . . ."

"You've got too much to worry about," Laura said. "It makes you feel smothered. You have to lock some things up and only worry about one at a time."

Kelly looked at her and nodded slowly. "You really do that, don't you? Is that how you stay so cool? God, Laura, I love you and I love having you here, but you make me feel so *sloppy*, all my emotions hanging out while you're so smooth and *together*, like one of those fortune-teller's globes that doesn't have any seams. Don't you ever let loose and scream or cry?"

Laura clasped her hands. "No."

"Everybody cries."

"Maybe if you concentrated on the resort and let things settle down between you and John—"

"Okay, you don't want to talk about crying. Concentrate on the resort? John gets jealous—can you believe it?—if I pay more attention to it than to him. And if I concentrate on him"—she spread out her hands —"he's loaded for bear, that man. You saw it just now; talking along nice and easy and—pow!—we're fighting. Even in bed, one of us says a simple word—well, maybe not always so simple—and that's it, no love-making that night, just another argument. And I tell you, that is not much fun."

"I know." *But I don't think about that. I don't miss making love; I don't want it; I don't even remember what it was like to want it. I know I used to think it was lovely but I'm not interested anymore.* "Maybe if you went somewhere, just the two of you . . . this is only the middle of March—we have two months until we get busy—isn't this a good time for you to get away?"

Kelly tilted her head. "You trying to get rid of us, my friend? Itching to take over and run the place yourself?"

Laura laughed and shook her head. "I wouldn't even try. I was thinking of you, not me."

"But you must want to run your own place," Kelly said probingly.

"Someday. We all have dreams we tuck away for the future."

"It's one big headache, you know. You're better off staying with us. Lifetime security."

They laughed, but inwardly Laura said no. The only real security was earning her way in a place of her own. Then no one could ever kick her out again.

"Think about it," Kelly urged. "I'm serious. We'd make you a partner."

"I'll think about it," Laura said, "if you think about a vacation. I still say this is a good time for you to get away."

"It would be if we could, but we can't. Cutting expenses, you cut your own pleasures first. You know about that; you've cut down a lot." She gazed at Laura. "That's one of the jackets you brought with you—and it's a Ralph Lauren or I'll eat my non–Ralph Lauren hat—and you haven't bought anything since. And there's that closetful of clothes, and those old leather-bound books I was looking at the other day. . . . Not that I'm prying"—she saw the involuntary smile that curved Laura's lips—"well, I am, but only a little bit. Mainly I'm interested in size, not cost, and I'm envious: every time I look at you I dream of being size eight instead of fourteen."

Laura smiled again, liking Kelly's openness and affection, thinking what a good place this was, and how lucky she was to be here, for however long she stayed. And then the telephone rang, and it was Ansel Rollins. The trial was set for July.

CHAPTER 12

LENI Salinger sat on the edge of the wide, satin-hung bed, leaning back, gazing beneath heavy eyelids at the bright red hair of the young man kneeling before her, his head between her thighs. She let herself float on slow waves of pleasure as he played his tongue on her sensitive flesh and thrust deep inside her wet darkness, and small shocks of sensation swept through her like iced vodka and warm honey, transforming her lean white body to a fluid line of feeling. She sensed rather than saw the brocade and velvet room, and the hypnotizing glow of a single lamp, and then her eyes closed as the young man suddenly lay on her, forcing her back on the satin spread, and thrust inside her, hard and deep. He moved within her, then raised himself so the tip of his penis caressed her small, hardened flesh, and then he plunged into her again so their bodies locked, and he pulled out and thrust again and again until the threads of Leni's body gathered together in a knot and then flew apart, giving her a few seconds of the ecstasy she kept locked inside her, waiting until she could find the secrecy and safety to release it.

The young man's breathing was as rapid as hers, and she put her arms around his muscular shoulders, pleased that he had found pleasure, too. But then she turned her wrist to see her watch. "I have to go," she murmured, and immediately he moved away so she could sit up. In the beginning, months ago, he had tried to keep her with him, but no longer: he knew if he wanted to see her again, he had to follow her lead.

"Let me help," he said; it was one of the games they played. He pulled on her hose and half-slip, fastened her brassiere, buttoned her sheer blouse, and tied the bow at her throat. Her body cooling, Leni drew her skirt over her hips, fastened a red snakeskin belt around her waist, stepped into gray snakeskin pumps, and picked up her jacket.

The young man was buckling his own belt. "Will you be here next week?"

"I don't know." She picked up the red Hermès Constance handbag she always used when she came to New York, and slung it over her shoulder. "I'll try, but I have four board meetings and that doesn't leave much time. Besides," she added lightly, "if I don't give you some free afternoons, when will you get your homework done?"

"At night."

"You should be dating at night."

"I don't date."

"All college students date."

"I can't. I can't even look at anybody else—"

"Tor," she said with a note of warning. "I would be very distressed if you changed anything in your life because of me."

"Well—" As always, he said what he had to say to keep her from looking for someone else. "I do go out, lots, I just didn't think you'd like to know. That's no problem, finding girls . . ."

"Then do your homework in the afternoon," she said gently, liking him, enjoying his infatuation more than she would admit to him or to herself. She stood before the full-length mirror. Pearl-gray shantung suit, white silk blouse, pearl silk gloves, a cherry red Adolfo straw hat tilted over one perfect eyebrow. Her mascara and eyeshadow were unsmudged. She freshened her lipstick; the case made a loud snap as she closed it. "I'll call you when I can get away," she said and kissed him briefly. In another minute she was in the brightly lit corridor of the Waldorf Towers, two steps from the elevator that took her to the lobby where she was one of dozens of well-dressed women spending their afternoons shopping, lunching, and perhaps adjourning for a couple of hours with a friend in the exclusive privacy of a high-priced hotel room.

The late afternoon air was warm and still; even the crowds on the streets seemed to move more slowly in the June afternoon as the sun slid lower in the sky. Leni stopped at Tiffany's, then caught a cab to the airport in time for the five o'clock shuttle to Boston. And by seven she was sitting at dinner with Felix, the French doors open, the blue and silver flowers on the French wallpaper seeming to sway in the ocean breeze. "I found the tie clip you wanted," she told him. "The last one Tiffany's had. It seems people now give gifts for Easter, especially jewelry."

"Good news for the merchants," he said absently, then, as if reminding himself, looked up and thanked her for the tie clip. "Did you have a pleasant day?"

"Very."

"What did you do besides shop?"

"I stopped in at the Waldorf."

His eyes took on a glazed look. "Ladies' lunches. I'm afraid I have no interest in what you did at the Waldorf. No matinee?"

"You mean the theater?"

"What else would I mean? Oh, concerts. There are none on Tuesday, as far as I know."

"Nor at the theater, either."

"Well, whatever you did, I'm sure you were able to amuse yourself. I assume you're amused; you're there most of the time, it seems, and it can't be for those deadly board meetings."

"They're not deadly; they make me feel useful." She took a second helping of veal and wild rice; she was always ravenous after a trip to New York. "How was your day?"

"Good. Very good. We saw a videotape of progress on the Elani in Honolulu; we should be able to open this fall. And I met with a group of bankers from Chicago about building a new hotel there, on the lake; we shouldn't have trouble financing it. They may even help us sell the old one; they think they know of a possible buyer."

"You can't sell that hotel; it isn't yours."

"It will be next month, after the trial. You wouldn't expect me to wait until then to make plans; I intend to be ready to move the minute that mess is settled."

Leni was silent.

"There's not much demand for small hotels—no real way to make them profitable—but some junior-college people are interested in Chicago, and a nursing home director in Washington. If things go well, all four of those relics will be off our hands within a couple of years."

She looked at him. "Owen took pride in those hotels."

"And so you're sentimental about them. He knew as well as anyone they can't compete with modern ones. I'm doing exactly what he would have wanted."

"That is not true," Leni said coldly. "He would have been extremely angry. He would have glared at you and called you a narrow-minded opportunist kicking aside the past just as you kick aside anyone who gets in your way." Her voice grew wistful. "And his mustache would have quivered like long wings on each side of his mouth, about to take off—" There were tears in her eyes. "I miss him. He was so alive. Paul said the same thing the other day, how much he misses that wonderful sense of life Owen brought to everything he did . . ."

Felix picked up the carafe. "More wine?"

"I suppose so. Yes."

"I didn't know you talked to Paul. Where is he?"

"Rome, I think. He doesn't stay anywhere very long; I've never known him to be so restless. I asked him if he was doing any photography and he said he'd met someone who wants to be a model and he's begun photographing her. I wish he'd find a woman he could love."

"He'd do better to find a job. He's been wandering around the world for months; nothing but a wastrel."

"I don't think so; I think he's trying to find something to believe in. It's the same with Allison. I know her trip to Europe was my idea, but I didn't think it would turn out the way it has: the way she's going from country to country, and dragging Patricia with her, it seems more like she's fleeing. Both of them, Paul and Allison, acting as if they're trying to get over a bad love affair. It's astonishing that one young woman could wreak such havoc. . . ."

There was a silence. "I had some of my father's things moved over here today," Felix said.

Leni frowned. "You took things from Beacon Hill? You're not supposed to touch anything involved in the court case—"

"I would appreciate it if you would stop telling me what I cannot do. I've done it, and what anyone says about it is irrelevant. I decided it was time we get some use out of those things; they've been sitting in that house for a year, with nobody there—"

"Rosa is there."

"She shouldn't be; she would have been gone long ago if you hadn't raised such an incredible fuss."

"I want her to live in this house, with us."

"I will not have her here."

"Then she'll stay in Beacon Hill."

"She will not. As soon as that house is mine, I'm going to sell it."

"You won't. Felix, you may succeed in taking those hotels from Laura, but I won't let you—"

"*I will take back what is mine! My father was terrorized into cutting me out of his will!*"

"Don't be ridiculous. He left you almost everything he had."

Felix's fist was clenched around the stem of his wineglass, and it suddenly snapped in his hand. A ruby rivulet ran along the dark mahogany table, staining the snowy place mat before him.

"Did you cut yourself?" Leni asked with faint concern. "I'll ring for Talbot."

"It's nothing." He wadded a napkin in his palm. "My father would never have done what he did if he'd been in his right mind. He trusted me, he cared for me more than anyone, he wanted me to keep his name as powerful after his death as it was in his lifetime. He knew I was the only one who could do that; he depended on me. He would never make a fool of me in the eyes of the world. The hotels were meant for me; his stock in the company was meant for me; his corporation was meant for me. And so was his house."

"If you win the case, that house will be ours," Leni said bluntly. "And it will not be sold."

Felix tightened his fingers against the linen napkin, pressing it into his throbbing palm. What the hell had happened to her? She'd been changing ever since Owen died and that witch had been sent packing in disgrace. Sometimes he hardly recognized her; she'd lost much of that charming passive serenity she'd developed over the years to mask whatever dissatisfactions she felt. Now, when she didn't agree with him, she told him so.

He had always dominated Leni. He used her elegance and style to make him feel powerful—the envy of other men—but his hold seemed to be weakening and it occurred to him that after twenty-two years of marriage he did not know her well enough to have any idea how to get it back.

Once he thought he knew everything necessary to make her his and to keep her. That was when she was nineteen, in hot rebellion against her wealthy, shipbuilding, churchgoing, publicity-shy family. Felix had met her on a street in Greenwich Village; she was with a man who glanced at him briefly, then, again, piercingly, and stopped him with his deep, gravelly voice. "By all the gods of the Salingers, if it isn't Felix the robber baron: Felix Salinger in the healthy and well-dressed flesh."

"Judd," Felix said flatly. He couldn't believe it: he never saw a familiar face in New York; it was an article of faith with him that the city made everyone anonymous. Yet here was Judd Gardner, whom he had long since wiped out of his thoughts, looking slightly seedier but otherwise not much different from years before. He would have walked away, but as he turned he got a good look at the girl whose arm was linked in Judd's. She was tall and spare, with tangled blond hair and sloppy clothes—and a way of holding her head, an elegance of style, that would have been at home in a palace. It was that elegance that caught Felix: he knew, with the same instinct that served him brilliantly in

business, that a man who owned that elegance would have the power
that came from the envy of other men. And he knew he would not
leave. "How are you?" he asked Judd.

"Barely," Judd said with a thin smile. "I barely am. But I see that *you*
very much *are*."

"Judd, I'm cold," said the girl.

The April wind was bitter; it whipped around the corner with a raw
chill. Felix was conscious of the girl's bare legs and his own fur-lined
coat, leather gloves, cashmere scarf. "Do you live nearby?" he asked.

"Around the corner."

"Then we'll go there."

Judd's eyes had been sliding from Felix to the girl and back again as
he saw Felix's fixed gaze. "Sorry, how rude I am. Leni Van Gris, Felix
Salinger. Felix is known for taking what he desires, Leni, so be on your
guard. Or perhaps I should be on mine. What do you think?"

"I think we should say good night and go home."

"But Felix wants a reunion," he said. "We can drink to old times.
Except that we haven't got anything to drink. We'll have to stop on the
way and get some supplies."

"We don't need any," she protested.

"We always need any," Judd said, and Felix realized he was in that
perpetual state of drunkenness in which alcoholics can function for long
stretches at a time before one more drink tips them into incoherence or
stupor. "And Felix will pay."

"Judd, let's go home. Alone."

"No, no, Felix will join us. Felix is Bacchus, god of wine. And here
we are."

The store was small and Judd was known there. Felix paid for wine
and whiskey, and soda for Leni, and they carried it to a nearby fourth-
floor walk-up in a brick building with a dry cleaner and pawnshop on
the street level. The apartment had three rooms along a narrow hallway,
like a train car, and Judd sat down in the front room in one of three
chairs around a folding table set with assorted china and a wine bottle
with candle wax dripping down the sides. One window was filled with a
piece of plywood where an air conditioner had once been installed; beneath it was a stain the shape of Africa. And everywhere, on the walls,
the furniture, the floor, were bright posters.

"The idea is to go somewhere," said Judd. He poured two straight
scotches and a soda, and handed a glass to Felix and one to Leni. "I'd
like to take this lovely child away from here. But in case I can't manage
it, we stare at exotic sights to swell our spirits with the wonders of a
world where beauty is all that matters."

"Judd, shut up," Leni said nervously. She sat cross-legged on a cushion on the floor beside Judd, the overhead light casting a shadow across her face that emphasized her cheekbones and the angular lines of her head and figure. Felix stood, staring down at her, knowing overwhelmingly that he wanted her and would do whatever he had to do to get her. It wouldn't be the first time, he thought dispassionately, that he had taken something he wanted from Judd Gardner.

Without being asked, he sat in one of the chairs at the table, across from Judd, and took a long look at him. Tall, blond, his hair falling to his shoulders, he was still good-looking, though not as extraordinarily handsome as Felix remembered him from the days when he had envied those golden classic features, and wished he himself were less dark. Judd's voice was still rough, but his eyes and mouth, when he talked to Leni, were tender. "Where do you want to go?" Felix asked him.

"Paradise. Where I can pick the golden apples of the sun and the silver apples of the moon and give them all to Leni, because, poor child, she thinks I'm romantic, since I'm poor and we met in an art gallery one rainy afternoon, and now she thinks she loves me."

"I do love you," the girl declared. "And you love me."

"Ah, if I could love you, my sweet Leni . . . if only I could."

"You will," she said. "I'll make you love me. You'll marry me and stop drinking and I'll find a way to get my parents to help you start another company all your own and we'll be happy."

"I had a wife. You'll find this interesting, Felix." Carefully he refilled his glass. "I had a wife and son but my wife kicked me out because I was drinking. Oh, and stealing, too—mustn't forget that. You see, once upon a time I owned a company. Owned it with a friend, but half was enough for me; I was so goddam proud of it. But it wasn't enough for my partner, so he stole my half." Once again he drained his glass and refilled it, this time pausing to hold it up to the light to admire its amber glow. "My friend stole it. Or, to be accurate, my un-friend. He wanted it so he stole it. So I stole too. That was after I found that I couldn't get it back legally, or even steal it back; all I could do was steal like an ordinary thief: breaking in and lifting a few things I could sell or pawn to keep going for a while and give money to my wife and son. He's eight now, my son, and I take him bowling and to Coney Island . . . fatherly things. I'm not much of a man anymore, but I can pretend, even if I have to steal to do it—so I do."

"Judd." Leni put her hand on his as he reached for the bottle. "You promised me you'd stop. You said when you finished what we had in the house you'd stop. And now we have all this stuff"—she glared at Felix —"and you know I hate it when—"

"Damn it, leave me alone! Sorry, I'm sorry, sweet Leni, but I'm talking to Felix and you mustn't interrupt."

She stood up behind Judd's chair and put her arms around him. "Will you please go?" she said to Felix. "I don't know anything about you, but for some reason Judd's getting awfully excited and it would be better if you left."

"You don't know anything about me? You don't know," Felix repeated, astonished at his good fortune. He looked at Judd's once-golden features in the circle of Leni's arms and thought he saw the first stages of a gaunt, hollow-eyed drunk. "Choose your paradise," he said to Judd, "and I'll buy your ticket."

Judd's eyes narrowed. "You want Leni."

"I want to help you find your paradise," Felix said.

"But not if I take Leni with me."

"No."

"What are you talking about?" Leni demanded. She moved away from Judd and spoke to Felix. "What the hell do you think you're talking about?"

"He's talking about taking you away from me," said Judd.

"Well, he can't do it." Leni stood with her head back, her hands at her sides, looking at Felix with the air of an empress. "I asked you to leave; now I'm telling you. Get out. We don't want you here. Anyway I don't like you," she added, suddenly sounding like a child.

"Let Judd tell me to go," Felix said.

"I might," Judd responded.

"Might!" Leni's voice rose higher. "Might! Judd, what the hell is *wrong* with you?"

"I might even talk about my past," Judd went on. His eyes were somber. "What do you think, Felix? Should I do that?"

Leni looked from one of them to the other. "When did you know each other?"

"In college," Felix replied.

"We were roommates," Judd added coldly.

"It was a long time ago," Felix said. "I don't remember it very well. Do you?"

There was a pause. The two men stared at each other. "No," Judd said. "I could remember, if I didn't get any money, but if I got some and went somewhere, the memory would no doubt stay very fuzzy."

Leni was biting her lower lip. "Judd, if you take money from this man I'm leaving you."

He nodded. "I know. But you would anyway. Don't you understand, my sweet Leni? You'd leave me anyway, one of these days, when the novelty of rebellion and poverty wears off. You'd leave me when you begin to want a young man with success ahead of him instead of a failed drunk who has nothing but bitter memories and a few lines of poetry to quote when you're hungry." Reaching out, he took her hand in his. "I have nothing to give you, and you deserve a kingdom. You don't belong here. I wish I'd had the strength to tell you that sooner."

"You needed a bribe," she said angrily.

"I needed a push. Someday you'll understand that."

She looked at him with the craftiness of a child trying to trick someone. "I warn you, if you leave me I'll go with him! That's what you'll remember: me and Felix. You'd hate that!"

"Yes. I would. But that's a choice you'll make for yourself." He looked at Felix. "How much?"

"If you go away by yourself, a thousand a month as long as you live."

Judd's head snapped back. "I'll be damned. I told you we should watch out for him, Leni. He just made our future."

"Not mine!" she cried. "Judd, I'm strong enough for both of us! I won't let you do this!"

He looked at Felix. "I need a six-month advance."

Felix pulled out his checkbook and unscrewed his pen.

"I wanted to take care of you!" Leni said furiously. "I wanted to make your life better. I wanted to make you happy!"

Judd stood and put his hands on her unyielding shoulders. "You can't remake people, Leni; you can't force them to be good or happy. I'm too full of hate to love anyone, but even if I could love, I'm not sure it would be you: you're quite exhausting to live with, my sweet."

Leni jerked away from him as Felix tore out the check. Judd took it and folded it into smaller and smaller squares. "But before my past blurred and I began to forget it," he said to Felix, as if continuing a conversation, "I told my son the name of the man who ruined me, what he did and how he did it. He'll remember; he loves me. And someday he'll get my revenge. Don't you think that was smart of me Felix?"

"I would have gotten your revenge," Leni said frantically. It was obvious she heard only some of what was said; her eyes were blank as she tried to understand what was happening. "But you wouldn't tell me anything!"

"I was trying to protect you from my hatred. Find someone strong and powerful, Leni; someone who can use your strength. You'll be happy then." He smiled, so sweetly that Leni began to cry, and both men saw the frustration and love behind her tears. "Now get out," Judd rasped. His smile had disappeared. "Go back to Mommy and Daddy and give them my apologies for stealing you away. Go on! *Get out of here!*"

Felix took Leni's arm and pulled her toward the door. She was crying stormily and Felix never knew whether she heard Judd whisper, "Goodbye, my lovely Leni," just before he kicked the door shut behind them.

Felix held her up as they walked down the four dimly lit flights. "I'm going to take you home." He tightened his hold as she tried to break free. "You have to go somewhere and I'm not taking you to a hotel."

"Why not?" she demanded. "That's what you want, isn't it? You want to fuck me; that's all you care about, shitty, filthy, rotten—"

He clamped his hand over her mouth. "Do you always talk like a stupid teenager? You'll have to change that before we're married."

"Fuck you—" she spat against the hand over her mouth.

"We will." He grinned: one of the few times Felix Salinger ever indulged in a full and gleeful grin. "As much as we want. Of course I want it; I've wanted you since the minute I saw you. And you won't try to make me better, the way you did that fool back there; you're going to be my wife and I'll be the one to make you better. And that's what you want, too, you little idiot: you haven't been satisfied by that pathetic drunk; you want to be dominated." She shook her head fiercely. "You're not a rebel," he said contemptuously. "You're a romantic. Rebels take up with other rebels and try to change the world; romantics take up with losers like Judd Gardner and wait for someone to rescue them."

She pulled away from him. "Bastard—!"

He kissed her. But it was a battle and he hated it. He hated violence; he hated foul language in women; he hated opposition. He was behaving contrarily to every rule of his life, and that astonished him, but he watched it happen and rolled with it. There was in Leni everything he wanted: the elegance of the mother he only vaguely remembered; a strength and a streak of coarseness that would help him defeat his father; the New York background that made her a stranger to Boston, so she would be dependent on him for friends and a social life. And as a bonus, she had belonged to Judd Gardner—a man Felix had never been able to stop envying.

He ended the struggle; it was disgraceful to try to kiss a woman who was uncooperative. "Where do your parents live?"

"I don't want to go home; I can't face them. We can go to a hotel. We can fuck all you want. You don't care about me or my parents, all you care about is my cunt—"

He slapped her, admiring himself for doing something he had never done. "You will not talk like that. Is that clear? Where do your parents live?"

"None of your goddam business."

He opened the lobby door and propelled her the three blocks to his car. It seemed a lifetime ago that he had parked it there to meet some business associates for dinner. Shoving her into the driver's seat so she would not be able to run away, he pushed her over as he got in himself. "Listen to me. This is what I'm going to tell your parents: that you and I ran away, that we were foolish and we know it now, but we were in love and we were afraid they'd object because you're only nineteen." Leni had become very still, her eyes wide as she watched him. "I imagine you don't want to go home because when you ran off you told them some nonsense about not liking their stuffy middle-class attitudes and not wanting to be like them. Am I right?" She was silent. "Am I right?" She nodded. "A lot of my classmates did that. Stupid asses. You can always defeat your parents if you stay close to them; what can you do from a distance?"

"I don't want to defeat them." Her words were almost inaudible.

"You want to go home," Felix said. He was feeling strong and satisfied.

She nodded and began to cry.

"Give me the address."

"820 Park."

He started the car. "I'm thirty-three years old; I've never been married or involved in a long relationship; and the Salinger hotels will be mine when my father dies. Your parents will be very pleased. Have I your permission to court you?"

She broke into wild laughter. And with that laughter, and the ride home beside Felix's powerful silence and satisfaction, Leni Van Gris took the first and irrevocable step to becoming Leni Salinger.

It was a memorable lesson in the uses of power. Felix never told Leni's parents about Judd but neither did he ever let Leni forget that he had made perfectly smooth her return to the family she loved and had longed for even at her most rebellious. And not long after performing that miracle, he had joined with Leni in a marriage that gave her social status, wealth, and a great deal of freedom.

"You don't love me," she said the night before their wedding.

"I need you," he replied. It was, for Felix, an astonishing admission, and Leni knew he would not have made it if he realized how much it told her about him. Because she knew now that no matter how powerful Felix Salinger was in the world of international business, he remained a little boy trying to find the mother he had lost, and to win his father's love, and since he never would succeed, the closest he could come to feeling like a man was to conquer and possess what other men would envy.

But though he conquered and possessed, he was not a man who could be close to anyone. And so Leni had more freedom than she had expected. As long as she was available to satisfy his sexual hunger for her, as long as she stood at his side at social functions, and as long as she was discreet, she could do what she wanted.

For twenty-two years, Leni had thought she understood Felix, even as she was in awe of his ability to master the uses of power. Especially after Owen died and Laura Fairchild was unmasked, Leni saw the extent of his reach, and was stunned at how little she had known. By then she had created as much power of her own as she thought she ever would have. She was no longer a nineteen-year-old clinging to a romantic dream, but a realistic woman. *I was interesting once,* she thought; *I was fiery and alive. And then I became a very wealthy, very dull wife.* She had no faith in herself anymore; all she could do was gather what little power she could within the boundaries of Felix's world, and that was what she did. Over the years, she grew close to Owen. When her sister Barbara was engaged to Thomas Janssen, Leni introduced them to Owen, who set Thomas on the path to becoming Midwest manager for Salinger Hotels, and brought him and Barbara and their son Paul into the summer compound at Osterville. And, finally, Leni found young men who adored her and made sweet love to her and gave her a kind of peace.

Imperceptibly, Felix and Leni achieved something of a balance. He would always be more powerful but he could not control her. He knew it without understanding it, but he never spoke of it or allowed himself to think too much about it. Because he could never let her go.

"Which of Owen's things did you take from Beacon Hill?" Leni asked, finishing her wine.

Felix looked up from his memories. She was as close as the other end of the table, but she seemed far beyond his reach. "Some furniture, some paintings; pieces I've liked for a long time."

"What furniture?"

"His desk. An armchair. A few tables. Why do you want to keep that house?"

"It's part of Owen. He wouldn't want it sold. I'm sure he wouldn't have left it to Laura if he'd known what she was, but he would have wanted it kept in the family. Besides, there's no reason to sell it. We don't need the money, and I like it. Why do you want Owen's desk?"

Felix pushed back his chair. "You bought it for him; I thought it should stay with the head of the company. It might become a tradition."

"You think I should have bought it for you."

"It would have been a nice gesture: a wife buying her husband a fine piece clearly meant for a powerful person." He walked toward the door. "Instead the wife buys it for her father-in-law. Most people would find that odd. Make sure you order another wineglass; I don't want to have a partial set; I don't like anything that is incomplete."

Leni watched him leave the dining room. Our marriage is incomplete, she reflected, and she thought of the many ways people disappoint each other: Judd's wife had sent him away; some shadowy figure had stolen Judd's company; Owen had never loved Felix as much as Felix wanted to be loved; and Felix had never been the son Owen wanted. And I disappoint, too, she thought: I disappoint Felix because I am not grateful enough for what he gave me, and because I have friends, and a daughter who loves me—and he does not.

And because I bought a Chippendale desk for my dearest Owen instead of for my husband. And in all these years, he has never forgotten it.

She rang for Talbot to clear the table, and then she went upstairs to see what Felix had done with Owen's desk.

CHAPTER 13

THE trial lasted two weeks. Each day spun by in scenes that briefly stood out, as if caught by a revolving spotlight, then vanished as the light moved on. The faces of the Salingers stood out first: it had been almost a year since Laura last saw them, and when they sat together in the courtroom they looked to her like cameos in a cluster of family photographs. They were exactly as she remembered them, but she had changed, and she saw Allison's surprise as their eyes met. She knew the change was more than her short hair; it was also the frozen look of her face, the careful calm she had practiced for a year and especially during the weeks before coming to Boston. And that was how she looked for the ten days of the trial, as, one by one, the Salingers came to the witness stand and their eyes and gesturing hands and moving lips all blurred in Laura's mind like a painting that had been left out in the rain.

Leni testified that Laura and Owen had worked together in his library; they had spent hours together walking on the beach; and, after his heart attack during a burglary in their house, she came with him to Boston and stayed with him day and night until he was well.

"Before his heart attack, and after he recovered from it," said Rollins, "he was strong and healthy?"

"Yes."

"No one questioned his mental faculties?"

"There was no reason to."

"Or his devotion to Miss Fairchild?"

"No."

Cheyne came back and faced Leni. "What did you think of Laura Fairchild when you first interviewed her for a summer job?"

"She was very pleasant and clearly anxious for work."

"And did she provide you with reference letters?"

"Yes."

"And did you form an opinion of them?"

"I thought they were faked," she said sadly.

Ansel Rollins remained silent in his chair. There was no sense in objecting; Laura had told him the letters had been faked.

When Felix testified, his words were measured. "We all were suspicious, especially after the robbery, but my father would hear none of it. He seemed positively mesmerized."

"Objection!" Rollins exclaimed, and the judge ordered it stricken from the record, but everyone had heard it.

Rosa sat upright in the witness chair and gave Laura a small, uncertain smile. "Those two loved each other," she said firmly in response to Cheyne's questions. "Whatever else you may say about Laura, I do believe Mr. Owen loved her, and she loved him."

"Tell the jury about her work in the kitchen," Cheyne said conversationally. "Did she plunge right in from the first day and take some of the load off you?"

"Well, I wouldn't put it that way."

"How would you put it?"

"She didn't know all that much about a large kitchen. But she learned very fast and she—"

"But at first. Did you think she had worked in kitchens of wealthy homes in the past?"

"I didn't. No."

"Did you think she was a liar?"

"Objection!" Rollins called.

The judge peered at Cheyne. "I think you'd better rephrase that, counselor."

"Did you have evidence that Miss Fairchild had been truthful about her past experience?"

"Well, no, but any youngster who really needed a job—"

"Just answer the questions, please. Mr. Salinger had a library in his home on Cape Cod. And Miss Fairchild took time off from the kitchen to work in it, is that correct?"

"Yes."

"Did Mr. Salinger talk to you about taking her away from her work in the kitchen?"

"Yes. In fact, that's where they were when the idea first came up."

"Mr. Salinger asked if Miss Fairchild could take time off to work in his library?"

"Well . . . actually it was Laura who offered and he said it was a good idea and suggested to me that we could work it out."

"*Miss Fairchild* suggested it?"

"Yes. She said she knew books."

"And what did you say?"

Rosa hesitated. "I said to Mr. Owen that I thought she wasn't always quite truthful about the things she'd done and could do."

Laura gripped her hands. *Dear Rosa. Fair, kind Rosa. It isn't your fault that everything is coming out wrong.*

On Friday afternoon, at the end of the first week of the trial, Allison was called to testify. "We were friends," she said. "We talked about everything."

"Including stories about your childhood?" asked Carver Cheyne. "Parents, school, boyfriends, slumber parties . . . that sort of thing?"

"Objection!" exclaimed Ansel Rollins. "This has no relevance to Owen Salinger's will."

"It has to do with Miss Fairchild's character," Cheyne said promptly. "And, especially in a case of this kind, character is relevant."

"I'll accept that," said the judge. "Objection overruled."

Cheyne turned back to Allison. "Did Laura Fairchild share stories about her past, Miss Salinger?"

"No. She said she didn't like to and it wasn't important."

"So she never mentioned to you her conviction for theft in New York City when she was—?"

"Objection!" Rollins thundered. He sprang to his feet. "If I may speak to your honor . . ."

The judge nodded and motioned Cheyne forward, too. Rollins, standing at the bench, handed the judge a stapled set of papers, the brief he had prepared in case this happened. "As your honor can see," he said, his voice urgent but confident, "the sealed record of a juvenile . . . not admitted as evidence . . . I've listed precedents for this—"

"Your honor," Cheyne said, as urgent and confident as Rollins, his own brief in his hand, "the conviction was only seven years ago. It is our position that such a history pertains to the character and motives of Miss Fairchild and her brother in becoming involved with the Salingers; it is also our contention that it is relevant and essential in judging Miss Fairchild's reliability when she describes her relationship with Owen Salinger and his wishes, especially during his illness."

There was a pause. The judge nodded. "I'll accept that," he said as he had before. "You may pursue that line of questioning."

Rollins's face turned a dark red. "Your honor, I make a motion for a mistrial," he snapped.

"Denied," said the judge. "May we continue, Mr. Cheyne?"

And so, as Allison left the stand and was replaced by a New York City police officer, while Rollins muttered furiously about the defeat they had suffered, the jury listened to a flat recital of Laura's arrest, her release on bail, her conviction, and then her release on probation in the custody of an aunt named Melody Chase who gave an address later found to be an abandoned building.

When he was finished, the courtroom was very silent. The judge struck his gavel once on his desk. "We will adjourn until Monday morning at nine," he said.

* * *

In the hot July afternoon, the weekend traffic leaving Boston was dense and crawling, and it was almost ten o'clock when Laura and Clay reached Darnton's. Laura had insisted on driving; Clay was in a rage and could barely sit still. "It's Ben's fault, damn him; he got us into that mess; got us caught and convicted—like stupid *criminals*—"

"He didn't," Laura said wearily. "We weren't even with him that night, and you know it. We thought we could do it ourselves."

"He shouldn't have let us. He should have been around, to take care of us."

"We shouldn't have been stealing."

"He taught us. He should have come with us."

"Oh, *should, should, should,*" Laura said angrily. "It's too late for *should*; we can't go back. And we can't blame Ben for everything."

"He was older."

That was true; silently Laura acknowledged it. Ben was older, Ben was smarter, Ben had been in charge of them. But he had been young, too, and he'd had a date, and hadn't paid attention when they said they were going out. Lots of times he hadn't paid too much attention, but in most ways he had been wonderful to them for years and years. "I don't blame him for anything he did back then," she told Clay. "He was wonderful. If only he hadn't robbed the Salingers we'd still be friends."

The great hall at Darnton's and the sweeping front lawn were ablaze with lights. The lodge had full occupancy, with nearly three hundred guests on the island. Some were still boating, others watched a film in the theater in the main lodge, others walked by the lake, and many of them were still strolling through the outdoor sculpture exhibit Laura had organized on the front lawn.

Kelly waved at them as they drove up. "Fifteen pieces sold today," she said. "Somebody from New York said it was as good a collection as he'd seen in—oh, shit, what's wrong? Was it a terrible week?"

"Not good," Laura said. Clay had left to see if the fleet of cars had been properly attended to, and she tried to be interested in the sculptures. "Fifteen sold? That's wonderful. No problems?"

"The wine coolers and champagne ran out; but John did some kind of deal in Jay's Landing and bought enough to last the weekend. We read about the trial; one of the guests brought a Boston newspaper with him. I'm sorry. Is there anything I can do?"

"You're the first I'd ask if I could think of anything." She managed a smile. "We haven't lost; we're just weaker than we thought we'd be. And I didn't like being there."

"In the city or in the courtroom?"

"Both."

"Well, you're home now. Why don't you go to bed and sleep off the whole week?"

"Thanks, Kelly, I think I will. I'll help you here tomorrow."

"I'll need you." She put her arms around Laura and kissed her. "We love you. Pleasant dreams."

But her dreams were turbulent, and she woke feeling almost as tired as when she had gone to bed. I'll be all right, she thought, standing for a long time beneath a hot, pounding shower. I'll think about sculpture exhibits and all the mail that's probably stacked on my desk.

But just after breakfast, she was stopped as she walked to her office. "Laura Fairchild?" The voice behind her was deep and faintly harsh. Laura turned and he held out his hand. "Wes Currier."

"Currier." She frowned slightly as they shook hands.

"I'll be at the Global Finance Conference in August; you wrote two weeks ago to welcome me." In the bright sunlight of the great hall, his look was quizzical.

Laura flushed. He was to be the main, and most prestigious, speaker at the most prestigious conference she had been able to book at Darnton's. "I'm sorry. I was thinking of something else. And I didn't expect to see you here until next month. Is there a problem?"

"Most likely not. But I don't leave things to chance. Since I've never been here, it seemed a good idea to stop by."

"And check us out. Of course."

"I wasn't really worried." His look was direct and unwavering, and Laura thought he could see how distracted she was but would not let that interfere with his own plans. "I liked your letter; I liked your voice over the telephone. And my first judgments are always right." He stood easily before her, his eyes on a level with hers, his compact, broad-shouldered form clothed in well-cut lightweight wool, his silver and gray hair neatly in place, like sunlit metal. He had a square face with gray eyes below thick gray brows, and his large head thrust slightly forward, giving him an aggressive look only partially softened when he smiled. "I do like to know where I'm going, however."

Laura nodded. She was having trouble thinking straight; she couldn't keep his face in focus, and she felt annoyed rather than flattered by the interest in his eyes. But Wes Currier couldn't be fobbed off on anyone else. "Would you like me to show you around?"

"Please."

They walked the length of the great hall, stopping when Currier examined a piece of sculpture or a painting, then into the library and dining room, as Laura made brief comments about the different functions held in each room. Even through her distraction, she was aware of Currier's energy; there was a magnetism in it that drew her on, as if he were leading and she were following. Laura found herself thinking that it was too bad they had met this weekend; any other time she would have found him attractive. Today, she only found him overwhelming.

They went through guest rooms, on the ground floor and upstairs, where maids were cleaning: spacious and bright, each with a fireplace, Early American wallpaper and furniture, four-poster or canopied bed, built-in bookshelves, desk, and a round table with four chairs—"in case you wish to eat in your room," she said. "Not many guests do."

"They like the noise and bustle?" he asked.

"They like the conviviality. Most people enjoy meeting new people, especially when they know they don't ever have to see them again after they leave here."

His brows shot up. "Do you say that to everyone?"

"No." She paused beside a tall window and gazed at a huge sycamore, its branches scraping the glass. "I'm sorry; I don't know why I said it."

"You said what you thought. I'm flattered. And you're very perceptive. Most people do prefer friendships that don't carry the burden of permanence. I'd like to talk to you some more, but I'll be leaving early this afternoon; will you have lunch with me?"

"I don't think I can. But please stay, as our guest; perhaps I can join you for coffee."

"Thank you. I'd enjoy that."

They had reached the office door. "One o'clock," she said. "Unless we have a crisis. I hope we don't."

"And so do I." He gazed at the door after she closed it behind her. Young, he thought, and probably beautiful if she could smooth out the pinched look in her face and the sadness in her eyes. But she had a shell around her that made her seem like a prisoner of her own defenses; what in hell had happened in her young life to make her so wary and with-drawn—and not the least bit interested in his interest in her?

He did not find out that day. Laura did join him for coffee, but she was on edge, and even though she apologized, telling him how much work she had after being away for a week, he felt piqued: when had Wes Currier come in second with a woman when his only competition was a job? "May I come back before August?" he asked.

She shook her head. "I'll be away part of the time on business, and this is the height of the season for us. We can't have much of a social life until September. That's a time for people who want to make friends instead of impermanent acquaintances."

He chuckled. "I'll remember that and come back in September."

She nodded, her attention already shifting to something else. "Is there anything more you want to know about Darnton's or the conference?"

"Will you be there?"

"I don't know. I'd like to; I'll try."

"May I make that a condition of my appearing here?"

"No." She smiled faintly. "But I will try."

When his taxi came, she watched it drive away, and thought again what a shame it was that she couldn't even flirt intelligently. But what difference does it make? she thought. I have more important things to think about: a trial, a jury, what to say about my past when I testify, what I'll do about the future if I lose.

And Wes Currier has nothing to do with any of that.

* * *

The air conditioning was fighting to keep up with Boston's July heat wave when Laura and Clay arrived at the courthouse and walked up-stairs. On the landing stood a small, wiry man, notebook in hand. "Yank Bosworth, of the *Globe*, Miss Fairchild. Hold on," he said hastily when her face changed. "I don't have a killer instinct; I only want a story. If you'd answer a few questions—"

"Fuck off," Clay said angrily. "We've got other things to—"

"Clay!" Laura put her hand on his arm. "Wait for me inside." She watched his face turn crestfallen. "I'll see you in a minute." When he had left, she let out a small sigh.

Bosworth heard it. "Brotherly protection," he said. "Not a bad thing."

"I know," she said briefly. "If you have some questions, I'll answer them, but I'd rather wait until this is over."

"Uh-huh. But I need a story to fill in, until the verdict." Rapidly he shot questions about where she had been over the weekend, how she felt about the Salingers, what she expected the outcome to be. "I'll get the rest from in there," he said, clipping his pencil to his notebook. "One thing, though: for what it's worth, I think you're getting a raw deal. The whole thing stinks, as far as I'm concerned. 'Course that's off the record."

Laura looked at him sharply and saw that he was not mocking her; he meant what he said. "I won't publish it," she said with a grave smile. "Thank you. It's good to know there are some friendly thoughts in the courtroom." She held out her hand and he took it and she felt comforted by the firmness of his grip.

"See you later," he said, and Laura went through the high door, pausing to touch Clay affectionately on the shoulder on her way to the table in the front of the room where Rollins already sat.

The courtroom had barely settled down when Rollins called Elwin Parkinson to the stand. He took the oath in a flat, nasal mumble and sat, folding his hands in his lap. A small twitch at the corner of his nose was the only sign of tension in his impeccably-pressed figure.

Rollins, relaxed and sure, led Parkinson through a description of his long association with Owen Salinger and his family, including the drafting of Owen's first will, five years earlier, and then Owen's demand that a codicil be added. Rollins took a step back and leaned against a table. "Did Mr. Salinger know exactly what he wanted in the codicil?"

"He did."

"He told you specifically what it should say?"

"That is correct."

"And you took notes as he dictated it."

"That is correct."

"And the next day you prepared the codicil in your office for his signature."

"I did. I deeply regret it. I did not serve my client well. I know now that he was not competent, that he was under great pressure, and I should not have—"

"Your honor, I want that stricken!" Rollins shouted. He had shot up from his relaxed position. "I want that stricken from the record!"

"This is your witness, Mr. Rollins," the judge said gravely.

"A hostile witness! Mr. Parkinson has just contradicted his testimony in deposition. I want that deposition made a part of the record."

"It will be done, Mr. Rollins."

"You are excused," Rollins said to Parkinson.

"Cross-examine," said Carver Cheyne.

"Your honor," Rollins said angrily, "we've had no time to prepare for a change in testimony. I request a recess."

There was a brief pause. "I think we should hear Mr. Parkinson's testimony," said the judge. "Mr. Cheyne, you may cross-examine."

"Exception," Rollins snapped.

"Noted," the judge responded.

Cheyne let a small smile curve his lips as Rollins returned to his chair beside Laura. His shoulders were slumped. "The son of a bitch sold out."

Laura's face was white, her eyes alarmed. "He didn't say that earlier. He said Owen was sure of himself. . . ."

"We'll appeal. The son of a bitch . . . how much money did it take, I wonder."

"Money? He was bribed?"

He shrugged. "It's not something I'd say in public."

"Mr. Parkinson," Cheyne said smoothly. He stood in the same position as Rollins had earlier, leaning against the table. "I'm sure this is difficult for you, but would you tell the jury more fully why you regret what you did?"

Parkinson touched the small twitch by his nose. "I knew Mr. Salinger was gravely ill, and it seemed clear to me he was not in control of his emotions, but I also feared I might make his condition worse if I argued with him, and so I acceded to his wishes. I put it out of my mind until after I had given my deposition, but that started me thinking about it, worrying about the ramifications of what had happened and how they affected my responsibility to Mr. Salinger as a man and a client and an old friend. I sought the advice of several eminent medical doctors whom I know and trust. I told them of Mr. Salinger's behavior in his sickroom and even before; I searched my memory and recalled bizarre behavior that I might have dismissed too easily—actions that seemed to me, on reflection, to indicate . . . fear, I thought, and a kind of helplessness, as if he were doing what someone told him to—"

"Objection!" Rollins bellowed. His face was flushed. "This is—"

"Counselor, this is becoming rather imaginative," the judge said to Cheyne. "Mr. Parkinson should speak only to what he actually saw."

Cheyne bowed his head. "You consulted some doctors, Mr. Parkinson. And what did they say?"

"Of course they had not attended Mr. Salinger, so they would not make a diagnosis, but as I described his rather strange behavior, they thought it was not inconsistent with a man who was not fully aware of what he was doing, who felt trapped, afraid of death, and completely dependent on other, stronger people."

No! Damn it, it's a lie! All lies! And you know it! Laura was cold, the same icy cold she had felt in the study when Felix attacked her.

"In short, stressed and agitated, as the doctors put it. I realized then I had made a terrible mistake—I had not realized what my eyes were seeing—I had failed my client."

"Mr. Parkinson, in making this admission, do you believe you are jeopardizing your career as an attorney?"

"I do. But the truth is more important. I made an error of judgment, and I owe it to the memory of Owen Salinger, and to his family, to do everything in my power to rectify it. As long as I know that my client, old, paralyzed, not competent, was badgered into changing his will—"

"Objection!" Rollins roared again. "Witness doesn't 'know' anything of the sort; these are wild fantasies!"

"Sustained," the judge said. "The jury will disregard the witness's last statement."

"You thought he *seemed* . . ." Cheyne prompted.

"Badgered," Parkinson said. "I concluded—and the doctors told me they saw this often in patients who had been powerful businessmen—that Mr. Salinger, a man accustomed to being in control, was confused because he didn't know what to do about his loss of control. He was old and helpless and sick, vulnerable to anyone who abused him or made him comfortable. Miss Fairchild did both, and in the end he was like a baby who learns to obey in order to be kept warm and comfortable—*seemed*," he added hastily as he saw Rollins about to object again. "I didn't realize any of that—I thought he was afraid of dying—who wouldn't be?—but I now know—*believe*— there was far more to it, far more. I believe he was not given a moment's peace—not allowed to die in peace—and I cannot tell you how deeply I regret my failure in not seeing it soon enough to spare him and his family untold grief. . . ."

Parkinson had not looked at Laura; now he swung his glare on her like a spotlight. Behind Laura, Felix rigidly looked the other way. Allison was crying. Leni closed her eyes and sat swaying slightly, as if she might fall. The air conditioning in the courtroom hissed; the outside temperature was close to a hundred degrees, and Laura shivered.

"Fucking bastard," Rollins muttered, losing the last of his Bostonian control. "They must have paid him enough to retire a dozen times over, to make him risk his career. . . . Admitting he wrote a document for a man he thought incompetent . . . cause for disbarment unless they believe his story . . . Bastard. Fucking, greedy bastard."

By the time Laura testified, she was sure they had lost. She sat rigidly in the witness chair and told again about the love she and Owen had found with each other. Her fists were clenched to stop her trembling, but she did not cry. The jury was waiting, everyone was waiting, for her to cry, but she could not. She looked small and vulnerable, and deep inside she was twisted with tears and pain, but her face was like stone. She's cold, the jurors thought. No feelings.

"Miss Fairchild," Rollins said after they had gone through the story of her years with Owen, "did you at any time intend to defraud or harm Owen Salinger in any way?"

"No!" she cried. "I loved him! I didn't even think about him leaving me anything in his will because I didn't want to think of him dying. I didn't want to think about it! And he wasn't a baby, he didn't act like a baby, he acted like a loving man who loved me and cared about me even when he was dying! He cared about me! And I cared about him! And no one has a right to try to destroy what he was!" She stared at the family. "And the way *all of us* remember him!"

When Cheyne began his cross-examination, his voice was very soft. "Miss Fairchild, you were convicted of theft some years ago."

"Yes."

"You were a thief."

"We were poor and I was very young and I stole sometimes, but I didn't like it; I—"

"Just answer the questions, Miss Fairchild—"

"I didn't want to be a thief! I wanted to change, and go to college and make something of my—"

"Miss Fairchild!"

"I'm sorry. But you make it sound—"

The judge leaned over. "I must warn you, Miss Fairchild, to confine yourself to answering counsel's questions."

Laura looked at him in contempt. He didn't care about the truth; he didn't care about her. "Yes," she said coldly.

"Now, Miss Fairchild," Cheyne said, as softly as before, "I believe you once knew a bookseller named Cal Hendy."

Small events of the past, the acts of a lifetime, done unthinkingly, without regard to tomorrow or next year—and long after we forget them, they appear like green shoots pushing through the earth, to change our lives.

Laura answered all the questions in a level voice, telling everything she had told Rollins. Cheyne never asked about Ben; she had been sure he would not. There was no mention of him in her records. Even in her high school files, she had listed a neighbor as her guardian because Ben thought, as he did later when she was arrested, that the city wouldn't let an unmarried young man be guardian for his brother and sister. And the building they had lived in had been torn down and the landlord had gone off, no one knew where. New York had a way of swallowing people up; it had swallowed Ben Gardner and no one knew of his existence.

At last Carver Cheyne gave his final summation. Standing close to the jury, he reviewed all the pieces with which he built his case of theft and deception, and then he lowered his voice until it sounded like a rumble of fate. "Think of your parents. Each of you: think of your parents as they are or were. Old, tired, wanting only comfort—the comfort they deserve!—as they lie helpless in bed. They have lived a long life—a hard, noble life—and now it is drawing to a close. They have a right to a peaceful end. *You* have a right to give them a peaceful end. BUT THINK! Think of them in the clutches of a clever, ruthless, conniving thief who wears a pretty mask of love and innocence—who comes into your home and *steals your parents from you!* This woman was a thief who came to steal—and stole! Stole a man from his family—stole his love—broke into the bonds of kinship—and robbed this close-knit family of a sacred tradition! Our society believes that a man works all his life, diligently and lovingly, to build an empire and leave it to his beloved family whole and intact. This is a family's rightful legacy—*unless it is stolen!* Ladies and gentlemen, a thief sits before you—not only a thief who breaks into the precious sanctity of our homes and makes off with those possessions we lovingly collect over the years, but *a thief who robbed the Salinger family of its father when he was too helpless to fight for his loved ones' rights!*"

The jury was out for three hours. When they returned, none of the twelve men and women would look at Laura. Rollins put his hand on her arm and she listened to the foreman's loud voice as he read in staccato syllables. "We the jury find for the plaintiff. . ."

Rollins let out his breath in a grunt of defeat. Laura sat very still.

"Pursuant to the jury's findings," the judge said in a matter-of-fact voice, "the codicil to the will of Owen Salinger is set aside."

In a flurry, the Salingers left the courtroom. At their head was Felix, the victor, on his way to take possession of his house on Beacon Hill and Owen Salinger's four hotels. Laura watched them, barely aware that the reporter, Yank Bosworth, had cut his way through the crowd and was at her side. "—a few more questions, okay?"

"Later," she said. She was watching the backs of the Salingers. "Just a few minutes . . ."

He perched on the edge of the table, unwilling to let her get away. "Listen." He waited until she turned to him, her eyes blank. "After this is over, if you ever need me, you know where to find me. You got a raw deal."

She nodded. It seemed so unimportant. She turned again to watch as Leni and Allison disappeared through the door. Rollins was watching, too. "We'll appeal," he said to Laura. "We have a good chance. I'm sure of it."

She shook her head. "I won't go through it again."

"Come now, you've done it once; you can do it again. You're not going to tell me you're willing to walk away from here with not a shred of what Owen Salinger left you."

"But I have a great deal that Owen left me." She looked at Rollins, her gaze level and clear. "I've had it all along: his love and what he taught me. And that's all I need to start again and get back the rest of my inheritance."

CHAPTER 14

EVERY room in the Amsterdam Salinger was full. The hotel swirled with visitors who spoke a dozen languages but shared the paraphernalia of tourists the world over: cameras, maps, guide books, dark glasses, crepe-soled shoes, a nervousness with unfamiliar currency, and running commentaries comparing everything with the way things are back home.

It was the end of August: the height of the season. The Kalverstraat was so crowded that people were carried along, rather than walking, from shop to shop; the daily flower market on the Singel was packed; people stood in line to visit Rembrandt's house; and everything from Shakespeare to striptease in the Leidseplein drew full houses and curtain calls.

"It is what they call in America a madhouse," the concierge told Allison and Patricia, beaming because he had everything under control —and it was his unbelievably good fortune that the daughters of Felix and Asa Salinger had, on the spur of the moment, chosen this busiest of all times to visit the hotel. They would, of course, report to their fathers on all the hotels where they had stayed on their trip through Europe, and the concierge had perfect confidence that the Amsterdam Salinger would get the highest marks of all. "The rooms are full, the restaurant is full . . . but for the Misses Salinger, of course, we have the royal suite."

"And if a king shows up?" Allison asked.

"We would put him in the furnace room."

Allison laughed, remembering Owen saying that a good concierge was a good politician. I miss Owen, she thought, following the rotund figure of the concierge through the packed lobby. A year ago this month we buried him, and I never knew how much I loved him until he was gone.

She missed Laura, too, but that thought she did not allow herself.

In the living room of their suite, she stood at the window while Patricia opened the bottle of champagne that had been delivered when they arrived. Below them the river Amstel cut a wide blue swath through the bustling streets and across the concentric rings of tree-lined canals laid out at perfect intervals in ever-widening U's around the city center. Block after block of closely-built buildings of gray stone and red brick, gabled, arched, many-windowed, often with bright orange roofs, stretched to the horizon, and Allison gazed at them, imagining families in each one: loves and hates, joys and fears, marriage and divorce. And none of them knew or cared about Allison Salinger, who had been Allison Wolcott for less than a year and now was right back where she started. At least in her name.

"What shall we do?" she asked abruptly. "How about a walk through the Walletjes while it's still light?"

Patricia made a face. "Ugly and depressing."

"It's just a neighborhood of self-employed women," Allison said mockingly. "And I'm interested even if you're not."

"Don't be cute." Patricia's voice was bored. "There's nothing interesting about looking at prostitutes sitting in the windows of their rooms, knitting and waiting for customers. I'd rather go to Cafe Reynders and meet some men."

"You mean instead of sitting in a window, knitting, you'll go out and grab the men yourself."

"How unpleasant you are," Patricia murmured.

"I know." Allison turned back to the window. Patricia was right: she was being unpleasant, and going to the Walletjes wasn't fun. Watching those women was like staring at caged animals in the zoo. But she didn't want to meet men; she didn't want to shop; there was really nothing she wanted to do.

Looking out the window, she felt ancient and world weary. It was being married and divorced, she thought; and on top of that finding out that your best friend was a thief who was out to rob your family. And on top of all that, doing your best to help a man—even marrying him!—and then finding out he was uninterested. Even worse, uninteresting.

Patricia was the smart one: nothing seemed to bother her; she never got involved; she just aimed at having a good time. I should be like that, Allison thought. What the hell, you do your best to help people and they don't give a damn. Well, fuck them all; I'll be like my cousin and just take care of me for a while.

The trouble was, she hadn't felt young or adventurous for the longest time. She wouldn't be in Europe this minute, running around like a teenage tourist, if her mother hadn't practically ordered her to go. "You've been mooning around for almost a year," Leni had said in June. "It's time for you to rediscover how big the world is. Go somewhere exotic; at least go to Europe. A healthy young woman of twenty-two should be thinking about possibilities, not failures."

And her mother was right. But her mother was always right: cool and competent; in control of her emotions and her whole life. Even when she had wept about Owen, she hadn't been messy; everything about her was elegant and perfect.

"All right," she said briskly to Patricia. "Let's go shopping. And I'll ask the concierge about the grand prix in Zandvoort; I think it's this month. I want to go there, anyway, to the casino."

"Shopping where?"

"P.C. Hooftstraat. And then you choose where we go for dinner."

"And then Cafe Reynders."

Allison hesitated. But Leni's voice came back: stop blaming yourself; stop blaming Thad; stop looking for blame. Look for fun instead. Try to have fun.

"Fine," she said. "Why not?"

Other shopping streets in Amsterdam were longer and more famous than P.C. Hooftstraat, but Leni had taught Allison, almost from the cradle, to gravitate to the faintly hushed atmosphere that settles like a silken cloak on those rarefied districts where nothing is offered that is not the finest the world can produce, and no salesperson offers it who has not raised attentiveness and expertise to an art. For hours she and Patricia browsed in the glittering boutiques where voices were as refined as the atmosphere, and when they returned to the hotel at two in the morning, after dinner and the Cafe, their purchases were waiting for them in their suite: dresses and coats, shoes and silks, purses and jewelry.

"Allison?" Patricia called suddenly as they undressed in their separate bedrooms. "Did you see that little vase I bought in Venice? I had it on the table next to my bed."

"The maid probably put it away with all your other treasures," Allison said from her room.

"Why would anybody put away a vase?"

"I can't imagine."

Patricia was opening and closing drawers. "Definitely not here. Somebody stole it."

Allison appeared in the doorway wearing a nightgown and a satin robe. "You're sure it's gone?"

Patricia gestured at the room and the open bureau drawers.

"It was worth something, wasn't it?"

"Only about fifteen hundred, but I liked it."

"Fifteen hundred is a lot of money to a lot of people." Allison went to the telephone and dialed the front desk. "This is Miss Salinger; would you please send someone from security to our suite?"

The voice at the other end, young and nervous, turned wary. "Security. Ah, yes, of course. But, please, if you could tell me what is wrong . . ."

"Something is missing from our rooms. I don't want to discuss it over the telephone; I want someone here. Now."

"Yes, now, of course, but also I will call the director of security; I think it is better—"

"Fine." Allison reached for a pencil. "What is his name?"

"Ben Gardner," said the boy.

* * *

Ben had just fallen asleep, his hand loosely cupped around the ample breast of his latest young woman, when the telephone rang beside his bed. "I wouldn't have bothered you," Albert apologized as soon as he answered, "but someone in the royal suite just called—about something being stolen. She said her name was Salinger, and I thought you would want to handle it your—"

"I would." He was already out of bed. "Which Salinger?"

"I don't know; she arrived on the day shift and I didn't take the time to look it up; I thought I should call you first."

"You were right. Tell her I'll be there in half an hour."

His voice had been steady, but his thoughts were churning. Something stolen. Royal suite. *Salinger.*

He pulled on dark twill pants and a white shirt just back from the laundry, knotted a somber blue tie at his neck, and grabbed his jacket on the way out the door. The young woman in the bed had not stirred.

Salinger, he thought, unlocking his bicycle. *Salinger. Something. Stolen.* He bent low, pedaling fiercely through the streets to the nearest taxi stand, the route so familiar he barely noticed it, concentrating on his thoughts.

Theft was a serious problem in hotels the world over, but not here; they'd been lucky or they'd been better than others, or both. He'd been at the Amsterdam Salinger for two years, helping to enlarge the security staff and overseeing the installation of a new system of door locks and safes in all the rooms. It had been his suggestion that guards be hired to patrol the loading dock—a suggestion that got him the position of director of security when the old director retired. And in those two years, not one major theft had been reported. A few minor problems, mostly packages taken in the lobby and restaurant, but nothing serious and nothing involving anyone influential. Until now. A *Salinger robbed in a hotel where Ben Gardner is director of security.*

He locked his bicycle at the taxi station and leaped into the first car in line. At two in the morning the streets were mostly quiet, and it took them only a few minutes to cross the bridges over the series of canals around the Centrum and past the slumbering shops on the Rokin to the Nieuwe Doelenstraat, where the Amsterdam Salinger stood in restored seventeenth-century grandeur. And where the assistant manager stood nervously at the entrance, awaiting him.

"I called Henrik," he said as Ben strode toward the elevators. "His wife said he is sick—"

"I'll take care of it." He kept going, noting that his breath and voice had sounded normal even though his heart still raced. In the elevator he tightened his tie, made sure his suit jacket was smooth and straight, and ran a comb through his hair. At the last minute he took from his inside pocket a pair of horn-rimmed glasses and put them on.

When Allison opened the door, their eyes met in silence. She was frowning because he looked familiar, but she couldn't place him. And even while she tried to pin down that elusive familiarity, she knew his hard face wasn't like anyone's she knew: the strong jaw, dark brows almost meeting above hard blue eyes, blond hair combed but still a little windblown, a tall, lean body standing at ease but the neck muscles taut for no reason that she could see. There was a contained fierceness in him that attracted her: she was curious about what was behind the sober respectability of his dark business suit and horn-rimmed glasses.

She held out her hand. "Ben Gardner?" At his quick flash of surprise, she smiled. "I'm Allison Salinger. I always get people's names; it's best to know who's supposed to be helping me." Their hands met with equal strength.

He knew of her. In the days when he read magazines and newspaper articles, looking for mention of the Salingers, he had read about Allison. Felix's daughter.

"Please come in," she said.

A young woman sat on the couch, and Albert was on a hassock nearby, a clipboard on his lap. But Ben still looked at Allison. He'd thought he knew what she looked like, from seeing her picture occasionally in a magazine or newspaper, but no picture had the impact of the woman before him. She was more striking than he had imagined, and more aloof, and he found himself wondering what she would be like when aroused. His eyes showed nothing, his face was impassive, but he was imagining the feel of that long, angular body and silken hair beneath his hands as he forced her to drop her cool facade and the small smile she wore as provocatively as her pale satin robe.

"My cousin Patricia Salinger," Allison said. "Patricia, this is Ben Gardner, the director of security."

Patricia looked up and nodded. A pale echo of Allison, Ben thought, with none of her style. Which means it comes from Leni. It had been a long time since he had wanted to confront the members of the Salinger family and make them pay for what Felix had done to his father; even a thirst for revenge diminishes as a boy of thirteen becomes a man of thirty-one. Now he found himself once again wanting to meet them.

"I've told him everything I know," Patricia said, tilting her head toward Albert. "It's astonishing that your security is so lax; have you been doing this sort of work very long?"

"Patricia is upset," Allison said quickly. "She ... bought the vase for ... as a gift for my mother. It was very special to her."

"Thanks so much, dear Allison," Patricia drawled. "But why make up a story? Why should you care whether a hotel employee thinks I have cause to be upset or not? I'm annoyed because it was a rather nice vase and I bought it for myself, not for the first maid who came along."

She could make trouble, Ben thought. But Allison, who had surprised him by trying to soften her cousin's harsh words, might keep her in check if she wanted to. "Do you have information about a maid taking it?" he asked evenly.

"Of course not; we weren't here. But the maids were; we'd been shopping and our packages arrived—" She gestured toward Albert. "He has all this; I don't know why I need to repeat it."

"You needn't, of course, if you've told Albert everything; I'm sure you'd like to get to sleep. I'll read his report and talk to you in the morning. If you'll call my extension when you get up we can discuss how we'll proceed."

He had not sat down. He bent his head toward Patricia in what was neither a bow nor a nod, but something in between, and turned to go.

"Why don't we talk at breakfast?" Allison asked.

There was the briefest hesitation. "We could do that. Eight o'clock?"

Patricia was crossing the room to her bedroom. "Allison, you know perfectly well I don't eat breakfast."

"I forgot," Allison said blandly, looking at Ben. "But if Mr. Gardner has breakfast with me, he can talk with you afterward."

"It's quite ridiculous," Patricia said from her doorway. "We'll never see that vase again; some crawly little maid has already sold it. I don't know why you even bothered to call . . ."

Her door closed behind her. Ben and Allison looked at each other. Finally Albert rose. "I shall type up my notes; they are not easy for anyone but me to read. . . ."

"I'll come with you; I have work to do." Ben's face was taut with the effort of keeping his eyes from betraying him when he looked at Allison. "Until tomorrow," he said to her and followed Albert into the corridor.

Looking at the closed door, Allison smiled. Breakfast, she thought. Not my best time of day, but a nice time to begin. And I get better as the day goes on; by the time we have dinner together, I'll be totally irresistible.

* * *

"For your cousin," Ben said at the breakfast table, and handed a box to Allison with Patricia's vase nestled in tissue paper inside.

Puzzled, she looked at it, and then at Ben. "It wasn't really stolen? Or you found it. Do you solve all your thefts so easily?"

"We don't have many, and our job is to solve them."

She waited. "And who is the villain?"

"One of the maids. We're still looking into it."

Allison let it drop; he wasn't ready to talk about it. The waiter came to take their order, and Ben met his thinly veiled surprise with a flat look. There would be talk in the employees' lounge about Ben Gardner and Felix Salinger's daughter, but it wouldn't last long and it couldn't hurt him. The staff paid almost no attention to the Salingers of Boston, so long as their salaries were good and they were left alone in the daily workings of the hotel they considered almost their own.

Allison ordered melon, apple bread, and coffee, and Ben said he would have the same, and then they sat back, the box on the carpet between their upholstered chairs. The restaurant was in muted shades of gray, mauve, and wine, and on every table was a fresh iris in a tall crystal vase.

"Do you know why this is here?" Allison asked, touching the iris with a gentle fingertip. Ben shook his head. "My grandmother was named Iris. When she died—years after she died—when my grandfather was able to think about living without her, he ordered all his hotel managers to do this: a fresh iris, every day, forever. Even my father wouldn't dare change that."

Ben drank his coffee, and looked out the window at the Amstel river and the pedestrians walking past the hotel. He didn't want to hear about Owen Salinger, not now; he wanted to ask about Laura and Clay and the five years since he had seen them. But of course he couldn't. How could he explain Ben Gardner, a hotel employee in Amsterdam, knowing that a Laura Fairchild and her brother, Clay, had been living with the Salingers?

He would wait. There was no rush. If he was careful and patient, he thought, he and Allison could go on for a long time.

"Where are you from?" Allison asked. "Tell me how you got here. I heard you speaking Dutch in the lobby; why would you bother learning it, when everybody in the whole country speaks English?"

"Because the language of the Netherlands is Dutch, and if I want to work here they have a right to ask me to speak their language."

"You're American, not British." He nodded. "In fact—New York?"

"Yes. You have a good ear."

The waiter placed pale green melons before them, then an array of plates filled with thin slices of cheese, sausage, and various breads, a basket of rolls, a tray holding small jars of honey, jams, and jellies, and a silver pot of coffee. "With the compliments of the concierge," he said to Allison. "He regrets the discomfort and displeasure you have experienced and hopes you will allow him to do anything in his power to repair the damage and make your visit one of perfection."

Allison laughed. "He said all that?"

"It sounds exactly like Henrik," Ben said. "Shall we ask him to join us?"

"No. Convey my thanks to Henrik," she told the waiter. "And tell him I'll see him after breakfast." She turned back to Ben. "You were telling me about your life in New York."

"I was telling you you have a good ear."

"Because of New York. Not a strong accent, though." She tilted her head. "You've worked at getting rid of it. Are you getting rid of memories, too?"

"About as many as you are."

"I'm not getting rid of them; I'm trying to understand them."

"So you can repeat them? Or to make sure you don't."

"To make sure I don't. How very easy it would be to repeat them."

"Especially if they involve other people."

"They don't."

"No one else? You made mistakes all by yourself?"

"I didn't say mistakes; I said memories. And of course other people were involved. But they have nothing to do with whether I repeat something or not. Will you tell me how we—"

"Was it a man? A woman? A friend? Someone in your family?"

"A little bit of everything. A death and a divorce and . . . a few other things. How have we—"

"Your grandfather's death?"

"Oh, you know about that? Well, of course, everybody in the hotels would know. That was part of it."

"And your divorce. Recently?"

"Last November; Thanksgiving, in fact. My ex-husband won himself an early Christmas present of a huge alimony—a very big payment for a very small performance—and went his merry way and I sold the apartment I'd bought us on the harbor and left town. Will you please tell me how we got to talking about me when I started out asking about you?"

"I have no idea," he said solemnly, and for the first time they laughed together.

Allison licked the tip of her finger and picked up crumbs of apple cake with it. "This is wonderful. Did your chef bake it?"

"No, your chef did."

She colored. "I wasn't making fun of you. You're part of this hotel."

"I work in it; you own it."

She frowned. "Why are you trying to make me uncomfortable?"

He paused. "I don't know. Why are we having breakfast together?"

"Because I want to get to know you. You're making it more difficult than—very difficult."

"More difficult than most men?"

She smiled. "Much more. I think we should start again."

"I'm sorry; I have to get to work." He pushed back his chair and stood. "I really am sorry."

"It's only nine o'clock."

"I start work at nine."

"And when do you stop?"

"At six."

"Then you'll be free at seven for dinner."

"Allison . . ." He saw her face change and heard her catch her breath at the rough caress in his voice. Allison Salinger, he reflected: heiress to the Salinger hotels and the Salinger fortune. Felix's daughter. Not the kind of pliant woman Ben had always preferred, but impressionable and still unskilled in hiding her feelings. And she wanted him. He relaxed. "Seven o'clock," he said, and put his hand briefly on her shoulder, feeling the shudder that rippled beneath his palm. "Shall I choose the restaurant?"

"Please."

"I'll call your suite at seven." He turned, then turned back and kissed her hand, neutrally, the way a European friend would do it. The lover comes later, he thought, and left the crowded restaurant to walk through the lobby to his office. And off and on, all day, he thought about Allison Salinger, and still was not sure what he would say to her when he phoned her just before seven and she met him in the lobby.

They walked to Dikker en Thijs in silence. Allison seemed withdrawn, and Ben, sensitive to the smallest signals, wondered what he had done wrong, and so they looked away from each other as they walked, only beginning to relax as they came under the spell of Amsterdam's clear golden light, slanting across the city from the low sun of early evening. It was the light that Rembrandt had painted; it was the light that modern tourists tried to capture with their cameras as it bathed the city's narrow streets, ancient stones, and stately buildings—turreted, gabled, arched, and topped with symmetrical clock towers and chimneys —in a glow filled with promise and hope. It was a light that had drawn Ben to stop his wanderings through Europe, and stay.

There had been other reasons for him to choose Amsterdam. Because even on days when lowering clouds and driving rain engulfed it, the city had a nervous, driving energy that reminded him of New York: people rushed through the streets instead of strolling, the theaters and concert halls were full every night, the shops were cosmopolitan, and the city's red-light district, strip joints, sex shops, and cabarets pulsed with a raunchiness that put most of Europe in the shade. It was a city where Ben Gardner could find anything and be anything; it was a city he could almost call home.

He had rented a room in the Jordaan, a district that attracted all the eccentrics of Amsterdam as well as working people and struggling young artists and writers; and he bought a bicycle to join almost everyone else in the city who had long since given up on finding a place to park and depended on two wheels instead of four. Within a week he had a woman and he had begun to learn Dutch; in less than a year he had moved to a nearby apartment and, at the Amsterdam Salinger, had worked his way up from porter to maintenance man and then to assistant director of security. And a year later, he got the director's job itself.

Now, walking with Allison, blending in with the throngs of visitors going to dinner and working people on their way home, he occasionally broke the silence by pointing out a particular building, or commenting on the stalls selling herring or pancakes, or asking her to stop for a moment to listen to one of the enormous street organs so heavy they had to be pushed along by teams of men while pouring forth waltzes and jazz on a weird mixture of cymbals, pipes, drums, wooden blocks, and plucked wires.

But even with the golden evening light and the distractions of street stalls and music, they still were awkward and stiff when they were seated at a window table in the restaurant. Neither the view of the tall homes along the Prinzengracht—"Princes' Canal"—nor the classic French luxury of the restaurant, nor the excellent wine Ben had ordered in advance eased their discomfort, until Allison, as if forcing herself to be natural, broke the silence. Looking at the canal flowing below their window in small, scalloped ripples, she gestured toward the long row of houseboats tied up along the far side. "Are all the boats in the city painted like floating farms?"

Ben followed her gaze. The boats were flat-bottomed, each with a rectangular house in the center brightly painted with cows and butterflies, windmills in fields of tall grass dotted with white and pink flowers, and birds in flight against a dark blue sky. Most of them had deck chairs in the stern, beside the steering wheel; on one of the boats, a small dog stood on a deck chair and eyed the passing scene. "They're all painted one way or another," he said. "Most people live on them because they can't afford anything else. So they paint them to look like the countryside to remind themselves of what they hope to have someday."

"I'd like to live on a boat," Allison said dreamily.

"Close quarters."

"Well, but cozy and comforting, too. And you could always go on land to get away."

"From the boat? Or the person living with you?"

"Oh, I'd only live on it alone. Unless I found someone I wanted to share it with. And then I wouldn't want to get away."

Ben raised his wineglass. "To 'someone.' I hope he finds you."

It was a curious way to phrase it. Allison studied him. "Thank you. I hope he does, too."

There was a small silence, more comfortable than when the evening began. "What will you do when you return to Boston?" he asked.

"Oh, no, you don't." She sat straight, one hand holding the wineglass, the other properly in her lap. "This time we're going to talk about you. Tell me about New York. Tell me about everything that led you from New York to Amsterdam."

It had been years since Ben talked about himself, but now he did. And he told almost the truth, walking the finest line between what he could say and what he couldn't. Because he had learned, during the past years, that while it was often better to tell all the truth than part of it, it was always better to tell part of it than none at all.

"My father owned a furniture company—he was a designer and a manufacturer—and he had a partner who supplied the start-up money and some customer contacts."

"What kind of furniture?"

"For hotels. It was a small company but it grew, and my father was proud of it. This was before I was born, but years later he told me there were three things he had loved in his whole life: me and my mother and that little company. When the war started—the Second World War—my father fought in Europe. I never knew how his partner avoided the draft, but he stayed home and ran the business. A few months before the war ended, my father was badly wounded. He came home in pain and anger, furious at a world that allowed the barbarity he'd seen, and he found his company gone. His partner had dissolved it and taken its designs into another company that he and his father owned."

Allison searched his face for emotion but found none. His features didn't seem as hard as they had the night before, when she had first seen him, but he showed no tenderness or sadness or anger. "Is your father still alive?"

"No."

The captain appeared and refilled their glasses. "Another bottle, sir?"

Ben nodded. "And the duck pâté." He contemplated the ruby wine in his glass. "He died when I was thirteen. My mother died eight years ago. She'd remarried, but I've been pretty much on my own since my father died, working around New York—"

"Doing what?"

"Clerk in a grocery store, waiter in various restaurants, selling antiques that I picked up wherever I could . . . Then, five years ago, I came to Europe and began working mostly in hotels. Porter, maintenance man, desk clerk, even bookkeeper one time in Geneva. I wasn't expert at anything; I didn't know what I wanted."

"And do you now?" she asked when he stopped.

A small smile played at the corners of his mouth. "I think so."

He watched the captain open their wine while a waiter arranged two plates of pâté, cheese, and crackers in front of them. He knew what he wanted.

A piece of the Salinger empire.

Because even though his early hunger for revenge had faded over the years, the craving to get something from the Salingers had not. But he knew now that what he had wanted when he was young had been childish and paltry.

He remembered his first wild imaginings of what he would do to get the revenge Judd had talked about more and more feverishly in the months before he died: send rattlesnakes into the Salingers' bedrooms, dynamite them at the dinner table, toss black widow spiders into their limousines. But to a thirteen-year-old the family seemed huge, remote, untouchable—and he did nothing. Then his mother remarried and Laura and Clay were born, and his anger and loneliness were eased by the adoration of those two babies who followed him around as they grew up, treating him like a kind of god. Eventually he stopped thinking about snakes and spiders and dynamite; they weren't practical. Neither was killing Felix or Leni or Owen. Because even though he had become a thief, like his father, he wasn't a murderer and never would be.

The only thing he could think of was to rob them, to make them feel the loss of something they loved, as he had. It was really Felix he wanted to rob, but Felix loved nothing but the family hotels. That left Leni's jewels, which Ben had read about: they were valuable legacies from her great-grandparents in Austria and, even better, they were much treasured by Leni. And Leni was as close to Felix as Ben could get.

But all that had been infantile, Ben thought as the waiter finished arranging their plates and pâté knives and forks. As childish as rattlesnakes and spiders. Because stealing treasures from a wealthy family was like pinching an elephant: it was only a momentary twinge that left everything exactly the same as before.

The way to get revenge and make a lasting change in the Salingers' lives was to become part of their empire. The only thing Felix loved was his hotels. Therefore, Ben would take as much of the hotel empire away from him as he could.

"You haven't told me what you want," Allison said as soon as the waiter and captain had left.

"I will." He contemplated her striking good looks. She wore a pale blue dress that left her shoulders bare; diamonds were at her throat and ears, and her blond hair, held with a diamond band, cascaded down her back. "But not yet. I want to talk about you. You haven't told me anything about your family."

Her eyes shadowed. "You want to know about the hotels."

He shook his head. "I want to know about the people who are important to you; the ones who make you happy. Or unhappy."

Allison smiled. "You want me to tell you all that in one evening?"

"As many as it takes. We're going to have a lot of evenings." He saw her quick flush. "But you can start. You had a grandfather and a husband. That's all I know. Except, of course, we all know about your father, since we work for him."

Allison sat back, taking small bites of the spicy duck pâté and sipping her wine. "Owen and Iris started it all. My grandfather was born in the last century, and he began the hotels and had two sons . . ." She described her family, lingering on Iris, who had died almost twenty-five years before she was born. "But it doesn't matter so much that I never knew her. The way my grandfather talked about her and how much they loved each other, it's as if she's part of my life, and I think about her when things go bad or I'm wondering what I should do and there's no one I can talk to."

"Not even your mother?"

"Mother is wonderful, but I can't run to her with everything. Some sadnesses you have to work out yourself, don't you?"

"Yes. What kind of sadnesses?"

"My grandfather dying . . ."

"That's one sadness."

"And my divorce . . . One hates to fail, you know, and everybody had told me not to marry him—Paul and Laura and Grandfather—and I did anyway."

"Laura?" The word sounded strangled and he cleared his throat.

"Paul and Grandfather tried to talk me out of it. Paul Janssen, my cousin. And Mother wasn't too happy either. But I ignored everybody, I thought I knew exactly what I was doing, and I was wrong."

Ben cleared his throat again. "Is Laura a cousin, too?"

"No. She's somebody I really don't want to talk about, Ben. I have lots of cousins if you really want to hear about them—you've already met Patricia—"

"I'm more interested in what makes you sad. Did Laura have something to do with it?"

Allison bit her lip. Once again she gazed through the window, absently noting the families chatting together on the decks of the houseboats. Other boats passed; people were cruising through the canals in the last of the evening light, looking calm and content. None of them looked as if they had secrets or would be miserable whenever they thought about the past. "Laura was my friend," she said abruptly. "She lived with my family for years, since she was eighteen; she worked in the kitchen and helped my grandfather organize his library. Her brother was there, too, but Laura was the one I cared about; we spent a lot of time together. She didn't know anything and I taught her to play tennis and dance and buy clothes—my mother and Aunt Barbara helped her, too —she was very pretty and we helped her be beautiful—and Rosa taught her to cook and I took her to restaurants so she'd learn how to order things, and we'd practice staring down rude waiters and laughing. . . ." She wiped her eyes with the back of her hand. "Sorry, I'm being silly, crying after all this time. But she was so much fun; she had a lovely laugh and she was wonderful at mimicking people, and she was loving and honest and smart . . . well, she wasn't honest, but for a long time we thought she was, and when I'd ask her advice on something she told me what she thought, and she was usually right. . . ."

"She wasn't honest?" Ben asked when she stopped talking. He was holding himself in, trying to see it all as Allison saw it, and also as Laura must have seen it, and all the time he was remembering Laura's smile and the way she once had looked at him with love and trust. "What does that mean: 'She wasn't honest'?"

"She was a thief," Allison said bluntly. "She'd been arrested in New York, and convicted—I don't know the details—and my father thinks she and her brother came to our house at the Cape to rob us. Actually, he's sure they did rob us because our house was broken into that summer and Mother's jewelry was taken, but he can't prove it and the police never arrested anybody for it."

"Do you think she did it? Maybe her brother did."

"I don't know. I don't care anymore. We loved her and trusted her, and she never told us the truth about herself and then, after my grandfather died—" She stopped and shook her head fiercely. "That's enough about her; let's talk about you again."

"No!" At her startled look, Ben said quickly, "I'm sorry, I didn't mean to yell at you. I got involved in your story and I wanted to hear the end of it."

She studied him. "You really care about it."

"I care about the things you care about."

Her quick flush came again. "My grandfather had a stroke and was very sick for about a month, and then he died. Laura was with him that whole month—most of the time, anyway—and just before he died he got his lawyer to change his will, leaving her his house and some stock in the Salinger corporation and four of his hotels."

"My God," Ben breathed.

"What?"

"It sounds like a fortune."

"My father said it was. He called her a fortune hunter. But I didn't think she was. I thought it was wonderful that she inherited the hotels and the rest of it, because she and Grandfather loved each other, and if he wanted her to have something after he was dead, that was his business." Once again she fell silent, her eyes staring unseeingly across the room.

"So she's a wealthy woman," Ben said. "But why does that make you sad?"

"Because she's not my friend anymore. She's not wealthy, either. I told you, she lied to us. For four years she told lies and kept secrets from us, while we were as open with her as we could be. And then, when Grandfather was ill, she did something—I have no idea what, but something that made him afraid or upset... something. His behavior was very odd after his stroke; he was restless, and he seemed angry or excited or unhappy—we couldn't tell which—and none of us could understand him when he tried to talk. Laura said she could, so we let her translate for us. It was awful to go into his room; I didn't know what to say to him. I thought Laura was magnificent because she'd be sitting there talking to him and listening when he made those garbled noises as if they were having an ordinary afternoon tea...."

"She sounds magnificent," Ben said.

"I don't know. Somehow, when she was alone with him she got him to add a codicil to his will, leaving her the house and stocks and the hotels. He hadn't done it when he was well; he hadn't even told anybody he was thinking about it; but somehow Laura convinced him to do it, even though he couldn't talk or think straight—"

Ben's eyes were narrowed. "How do you know she convinced him?"

"I don't, not for sure; I wasn't in his room as much as I should have been—none of us was, we let Laura do it, and I don't admire us for that. But the lawyer who drew up the codicil testified that—"

"*Testified?* In court?" There had been vague talk, he remembered, about a contest over Owen Salinger's will, but it hadn't affected the Amsterdam Salinger so no one paid much attention.

"My father sued to get the codicil thrown out; in the original will, he and my uncle got everything."

"And what happened?" Ben asked; he was trying to mask his impatience.

"My father won. We did, if you want to look at it that way. The jury decided that Grandfather wasn't in his right—wasn't able to think clearly when he dictated the codicil."

"So she doesn't have anything."

"Not from Grandfather. I don't know what else she has. My father forced her to leave after Grandfather died, and I didn't see her again until the trial last July, and I didn't talk to her then. I wanted to, but she was so cold and distant, and I guess I was still so angry I didn't make the effort. I don't know where she is now or what she's doing. All I know is that we gave her everything and she threw it in our face, lied to us, took advantage of my grandfather. . . . And damn it to hell I still think about her all the time and miss her and I wish we could undo everything and go back where we were, being friends, almost sisters . . ."

Her voice trailed away. The sounds of the restaurant drifted between them.

Ben was leaning back in his chair but, hidden by the tablecloth, his hands were gripped together in his lap. *My father forced her to leave after Grandfather died.* Triumph had surged through him as Allison said those words. Well? he demanded silently of Laura. Not such a perfect family after all, are they? I warned you, but you wouldn't listen. You wanted them, and you turned your back on me to get them. And they kicked you out. It serves you right.

He was angry at her, too. She could have told him; she could have asked for his help. She must really hate him, not to turn to him at such a rotten time in her life.

But then he felt a rush of pity. He still remembered the feel of her delicate shoulder bones the last time he hugged her good-bye. Damn it to hell, she was a little girl who'd never harmed anyone, and that fucking Felix Salinger had thrown the whole legal system at her.

With grim amusement, Ben reflected that now he had two scores to settle with Felix. "What?" he asked Allison as she looked at him, her head tilted. He sat straight and drank off the wine in his glass. "I'm sorry; I was thinking. About your story."

"I said I don't want to talk about it anymore." Briefly, she put her hand on his. "You're a wonderful listener and I appreciate your being so interested, but it's so hard for me. . . ." She gave a small laugh. "It was easier getting over my marriage than getting over Laura. Let's talk about you again. You still haven't told me what you want."

Her eyes were direct and curious. She was fascinated by him, and almost as trusting as Laura. Ben caught the tantalizing scent of her perfume; the touch of her fingers lingered on his hand. Felix's daughter. She had style, she was strikingly good-looking, she wanted to prove she wasn't a failure at marriage, and she was still young enough to be malleable. She was everything a man could want.

"Tell me what you want," Allison said again, softly.

"Love," he said. "And work. I'm not much different from other men: I want a woman to believe in; an empire, or a piece of one, for myself; and a family to fulfill the dream of the one I never had."

His words settled around her like a familiar cloak, warm and fitting her as if made for her. And once again, as so many times before, Allison Salinger thought to herself, I could be that woman; I could make his life what he wants it to be. I could make him happy.

CHAPTER 15

W ES Currier was a financier who had moved beyond the sky-scrapers of New York and Chicago to roam the world as consultant to international corporations that straddled geographical, political, and religious boundaries, and even raging wars. He had been on the move through three marriages, and now, at fifty-five, with half a dozen homes in Europe and America and memberships in as many exclusive clubs, he was known as a master of mergers and acquisitions; a generous supporter of the arts and of young people starting their own companies, and one of the most eligible bachelors on two continents.

No one really knew him. After his second divorce, a reporter had written a breathless book about him archly titled *Currier's Lives*, but it had been nothing more than a pastiche of newspaper articles and secondhand gossip that disappeared almost as soon as it was published. Even a good reporter would have had a hard time with Wes Currier, who had made his fortune by following his hunches and never showing his hand; who nurtured his reputation for unpredictability; and who had no intimate friends. And while everyone in the financial world tried to keep one step ahead of him, no one would lay odds on being able to do it, and no one else had begun another book about him.

"Though I'm told a couple of journalists are collecting information for one," he told Laura carelessly as they sat in the dining room of

Darnton's on a hazy morning in September. It was the Labor Day weekend, the lodge was full, and they were having breakfast together before
he gave the opening talk at a conference on international trade. It was
his second talk at Darnton's, following the one he had given three weeks
earlier. "I can't believe they don't have more important things to do with
their time."

Laura looked at him quizzically. "You don't mean that. People want
to know how you shape their lives."

"I don't shape; I influence."

She shook her head. "You know how powerful you are. You help
determine the future of the companies people work for, the products
they buy, the stock they own—"

"I influence external forces. But as for shaping—we shape our own
lives; no one does it for us."

Impatiently she looked away, disliking his arrogance. Automatically,
as soon as her attention changed, she found herself making a quick
survey of the dining room. All the tables were occupied, and guests were
waiting in the lounge; coffee cups were being refilled promptly; tables
that were vacated were cleared without delay and as quickly reset with
the dusty rose cloths and stoneware dishes that were used for breakfast
and lunch, and would be replaced, for dinner, with white linen, crystal,
and china. Bending down, she reached out to pick up a napkin a de-
parting guest had dropped from his ample lap, and laid it on the table for
the busboy.

And then, knowing everything was in order, she turned back to Currier. She had had dinner with him in August and again on this trip, and
she found him attractive and intriguing, but in his very success he was
also exasperating. "You assume everyone has the same luck or skill you
have. Most of us don't control fate the way you do."

"I make it, my dear; that's far better than controlling it." He drank
coffee and gazed at her. "I'm curious to know why you think you haven't
been in control of yours."

"I'm in control as long as all our guests get breakfast on time," she said
lightly, ignoring the flash of irritation in his eyes: he was a man who
didn't like being put off. "And if I can get away this morning to listen to
your talk. I hope I can."

"You heard most of it last month."

"I like to watch you; you're very good with an audience."

"Thank you. You're very good at changing the direction of a conversation."

"Thank you." They smiled and Currier acknowledged to himself that her reserve was going to be harder to breach than he had expected.

"You'll have dinner with me tonight?" he asked. "We can eat on the mainland if you can recommend a good place."

"The Post House is good; almost as good as here. I'd like to have dinner with you if I'm able to get away."

"You can always get away. The sign of a good executive is a good staff."

"I'll remember that," she said evenly.

"I'm sorry," he responded quickly. "I have no right to tell you how to do your job. It was a poor attempt to make sure of you for dinner."

"I'll do my best." They stood, and as they walked through the room, Laura nodded to the guests and noted the trays the waiters were carrying: smoked trout and scrambled eggs seemed to be heavy favorites this morning. "And I will try to get to your talk."

They parted in the Great Hall as Currier left for the conference room and Laura went to her small office adjacent to Kelly's. Her desk was covered with stacks of bills to be verified, samples of drapery fabric from which she and Kelly would make final choices for redecorating some of the rooms, and letters of confirmation to write to designers showing in a fashion show to be held at the end of the month. But she was having trouble concentrating, and shortly before nine-thirty, she pushed back her chair and walked down the corridor to the stairs that led to the lower-level conference room, greeting guests by name as she passed them, and feeling pleased at their delight in being recognized.

She had missed Currier's talk. In the windowless, brightly furnished room, he sat in an armchair at the head of the long rosewood table, answering questions from those who had not yet left for the day's recreation. He smiled at Laura as she came in, thinking how lovely she was but wondering at the same time why something always seemed to be missing in her beauty. She stood in the doorway, slender and as poised as a dancer in a blue, full-skirted dress; her delicate face was framed by springy chestnut hair, her enormous dark blue eyes were long-lashed above faintly shadowed cheekbones and a mouth meant for laughter and love—but her beauty was dimmed by the firm line of her lips and the tight control she kept over herself. When occasionally she let a smile of delight or a mischievous laugh break through, Currier caught his breath at the promise she gave of unfettered beauty and a vibrant woman.

"Please join us," he said, and, like a host, indicated the sideboard. "Coffee and croissants. Darnton's has an excellent management that takes care of our every—"

The lights went out. In the absolute darkness there were mumbled curses and the rustling sound of chairs being shoved back on the carpet.

"I think we should stay where we are," Currier said calmly. "Laura, is there a flashlight?"

"I don't think so. But there are candles; we use this sometimes as a private dining room . . ." She felt her way to the closet in the corner, and her hand found a stack of cardboard boxes. Taking one down, she moved along the wall to where she thought Currier sat. "Wes? If you talk to me I can find you."

"A good definition of love," he said good-humoredly. "If we talk to each other we can find each other." He felt her hand brush his shoulder with the sensitive probing of the blind, and reached up to clasp it with his. "And so we have," he added quietly. Then he raised his voice. "Now if someone has a match . . ."

"I would have lit it," came a sarcastic voice.

There was a pause. "Not a match in the room?" someone said incredulously.

"Of course there are matches," Laura said quickly. "I forgot to get them. Wes, please take these . . ." Putting the box of candles in his hand, she found her way back to the closet. A minute later she struck a match and saw everyone blink as the flame flared. "If you'll be patient, we'll get the lights on right away." She left the matches with one of the guests and was out of the room and in the corridor before the match burned down to her finger.

But instead of lights, a bellboy brought a flashlight and led Currier and the others into the blackness of the corridor and up the stairway to the sunlit Great Hall. A few guests were there; most had left for the day. Currier saw Kelly Darnton through the open door of her office; she was standing beside her desk, a telephone cradled on her shoulder. "The whole fucking *island* is out," she said, then, with a quick glance at the guests in the Great Hall, lowered her voice.

Currier went to her office and pulled the door shut behind him. "Perhaps I can help," he said quietly.

She covered the mouthpiece with her hand. "Thanks; why don't you ask Laura? I've got to deal with the electric company . . . What?" she shouted into the telephone. "*Twenty-four hours?* Are you out of your mind? There are *two hundred people* here who paid good money—"

Currier opened the door to Laura's office and closed it behind him. She, too, cradled a telephone on her shoulder while making notes. "They got you out," she said to Currier with a smile. "Poor man, it must have felt like a dungeon down there. . . . You have a hundred pounds?" she said into the telephone. "Wonderful; if you could bring it right away . . . Of course, if you have more, bring it; how can we have too much dry ice when our refrigerators are off? Oh, one more thing, Bill. Would you stop on your way and buy all the flashlights in the hardware store? Charge them to our account. No, as many as they have; I just heard Kelly say this is going to go on all night, and we don't have a hundred flashlights..." She stood up. Currier saw how anxious she was to end the call, but she kept it out of her voice. "One for each guest room. Illumination is one of the amenities that makes Darnton's a high-class place." Currier heard Bill laugh and Laura gave a small smile. "Thanks, Bill; you're a good friend."

A lot of men, Currier thought, would go out of their way to hear Laura Fairchild's low, lilting voice say they were her good friend. "What can I do to help?" he asked as she hung up.

"I don't know. I haven't had time to think about assignments."

"What happened? A transformer?"

She nodded. "And for some reason it can't be fixed before tomorrow, which means we have until sundown tonight to get ready. John went to get some generators in Burlington, but we can't rent enough for the whole island, so we have some organizing to do."

Currier sat in a chair in a corner of the small room. "Let me know when you have my assignment."

She nodded, already dialing again, this time an in-house call. "Roger, the dry ice is on its way; you'll keep the refrigerators closed until then? ... Yes, soup and sandwiches would be fine for lunch... I don't know about dinner; we'll think about that after lunch." They talked some more, then hung up. "Thank God for gas burners," Laura murmured, then looked at her list and picked up the telephone again.

For two hours, Currier watched her. He sat without moving, and Laura seemed unaware of him. Now and then she gave an absent look in his direction, but her thoughts were elsewhere. Talking to Kelly and other staff members who appeared in her doorway, disappeared and then reappeared, she made telephone calls and wrote pages of notes.

As she finished one of the calls, Clay burst in. "Do you know they're saying in town that we've shut down? I was in the Landing drugstore and somebody said there's no power here and we're closed."

"My God." Laura began to dial another number. "Did you tell them we're open?"

"I told them they're crazy. What's the problem with the power?"

"A transformer went. Tim," she said into the telephone, "it's Laura, at Darnton's. Would you do me a favor? Put a note in the airline lounge where our guests get the limousine, saying we're open and ready for everyone who has a reservation. I'm worried about people flying in and then hearing rumors about our being closed...." She drew squiggles on the paper before her. "Of course not. Everything is fine, and nobody will feel cheated. We'll always give them plenty for their money."

Currier saw a sudden brightness in her eyes. Curious, he watched her pencil stop its random marks on the paper, and her mouth curve in a faint smile. "I just had an idea," she told Clay as she hung up the telephone. "Do you know how to make a campfire?"

"How the hell would I know that? I grew up in New York."

Kelly came in and perched on the edge of Laura's desk. "Roger planned lobster coquilles for dinner. They require ovens. He has electric ovens which, of course, are stone-cold."

"I have an idea about that," Laura said. "What would you say to eating outside? Campfires and big cast-iron pots—can you boil water that way?—I wish I'd been a Girl Scout; well, let's assume we can. We'll call it Lobster Primitive. Baked potatoes—in foil?—we really need an expert—cooked in the coals. Roger can make a magnificent salad and ice cream for dessert; we have to eat it; we aren't going to have enough dry ice to keep it— You're shaking your head."

"You've forgotten we're not supposed to be rustic anymore; we've been pushing elegance ever since you suggested it. An Adirondacks lodge with the luxury of a Park Avenue mansion. You do remember saying that?"

"Yes, but I'm rethinking part of it. Kelly, everybody likes to play at being rustic once in a while; even people who wear silks and black tie to dinner. If we make it lavish, I think they'd love it."

" 'Think' is an uncertain word. What if they hate it?"

"Then we have a problem. But I'll bet lobster under the stars, with lots of good wine, would be a hell of a lot more fun than the same meal in the dining room."

"I'll bet so, too," Currier said quietly.

Kelly and Laura looked at him. "You really do?" Kelly said.

He nodded. "I'll crack the first claw. I'll offer a prize for the most perfectly dissected lobster. I'll help make the fires."

"Do you know how?" Kelly asked.

"No, but I can follow orders."

She stood up and went to the door. "I'll talk to Roger. It may be a good idea. Clay, would you check on the boats?"

As Kelly and Clay left, one of the maids came in. "How do we do the rooms, Laura? We can't vacuum."

"Try a broom," she said absently. She was gazing out the window.

"How do you use a broom on carpets?"

"The same way you use it on the floor. It really works, Beth. Brooms were invented long before vacuum cleaners."

"Well, I guess I can try. Just don't expect very much . . ."

"I have absolute confidence that you'll do a very good job."

She shook her head as the maid left. "I never had a vacuum cleaner until I was at the Cape," she murmured. She went to the door of her office. "Kelly, there's a man named Pickard in number eighteen."

"If you say so," Kelly said. "You remember their names better than I do."

"He's an IBM executive and an actor in his spare time."

"So?"

"How about a ghost story at the campfire? Edgar Allan Poe or Robert Louis Stevenson . . . something wonderfully terrifying."

There was a silence. "*That* idea I really like. What did you say his name is?"

"Eric Pickard."

"I'll call him."

"He plays golf, but he'll get a message."

"How the hell do you remember all those things?"

"It's a Fairchild talent," she said lightly and came back to her desk. "Do you sing?" she asked Currier, and he realized she had been aware of him all morning.

"I follow a good leader," he replied.

"I'll bet that's the only time you do."

"You'd lose. I follow those who do things superbly. I would follow you."

She flushed. "I don't do things superbly. I improvise when I'm in a tight spot. That's a Fairchild talent, too."

"I'd like to hear about it."

She gave him a long look. "You might. Sometime."

Kelly walked in. "Clay just called; he's putting a hand pump on the gas tanks at the marina, so we don't have to worry about dry-docked boats. They're doing massages by candlelight at the spa; everything else is outdoors, and if you walk around out there you'd think it was an ordinary day; not one sign of trouble. Isn't it amazing how John got out of here right at the start? You'd almost think he practices avoiding crises. But you've been wonderful, Laura; I would have been lost without you. Why don't you take off for a while? You look frazzled."

"A boat ride," Currier said, getting to his feet. "Since we don't have to worry about running out of gas."

Laura was about to refuse, then changed her mind. She had been making decisions all morning, with Kelly's encouragement, but now it was time to recognize Kelly's supremacy at Darnton's. She owned it; she employed Laura; she had just told Laura to leave for a while. *When I have my own hotel, I'll be able to make all the decisions I want.*

"And lunch," Currier added. "Would Roger pack something for us?"

"He's probably too busy; I'll do it," Laura said. "Is a couple of hours all right, Kelly?"

"Fine. Take as long as you want."

In the kitchen, Currier watched Laura pack cheese, French baguettes, nectarines, and white wine in a basket. She stood at a corner of the work area away from the bustle of the large kitchen staff, working as coolly and efficiently as she had in her office. He had no idea what she was thinking or what she had felt during that frantic morning, whether she had been worried or enjoying the challenge or simply absorbed in doing a job. No, he thought, she's got more fire than that. She's very young— she can't be more than twenty-eight or nine—young enough to feel the excitement of knocking down problems and watching people hop to her suggestions.

"How old are you?" he asked as they walked across the broad lawn toward the marina. When she told him, he stopped short. "*Twenty-three?*"

"You thought I was younger? Older?"

"A little older." He fell silent until they reached the dock, where he and Clay selected a speedboat.

"I'm going to town to pick up the first batch of golfers," Clay told Laura. "Do you need anything?"

"Check with Kelly," she said and waved good-bye as Currier started the engine. The powerful boat leaped forward, trailing a long wake that furled out from the center and then smoothed out, leaving a faint feathery V on the surface that reflected the few puffy clouds in a brilliant sky. Laura thought of the ocean off the Cape, its swells crashing on the shore where she and Owen sat, or hurling themselves toward the dunes where she and Paul walked. She closed her eyes and put back her head to let the wind blow her memories away.

Currier steered the boat away from others on the lake. When they were alone, he reduced the power and they slid slowly along the shore, the forest almost within reach, birds and wildlife visible among the trees. He glanced at Laura. She was pushing her hair back with a precise movement of her hand, as controlled as her voice and face, and he was aware once again of the challenge she presented. He had never met anyone, man or woman, who could calmly allow a silence to stretch out for many minutes without bursting into nervous chatter to fill it. She was silent now, and he reduced the power further, cutting down the noise so they could talk.

"Do you ever make an effort to impress someone?" he asked.

She looked surprised. "Of course. What an odd question. I want people to like me and admire me... it makes it easier for me to like and admire myself." She smiled, a little embarrassed. "Don't you do that? I think most people do. Make others a mirror, I mean, so that what we look like to ourselves depends on how we look to them."

"Clever," he said. "I like that. But I haven't seen any signs that you do that."

She gave him a level look. "You mean, since I haven't tried to impress you, and since most people do—certainly most women do—there must be something peculiar about me."

"Something unique," he corrected with a laugh, though she had given him a moment of self-consciousness that was almost discomfort. "But you're right about people trying to impress me, show me their tricks, whatever they are; I didn't realize how much I've come to expect it."

She smiled faintly. "You saw my tricks this morning."

"But you did them for the lodge. And to satisfy yourself."

She reflected. "But I need that, too. Don't you? If you depended on other people to tell you how good you are, you wouldn't have enough pride in yourself to get past the times when people are cruel."

He was watching her closely. "Did it happen recently, that someone was cruel to you?"

"We all know cruel people." She caught a glimpse of a deer bounding away from the sound of their boat. "Don't even cruel people show you their tricks to impress you?"

He nodded. "Cruel, crooked, selfish, bigoted, weak... they'll all perform if it helps them do a deal and be on top, with the deck stacked against everyone else."

Still gazing at the forest, she said, "I know someone like that."

"Only one?"

She turned back to him. "Do you know so many?"

"Hundreds. Thousands, probably. I take them for granted."

"I don't."

"That's one of the reasons I expect to be here often."

"And the other reasons?" she asked after a brief pause.

"I like the adventures you arrange for your guests."

They laughed together, and Laura said musingly, "I wonder if we can make that work."

"I think you can make anything work," he said quietly. He turned the wheel, guiding the boat into a small cove. "Time for lunch. And you can tell me about Cape Cod and the first time you had a vacuum cleaner."

* * *

All through the fall—when electric power had long since been restored and guests again wore silks and black tie to dinner while recalling
the charm of that evening under the stars when the lobster tasted better
than ever before and the tale told by Eric Pickard made chills run
through them even in the heat of the campfire—whenever Currier was
not in Europe he spent the weekends with Laura. They rode horseback
and played tennis, took boats on the lake, swam in the outdoor pool,
and explored the small towns of the Adirondacks. They talked about the
Europe Currier knew, his world of finance, his friends, his wives. They
talked about Laura a little at a time; she was uncomfortable when he
questioned her, and after a while he was willing to let her find her
confidence with him at her own pace. He was not giving up, only spinning out his forcefulness more slowly. After their first time on the lake,
when he had asked her about Cape Cod and she had instinctively with-
drawn, he had recognized how deep her reticence went. Her actions
were automatic, he realized: she concealed from habit.

Still, as the days grew short and chilly, and they spent more time
indoors, before the fire, she gradually told him bits of her life, describing
the university, mimicking her professors as she once had mimicked Jules
LeClair for Paul, and talking about her part-time jobs as assistant concierge at the Boston Salinger and companion to an elderly widower.
"And then Clay and I came up here," she told him as they sat in a
corner of the Post House in Jay's Landing. It was a small tavern with
leather wing chairs, gas mantles hanging from the low, beamed ceiling,
and prints of Revolutionary War battles on the walls. On a weekday
afternoon in November, they were the only guests. "Kelly and John
offered us jobs and it's a wonderful place for me to learn. I've been here
a year and I've done everything from filling in as hostess in the dining
room to managing the whole place whenever I'm able to convince Kelly
to convince John it's all right for them to take a vacation."

Currier was watching her closely. "The elderly widower—"

"He was my friend," she said briefly, wondering what had made him
pick up on Owen. Something in her voice or her face . . . Suddenly she
felt a wave of revulsion at the lying that had become almost a way of life.
She was so sick of picking her way through the mine fields of her own
lies—and Currier was so sophisticated, she thought; surely he was
beyond being shocked or censorious—that she almost told him everything. But the words never came; the habit of secrecy was too strong.
"He died and I . . . miss him very much. I worked in his kitchen, too,
with a wonderful woman named Rosa"—her voice wavered and quickly

she took a sip of wine—"and learned how to cook. Do you cook? Somehow I can't imagine you in the kitchen."

"I have six cooks, one for each of my houses, but I make a wicked hamburger. I'll make one for you when you come to New York."

"I'd like that."

He gazed at her. "When are you coming to New York?"

"Not for a while, but someday, I think. What else do you make besides hamburgers?"

"Martinis. Will you come to New York with me?"

"Not yet," she said easily. "But I promise to eat hamburgers in your kitchen when I do. And I'll make dessert. What would you like?"

"Tarte Tatin."

"I make a wicked tarte Tatin." They smiled together, and he was surprised, during the following week, as he sat in meetings and flew across the country, how often he saw her smile and heard in his memory her promise to come to New York. He was still remembering when he returned to Darnton's the next Friday.

"Almost through?" he asked.

"Almost. Are you here for the weekend?"

"Just tonight. I'm sorry, but I have to be in Washington tomorrow."

"I'm sorry, too." She signed letters and folded them in their envelopes. "Ready. Shall we have a drink on the porch? It's been so warm today; it doesn't feel like November, does it?"

The weather was warm, but she was cool, as always, and Currier felt a flash of adolescent anger: didn't she appreciate what he was going through to see her—dragging himself to the Adirondacks ten times in three months? And what did he get for it? A lilting voice saying 'I'm sorry, too.' Fuck it, he thought as they sat on a cushioned sofa on the long front porch. I don't need her; the world is full of women.

"Laura," he said, "I want you to marry me."

The silence was sudden and complete. All around them, as the sun set, the sky was an ocean of flame streaked with islands of thin, purple-gray clouds. "How can you marry someone you've never slept with?" she asked lightly, then added quickly, "I'm sorry, Wes, that was foolish. I'm ashamed of myself. You took me by surprise."

"And you said the first thing you thought of."

"I apologize. It was crude."

"But you aren't crude, and I know it. And I did indeed take you by surprise, so I apologize, too. As for my sleeping with you—"

"Please, I've said I'm sorry. It's not important."

"It's very important, at least to me; I've wanted you in my bed for a

long time. But I'm a patient man, Laura, and I always get what I want.
And I'm not worried. Are you? One of these days, as soon as you vanquish your demons, you'll want more from me than companionship and
my presence at conferences and then—"

"That's unfair." Her face was flushed.

"It was and I apologize." He held her face between his hands and
kissed her lightly. "This is the damnedest proposal; all we're doing is
apologizing. Laura, I want to marry you and take care of you. I don't
want you to look the way you did when you told me about the old man
you took care of when you were working your way through college, the
one who died—"

"How did I look?"

"Brokenhearted," he said briefly. "Not for long—you have a remarkable spirit—but I don't want you to feel any sadness, ever again. You
deserve happiness and luxury and a life free of worry, and I can give you
that. I can give you everything. And I want you with me wherever I go;
I'm even going to ask your help in some of my work. You have a way of
striving for order that I admire, and you're very precise in what you say
and what you don't say. In a marriage that might be a problem, but in
business it's invaluable."

She smiled. "You mean you'll take the lumps in marriage because the
business will prosper."

"*That's* unfair." He studied her face. "You won't always be so careful
with me; if we love each other—"

"Love," Laura murmured. "Does that enter into it?"

He laughed. "Yes. I should have said that first, not last. But I'm not
always sure whether my love may not be suspect. Three times it's ended
in divorce. I thought you might prefer a simple proposal without the
fluff of an emotion that might sound a little frayed around the edges."

Laura laid her head briefly on his shoulder. "A girl likes a little fluff
now and then, even if she has to say no."

He hesitated only a fraction of a second. "Then I'll use more of it next
time."

They were silent. The sky had darkened to a deep bronze so rich it
turned to orange the shadowed grass and tall pines in front of the lodge.
Currier put his arm around Laura, his fingers caressing the short springy
hairs at the back of her neck. Vanquish your demons, she thought. Of
course I will. I've stopped missing Ben, except when I'm really lonely,
late at night, and then I wonder what kind of life he has in Amsterdam
and if he ever thinks of me anymore. And it's just a matter of time before
I forget Paul and stop having dreams about Osterville and Boston, Leni

and Allison, Paul's parents, even the cousins who were always in the background, making everything seem more alive, more like a storybook family.

It will all seem like a story if I wait long enough; like something I read once and put away. And then maybe I'll be able to make love to Wes Currier instead of knotting up inside every time he kisses me.

"Still," he said musingly, as if continuing a conversation, "you're not as brittle as you were four months ago. You may be breaking out of this cage you've made for yourself."

She stirred. "What does that mean?"

"I'll tell you a story. When I was twenty-five, a year after I'd made my first million, my wife left me. I fell into a funk that wouldn't go away. Something I cared about, something that was safely mine, had been stolen from me. All I could think was that some vicious mythical beast was punishing me for having everything I wanted." He paused. "I think someone took something away from you, something very precious, and you've been feeling like a victim ever since, with the forces of nature and mythology stacked against you. The logical reaction to that is anger, and building a thick shell around yourself, and no sex."

She smiled. "Probably." But her eyes were focused inward. "You think a shell is like a cage."

"It was for me. I was locked into my anger because I'd been robbed, and I was determined to defend myself so no one could rob me again. That was my shell and that was my cage." They were silent. Within the circle of his arm, Currier felt Laura's taut muscles, and he spoke quietly but with an intensity that struck to the heart of her memories. "I'd earned what I had—that was what made me angriest. I'd worked hard and I'd given love, and I deserved the good things I had. Other people got what they wanted; why shouldn't I? I was as good as they, maybe better. But in a way that was the worst of all: I'd known what it was to have the happiness I wanted and then it was taken from me before I could enjoy it. So I locked myself in even tighter, like a besieged general."

"And how did you break out?" Laura asked after a moment.

"Oh, that's the dull part of the story. I remembered what I'd always known: that life isn't fair and we're never promised that it will be. Too many people spend their time looking for someone to promise them happiness or beauty or wealth, instead of fighting to carve out their own. I'm still fighting, but I'm almost there; I have most of what I want and I'll get the rest. I told you, I always do."

The last faint hues vanished from the sky. The first star flickered just above a grove of pine trees; amber lanterns lined the curving driveway and front walk. Behind them, Laura and Currier heard the chatter of guests gathering in the Great Hall for cocktails, and the soft strains of classical guitar from the tape John Darnton had just put on. "Wes," Laura said thoughtfully, "if I asked you to back me in buying a hotel, would you consider it?"

He masked his surprise and the instinctive refusal which sprang to his lips. He wanted a wife, not an entrepreneur. But he was patient, and he knew the advantages of having someone in debt to him. "If you knew what you wanted, of course I would. Do you have a specific hotel in mind?"

"The Chicago Salinger," she said.

* * *

Myrna's legs were clamped around Clay's hips and he thrust deep inside her. He heard her little kittenish cries that meant she was coming, and then let himself go. The surge tore through him like a torrent bursting through exploding floodgates. He couldn't see, he couldn't hear, for that incredible instant when everything in him felt free and absolutely perfect, and even when he heard Myrna's voice murmuring, "So lovely, Clay, you are a lovely lover," and opened his eyes, he still felt the tremors all through him and her warm wetness clinging to his penis. He lay flat on her surprisingly cushiony body to stay inside her as long as he could, and reached back to pull the sheet over them; in the midnight air, his skin suddenly felt chilled. "Lovely lover," Myrna whispered, turning her head and flicking her tongue deep into his ear. "My wonderful lover..."

Little sparks shot from her probing tongue all through him. Her hands grasped his buttocks and he felt the quick sharpness of her finger pushing into him and then he was hard again inside her; he was moving again inside her; and again they found a rhythm that could last, as far as he was concerned, forever.

Of course he wouldn't say a thing like that, then or later, when, finally, he was pretty sure he couldn't get it up again even if he had the energy to think about it. Myrna didn't seem tired—Myrna never seemed tired, whether she was teaching on Darnton's tennis court or swimming in the pool or shopping all day for presents for her family somewhere in Nebraska or screwing all night in her little rented house in Jay's Landing. Crazy lady, he thought, and I'm crazy about her—but sometimes she scares the shit out of me.

He thought that every time he got to this very dangerous moment: three in the morning, sprawled on her bed in ecstatic exhaustion, his mind numbed with gratitude and satiety. And as always, he gathered caution around him like a winter coat and did not ask her to marry him or even live with him, though it did occur to him that there were advantages to knowing she was off the market and definitely his.

Later, later, later, he thought, but at the same time part of his mind was listening to the satisfied hum of his body, telling him to wrap her up and make sure of her. Caught between two pieces of contradictory advice, he fell asleep.

Myrna Appleby was twenty-seven and had been a tennis instructor for almost ten years. She didn't mind that Clay was only twenty-one; he was taller than she: blond, handsome, with a neat mustache and a kind of permanent boyishness that led her to believe she could turn him into the kind of man she wanted. She'd just about given up hope of finding one.

The problem was, most men were afraid of her. They called her bold when they were being kind, and aggressive when they weren't. But Clay liked it when she took command. At first she thought he didn't have much backbone, and in that case he wouldn't be right for her at all, but then she decided it was just that he'd gotten so used to his sister making decisions that he pretty much took it for granted when Myrna behaved similarly. He'd probably been looking for a woman like that all along, she reflected as she set her alarm, and then she, too, fell asleep.

She woke him at five in the morning so he could get to work on time. If it weren't for her, she thought, he'd likely lose his job and go wandering off with no real skills except chauffeuring and being a desk clerk, and how far would that get him? She had no idea what he'd do without her, especially since Laura was working eighty hours a week and spending the rest of the time with Wes Currier. Clay had nobody but Myrna. "Rise and shine, darling. I'll fix breakfast."

"Just coffee," he mumbled, his head under the pillow.

Myrna stroked his long, boyish back and felt a rush of tenderness for him. Men were so vulnerable, when you thought about it; terrible at the basic necessities like cooking and doing laundry and buying socks; they didn't even know how to eat properly. "You'll need more than coffee," she said decisively. She ran her fingers through her straight black hair, pulled on a kimono, and went downstairs to the kitchen.

"What are we doing tonight?" she asked when he was at the table plowing through fried eggs and toast. "There's a film at the—"

"Can't see you tonight," he said. "We can go to the movie tomorrow if you want."

A flicker of alarm appeared in her gray eyes. "I thought we had a date."

"Not that I remember." He looked up, worried. "Did we? I didn't think so. Anyway, it doesn't matter, does it? The movie'll still be there tomorrow night." He returned to his eggs. "Terrific breakfast, babe."

"What are you doing tonight?"

"Playing poker. Want to tie a ribbon around my arm for good luck?"

"Knights in armor did that before they went into combat."

"Good for you. I didn't know you knew that."

"Are you going into combat?"

"Who knows? These guys are good. I may bet some real money."

"Does Laura know you're going to play?" His face tightened and she knew she had made a mistake. "Well, it doesn't matter," she said in a rush, adding carelessly, "Have fun and buy me something beautiful if you win."

"Thanks, babe. Talk to you soon." On his way out, he kissed her on the cheek, and a minute later, as he backed out of her driveway, he offered a prayer of thanksgiving that he hadn't given in to his mellow mood the night before. He wasn't ready to make a commitment. Most of the time he was happy as a clam, just the way things were. He still missed the excitement of stealing: scaling walls; moving like a shadow through other people's houses, as if he controlled their lives for a little while; he even missed picking pockets in the subway with Laura. But he'd stopped that small-time stuff a long time ago—not exactly when Laura stopped, but soon after. Everything seemed to peter out after she wouldn't share it with him, especially when she started saying things that made him feel . . . *small*, sort of . . . like he could do better things than rip off people who weren't there to fight back, or pick the pocket of some ass who didn't know enough to keep his wallet inside his jacket when he took the subway. Big deal, she kept saying sarcastically. My big hero. After a while it got to him, and he told himself he didn't want that piddling stuff anyway; she was right, he was meant for bigger things.

Of course, by then he was earning money, first in Philadelphia and then at Darnton's. And things were better at Darnton's than he'd expected. He got restless for New York, and one of these days he'd get back there, but he was having an okay time right here. He was driving people around in classy cars he could pretend were his; he was working half-time on the front desk and helping with the payroll; he got along with Laura in their apartment, though he wasn't there a hell of a lot anymore; he had Myrna whenever he wanted her; and then, a couple of months ago, he'd discovered some all-night poker games in Jay's Landing and nearby towns, organized by the chauffeurs, butlers, and chefs for the wealthy New York socialites who had vacation houses in the Adirondacks. Decent guys; most of them a lot older than him but willing to let him join in whenever he wanted. And they had respect for him; he could tell. After all, he was a chauffeur, too.

The only problem was, their salaries were double or triple his, and they played for higher stakes. But what the hell, he thought as he drove over the causeway to the island, when I get on to their tricks, and everything starts clicking... then they'll see what I can do. Because I have it all figured out: Clay Fairchild is really going to clean up.

* * *

In the airline club at O'Hare, Currier found an armchair in a quiet corner, pulled the telephone to him and dialed Laura's number at Darnton's. "I miss you. I called you from San Francisco last night but no one knew where you were."

"I was helping Kelly and John look for a four-year-old who stomped out of the dining room when his parents told him he couldn't have dessert. They didn't go after him because they said he needed to be taught a lesson—I don't know what the lesson was supposed to be—and an hour later they couldn't find him anywhere."

"And you were annoyed."

She gave a short laugh. "Furious. That poor kid was at the marina, sobbing because he thought he'd have to sleep in a boat since his parents didn't want him back."

"Because he walked out of the dining room?"

"Because he didn't finish his trout with ravigote sauce, which was the reason he was denied dessert. Why do people do that to children? Why do they make them stuff down food they don't want and then punish them by taking away their love?"

"Damned if I know. Does a bloated stomach make a more lovable kid? I'm not an expert; I never fathered anyone. Did you carry him back with his arms around your neck and his head on your shoulder?"

"Yes; why?"

"Because I envy him."

Her low laugh came over the wire. "Are you still in San Francisco?"

"Chicago. I looked at the Salinger."

"Oh."

"It's in bad shape, Laura."

"We knew—I knew that. It's been neglected for years. Did you find anything else wrong?"

"Not in a quick tour; we'd need to have studies done. How important is this to you, this particular hotel?"

"It's the one I want. I've seen reports on it, Wes; it's in a perfect location, there's a good market for what I want to do with it, and the basic structure is sound."

"You can't know that until we have engineering studies made."

"It was sound a little over a year ago; I told you, I saw reports on it. If all it needs is renovation—"

"Ten million dollars' worth. At a guess."

There was a silence. "That's what we thought the purchase price would be."

"If the Salingers even want to sell. I'm going to have one of my staff sound them out."

"Wes, please don't do anything that connects me with it."

"Because the financing will come from me? My dear, it doesn't bother me to be behind the scenes; I usually am when I finance a project. This is yours; the publicity should be yours. All I ask is that you make money."

"I don't want publicity. I'm going to be an employee of the corporation I'm forming to own all the hotels—"

Her voice abruptly stopped and he frowned. "How many hotels are we going to buy?"

"I've only asked for your help with one."

"But others are on the horizon."

"Aren't there others of everything on your horizon? Isn't that how you got where you are?"

"How many hotels is your corporation going to own?"

"Four." There was a pause. Then, as if she had made a decision, she said, "Wes, I'll tell you all about it when we're together. Are you coming back soon?"

He waited for her to say she'd missed him, as he missed her, but she did not. "I'll be in New York tonight; I should be with you for dinner on Friday. Or—I have a better idea. Why don't you meet me in New York?"

This time the silence lasted only a heartbeat. "I'd like that," she said easily.

Currier was amazed at the exultation that filled him; he felt like a schoolboy. But he kept his voice casual. "Friday afternoon, then. Meet me for drinks at five-thirty at the Russian Tea Room. Call my houseman with your flight number and he'll have my driver meet you and take you to my apartment and then the Tea Room. If you don't get a chance to call—"

"Wes." She was smiling; he could hear it in her voice. "I can find my way. I'll be there."

"Friday," he said.

"Friday," she repeated, and when she put down the telephone she let out a long shaky breath. She had to take the chance; she had to tell him. She couldn't have secrets from Wes: they would be working together and he was going to trust her with twenty million dollars. For a start. And it would be all right. He was a businessman, and he'd just said, a few minutes ago, that all he asked of her was that she make money.

It wasn't true; he asked considerably more. But even that would be all right. Because there was excitement in Wes Currier. He was at the center of great events and had a part in shaping them on the world stage. And that made all the greater the excitement of his desire for her. Maybe I'm ready for excitement, she thought. And a man who takes crooked people for granted. Maybe it's the perfect time for me to be honest.

But her shakiness came from something else, as well, and she knew it. She'd known it when she heard Currier talk about the Chicago Salinger. For all its problems, he'd decided it was worth pursuing. He wouldn't have talked about making studies if he thought studies were a waste of time, or if he thought the idea of buying the Chicago Salinger was a foolish one, or if he thought she couldn't handle it. He was taking it seriously, and that meant it was going to happen.

Owen, she said silently. We're going to buy back your hotel.

* * *

A hard October rain was falling when the taxi pulled up in front of St. James Tower, so Laura had no more than a blurred glimpse of the building before the doorman whisked her inside and into the elevator that took her to Currier's apartment. She was late—the plane had been late; traffic from LaGuardia had moved at an agonizing crawl—and she barely had time to unpack in his bedroom and wash up in his black and silver bathroom before it was time to leave. "Mr. Currier's driver will take you wherever you wish to go," the houseman said, helping her into her raincoat. "If you will wait here, or in the lobby, it takes him about five minutes to get here from the garage."

She had planned to walk crosstown to the Russian Tea Room, taking a few minutes alone before she met Currier to rediscover the feel of the city she had not seen in almost six years. But her lateness, and the rain, and the promise of a dry car with someone else to drive it changed her mind. "I'll wait here," she said, and as soon as he left to make the call she took an unashamed look around. The rooms were large and comfortable, with deep sofas around low, square coffee tables, and Italian floor lamps of stainless steel with black steel pivoting arms. Everything was modern, expensive, and almost unlived in. It needs some clutter, Laura thought, and some wrinkles in the cushions. But of course a good houseman would not permit that.

She looked into the dining room, its twelve chairs surrounding a gleaming table that would have been at home in a conference room, and then into the study, Currier's office, and once again into his bedroom. It was then that she felt her first moment of anticipation. Until now, she had been in too much of a hurry to think of anything but the plane circling the airport in the rain, the taxi driver changing lanes in a futile attempt to speed up, the need to wash and change quickly so she would not keep Currier waiting. But now, gazing at his sleek ebony bureaus and nightstands, and his wide bed beneath a black and white comforter, she shivered with the anticipation of change.

And then the houseman was in the doorway, saying the car was downstairs, and she turned to go.

Currier was there before her, chatting with the maitre d' even though the small waiting area was jammed with damp, vociferous groups waiting for tables. "Just in time," he said with a smile as she joined him. Holding her arm, he kissed her cheek. "We couldn't have held off the hordes much longer." And in another moment they were seated in a red leather booth in a room as colorful as the oil paintings on the walls. "You look very lovely," he said, taking her hand between his. "I wondered if you might change your mind and not come."

"It never occurred to me," she said simply. But she was distracted by the activity around her, and Currier, after ordering wine and caviar with blinis, waited for her to turn to him with an awed comment about the luxury of the room, the number of stars and other celebrities she recognized, and the delights of being in New York with him.

When she spoke, he leaned forward, smiling, to hear her amid the high pitch of conversation and the clink of silver on china. "I don't see how I can go to bed with you," she said thoughtfully.

His head snapped back in surprise. "Why not?" he said and then was annoyed at himself because he sounded more like a feeble teenager than a man accustomed to dominating.

She gave a small private smile and he knew she understood him, even if he did not yet understand her. "You've just agreed to back me in buying a hotel. And I'm grateful."

His face hardened. "I don't want your gratitude. I expect you to make money for me. Listen to me." He leaned toward her. "I don't buy sex; I've never had to. I never believed the infantile fantasy that a prostitute is the perfect teacher for a young boy; I never believed I couldn't attract my own women, at any age. I do what I want and I do it honestly. And I never barter."

"I didn't say that to insult you," Laura said without apology. She looked at his hands clasping hers. His fingers were short and very strong. Then she looked up and met his hard eyes. "I know it wasn't a trade. But it might have seemed like one."

"To whom? No one knows anything about us."

"I do. I act for myself, not because of what others might think."

"Then you should have known me better."

"I wasn't worried about you! Can't you see? I was trying to understand my own feelings—how much is gratitude and how much is desire."

Once again surprise showed in his eyes. "It doesn't matter. I want you. I don't ask why; I'll discover that as we enjoy each other. If I don't discover it, we won't last long. But I don't think that will be a problem."

They were interrupted as their wine was poured and a waiter wearing a green Russian shirt served thin pancakes with caviar and sour cream on large plates that reflected the bright lights of the room. Nothing in that famous place was done in shadow or done quietly: it was a room in which food and people alike were to be seen and remembered.

But Currier's eyes were on Laura. "You came to New York because you knew it was time for us to begin."

She nodded, remembering her shiver of anticipation. "I thought so. But I wasn't sure. . . ."

"Because of your gratitude? Or because of the man you're trying to forget?"

"Both." Her eyes were steady on his. She did not ask him how he knew; a sophisticated man would assume there had been a past she was trying to forget on that island in Lake Champlain. Then she smiled. "But my gratitude is more recent."

He returned her smile, admiring her quickness. He lifted her hand and kissed it. "I promise we'll keep business and old loves outside our bedroom. I'll help you forget them both. Do you want to eat your caviar or shall we leave now?"

She gave a low laugh. There was something wonderfully comfortable about giving in to Currier's supreme self-confidence, as if she were sinking back into a deep sofa that embraced and supported her and muffled the clamor of the outside world. "Do you mind if we wait? I didn't have a chance to eat today and I'm famished." He laughed with her but then she grew serious. "I want to talk to you anyway; there are so many things I'm trying to forget, and I want you to know what they are."

"I want to know, too, but not tonight. Do you mind? This is a beginning for us; I'd rather not start with the past."

It was a reprieve. "Whatever you want. But sometime this weekend . . ."

"Tomorrow. Or Sunday." Silently they touched their wineglasses, then turned to their food, savoring it while he told her about the New York in which he had grown up, describing places long since torn down, telling anecdotes about his neighborhood and the people who had kept an eye on him while his parents worked. He had always been on his own, and Laura began to understand his need to dominate: the only way he had ever been able to feel secure in a world where no one paid much attention to him was to control events around him, to know what was happening because he was making it happen.

They finished their blinis and wine, and because his driver had the limousine parked in front of the restaurant, it was only a few moments before they were in his apartment.

He took her in his arms as soon as the door closed behind them, and they dropped their raincoats on the floor. "Do you know when I first wanted you?" He kissed her, holding her tightly to him, his tongue taking possession of her mouth. "Our first breakfast at the lodge." His lips brushed hers as he spoke. "The whole time we were together, you were looking around to make sure the dining room was running smoothly. I wanted to hold you in my arms and make you think I was more interesting than that goddam lodge."

Laura laughed deep in her throat, then brought his head to hers again and kissed him as greedily as he had kissed her. It had been so long, she had ached for Paul and then felt no desire at all for so long, that the first touch of Currier's lips, and the excitement of being held and loved again, split her thoughts apart, one part still caught in the past, the other aware only of the man holding her, the feel and voice of Wes Currier, the faint scent of his after-shave, the softness of his cashmere jacket, the crushing pressure of his mouth. She felt she was coiling upward, her weightless body responding to the demands of his hands and lips as they pulled her out of the shell she had kept intact for two years.

"And then," he said, his lips again just above hers, "in the dark that morning, when you said if I talked to you, you could find me . . ."

"And I did." The words were almost a sigh. Together, they turned and walked down the hall to his room, where the houseman had turned down the bed. A single floor lamp cast its light upward, its indirect glow softening the blacks and whites of the room and making it seem like a shadowed cave as rain pounded the windows. Currier slipped off Laura's suit jacket and took her in his arms.

"I want to make you forget everything else," he said, his voice almost harsh. "That look you have, of thinking of other things, other people, not even aware of me—"

Laura's quick fingers were unknotting his tie. "Don't talk about it. There's no place like bed to forget—"

"Not only bed! Damn it, don't you understand I want you to want me everywhere; I want you to think of me so there's no room for anyone else. . . ."

"Wes, don't talk; make love to me. Please. We'll talk later." She kissed him, willing him to sink into lovemaking as she wanted to do. His mouth opened beneath hers, his tongue responded to hers, and then his hands were once again urgent and demanding, undressing her, not allowing her to help. He untied the bow at her throat and opened the pearl buttons of her blouse, pulling it off and unhooking her brassiere almost at the same time. Laura felt the freedom of her unconstricted breasts and then Currier's hands cupped them and his mouth enclosed each nipple and she closed her eyes and let herself be engulfed in the heat that flowed from his touch.

His mouth lingered on her breasts as he slipped her skirt over her hips. Laura reached down to unbutton his shirt, to help him, but he refused; instead, he pulled away. She opened her eyes and saw him peeling off his own clothes, and she realized with surprise that she felt cold and lost without his body close to hers, and his hands and mouth on hers. But in a moment he was holding her to him, pressing her body along his, turning her toward the bed. Laura let him; her hunger was so intense she barely noticed he was the one setting the pace.

Currier stretched out above her on the bed, brushing her skin with long strokes that left a trail like an electric current. His fingers reached the small triangle of chestnut hair between her legs and then explored her dark, wet center, reaching deep inside; his mouth was on her breasts again, sucking and licking her hard, erect nipples. Laura's breath came out in a lingering sigh, almost a moan, and she tried to pull him onto her, but still he would not yield; his fingers and mouth possessed her, drawing her up and up like a long flame until there was nothing but fire, a burning luster, that blocked out everything else. And then he moved and covered her and Laura felt the wonderful warmth of his full weight upon her; she raised her hips and pulled him into her, the plunging hardness of him, the sureness of his movements—a sureness she knew she was beginning to count on. Her body moved with his; she was filled with a man. Briefly she wondered how she had gone so long without missing it before she stopped thinking. She only felt. And her body came to life.

* * *

A good part of the weekend was spent in bed. But they walked, too, once the rain stopped, exploring the city that Currier knew, so different from the one in which Laura had grown up it might have been on a different planet. His limousine followed them when they walked; it waited at the entrances to shops and galleries and restaurants in case they wanted to be driven to the next location. They went into boutiques smaller than Laura's old tenement apartment where the price of a dress was more than their rent had been for a year, and galleries where paintings sold for twenty times as much as Ben had made in years of stealing.

But all that seemed far away. Laura and Currier were fawned over as they browsed, and New York was transformed into a city of treasures whose beauty could be admired and held—and even owned when Currier convinced her to let him buy her a pair of leather gloves with pearl buttons—without fear or guilt or danger.

"Now," he said on Sunday afternoon as they sat in his study two hours before Laura's plane for Burlington. The rain had begun again and the houseman had lit a fire; they sat in deep chairs before the fireplace, sherry and raisin scones on the table between them. "Let's hear your story. I'm prepared for anything. Did I tell you what this weekend means to me?"

"Yes." She smiled but she was abstracted, thinking of how to begin. "It was wonderful. Much more than—"

"Than you expected," he finished when she stopped. "Well, who is he?"

"Paul Janssen." The name sounded almost foreign in Currier's room. "A great-nephew of Owen Salinger."

Currier's eyebrows went up. "You were involved with the whole family."

Laura had been about to go on, but the words fell away and she stared at him. "You know all about it. You've known all along and never said anything."

"It wasn't for me to say. It was your story and I knew you'd tell me when you were ready. My dear"—he leaned forward and took her hand— "I have people in most cities whose job is to keep me informed about the finances of major corporations. There was no way I could miss hearing about that trial. And it was in July, the month I met you, when you were so distracted you were barely aware of me: if nothing else, that would have made me wonder about you."

Laura smiled faintly. "I used to know how important you are. I guess I forgot. You started acting like a lover and I stopped thinking about your international reputation."

"You were supposed to. I didn't want you going to bed with a reputation. But you must have known that the trial would be in the Boston papers and others, too, especially New York and Los Angeles."

"I didn't want to think about it." She took her hand from his and sat back. "I pretended no one knew. No one talked about it at Darnton's."

He poured sherry into their glasses. "Tell me now."

"You know the story."

"I want to hear it from you. Start with New York. Were you really a thief?"

Laura flushed. Most of the drama had gone out of her decision to be honest for the first time. "Yes."

"A good one?"

Involuntarily, she gave a small laugh. "Not good enough; I was caught. But I wasn't a thief at the Salingers'." She skipped over the years in New York, telling him instead about her love affair with the Salinger family—about having a place to belong, and people to care about, and a world of comfort and dreams of a future. She told him about Owen and their plans for his hotels, about his death and the will reading, and the trial.

But Currier was a man who paid as much attention to what people did not say as to what they did. "Why did you go to the Salingers in the first place?"

No one had asked that at the trial. Rollins had told Laura why: Felix wanted her background revealed in order to undermine her credibility, but there was nothing they could prove about that early robbery, and so they left it out. But Currier, who missed nothing, brought it up. "We went there to rob them," Laura said evenly. "But we never did; we couldn't. They were too good to us, too important . . ."

"Why the Salingers? Why not someone else?"

She took the last plunge into the truth. "Because my older brother sent us there."

Currier's look sharpened. "You didn't mention him in the trial."

"He didn't have anything to do with Owen's will, and we didn't want them to know we'd been secretive—deceptive—about something else all the years we were with them."

"Where is he now?"

"In Europe; he's been there for years."

Currier contemplated her. "He may not have had anything to do with Owen's will, but he had something to do with Felix's accusations."

Laura returned his look. "You would have made a better prosecutor than Carver Cheyne. Yes, he had something to do with it. That summer, a couple of months after we got there, he robbed the Salingers, exactly as we'd planned. I asked him not to, but he did. At the will reading, Felix accused us of the robbery and said we'd stayed on afterward to rob them again by manipulating Owen to change his will."

"And the family believed him. And forced you to leave. And then took back what Owen left you."

She gazed into the fire, her face like stone.

"And your brother fled to Europe. You haven't seen him since?"

"No."

"Nor missed him?"

"I've missed him," she said after a moment, her voice low. She turned back to Currier and told him how Ben had taken care of the two of them. "I've wanted to see him again for a long time, but every month that goes by makes it harder. I was so angry and hurt, and then I was so much a part of the Salingers—and he'd warned me, you see, that they didn't really care about us—there just didn't seem any way we could be brother and sister again."

"I'll take you to Europe," Currier said. "You'll have a grand reunion and forget the past."

She smiled. "Thank you, Wes, what a lovely idea. I'd like to go to Europe someday, though I'm not sure about a reunion. . . . But first we have to buy a hotel. If you still trust me."

He stood and came to her chair, raising her to stand with him. "I believe in you. I trust you. We'll get your hotels back from that son of a bitch, and then—"

He kissed her with a passion that revived the weekend and convinced her he meant it: he believed her. And Laura responded, her passion matching his. Then she forced herself to pull back. "Wes, I have a plane to catch."

"I'll take you in mine." His voice was rough. "You wanted to come here on your own, but you'll let me take you back."

She hesitated only a moment. "I'd like that," she said, and they kissed again. And as he held her to him, Laura realized that this was the first time in years she was hiding nothing. She could say what she felt and be what she wished. Never again would she have to tread the mine fields of her lies. Gratitude for Currier filled her, another kind, a better kind, than for his help with the hotels. It could almost be confused with love. But she didn't want to think about that now; it was too soon. It was enough to feel, to be alive, to enjoy him as he enjoyed her. And in the last clear moment before she let herself sink once again into the touch of his hands and mouth and the promise of his body, a thought came to her with a surge of triumph and relief.

She was finally free of the past.

CHAPTER 16

ALLISON and Patricia walked once through the apartment and then back again while the landlord turned on lamps against the darkness of a rainy October afternoon. The apartment was on the third floor of a tall, narrow house on the Prinsengracht, once the residence of a large family but long since converted to five apartments, one on each floor. "Definitely not for you," Patricia declared. "Very small."

"So is Amsterdam and I like them both." Allison turned to the landlord who watched from the doorway. "It's fine; even the furniture is perfect. I'll take it for a month."

He shook his head. "I'm sorry; I need a minimum of six months."

"I never plan that far in advance." She began to write a check. "I may be here that long, but I can't guarantee it. I might even stay a year," she added with nervous gaiety, causing her cousin to give her a swift look.

"You wouldn't stay that long. Your mother would think you were involved with someone and she'd drag you—"

"She'd be right," Allison said, still with that nervous excitement that made Patricia frown.

She handed the check to the landlord. "You will take this, won't you? I'd like to move in tomorrow."

He studied the check. "Are you related to the Salinger Hotel?"

"Intimately." She broke into a giggle. "The hotel and I are intimately related."

Patricia took her arm. "You're acting very oddly. Come on; I'll buy you a hot chocolate, or something stronger."

"You *are* a member of the Salinger Hotel family?" the landlord asked.

"My father is president of the company." Imperiously she waved toward the telephone. "Call the manager of the hotel; he's my reference. And I'll move in tomorrow."

"I suggest you call first, to confirm that all is satisfactory."

Allison sighed. "I wouldn't have this trouble in Boston." But she knew she would; landlords were the same everywhere. It was just that she wanted everything about this apartment to be as magical and exciting as all of Amsterdam, as all her times with Ben.

"I suppose you're seeing him again tonight," said Patricia as they left the house and stood in the doorway, partially protected from the downpour beating on the cobblestones and the gray water of the canal. She opened her umbrella with an angry snap and waited for Allison to open hers. "You're ignoring me in the middle of a foreign country."

Allison burst out laughing. "You know Amsterdam as well as I do." They walked along the Prinsengracht, their umbrellas merging with dozens of others in a fanciful, undulating black roof. "And you've spent the last three weeks with some American college man, and I also heard you say you're bored and want to go to Paris. Anyway, I did ask you if you minded my going out with Ben."

"The first two times, you asked me."

"And you said you could take care of yourself and I didn't need to ask permission as if you were my spinster aunt. Oh, let's not quarrel; I'm feeling too happy."

"You don't know anything about him and he has shifty eyes."

"He doesn't have—"

"I'll bet he can see perfectly well without those glasses; he just wears them to hide his eyes."

"Patricia, you're being a bitch."

"And you're being gullible."

"Fuck it," Allison muttered. "I really was feeling happy." She stopped walking. Rain drummed on her umbrella as she stood still, looking at one of the brightly painted glass-enclosed excursion boats that plied the canals, giving visitors the best tour of Amsterdam. Her grandfather had taken her on one of those the first time she was in Amsterdam, when she was eight. They'd laughed and made jokes, she remembered; it had been a lovely day. She sighed. It was easier being a child.

"I'm going back to the hotel," she said to Patricia who was standing indecisively nearby. "I'm also going out with Ben tonight."

Patricia shrugged and walked beside her. "We should have taken the hotel limousine," she said after a moment. "My feet are soaked."

"I didn't feel like it."

"We could take a taxi."

"I don't feel like it."

They walked the remaining six blocks, rapidly, without speaking, and once inside the hotel stood in the lobby, catching their breath and dripping quietly on the Oriental carpet. "Are you going to sulk?" Patricia asked. "I was only warning you for your own good; you're just so damned infatuated—"

"Hello," Ben said, coming up to them as he crossed the lobby. "Shall I bring towels?"

"For us or the carpet?" Allison asked, smiling.

"I was thinking of you." He looked at Patricia. "Can I get you something, Miss Salinger?"

"No. Thank you. Allison, I'm going upstairs and have tea sent up. If you care to join me—"

"Paul!" Allison cried and dashed across the lobby. Heads turned, and frowns followed her squishing shoes and loud greeting. "Paul, for heaven's sake, what are you doing in Amsterdam? Did you just get here? Are you staying here? Oh, how wonderful to see you—!"

He put his arms around her and they hugged each other. "You look damp but healthy," he said, holding her away from him.

"You're getting gray," she responded accusingly. "And you look older." She touched the lines at each side of his mouth. "These are new."

"I am older," he said with a smile. "Your mother wonders why she hasn't heard from you."

"Oh, God, you're a missionary."

He shook his head. "A simple tourist. Hello, Patricia."

"Hello, Paul. What a surprise; did you know we were here?"

"Leni told me. She was at my mother's when I called the other day, from Geneva—"

"—and she asked you to be a good Boy Scout and check up on Allison."

"—and she said if I had any plans to be in Amsterdam of course I'd want to see both of you. I told her I wanted very much to see you, so here I am. Are you free for dinner? I want you to meet someone."

"Actually not," said Patricia. "I have a date."

Allison shot her a look. "You didn't mention that earlier."

"You'll come, won't you, Allison?" Paul asked.

"Yes, if I can bring someone. Whom do you want me to meet?"

"Emily Kent. She found me in Rome about six weeks ago. I knew her years ago in Boston; you might have met her."

"I've heard the name." She tilted her head. "Is it serious?"

"I don't know. It's too soon to tell."

"Where is she?"

"Upstairs in our room, changing. She seems to do a lot of that. Who's *your* friend?"

"Ben Gardner." She turned and looked across the lobby. "Damn, he's gone. That was rude of me; I ran off and forgot him. Do you mind having dinner with a stranger?"

"Not if you don't."

"Then you and Emily come to our suite at seven. We'll go to Excelsior—unless you don't want French?"

"That's fine; Emily will love it." He kissed her on both cheeks. "You look a lot happier than you did at home."

"I am a lot happier. Everything is wonderful. What about you?"

He shrugged. "Not wonderful." There was a pause. "Have you heard from Laura?"

"No."

"You don't even know where she is?"

"I don't want to know. I'll see you at seven."

We all act like betrayed lovers, Paul thought as he went to the elevator. But he wondered how else they could have acted. If only she'd trusted us and told us the truth; we all loved her enough—

Bullshit, he said silently as he reached his floor and walked to his room. How much would we have loved her if she'd told us she came to rob us, and then stayed on to get what she could from Owen?

Laura Fairchild wouldn't do that. Not the Laura Fairchild I knew.

And that was where his thoughts always stopped. Because Felix had proof. And Laura had admitted he was right. Which meant Paul Janssen, like everyone else in his family, had been made a fool of by a very clever actress. A very lovely, very loving actress, Paul thought, the pain like a fist in his stomach. He didn't want to believe it, but it always came back to that in the end.

"Hi," Emily said as he unlocked the door and walked in. She was sitting at a desk, her slender blond head silhouetted against the window. Paul's photographs of her, taken over the past month, were spread out on the desk and propped against the wall. There were almost forty of them, with Emily posing in evening dress, business suits, hiking clothes, and filmy nightgowns: professional poses, outdoors and in, with the ancient buildings, modern skyscrapers, mountain ranges, and deep forests of

Switzerland as backdrops for her cultivated beauty. Emily dropped the one she had been studying and stood up and they kissed lightly. "Guess who just telephoned."

"I can't imagine. Does anyone know we're in Amsterdam?"

"Barry Marken does. The luckiest chance: I saw his name on the guest register and called him this morning, and he just called back. We're having dinner with him tonight."

"I've already made plans for dinner with my cousin."

"Paul, we can see her anytime. Barry is leaving tomorrow."

"Am I supposed to know who he is?"

"He's your friend! Isn't he?" she asked with sudden nervousness. "You were the one who told me about him; I'm sure you've mentioned him at least twice, that's why I called him. And he was very polite. . . . Paul, he *is* your friend, isn't he? The publisher of *Eye*? He owns the Marken Agency."

"I remember. We've met a few times in New York. He's an acquaintance, not a friend."

"I shouldn't have called him." Her voice was anguished. "It wasn't proper."

"I wouldn't worry about it; he obviously wasn't insulted since he made a dinner date. But why don't we invite him up here for a drink? You want him to look at these photographs, and he won't do that at a dinner table."

"No, but I want more than a working relationship with him; I want a proper friendship. It's not enough for him to think of me as a fabulous model and you as a brilliant photographer."

Amused, Paul said, "He could think of us in worse ways." Then he shrugged. "All right, I'll call Allison; we'll make it another night."

"Thank you, darling." She smiled at him and, as he made his telephone call, he acknowledged her perfection. There were no flaws in Emily Kent. The only child of a wealthy, adoring, old Boston family, she had everything. She had few friends, which Paul found puzzling, and had not married, though she had been linked to several prominent men in Boston and New York, but her singleness could be exclusivity: a trait she cultivated. Like Paul, she was almost thirty, though her beauty was such that it was impossible to guess her age: neither the sun nor laughter nor worry had left traces on her alabaster skin, rounded cheeks or small moist mouth. She had perfected a slight tilt to her head that kept her sleek blond hair partially over one eye: a racy look that seemed at odds with the ingenuous, slightly startled expression in her light blue eyes. It was that contrast that Paul had highlighted in his photographs of her.

For years her hobby had been modeling in benefit fashion shows. After her twenty-seventh birthday, when no one acceptable had offered to be her husband, she began to take modeling seriously, and so a hobby became a career.

"We'll have a drink with them," Paul said, hanging up the telephone. "Allison's friend is going out of town tomorrow, and she's anxious for us to meet him."

"Who is he?"

"Ben Gardner."

"From where?"

"She didn't say. Five-thirty for drinks. What time are we meeting your friend Market?"

"Mar*ken*, darling. And he's our friend—or he soon will be. Seven o'clock. Where are we having drinks?"

"Here in the lounge."

"Good, I can change for dinner after we shop." She pulled on her rain hat. "Paul, I don't mean to criticize, but you won't forget Barry's name again, will you? Especially in front of him? It's not flattering to do it with anyone, but Barry can be so enormously helpful to me. And to you, too. That is what you want, isn't it?"

"It's more important that he help you, if he can." He was silent as they took a taxi to Beethovenstraat, where Emily had heard of a new shop. He wasn't sure what he wanted. That was the heart of everything: he didn't know and didn't much care. Nothing tantalized him; nothing aroused his passion, either for work or for play. It was as if something inside him refused to make any connection with the rest of the world, because he'd been hurt—and because he had inflicted hurt.

In the satin-draped Valois boutique Emily tried on hats while Paul watched. Sprawled in an armchair nearby, he saw her image in the triple mirror: full face and two perfect profiles, like framed pictures, and automatically his fingers curved as if he were picking up his camera. Making a circle of his thumb and forefinger, he held it up to frame Emily's triple image. She smiled at him in the mirror, knowing what he was doing. "What a shame you didn't bring your camera; you don't often get three of me at one time."

He lowered his hand. "I'd like to try some new pictures of you."

"Of course, darling. Anytime."

She was the perfect model, he reflected. She would stand or sit for hours in whatever pose she was given, because that was where she was happiest: at the center of someone's view, or viewfinder. She hadn't even asked what would be new about the pictures; all that was important was being photographed. But to Paul, the challenge of photographing triple-mirrored Emily to show simultaneous images of perfection brought a spark of interest that he knew would cut through his restlessness and boredom, at least for a while.

"Do you want me to wait while you get your camera?" she asked.

"No, we can come back tomorrow." He looked at his watch. "I want to buy a gift for Allison."

"Is it her birthday?"

He was amused. "I don't think so. I want to buy her something because I love her and I'm glad to see her."

"How erratic that sounds. Gifts are for special days."

"This is one," he said shortly. He waited while Emily paid for her hats and gave instructions for them to be delivered to the hotel.

"You're not angry with me, are you?" she asked as they ducked through the rain into the waiting taxi. "I didn't mean to criticize you."

"You can criticize me whenever you like; it's not forbidden. And I'm not angry."

She moved close to him on the back seat and took his hand, and began to talk about changes in Amsterdam since she was last there. In a minute they were laughing together and his irritation was forgotten.

Paul knew he had to guard against the seductiveness of Emily's pliancy. He wanted companionship, not servility, yet he could not deny how soothing it was to be with a woman who enveloped him in agreement, flattery, and deference. It was like a drug, he thought; a man could become addicted to being stroked.

That was the sort of thing Allison scorned. He saw it a few minutes after they sat down at a table in the Salinger lounge. The din was tremendous, conversations in a dozen languages shouted by men and women wearing wildly dramatic designer fashions from Milan and Paris. Allison ignored them all; she was talking to Emily. "You don't ever disagree with Paul?" she asked in exaggerated surprise. "Isn't that awfully dull?"

"Paul is never dull," Emily said seriously. "And there are ways he can be . . . convinced."

Allison gave her a sharp look, and Emily told herself to be more careful; after all, this was Paul's favorite cousin.

"Where's your friend?" Paul asked. "And Patricia?"

"Patricia decided not to come. Ben should be here; he must have been delayed."

She was wearing a long sleeveless dress, in black, with diamonds at her ears and throat. Paul admired her angular beauty; it almost dimmed Emily's soft roundness. "Ben Gardner," he said thoughtfully. "American? British? What's he doing in Amsterdam?"

"American. He works here."

"In Amsterdam?"

"In the hotel. He's the director of security."

Her color was high; she was waiting for him to make a comment. But he did not, and neither did Emily after a swift glance told her Paul would not be pleased if she said what she thought about a Salinger socializing with an employee.

Allison stood abruptly as a tall man made his way to them. "Ben," she said, her voice a little higher than usual. "My cousin Paul Janssen. And Emily Kent. Ben Gardner."

They shook hands. The two men were the same height and had similar lean, muscular builds, but in all other ways they were different: Ben very fair, with blond hair and blue, heavy-lidded eyes behind horn-rimmed glasses; Paul very dark, his black hair thick and unruly, his black eyes deep-set and intense, his hands thin and restless. "I'm glad to meet you," Ben said, wondering about him. Paul Janssen. What did Laura think of him—and he of Laura? "Allison told me about you but I didn't know you were in Europe."

"My fault, I'm afraid. I've lost touch with a lot of people. Have you lived here long?"

"Two years in Amsterdam, five in Europe."

"A long time to be away from home."

"For you, too."

Paul shrugged. "I've always traveled. Where did you live before you came to Europe?"

"New York. Allison says your home is Boston."

"It was. I'm not sure where I'll go from here. It might be New York. Will you be going back there?"

"I don't know."

"What about your family?"

Ben spread his hands.

"He hasn't any," Allison said. "I can't imagine what that would be like."

"It wasn't large to begin with," said Ben. "Then some of them died and others . . . vanished."

"That's very dramatic," Paul said with a smile.

"It was. We had some stormy times."

"And so you came to Europe."

Ben nodded. "And you? Did you leave because of family storms?"

"I told Ben something about us," Allison said to Paul, almost apologetically. "But not about you and . . . Not much about you. If you want to tell about yourself, it's up to you."

"I'd like to hear it," Ben said.

Paul shook his head. "Past history. It's not something I talk about. I'd like to hear about yours, though; it's not often an entire family disappears because of a . . . was it a quarrel?"

"Betrayal," Ben said, and saw the quick look of surprise, and then despair, that shadowed Paul's eyes. "The same thing that happened in your family."

"Maybe it's a trend," Allison said with a nervous laugh.

"I hope not," Ben said somberly.

Paul found himself drawn to him. He was a little too curious about their family, but he could be forgiven that by anyone who saw the intensity of his eyes when he looked at Allison. He had a kind of boldness that Paul admired, as if he were taking the measure of a world he intended to conquer, but there also was something of the searcher in him, looking for things lost or not yet attained. That was probably what drew Allison to him, Paul reflected. He hoped she wasn't rushing into yet another project to make someone's life better, but he thought it likely that she was. And for that reason, and because he already liked Ben Gardner, he wanted to know him better.

"Can we have lunch one day?" he asked. "Can you take time from the hotel?"

"I could, but I'm going to London tomorrow for two weeks."

"Damn. We're not staying that long."

"Well, next time you're in Amsterdam—"

"Oh, Paul, stay here longer," Allison said. "What else do you have to do?"

"Paul wants to work," Emily said. "We both want to work."

"Work? Paul? Since when?" Allison saw Paul's quick frown. "I'm sorry, have you reformed?"

"I'm thinking about it," he said mildly, and looked at Ben. "How often do you visit the States?"

"Now and then; not often. But I think that may change."

"If it does, look me up." He took out a business card. "This is my answering service in Boston; they'll know where I am."

Ben took out his own card. "If you get back to Amsterdam first." They smiled, liking each other, and Paul and Emily stayed longer than they had planned, the four of them talking of Europe, drinking wine, nibbling on Dutch cheese and crackers, until Emily said firmly, "Paul, we're expected," and they all rose and made their farewells.

Outside the hotel, Paul and Emily took a taxi, and Ben and Allison walked along the Rokin, their hands clasped between them. The rain had stopped and the air was fresh and chill. "You didn't tell them you're joining me in a few days in London," Ben said.

"There's time. I could tell that Paul thinks I'm rushing into something."

"And are you?"

"Possibly. I have something to tell you."

He felt a moment of alarm and stopped walking. "Has something happened?"

"You mean something bad? Of course not. You do that a lot, Ben; think about bad things happening. I want you to think of happy things." She took a breath. "I rented an apartment today."

His look sharpened. "*You rented—*"

"On the Prinsengracht. Very pretty and very small, but big enough for the two of us to get to know each other much, much better."

He was smiling; the smile broadened. "An American woman. You take things in your own hands."

"Is that all right?"

"It's wonderful. I've lived in Europe so long I've forgotten how wonderful it is. But what about Patricia?"

"She's going to Paris. She says six weeks is more than enough for Amsterdam. I don't agree."

Ben put his hand beneath her chin and searched her eyes. "This isn't a whim? This is something you really want?"

To herself, Allison said, *You're* what I really want. Aloud, she said lightly, "Maybe it is a whim. But if it is, we ought to enjoy it while it lasts."

His look held for a minute. "I'd like to buy you something," he said. "I've wanted to for some time. Let's do it now, before dinner."

"I don't want anything," she protested. "Just for us to have more time together."

"You've taken care of that. Let me take care of this." He took her arm in a decisive grip, walking briskly down the Rokin.

"Ben, nothing is open now."

"They close in fifteen minutes. If we hurry we can make it."

"Who closes?"

He only smiled and walked faster, and in a few minutes Allison found herself beneath the huge marble arched entrance to the Amsterdam Diamond Center. Some of the cutters were already going home, but the managing director greeted Ben with a warm handshake.

"May I present Miss Salinger," Ben said. "Allison, this is Claus Cuyper. Are we too late to buy something for Miss Salinger, Claus?"

"As long as you do not want the guided tour there is time."

"Good. Allison, do you want to choose?"

She shook her head. She was uncomfortable. From the moment she had told Ben about the apartment, everything had speeded up, and under Ben's direction, not hers. She didn't know if she wanted a diamond from Ben—at least she didn't know if she wanted one yet; she wanted to think about it. But she couldn't embarrass him in front of Claus Cuyper. "I'll watch the cutters," she murmured, and drifted off, leaving the two men to confer in private.

In the blindingly lit room, smocked men and women sat in armless secretary's chairs at long tables, cutting and polishing the diamonds that had been classified by examiners for weight and color and the way they would be cut. Allison watched some of the workers sawing the carats, others shaping the sawed gem by hand, and others polishing its facets.

"I hope you'll wear it," Ben said, breaking her reverie. "Claus had one already set and it was what I had in mind." He opened her hand and put the small piece on her palm. It looked like a Crystal, faintly tinted white, less than a carat, and nestled in a silver filigree as airy as lace.

"It's lovely," she said softly. And she knew she could not refuse it. It was modest, in perfect taste, and it was a pendant, not a ring. It was the gift of a good friend who had every reason to believe he would become a much closer friend. And it was the gift of a man who was happy. He is happy, Allison thought. Much happier than when we met. I've done that for him already. She fastened the silver chain around her neck. "Thank you. I'll probably wear it so often you'll get tired of seeing it."

"By then I'll have bought you another." He took her face between his hands and kissed her, briefly, because he was not a public person. "I love you, Allison," he said.

* * *

Carolers sang outside the Manhattan office of the fashion editor of *Eye* magazine, and in his reception room a polystyrene Christmas tree was hung with dozens of papier-mâché eyes, pupils gleaming red, green, and white from tiny light bulbs tucked inside. Emily had glanced at them once, seen that they were in dreadful taste, and looked the other way.

"Barry wanted me to come directly to you," she said to the fashion editor, who had been Jock Flynn in Little Italy but, on moving uptown to Rockefeller Center, had become Jason d'Or. "He said he wouldn't dare impose his wishes on you."

"He also told you not to tell me he said that," Jason said with a tight smile; his voice vibrated with a thin whine. "But you decided to because you thought it would establish a camaraderie between us."

Emily was silent. He was right, but he was in as bad taste as his reception room.

"Well, let's see what you have." His voice had turned brisk. "Barry doesn't send people to me with his bad jokes unless he's truly impressed." He opened the leather portfolio Emily had insisted on bringing over herself, even though Barry had told her it should come from his agency and she should stay home.

"I can't stay home," she had protested. "I do best with the personal touch. Look how well I did with you in Amsterdam."

"Your friend Paul's photographs did well with me in Amsterdam," he had growled. He wanted to sleep with her but she stayed faithful to Paul, even though they were only living together. "The personal touch had nothing to do with it."

"You can't be sure. You were influenced by me. And Jason d'Or—my God, what a name—will be, too."

"Don't tell him you don't like his name. Or his Christmas tree."

"What's wrong with his tree?"

"You'll see."

Jason finished the portfolio and went back to the beginning, turning the pages slowly. "You're fortunate in your photographer," he said at last. "He's damned good."

"The photographs or the model?" Emily asked before she could stop herself.

"Both. There's a nice ingenuousness here, as if you're only pretending to be sophisticated."

"Or vice versa," she said gaily.

He shrugged. "I assume Barry told you we have models we call on regularly."

"He told me you're always looking for new faces."

"So we can call on them when the need arises."

Emily waited. "And when will that be?" she asked, struggling to hide her growing anger.

"I have no idea." He closed her portfolio. "At the moment we're working on the May issue; I can't say what we'll need for June. We might be calling you." He opened the door to the reception room and stood there, holding it for her.

Stiffly, Emily picked up the portfolio. "Thank you for your time." She was properly correct, but inside she seethed.

"How dare he?" she raged to Paul when she returned to his apartment where she had been living since they came to New York from Europe. "Barry recommended me; I didn't come begging. And I'm a Kent from

Boston, not just somebody who walked in off the street. Who does he think he is, treating me like that?"

Paul was holding a match to the fire; when the flames leaped up he pulled shut the glass fire doors and put his arms around her. Reluctantly, she kissed him. "Did you hear me?" she asked.

"I did." He moved away. "A drink might help." At the small bar tucked into an alcove, he mixed two martinis. "Now come and sit down. It sounds as if you walked into the middle of a battlefield."

"What does that mean?"

"Your old friend Barry and your new friend Jason may be at war over who makes decisions, and Jason didn't appreciate Barry's sending you to walk in on him, instead of following the usual procedures."

"What usual procedures?" But she knew, and it showed in her face.

"Barry told you the agency should send over your portfolio."

Her mouth was stubborn. "With civilized people a personal approach is infinitely superior."

"You may be right. But he did warn you. Are they lovers?"

"I doubt it. Barry wants me."

"Does he? What a sensible fellow."

She laughed, feeling better. "He can't compare with you and he knows it, or at least he knows I know it. May I have another drink?"

He went to the bar. "I made reservations for dinner at Le Cirque."

"Impossible. You would have had to call three weeks ago."

"Two weeks."

"You really did? Is it an occasion?"

"Your birthday next week. Christmas three days after that. Do we need any more?"

"You might have wanted to ask me to marry you. Sorry," she added quickly. "That was as much in bad taste as Jason d'Or."

"You're never in bad taste, my dear," Paul said quietly.

Emily was silent and he stood at the bar, watching her as she gazed at the flames. She sat on a dark suede couch in the paneled library he had hung with Audubon prints and three of his portraits of Owen. A Bokhara in taupe and black was on the floor; the shelves were filled with leather-bound books. In that dark room, illuminated only by the fire, Emily's fair beauty seemed to shimmer in its own halo. But as Paul contemplated her, her features subtly changed in the shadows thrown by the dancing flames, and he saw the other faces behind the public face of Emily Kent.

Her anger was still visible in the tight corners of her mouth, but then it seemed to become willfulness, then arrogance, then, as swiftly, doubt. It was as if he were looking at a map of her emotions. He stepped back, increasing his distance and angle from the couch, and her face changed again, first calculating, then promising passion. And, as a log fell, sending sparks against the glass fire doors, he thought he saw sadness.

And in that instant, Emily's face became Laura's, the corners of her mouth curved in sorrow.

Shaken, enraged, Paul flung his glass across the room where it shattered on the stone hearth. Emily cried out but he barely heard it. God damn it, a year and a half and he couldn't get her out of his mind. Every affair had an end; theirs was over. What the hell was wrong with him that he couldn't go on to other women without seeing her wherever he turned?

"Paul!" Emily was staring at him, and Laura's face vanished. "What in heaven's name is wrong? This isn't like you."

"Breaking glasses or thinking of something besides you?" he asked brutally. When she winced, he went to her, handing her her drink as he sat down. "I'm sorry. But you'll notice I threw my own, not yours. So I really was thinking of you, even in my most uncivilized moment."

"What were you thinking of besides me?"

"An old friend. And taking photographs."

"Of me?"

He never had to fear, Paul realized, that Emily would probe very deeply into his thoughts; she was too absorbed in herself. In a way, it was refreshing: she could never be accused of pretending to be something she wasn't. "Of course of you," he said. "My favorite model."

"And companion."

"Yes." He was thoughtful. "That's true." Abruptly, he stood. "Let's have dinner."

"What time are our reservations?"

He had forgotten them. "Eight, but I feel like walking."

"What a good idea." She jumped up. "I'll get my boots; it was snowing when I came in."

Paul smiled as he watched her leave the room. He knew she didn't want to walk from Sutton Place to the Mayfair Regent, especially in December, especially in the snow. But part of Emily's charm and skill was perfect intuition. When she put her mind to it, she knew exactly which of his moods and desires was important enough to outweigh her immediate comfort. And Paul, knowing how rare that was, appreciated it and was grateful for it.

They walked along the river and turned the corner at Fifty-seventh Street. Emily's face was outlined in fur, her fur-lined boots left small prints in the snow that drifted silently past streetlights and Christmas trees in apartment windows. The buildings all seemed to duplicate Paul's—closed-face high-rises, each with its own gold-braided doorman and glimpses of private lives through draped windows. He had bought his apartment years before, and the one-bedroom apartment adjoining it, as well, converting it to a studio and darkroom. After outfitting it, he seldom used it, but he lived in the apartment when he was in New York and loaned it to friends at other times. He and Emily had been living there for a month, and for the first time Paul was using the darkroom every day.

They had traveled together in Europe, Africa, and India for a month after leaving Amsterdam, and Paul had taken hundreds of photographs, mostly of Emily. For the first time he had used scenery, indoor settings, and other people as contrasts to her ingenuousness and sophistication, which he captured in a series of brilliant photographs—and he had felt a rush of pride when Emily told him Jason had seen it. He isn't as much a fool as she says, Paul thought wryly, if he understands what I was trying to do in those photos. And the sensual pleasure he felt in working, and the ability to lose himself in it, had lasted through most of that time.

Over the years his desire to work at photography had flared and died, like the flames of his fireplace, always giving way when his restlessness returned or his motivation disappeared: the children building the sand castle went home and did not return; Laura was gone; Owen was dead; his college friends, whom he had photographed at play and at their studies, had scattered. Now, walking beside Emily on the quiet street, glancing at her shadowed features, he thought of the many moods he had seen in the firelight of his study, and suddenly he felt a hunger to be better than he had ever tried to be, to take photography beyond the narrow boundaries he had lazily explored all these years when he was content to be little more than a dilettante.

He wanted to show what was behind the public facade of people and events; he wanted to photograph secrets: the faces behind each face, the scenes behind each scene. He wanted to make photographs in which people could find themselves and understand something new about themselves and their worlds.

For the first time, Paul wanted to do more than satisfy himself. He wanted to reach others. And he wanted it with a passion that would have delighted Owen Salinger.

Emily turned up Third Avenue and he followed, content to let her linger when something in a shop window caught her eye. The street was brightly lit and crowded; a solid stream of traffic moved in honking fits and starts, and the sidewalks on both sides were lined with attractions ranging from hot dog stands to movie theaters, yuppie bars to Bloomingdale's. In some small shops wreath-hung doors swung open as Christmas shoppers and tourists came and went, and outside the bars, well-groomed young professionals talked of the evening's entertainment. In silence, Paul walked absently beside Emily; window-shopping bored him, and he paid more attention to the crowds, the sidewalk peddlers, and the bell-ringing Santa Clauses and trombone-playing Salvation Army troops on the corners.

They turned up Sixty-third, where it was again quiet, the rows of solemn brownstones like a gathering of old Boston families shutting out the clamorous world, and soon reached Park Avenue. Emily was talking about antique picture frames when they came to the Mayfair Regent and Paul stopped short.

Leni Salinger was walking out of the hotel, smiling up at a very young man who was holding her arm.

They all saw each other at the same time. "Well, Paul," Leni said brightly, and Paul realized this was the first time he had even seen her flustered. "And Emily. Strolling in a snowstorm, how charming, somehow I didn't expect to see anyone . . . anyone walking on a night like this, though it isn't cold, of course, just . . . Oh, I'm so sorry. Tor Grant, Paul Janssen, Emily Kent." In the brief interval as the men shook hands she regained some of her poise. "I'm quite late or we might have had a drink together. Are you on your way to dinner?"

"Le Cirque," Paul said.

"Well, we mustn't keep you. Perhaps we'll have a drink another time. I'm in town fairly often; we're looking for an apartment."

Involuntarily Paul's eyes moved to the young man's face.

"Felix and I," Leni said evenly. "We've talked about a place in New York for a long time. It does seem a slow process, though; how wise you were, Paul, to buy your apartment when you did. I'll call you one day and we'll have tea or drinks. Emily, how nice to see you; have a pleasant evening. Paul dear"—she reached up and kissed his cheek—"I'll call you soon. Tor?"

Once again the men shook hands. "Ridiculous custom," Paul muttered as Leni and the young man walked away. "Why do I shake hands twice with a man I don't know and have not exchanged one word with and, if my aunt has anything to say about it, will never see again?"

"She's a little old for him," Emily said carefully.

Paul gave a short laugh. "He's a little young for her."

"I don't understand."

"He's besotted. Did you see the way he looked at her? I didn't know Leni was finding other men, though God knows she deserves them, but she needs someone who can match her in sophistication and brains, not some poor kid who's having the sexual adventure of his life."

"How can you know all that? You saw them for two minutes."

The scenes behind each scene. "That was my feeling."

They walked the few steps to an unobtrusive door beside the hotel entrance and went into the restaurant. "Poor Leni," Emily said suddenly. "I think it's very sad."

Paul gave her a quick look. "Why is it sad?"

She took off her boots and handed them to an attendant, and slipped on her evening shoes. "Because she should have what she wants; not what she can get. Nobody should have to settle for that."

"But if she has no choice?"

"Well, we don't know that, do we? Anyway, if women wait long enough, their dreams come true. I believe that."

The maitre d' greeted Paul by name and led them to their table. "You mean," Paul said, "they make them come true."

She shook her head. "There's no need to be masculine and aggressive; the proper way for a woman to behave is to wait and to believe that everything she wants will come to her. Of course she has to be smart enough to recognize what it is she has in the palm of her hand, and sometimes she has to help things along once they've begun, but mostly it's waiting and watching."

Paul thought of Laura, and wondered what she was doing. Whatever it was, he knew she would not be waiting. She would be making things happen.

But Emily had a point, he thought. After all, she'd waited in Rome until he found her; she'd waited until he was ready to photograph her, and she accepted his decisions on the kinds of photographs to take; and, largely because of him, she might be on the brink of a modeling career with *Eye* magazine and the Marken Agency.

Then he had another thought that made him smile.

"What?" she asked.

"I was wondering if you think I'm in the palm of your hand."

She flushed. "I'd rather have you in my heart."

"Well done," he murmured. The captain brought a bottle of Dom Perignon and Paul watched absently as he opened it. "I'm going to invite Leni to tea," he said.

"Do you want me there?"

"I don't think so." He looked at her thoughtfully. In pale blue silk, wearing a sapphire necklace he had bought her in Paris, she was perfectly at home in the sybaritic luxury of the room. Self-absorbed, and willful, she still could show that instinctive sympathy for others that made her even more desirable than her pliancy and charm. She was especially desirable at that moment, as Paul reflected on the image of his aunt leaving a New York hotel. Emily was right: there was an awful sadness about it, and also, Paul knew, the cruelty of long, lonely days, perhaps years, of waiting for something better, something good, something right. "But I'll tell you what I do want." He reached across the table and took Emily's hand. "I want you to marry me," he said.

CHAPTER 17

THE Ninety-Fifth restaurant hovers over Chicago like a great eagle, ninety-five stories above the city at the top of the sloping John Hancock Center. From that lofty perch the lights of the city, orange and garish from the ground, become amber garlands laced together in grids and long diagonal strokes that stretch from the horizon to the dark, restless waters of Lake Michigan. And it was at the top of the Hancock that Wes Currier hosted cocktails and dinner for two hundred to celebrate the New Year and, more importantly, the purchase of the Chicago Salinger by the OWL Development Corporation.

The name was Laura's idea. Currier had objected. "It sounds like a joke, and that's a red flag to bankers when you come to them for financing. You want something serious and conservative and faintly dull."

"I like it," Laura said firmly. "Especially because it is a joke, my joke, and it's important to me."

Currier contemplated her. "OW from Owen," he said after a moment. "And L from Laura. I can see why you like it, but this isn't a time for games; the stakes are too big."

"Please, Wes," she said. "Symbols are important to me. I'd like to keep this one." And so the name stayed.

Once he accepted OWL Development, Currier helped Laura through the legal steps that made the company a corporation, and then he arranged the financing for the purchase of the hotel by investing nine million dollars.

The money was divided. Currier bought fifty percent of the equity in the hotel with four and a half million dollars, loaning Laura another four and a half million to buy the other fifty percent. Their investments also gave each of them fifty percent of OWL Development Corporation. So Laura's first debt was to Currier, for four and a half million dollars.

Currier arranged his travels so that once Laura moved to Chicago he was frequently with her, involved with every step of her work. They had spent two weekends in New York after their first one, and then Laura began traveling between Chicago and Darnton's, where she was helping Kelly and John train a new assistant manager. Currier and Laura had hired an architect, and when she was in Chicago she worked with him on drawing blueprints for the renovation of the hotel from the detailed plans she and Owen had worked on together. And then Currier and Laura took the blueprints to a banker he knew well, who approved the mortgage and construction loans for the purchase and renovation of the Chicago Salinger by the OWL Development Corporation. So Laura's second debt was to the bank, for twenty million dollars.

Once the money became available, Currier had his assistant take over the negotiations to purchase the hotel so Laura's name would be kept out of it.

It was well known that Felix had been seeking a buyer for the hotel since early summer, even before the court case over his father's will was settled. But two potential purchasers had bought other buildings, and by late fall he was angry at his Realtor, short with his banker, and impatient with what he called the dead Chicago real estate market; that was well known, too. And so, when Currier's assistant negotiated with Felix's Chicago Realtor, he was able to buy the Chicago Salinger for nine million dollars rather than the ten Currier had thought it would cost, with immediate possession; the building had been empty since Felix closed it six months earlier.

Laura's name did not appear in any of the negotiations, nor on the purchase documents. Her Chicago lawyer represented her at the meetings with Felix's Chicago lawyer, everything was done in the name of OWL Development, and when Currier introduced her to Chicago financiers, he told them she was the manager of OWL Development's hotel. She knew that Felix would find out eventually who owned the corporation, but for now it was a secret. And she intended to keep it a secret for as long as possible, while she tried to think of ways to get control of Owen's other hotels.

"You understand the name of the hotel must be changed," Felix's attorney told Laura's attorney as they signed dozens of documents for their respective employers. "OWL Development cannot use the Salinger name at any time."

"We have no intention of doing so," he replied.

"And what will the new name be?" Felix's lawyer asked idly.

"It hasn't been chosen yet."

It had been chosen, but only Currier and Laura knew it. From the beginning, she had known it would be called The Beacon Hill. And every hotel she managed to buy, from then on, would be given the same name. The only difference among them would be the name of the city.

So, on Currier's orders, the chef of the Ninety-Fifth baked a cake for dessert on New Year's Eve in the shape of the old Chicago Salinger, with *Chicago Beacon Hill* lettered on the marquee in gold, and an owl perched protectively on the roof. The cake stood on a table in the foyer; it was the first thing guests saw when they arrived at ten o'clock. Men in black tie and sleek women with gems sparkling at their throats and ears hovered over the square, white-icinged edifice like children at a toy-store window, and they had to tear themselves away to greet their host who stood with Laura and Clay at the entrance to the dining room.

Clay was whispering to Laura. "The owl was my idea, but that's just between us. Wes thought up the gold letters. He thinks of gold at the drop of a hat."

"It's very sweet," Laura murmured while waiting for another stranger to come forward to be introduced. "Thank you, Clay."

"A small gesture," he responded modestly. "Since I'm going to be the assistant manager of the very posh Chicago Beacon Hill, I have to keep my boss happy." He caught Myrna's eye across the room and winked at her. He was feeling very good.

"Laura, may I present—" Currier said, introducing her to one of his Chicago friends as the manager of the future Chicago Beacon Hill, and Laura shook hands and smiled.

"Lovely, my dear. Exquisite," the guest said, holding her hand in his and peering up into her face. "You, too, Wes; you look fine. Wish I looked as spiffy as you in black tie, instead of like a dead cockatoo with the color washed out. You really carry it off. I like your lady. I do like your lady." He tilted his head, appraising her, and Currier, for a moment, saw Laura through the other man's eyes.

She looked lovelier than at any time in the six months he had known her, not quite as thin, though still thinner than he preferred, and her face more lively, though too often still reserved, even distant, when what he wanted to see there was pleasure, delight, laughter—and love. She wore a close-fitting dress of white satin, long-sleeved, the neckline plunging in a deep V, with a necklace of irregularly-shaped amethysts, and, at the point of the neckline, a pin that was a single iris carved of blue-violet opal with a center of gold. Currier had given enough jewelry to his women to know a good piece when he saw one, and Laura's pin was very fine. He had not asked about it—it was a rule of his never to ask where a woman's jewelry came from—but Laura had told him Owen had given it to her. As a gift, it could not be compared with the inheritance he had left her, but because it was more intimate it made clear to Currier, more than anything else, the depth of Owen Salinger's love.

He put his arm around Laura's waist with a proprietary gesture that no one could miss. And when Laura leaned back slightly against him he felt the swell of pride and possession that he had not felt for a woman for a long time. He wanted to give her everything, do everything for her, take every burden from her and solve every dilemma so she had nothing to do but lean against him and shed, forever, the guarded look that froze her features and kept her just this side of true beauty.

"Well, now, Wes." The guest, seeing Currier's arm around Laura's waist, finally relinquished her hand. "Good to see you again. You in town for long? How about lunch?"

They made their arrangements while Laura looked through the doorway at the wall of windows in the dining room. When the guest moved on, she said, "Would anyone mind if we took time out to look at the view?"

"It's your party; you do what you want. Anyway, I think everyone is here." His arm still around her, he led her into the dining room where groups of people stood among the tables set with crystal and silver-rimmed china, with a spray of hibiscus in the center of each, and individual flowers at the women's place settings. Most of the guests had congregated in the dimly lit Sybaris Lounge a few steps up from the main room, where a pianist played show tunes and two bartenders mixed drinks. But Laura was drawn to the windows, almost floor to ceiling, giving a panorama of orange street lights, blue office lights and white apartment lights, like a glittering toy city sharply sliced off along the side that was the black expanse of the lake.

"You're part of it now," Currier said. He was standing behind her, his hand just below her breast. "And you'll make it yours."

Laura leaned back as she had before, letting herself rest against his solid strength. He had none of Paul's lean, nervous, searching energy; almost twice Paul's age, and self-made, he was methodical and rock-like, self-directed and absolutely sure of himself.

And if he was sometimes too domineering for Laura's independence, too deliberate for her impatience, too predictable for her enjoyment of the complexities in people, he was a powerful friend, steady and trustworthy. And she knew nothing was more important or valuable in the long run, especially if she ever wanted someone to whom to cling.

He was even good for Clay, Laura thought, glancing across the room at her brother, who was lifting his champagne glass in a toast with Myrna. Currier had little tolerance for young people who did not meet his standards of maturity and responsibility, but because of her he was teaching Clay some of the mysteries of international banking and trade, and Clay, fascinated by the size of the deals if nothing else, was absorbing it all. And, for Laura, he was doing even more: he was studying.

For the first time Clay was willing to read a book, or a dozen books if that was what Laura wanted, and he even submitted when she quizzed him on what he read. He did most of the things she told him because she had promised him the assistant manager's job in the new hotel, but only if he could learn enough, fast enough, adding to what he had learned in Boston and Philadelphia and at Darnton's. So he read and studied and didn't mind it too much, partly because of the job and Laura's pride in him, but also—he had to admit it—because Myrna was really proud of him and kept telling him so. "I'll make you a tycoon yet," she exulted, and Clay didn't mind her taking the credit for his new job because as soon as she heard about it she became more passionate than ever.

For what was probably the first time ever, Clay wasn't envying anybody; he didn't feel he was just marking time until something bigger came along. I guess I'm happy, he thought.

Everyone is happy, Laura reflected, looking again at the lights of Chicago and listening to the piano music weaving through the conversations in the restaurant. Everyone is happy. In her mind she saw Owen's smile and felt the touch of his hand on her hair. *Dear Owen, this is your party; you should be here to see your dreams come true.*

"You're a long way off," Currier said, his lips close to her ear. "Tell me what you're thinking."

"About dreams," she replied. She put her hand on his, her fingers lying along his short, strong ones. "Owen's and mine."

"And mine," he said. "Don't shut me out, Laura."

"I won't."

But, still, it was Owen's dream, it had been theirs together, and she longed for him. She wished she could watch him move among the guests, towering over them, his mustache waving as he spoke, his eyes weighing everyone, memorizing their quirks and phrases so he and Laura could joke about the party later, as they had done so many times in Beacon Hill and at the Cape.

But that was another dream he had: to share his last years with some-one he loved and could teach, who would make his other dreams real after he was gone. He died believing that. I did that for him.

And so, at midnight, when Currier kissed her she smiled at him with an openness he had not seen before. "Happy New Year, Wes. With all the wonderful things we have to look forward to."

"Together," he added. "Everything. Together." And when they kissed again, he thought she understood he was talking about marriage.

Laura didn't realize it until late the next morning, the first day of the new year, as she woke slowly in her suite in Chicago's Mayfair Regent. Her eyes still closed, she reviewed the party in her mind. She felt again her flush of excitement as the guests toasted her and she stood alone beside the piano, a few steps above them, her white satin dress catching the light and glowing almost like a blue-white diamond. She saw again Clay watching Myrna with mesmerized eyes, the architect circulating among the guests talking with professional satisfaction about the brilliant hotel they would soon create, the investors who, even at a party, talked about cost per room and compared the Beacon Hill to other hotels recently renovated on Chicago's Gold Coast. And she remembered the New Year kiss she had shared with Currier, passionate and affectionate, with thoughts of the future. Together.

She opened her eyes. The first thing she saw was the lake, deep blue under a clear, cold January sky. The room was cool, and Laura stretched out in the warm bed, enveloped in the comfort of the room's muted colors and soft fabrics. Currier had rented the suite for a month so she could stay there while looking for a place to live. The rooms overlooked the deep curve of the Oak Street Beach and the Outer Drive, stretching north, one side bordered with beaches, parks, and the high waves of Lake Michigan, the other lined with a solid wall, miles long, of apartment buildings. Gazing at them from the elegance of her room, Laura thought of the Beacon Hill. She couldn't believe Currier assumed she would give it up to marry him. She moved restlessly. He must know she wouldn't. Which meant he thought they would be married and she would stay with the hotel. Well, why shouldn't she do that? Because he would want her to travel with him and, slowly, a trip at a time, she would lose touch with the hotel in Chicago and never get to the other three.

But that wasn't even the most important reason. I don't want to marry

Wes, she thought. I don't want to marry anyone. I have something to do that's more important than anything else, and I wouldn't marry anyone...

Not even Paul? If Paul came back, the warmth in his dark eyes embracing her, his deep voice saying, "I'll be one of those husbands who happily follows his wife from job to job..."?

She pulled herself up in a tight ball, to stop the pain that still struck her when she let herself remember. *I have to stop this. It's the first day of a new year, a time to turn to new ideas and new thoughts. A time to turn away from old ones.* But just the week before, she had finished reading a book that haunted her, especially one line, about a woman who cannot have the man she loves. "There would always be a little dry patch in her heart, hungry for the sweet summer rain of his voice." The words stayed with her; she recognized herself.

Well, then, there will be that dry patch, she thought. And Paul will be part of it. And everything I do from now on will circle around him because he will not leave.

Or perhaps I am holding him there because I want to believe that love endures, even a love that brings pain. Even a love that lives in a desert, and must be circumvented, because I have to make a new life.

A new life. A new year. New thoughts and feelings, new friendships and sex and work. She thought of the Beacon Hill and all she had to do. And, beyond it, the New York Salinger, the next one she intended to buy. And after that...

She stretched restlessly. Once again she was part of the present and thinking of the future. And she wanted to get started. She had so much to do, so many plans, so many steps to take to get back what Owen meant her to have.

Half-awake, Currier put his hand on her breast. "Too early to get up."

"It's getting late; almost five-thirty," she said slyly.

His eyes flew open. "You woke me at five-thirty on New Year's Day?"

"I wanted to ask your opinion about the new plumbing in the Beacon Hill bathrooms—"

"God damn it, Laura—" He saw her mischievous smile, and he laughed as he pulled her to him. "You had other kinds of plumbing in mind."

"I must have," she murmured and came to him with a passion that was as much a determination to live a new life as it was gratitude for his love and what he gave her. He knew how much she had to do, and he knew she wanted him to share it; he would understand why she couldn't marry him. He always understood. She was beginning to count on that.

"No work for you today," he said later as he stepped from the shower in his bathroom. "It's a holiday, and we're going for a walk."

"Where?" She was in the other bathroom, pulling on the heavy terry robe the hotel provided for the use of its guests. How many of these are stolen? she wondered. I'll have to ask the manager.

"Wherever real tourists go."

By day and night, the trees that lined north Michigan Avenue sparkled with festoons of tiny white Christmas lights. The stores were closed, but still there were crowds strolling past the glittering windows of Marshall Field's and Saks; gazing at the haughty mannequins in I. Magnin's and the jewelry at Tiffany's; photographing the old water tower, a survivor of the Chicago fire silhouetted against the modern gray marble of the Ritz-Carlton hotel; and riding in horse-drawn carriages driven by top-hatted, black-caped coachmen. Currier and Laura walked up the avenue to the river, bending against the wind that whipped their coats about their legs, then turned back. A block from the Mayfair Regent, though they were chilled, Laura turned east, to the empty building that had been the Chicago Salinger.

They stood in silence, contemplating it. "It's a lot more attractive with icing," Laura said with a small smile, thinking that few things are as sad as an empty building, brooding in the midst of a city's vibrant life. "But wait," she added. "In a year no one will recognize it."

"Not even the plumbing," Currier agreed, smiling. He put his arm around her. "Each time I see the plans I'm more impressed. Owen was a visionary. And so are you."

She shook her head. "I don't know enough to be one; this hotel will be Owen's vision. And my fantasies, brought to life."

He looked at her thoughtfully. "If you really do that, you'll be a brilliant success."

Laura hugged his words to her in the next weeks, as the plans were finished and bids were let and work was begun. In mid-January she rented an apartment in a graystone Victorian six flat in the DePaul area. Its windows looked across the street at other Victorians, and when the wind shifted she could hear the rumble of the elevated train two blocks west, but the apartment had large rooms with high ceilings and carved moldings, a real fireplace, and an extra bedroom for her office. Best of all, she liked the DePaul University neighborhood. The faculty lived there, and working couples, and the area was always alive with people whom she came to know: young families with small children in strollers, older children building snowmen, teenagers walking from the nearby high school beneath tall, winter-bare elms to sit on creaky swings on their front porches or temporarily take over their parents' living rooms. It was more like a small town than a city; in many ways it reminded Laura of

Beacon Hill in Boston and the small village of Osterville on Cape Cod. And when Clay and Myrna rented a two-room apartment less than a mile away, it became home.

"Why don't you like Myrna?" Clay demanded soon after they moved into their apartment. He and Laura were riding the bus along the lake to the hotel, and she had been scanning a list of suppliers she had appointments to see.

She tucked the list into her briefcase. "I do like her. I don't love her."

"Why not?"

"Do you?"

"What difference does that make? We're talking about you."

"Do you love her, Clay?"

"I'm living with her."

"Clay."

"Well, I probably do. I mean, it's hard, isn't it, to know whether you're in love with somebody or just excited about her? Are you in love with Wes?"

"No, but I like him, I like being with him, and we're working together, in a way. Do you like Myrna?"

"Sometimes. She pushes a lot, you know, and that's a pain in the ass, but she's fun to be with, and she lights up like a little kid when I buy her presents, and she gets *very* grateful—"

"You buy her a lot of presents, don't you?" Laura asked.

His voice grew wary. "Why shouldn't I?"

"You should, if that's what you want to do." She had meant to ask him where he got the money, but she changed her mind. She thought about it frequently, knowing what he had earned at Darnton's and what she was paying him through OWL Development, but he was twenty-three, and even though he often acted younger than his age, she couldn't press him with questions as if she were his mother or guardian. "But I don't hear much about any presents she buys you," she said.

"She doesn't have to buy me things. She knows how to make me happy. She really does care about me—and who else does, except you? I remember a long time ago Ben said he'd always take care of us, and I thought, so what's the big deal; when I grow up I won't need him. But you always need somebody, don't you?"

"Yes." The bus lurched to a stop in the heavy traffic, and Laura was thrown against him. "Especially somebody with a strong shoulder," she said with a smile.

"You heard from him lately?"

"No. I will, though. I always get a card on my birthday."

"That's next week. Does he know we're in Chicago?"

"I wrote to him about buying the hotel, and I sent him my address. And I told him you said hello."

"What for, damn it! I didn't tell you to do that."

She was silent.

"I don't want to have anything to do with him!"

"Then all these questions are a little odd," she observed.

"Well . . . shit." He shrugged. "You don't just forget somebody . . ." His voice trailed off.

"You don't forget your brother," said Laura. "No matter what he's done." The bus reached their corner, and they jumped up and pushed open the center doors to alight.

Each day, as they approached the hotel from Michigan Avenue, it looked new to Laura, as if it were being transformed, and more her own. In fact, except for the new windows that had been installed, the outside always looked the same; cleaning the bricks and limestone and putting in new doors and the marquee would come last. Now everything was happening inside, where walls had been torn down, and plumbing and electrical wiring were being relocated, to transform two hundred and fifty rooms into one hundred large bedroom–sitting rooms, thirty suites, and a penthouse suite with its own terrace. This day, as they walked the block from the bus stop, Clay exclaimed, "The marble's here!" and they stopped to look at the wrapped slabs that would line the walls of the bathrooms and form countertops and whirlpool tubs. All the marble was the same: a soft dove gray shot with dark green and blue; the fixtures would be white, the towels blue. Every room would have two bathrooms, but they would be identical—"so either a man or a woman will feel comfortable in them," Laura had told Christian DeLay, the president of the design firm she and Currier had hired. "I don't want one of them to be a pink and gold boudoir, and the other one to look like it belongs to the Chicago Patriots football team."

"Chicago Bears," DeLay corrected her scornfully.

"Bears," she repeated thoughtfully. "I'll remember that. I've been living in New England, and I got used to the Patriots. Perhaps you'll tell me other things about Chicago, too, so I won't feel like an outsider."

He resisted her smile. She *was* an outsider, and she was making too many design decisions on her own, instead of deferring gratefully to his expert advice. "Many people don't like blue towels," he said, returning to the subject of the bathrooms. "They think only white looks clean."

"But I talked to the salespeople at Marshall Field's," Laura said, "and they told me they sell more towels and sheets in colors than in white, so that must be what people like."

"In their homes, perhaps. Not in their hotels."

"But this isn't their hotel. It's mine. And I think blue will do very well."

He frowned, breathing annoyance, thinking someone should have taken a strap to this young woman when she was young. "Just as you like," he said.

Laura gestured to one of the straight chairs in her temporary office. "Would you sit down for a moment? And tell me something. You own your design firm, is that right?"

Still standing, he nodded stiffly. "And Mr. Currier recognized our excellence by bringing us into this job—"

"Mr. Currier and I made that decision together." Her voice was gentle. "I'm trying to make a point. You own your company and you're proud of it, and you don't like others telling you how to do your job."

"Exactly. My point exactly."

"And mine," Laura said even more softly. "I've never owned anything in my life, you see, until now. And I'm so proud of this hotel, and so excited about what we can do to make it perfect, that I want to be part of everything in it. I care about all the decisions, from toilet paper and towels to carpets and the concierge's desk." She smiled, a little wistfully. "I can't help it; it's a dream come true for me and I'm afraid of missing any of it. But I do need your help. I want to learn; otherwise I can't really be part of everything, and it won't be like a dream at all. . . ."

DeLay melted. He sat down. He smiled.

"And also," Laura added, "I plan to buy three more hotels in other cities. If we work well together, I see no reason why you shouldn't design all of them."

He sat straighter. What a pleasure it was to do business with her. "Perhaps we might begin with upholstery samples," he said. "There is a wide selection."

Laura gave him a smile he remembered the rest of his life, and his answering smile was still warm on his face as he spread large squares of fabric on the desk and a worktable standing at a right angle to it. Decisively, Laura rejected twenty of them. "What I have in mind is the same thing I said about the bathrooms: I want to stay away from stereotypes of masculine or feminine. If we could combine them in some way—very bright, very bold, and comfortable for both men and women so everyone will feel at home . . ."

He nodded sagely. "An interesting idea. Something neutral, then, like this one, simple gray and blue."

"Perfect for soldiers in the Civil War," Laura said with a smile. She took scissors and a box of crayons from her desk. "May I cut these samples into pieces?" Without waiting for an answer, she began to cut the fabric into strips. "If we could put some patterns together..."

In the end, the carpets were custom-made by Couristan in silver gray with an overall pattern of violet and gold fleurs-de-lis, similar to an iris but not floral, and DeLay sent the same design to Essex to be made into matching draperies. From then on, each morning, he appeared in the old manager's office Laura was using until it fell to the workers' sledgehammers, and the two of them reviewed samples, met with suppliers, and made hundreds of decisions, large and small, that determined the furnishings, the design of each room, the look of the lobby and restaurant, and the decor of the tea lounge a few steps up from the lobby. With DeLay's advice, Laura chose Henredon furniture upholstered in a lustrous, tightly woven fabric of silk and wool in solid colors of blue violet, white, old gold, and dark green—the colors of the iris. The other furnishings were antiques brought in by dealers who spent hours with Laura and DeLay, and then hours more alone with Laura, bargaining on prices.

Other representatives came from Hermès, Clinique, Sebastian, and half a dozen other companies to woo her so she would choose their specially packaged products for the bathroom/dressing rooms: shampoo, conditioner, hand lotion, tissues, emery boards, bath gel, toothbrush, razor... the lists grew longer as Laura asked for more and the salespeople promised more in order to get their products into the European-style hotel that was already the talk of Michigan Avenue. The rumors were that the owners were sparing no costs to make it intimate and luxurious, providing decor and service far more personal than that offered in the Hyatt or Marriott or any large chain hotel, and that the costs would require its room rates to be so high only the wealthiest could stay there.

Other manufacturers came when Laura sent for them, and from the best she chose television sets, radios, and videocassette players, terrycloth robes, carafes and tumblers for bedside tables, hairdryers and built-in makeup tables with illuminated makeup mirrors for the dressing rooms, and built-in refrigerators to be stocked with cheeses, pâtés, soft drinks, wines and liquor.

Restaurant suppliers came and Laura chose, for the Beacon Hill restaurant, Villeroy & Boch china, Sambonet flatware, and Lenox crystal. The cost was close to three hundred dollars a place setting. "Do it right," Currier had said; he did not believe in spending millions and then cutting corners on small items, especially in a highly visible place like a dining room that he anticipated would become one of the city's top restaurants.

Finally, Laura and the design consultants worked out the plan of each room. She knew what she wanted: each one had to remind her of her rooms in Owen's house. They were the first to fulfill the fantasies of space and beauty she'd had in the tenement she had shared with Clay and Ben, and she still remembered the warmth that engulfed her each time she entered them. It was that warmth and spaciousness she wanted to give her guests.

"It should feel like a home," Laura said to Currier one night in February as they dined at Le Perroquet. It was her twenty-fourth birthday, and they were sipping Dom Perignon and sitting close together on a banquette in a corner of the long room. "It doesn't matter whether it's for a few hours or a week or a month. It should feel like home."

"Do you think people really care?" he asked. "They're not fooled, you know; they know the difference between a hotel and a home. All they want is to be comfortable."

"I don't know. . . ." With her fork she swirled a tiny bay scallop around her plate to pick up some of its lobster sauce. "Name your favorite hotel," she said.

"The Mayfair Regent," he replied promptly. "But I don't remember what it looks like, only that you were with me."

She smiled. "Name some others."

"Other favorites?" He reflected. "The Ritz in Paris, 47 Park Street in London, the Salinger in Amsterdam, Stanford Court in San Francisco. And the Beacon Hill."

"You haven't stayed there."

"And I don't intend to, unless my welcome wears out in the DePaul neighborhood. What does that have to do with its being one of my favorites?"

She smiled again. "What do they all have in common?"

"Small size, superior service, comfort, serenity."

"Just like a well-ordered home."

He looked at her thoughtfully. "Is that what our home would be like?"

"It's what every wonderful home would be like," she said calmly. He had not mentioned marriage since New Year's Eve, but occasionally, especially since she had moved into her apartment and made him part of it when he was in Chicago, he found ways to let her know he had not forgotten. But neither had she forgotten what she intended to do. And so she did not let the talk turn to marriage.

Currier refilled their glasses. "We haven't toasted your birthday." The soft lights of the tranquil room decorated with arrangements of fresh flowers turned the pale champagne to gold, its tiny bubbles glinting as they burst to the surface.

"Thank you," Laura said. "You've made it a lovely birthday."

"How can that be, when you don't yet have your present?"

"I got my present in December. You gave me a chance to do what I most wanted to do."

"I gave you the chance to work a hundred hours a week."

"But that's what impressed me," she said, her eyes dancing. "You could have given me a microwave oven, or a featherbed, or something else to make my life easier. Instead you invested ten million dollars in me so I could borrow twenty million more and work harder than I ever have."

He chuckled in appreciation. She had a way of deflecting the points he tried to score, and she did it without making him feel diminished. That was rare in anyone, especially in a woman as young and inexperienced as she. And what a pleasure, he thought, to enjoy a woman outside of bed as well as in; to find her challenging and independent even as he pressed her to become more dependent on him. "I bought you a ring," he said. "Will you wear it?"

She shook her head. "I'm sorry."

He had expected it. "Fortunately, there is an alternative." He laid a small velvet box on the table. "To remind you that I want you to save some time for me."

Laura opened it and took out a slender gold watch, its face outlined in tiny diamonds, two diamonds forming its hands. "How beautiful," she whispered. She fastened the small gold clasp and turned her wrist to catch the light. "I've never seen one like it."

"The ring is in my other pocket," he said, watching her.

Once again she shook her head. "Don't press me, Wes; we'd both be unhappy if you did. Let me just thank you for the watch. You do mean so much to me. . . ."

He smiled and deferred to her. She would marry him, and it would take no pressing. He had known this was not the right time, even though he couldn't let the evening go by without trying; she had to get closer to the completion of her hotel. There was something mystical about it, he knew, that went beyond her need to get back what Felix had stolen from her: it had to do with Owen Salinger, what he had done for her, how he had made her feel about herself, how she wanted to feel about herself in the future. She wanted revenge on Felix and to be worthy of Owen's trust. Currier would not fight such powerful needs; he would wait. Wes Currier was known throughout the world for his patience—and also for his triumphs.

They talked like close, comfortable friends through the perfect courses of the meal. Currier had ordered Laura's favorite raspberry soufflé for dessert, and the chef served it himself, with a small silver candle trembling in the center. She bent over it. But suddenly all she could think of was Ben. She always thought of him on her birthday, remembering how he had tried to make it cheerful for her in the dark years after her parents were killed. And even after they had parted in anger after the robbery of the Salingers, he always had sent birthday greetings, with bits of news about himself. This year there had been nothing. So she thought of Ben, and as she blew out the candle, her wish was that someday they would find a way to be brother and sister again.

And when she and Currier got home at midnight, a cable from Amsterdam was on her front porch, with a note from a neighbor saying that he had accepted it for her.

"I didn't know you knew anyone in Amsterdam," Currier said.

"Ben. My brother . . . I told you about him . . . I usually get a letter on my birthday, not a cable. . . ." Oddly, her hands were shaking as she tore it open, and she sat on the sofa in the living room to read it.

Happy twenty-fourth—hope it's a great birthday and wonderful year—lots of news—I'm Security Director at hotel and marrying Allison Salinger—how's that for first step to sweet revenge—love Ben

She stared at it, rereading the few words again and again. The paper quivered in her hand.

"Is there anything I can do?" Currier asked.

Laura looked up, barely seeing him. "What? Oh, I don't think so. Yes, there is. How do I send a cable?"

"To Amsterdam?"

"Yes."

He reached for the directory, found the number and wrote it down. "Shall I wait for you in the study?"

Through the turmoil of her thoughts, Laura felt a rush of affection. "If you would. Thank you, Wes." And then she turned again to the cable in her lap. How did he meet her? The world was so big, how could Allison and Ben meet? And fall in love? But he wasn't in love; he wanted revenge. What for? What could be so terrible he would—? But it made no difference what it was. Ben wanted revenge. He always had. That was why he had robbed the family so many years ago.

She sat still, letting memories engulf her. Allison on the tennis court, her arms around Laura as she taught her how to hit backhand and forehand and how to serve; Allison in restaurants, translating menus and listening to Laura repeat the phrases until she was perfect so no tuxedoed waiter ever would look down at her with the scornful hauteur that could wither inexperienced diners; Allison darting in and out of the boutiques of Newton and Boylston streets, trying to find the perfect blouse

for Laura; Allison crying furiously—something about Thad—her head
on Laura's shoulder, thanking her for listening and not calling her a
damn fool; Allison's bewildered face in the library as Felix hurled his
accusations and Laura did not fight back.

She felt empty inside. *Allison, I miss you.*

But Allison had turned away. She'd turned her back on her friend.

So what? She felt betrayed. Just as I did.

*She could have waited. There's always time to turn away. She could
have waited.*

Well, she didn't. But that didn't wipe out all the years when she'd
been a friend, a sister, a teacher to Laura.

Nothing Allison Salinger had done deserved her being used as a
weapon of revenge—for whatever reasons—in Ben Gardner's hands.

Laura shook herself as if waking up, swiftly wrote a message on the
pad of paper Currier had left her, and picked up the telephone. "To Ben
Gardner," she said and gave his address in Amsterdam.

Allison was good to me—don't hurt her—whatever happened so long ago
can't be important anymore—can't you forget about revenge—Laura

* * *

The Chicago Beacon Hill was scheduled to open for Christmas, one
year after the party at the Ninety-Fifth. In early November, while the
wind swirled powdery snow in small vortexes along Michigan Avenue,
and Christmas shoppers scurried from store to store, heads bent against
the cold, Laura sat in her newly furnished office at the hotel, working
on menus for the private opening, while her secretary addressed invitations. A select list, from Europe and America, was being invited for a
weekend stay as guests of the Beacon Hill before the hotel was open to
the public. The dining room would be open for every meal; afternoon
tea would be served in the lounge; and limousines would take guests to
the opera, symphony, museums, and shops.

Currier had assembled the guest list from friends, acquaintances, and
business associates, and Laura had designed the invitations, printed in
gold on heavy linen, with *Beacon Hill* in gold on the envelopes, just
above the hotel crest, the outline of an iris in blue and gold. As the
secretary addressed them, she stacked them on Laura's desk unsealed;
Currier would add his handwritten invitation to many of them.

Three hundred names were on the list, and all but fifty had been
addressed when Laura's telephone rang. Still writing the menu for Sunday brunch, she picked it up. "Laura Fairchild."

"Laura Fairchild," a woman's voice repeated in an unmistakable

Texas twang. "My oh my, isn't it a very small world? This is Ginny Starrett."

Ginny Starrett. The name, and the accent, brought back a vivid scene: the lobby of the Boston Salinger, a woman's scream, Virginia Starrett lying on a couch, her heavy makeup streaked with tears, and Laura bending over her, wiping away the smeared mascara and ordering Jules LeClair to bring tea. Ginny Starrett. Laura had taken her upstairs, to her room, and they had talked, and Jules had scolded her for being away so long.

"Ginny, how wonderful to hear from you . . . where are you? How did you find me?"

"New York, and I found you because your friend Wes Currier—excellent taste in friends, my dear—told me he was sending me an invitation to your grand affair next month. He neglected to tell you about it?"

Laura glanced at the unfinished invitations. "We're still addressing them. Wes made up the list; I didn't know he knew you. Can you be here? I hope you can. It would be so good to see you again."

"Wouldn't miss it on a bet. How could I stay away from your coming out, or whatever you call it? I owe you so much this won't begin to pay it back."

"You don't owe me—"

"Pish-tush, child, don't tell me what I owe. I'm up there with the world's debtor nations; people are always doing me favors and I'm always vowing to repay them. Trouble is, I'm usually so busy making Ginny Starrett happy I don't have much time for anybody else. I didn't forget you, though; I looked for you, oh, about six or eight months after that boxing match Wylie and I had in your lobby, but you were gone and nobody knew where. You'll have to tell me your adventures, and about Wes. Is he behind the hotel?"

"Yes."

"He's a good man. Rides roughshod over people sometimes, but he frequently ends up making them rich so they don't stay peeved too long. Can you put me in one of your suites?"

"You'll have the penthouse." Laura's heart was pounding with excitement and at first she didn't know why. But then she did. Ginny Starrett was from her past, and Laura was starved for the past.

"It's too late for me to get the penthouse," Ginny was saying. "Wes promised it to some friends of mine. He didn't tell you that, either?"

"No, but he's in New York and I haven't talked to him today. We have other wonderful suites. Is it just the two of you?"

"Just the one of me. Wylie and I fought our way through a divorce right after that day in Boston. I have you to thank for that, too. Do you recollect our talk together? Right after you wiped my tears and found me a room? Something you said that day sent me to a divorce lawyer. Know what you said?"

"I can't believe I would have told you to get a divorce."

"No, no, it was much more interesting than that. There I was, over-weight, over-bleached, drinking more than was good for me, wearing enough makeup to float an Estée Lauder factory, moaning and groaning about that jogging jackass I was married to and saying I deserved better, and you said, 'Isn't it odd how we give terrible people so much power over us?' And I thought to myself, that little girl is just about the smartest person I have met in all the hellish years I've given Wylie Starrett the power to make a mess of me. So I went to a divorce lawyer who squeezed a few millions out of his skirt-chasing hide, and then I went to a spa—twenty-four spas, to be exact—and here I am, one of Manhattan's few hundred thousand thin, single women looking for a good man. I may bring a friend to your shindig; he's fun in small doses and, after all, there's no way I can go to movies and hotel openings alone . . . oh, by the way, speaking of going places alone . . . but you're probably not interested in gossip about the Salingers anymore."

Laura frowned. "I didn't know you knew them."

"Oh, just a tad. I see Leni and Felix now and then at benefits, and we smile ever so politely. But when I'm around Boston and New York I hear about them; people love to talk, you know. There was that publicity over Owen Salinger's will—you probably know more about that than I do; I was in Europe when it happened. I'll bet if it had been a trial about Felix finding Leni with somebody—or vice versa, but who can imagine Felix romping in the hay with anyone but another hotel?—well, *then* there would have been lots of talk, the way there is now about Allison Salinger engaged to an absolute unknown, somewhere in Europe. They're getting married this Christmas, and it seems her parents haven't even met him! And that's not all; it's been a bumper year for—"

"Wait." Laura's voice was husky and she cleared her throat. "Do you . . . do you know the name of the man she's marrying?"

"I didn't pay much attention because nobody ever heard of him. I believe he works for one of her father's hotels. Manager? Something like that. I'm afraid I didn't listen as closely as I might have, because I heard it about the same time I heard about her cousin getting married, and I was surely much more interested in that, because I know the lucky lady."

Laura's stomach contracted. "Which cousin?"

"Paul Janssen. He married Emily Kent, an absolutely gorgeous and very proper Boston girl. If I were the betting kind, I'd put my money on Paul. Allison's taking a real flyer, but Paul knows exactly what he's getting into: found a girl from his own background so he doesn't have to worry about bombshells."

There was a silence. "Oh, my," said Ginny. "I've talked your ear off, and you're at work and all. I do apologize; am I forgiven?"

"Of course," said Laura automatically. She was leaning over the desk, her head resting on her hand, her eyes closed. "Please let me know when you'll arrive, so we can have a drink together."

"I surely will." She paused. "You sound a mite upset, honey. I didn't say anything out of line, did I?"

"No." She tried to make her voice natural. "Thank... thank you for coming to the opening; it means so much to me. I'll see you soon."

When she hung up, she was dizzy, hot and cold by turns. I'm going to faint, she thought. But I've never fainted. I don't even know what it feels like to be about to faint.

She clutched the edge of the desk. It's just that what Ginny said was such a surprise.

Surprise. Surprise. The word echoed. *A long time ago I asked Ben not to rob the Salingers—and he did. Last February I asked him not to marry Allison, and now it's November and he's set the wedding date.*

She closed her eyes, thinking about Ben. It was easier to think about Ben than about Paul. *Just when I thought we might find each other again, after so many years...*

Surprise. Surprise. The word jeered. But it wasn't about Ben; it was about Paul. She couldn't keep her thoughts away from him. Emily Kent. Paul and Emily. Paul and Emily Janssen.

Damn it, it was supposed to be me! Damn it! Damn him! And damn his whole family!

But why shouldn't he marry? A man wants a woman and a home and a life without bombshells. A man wants children.

They were supposed to be our children.

She sat at her desk until the dizziness receded and her thoughts slowed. Automatically, she straightened the piles of papers and books on her desk: plans for the opening weekend, the stack of invitations, invoices, catalogues. So much work to do, such a full life to lead. Her life, in the present.

Wes. Clay. Kelly and John. Memories of Owen. The Chicago Beacon Hill. And three other Salinger hotels that were going to be hers.

A full life to lead. The doors had closed on what had gone before.

Once she had thought she was free of the past. She knew now she never would be. The past was part of her: part of her heart, part of her thoughts, part of her future. But the doors had closed on it, and she would not look at it again. She would look only at today and tomorrow. The past was done.

Part IV

CHAPTER 18

"MY oh my," Rosa marveled, surveying the guests in the lobby of the Chicago Beacon Hill as Laura came to greet her. "What an impressive way to celebrate a hotel opening; I must say, the Salingers never did anything like it. Hello, my young miss; it's wonderful to see you again."

Laura kissed her soft cheek and closed her eyes for a brief moment as Rosa's plump arms encircled her. "You still smell like fresh bread," she said, smiling but somehow also looking sad. "I'm so very, very glad you're here."

"Well, and so am I; I wouldn't want to miss this elegant party." She took a step back and eyed Laura critically. "You've changed. Grown up and gotten all sophisticated and smooth."

"Outside," Laura said. "I'm still having trouble with the inside."

"Good. At my age, I get confused by too many changes at once." She patted Laura's hand. "I do thank you for writing to me; I've so wanted to talk to you but I confess I didn't know how. After that snake-in-the-grass lawyer made me sound so mean in the courtroom, I kept thinking I'd call you and say I missed you but I didn't know if you'd talk to me."

A young couple interrupted as if Rosa were not there. "Lovely job, Laura, our rooms are just perfect, such a good idea to have a weekend like this, we're looking forward to all of it."

"Thank you," Laura said. "May I introduce—"

"We're having a New Year's Eve get-together at our place in Lake Forest; is it too late to ask you? Do come—so many people you'll just love, and if you're going to be part of Chicago there's no better way to get the right start. Otherwise you could waste months meeting the wrong kind of people. We'll send our chauffeur to pick you up, if you'd like. We'll talk about it in a few days, all right? Such a lovely weekend . . ."

They drifted off. Laura and Rosa looked at each other. "I've fed those two a dozen times at parties Felix and Leni gave," Rosa said thoughtfully. "In fact, I've fed more than half the people here. I'm afraid I belong on the other side of the kitchen door, my young miss."

"You belong here," Laura said firmly. "This is my party and I've invited my special friends. The rest of the list was put together by a friend of mine."

"Well, they're all lovely people, just perfect, such a good idea to have them," Rosa said with a twinkle. "I'm proud of you, you know; you got them to come for a weekend in December—a busy social month, you know that—and you've got photographers here; my goodness, everyone must think this is going to be a major hotel. And you're the manager! What a good job for you to have!"

Laura nodded, feeling guilty because she had lied—again—to Rosa. But she still was keeping her ownership a secret, especially from Felix, and she would as long as possible.

"So when you sent me the invitation," Rosa said, continuing the conversation that had been interrupted, "I told myself, She does want to talk to me. She's forgiven me for messing up her case in court. But I don't want to talk if you're going to start with a lot of explanations. You never did me any harm, my young miss; you loved me and I knew it, and I've missed you something fierce. And if I don't ever know the absolute truth, it doesn't matter any more. It was so long ago, and I've always known, from day one, you were telling some lies and some truths, and since everybody does that why shouldn't I just go on loving you the way I always did?"

"Thank you," Laura said, her voice husky. She looked around as Clay came up behind her.

"Small problem with a table seating. Could you help?"

She nodded and hugged Rosa—almost clinging, it seemed to Rosa—and kissed her again. "Cocktails in the lounge and dinner at eight. I'll try to get back to you, but there's so much to do . . ."

"Go on, go on," Rosa said. "I've done it in my time; I know it's the little things that can ruin a party or make it perfect. I'll be fine; I'll just look around and be impressed."

It *was* impressive, she thought as Laura left with Clay. And so were the two of them; Clay had grown a mustache and looked positively handsome, his blond hair smoothly waved, and Laura glowed with a polished beauty she'd never had before. Walking through the lobby, Rosa wondered what was behind it: if she was happy, if she had friends and a new lover, if she'd gotten over everything that happened. Maybe she has, she thought; she's certainly got a peach of a job, and if she helped with the decorating she's got more talent than I ever knew.

In the lounge, she found a wing chair beside the fireplace, and that became her vantage point for the weekend, as she watched the guests and kept her eye on Laura, who rushed about from one task to another, never sitting down and resting. She never looked flurried or anxious, but she never relaxed, not even at dinner on Friday night. While two hundred guests feasted on caviar, pheasant, and raspberry sabayon prepared by Enrico Garibaldi, the Beacon Hill chef, Laura was everywhere, taking care of hundreds of small details. On Saturday it was more of the same. There was a lunch of northern Italian specialties that Rosa, the experienced chcf, much admired, and then everyone was chauffeured by limousine down Michigan Avenue to the Chicago Art Institute for a private showing of the year's most sensational exhibit: a treasure trove of gold, silver, and gems found in an Italian trading ship that had sunk off the coast of Spain four hundred years earlier. Currier had been a major investor in the search expedition that found the ship and brought up its treasure, and he had arranged with the Art Institute to have the private showing a day before the exhibit opened to the public. The magazine photographers who were covering the Beacon Hill weekend for *Town and Country, Vogue, Eye,* and a dozen other magazines dedicated to the glossy doings of the rich and famous were there, too, posing television stars, countesses, and corporate magnates beside glass cases gleaming with goblets, coins, and fabulous coronets. They paid no attention at all to Rosa. She had been personally invited by Laura Fairchild, but that didn't impress them; all they knew was that she was small and round and her shoes were sensible, and they'd never seen her before.

Kelly Darnton received the same glazed looks of nonrecognition. She arrived on Saturday morning, and after the guests returned from the Art Institute to the Beacon Hill lounge for tea and cocktails, she joined Rosa at her post beside the crackling flames in the fireplace. "It's obvious we're equally non-newsworthy," she said, and held out her hand. "Kelly Darnton."

"Rosa Curren." Rosa took her hand, liking its strength and the direct look in her dark eyes. "Laura told me about your lodge. And she says wonderful things about you."

"All true, probably. I hear good things about you, too. When Laura likes somebody, she's generous with her praise."

"And when she doesn't like someone?"

"She gets very quiet," Kelly said. "Isn't that what she did when you knew her?"

"She was very young, but she was never very big on showing her feelings."

"Well, God knows, she's still like that. Hello," she said, looking up as Ginny Starrett joined them.

"I wanted to meet someone new," Ginny said, taking the third chair at their rosewood tea table without being asked. "I do get tired of seeing the same people at every party." She introduced herself, noting Kelly's callused palm and Rosa's soft one as they shook hands. "Laura is still like what?" she asked, having heard the end of Kelly's sentence.

"Private," said Kelly. "Doesn't talk about her own feelings, or anyone else's, either. To anybody."

"But she must have made friends," Rosa protested.

The three of them looked at each other. They all thought of themselves as Laura's friend; Ginny and Kelly had confided in her; Rosa had talked to her freely about the Salingers and her feelings about them. But they were the ones who had done the talking; Laura had never really been open with them. They loved her, they knew she cared about them —but none of them knew her intimately.

Rosa sighed. "Is she happy, I wonder? She's got a good job here, and it's such a perfectly beautiful place. . . ."

A hostess stood at their table. "I'd like more sherry," Ginny said. "Kelly? Rosa?"

Kelly nodded. "Tea, please," said Rosa, and then looked about the room. "She was always very big on beautiful things. And I knew someday she'd find a way to make something beautiful of her own."

Her own, Ginny echoed silently, and she knew then what it was that was special about the Chicago Beacon Hill: its beauty was very personal. The lounge where they sat was a large room with soft lights and colors that made it a soothing oasis on a gray Chicago weekend. Along one wall, mirrors reflected the fleur-de-lis carpeting used throughout the hotel and large panels of French tapestries on the opposite wall. A sky blue ceiling with gilt scrollwork from another age arched over the guests sitting in pale blue armchairs and sofas around small round tables. On a raised platform, a harpist played baroque music, the delicate melodies weaving through the hum of conversation that rose and fell throughout the room. Hostesses served from glass and silver carts, and Laura moved from table to table like a slender flame in a long gold dress that glowed amid the soft colors of the room.

Ginny sighed with envy, remembering a time when her own face had been fresh and smooth, her color high and her eyes large without the help of makeup, her hips slim and her waist narrow without inhuman diets and diabolical exercise equipment. But her envy faded. It was absurd for a woman of sixty-one to envy a girl of twenty-five, but also, in all honesty, she had to admit that even at her best she wouldn't have looked like Laura in that dress: she didn't have Laura's catlike grace that made the fabric flow like liquid gold when she moved.

The hostess brought their drinks and, for Rosa, an English porcelain teapot with a matching cup and saucer. Beside them she set a George V silver tea strainer fitting snugly in a silver receptacle. She opened a polished wooden box divided into small compartments filled with tea leaves and, when Rosa had chosen the kind she wanted, she spooned the leaves into the teapot, closed it and covered it with its own quilted cozy to steep. Finally, she arranged a plate of cookies and a basket of fruit in the center of the table, and set out fruit plates with mother-of-pearl fruit knives at each place. Rosa sighed. "There aren't many places where that's done so well. She's remembered everything I taught her, and then some."

A dog barked. The sound was so startling that all conversation stopped. Heads came up, glances darted about, the barking grew louder and more frantic, and then everyone realized it was not a dog but a man, sitting on a love seat near the harpist. His head back, his mouth wide, the muscles of his neck rigid, he growled and woofed and yelped while his companion, a young girl, by now in tears, tried to shut him up.

"Son of a bitch," Ginny muttered. "Britt Farley. Coked to the gills. He never could hold it, especially when he drinks."

"Who?" Kelly asked loudly, competing with the barks and yowls.

"Country-rock singer; hit it big in one of those television series." She stood. "He went to high school with my ex-husband; they both liked to drink and screw. Maybe I can get him out of here before he messes up Laura's weekend."

But as she started toward Farley's table, she saw that Laura was already there. People were talking again, their voices raised in outrage or embarrassment; dishes and silver clinked, the harpist played rapid trills and runs, and everyone tried to pretend nothing was amiss. As Ginny reached Farley's table she saw Laura sit beside him, her arm around him, talking to him with her lips close to his ear. She talked steadily, without pausing, her fingers digging into his shoulder. And all the while his young companion was sobbing beneath the barking that had begun to quiet down: "I *asked* him not to do any coke. See, they all think he stopped; he told them he did after they said if he didn't they'd write him out of the show, have his character run over or something, and he couldn't stand that, he couldn't stand it if they killed him off, and he promised them he'd stop, he promised me he'd stop, but he doesn't pay me much mind usually, I mean, he thinks I'm like a little girl—that's what he calls me, his little girl who's silly enough to stick with him. . . ."

Her voice trailed off. Ginny bent down beside Laura, listening. ". . . good, you're very good," Laura was saying, her voice a steady hypnotic monotone. "Good sound, good timbre, good volume, but no one appreciates it; there's no market for it, no market for country-rock singing dogs in television—"

A giggle broke from Ginny. Laura flashed her a look of warning, and she cut it off.

"—or romantic ones, either, and you're so good at country-rock and romance, they wouldn't let you change even if they appreciated you. Maybe someday, someday soon, someone might recognize your other talents, but right now you're so big the way you are, so good, so important to the network they couldn't let you change, they couldn't let you be anything but the hero you are. . . ."

Slowly, as she talked, she eased him up, her arm still around him, her lips still beside his ear. He was much taller than she, and she had to walk on tiptoe, talking, talking as she led him through the room. Trancelike, his eyes half-closed, at last completely silent, he went with her.

Laura glanced back at Ginny and made a small gesture with her head asking Ginny to stay with the young girl, and then, as some of the guests watched and others turned away, she led Britt Farley from the lounge, down the two steps to the lobby, and into the elevator.

"I'm taking you to your room," she said, her voice like ice. At her abrupt change, his eyes flew open. "I'll have dinner sent to you there. I don't want to see you downstairs until you're sober. If that means brunch tomorrow, and I think it probably does, then you won't come downstairs until brunch tomorrow."

They stood close together in the richly paneled elevator while Laura tried to control her fury. *This is my house, the first I've ever had that's really mine, and I have guests here, and this damn fool dares to get drunk! And bark! Who the hell does he think he is, to come into my house and make my guests uncomfortable?* The elevator reached the eleventh floor and she held his arm, propelling him down the short corridor to his room. "Hold on," he said thickly, trying to come to a stop. "Can't force me to leave the party . . . paid my money. . ."

"Not this time, you didn't; you're here as my invited guest, and you'll do as I say. Give me the card for this room." He hesitated. "Give it to me, Britt. You're in real trouble if you don't."

He squinted at her. "Britt doesn't get into trouble; Britt makes trouble."

"Call it what you want; if you don't unlock this room or let me do it, I'll call the police and have you arrested for disturbing the peace."

"Oh no. No siree. Wes wouldn't let you do that. Knows me from way back. Bad publicity for hotel."

She looked at him with contempt. "Try me."

He tried to stare back, but his eyes wandered, and after a moment his shoulders slumped. "Fuck it." He took from his pocket the plastic coded card that fit into a narrow slit in the door, releasing the lock. Laura used it and pushed him inside. The room looked as if a tornado had ripped through it: in the hour between returning from the Art Institute and going to the lounge for cocktails, Farley and his girl had flung clothes and shoes in all directions; scotch and bourbon bottles were on tables and amid the tangled sheets on the bed, and white powder was scattered over the dressing table, along with a deck of cards, men's and women's jewelry, and the girl's cosmetics. "And I worried about which room style you'd like best," Laura murmured. "Get undressed, Britt," she ordered bluntly. "Get into bed, sleep it off. I'll call later to see if you want dinner sent up. And don't worry about your friend; we'll take care of her."

"Silly little slut," he murmured sleepily, trying to unbutton his shirt. "Hangs around when nobody else cares whether I shit or shine. Even when I bark. You were right, you know; I'm good at it. Makes everybody pay attention to me. You see their faces? Ha!"

Gently, Laura pushed aside his fumbling fingers and unbuttoned his shirt. He stood quietly, his large body slack as she undressed him. Once, automatically, his hand came up and clutched at her breast. She pushed it aside without fuss, as if it were a fly, and he made no protest; he acted from habit, not desire. She pulled back the tangled sheets. "Sleep well, Britt," she said quietly, and left the room, his heavy breathing filling the silence even before she closed the door.

Our American hero, she thought caustically as she walked back to the elevator. But though her anger had faded, she was shaken. What had occurred would do more damage to Britt Farley's social reputation than to her hotel, but what shook her most was the gross falling away of the facade of Britt Farley. She had met him once in New York, with Currier, and had seen only the public man: a rugged, swaggering figure who had built himself into a mythic hero whose songs were about the dreams of everyday people and the ways to make them come true against all obstacles.

But then there was the man she had just put to bed: weak, frightened, probably on his way out of a job.

Every face has another face behind it, she thought as she took the elevator back to the lobby. Every scene has another one that's hidden until something reveals it to us.

She thought of Paul's photograph of the three children and their sand castle: a peaceful scene—but the children were quarreling. If Paul photographed Britt, she thought, he'd know how to show the face behind his public one.

Paul. She stood in the lobby, alone in the empty space, wanting him, remembering the times in the past months when she had longed to share with him anecdotes about the people who worked on the renovation, neighborhoods she was discovering in her solitary explorations of Chicago, and the men and women of other cultures whom she met in grocery stores and restaurants where she could not speak their language, nor they hers, but somehow they communicated and laughed together. She was alive, she was busy, she loved what she was doing, but none of it was as rich as it might have been, because she could not share it with Paul.

She wanted him so overwhelmingly she ached all over. She could feel his arms around her, she heard his voice inside her as clearly as if he stood next to her in the lobby, she felt the wonderful security and completeness she had felt whenever they were together.

She crossed her arms over her breasts, willing the pain to stop. *It's over. He's married, I have a whole life of my own, what we had is ended. Damn it, affairs end all the time; why can't I get used to the fact that ours is over?*

One of the guests bumped into her; someone else adroitly stepped around her. "Sorry," she murmured, and moved away from the elevator.

"No problem," said a tall, bearded man, one of New York's leading Broadway producers. "I'm glad to have a chance to tell you what a splendid job you've done here."

Laura smiled, grateful to him for bringing her back; she belonged here, in this lobby, not in her memories. Praise was as good as a fur coat, she thought wryly; it makes one feel warm and admired, no matter what else is going on.

She walked across the lobby and saw Currier waiting for her. "Well done," he said, putting his arm around her waist. "Ginny told me all about it; I'm sorry I wasn't there to help you."

"Where were you?" she asked. *This is where I belong: in this hotel, with Wes, with the life I'm making for myself.* "There was a small problem in the kitchen. Nothing serious."

"What problem?"

"I told you, nothing serious. The chef had a small tantrum and I took care of it. You got Farley to his room?"

"Yes; he's asleep. I'll have to rearrange the seating for the show tonight; I don't want his girlfriend to have to sit with someone who'll tear Britt apart."

They walked up the two steps to the landing at the entrance to the lounge, and Laura smiled at the young woman who stood behind a long table at one side of the landing, wrapping Christmas gifts the guests had bought that day on Michigan Avenue. It was one of the services Laura would be offering until Christmas to guests of the hotel. She glanced at the long rolls of garlanded and tinseled wrapping paper. "It looks like you'll need more, Mary. And ribbons, too. I'll make sure it's here by morning."

In the lounge, guests stopped her to ask about Farley and compliment her on getting him out peacefully. Others stopped her to invite her to dinner parties in their homes. "And Wes, of course, if he's in town," they all said. She talked to each of them for a few moments, making her way closer to the fireplace. When she reached it, she sat on the arm of Rosa's chair. "How wonderful that three of my favorite people are getting to know each other."

"Getting to be friends," Kelly said. "And Ginny's filling us in on all the gossip. She wasn't surprised by your barking actor; he's done it before."

"I wish I'd known," Laura said. "I'd have bought a leash and a muzzle, to be ready."

"You did fine," said Ginny. "He's been known to knock heads together." She contemplated Laura. "Are you enjoying your party?"

"Of course." Laura's eyebrows rose slightly. "Don't I look as if I am?"

"You look beautiful and calm. You ought to look beautiful and triumphant. You've got this crowd smiling like a happy bunch of Eagle Scouts who just discovered what it's like to feel up a girl. Do you have any idea how miraculous it is to make them look happy about anything?"

"I'll look triumphant when I know I am. Ginny, it's only five o'clock on Saturday. We still have to get through dinner tonight, and then the Jacques Brel show at Chez Fromage and tomorrow's brunch."

"You can't miss; you're on a roll. There's a kind of rhythm to these things—trust me, this I do know—and once all these too-rich, too-finicky folks decide they're having a good time, they stop looking for things to complain about. Last night's dinner was a gem, and so was that knockout show of gold this afternoon. You're doing everything right, honey; you've made them light up like a Las Vegas strip."

Laura smiled and looked about the room. Ginny watched her, knowing that there still was something unexplained about the magic she had worked with her guests. They'd come, these two hundred blasé, demanding world travelers, because of Currier, or because of friends of friends, or because of the curiosity that sometimes sparks from the ashes of ennui, but Ginny knew they also had come to pass judgment and criticize. And somehow, before they could gleefully tear into the newest hotel on the scene, Laura had made them feel part of her celebration, part of her success.

It isn't just that they're being catered to and coddled with little innovations they haven't seen anywhere else, Ginny decided; it's because of Laura. They look at her and see a sophisticated beauty, and then, almost hidden, there's a little girl who isn't part of them, and who won't be. She's separate, cut off from all the bustle of people attaching themselves to other people. They may not understand that that's what they see, but whether they do or not, they want to help her to succeed, to belong, to be one of them instead of standing outside, peering in.

And besides, she was damned good at what she did. "Tell me something," Ginny said to her. "How do you remember all their names and their kids' names and their favorite vacation spots and all that other stuff you drop like little dribbles of perfume when you talk to them?"

Laura smiled. "Dribbles of perfume," she repeated.

"Well, literary I'm not. But it's like perfume, you know: it makes their nostrils quiver; they pay attention and feel good. I've watched them when you do it: first they're surprised, and then their eyes light up, and they look like little kids whose mommy just kissed them for making it to the potty on time."

"Ginny." Laura was laughing. "If you tell my guests that's how they look in the Beacon Hill I'll be ruined."

Unexpectedly, Ginny felt a rush of delight. She'd made Laura Fairchild laugh; she'd made the cool reserve vanish from that lovely face and had brought back, for a moment, the warmth and liveliness she remembered from four years earlier. She was astonished at how good that made her feel. This child needs taking care of, she thought; she needs a woman friend who's like a mother, somebody who can help her relax and take the bumps without always getting bruised. She needs me. Of course, I've never had a daughter, only a couple of sons, but I don't know why that should stop me. I'd never been divorced, either, but I went ahead and did it, and I've been a hell of a lot better for it ever since.

Her thoughts had taken only a few seconds. "Honey," she said promptly, "I'll tell every one of 'em they look like royalty in a Persian palace. You think that'll bring 'em back fast enough?"

"I'm sure it will." Laura had been watching the door as they talked— unobtrusively, Ginny noted approvingly, but watching nonetheless— and now she stood. "Carlos Serrano just came in; he'll want tequila and someone to talk to about oil prices and someone else to share his bed. I'm sure I can provide the first two. If you'll excuse me—"

"You could relax for five minutes," Rosa fussed. "Your boss wouldn't fire you; he'd never find another manager as good as you."

Laura smiled absently, regretting, again, that she couldn't tell Rosa the truth. "I'm not afraid of being fired," she said and leaned down to kiss Rosa's cheek. "I just want to do a good job, the way you taught me. I'll be back soon."

They watched her as she reached Serrano's side. He kissed her hand and talked animatedly as she led him to a table with Sid and Amelia Laughton. Ginny nodded with approval. "Sid Laughton's begun invest-ing in drilling equipment companies, and he owns half a dozen banks in Oklahoma and Texas," she said to Rosa and Kelly. "Carlos will have somebody to talk to about oil, OPEC, Washington, the whole bit, from a different angle. It'll keep him more perked up than somebody who owns wells, like he does. Clever," she added, as proud of Laura as if she were her mother.

Still watching, she saw Currier come up to Laura, and thought what a striking couple they made, each of them commanding attention in a different way. She contemplated Currier. Smooth, suave, wealthy, pow-erful: most women's dream. Not mine, she thought. But if I wanted to be dominated and protected by a guy who's plenty nice even if he likes to run the show, and who has that stubborn kind of patience that means he's probably great in the sack, then I might find him irresistible.

Laura might. Ginny gathered, from a very few confidences, that Laura had had a rough time and might want to relax in somebody's strong arms. And she had a loyalty that impressed Ginny, who came from a world where loyalty often clashed with the business of making money, and money won. But here were Rosa and Kelly, who weren't part of the international set but had been invited simply because Laura liked them, felt grateful to them, and wanted them to be part of her new job. It was impressive, Ginny thought, except that that loyalty might tie her to Currier even more.

No question about it, she decided firmly, Laura needs a woman to watch over her. Looks like I'm going to be in Chicago a lot more than I planned.

Laura and Currier had gone to Farley's table, where the young girl huddled with a woman Ginny didn't know. She watched them talk to her, saw her face begin to clear, and watched as they walked to other tables, chatting with the guests. When they were a few feet from her chair, the concierge came to them. Ginny leaned forward to hear what she could. "So sorry to bother you... I tried, but... kitchen staff... chef... delicate matter..."

Laura was walking toward the door before he had finished, with Currier and the concierge keeping pace. "I told you I thought it was settled," Currier said. "He's more stubborn than I thought. Don't worry about it; I'll take care of it once and for all."

Laura shook her head. "I'll do it, Wes. I wish I'd heard about it the first time." She glanced at the concierge, who bowed his head. Next time he would come to Laura. Men take problems to men, she thought; it takes a long time for them to get used to taking them to women. "And I'd like to talk to him alone," she added firmly to Currier. "It's confusing if the staff doesn't know who's in charge, don't you think?"

It was a line Currier had used in describing his skills in arranging mergers and acquisitions. He acknowledged it with a small smile. "If you need me, I'll come right away."

"Thank you," she murmured, then walked through the small lobby. It was not a place to linger, but a sumptuous space, like the foyer of a mansion, with the lounge on one side, the restaurant on the other, and two paneled elevators at the back. In a recess along one wall was a mahogany reception counter; opposite it stood the concierge's antique desk; and in the middle of the lobby, beneath the gold and crystal chandelier, was Myrna Appleby, in a mink coat.

She was walking away and did not see Laura. "Hi," Clay said, appearing at Laura's elbow. He followed her gaze as Myrna went through the wide glass doors that led to Walton Street. "Christmas present," he said. "Doesn't she look sensational?"

"Did you steal it?" Laura asked bluntly.

He reared back. "Goddam it, what the hell way is that for you to talk to me? I'm your brother—remember?—and I love you. I also happen to be your assistant manager, and it's a hell of a thing for you to talk to me that way."

"I asked you a question. Did you steal it?"

"Shit, Laura, if you haven't got any faith in me—"

"Where did you get the money for that coat?"

"I earned it."

"Not in this hotel. Not working for me."

"You don't know how much I save."

"I know what your salary is; I know what your rent is because I helped pay it a couple of times before Myrna found a job; I know the high-priced places where you buy your clothes. Where did you get the money for that coat?"

After a moment, he shrugged. "At Sy's loft in Printer's Row. I had a lucky week."

"At poker."

"Mostly. We throw in some blackjack now and then so things don't get dull."

"And you play for big stakes; big enough for fur coats."

"It takes big stakes to keep Myrna interested."

"Don't be ridiculous; she wouldn't leave you. She's been trying to get you to marry her for almost two years."

He shrugged. "It takes big stakes to keep *me* interested."

"I didn't know you were bored."

"Not with you," he said quickly. "You've got a lot going on, and I like being part of it, but, what the hell, Laura, you've got to admit it's just a job—even if it is your hotel and terrific—and everybody needs something more than that, something risky or free or whatever. I mean, everything seems different when you're risking a lot and you don't know how it's going to come out. Do you know what I mean?"

I'm in debt for five million dollars and you're asking if I know what you mean.

But it isn't the same, she thought immediately. I'm gambling to get back Owen's dream and build my future. Clay gambles for excitement and money.

But what if he does? He's twenty-four years old, he's holding down a job and doing it well, he's living with a woman, he attracts friends and he's generous with them, and with me, and if he chooses ways to play that I wouldn't choose, that's his business. He's a man who's living his own life, and I'm not his mother. "Just so you know who's across the table," she said lightly. "It's dangerous to play with strangers."

A broad grin, mostly of relief, creased his face. "For that, my dear sister, *you* get an early Christmas present, too." Reaching behind the reception desk, he whipped out an oval box wrapped in silver. "Open it now; I hate it when women open my presents without me being around to see their faces."

Laura slipped off the paper and lifted the hinged lid. Inside, coiled to fit the oval box, was a belt of gold mesh, the buckle an oval tigereye that matched her chestnut hair. It was exactly the kind of dramatic accessory she had begun to wear after she had learned how to dress. *A lucky week in Sy's loft in Printer's Row. What the hell has Clay gotten himself into?* She reached up and kissed him. "It's beautiful, Clay; the most elegant belt I've ever had. Thank you. I love you."

"Runs in the family," he said, his grin now one of pleasure. "I love you, too. How's the big party going in there?"

"The party's fine; the chef seems to be acting up. I have to get to the kitchen. Would you check on the limousines for tonight? I told them quarter to ten, to make sure we get out of here on time; the show at Chez Fromage starts at ten-thirty. Oh, and call the First District station again to make sure they've told the police on the street we'll have cars lined up for the whole block at quarter to ten and between twelve-thirty and one."

Clay gave her a mock salute, then bent and kissed her cheek. "You're a hell of a lady," he said, and as she walked away she was smiling, feeling good about Clay once again. It was easy to love Clay, she thought as she reached the restaurant and walked toward the kitchen between the tables set for dinner, each with a single flaming ginger flower in the center. As infuriating as he often was in his persistent childishness, he could always disarm her with his sweetness and by reminding her that he was her family and he loved her. And the gambling wouldn't go on forever, she told herself as she swung open the kitchen door. Even his need for excitement would take new directions. One of these days Myrna would get her way: they'd be married, and Clay would settle down. Myrna would see to it.

"No one lectures Enrico Garibaldi on how he is to create!" the chef thundered the moment Laura appeared in the gleaming stainless steel kitchen. "Enrico Garibaldi, chef to popes and kings, is not one to be lashed with the tongue by a focking accountant who thinks a *veau aux champignons* is as ordinary as one of his focking bottom lines!"

Laura's lips twitched, and she forced them to seriousness. "Banker," she said gently. "Mr. Currier is an international banker, not an accountant, as you well know, Enrico." Enrico hadn't ever been a chef to popes or kings, either, but she let that pass. "No one wants to lecture you; we admire you and rely on you. Now tell me what is the problem."

"Money!" he roared, unmollified. "The focking almighty dollar! I discover only two hours ago what it is that the concierge, that focking Frenchman, earns per month, and it is almost as much as Enrico, who is a genius, and the focking concierge will get tips and I do not, and therefore he will be making more than Enrico and I am enraged!"

"I see that," Laura said. She was aware of the sous chef and the pastry chef, standing quietly to the side, ready to demand more money if Enrico got more. But of course Enrico would not get more. "You picked a poor time to discuss salaries, Enrico. If you want to come to my office on Monday, after the guests leave—"

"I pick the time and I pick now," he said flatly. "Enrico does not wait."

"And I do not let anyone hold me up three hours before I give a dinner for two hundred guests! You may ask my secretary for an appointment on Monday." She turned to go.

"No, no, no, you do not walk out on Enrico! I can walk out, too!"

"We'll talk about that on Monday," Laura said icily. "We may decide it would be best for you to do that."

"There is no need! It is just a matter of money!" A frantic note in his voice convinced Laura he wanted to stay at the Beacon Hill; his instinct probably told him its restaurant would be more prestigious than the one he had left. "We can agree on money and then all is serene! We can talk; we are alike, you and I. Yes, yes, it is true! Listen! Enrico was poor and hungry as a boy, dreaming of fame and fortunes, and this you can understand better than others because you knew poverty and hunger, too—I know, I have heard from my friends in other hotels—you knew poverty, you stole and went to jail and robbed people you lived with because you were hungry and—"

"Stop! How dare you! *How dare you?*" Laura's face was burning; her nails were cutting into her palms. *I have heard from my friends.* Who else knew? How much did they remember of newspaper reports from almost three years ago? What whispers were trailing her like long shadows that might make powerful people turn away rather than take a chance on her?

The kitchen was filled with a blood-red light. Enrico's face wavered before her like a detached balloon with a tall chef's hat that wobbled absurdly and thin lips that were saying something she could not hear. *Get him out of here!* Everything else fell away. *Get him out of here!* She wouldn't let the past ruin the life she was making. Nothing was going to ruin it, not a stoned television singer, not a blackmailing chef—nothing was going to stop her now that she'd gotten started. This was her home, her real home, and she'd do anything to keep it free of the tentacles of the past that reached out to choke her when she least expected them. "None of that is true—not one word! Lies! Lies! But it doesn't matter; you're through here! Get out!"

"But—wait—you must understand! I tell this to no one! I keep your secrets! We can talk and agree—it is only money! We settle it, we keep our secrets, we understand each—"

"No! God damn you, you whining, blackmailing son of a bitch, get out of here!" Her voice shook with fury. "We'll send your money— whatever we owe you—but you're through! Get out! And stay out!"

"But you cannot—! You need me! You are desperate without me! At eight o'clock is dinner—" He saw Laura's face and took a step back. "Hungry people in the dining room—!"

Almost blindly, she strode across the room and picked up the telephone. "I told you to get out! If you don't—if you're not out of here in one minute—I'll call the police and have you arrested for attempted blackmail."

His mouth worked as he tried to decide if she was bluffing. But he couldn't; he couldn't be sure. A minute passed. Laura began to stab numbers on the telephone. "Bitch!" he blurted, and without a glance at the sous chef and pastry chef who were trying to make themselves invisible in the corner, he turned on his heel and marched down the room and through a back door to the locker room. Laura waited until she heard the outer door open and slam shut. She hung up the telephone. "See if he's gone," she said to the two chefs in the corner.

They scurried to the locker room and in a moment were back, nodding.

Laura's breathing was becoming more regular. Her face still burned, but the redness had faded from the room; once more its white tiles and stainless steel were crisp and cool. Along one wall, on three Garland ranges, tall pots gently burbled, giving off fragrant tendrils of steam; oven lights clicked on and off like small spotlights; a pair of industrial Cuisinarts and two KitchenAid mixers were poised for action on a counter that was a patchwork of utensils, spices, and ingredients. "Can you finish his dinner?" she asked the chefs.

"I only make dessert," said the pastry chef.

"I don't do the whole show," said the sous chef.

"Some of it's done," added the pastry chef. "Three pâtés as a first course, and the scallop bisque. And there's a sauce . . ." He shrugged. "Enrico likes to keep some tricks close to his chest."

Where she had been hot, now Laura was cold. Two hundred people for dinner. Two hundred people who were supposed to depart smiling at the end of the weekend and tell their friends all over the world about the very special, superbly run Beacon Hill hotel, where everything was done perfectly, for their pleasure and comfort.

Hungry people in the dining room.

And Laura Fairchild's temper in the kitchen.

"Go on with the desserts," she told the pastry chef. "And you can do the salads," she said to the sous chef. "You can do the salads, can't you?"

"Sure."

"Do you know what the entrée was to be?"

"Veal with mushrooms. And red pepper mousse... I think... with some kind of sauce. And wild rice with something."

Laura nodded. *Wonderful to start with such a wealth of information.* "I'll be back as soon as I can."

She almost ran across the lobby. She had to find Currier. He would know someone to call. Was there an agency for temporary chefs who could step in three hours before dinner? Or maybe he had a friend; he had friends everywhere. Oh, God, I've ruined it, she thought. I've thrown it away. Everything was perfect, they were having a wonderful time, and now it's going to be terrible, and that's what they'll tell everyone. Laura Fairchild can't run a hotel; she's still a little girl from the slums of New York, with a lousy temper, trying to make people love and admire her. Trying to con them out of their love. She's still a thief. She's still a failure.

She paused beside the table where Mary was wrapping the last of the day's Christmas gifts and looked into the lounge. Conversation and laughter flowed through the tranquil room, punctuated by an occasional guffaw and the clatter of china and silver. Some guests were beginning to leave, to dress for dinner. Beside the mirrored wall, the harpist played tunes from the Jacques Brel show they would be seeing later that night. And, at a small table beside the fireplace, Rosa and Kelly smiled at each other with the comfortable look of a new friendship that was going to work.

Rosa looked up and saw Laura's face and her smile faded. Kelly followed her gaze, and the two of them shoved back their chairs and reached Laura in a minute. "What happened?" Rosa said. "Who died?" Kelly demanded.

Rosa.

Laura shook her head. Of course not; it was ridiculous; it only showed how desperate she was. She couldn't put Rosa to work; Rosa was her guest. And besides, she was used to family parties, not a dinner for two hundred.

"What does shaking your head mean?" Kelly asked. "Nobody died? Nothing happened?"

"I just fired the chef," Laura said. "The worst possible time, but he said something and I got angry and... kicked him out."

"That temper again." Rosa nodded wisely. "I warned you and warned you. Ah." Her face grew thoughtful. "At a guess, I'd say you were shaking your head because you can't trust his staff. Yes?"

"There's nothing to trust. They don't know much... or they're pretending they don't; I think they don't want the responsibility. I'm looking for Wes; have you seen him? He may know someone I can call."

"Well now," said Rosa slowly. She looked at Kelly, then back to Laura. "Dinner is at eight o'clock?"

"Yes, and I can't hold it; we leave at ten for a ten-thirty show." She looked beyond them. "I thought he was here. I'm sure he'll have a name I can call. A lot of the work is done, but someone has to know how to put everything together and get it served properly."

"Exactly what I was thinking," Rosa said. Her eyes were bright, and she looked at Kelly again with a smile.

"Strange," Kelly chimed in lazily, "it's what I was thinking, too. Of course, far be it from me to tell you how to run this joint, but you do seem to need some talent, and Rosa tells me she's a high-class chef, and I'm pretty good at giving orders. Between the two of us we'd have your kitchen humming in no time and give you service you could be proud of."

"You're not here to give service." Laura put her hand on Kelly's arm. "Thank you. I did think of Rosa, but it isn't fair. You're here to have a good time, not work."

"If I want to work, young miss," Rosa said huffily, "it's not for you to tell me what I'm here to do or not do."

A laugh broke from Laura. "You're right. But I still can't ask you to do it. You're used to a family kitchen, Rosa, not a place that serves two hundred. This isn't a home, it's a—"

"I am perfectly aware what it is." Rosa drew herself up. She came only to Laura's chin, but her head was high. "I told you I've cooked for a lot of these people—a few of them recognized me even though they thought they weren't letting on that they did—and I've cooked for two hundred at dinners in the tent. What's the menu?"

"I don't think—"

"All I asked for was the menu, my young miss."

"Veal with mushrooms and red pepper mousse."

"Well, in some ways he's not so dumb. That's easy and impressive. Veal with morels, I'd bet with great confidence, and the mousse is something any self-respecting cook has known for years. I could do it with one hand tied behind my back. Probably blindfolded, too. I've made this very menu, young lady, and if you don't think the people who ate it at Mr. Owen's table or Felix's and Leni's weren't as finicky as these you've got here, you've got another think coming."

"There's only one thing," said Kelly. "I draw the line at cleaning up. I want to see Jacques Brel and drink champagne and feel frisky. I owe it to John: I promised him I'd do some serious playing since he had to stay home and mind the lodge. But until showtime, it sounds like fun, and as far as I'm concerned, Laura, since we're here and nobody else is offering, how the devil can you resist?"

"Resist what?" Currier asked, coming to the lounge from the lobby.

"Turning her kitchen over to us," Kelly replied before Laura could stop her. "The chef is gone, and we're going to finish dinner if Laura allows us."

His look fastened on Laura. "*Gone?* You let him quit?"

"I fired him. I'm sorry, Wes, he said . . . well, it doesn't matter what he said. I shouldn't have done it, but I did, and then I came to ask if you knew someone we could ask—"

"Of course I do. Just a minute." He was holding his anger in; they all saw it. "A couple of restaurants folded recently, and I knew the chefs at both of them. I'll call; we'll have someone here in half an hour."

"And if you don't?" Kelly asked. "If they're out of town or in bed with the flu?"

"Then we'll find someone else," he snapped. "This is a hotel, not a sorority. We hire professionals whom we can rely on—"

"Unless they turn to blackmail," Laura murmured.

"What's that?"

"It's not important. Wes, I've made up my mind. I want Rosa and Kelly to do it. Kelly knows as much from Darnton's as anyone we could hire, and Rosa can finish what Enrico started; I know she can."

"Without any doubt," Rosa said. "Seventy-four years old and there isn't a kitchen in the world I can't handle. But you're making it harder for me, keeping me here chattering instead of getting to work. I'm very big on plunging right in and doing instead of talking, as Laura can tell you, Mr. Currier, and I do know my way around a kitchen." She stood before them, round and determined, her color high.

"That isn't the issue," Currier said. "This is an important dinner; we aren't going to take any chances with it."

"Yes we are," Laura said. "I'm sorry, Wes, but I want to do this. I believe in Rosa and Kelly, and they believe in me, and I'm going to go with that. It may turn out to be a lot more reliable than professionalism, whatever that is." She held out her hands to Rosa and Kelly. "Thank you. Whatever you need, let me know. Rosa, I wish I could come in and help you; it would be like—well, I can't; I have too much to do out here. I'll leave it to you and Kelly. And thank you both. I can't tell you how much—"

"Tell us later," Kelly said easily. "This is going to be a blast. How about Farley? Shall we cook up some dog food for him?"

"What a thing to joke about," Rosa said reprovingly. "We'll save him some veal; he'll wake up starving and thoroughly ashamed of himself. Come on, come on, I can't wait to get to work."

Currier and Laura watched them walk through the lobby and disappear through the restaurant door. They made an odd pair: Kelly tall and big-boned, black hair fanned out in a wild halo, her stride long; Rosa small and round, almost waddling as she tried to keep pace, her gray hair pulled into a neat coil at her neck, her head tilted up as she talked to Kelly.

"That wasn't smart," Currier said coldly. "It wasn't good business; it wasn't even good friendship. If they ruin your evening, the friendship is ruined, too."

"We're all taking a chance. But they won't ruin it, Wes."

"That's blind faith and nothing else. What in God's name possessed you to fire Garibaldi?"

"He told me he'd heard I'd been a thief, and in jail—"

"He tried to blackmail you?"

She nodded.

"Damned idiot. But that's no reason to fire him three hours before dinner."

She did not answer.

"I told you when you insisted on using the name OWL Development that sentiment has no place in business. Neither does emotion. If you can't bring yourself to keep them separate, you'll destroy yourself."

"No. I won't do either." She looked at him with clear eyes. "I don't allow myself much sentiment these days, Wes, but when it's important enough I do. I don't think I'll do it to the point of destruction, but you'll have to trust me on that."

He met her look. Or what? he wondered. If I don't trust you, will you tell me to get out of your life? You can't; you're tied to me financially. If I push the issue, will you give in?

He gave it only brief thought. It was not the time or the place to have a confrontation; they'd have to wait until after the weekend. After Rosa's dinner. Christ, what a half-assed gamble. He hadn't thought she was capable of anything so stupid.

Guests passed them as they left the lounge to dress for dinner and the nightclub show. They stopped to remark on the furnishings, the service, the food, and especially the smooth operation. "Amazing, for a new hotel!" Amelia Laughton exclaimed as her husband, Sid, nodded. "Such attractive surroundings," said Carlos Serrano, kissing Laura's hand. "Exquisite taste," said the Italian couturier Flavia Guarneri, showing all her teeth as she smiled. Laura thanked them warmly, thinking it could either blow up in three hours, or she would have another triumph. She thanked everyone who praised her, on and on, until they were all gone and only she and Currier were left.

"We haven't had a minute alone for the past three weeks," he said. "On Monday we'll take off for a few days. I've made reservations at a place I like on St. Thomas."

"I can't, Wes, not yet. We've got bookings for the next three weeks, and Flavia told me she'll be back for a showing at Ultimo next month, and she's bringing friends—"

"You have a staff. You have your brother. You can't be here every minute."

"I can be here when I'm needed. When did you ever leave a project in its first week?"

"I left it at night so I'd have some energy for my companion."

That was fair, Laura thought; she'd been too tired lately to make love. "You're right; I haven't been much fun to be with. Can I have a few days to settle down? Then I promise I'll be back to normal."

"But not ready to go away, I gather."

"Not yet. Maybe . . . maybe in the spring."

He started to say something more, then changed his mind. "I'm going to change for dinner. Are you coming?"

"In a minute. I'll join you upstairs."

He left for the suite they had taken for themselves for the weekend, and Laura stood still, savoring the brief privacy and the quiet, broken only by the sounds of the waitresses clearing the tables. She'd have to change her schedule; she owed Currier energy and attention. They wouldn't be having so many clashes if she gave him more time instead of letting the hotel absorb her almost every minute of every day.

But it wasn't just the Chicago Beacon Hill that filled her thoughts; already she had begun to go beyond it. She hadn't told Currier, or anyone, and of course there wasn't much she could do for at least a year, until she'd proven herself here, but her imagination was already soaring past Chicago, to Owen's other three hotels, and his plans, and her own, for transforming them. She didn't know exactly how she'd do it: where the money would come from, how long it would take to buy all three of them—even *if* she could get them, the most troubling thought of all, since Felix might sell them before she could get the money, or she might not be able to find the money at all—but she had to believe she could make it happen. Somehow, whatever it took, she intended to do it all, as fast as she could, and she wasn't going to let anything stop her.

The New York Salinger, she said silently, then swiftly changed it. The New York Beacon Hill. The Philadelphia Beacon Hill. The Washington Beacon Hill.

Felix, I've got my start now. And one of these days you and your family are going to know I'm here. I'll own the hotels you stole from me and swore I'd never have; I'll fill them with the kind of famous, wealthy, powerful people you admire most; and I'll make them pay.

She turned and left the lounge to join Currier and dress for dinner. She was smiling to herself. And then, Felix, you'll know that Owen and I beat you after all.

CHAPTER 19

"**H**E can be vice-president for security," Felix snapped to his daughter, who was calling from Amsterdam, and his wife, who was on an extension telephone in another room of the house. "I told you that a month ago, and I haven't changed my mind. I also told you it's tentative. We don't know anything about him except the reports I've gotten from the hotel's management—"

"I've told you all about him," Allison said. "I've been telling you about him for over a year."

"You've been giving us romantic twaddle for over a year. And you refused to let us meet him; when you came home to visit, you came alone, and you told us you didn't want us there. And your cousin Patricia thinks he's a fortune hunter. I shouldn't be promising him a job at all; we're cutting back, not expanding, and I can't think of one good reason why he should get an executive's desk without working his way up from the bottom."

"He did that in Amsterdam. And he's going to be your son-in-law."

"That's no reason. Thomas Janssen is my brother-in-law, but he doesn't work for the company anymore."

"He left on his own," Leni put in quietly. "As soon as Owen died. And he's still a shareholder and member of the board."

"I'm asking you to do it," Allison said. "Is that a good reason?"

There was a pause. Like mother, like daughter, Felix thought: cold and independent. They don't ask for love. No wonder I don't love them.

But he still felt the same pride in them he had felt for twenty-four years; it had never waned, and by now he thought of it as a kind of love. When he saw them together, their striking angular elegance causing passers-by to turn as they walked down the street, he had the same sense of achievement and possession he had when he walked through one of his hotels. He became larger, more visible, more envied: Felix Salinger, who had outstripped his father in vastly expanding his hotel empire, who was changing the kind of empire it was by getting rid of its small properties and concentrating on mammoth ones, who had even outdone his father in his family life—his father's wife had died after ten years of marriage, but Felix still had his wife.

And now, listening to his wife and daughter talk over the telephone, their clear Boston accents filling his head, he was swept again by a sense of accomplishment, because it was through his largess that they were what they were: wealthy, world-traveled, sophisticated—and Salingers. They weren't soft and pliable, but they were part of his empire; they were essential to his whole being. And since, in the past year, the Salinger hotel chain had begun to show certain signs of trouble, Felix needed his wife and daughter more than ever, as proof that he always triumphed in the end.

He gazed at the December blizzard that swirled beyond the window, obscuring the homes across the road. A white Christmas, he reflected. A white Christmas wedding. Pity my daughter isn't a virgin; it would be so appropriate. But not only isn't she a virgin, she isn't even making a pretense at respectability: openly living with a man nobody knows, announcing their engagement in a telephone call at Thanksgiving, planning their arrival in Boston one week before the wedding. What does she have to hide? "What are you hiding?" he asked abruptly.

"You keep asking me that. Nothing. Ben is wonderful; everything is wonderful. I just wanted to have lots of time for us to be alone, to get started by ourselves, without anyone around. There were so many awful things that had happened at home—Thad was a hideous mistake, and then Grandpa died and then that mess with—with his will . . . I couldn't stand the thought of something else going wrong: I wanted everything with Ben to go right." There was a silence. "Can't you understand that?"

"Yes," Leni said. "But it would have been kinder if you'd said that months ago. You've been secretive for such a long time, keeping everyone away: I would have liked you to share it with me—with us."

"I know." There was another silence. Felix listened to the faint hiss of the thousands of miles between them. "Well, but that's past," Allison said tranquilly. "There aren't any more secrets. We're coming home, and we'll live in Boston and see you all the time. I just wanted to make sure Ben had a job. He said he'd look for one when we got there, but why should he? We have a company and he belongs in it. And he's satisfied with being vice president for security; you mustn't think he's complaining about it. I'm the one who thought he should be in charge of something bigger. Finance, or something like that. More important. And paying a lot more."

Felix stirred in his chair. "There's been no talk of salary. And I will not be forced into discussing it now."

"I wasn't forcing. I just thought I'd mention it because Ben won't. He'd never say anything, but I know it bothers him that I have so much more than he does."

"Then he'll learn to accept it or find a way to make more money on his own. He'll get no special treatment from me. Is that clear?"

"Yes, indeed," Allison said crisply. "It's all business in our family. No sentiment allowed. Actually, Ben will like that: he's not a very sentimental person. The two of you will probably get along fine."

"I'd like to talk about the wedding," Leni said before Felix could respond. "We'll have dinner here the night before, and lunch after the ceremony. Of course, it's only the family, but it's not often we're all together anymore . . . unless you'd like me to call some of your friends?"

"No, just the family," Allison said. "Ben really is adamant about keeping it small and absolutely no publicity; he's the most private person I've ever known. Did Rosa call you? I wrote and asked her if she'd come out of retirement long enough to make our wedding dinner."

"Yes, she called, so pleased that you wanted her."

Felix listened to the talk about menus and the small ceremony in their living room and the shopping Allison wanted to do as soon as they arrived. Ordinarily he would have hung up at this point but today he listened, confused and a little disturbed at the new confidence and composure in Allison's voice. She had been unsure of herself for such a long time, drifting from one man to another, one hobby to another, even one country to another, that now she sounded almost like a stranger. This business of gaining a son was sentimental horseshit, he thought: he wasn't gaining anything; he was losing the daughter he thought he knew. A wave of anger at Ben Gardner swept through him; she'll even change her name to his, he thought.

"Good-bye, Daddy," Allison said. "I'll see you next week. And Daddy"—her voice changed, becoming younger and more tentative—"please be nice to Ben. To both of us. I'm sorry I didn't want you to meet him, but it was all so special and I wanted it to stay that way, and Patricia was such a bitch—"

"Allison, she's your cousin," Leni said.

"Sorry. But she was snide and kept hinting at awful things just when I felt happiest, and I didn't see why I should have to go around defending the man I love to people who don't know a damn thing about him, so I just kept everybody away. It seemed a lot simpler at the time. I know I hurt your feelings and I'm sorry, but it's over now and we're all starting again, and I hope you'll be . . . nice."

"I am always civil, Allison," Felix said evenly. He knew she had started to ask him to be loving, but had evidently thought better of it. "We'll all be glad to see you next week."

"Next week," Allison echoed, her voice subdued, and Felix hung up, satisfied that his daughter had come begging to him and he had cowed her by being in better control of his emotions than she was of hers. He was always in control, he thought, turning to the paperwork on his desk. He assimilated information and then acted on it without second thoughts or puerile shilly-shallying. The ability to make swift decisions was his strength, and he relied on it even when he felt beset, as he did occasionally with the troubles at the company and this damned business with Allison.

Her new marriage would do nothing for him. It would not bring prestige or an infusion of wealth into the family; it would not even make him father-in-law to a pedigree like Thad Wolcott's, who, even though he turned out to be in debt, could trace his descendants to the Mayflower. His daughter was marrying a nobody, a nonentity they'd have to stumble over in the executive offices until she shed him the way she'd done with Wolcott, and then he could fire him. And if he could speed up that day, he'd damn well do it. In the meantime, to keep her and her mother happy, he'd go along with them as sociably as he did everything, even playing the proud father at the wedding. None of it would take much of his time. And none of it would last long.

I knew a Gardner once before, Felix thought. He was a nothing, too.

* * *

Paul flew to Boston a week before the wedding, scheduling his flight to arrive close to the time Ben and Allison were to arrive from Europe. It was the first time he had been back since his own wedding, eight months earlier, and as his plane flew out over the ocean and turned to come in low over the islands and bays and curving necks of land crowded with houses that formed the Massachusetts coast, he reflected that almost nothing in his life was the same as it had been when he last flew over that landscape. Then, he and Emily were poised at the edge of the extravagant success they would soon achieve. Emily had appeared twice in *Eye* magazine, in small spreads, and had just heard from Barry Marken that the fashion editor of *Elle* wanted her in Paris for a feature on new young designers; and Paul's portraits of three of Manhattan's most prominent hostesses had brought him calls from their friends and from two of their publicity agents: the swiftest road to fame. And in those early months after they had settled into Paul's Sutton Place apartment, they had been "discovered" and had soon become one of the hottest couples on the city's social scene, invited to dinner parties, charity balls, and discos, and sought after for all the fund-raising boards in town.

It was a whirlwind of black-tie affairs by night and work by day that stopped only briefly when they went to Boston in May for their wedding, then picked up as soon as they returned, because their marriage made them even more enchanting in a time when every social event became an occasion to learn who had divorced whom, or moved out or in with whom, or was sleeping with whom, or had wed whom.

Paul became one of the chroniclers of this scene, photographing its wealthy, powerful leaders with an eye for angle, lighting and pose that made every woman look as stunning as a dream and every man as sleekly powerful as he imagined himself to be. And Emily was a symbol they all wanted to claim as one of them, because she was the woman who had everything: wealth, background, youth, beauty and fame, and her presence was like a promise of hope to those who had not yet achieved so much.

But her fame really rested on Paul's photographs of her; they gave Jason d'Or and photographers at other magazines ideas on catching her beauty at its most tantalizing. In modeling, as in any field, there are fads that are seized by the quick and promoted by the clever, and Emily's ingenuous sophistication became the rage of the year on both sides of the Atlantic, her looks imparting a tantalizing blend of innocence and knowledge to whatever she modeled so that it looked as if it could be worn by everyone from hesitant virgins to jaded women of the world. By the time the Manhattan social season revived in October after its summer lull, Paul and Emily Janssen were the center of its spinning days and nights—the perfect couple: talented, beautiful, ideally matched. And if they quarreled, they never did it in public.

It was not until Thanksgiving that Paul took a night off to be alone and think. Emily was in London on an assignment for a consortium of British designers, and he hadn't felt like going to Boston for the holiday. Allison had called the day before, from Amsterdam, to tell him she and Ben would be married at Christmas, in Boston, and he had felt a sharp surge of longing, the same kind he had felt a year earlier, when he had seen Leni and her young man outside the Mayfair Regent. And he remembered what Emily had said: *She should have what she wants, not what she can get. Nobody should have to settle for that.*

What have I settled for? he wondered. He sat in his library, where he had watched Emily's face by firelight, and thought back over the past frantic months of work and social life. His portraits of social leaders hung in Park Avenue apartments and homes throughout the world, and they illuminated commercial and charitable advertisements in magazines of a dozen countries. But no art or photography gallery carried them, and Paul knew why: they all looked the same and, though they were excellent, they were not art.

For months he had been telling himself that soon he would move beyond the obvious: change the lighting to heighten shadows, not disguise them; refuse to brush out the lines, creases, and pouches that made faces distinctive; and try to recapture his earlier vision and brief moments of passion. But the months had gone by, and he had done more of what people wanted, avoiding controversy, as he always did, accepting their praise in an increasingly moody silence that was hailed as refreshing modesty.

It doesn't make much sense, he brooded, sitting in his library and thinking about what he had settled for: fawning adulation, a wild social scene, and more commissions than a serious artist could accept. Owen wouldn't be impressed, he thought. In his memory he saw Owen, tall and a little stooped, his long mustache curling at the ends, his eyes dark as he scolded Paul for his restless wanderings. "I'm finding myself," Paul had always declared, young and sure of himself, and Owen had shaken his head. "It'll take you a hell of a long time if you keep cluttering up your life so you never have time to do anything but make more clutter."

Clutter, Paul thought. All his ambitions to do great photography, drowned in the clutter of making flattering pictures of people who had an insatiable hunger for recognition, whether in a silver frame in their drawing rooms or in national and international magazines. He sat in his library, thinking about clutter, and the next day he asked his secretary to cancel all his photo sessions, saying he was ill.

It wasn't any one thing, he told himself that unexpectedly free day, and the days that followed. He walked in Central Park, drove to the Cloisters and sat for hours staring at medieval tapestries that showed the struggles of armies and kingdoms and made his own agonizing seem very small, and he wandered through the angled streets of Greenwich Village and SoHo and TriBeCa, watching the faces around him and wondering when he would have the guts to believe he could make art from real people.

"I don't believe in myself, whatever that means," he said gloomily, after a week of gloomy wandering around New York. He said it to Larry Gould, a friend from college, as they sat at lunch in Los Angeles, where he had gone to meet Emily. Paul and Larry had been roommates and partners in class projects, making films together that were raw and tentative, but that eventually led Larry to a phenomenally successful career in television commercials. He had been a scholarship student from three generations of Indiana steelworkers; by the time he was thirty, Gould Films was the top commercial studio in the country. "You probably know what it means," he replied to Paul as he sprawled in his chair on the outdoor terrace at La Chaumière. "All those philosophy courses in college about who we are and where we're going. Or have you forgotten them?"

"I think I've forgotten everything except how to make prominent people happy." Paul touched a deep red bougainvillea on the vine beside their table. "I never get used to these in December. Most of them are fakes. The prominent people, that is, not the bougainvillea. Some of them appear in advertisements for homeless children or heart research and care a hell of a lot for what they're doing, but then there are all the rest, who don't give a damn but like to see themselves in glossy color. It's their little ego trips: national exposure to show what good people they are, when the truth is they don't lift a finger or give a damn about the people they say their hearts bleed for."

"So what?" Larry watched the waiter serve their crabmeat salads. His sun-bleached hair was almost white, his long face was tanned and melancholy, reminding Paul of a basset hound wearing a blond wig. He looked lazily at Paul. "What do you care how people are separated from their money? The dollars buy the same homes for orphans or heart research or whatever, whether somebody in an ad is faking compassion or not. What's to get excited about?"

Paul shrugged. "I don't like frauds and liars. If it's a decent cause, there ought to be decent ways to get money for it."

Larry sighed. "And presidents should always tell the truth, stockbrokers should be honest, and spouses should love each other. Manhattan addled your brain? Or you just want to revert to childhood and live happily ever after in your playpen?"

Paul gave a grunt of laughter. "Right. I'm an ass." He picked up his fork and toyed with his salad, pushing aside the crab legs framing it. "I'm sick of the whole scene, that's the problem. I'm not even sure how I got mixed up in it. A year ago I had visions of being a hell of a photographer, seeing the hidden faces we all keep from the world, the scenes behind every scene . . . as if my photographs could be like a telescope, giving people a new view of the world, clearer, more intimate than the one they're used to . . . I don't know if this makes sense to you or not."

"You know damn well it does. What do you think I do for a living?"

"Make commercials, my friend. That's hardly photography."

"Filmmaking doesn't use a camera?"

"It has sound and action; it doesn't have to rely on a single frozen moment in time. It doesn't even have the same goals."

"Oh, he knows it all, he does. You ever direct a film, my friend, outside of those half dozen we did in college?"

"No."

"Then you're making a lot of noise for somebody who doesn't know what the fuck he's talking about."

Paul smiled. "Could be. Maybe I'll tag along on your next job and learn something."

"Why don't you? In fact," Larry said casually, "I think you ought to come to work for me."

Paul raised an eyebrow. "Do I look that desperate?"

"More than you should. Out here in the West we believe in happiness. I think you can find happiness in making films. Now listen." He leaned forward, the flippancy gone from his voice. "That speech you gave about hidden faces, and scenes behind the scenes—shit, Paul, that's what we all dreamed of in college. Right? You with your photos and me with films. But then I got the idea that life would be more fun if I got rich. And I was right. You know all about that; you were already there when you were in your cradle. But somewhere along the way to getting rich, I lost sight of all the wonderful films I'd wanted to make so I could give people a telescope to see the world in a new and intimate way. Are you following me?"

There was a pause. "You want to start another company."

"You got it." Slowly, giving Paul time to think, Larry buttered a chunk of French bread. "I think you need something new, and I know you're what I need: somebody with plenty of time and plenty of money, somebody who doesn't have to earn a living and can work like hell on a project because he loves it, not because he's praying it will make money —because usually it won't."

"Could I have a vague idea of what we're talking about?" Paul asked.

Larry chuckled. "Documentaries. I want to form a company to make brilliant documentaries about hidden faces and scenes behind scenes, and I want you to run it."

"You're dreaming, friend. I don't know the first thing about films, as you yourself pointed out. You can't start another company and put an amateur in charge. Unless—" A thought struck him. "Unless you're looking for an investor to fund it."

Larry nodded. "That, too. But I'd take you without money, because I think you're damn good. We'd make the first film together. That's a benefit of success: I can take a leave from my company. You wouldn't be an amateur for long; I've watched you in action, and I know how fast you learn." He sat back. "Remember how we talked in college? We had the same ideas, the same dreams. Only you had too much money; you weren't ever forced to see if those dreams could really work. Now here you are, bored and weary and feeling old, looking for something new. Something different. If you don't mind hard work and taking orders— and I don't fart around, you know; when I give orders my assistants jump—then I don't mind dragging you around for a while. Look, damn it, you have vision, my friend, and the world is pretty fucking short of vision these days. I want you with me, money or no. If you want a job, you've got it." He paused a fraction of an instant. "Of course, the money would help."

Paul burst into laughter. "How much?"

"A couple hundred thousand ought to do for a start. But it wouldn't be an investment, Paul; it would be more like a grant; you wouldn't get it back. These films don't make money. They might make you famous, but that doesn't pay the rent."

Paul toyed with one of the crab legs on his plate. Unexpectedly, he recalled another plate, in another restaurant, with red shells lying beside white meat. *You're the only woman I know who can crack open a lobster without turning her plate into a disaster area. Wonderful fingers; you'd make a good magician. Or a pickpocket.*

"—subject matter," Larry was saying. "It would be a joint decision once we—"

Paul shoved his plate aside. Something new, he thought, something different but not so different it's completely foreign. Something I can be proud of. Emily won't mind living here; she can live anywhere and still get work. And we'll be better off away from that damned merry-go-round we've been on, with no time to ourselves, no time to find out what it is we've got together. I owe it to her to make the best marriage we can, and I owe myself a life I can be satisfied with. And if I do all that, and do it well, there won't be any room for the past.

He finished his coffee. "Sorry, Larry, I didn't hear that."

"I said we'll choose the subject matter of the films together. I just happen to have a few story proposals in my pocket, but anything you want to add we'll talk about; I'm open to anything as long as it's controversial and visual and, of course, brilliant."

And so, because of high society in Manhattan and a crab salad in Los Angeles, Paul Janssen became a documentary filmmaker.

That week, while he and Emily were in Los Angeles, they bought a house in Bel Air, high above the city; lawyers began drawing up the papers that would make Gould-Janssen Productions a reality; and two weeks later work was already under way on the company's first outline when Paul flew to Boston for his cousin Allison's wedding to Ben Gardner and found the family waiting in the terminal at Logan Airport.

"Quite a reception," he said as his mother kissed him. "But I gather it's for Allison and Ben."

"Mainly," said Thomas, putting his arm around his son. "But we came early to meet you."

Paul counted his relatives, including some cousins he had not seen in years. "Eleven. It looks like a show of force."

"Morale boosters," Thomas said. "Your Aunt Leni thought it was necessary, since Felix is less than enthusiastic."

"Felix," said Paul, looking for him.

"He's making a telephone call," Leni said. She hugged Paul. "I'm so glad you'll be here for a few days; we'll have a chance to talk. When does Emily arrive?"

"In three days. Four at the most."

"Where is she?" Patricia asked.

"Scottsdale. A spring feature for *Vogue*. She's been there for two weeks; she's almost finished."

"On time, I see," Felix said, returning from the pay telephone. He took charge of the family. "We'll wait in the airline lounge; I told Allison to meet us there when they get through customs." Shepherding them down the corridor, he seemed to Paul to be nervous and even vaguely alarmed.

"Bad news on the telephone?" Paul asked casually.

"Of course not." The answer was automatic. "Some confusion at the office; this is a transition time for us, and it's difficult to get people to follow orders."

"Transition?"

"Everything changes," Felix replied obscurely. "Those who don't realize that and act on it fall by the wayside." He stopped beside an unmarked door and pressed a tiny, almost invisible doorbell. The door swung open, and he led the way inside, to a far corner where upholstered chairs were grouped around a table shaped like an airplane wing.

"Drinks?" he asked, and relayed his family's requests to one of the retired stewardesses who staffed the airline club.

"I didn't quite follow that," said Paul as the others began to talk among themselves. "Do you mean you're changing the way the company operates?"

"We're getting rid of dead wood," Felix said. "Old properties, old people, stale staff. We'll end up leaner and more efficient, and bigger than ever."

Paul took the drink being offered him. "How many are you laying off?"

"Twenty percent overall, including—"

"Twenty!"

"—natural attrition. Why not twenty, if it makes us more efficient? Your stock will go up when our balance sheets show it."

"How many of those people are longtime employees?"

Felix shrugged. "We've been in a rapid expansion program; we have to cut overhead. Some people always get caught by progress."

"I heard about the expansion," Paul said musingly, recalling letters from his parents. "You're tearing down the old buildings? Or renovating them?"

"I told you: we're getting rid of them; the lots are too small for what I want to build, and I won't be saddled with a style of building that may have mesmerized my father but doesn't impress me. We sold off the Chicago hotel a year ago, and I've had queries on the ones in New York and D.C. That only leaves Philadelphia and a couple more in Memphis and Fort Worth that the company picked up somewhere, God knows where; I've already got an offer on them. And we've been building steadily; I'm projecting ten new hotels in the next five years."

"Impressive," Paul murmured, hearing the defiance in Felix's voice and tying it to the other things he had heard: *transition . . . leaner . . . twenty percent . . . cut overhead . . . rapid expansion.* He wondered if they were in for stormy times. He had a lot of money at stake; his income depended mainly on the trust Owen had established when he was born, and a good part of it was stock in Salinger Hotels Incorporated.

The door to the club opened and, in a rush, Allison was with them, kissing Felix and Leni, reaching for Paul. He had time to see her radiant smile before she was in his arms and they were holding each other tightly. "Welcome home," Paul said softly, and as the others pressed around them they smiled together and became part of the crush. But Leni stood apart, frozen, her gaze fixed on the man who had followed Allison through the door and stood apart: tall, golden blond, with classic features and blue eyes behind horn-rimmed glasses. His mouth was hard; his gaze flicked rapidly over the circle around Allison. "Judd," she breathed. His eyes met her stunned look and held it. Allison, standing within Paul's arm, held out her hand, and Ben came and took it, shaking hands with Paul with the other. Then he turned to Leni and took her hand between his. "At last," he said. "I'm so glad to meet you. Allison's kept us as a surprise for each other for a long time."

"Yes," Leni said. She was ensnared in memories and could not speak.

Ben frowned, then he smoothed it away. "Allison didn't want us to meet earlier. I went along with that, so the responsibility is mine, too, but I hope you won't hold it against us. She said her father wasn't happy about us, but I hope you'll wish us joy."

"How do you do," Felix said thinly, his hand out, forcing Ben to turn from Leni. He was annoyed that Ben had gone first to Leni, he was annoyed that Ben was young and had the kind of golden blond looks he hated most, he was annoyed that his daughter was greeting everyone as proudly and happily as if she had brought home a member of European royalty instead of someone who dropped out of the sky and *was satisfied with being vice president for security*. Who the fuck did he think he was—being *satisfied* with a top-level job he would have groveled for, and been refused, if he'd been on his own? "And Allison," he said as she put her arms around his stiff shoulders and kissed him. "One of my staff is here; he'll bring your luggage; we'll go on in our car."

"Fine," said Allison. "Ben, you haven't met my cousins...." She introduced them in a blur of names and then stood expectantly, ready to leave.

Ben was gazing at Leni with a puzzled frown. "I hope we'll have time to talk today, to get acquainted."

"I'm sure we will." Leni's face once more was serene, her hands clasped before her. He really didn't look like Judd at all; she couldn't imagine what had gotten into her. His face was more rugged, less sensitive than Judd's; his jaw was more square, his forehead not as high, his hair less wavy. In fact, when she thought about it, the resemblance was really very slight. "Please forgive me for being rude; I get nervous in crowds. We'll have tea when we get home, and you and I will have a quiet time to become friends."

Ben's face cleared. "I'm glad. I was afraid I'd done something to offend you, and I would have hated that; I already feel so close to you, as if I've known you for a long time."

A wave of dizziness passed over Leni, and she put her arm through Ben's as they all walked down the wide corridor toward the parking garage. Of course there was a resemblance, she thought; she couldn't talk herself out of it; it was real. And there was something else: an odd blend of gentleness and toughness, almost cruelty, that jarred her memory and made her nervous. Because if he really was Judd's son—and she didn't know who else he could be—she had no idea whether or not Judd had told him about her. She didn't understand how it could come about that he had found their family, or what he would do now that he was here, or what he wanted from them.

Perhaps nothing, she told herself as the chauffeur held the doors for them while the rest of the family went on to find their own cars. The world is full of coincidences that make us look for meanings where there are none. If he wanted to go into hotel work, the chances of his finding us were very good. And I'd be very surprised if he knew anything about me; he was nine when I last saw Judd; he wouldn't remember even if Judd had been so lonely for companionship he told his little boy about us.

"Your parents," she said, clearing her throat as she turned to Ben. He was on the jump seat in front of Allison, who sat with her parents on the wide, deeply upholstered seat. "Allison told us they're dead."

He nodded. "My father died when I was thirteen, my mother some years later."

Judd, Leni thought, trying to recall the look in his eyes when he lay on her and told her he loved her. Dead. She had never thought of him as dead. When she allowed herself to think of him, she remembered the line of poetry he had quoted when Felix asked him where he wanted to go—*Where I can pick the golden apples of the sun and the silver apples of the moon*—and she would picture him in a misty paradise filled with luminous gold and silver apples, and peace.

Judd, Leni thought, with a painful longing she'd thought she had banished forever. What we had wasn't right, I know that; it wasn't right for either of us and it couldn't last, but, oh, it was so lovely when it was good, it was such pure joy... I think I've been trying to rediscover it ever since.

Ben's color was high, and she realized she was staring at him. Abruptly, to fill the silence, she said, "Felix and I have decided to give the two of you Owen's house as a wedding present."

"Oh, Mother!" Allison cried. She leaned across her father to kiss Leni's cheek, and then Felix's. "Thank you, thank you! Ben, wait until you see it—it's a wonderful house. We'll have Grandpa's rooms...of course they're a little dark; lots of mahogany and dark velvet drapes; we'll have to redo them...."

"How big is it?" Ben asked.

"Twenty-two rooms, thirty-three thousand square feet," Felix said.

"We don't need that much room."

"Not yet," Allison said serenely. "But it's a wonderful place for children."

"And we can't afford to maintain it," Ben went on.

"Of course we can; it won't be that expen—" She stopped. "We'll talk about it, all right? It's worth talking about. And you really should see it before we decide. We'll go there tomorrow, is that all right? Just to look at it?"

After a moment, Ben shrugged. Allison's eyes met Leni's, both of them thinking they'd talk to him and work it out. Because Leni wanted them in that house, and Allison wanted to live there. And Ben would agree, Leni reflected, because Allison was determined and because he would love it. She didn't know how she could be so sure of that, but she knew Ben Gardner would love Owen Salinger's house and would want to live in it as much as his bride did.

They'll be all right, Leni thought, sitting back and watching the gray coast flash by as they drove north to Beverly. Whatever Ben wants, it can't be to harm Allison; it's clear he loves her and she adores him. It will be good for all of us to have him here; we need someone fresh, an outsider, in the family and in the company, too. Her thoughts caught on a memory. Did Owen think that, she wondered, when he brought Laura into their midst? Someone fresh, an outsider . . . and it proved to be disastrous.

What *did* he want? It really was hard to believe his meeting Allison was accidental; it seemed more likely that he had sought them out. It didn't make sense, and it might turn out to be a coincidence, but just then she couldn't think of any other explanation.

And I can't ask him about it, she thought. All I can do is watch him and try to figure him out. I'm sure nothing disastrous will happen. Why would it? They love each other, they're young and happy, and I won't do anything to ruin what ought to be a happy time. Anyway, Ben isn't really an outsider; he and Allison have been living together and she knows him. They're going to be very happy, and so are we all.

The car came to a smooth stop in their driveway. Ben opened the door before the chauffeur could step out and do it for him, and held out his hand to Allison. The sky was dark, with a sliver of a moon, and Ben's face was strangely contoured in the light from the car. Leni could not help herself; she shivered.

It really was such a strange coincidence.

CHAPTER 20

THE first theft was in New York. Few people other than Flavia Guarneri's friends, her insurance company, and the New York Police Department paid much attention; it was shortly before Christmas, and everyone was busy. But Flavia took action: she fired her maid and butler. They hadn't been in her Fifth Avenue apartment when it happened—she'd given them a month off while she visited relatives in Chicago, San Francisco, and the south of France—but since there was no sign of forced entry into the apartment, who else could be responsible? So she fired them, gave the police and the insurance investigator all the information on the three Toulouse-Lautrecs that had been stolen, and went to an auction at Sotheby's and bought herself, for Christmas, three new paintings to fill the blank spaces on her walls.

And Clay delivered the Toulouse-Lautrecs to the broker who had hired him to steal them, netting himself a nice pile to pay off a few gambling debts, buy a fur-lined leather jacket he'd been wanting for a year, and get Myrna and Laura something grand for Christmas.

* * *

Laura heard about the theft from Currier the night they arrived in New York for a vacation, the first she had allowed herself since the Chicago Beacon Hill had opened a year earlier. "I talked to Flavia yesterday," Currier said after reading the paragraph in the morning *New*

York Times. "She says the police haven't a clue, and those were three of her favorite paintings, but I think she's far more concerned about finding a new maid and butler."

Laura smiled absently. She had picked up a Chicago newspaper from the stack of papers from five cities Currier had delivered to his apartment every morning, and was reading an item on the society page.

> The Place To Be Seen these days is the Chicago Beacon Hill, an *intime* hotel with a clubby bar that's a haven for the famous (when you go, don't gawk; just soak up the ambiance of power and wealth), a restaurant with continental cuisine that's to die for, and guests straight out of the rarefied heights of international society, culture, and mega-corporations. If you want to impress your visiting in-laws, buy them a weekend in one of the heavenly suites with decor supervised by general manager Laura Fairchild, who keeps the place running as silkily as a sybaritic spa. But be sure you book at least two months in advance; otherwise you haven't a prayer of getting in.

Laura handed the paper to Currier. "A little coy," she said dryly.

He skimmed it. "Perfect. She spelled the names right, yours and the hotel's, she got in the bar and the restaurant, and she gave you the credit. It couldn't be better."

"I wonder." The butler was pouring coffee and serving hot croissants and spiced pears, and Laura gazed out the window at Manhattan's spires and domes and rooftop terraces that seemed to sprout evergreens and winter-bare trees. Here and there a network of girders was visible, hinting at a new office or apartment building that soon would be completed, then occupied, then taken for granted as newer buildings appeared, seemingly overnight, like plants thrusting up to reach the sun. The whole city was like that, Laura reflected—eager, restless, pushing up and out, and at the same time pulling newcomers in, daring them to keep up with it, match its aggressiveness, master its intrigues, and keep on growing, like the city itself. I have so much to learn, she thought. About hotels, about business, even about New York. I was born here and grew up here, but I never saw it from this angle, and I don't think I know it at all. "I wonder," she said again, turning to Currier. "Our guests want privacy. If I were paying five hundred dollars a night, twenty-five hundred for a suite, I wouldn't appreciate this sort of thing."

He shrugged. "If you had the money to pay those prices, you'd be used to it; you'd ignore it. The people who pay attention are the ones who don't have that kind of money. They'll never stay at the Beacon Hill, or put their relatives there, either, but they'll damn well make sure they *visit*, to rub shoulders with the mighty, and they're the ones who'll keep your bar and restaurant profitable when the hotel has slow periods." He broke apart a croissant and spread honey on it. "As good as money in the bank. It has been, from the first weekend."

When Rosa and Kelly produced a superb dinner, and no one ever suspected the evening might have been less than perfect, Laura thought. But she did not say it aloud. Currier had thanked them and praised them afterward, at the nightclub, and the two of them had been as pleased with themselves as if they'd been understudies who saved a Broadway play, so Laura never worried that they hadn't had a good time at her opening. But Currier never mentioned it again, and neither did she. They both knew it was luck, not professionalism, that had pulled the evening off.

"It was a good beginning to a wonderful year," Laura said, thinking that it also had brought her the friendship of Ginny Starrett, who had taken to drifting in and out of Chicago like a southern breeze: unexpected, warm, and embracing. They were still getting to know each other, because Ginny couldn't bear staying in any one place for long, but by now Laura knew she would be back after every excursion to some part of the world, and soon she found herself looking forward to Ginny's return as much as she did Currier's. And in between, she had her privacy. The best of all worlds, she thought, and was taking a croissant on her plate when the butler came to the door to say there was a telephone call for her from Chicago.

As soon as she picked it up, Clay began talking, his voice pitched high with excitement. "Listen to this. We just had a call from Felix's office. They thought we might be interested in making an offer on the New York Salinger. They're ready to come here to talk to us about it."

Laura closed her eyes for a brief moment. *He came to me. He's asking me to buy Owen's hotel.* She smiled.

"What is it?" Currier asked.

"Felix thinks OWL Development might want to buy the New York Salinger." She tilted the telephone away from her ear so he could listen. "Did you make an appointment?" she asked Clay.

"I said Thursday morning. Is that okay? I thought we shouldn't sound like we were jumping at it."

"That's fine. It gives me time to take a look at the hotel and fly to Chicago Wednesday night."

Currier stirred and started to say something, then changed his mind and contemplated the view.

"I'm sorry," Laura said as she hung up. "I know this was supposed to be our vacation, but I can't pass this up. You wouldn't want me to.

Would you? Wes, you know how long I've been thinking about it."

"Since the day the Chicago hotel opened."

"Even before that. I didn't make a secret of it."

"But you kept it in perspective. You had a job to do, and you concentrated on it."

"And I did it."

"You're through with Chicago? You have nothing more to do there?"

"I could always find more things to do. But why should I?" Caught between puzzlement and anger, she gestured toward the Chicago newspaper. "This says we've done something right, and I can hire a top manager to keep it up. Why not? I've watched you make plans for a new project while you were still finishing an old one and your staff was researching a dozen more; why is it all right for you to look for ways to get bigger and more powerful, but not all right for me? You've known from the beginning that I wanted all four of those hotels, and now, when one of them almost falls in my lap..." She gazed at his tight lips and felt her anger spark. "You thought I'd be satisfied with one. Am I right? You thought I'd get it out of my system, and then marry you and travel with you and spend my time and energy on Wes Currier instead of something as unimportant as a little hotel in Chicago."

"I never said it was unimportant."

"You're right; I take that back. You helped me; you made the whole thing possible. But now that it's a success, you want me to walk away from it and forget everything else I want to do. Why should I? You're not changing your plans; why should I?"

"Because my plans, as you call them, are a solid business, and yours are dreams and fraught with risks. Because I can take care of you—"

"If they are dreams, they've started coming true, and I'm not afraid of risks."

"You don't build a life from one success."

"You did. You told me you arranged one merger and then staked everything you had on funding your own company."

"It was a long time ago, and now it's behind me. All the groundwork, the scheming, the anxiety about success or failure, the crazy hours and priorities... it's all in the past. Why should you waste years going through the same things when you don't need to? I can take care of you, I can spend as much time with you as I want, we can go anywhere in the world that pleases us. The struggle is over. I don't want to go through it again; there's no reason to."

"No reason to," Laura echoed. "You don't want to go through it again. Isn't that too damn bad!" She shoved back her chair. Tense with nervous energy, she walked around the room, picking objects up and putting them down. "Your struggle is done, so I don't need mine—or the victories either, of course! You thought it was all right for me to have one success—how generous of you!—but that's it; now I'm supposed to let you take care of me. And you're going to spend all the time with me you want. My God, how flattering! What if I don't want to spend that time with you? What if I want the struggle and the anxiety and the crazy hours? What if I like the priorities I've set for myself? What do you think I am, a company you're planning a merger with? You set up a time schedule, you decide who does what and when, and then at the proper time you announce it and wait for the troops to fall into line."

"Sit down," Currier said calmly. "When are you going to learn to control that temper? If you're not careful, you'll fire me, the way you fired the chef, and then you'll be in terrible trouble."

"Will I? What makes you so sure?" Breathing rapidly, her head high, she stood near the window, challenging him. Behind her was the pale winter sun and the rooftops of New York; in front of her was Currier's starkly elegant dining room and his commanding presence. It seemed to Laura that she stood between two choices: the city where she wanted to make her mark and the man who wanted to make her his.

"You're being exceedingly foolish," Currier said. His voice was not as calm as before; Laura heard an edge in it that could have been impatience or worry. "I can't force you to do anything, not even to live a life of luxury instead of struggle. And I don't set time schedules for you; on the contrary, I've been following yours since you told me you wanted to buy that hotel in Chicago; it doesn't seem too much to think you might follow mine for a while. I've backed you from the beginning, I believed in you and I proved it, and I have a goddam right to ask—" He stopped.

"Right?" she echoed coldly. "Right? Because of money? We are talking about money, aren't we? Even though we decided a long time ago it was never going to be part of our personal relationship?"

Currier threw down his napkin and went to her. "I'm sorry." He put his arm around her but she took a step back, and he let out a sigh of annoyance. "Damn it, listen to me. What I meant was, I'm part of your life now, part of everything you do, and I expect to be consulted when you're making new plans. I won't be ignored or bypassed, Laura. I'm saying that as an investor and your lover and your husband—"

"You aren't my husband."

"I will be; you know it as well as I do."

"No." Involuntarily she took another step back. "I won't marry you, Wes. I've never said I would, but you pretended I just needed time—"

"I *knew* you needed time, and I didn't mind giving it to you. But I know how brutal business is, and I knew once you found out for yourself, you'd be ready for the kind of life I could give you."

She shook her head. "You just won't understand. I *want* the brutal part. I want it all. Damn it, I have a right to it if I want it! Why do you think men are the only ones who can struggle and win, or lose and get up to struggle again? What do you think you're protecting me from? A few bruises? I've had them; I can survive a lot more if I have to. This is my dream, Wes, mine and Owen's, and I don't see any reason why I'd turn my back on it just because you tell me life can be a lot easier. I'm going to Chicago Wednesday night, and on Thursday I'm going to do my damnedest to buy the New York Salinger, and as soon as I do, I'll be back here to start work on renovating it and to find an apartment I can afford in Manhattan—and that's probably going to be the hardest thing of all."

Reluctantly, he chuckled. "Probably. But I can help you; I know some management agents—"

"Wes, I'm trying to tell you I'm not asking for your help; I don't want it."

"That's idiotic. Of course you do. This has nothing to do with marriage or even living together. We're partners in OWL Development, and I intend to protect my investment. We're also friends, and I'd like to protect that. In any case, you need me. How do you expect to buy the New York Salinger? You won't get a bargain, the way you did in Chicago, and you've borrowed to your limit; you couldn't get the money to buy it at any price."

"No, but we have people who want to be investors." She gave him a clear look. "You told me about them a couple of months ago; did you think I wasn't paying attention? Some bankers and developers, you said, who want to buy into a Beacon Hill chain."

He nodded. "But they came to me, not you, because they trust my judgment and they know I'm behind the corporation. Do you think they'd offer you the same money and the same terms?"

"One of them might. And then the others would follow; it would be the same as following you. I haven't talked to any of them yet, but now that Felix has called, I guess I'll have to get my act together. I think I can swing it: the balance sheet is good, and the auditor's report was excellent; you were the one who said what a good year it's been since that first weekend."

The room had darkened as a bank of clouds obscured the sun. Snowflakes flew past the window, blown straight up and sideways in an erratic dance. Currier moved to a wall switch and turned on a row of ceiling lights. "Did I teach you that confidence?" he asked.

"A lot of it. But mostly it was the success of the hotel: the letters I get, and the comments from people when I talk to them in the lounge and the restaurant, and our occupancy rate—a few times we've had the highest in Chicago. And the people who come back. It makes me feel appreciated."

"Loved," he corrected.

"Appreciated." She smiled. "You make me feel loved."

He raised his hands and dropped them in exasperation. "You're the damnedest woman. Why the hell do you get on your high horse and force an argument? You could have married me and had fifty hotels; I would have given you everything you wanted."

"I don't want to marry you," she said with an honesty that Currier admired and loved, even as he felt he'd been struck in the gut. "And I don't want you to give me everything. I really do want the struggle, Wes. I want to win. It wouldn't be the same if you dropped all the victories into my lap, ready-made."

He contemplated her for a long moment, then returned to the table and took the coffee carafe from its warming plate. "More?"

"Yes. Thank you."

"How about this?" he asked casually, filling their cups and not looking at her. "When you move to New York, you'll live here. It's empty most of the time, and you might as well use it. I'll help you talk to those investors; we'll put together a financial package for the New York hotel and build into it something we can draw on for the other two as soon as we can get them. For the rest you're on your own. We'll expect the New York Beacon Hill to be as successful as the one in Chicago; you'll submit the same monthly reports to us as you do now, and keep us advised of major upheavals, such as the firing of a chef, or any security problems, or adverse reports from guests. And you and I might dine together now and then or go to the theater, if the mood strikes us." He handed her the full cup. "Is that satisfactory?"

Laura held herself back from going to him and putting her arms around him. "You're a good friend, Wes," she said quietly. "Thank you." She smiled wryly. "I really didn't want to go to any investors without you. I'm so grateful . . ." She went back to her chair at the table and he joined her there. "But I can't live here. I know how crazy that sounds, to turn down any apartment in Manhattan, much less a palace like this, but I think I'd better live alone. I'd love to have dinner with you, and go to the theater; I want us to go on being friends. But not lovers."

After a moment, he put his hand on the table and she put hers in it. "We'll see how that works out," he said, and they sat quietly, finishing their coffee and watching the papery snowflakes whirl faster and more thickly in the gray light. It was good enough, Currier thought. He'd gotten past the worst of it, when she was ready to throw everything to the winds and rush off on her own: they were still working together, they'd see a great deal of each other, and she'd still be largely dependent on him. And they'd go on from there.

He was no longer as surprised as he had been at his persistent desire for her, but he hadn't expected that his desire would grow as his own successes multiplied. In the complex arena of international mergers and acquisitions where he maneuvered and manipulated, he went from triumph to triumph, skillfully satisfying both sides in every negotiation, and delighting stockholders. He would fly home to Laura with satisfying memories of arranging people and their money into new patterns, like an artist designing a mosaic; but then, in her apartment, he would discover anew that while he could arrange others, he could not arrange her. He could not even fit her into a predictable pattern. She veered from affection to aloofness, warmth to reserve, carefree laughter to stubborn determination. And Currier, accustomed to leading the way, found himself following her, because it was precisely her stubbornness and aloofness that he loved the most, even as he wanted to tame them, or at least tone them down.

Laura stirred in her chair. "You still think I'll give it all up," she murmured.

He smiled. "No. It's hard to hold on to that kind of blind belief when you keep knocking it down."

"What do you think, then?" she asked, and he thought it was almost as if she were asking him how a book would end.

"I think we'll find a way of pleasing each other," he said, and at that moment he believed it with the same kind of assuredness that had won him an international reputation. "I won't ask you to give everything up, and you won't ask me to be a friend who loses out on a vacation because you decide to buy a hotel. One way or another, we'll work it out."

She glanced at him. "Are you in a hurry?"

"Of course not," he said promptly. "Take your time." And they laughed together, more relaxed than they had been all morning.

Of course, Currier mused, there was the question of other men; neither of them had brought it up. But if she was living alone, not engaged, not even pledged, she was free to see anyone she liked. Not if I can help it, he thought. Not if she's so busy she doesn't have time. Not if she's with me much more than she anticipates.

"How about an inspection visit to the New York Salinger?" he asked. "We can pretend to be young lovers looking for a morning toss in the hay."

Laura laughed. "More likely they'll think we're narcotics agents with a lousy cover story. But I do want to go; I've only seen the lobby so far."

Currier stood. "Another thing," he said casually. "I'd like to invite Flavia to dinner one night. She's probably more upset about that robbery than she's admitting, and it's a good time to get her together with friends. No more than twenty or thirty guests; will you be my hostess?" When Laura hesitated, he added, "I know you'll be finding your own apartment, and I won't pretend to anyone that we're more than friends. But Flavia likes you; I'm asking you to do it for her sake, not mine."

She laughed again. "My generous Wes. Of course I'll do it, for Flavia and for you." She stood with him. "I do like to be with you, Wes."

He nodded and put his arm around her. He was counting on that.

* * *

Felix had not looked at the New York Salinger for years. He'd never liked it, and once he began building towers of glass and steel in other cities, it rankled him that the Salinger name in Manhattan was on a narrow old building of dark brick, stuck like a sliver between two office buildings in the shadow of the Plaza Hotel. Owen had built it when he was young, and it was in the *grande dame* style of its day, but after Iris died and he withdrew into his grief, the hotel settled into middle age, like a respectable matron who reminds everyone of another generation. That was when architecture was turning to stark, unornamented facades, towering skyscrapers that reflected the passing clouds, and lobbies like train stations, where conventions could come and go and still leave room for business travelers and a few families. The New York Salinger slipped into obscurity. Even when Owen returned to the company, there was too much to do to keep up with other hotel chains at a time when everyone was reaching for modernism as if it were the golden fleece.

Still, he never abandoned the old hotels; they were impeccably maintained, and after a while the New York Salinger gained a permanent listing in Manhattan guide books as a comfortable, relatively inexpensive hotel for visitors or businesspeople on a tight budget. It never lost money. Its location near the Plaza made it an easy walk to theaters, shopping, and major office complexes; there were always people looking for a low-cost, pleasant room in the center of town; and, after Owen's death, Felix cut back on staff and services enough to ensure a profitable operation until he could get rid of it.

But it hadn't sold, partly because for a long time no one thought a one hundred and ninety-room hotel could make money, especially in Manhattan, and partly because mortgage rates had gone up. Felix could have lowered his price, but he had paid an exorbitant amount for land on the

West Side, near the new convention center, and his board of directors was growing concerned about what some of them were beginning to call overextending themselves. He was reluctant to lower the price, anyway; he balked at the idea of giving away a hotel in one of the most desirable locations in Manhattan. So he waited, growing more impatient, worried that his board might try to slow down the rapid expansion he had vowed he would undertake the day his father died. And finally, bypassing his real estate agents, he had one of his staff call OWL Development in Chicago.

It was a piddling company with only one hotel—that had been a Salinger hotel, too—but Felix knew Wes Currier was the financial backer, which meant their money was good, and, probably, their aim was to expand. And soon he was congratulating himself on his good instincts: OWL's offer was below what he'd thought he'd have to settle for, but in the negotiations he got them to go up enough to make a satisfactory deal. By the middle of February, much sooner than anyone had predicted, the New York Salinger had changed hands. An item in *The Wall Street Journal* reported that the hotel, now called the New York Beacon Hill, would undergo extensive renovation and open sometime the following December. But Felix barely noticed; it was off his hands. He celebrated by taking Leni and Ben and Allison to Loch Ober's for dinner, and was more expansive than usual in talking about business outside the office.

"I wonder, though," said Ben ruminatively. "Maybe it's not a good idea to get rid of those hotels and put everything we've got into the huge ones; we may be going against a new trend in this country."

"A new trend," Felix echoed contemptuously, raising his voice in the close-packed room where the din of conversation forced everyone to speak louder, increasing the noise even more. "You've been here fourteen months, hardly enough to be an expert on a country and its trends."

"Maybe Ben's been paying attention," Leni said mildly. "You can learn a lot about any place in fourteen months if you pay attention."

"What trend?" Allison asked.

"Small and elegant," Ben replied, ignoring Felix's contempt. "People seem to be turning away from massive things. It's as if they're reaching out for a way of life that lets them feel more in touch, more in control of their world. Small dinner parties, small movie theaters and boutiques; maybe small hotels."

"Very fanciful," Felix said. With his napkin he dabbed scotch from the mustache he had grown soon after Owen died. "Dinner parties and movie theaters may be able to survive if they're small; hotels can't. With the costs of building—"

"Renovating is cheaper. That's why I think we shouldn't be in a hurry to get rid of—"

"*With the costs of building*," Felix repeated, to ensure he would not be interrupted again, "we've got to get the highest possible return per square foot. But it's not only building costs, and you know it: you've heard me say it before. The public doesn't want small and elegant; most people wouldn't know elegant if it bit them. They want big, splashy buildings, bright lights and noise, swimming pools, video games, heated garages, and a place big enough to hide for a quick afternoon with the secretary."

"Oh, Daddy, for heaven's sake," Allison said. "There aren't enough men like that to keep us in shoes."

"You know all about it, of course. Hotels are full of men—and I daresay women, too—looking for a quick lay between lunch and going home to the family."

Leni was watching Felix intently. "Is that true?" she asked.

"I said it was."

"You don't like people, or trust them, either," Allison said.

"I understand what they want. And what they want has to do with quick and easy; it hasn't a damn thing to do with elegance."

Ben shrugged. "The Regent International chain wouldn't agree. And that new hotel in Chicago, the Beacon Hill—it used to be ours, didn't it? And now it's got one of the highest occupancy rates in the city, with the highest room rates. Somebody must like it."

"And no one likes Marriott," Felix said sarcastically. "Or Hyatt or Hilton."

"I didn't say stop building the big ones; I only said I thought we might do both."

Felix preserved a disapproving silence as their dinners were served, and then Leni changed the subject.

Ben watched her as she talked about the apartment she and Felix finally had bought in New York, after two years of looking and never being able to agree on one. Her face and voice were serene, but he thought she seemed uncomfortable. It was difficult to be sure about Leni; Ben didn't understand her at all. Whenever he asked her questions about her background, she changed the subject, and he wondered about it: why she had married Felix and what their marriage really was like. He wondered what she thought of his marriage to Allison; he wondered what she thought of him. She treated him warmly, but often he found her watching him with puzzled eyes and a strange kind of longing, as if she would have been different with him, somehow, if he did—something. He didn't know what she wanted him to do. He didn't know what she wanted him to say. He would have done it or said it if he could have figured it out, because he wanted her to be his ally, but all these months had gone by and he still didn't know whether she was watching him because for some reason she didn't trust him and was waiting for him to trip up, or because she just wanted to figure him out and he didn't talk about himself very much.

Felix was easier—and more difficult. His contempt stung Ben and made him want to strike out, but he forced himself to shrug it off. He was unfailingly civil, reminding himself every day that Felix was his father-in-law and his employer and he couldn't afford any kind of breach, but his hatred for Felix must have shown in ways he wasn't aware of, because from the first day, it was clear that Felix hated him and could barely hold it in.

Maybe I remind him of my father, Ben thought, as he often had since arriving in Boston, but on balance he didn't think he did. It had been over thirty years since Felix had stolen the company from Judd, and Felix seldom paid much attention to people he used, or abused. Ben thought it unlikely he'd ever given Judd much thought after Judd came back from the war and found his company gone and Felix's door closed to him.

But the main reason Ben didn't know if he reminded Felix of his father was that he couldn't remember exactly what Judd had looked like, and he had no pictures of him. He had some of his mother, and he knew he resembled her, but how much of him was Judd? Every time he got to this point in his thinking, he gave it up. He couldn't know. Anyway, even if he did remind Felix of Judd, so what? Nothing would come of it, because he and Allison were married, and now that she was pregnant he was more a part of the family than ever. He was also damned good at his job and everybody knew it.

From the day he moved into his new office, he'd acted fast, knowing he had to make a place in the company as secure as his place with Allison so no one could force him out the way they'd forced out Laura. And within a year, with a speed that impressed hotel experts, more than half the Salinger hotels had new key locks, safes in the rooms, national computer checks on maids and lobby personnel, television cameras in the corridors, and expanded plainclothes staffs. Ben had made special trips to the hotels to talk to the newly enlarged security staffs, sitting in on their lunch breaks, making suggestions on what to look for, and where. Felix heard about it in monthly reports from the managers, who said that, thanks to Ben Gardner, they had higher morale, tighter security, and fewer problems to report.

And whether he liked him or not, Felix had given Ben two raises, bringing his salary to sixty thousand dollars a year. Ben nodded somberly when he heard about the second raise, and Felix, irritated, said, "You might be appreciative."

"I am. I hope you are. I thought my work was good."

Felix struggled with his inclination not to praise anyone. "It is. You've read the reports."

Ben smiled briefly at his small victory. "I've been thinking it's time for me to move out of security. We have no vice president for development, and I'd like to create that position."

"We have none because I handle it; if you have any suggestions for new properties you can bring them to me. You'll stay in security; as you yourself said, you've done a good job."

"I'd like you to consider the new post; perhaps we could bring it up before the board."

Felix heard the threat behind the words and his face tightened. "I've considered it; I've rejected it. You've just been made a member of the board, and that's enough for now. And I think it's time you got back to work."

In his own office again, Ben thought about his next step. He wanted the new position because development was at the heart of a large corporation and would put him in the best possible position for the future. But he also wanted it because development commanded higher salaries than security. Money was not a subject he could discuss with Felix, but it was something he thought about all the time. He didn't feel secure, and money was a big part of the reason, though there were others, too, mainly his worries about Laura.

He felt her presence in the house, and sometimes he went into the rooms that had been hers and sat there, thinking about her. Allison had told him the whole story while they were in Europe; he'd read the trial transcripts as soon as they got to Boston; and he kept thinking about calling her. But he didn't know how. He was having enough trouble knowing how to behave with Allison and her family; he couldn't deal with Laura, too, not right away, anyway. And so the time slid away and he didn't call, and finally, in desperation, he wrote a long letter. It was easier to talk to a piece of paper than to talk to his sister and hear the anger he remembered in her voice while trying to say everything he wanted to say without interruptions or having to defend himself. So he wrote. He sent it to the Chicago Beacon Hill—he'd read in a hotel magazine that she was its manager—but he never received an answer.

The hell with her, he thought, and didn't write again. But her presence was still in his house. It seemed nothing would change that.

Even her rooms weren't changed. As angry as Allison was about Laura, she didn't redecorate her old rooms. She did the rest of the house, spending a small fortune on what Ben thought was just fine the way it was, but she left Laura's rooms alone. And then one day she asked Ben, "What do you think about putting the baby in here?"

"And redecorate it as a nursery?"

"No, it's fine. If it's a boy we might move him later to make room for his sister. If it's a girl, she can stay here. And the nanny can use the sitting room; we can get a daybed in there without any trouble."

"Sure," Ben said casually, and that settled it.

He and Allison agreed on most things as long as they weren't talking about money. It was when she started talking about all the things they would do that he got tight and edgy. She wanted more children; she wanted to travel—children, nanny, and all; she planned to enroll their ten-week-old fetus in Stoddard, the private school that would be full if they waited too long . . . and on and on while Ben calculated costs and knew he could never keep up.

Even with his second raise, Allison's income from her trust was ten times his. He wasn't pulling his weight, and he told her so, over and over. She'd even sold him some of her shares in Salinger Hotels Incorporated for a token sum because Felix hadn't yet offered him any, and Allison insisted that he should own at least a small amount. But he knew what they were worth and what he had paid, and that was another example of his not doing his part. And however much she waved all that aside, it nagged at him: he knew it would get worse as the years passed and their expenses increased and his salary lagged farther and farther behind. And it wasn't just the children they would have or the trips they would take as soon as Felix let him have decent vacations; they were becoming part of a young crowd that was fast-living, worldly and very wealthy, and that meant clothes and gifts and club dues and a host of expenses he hadn't dreamed of when they lay in bed in Amsterdam and talked about getting married.

Of course he'd known that money would be a problem, and once they were settled in Boston he'd tried to do something about it, but the problem seemed to grow faster than the solutions he could think of. It all came down to a very simple fact: he knew he would never be comfortable as Allison's husband, or as one of the Salingers, unless he found a way to get more money.

So, although he disagreed with Felix about ways to run the Salinger hotel chain, he seldom argued with him for long; he couldn't afford to.

Even when Leni and Allison seemed to be on his side, as they were at Loch Ober's, celebrating Felix's sale of the New York Salinger, he let it go. They shouldn't have sold it, he thought, but it was gone. He would have liked to say they should seriously consider keeping the ones in Philadelphia and Washington, D.C., but he kept silent and he was quieter than usual for the rest of the dinner, at the same time that Laura was being unusually quiet with Currier, in New York, where they were dining at Lutèce.

"You're very quiet," Currier said as the wine captain decanted the rare burgundy he had ordered. The airy room was like a garden, its trellis-work, white columns, and palms in brass pots bringing thoughts of summer rather than the raw February night held at bay by the high dome above. The diners spoke in low voices, the waiters moved efficiently and murmured as they discussed menu and degustation items, but as quiet as the room was, Laura's silence was noticeable, and Currier studied her when the wine captain left them. "What happened to the excitement you had when we bought the Chicago hotel?"

"It sank in a sea of reality," she said with a small smile. "This time I know how much work is ahead."

And how much money.

"I've been thinking about the work," Currier said. "I have a heavy schedule coming up, and I won't be able to get as involved as I'd like. I'll be in town as often as I can, but the more we get done this month, the better. Those architects we interviewed, for example..."

I owe three million dollars to the three investors who came in this week.

"I liked Simons best, but I think we ought to see him and Brewer again; see how they react to your idea of making the hotel all suites."

And I already owed Wes five million dollars.

"It hasn't been done in mid-Manhattan, but it's the perfect town for it and probably the perfect time, with the swing back to older buildings."

And to get the three million this week I had to give up control of OWL Development; the three investors could outvote Wes and me. And I used my stock in OWL as collateral for that loan; if the hotels do badly, if I miss a payment on my loans, I lose it all.

"If we choose an architect in the next couple of weeks, there's a good possibility we can open around Christmas, just as we did in Chicago. We might be starting a tradition—part of your good luck."

Wes warned me; he told me not to think about the other hotels, not to give up control. He wouldn't have gone along if I hadn't insisted. But I can't stop now. If I'm risking everything, then that's how it has to be. I'm halfway there, and nothing's going to keep me from finishing what I've started.

"On the other hand, your good luck could be finding a dinner companion who's willing to carry on a monologue while you're so wrapped up in your thoughts you don't hear a thing he says."

Laura's look focused on him. She gave a small laugh. "But I did hear you. You want to interview Simons and Brewer again, and old buildings are coming back. And you want to open a new hotel every Christmas."

"God forbid. And what about my idea for a restaurant on the top floor of the New York Beacon Hill?"

She frowned uncertainly. "I don't . . . did you talk about that? I'm sorry, Wes, I didn't hear it."

He smiled and shook his head. "I didn't. Somehow, and amazingly, you got most of what I said." He put his hand under her chin. "What are you worried about?"

"Money."

"Good. Smart businesspeople always worry when the numbers are large and the chances for success significantly smaller. It doesn't stop them; it just keeps them somewhat realistic. You're off to a good start." He lifted his glass and waited for her to do the same. "To the past and the future," he said.

A little startled, she shook her head. "I never drink to the past; I thought you knew that."

"Not the distant past," he agreed, "but the nearer one. The Chicago Beacon Hill, our partnership, our friendship . . ." He raised an eyebrow. "Not worth a toast?"

"Of course," she said and drank some of the smooth wine. But once again her thoughts intruded, and when the waiter handed them menus, she held hers absently, half listening as he and Wes discussed the chef's specials. She was thinking about Ben.

Ben was the distant past, and the near past, too. Because he had written to her months ago, a few months after he arrived in Boston and was married.

"I wish you'd been there," he wrote in his letter.

I thought of inviting you, but from what Allison told me, I figured you wouldn't want to be part of a small Salinger family gathering, and I'm afraid they wouldn't have made you welcome. They've got to change their minds about you—I'm going to make damn sure they do—but it'll take a while, and I have to be careful because they don't know I have a sister, much less who she is, and I can't do anything to make them suspicious. I hope you understand that: I really can't take a chance and make them suspicious of me. I wish I could move faster and do this for you, Laura, but I can't. So far they've all been cool but civilized to me, except for

Leni, who's mostly friendly and warm, and Felix, who's a cold, fish-eyed son of a bitch I wouldn't trust for a minute. He acts like he doesn't trust me, either, which makes it kind of tense around the office. I'm vice president for security for Salinger Hotels—not a bad start, wouldn't you say?—with a fancy office down the hall from Felix's. It's a good job and I like it; the company is so big there's always a crisis going on somewhere and it's like solving a different puzzle every day, and that keeps me on my toes. The only problem is money, but I'm figuring out ways around that. No, there is another problem: you. I want to see you, Laura; I miss you a hell of a lot. Everything's changed in our lives, and I guess we have, too, but I don't know how much. When I got here at Christmas, and we went to the Beacon Hill house—you probably noticed from my stationery, that's where we're living; Felix and Leni gave it to us as a wedding present—and when I saw the rooms you'd lived in, I couldn't believe how beautiful you'd made them. Remember when you used to say you wanted a place of your own away from me and Clay? You really got it; when I saw your rooms I knew why you never wanted to come back to live with me. But I wanted to cry, because they weren't yours anymore, and that's when I knew somehow I'd get you back here. Not to live, of course; you've made a new life, the way I did a few years ago, and you probably have another beautiful home now; but you ought to be able to come and go in this house and not feel you couldn't ever see it again, with all its memories. What I'm trying to say is, I could tell from those rooms how much you've changed, and your life has changed, but I don't have any idea how you feel about me now. Maybe you've changed enough to change your mind about never wanting to see me again. I've changed, too; I'd like to talk to you about it. Maybe we've changed in the same ways. There's a lot I'd like to explain and talk to you about; it's very strange being here, and I need somebody from outside, especially somebody I care about. Laura, we loved each other once, and that doesn't ever really disappear, does it? Could we get together and see if we still do? Or could again? I wouldn't ask you to come to Boston; I'd come to Chicago (I read about you in *Hotels Today*; it sounds like you've got a good job, and I'd like to hear more about it). Please write to me; I really want to see you. And Clay, too, of course, if he wants to.

The Beacon Hill house. Laura turned back to the first page of the letter. The imprinted address on the stationery was Owen's, and it had been hers. Staring at it, she began to tremble.

Everything she had loved and dreamed of and lost, Ben had won. He was living in the Beacon Hill house. He owned it. He had married into the Salinger family. He was an executive in the Salinger hotel chain.

He had destroyed her chances for all of that, and then he had grabbed it all for himself.

Get together with you? And have you invite me to your house? It's my
house! Owen left it to me! If you think I'll ever go there and have you
greet me as its owner...

She crammed the letter into a corner of her briefcase and carried it
with her, thinking someday she might think of something to say and
answer it. But every time she thought about it, she remembered a different part. *'I need somebody from outside'... Who the hell does he think he*
is, to remind me I'm an outsider there?

Finally, on a golden day in early fall, when she'd taken a weekend off
to hike at Starved Rock, she sat under an oak tree and read Ben's letter
one last time.

We loved each other once, and that doesn't ever really disappear, does
it?

She rested her head against the rough bark of the oak tree and let
herself remember Ben when she had adored him and counted on him to
take care of her in a frightening world. And she knew that no matter
how angry she might be, somewhere inside her she would always love
him because he was so much a part of her, no matter how high the walls
between them seemed. And then, as smoothly as one wave following
another, she thought of Paul; she could hear his voice and see his smile
and the way his eyes darkened when he looked at her, and remember the
feeling of belonging she always had when they were together.

No. That doesn't ever disappear.

She tore Ben's letter into small pieces and dug a small hole in the moist
earth, burying the pieces as deep as she could. Black soil was under her
polished nails; she thought of Clay working in the greenhouse on Cape
Cod, and wondered if she could ever escape from her memories. Then she
filled in the small hole, brushed off her hands, and went home.

"I'll drink to the future," she said to Currier. It was February, now,
more than a year after the Chicago Beacon Hill had opened, more than
a year since Ben had married Allison. It was time to look ahead. The
waiter had just left; Currier had ordered for both of them—he liked to
do that. Laura lifted her glass. "To our past and the future."

Currier smiled at her seriousness. Whatever had suddenly preoccupied her was gone, and once again she had turned to him. That always
would be their pattern, he thought; she really had no one but him.
Ginny Starrett was only a friend, though she seemed to be giving Laura
more attention than she gave her other friends, and no one could call
Clay someone Laura could count on: he seemed to be having a good
deal of trouble deciding to grow up. "To our past and our future," Currier said, changing one word, and their glasses touched with a singing
tone of perfect crystal.

And then, as they drank, Laura's seriousness was replaced by a smile of self-mockery, almost as if she were chastising herself for what she was about to say—worried as she was about money—but she couldn't help it, she couldn't stop. "Speaking of the future, Wes: about those other two Salinger hotels, in Washington and Philadelphia . . ."

* * *

A drenching May thunderstorm was blowing against the office windows the day Felix learned that Laura Fairchild was a major shareholder in OWL Development. It was reported to him by his Realtor in Philadelphia, who had called with OWL's offer for the Philadelphia Salinger. "I heard it from a friend in Chicago; he's pretty sure it's true."

"She's the manager of the Chicago hotel," Felix said tightly. He'd known it for over a year, ever since stories on the Chicago Beacon Hill began appearing in hotel trade magazines, but however much he detested it, he'd known there was nothing he could do but ignore it. The bitch was determined to claw her way into a Salinger hotel, just to get back at him, even if it didn't belong to the family anymore, but it had nothing to do with him. She could rot in Chicago forever; he wouldn't lose any sleep over it. That was what he had thought for the past year.

"She did manage it when it opened," the Realtor said. "I assume someone else is doing it now. All I know for sure is what I heard: that she and Currier started OWL Development, and she owns a good chunk of the stock. Does it matter?" he asked when Felix was silent. "They've made the only respectable offer we've had in two years. I'd like your permission to counter with eleven million and settle at ten. It's not what we'd hoped for, but the Philadelphia market isn't hot right now. I guarantee you they'll pay ten; we can have the whole thing wrapped up in an hour."

"Find another buyer." Felix could barely speak through the rage that was sweeping through him like the rain that swept his windows. He'd called her insignificant; he'd almost forgotten about her. And now, to hear that she was a major stockholder in a corporation with which he'd done business! He couldn't tolerate it; it destroyed the orderly pattern of his thoughts—as if a person he'd been told was dead had been seen shopping at Copley Plaza. He prided himself on being in command of information and knowing exactly what to do with it; his fury was greatest when he had to admit he'd been mistaken or kept in the dark. "Go back to the other offers we've had. Negotiate with the best of them. Don't argue with me," he snarled when the Realtor began to protest. "Get back to me in a week. I want that hotel sold."

In the conference room at the other end of the corridor, the board members were waiting for him to begin their monthly meeting. Let them wait; he couldn't go in yet. Rage weakened him, and he had to be in control. He sat still, willing himself to calm down. It was getting harder to control his rages, especially when he had to hide them from others. And he knew he would have to defend his actions calmly and reasonably when he told the board about the offer for the Philadelphia hotel.

"Turned it d-d-d-down?" Asa said at the end of the meeting when Felix reached the last item on his agenda. "Turned down a t-t-t-ten million dollar offer for that d-d-d-d-dump?"

"They haven't made it yet."

"But your Realtor said they would," Cole Hatton said. One of three board members who was not a member of the Salinger family, he was the most outspoken and difficult to intimidate. "Who else came close to ten? Anybody?"

"Not yet," said Asa. "Right?" he asked Felix. "Nobody came c-c-c-close to ten? One was as low as seven. Right?"

"We aren't talking to the one who offered seven." Felix sat rigidly in his leather chair and let his look slide around the table, from Asa on his left to Cole Hatton and the two other outsiders, then to Thomas Janssen, who retained his seat on the board though he no longer worked for the company, and finally to Ben Gardner, his son-in-law, still there, still married to Allison, and showing no signs of leaving. "We'll push the others higher and get as close to ten as we can."

"Why bother?" Cole Hatton demanded. "You have a buyer."

"We shouldn't give the place away if we can get a decent price," said the man next to him.

They began to talk to each other, and Felix looked beyond them at the gray sheets of rain lashing the conference room windows. They made the distant outline of Beacon Hill look blurred and wavering.

That bitch will never own a Salinger hotel.

He shook his head. What was he thinking? She already owned two. *Two of my hotels.* Conned some money men—probably old men, like my father—sneaked in, and got two of my hotels.

But she'll never get another fucking thing that's mine.

"I don't intend to give it away," he said harshly, "but I don't like OWL Development—I won't deal with them—and that's a sufficient reason—"

"Not for me," Thomas Janssen said. His dark eyes were puzzled behind his round glasses. "If we're rejecting a qualified buyer, I'd like to know why."

"M-m-maybe they're not qualified?" Asa said tentatively.

"For Christ's sake," Hatton exploded. "Not qualified? They bought our Chicago and New York hotels, they've gotten mortgages and construction loans, and the Chicago hotel is wiping the floor with the competition. Shit, not qualified? Call your man back," he said angrily to Felix. "Tell him we'll take ten million. I don't care what beef you've got with OWL Development; get rid of that damn hotel. We've been farting around with it for over two years, and we've got to get started on the new one in New York. It's the only one I'm absolutely sure we *should* be building."

Felix's lips were a thin line; his muscles were tensed as he fought to contain his rage—at Laura Fairchild, at his board for opposing him, at his father for building the damned hotels in the first place. "I've already made this decision. We'll find another buyer."

"What's wrong with OWL?" Ben asked. "Odd name; I've wondered about it. It sounds almost like a joke, doesn't it? What's wrong with them?"

"I don't like their way of doing business," Felix snapped without bothering to turn his head. "I already said the decision is made. And we've debated it long enough."

"I'd like an answer to that question, though," said Hatton. "What's wrong with them? It didn't come up with Chicago and New York. Something changed over there? Who runs it? Who we dealing with?"

"Wes C-C-C-Currier," said Asa.

"Good man," Hatton declared. "Handled a merger for me. Something wrong with Currier?" he asked Felix.

"No," Felix said shortly.

"Who else, then? Somebody you don't like. Somebody you don't like a lot, to queer a good deal like this. So who is it?"

The door opened and a secretary came in, walking the length of the table to whisper in Ben's ear. Immediately he stood. "I'm sorry," he said, a grin breaking through his cool demeanor. "My wife is on her way to the hospital, and I want to be with her when our baby is born. If you'll excuse me—"

A chorus of good wishes rose from the table, and Thomas Janssen jumped up and put his arm around him. "Give our love to Allison. And you'll let us know right away—?"

"Of course. Thanks." Ben turned and walked toward the door.

"So who don't you like?" Hatton pressed. "If you think I'm going to let a good deal fall through because you've got a flea up your ass—"

"A stockholder," Felix burst out, his rage breaking through. "I just found out. A major stockholder. Laura Fairchild. A scheming, lying—"

Ben tripped and crashed against the doorjamb.

"Good God—!" Thomas exclaimed and started toward him.

But Ben was already getting up from the floor. "Chair," he said hoarsely. "Bumped it. Sorry—"

"It's hard to be a father," Hatton said jocularly. "Even if you aren't one yet. Better take a cab to the hospital; might not be able to trust yourself driving."

Ben nodded. Numbly, he looked at the conference table: everyone was standing, casting covert glances at Felix, who sat rigidly, staring straight ahead. Thomas had come up to Ben. "Sure you're all right?"

"Fine." Ben lowered his voice. "When I call about the baby, you'll tell me about the rest of the meeting?"

"Of course."

"*All* about it." Thomas nodded, but as Ben opened the door to leave, he was not sure how much he would hear, especially if Thomas and Asa managed to have a private conversation with Felix.

"What the fuck difference does it make who she is?" Hatton was demanding while others around the table began to raise their own questions. "Money's money; who gives a damn where it comes from? You thinking of what's best for the company, or whatever's eating you?"

The questions were cut off as Ben closed the door behind him and strode down the corridor, his thoughts racing between two poles.

Laura Fairchild. OWL Development.

Allison should be at the hospital by now.

How did she get to be a major stockholder?

I won't drive; Hatton's right; better take a cab.

She always was the smartest of us all, but how did she do it? Where did she get the money?

The doctor said everything was fine, but things can go wrong; my God, if anything happens to Allison—

And where the hell is Clay?

Nothing will happen; she's fine; the baby's fine—

I have to see Laura. Find out what she's doing . . .

"Mr. Gardner," the receptionist said, "I told them to hold a taxi downstairs; I thought you might want it."

"I do. Thanks," he said. "Thanks for thinking of it."

He stood in the elevator feeling he was being sucked into a vortex. Laura. Allison. Our baby. Felix losing control.

And if he does that once too often . . .

And I keep mine . . .

The Salinger hotel empire will be at the tips of Ben Gardner's fingers.

He ducked into the taxi as the doorman held the door, and sat back, letting his thoughts spin, unaware of the honking and screeching of the traffic on rain-slicked streets, or the driver's muttered monologue directed at everyone who drove or walked. At the hospital he asked the way without being aware he was doing it, and so found himself in a room with Allison before he had time to shut out thoughts of the meeting and think only of her.

"You look fierce," Allison said as he bent to kiss her. She lay on a narrow bed and smiled up at him. "Was it the board meeting? Hold my hand and stop thinking about it. Think about being a father. I'm trying to think of us being parents in a few hours, and all of a sudden I can't imagine it. I don't have the faintest idea how to be a parent. Do you? Do you believe in spanking children?"

"No." He pulled up a chair and sat beside her, holding her hand. "I believe in giving them lots of attention and never leaving them."

"Not even for a vacation?"

"We might be able to manage that."

"We've hardly talked about it. Isn't that odd? I think we spent the whole nine months choosing names." She took his hand and held it on her breast. "It's been a wonderful time, hasn't it?"

"The best I've ever known. But it isn't ending, you know; it's just going to change."

She smiled. "Ever since I found you, I haven't wanted anything to change. Everything, the whole family, has been perfect." Without warning, a gasp broke from her and her face grew pinched. She drew up her legs as if trying to keep the pain from bursting through. Her breathing was shallow and quick and her hand gripped Ben's with a strength he had not known she had. "Damn," she gasped. "Why... isn't it... fun? So much... fun... making it."

He grinned. "Breathe. All those exercises, remember?"

She grimaced. "Easier when it... didn't hurt."

"I'll count," he said, trying to be casual. He hadn't known what it would be like to watch Allison in pain. "Try to remember: deep, slow..."

"Good," approved a nurse, appearing at the bedside. "So many of them forget. Mrs. Gardner, you're doing fine."

Allison nodded, her eyes still closed. "Because of my husband."

"Fine," said the nurse absently; she was taking Allison's blood pressure.

"Is she all right?" Ben asked. He told himself not to be a fool: he'd been through all the classes with Allison, he knew what to expect, he shouldn't be worried. But it was one thing to share talk and exercises with a group of pregnant women and their husbands, and another thing to sit in a hospital room and watch Allison's face and body tensed in pain. *Is everything all right?*

"Hush," Allison said. "Ben, darling, don't yell at the nurse; she's just doing her job."

"Everything's dandy," the nurse said. "Hang in there and keep up the breathing. You're both just great."

"Does she have to be so goddam cheerful?" Ben growled.

Allison made a sound that was part grunt and part laugh. "You're supposed to pay attention to me and nobody else. Just stay close and talk to me and everything will be wonderful. . . . We're going to be the happiest threesome in the world."

Ben held Allison's hands with both of his, and neither of them looked up when the nurse left the room. "You're wonderful," he said. "And I love you."

"Hey," Allison said with a smile. "You sound surprised. You should never sound surprised when you tell your wife you love her." She closed her eyes. "Having you love me is the most perfect thing that ever happened to me." She lay quietly, her body waiting for the next contraction. "I'm so glad we have everything ready at home. The bed for the nanny. . ." The pain was building; Ben could see it in the pinching of her face. "Call her later, Ben . . . don't forget . . . tell her we'll want her in a couple of days. . . ."

"Stop talking and breathe," Ben ordered. "And listen to me count." He held her hands and counted rhythmically, breathing with her, and as he did, everything else faded away. Felix's hostility, a new vice presidency, money, Laura, the desire to avenge Judd—they all faded to nothing. He stroked the taut, trembling mound of Allison's womb that held their child, and leaned down to kiss her breast through the thin hospital gown, his blond hair merging with hers, long and ash-blond. He had a deep sense of safety. He had a wife who loved him, he had a home, he had a family of his own.

Laura had never answered his letter, and after he'd stopped watching the mail for it, he'd decided to wait until the baby was born and then try again. But even if she refused to have anything to do with him, he was finding a new life that gave him almost everything he could ever want: love, a place to belong, a future. Even his drive to gain power in the Salinger empire, to settle the score with Felix, seemed unimportant as he sat beside Allison. He knew it would probably return later, but for now it was enough to love his wife and cherish what they had together. He hadn't expected to feel this way—he hadn't dreamed he could, about anyone—but now that he did, there was only Allison: her pale face, her eyes fixed on him, her hands gripping his as no one had since Laura had clung to him in the months after their parents were killed. Today there was only Allison and their baby.

"I love you," he said again. His voice was low and, oddly, he felt like crying and rejoicing at the same time. "More than I ever thought I could love anyone, or need anyone. You taught me that. I love you, Allison, and I promise to take care of you. I'll always be with you, I'll never leave you, I promise you'll never have anything to be afraid of, ever."

He kissed her and held her hands while the pains surged through her, and he stayed there as the nurse returned and left and returned again, and was replaced by a different nurse when the shifts changed. At eleven that night, Allison's contractions were so close she barely had time to catch her breath between them, and it seemed to the two of them that the whole world had narrowed to that white room and Allison's determination to breathe properly while everything inside her felt as if it was twisting and pulling apart. Ben talked and talked, trying to distract her. And then her doctor arrived, beaming at her because she was doing fine and the baby's heart was strong and it wouldn't be long now.

And less than an hour later, just after midnight, while Ben sat beside Allison in the delivery room, still holding her hand and telling her he loved her, his son, Judd Gardner, was born.

CHAPTER 21

THE second theft was in Paris, where Britt Farley, returning from a concert tour in America, unlocked the door of his apartment and found an empty mantel over the fireplace where his three rare Remington sculptures had stood. Nothing else was touched; there were no signs of forced entry, nor were there any clues. Clay's copies of Farley's keys had worked smoothly, and he had had all the time he needed, since he had learned from Farley's pocket calendar how long he would be in America and when he would return to Paris. He left the apartment exactly as he had found it, except for the three very fine Remingtons; delivered the sculptures to his broker, who commissioned all his jobs for private collectors who could not acquire certain works of art any other way; and was on the Concorde and back in New York before the weekend was over. And there was no information Farley could give the Paris police and his insurance company. The case was filed away before an investigation even had begun.

Farley had been living in Paris for almost a year, trying to kick his alcohol and cocaine habits while his manager looked for a new television series for him. For twenty-five years Britt Farley had been a singer and actor who made audiences love him. He was the country boy in the city, the innocent young man looking wide-eyed at the big wonderful world; he was naive and not too smart, but a ruggedly handsome hero with a lopsided smile that made parents think of their children when they were young and lovable, and women remember what they had once dreamed their husbands would be like. But then his skid began, and soon a reputation for alcohol, drugs, and women hung over him like a miasma. "They won't promise us anything," his manager told him on one of his visits to Los Angeles. "Not a television series, not even a concert appearance, until you've proved you can stay clean for a while —say a year. Unless..." He cocked his head. "I did have an idea. How about this? The new Britt Farley does a concert tour to raise money for the poor and hungry of the world."

"It's been done," said Farley.

"So is the whole world fed and happy?" His manager's name was Louie, and he prided himself on knowing how to handle temperamental geniuses. "There's enough starvation around to keep a thousand singers in business for a thousand years. And where else do you think you'll get publicity like that? Prove you're back: the one and only Britt Farley— singer, actor, humanitarian. You got something better?"

Farley shrugged. And so the tour was organized, with a major band and three lesser-known groups as backup. It became the sensation of the year. FARLEY FIGHTS FAMINE! read headlines around the country; television specials bloomed on refugee camps and slums where gaunt children stared into cameras; sponsors lined up to help pay for the tour; world distribution rights were negotiated for recordings of the tour theme song and videotapes of the final concert, to be held on the mall in Washington, D.C.

Ticket sales set records. BRITT'S BACK! shouted Newsweek, People and Time, but all of them also wondered how much money would actually get to the needy. "All of it," Farley declared on a radio call-in show. "Well, not all of it, a'course, there's expenses and such, but every-thing else goes to all those folks who need it. We're saving lives, not getting rich, you can count on that. But a'course we're getting"—he found his place in his script—"genuine satisfaction from it. Believe you me, we're loving every minute of it!"

FARLEY FEVER! boomed the headline in the New York Daily News, and soon everyone believed Farley had done it: a short time ago it had seemed he was through—addicted, discredited, out of work, and broke—but now he was adored again and back in the spotlight. It was the enduring magnetism of those twenty-five years in front of audiences; all it took was a reason to love him again.

Over two million dollars was raised from the first four concerts, through ticket sales and donations. Then the group took two weeks off before beginning the next set of concerts. Farley went back to Paris—and found his apartment burglarized and his Remington sculptures stolen.

A few days later, a gossip columnist in Los Angeles reported that Britt Farley was back on the party scene after months of being a model citizen, and had been in a scuffle in a Parisian nightclub. His agent had been discussing a new network series; its future now was uncertain.

"He fucked it," said Larry Gould, handing the newspaper to Paul. "He'll be lucky if the sponsors stay with the tour. Best thing in years he had going for him if he could have stayed clean; it's hard to believe anybody'll do a fucking thing for him now."

Paul skimmed the column. "I'd like to do a film on him," he said thoughtfully. "The rise and fall of an American hero. If he'd cooperate."

Larry narrowed his eyes, thinking about it. "It's an idea." They looked at each other across Paul's cluttered desk, and slowly the idea took hold. "It's got everything," Paul said, excitement growing within him. "Everyone's fantasies of making it big and everyone's fear of failing."

"And a real star," Larry said, his voice rising with his own excitement. "People know him; they can identify with him." Then he put back his head and looked at the ceiling. "Unless it's too much of a downer; you might have audiences staying away in droves."

Paul shook his head. "Not if we do it right. It's one of the oldest ideas in the world, and it never stops fascinating people."

"What: failure?"

"Not just failure. Spectacular failure. The fallen idol. The king who's brought down. The billionaire who loses it all. Do people stop reading the story of Agamemnon because it's a downer? Or Oedipus? Or Lear? All the way to guys like Stan Kenton and John Belushi, it's—"

"You convinced me. You're right. I never thought of Britt in terms of kingly fate, but there is something there—a kind of tragedy—to climb so high, and then fall . . ." He reached for the newspaper and reread the gossip item. "What if I was wrong, though, and he doesn't fuck up? What if somebody gets to him and he makes a quick recovery?"

Paul grinned. "We do a film on the fall and rise of an American hero, and we have a very upbeat ending."

They laughed. "Either way," Larry said. "By God, I like this! It's not just one hero; it's every hero—"

"And it's all of us: the audiences who prop celebrities on a throne and then turn away and let them topple when they turn out to be human after all."

"It gets better and better." Larry sat back with his feet on the desk. "So you'd film the tour, follow him around, film him in his hotel rooms, dressing rooms, restaurants, waiting for him to fall apart—"

"I wouldn't make it a hatchet job," Paul said absently. His thoughts were racing ahead, the film taking shape as they talked: he could see the scenes weaving together, the different voices, the images, the concert tour building to a climax. "If," he said, slowing down. "If he co-operates."

"Why wouldn't he? What else does he have going? Anyway, he's a little dim upstairs; he'll probably jump at the publicity. Do you know him? I've met him, but I doubt he'll remember; I'll call his manager tomorrow. You might want to fly to Paris this week to talk to him. Would Emily mind?"

"They're shooting the next *Fashions of the Times*," Paul said absently. "She'll barely know I'm gone."

"Well, then, how about an outline? I can give you a little more of my exceedingly valuable time, though not much. Christ, I wish I was going to do this instead of the dramatic thirty-second story of how a marriage is saved by the right detergent. I get ecstatic moments of squeaky-clean collars, while you get the great myth of the American hero. Shit, you have all the fun. Okay, I have an hour. What do you know about Farley besides drinking, drugs, and barking at the moon?"

"I didn't know he barked."

"He's done it for a couple of years, at odd times. I hear he does a respectable Irish setter. Or maybe it's a dalmatian. Somebody told somebody he made a scene in a hotel—New York, Chicago, something like that—it was more than a year ago and it never really got talked about. I don't suppose he'd let you film that, though."

"Not a hatchet job," Paul reminded him. "I'd rather have the audience feel sorry for the guy. He got caught in something and doesn't know how to get out."

"Even if he knew how, one slip and he's back again. He'll never really live down his reputation."

"He might, if enough people helped him."

"Probably not even then. Most people carry their past around like a load of luggage, and it just gets heavier the older they get." Paul was silent. "Well, where would you start? Paris, probably. Lonely guy in the city of lights. You suppose he has a girl with him?"

"No idea."

"Let's hope he doesn't. Lonely is better. And then this tour: trying to pull himself up, desperate for attention and love, power over the audience..."

"Clips of his audiences," Paul said. "I've seen them: masses of adoring faces. Then back to him, in a taxi, going to his hotel room, all alone

. . . Or maybe he's never alone. Aren't there always girls?"

"Maybe he's different in Europe. If he's got a girl we could bribe her to go home and leave him by his lonesome. Why is it I like scripts better than real life?"

"You control the ending."

"And the beginning. And everything in between."

They chuckled together, then Paul said, "I'd like to call Farley's manager now; I can put together a rough outline today and talk to him about it tomorrow."

Larry grinned. "I like that enthusiasm. Go ahead. And I have another idea. There's a guy in public television who reads Greek tragedy in his spare time. Get me a copy of your outline, and I'll pitch it to him; if they help fund it, you'll have a hell of a budget." He stood. "I'll be in my office if you need me."

Farley's manager, Louie Glass, was hesitant. "I'm off for Paris tomorrow on the Concorde," he said. "You wanta come? No promises, but we can talk on the plane."

He'll do it, Paul thought. In spite of himself, Louie had sounded eager. The news about his client was bad, and he needed something.

He sat back, going over in his mind the scenes he had imagined while talking to Larry. They were as vivid as if he had really seen them. Everything about film was vivid; that was the amazing thing to Paul. After a lifetime of using a still camera, he had discovered the exhilarating freedom of movement and sound and the ability to show simultaneous events. No matter how much emotion he had packed into the best of the photos he had made before becoming a society photographer, it couldn't compare with the drama of film. It was as if he had left a large house, and now had the vastness of the whole world in which to create.

The first film from Gould-Janssen Productions had been finished a year and a half after the company was formed. It sank with barely a ripple. A few theaters carried it, a few reviewers mentioned it, a few people saw it but left the theater talking not about its brilliance, or even its faults, but where they would go for a drink or whether it would be her bed or his afterwards.

A month later, Paul and Larry watched it again in the screening room in Larry's house. "The audience was right," Larry muttered. "I'd rather talk about whose bed I'm going to fuck in, too."

Paul did not smile. He was not used to failure and was angry with himself. "Why the hell did we release it?"

"Hypnotized by our own brilliance," Larry snorted. "It used to happen to me all the time when I was a smart-ass genius starting out in commercials. Shit, it still happens now and then. I'm surprised it did with two of us, though; you'd think one of us would have noticed we were coming up with a bomb." The film ended and the lights came on. They brooded in silence. "Look at it this way: it wasn't a total waste. You did your apprenticeship, learned a lot... what the hell, you learned to work. For a guy who never held a job in his life, you did okay. I have no problem letting you do the next film while I go back to the shit that pays our bills. 'Course I'd hang out with you as much as I could. Beer?" He held out a bottle and an opener.

"Thanks." Paul stretched out his legs. "One thing I've learned. I need to narrow things down a little. There's something to be said for still photography, after all."

"Meaning?"

"Meaning when I make a photograph of something, what I'm really doing is pulling it closer so I can see what makes it unique, and find a way to show that uniqueness to others. I want to do the same thing with film: pull something closer and show why it's unique. There's too much going on all around us; how can anybody make a film from chaos?"

"That's the world, my friend. Most of us learn to cope with it."

Paul smiled. "So do I. Most of the time."

"So what do you want to do?"

"Make profiles. Build each film around one person, and use his or her story to tell the story of a city or a profession or whatever we want, even an entire country. It would give me something to focus on. And it would give the audience a person to identify with—or hate."

Larry looked thoughtful. "Let's kick it around awhile."

He had liked it more the more they talked about it. They were talking about it the day they read the gossip item about Britt Farley, and it fueled their excitement: Farley's story could tell the larger story of celebrities in show business, and the still larger one of heroes who rise and fall and, perhaps, rise again.

The day after he talked to Louie Glass, Paul flew with him to New York and then, on the Concorde, to Paris. They used the time to get acquainted. Louie talked about Farley, especially how upset he'd been by the burglary of his apartment, though he'd recovered by now, and then they went over Paul's outline. By the time they were approaching Paris, Louie had approved the idea for a film and, in general, the outline.

When they reached Farley's apartment, he was waiting for them. Louie had talked to him the evening before, on the telephone, and told him about the film. "You're talking about a documentary, right?" he asked as he led them into his living room. His voice was deep and dark, like velvet. One of his wives had said listening to it was almost as good as going to bed with him. After the divorce, she said listening was better. In a corner a young girl with startled eyes was curled up in an armchair. Farley did not introduce her, and she sat in silence the whole time they were there.

"Documentaries," he said, drawing out the word. "Those friggin' things we had to sit through in school: labor unions and how to build a cathedral. And those cute things about polar bears fucking on the ice. You putting me in with polar bears?"

"We're putting you with celebrities," Paul said easily. "Audiences like to know the inside story of their favorite stars."

"Audiences are too stupid to know inside from outside," Farley said carelessly.

"You didn't hear him say that," said Louie Glass. Farley shot a look in his direction, but he stayed silent; he depended on his manager to get him out of any mess he made with his loose tongue.

"Nice apartment," said Paul, looking at the long room crowded with tufted furniture. The tall windows were open to the soft June morning, and he caught glimpses, through the trees, of the Avenue Foch three floors below. "It's hard to believe it was broken into, this high off the street."

"It wasn't through a window." Farley's voice fell to a growl. "The son of a bitch came through the front door, like he belonged here. Nothing pried open, nothing scratched, nothing moved out of the way. He had to have a key, the fucking son of a bitch. Came right in as if he belonged here . . . *my* house, where I live! Invaded *my* house, where I—" He stopped abruptly.

Hide, Paul thought. Your house, where you hide. And when he did that you felt vulnerable; no place to hide. So you started snorting coke and drinking again. It had been five days since the robbery, and Louie had said he'd recovered, but that wasn't exactly the truth.

He met Louie's eyes and thought they probably understood each other. Farley wasn't especially stable, but he'd been in good form for the first four concerts of his national tour, and Louie and his staff probably could keep him going for the rest of the tour and long enough for Paul to finish his film.

"Let's talk about our film," Paul said, his voice relaxed. "We want to show you in your daily life, get a feel for how you work and play and talk to your friends, other singers and actors, whomever you see socially. How you get your ideas and create, so to speak. What we want to do, if you don't mind, is follow you around, sit in at your meetings and rehearsals, be with you in nightclubs"—at Farley's look of alarm, he changed it—"restaurants, and backstage at your performances. After a while you'll forget we're there. We'll use clips of your television shows for background, and we'll interview people who've known you over the years. Sound all right?"

"'Scuse me," Farley said abruptly, and made for the bathroom.

Louie put out a hand to stop him, then pulled it back with a small shrug. "Stomach problems; something he ate," he said to Paul.

They were silent until Farley returned. "Sorry, don't like to leave guests, but when you gotta you gotta." The underside of his nose was pink. "You were saying—?"

"I was talking about interviews with people who—"

"Right. Interviews." He nodded, smiling broadly. "No problem. Long as you interview people who like me. No way are you going to talk to anybody who's got it in for me."

Paul bowed his head and Farley took it for agreement. They began to talk about the tour that would resume in a few days, with Paul and Louie trying to keep Farley to the subject when he wanted to wander into a reminiscence or anecdote. It was like being a sheepdog, Paul thought: nudging Farley to prevent him from getting lost in the thickets of miscellany cluttering his mind. It took another two hours, but at last Farley, Louie, and Paul were initialing an informal letter of agreement, and then standing and shaking hands. "I'll see you first thing in the morning," Paul said.

"It'll take—how long?" Farley asked. His voice was raspy and his eyes bright. Paul tried to remember if he had returned to the bathroom twice or three times as they had talked, but he wasn't sure.

"As long as you want to talk," he replied. "I'm a good listener, and we have forty years of your life to cover."

"Thirty-seven," Farley said automatically. There was a pause. "Well, one thing," he declared cheerfully, "I don't have any trouble talking about me. Never did; I'm a subject close to my heart. A'course I've had a life bigger than life, so there's plenty to talk about: a real trip. And this tour we're doing! Biggest thing to hit hunger in a couple thousand years. You wait, you got enough in me for a twenty-hour miniseries; big stuff. And I tell it all. Total honesty, that's my creed." He grinned his world-famous lopsided grin. "Everybody else has mottoes; I have creeds. And I live up to them a thousand percent. Long as I have a little help along the way," he added with a wink.

In the taxi, Paul scribbled notes to help him remember the conversation until he could write it all down. Can't trust him, he thought, remembering Farley saying they couldn't talk to anyone who had it in for him. He wants a public relations film, not a documentary.

But he was amused, not annoyed; Farley wasn't the first, or the last, to try to hide his warts from the public. They'd find plenty of people to interview, on their own, without relying on the names he and Louie gave them.

Thinking about it, making notes, he felt the excitement of beginning a project, of working toward a goal. It was still new to him, this pleasure in getting involved and putting ideas and images together to create a whole picture, good and bad, fantasy and reality, the ordinary and the exotic; it was as stimulating and satisfying as anything he had ever done. This is what I want, he thought. To bring people to life on the screen, to show the faces and scenes behind the ones they show the world, and make their stories real for everyone.

In the next days, the film grew more engrossing, more solid in his mind as he interviewed Farley. They would sit in his living room, with a cameraman filming quietly in a corner, and the interviews would go on all day, every day. By the time he returned to California, he had a much more complete outline of the film, with wide spaces left for the unexpected. It was held in a loose-leaf notebook with his notes and the list of names of people to interview that his secretary had prepared. When filming began two weeks later, in Nashville, he had the beginnings of a fat notebook that would grow and change and become dog-eared and be joined by others as the months passed. When the film was finished, the notebooks would be, too: a complete record of the film, including mustard, relish, and coffee stains from lunches eaten on the run.

Larry took time off to go to Nashville with Paul. "We had to delay the detergent commercial," he said as they drove to the hotel from the airport. "The five-year-old who's supposed to watch his squabbling parents coo like doves when they discover how they can get his collars clean got some dread disease. Chicken pox, I think. So we'll wait, or they'll find a healthier kid. Whatever; I get a few days off. Emily didn't mind your leaving again so soon?"

"She's very busy," Paul said vaguely. Then, remembering that he lived in Los Angeles where everyone talked, even close friends and business partners, he added, "We're going away for a few weeks when the film is finished. We've missed being together."

"Nice," Larry murmured. "I keep thinking I ought to get married, but there isn't anybody I miss."

"You're living with Bonnie," Paul pointed out.

"And I like her. But I don't miss her. So why would I marry her?"

Paul was silent. The only woman he missed, even now, was Laura.

"We can celebrate tonight," Larry said. "I haven't had a chance to hoist one with you since the word came from PBS that they'd fund us.

Big news for you; I hope you know it. They only do this once in a blue moon."

"It means they'll schedule it as soon as they can," Paul replied. "That's the most important thing to me." He picked up his notebook as they reached the hotel. "Time to get to work. I hope the star behaves; it's going to be a hell of a chore if he doesn't."

But, as they learned that morning, it wasn't only Farley they had to worry about, it was the carnival that followed him wherever he went.

It had begun during the first four concerts, before Paul arrived; by the time the tour went to Nashville, and then to Dallas, Denver, and Salt Lake City, it had taken on a life of its own. Always, now, Farley was surrounded by a crush of people: fans holding out scraps of paper for autographs, calling "Britt! Way to go, Britt!"; hangers-on trailing after him; curious crowds milling in the street outside his hotel and surrounding him when he emerged; anonymous hands reaching out to rip a piece off his shirt, a bandanna, a bola (Farley stopped wearing them after he was nearly strangled by someone trying to yank one off); shouts and screams and, always, someone singing, perhaps thinking it was a good time for an audition. BRITT'S BACK T-shirts were everywhere; a fast-thinking businessman made a yo-yo emblazoned on one side with "Down with hunger" and on the other with "Up with love"; someone threw a rose at Farley when he was bowing low in a curtain call in Dallas and it drew a tiny fleck of blood on his forehead, which in turn drew a headline proclaiming BRITT BLEEDS FOR THE POOR; a young girl was knocked down in the jostling crowd in Denver and an alert press agent brought her to the stage, where Farley held her hands and sang a love song directly to her and it made the front page of a hundred papers the next morning.

Everything Farley did made the news, either locally or on one of the television networks. The tour was becoming the biggest event in the cities where he appeared, and Farley, the sun at the center, smiled and waved and sang, he threw kisses at the crowds, and gave parties where he was stroked, nuzzled, and kissed. "They love me," he said to Paul. "They never stopped, you know; they always did and they still do. Love Britt." He took strangers to restaurants and picked up the tab for two dozen, three dozen dinners at a time. He had a companion every night in bed and the next morning gave her perfume and chocolates. "They love me," he said, with a wink at Paul. "A fuck a minute. A'course you didn't hear me say that. How about 'greatest lover of the Western world'?"

"Where's the money coming from?" Paul asked.

"Around," Farley said vaguely.

"What's paying for the parties and the perfume and the dinners?" Paul asked Louie Glass.

"Britt's a wealthy man," Louie replied instantly. "Saved a lot when he was on top."

"I'm on top now," Farley said, coming into the hotel room where they were talking. "Never higher. Never better." He looked at Paul. "This is how a king feels. I'm a king again." And he turned to his stash of cocaine and his cache of gin.

"Hey, fella, you got a show tonight," Louie said gently. "How about skipping this one?"

"I skipped the last one."

"When was that?"

"Five minutes ago."

"Very cute." He put his hand on Farley's arm. "Lay off till after the show."

"Get your fucking hand off me." Louie dropped his hand. "I don't like being told what to do, Louie, you know that. I'm a big boy, just had a birthday—thirty-seven," he said to Paul. "Old enough to do my own thing."

Paul picked up his jacket. "I'm going to dinner. Come on, Britt, I'll buy you a steak."

"I'm not hungry; I'll just stay here."

"You don't eat when you're on that stuff," Louie said bitterly.

Paul shot him a glance. "Come anyway," he said to Farley. "I don't like to eat alone."

"You're just trying to get me to eat. You'll get me in the restaurant and throw a steak at me."

"I might. If you catch it, it's yours."

Farley chuckled. "I like you, Janssen. You don't lie to me."

"Come on; I'm hungry, even if you're not. You can tell me about high school, when you were the star of the senior class play."

"I was the star. How did you know that?"

"Your high school advisor told me. But I want to hear it from you."

"Right. I don't mind talking about that. Those were good times." He turned and walked out of the room into the corridor.

"Can you get some food in him?" Louie asked Paul in a low voice.

"That's what this is all about," Paul said and followed Farley.

Each day it was a game: getting Farley to eat, getting him to sleep when he said he was wide awake and full of energy, keeping him in shape for the concert. They all worked at it, Louie, Paul, the staff. They dressed him and undressed him, tried to keep him from spouting too many personal opinions in public, got him on and off airplanes and onto the stage for his performances. And much of it Paul had on film. No matter how blurred Farley's thinking was on some things, he never forgot Paul was making a film on him. For eight or ten or fifteen hours a day, he and Paul and the cameraman were together, and whenever Paul gave an unobtrusive signal, the cameraman would begin filming: Farley at rehearsal, Farley talking to the other musicians about an upcoming concert, Farley reminiscing with Louie, Farley alone, sitting at the piano, humming, singing, making sure his voice was all right. Now and then he would order the cameraman out, saying he needed privacy, but mostly he wanted him around. He was beginning to live each day for the camera.

Finally, when all of them thought they couldn't get through one more day, they had a week's rest, and Paul went back to Los Angeles.

"Emily?" he called as he opened the front door. The cool silence of the house wrapped itself around him. He took the stairs two at a time to the long, glass-walled living room, then passed through it to the deck cantilevered over the scraggly grass cliffs that separated each layer of houses from neighbors above and below. For a long time he stood there, gazing at the sprawl of Los Angeles in the distance, pale and hazy beneath a slanting July sun struggling to cut through the afternoon smog. Little by little he began to relax as the silence soaked into him and the tension that Farley seemed to generate faded away.

He paced the length of the deck, admiring the maintenance man's upkeep of the lush beds of vivid flowers whose names Paul had never learned. But Emily doesn't know them either, he thought, and it occurred to him that they used the stunningly decorated and immaculately maintained house as if it were a hotel. We don't behave like homeowners, he reflected. Or homebodies.

"You're back!" Emily said, her voice high with surprise. She stood in the doorway in a light shift and sandals, her blond hair wildly teased for the day's shoot, her light blue eyes glad to see him. "You didn't call."

Paul went to her and took her in his arms. "I called last night. You look lovely but I'm not crazy about the hair."

She laughed. "I was in full-length Russian sable, walking barefoot on the beach, with my hair looking like I'd just gotten out of bed. Somebody's idea; they didn't inform us. Don't you think I can sell furs, looking like this?"

"I think you can sell anything."

He kissed her but in a moment she pulled back. "I was out with Barry Marken last night. He was only in town for a short time, so when he invited me I said yes. I was home by ten."

"I wasn't asking for an explanation," Paul said gently.

"You have a right to know where I am when you're gone. You have a right to ask me not to have dinner with Barry again."

"I don't have the right and I wouldn't do it. I'm not your jailer, and it's not flattering knowing you think I am."

"You're angry. I'm sorry. It's been an awful day, really; I shouldn't be held responsible for what I say."

"How about a drink? Then you can tell me about it."

"Oh, good. Vodka, please, with ice." She stood aimlessly until he returned with their drinks. "There's not much to tell. Modeling is dull, you know; or maybe you don't. Nobody knows, until you do it. It has nothing to do with talent, or intelligence, or even being interesting; it's just being in the right place when a new fad comes along."

Paul heard the faint tremor in her voice. "Is there a new fad?"

She gave a brittle laugh. "They don't tell us. But this morning the art director told me my hips were too big."

"You told me they always make comments like that."

"This time it sounded different." She perched on a low stone wall between two flower boxes. The setting sun was behind her and her face was shadowed. "It's not orderly. There isn't any correct way to do things or plan things. You never know what they're going to want next."

"You mean which model they'll want next?"

"Which kind of model. Of course I'm not worried that it will affect me, but it's very dull to be part of something so disorderly and uncreative."

Paul knew how she hated not knowing the rules, because that meant she didn't know how to tailor her behavior to fit. "Has it really changed?" he asked. "A couple of years ago you didn't think there was anything wrong with it. You wanted it more than anything else."

She shrugged. "I know more about it now than I did then."

It suddenly occurred to him that she wouldn't stay in modeling long, and he thought how strange it was that their lives had become reversed. When they met, Emily had known exactly what she wanted—to be a model, to be married—and he had been wandering around Europe, restless and dissatisfied. Now he knew what he wanted, at least in work, and she was the one who seemed to be drifting.

Nearby, a bird sang out and was echoed by another. In the late afternoon stillness they heard the clink of glasses from the house below. "You haven't asked about my trip," Paul said.

"Oh. How was it?"

"Fine."

She ignored the shortness in his voice. "Good. Did you finish?"

"The tour? I thought I told you there are four more weeks."

"I remember you said something about it, but I can't imagine why you have to go to every concert. They're probably all the same; *he's* probably the same wherever he is. And I hate having you away."

"I don't like being away. But I have to do this."

"You like doing it. You love doing it. You love making movies."

He gazed at her angry eyes. "I thought you understood that. I've told you how I feel."

"You never used to feel like that about anything. Except me."

"I still feel that way about you," he said, almost reflexively.

"But work. You never felt that way about work."

"I wanted to." He wondered how much to tell her. They almost never talked about his work; it was her own career that most interested her. "I was always waiting for something to come along that I could care about. It didn't occur to me that I ought to be looking for it, that things might not always fall in my lap." He smiled ruefully. "Amazing, how long it took me to learn that; it comes from being brought up with too much money."

"That's just plain nonsense. Things do come, if you're patient. Larry offered you this work; you didn't go hunting for it."

It gave him a moment's pause. "You're right," he said. "But it would have died, like a lot of other things, if I hadn't worked at it, studying and following Larry around like a baby learning to walk. Maybe it was just timing: I needed something to care about."

"Well that's all right as long as it wasn't some*one* you needed," she said brightly. But then she added wistfully, "I wish I felt the way you did. About anything." She was looking over the parapet at the view of Los Angeles and did not see Paul's startled look. "I guess I will someday. Everybody does, don't they?" There was a silence. "How long will your movie take?"

"Four to six months. And I promise we'll get away then; we'll take a long trip and—"

"And then what will you make?"

"What film?"

She nodded.

"I don't know. We'll find a subject that interests us."

"How about me? You're interested in me, and Larry thinks I have a fascinating face; he told me so. You could make a movie about me."

He frowned, then quickly erased it. "I could. Someday I might. I'm going to get another drink; would you like one?"

"Yes." She followed him into the house. "It could be very helpful to me, Paul."

"A film? How?" He smiled at her. "You're one of the top models in the country. A documentary on the bright and dark sides of the modeling business doesn't sound helpful to me."

"You don't have to do the dark side."

"We have to do both; that's one of the things that makes a documentary different from fiction." He put his arm around her. "Helpful how?"

"Any exposure is helpful."

Her voice was evasive, and Paul tilted her face to look at her. "That's not it. What is it?"

She snuggled against him, hiding her face against his shirt. "I'm just not happy. I want . . ."

Paul held her close. *I want.* It struck him how many of Emily's sentences began with those words. "What?" he asked.

"To be happy."

Paul felt a moment of helplessness. "I thought you were."

"Sometimes I am. I try to be. It doesn't always work." He held her, wondering what to say, wondering what the hell it was she wanted and how much he could do for her. "I just thought, something that showed I was different from the others—more interesting—so they'd want me for more than my looks . . ."

He heard the tremor in her voice again and wondered what his life would be like if he had only his face to depend on. "I'll think about a film," he said gently. "I can't promise anything."

Emily turned within his arm and brought his head down to kiss him. "Thank you, darling. I know you'll do your best for me. I do trust you."

And we'll live happily ever after, Paul thought wryly. But the thought faded. Emily was holding his head to hers, kissing him again, her small tongue darting in his mouth like a flame. "Missed you," she murmured against his lips and stretched against him on tiptoe, pushing one leg between his.

Beneath Paul's hands her body was soft and yielding, and the warmth of her skin penetrated the light shift she wore. His hands tightened until her slenderness seemed to fit in his palms. "Missed you," she said again, holding his head to hers. One hand caressed his neck and slipped inside his open shirt collar; swiftly she unbuttoned the shirt, and her fingers were warm in the dark hairs on his chest and the smooth skin beneath his belt. "Every night," she breathed. Her leg moved rhythmically between his, and as Paul pulled up her shift, his fingers sliding along her breasts, she turned, leading him down the hallway to the bedroom.

She was always able to mask her self-centeredness with the heat of their bodies.

* * *

"So," Larry said when they were on the plane for Minneapolis, "was it a honeymoon?"

"It's always a honeymoon," Paul said lightly. He had never understood the male need for sexual recapitulation, unless the night or weekend had been such a failure it could only be erased by lying about it. But the truth was, his week with Emily hadn't been a honeymoon, except in bed; they hadn't had enough to talk about, and when they did talk, they often seemed to be talking about different things. After two days, Emily managed always to be working or shopping or meeting friends for lunch. The truth, which Paul acknowledged reluctantly, was that, whatever kind of carnival awaited him on Farley's tour, he was glad to be on that plane. "And I got some work done," he added.

"Good. So did I." He handed Paul a folder. "Outline of Farley's life."

Paul chuckled and held out his own folder. "Outline of the film. Fifth draft."

"God damn. Good for you. Well, let's see."

They read in silence, then worked for the rest of the trip on lists of people to interview, sites to film or stock shots to rent, and scenes with Farley. "Where's he been this week?" Paul asked.

"New York and L.A., seeing art dealers about finding new Remingtons to replace the ones that were stolen. He's hung up on cowboys; they're his role models or something. And he talked to some insurance investigator who's working on the robbery. I called him last night and he was okay; coked up, but I don't think anybody'd notice if they didn't know what to look for. My bet is he cares about the tour and our film enough to keep some kind of control over himself. After that, all bets are off."

Larry stayed through the concert in Minneapolis, then left once again. "I'll try to get back for the biggie in Washington," he said as he and Paul had breakfast before he left. "Should be a smash. They sold out the bleachers at two thousand bucks a head, and they expect a quarter of a million on the rest of the mall. 'Course those are freebies, but still, live TV, money pouring in . . ." He shook his head. "They started with zilch and they've built it into a first-class circus."

"Who knows, it might even make some money for the hungry," Paul said dryly.

"Who?"

They laughed ruefully. "Nobody but the hungry remembers what this tour is all about," Paul said. "How much of the money do you think they'll get?"

Larry shrugged. "Ten cents on the dollar? I never looked into it. They sure as hell don't get much. I have to go; I hope I'll see you at the grand finale. Good luck with Farley."

The tour moved across the country to Detroit, Buffalo, and Pittsburgh. Buffalo was almost a disaster: Farley had a bad night, forgetting the words to his songs, stumbling over his patter with the other musicians, telling a joke that rambled interminably, then petered out with no punch line. "Goddam it," Louie exploded afterwards. "You forgetting every fucking thing I told you? Your *life* depends on this tour! You gonna shit all over it because of a lousy habit you could kick if you really wanted to?"

"I know," Farley said humbly. "I know, Louie. I'll be okay. Things just got a little out of hand. I'll be fine."

"Get to bed," Louie ordered. "Relax. Cogitate. You need a couple days to recover before the next concert."

Farley shook his head. "I need company. It's hell when I'm alone." And that night and the next, there were parties, as there had been in every city, and dinners bought for hangers-on, and gifts for the women who shared his bed. "I'll be fine," he mumbled when Louie scolded, but he could not finish the concert in Pittsburgh: he wandered off before the last number, and the other musicians performed in his place.

"I was okay," Farley said to Paul the next day. They were in his hotel room in Washington, watching a television commercial for the final concert of the tour, to be held on the mall stretching from the U.S. Capitol to the Washington Monument, and he was nervous. "Up to the last two it's been good, you know. Hasn't it? I mean, *good* good, not just some shit that fills the seats because some second-rate fart papers the house. I mean, we've been *selling tickets!* And *raising money!* Right? We've had *audiences!* On the name Britt Farley. And the talent. Right?"

"Right." In a corner, the cameraman was quietly filming. Paul wondered if Farley was aware of it.

"But that was small potatoes. I mean, what's Salt Lake City, when you think about it? A pimple on the desert, right?" He paused, thinking. "You didn't hear me say that. It's a very fine city. But what I mean is, how many celebrities ever performed for three hundred thousand people on the mall in Washington, D.C., the capital of our country? Awesome, right? An awesome responsibility. My agent says that's what it is. Tell that guy to turn off his camera."

Paul nodded to the cameraman.

"He can go get some coffee, too."

Paul nodded again, and the cameraman left the room.

"Un-huh." Farley opened the desk drawer near him. "Got a stash here

unless some gremlin ripped it off..." It had been a long time since he
hid from Paul. "You're family now," he had said, "and my coke is your
coke, as long as you pay for what you use and don't overdo it."

He poured the white powder in a straight line on the desk, his hand
steady, and then breathed it through a straw deep into his nose. "Three
hundred thousand people," he repeated. "I'm a king again." He met
Paul's eyes. "Sorry, rude of me. You want some? Appetizer before
lunch."

"No, thanks. I was just thinking—"

"You don't have to be polite, I got plenty and I like you." He held out
his hand, but Paul smiled and shook his head. "You always turn me
down. You do *do* this, don't you? I mean, shit, am I telling my life story
to Mary Poppins? What do you like? I'll get it for you. I can get anything
you want—no, wait, you didn't hear me say that. Goddam it, tell me
what you like!"

None of them likes to be the only one, Paul thought; they have to
believe everyone does what they do. "I don't talk about it," he said easily.

"You can trust me!"

"I'm sure I can. But it's a habit; I just don't talk about it."

"And I can trust you, right?"

Paul's glance sharpened at the new note in Farley's voice. "I hope you
trust me. Are we talking about anything special?"

"Not a big deal." There was a pause. "Just a small loan."

Paul kept his face calm. "How much?"

"Couple thousand? Three, if you got it."

"Not in my pocket. I can get it. How soon do you need it?"

"Pretty soon. This afternoon."

Paul hesitated, then, very carefully, he said, "I wondered about the
parties and the presents. Is that where it went?"

Farley shrugged. "A king has expenses. I'll pay you back."

"I'm not sure you can."

"Damn right I can! I got resources! I can figure things out!" When
Paul was silent, he leaned forward. "Listen. One thing about this pretty
white stuff—it opens my mind. I can solve problems—think up new
ideas—you name it I can do it. Everything's so goddam clear and easy!
No limits, that's what this little friend does for me. It's the only friend
that does it. You got a wife? I had a wife, a whole bunch of wives. But
they're no good. This stuff, now, this stuff is fine! It won't talk back,
won't walk out on you, won't get smart. I'm not much for smart women.
You like smart women?"

"I like them to be as smart as I am."

"Well, that's okay. That's right. But most of 'em think they're smarter, think they can take over your life." His face took on a brooding look. "There's one little lady I truly love with all my heart. I told her so, but she said she doesn't want to settle down. I did something once, almost spoiled a party she was giving—I wasn't nice—and she told me off and made me go to bed. But she didn't kick me out of her hotel, you know? Sat with me at brunch the next day, this gorgeous lady, soft and friendly, not a smart ass telling me how to run my life. And I thought, shit, this is a real lady, she takes time to be nice to people. I tell her that every time I see her. Laura, I love you and I'll always stay in your hotels and never bark at you again because you are a kind and lovely lady and you make me feel good. But she's the only one, you know. Everybody else wants something from me. And that I definitely do not need. Like I was saying. What did you ask me?"

Paul was staring out the window. Farley followed his gaze to see what held his attention, but all he could see was another Washington building across the street. "Hey, fella, you still with me?"

Paul turned to him. "I was thinking about the lady in the hotel."

"Laura. You'd like her. Soft-spoken even if she is smart. She's smarter than me, but it don't seem to matter; she's . . . gentle."

"What's her last name?" Paul asked.

"Fairchild. Fair child. Nice, huh? I figured it out; it fits her. You know what? You'll meet her! I'm throwing a party when the tour is over—celebrate all these great things we've done—and I'm inviting Laura. So you'll meet her. But first we got this other thing. You'll get me the money, right?"

"Right."

"Thanks, buddy. I knew I could talk to you."

"I'll be back," Paul said. He left the room and went to Louie Glass's room, one floor down. "How broke is Farley?" he demanded.

"Not broke. I told you, he's rich."

"He may have been once; he's not now. He's asking me for money." He watched the lines deepen in Louie's face. "I asked you before, Louie: where's the money been coming from all these weeks?"

"I don't know, Paul. I wondered, just like you, but I don't know."

"Bullshit. There's nothing about Britt you don't know; it's your job to know everything. Where does it come from, Louie?"

"Look, why don't you just run your camera and make your movie? This has nothing to do with you."

"It has to do with Britt. And that's what my film is about."

Louie shook his head. "Not this part. Some things are off limits."

Paul perched on the windowsill and watched Louie pace. "He's taking it from the tour, isn't he? Using money from ticket sales and checks coming in—"

"Leave it alone! It's not your problem where he gets the money! What the fuck is it with you? You a crusader or something? All you're doing is making a movie about a singer; the rest of it—it's all separate. You've never asked one lousy question about how the tour worked, you never gave a damn—"

"Well, I'm beginning to give a damn. This tour is a good thing in a world that doesn't have enough good things, or people to do them, and I want to know what's happening to it. And you're going to tell me."

"Not me. The accountant may be sloppy; we'll check that. But I don't know a thing for sure."

"That's a lie."

Louie shrugged.

Paul slammed out of the room and went to his own room where he called the New York office of Britt Farley's Music for the Hungry. "I need some numbers before the final concert," he said to the accountant, his voice mild. "Just background for the film. Can you give me total tickets sold, total revenue, and total expenses to date?"

"Can't do it," the accountant replied. "Not now, anyway. There's a lot going on here, you know, they won't get me an assistant, it's a fucking mess with everything happening at once and nobody really keeping track—"

"That's what you're there for," Paul said sharply. "What the hell is your job if it's not keeping track?"

"Goddam it, it's not my fault!" The accountant's voice rose to a screech. "Don't tell me what my job is! I know what my fucking job is! It's keeping that junkie happy! That's what Louie said: keep him happy! Pay his bills, send him money when he—" His voice stopped. "I mean . . ."

"I know what you mean," Paul said. "Does anyone else know?"

"Listen, are you gonna put this in your movie?"

"Does anyone else know about it?"

"Louie."

"Besides Louie."

"I don't think so. God, I hope not. But listen, are you gonna put—?"

"How much has Farley used?"

"Look, I don't have to tell you—"

"You haven't any choice; Louie's already saying you may be sloppy in your accounting. How much has he used?"

"He said that? The son of a bitch said—"

"How much?"

"Son of a bitch. A couple hundred thousand. Two hundred twenty thousand, five hundred sixty-one dollars, to be exact. But I couldn't tell him no! I mean, Louie said to keep him happy, and Farley said he'd pay it back! You wouldn't put it in your movie, would you? I mean, I got a job to worry about, a family, and it wasn't my fault! I just followed orders! You don't want to ruin Farley either, do you? I mean, even if you don't love him, there's all those people who think they're gonna get money or food or something... you say something, it hurts the cause, all those people. Right?"

Right, Paul thought. That stupid bastard; he had a chance to do something decent and pull himself up at the same time. "I don't know what I'm going to do," he told the accountant. "I'll talk to you later." He hung up. The stupid bastard. He doesn't care whom he destroys. Including himself.

In eight weeks, from ticket sales and televised coverage with pleas for money, they'd raised five million dollars, and they expected more than twice that from the concert on the mall, the climax of the tour, to coincide with the biggest fund drive. Two hundred thousand was a small part of that, but that wasn't the problem: if word got out that any of the money was going into Farley's pockets, they would lose their tax-exempt status and television sponsorship, and also permission to use the mall. And thousands of people would demand their money back.

Paul had never been under any illusion that Farley cared about the poor and hungry of the world, but, as Louie said, he'd ignored it: it wasn't his problem; he was only there to make a film. But in the past weeks, in spite of the circus atmosphere and the phoniness of the whole thing, he'd gotten involved with it. Just in time to find out that this stupid bastard had done the one thing that could scuttle it.

The concert on the mall would be held in two days. Or it would be canceled.

Farley was sprawled in a chair in his room, staring at a soap opera on television, but he leaped up when Paul came in. "You got it? I knew you would. Have a drink. What's your poison? How much did you get?" He held out his hand.

"I haven't got it."

"Haven't—! Jesus, fella, you playing games? You promised!"

Paul pulled out a desk chair and sat down. "I wondered how you'd pay it back."

"I'll take care of it! Britt Farley is an honorable man! I'll pay it back!"

"Before or after you pay back the two hundred twenty thousand you've taken from this tour?"

"What the fuck are you talking about? Take? I didn't take a fucking thing!" Paul was silent. "I sent some bills to New York to be paid—you talking about that? Shit, it was a few hundred bucks, it wasn't..." He moved his head as if a collar were binding his neck. "What's-his-name, that Minnie Mouse accountant, you been talking to him? He said he wouldn't talk to anybody. Promised he wouldn't. Anyway, he's a liar." Paul sat still. "Well, fuck it, what difference does it make? We finish this thing with a bang in D.C. and take in a few million, who's gonna notice a few measly bucks aren't there?"

Suddenly he swung around and looked at Paul, his eyes sly and bright. "I forgot. I had it all figured out. There's lots of time to put it back. All those people have to prove they're hungry, right? And there's bookkeeping and the eternal revenue boys, and then they gotta decide who gets the money and then they gotta *get* it there. Shit, it could take a year for all that. By then I'll have a series, be making good money; I'll put it all back. Nobody'll know. Except you, but you're family, so that's all right. And"—he swiveled his head—"there's nobody running the camera."

The door was flung open and Louie hurtled into the room. "He called the IRS!" he burst out to Paul. "You really fucked us, you know that? The little shit says he isn't gonna be anybody's fall guy, and he called them and they're coming tomorrow for a field audit. Field audit! Tomorrow! You hear that?"

Farley looked from Louie to Paul. "What's going on?"

"What's-his-name, the accountant!" Louie yelled. "Says we told Paul and he doesn't trust us, and now the tax boys are gonna be all over us and we've been fucked!"

"Hell no," Farley said wisely. "They take forever; everybody knows that. They'll fart around for a few months, playing with numbers. We got plenty of time."

"You poor fool," Paul said. "The only thing that makes this tour work is people's confidence. As soon as word gets out that you're being audited, you lose that. The tour is through and so is your comeback, if you can call it that. You haven't got—"

"I don't wanna hear this!" Louie shouted. "Nothing's through, you hear? We'll figure something out! I got contacts, they'll talk to the IRS, hold 'em off—"

"You're going to make sure people talk about it," Paul said.

"Wait a minute," Farley said. "You guys crazy or something? My fans love me; they'll come no matter what. They don't know from field audits; they want to sit out there and love Britt! There's no problem! Everything's gonna be fine!" Behind him, his hand had been groping; it touched the drawer handle and pulled it open while he kept his eyes on Paul and Louie. "You stick with me and everything'll be just—"

"Leave that stuff alone," Paul said.

"I pay attention better if I have some. You'd understand if you weren't a fucking Mary Poppins—"

"If I don't ask my contacts for help, who do I ask?" Louie said, almost to himself.

Paul reached out and clamped his hand over Farley's. "Leave it alone. Now listen. I'm not going to let this whole thing go down the tubes."

"What are you gonna do to stop it?" Louie asked.

"I'm thinking about it. But first I have to know that Britt can perform."

"'A-course I can perform! I told you, my fans love me! Doesn't matter what I do: I don't have to be top-notch; I could howl like a hyena and pee on them from fifty yards, and they'd scream and say I'm awesome. 'A-course I can perform . . . no question!"

"That's not what I had in mind," Paul snapped. "You're going to give that concert, and you're not going to howl or pee or do anything else except sing and make it the best you've ever done. Did you get that? I'll stay with you every minute between now and the time you go on that stage, and you'll be as clean as I can get you—"

Farley barked. His head back, he let out a series of high yelps that turned his face red. Paul waited it out, his hand still clamped on Farley's until the yelps faded away. "And when you're clean," he said quietly, "and you've given that concert, and the tour is over, we'll talk about how we finish the film."

"Jesus H. Christ!" Farley's voice was a rasp. "*I can't go on if I'm clean!* Are you so fucking stupid you can't get that? I've gotta have something or I fall apart. Can't sing. Can't talk. No voice. Whatcha gonna do about that, old buddy?"

Paul was silent. He didn't know if it was true or not.

"What difference does it make?" Louie asked. "If the IRS puts us outa business—"

"Tell you what," Farley went on. "Louie can stay with me. He's made me cut down other times; it only works if I ask him. It worked in Salt Lake; you remember how good I was there? So you don't have to worry; you'll have your concert. And we'll have a movie, too. Right? Louie'll take care of the money—he has these contacts who know their way around the government, they get lots of favors—and he'll take care of me, too; I gotta have somebody take care of me, y'know; I don't like being alone. But there's one thing. Listen, I don't have the money, you know, to pay it back? And I don't know just when I will. You never know how long a series takes to get off the ground. So I can't do it. I'll give you a hell of a show in D.C., but I can't do the money. Okay? I can't handle it."

Paul contemplated him. Our American hero, he thought caustically. A frightened little boy, weak and going downhill fast, on his way out of a career. "I'll handle it," he said at last. "I'll put the money in if you give me your word—"

"What money? In where?"

"Sorry, I didn't make that clear. I'm putting two hundred twenty thousand dollars into the fund. Nothing will be missing when the books are audited."

A strangled sound came from Louie. He stared at Paul, his eyes bulging.

"Where you gonna get that kind of money?" Farley demanded.

"I'll get it," Paul said briefly. "Your problem is keeping quiet about it. Can you? Can you keep your mouth shut so this whole thing doesn't blow up in your face?"

"Hey, shithead, this is Britt Farley you're talking to—"

"I didn't hear you say that," Paul said, his voice like steel.

Farley reddened. "Fuck it. Okay. Yeah. I can keep it quiet."

"You'll give me your word you'll keep it quiet."

Farley looked at him for a long moment. "For what it's worth," he said in one moment of honesty. "On my word."

Paul stood and put his hand briefly on Farley's shoulder. He had an odd liking for him, part pity and part sorrow over the waste of what he had been, and could have been again. "I have to make a phone call. I'll see you later."

"Sure. Hey, buddy," he said as Paul turned away, "if you're gonna ask somebody for that money, ask real nice."

Paul gave a brief smile. "Thanks for the advice."

"Wait," Louie said. "I'll walk you to the elevator. Right back," he said to Farley and followed Paul into the corridor. "You really can get the money?"

"Yes."

"Why? You gonna go into debt for a *concert?*"

Paul laughed. There was something so gross about Louie that he was almost impressive. "I thought I was doing it for a lot of hungry people," he said.

Louie ducked his head. "You must think I'm some kinda monster."

"No; I think you're scared, like our singer in there. Go back to him, Louie; you've got your job cut out for you. Two days. Get him as clean as you can. Go on. I'll see you at dinner."

In his own room, he called his broker in Boston and told him what he wanted.

"Two hundred twenty thousand," the broker repeated. "Transferred to your personal account?"

"No. Wired to me here." He gave the address of his hotel. "And make sure you get it out today." Tomorrow he would send it to the office of Music for the Hungry, under Britt Farley's name. It would appear on the books as a simple repayment of an advance.

As soon as he hung up, he went downstairs to the bar. He found an empty booth in the corner and sat there, drinking scotch and watching the people who came and went. Every one of them had a story; each could have been part of a novel or a film. Farley wouldn't have believed that. He thought he was unique.

But he's just like so many others, Paul thought. Emily and Louie and Britt, all wrapped up in themselves, with not a lot of time or energy for the rest of the world. He knew, as he thought it, that he had been like them once, seeking only his own satisfaction and comfort, refusing to get involved in anyone's problems. But something had changed. *I'm beginning to give a damn.* He'd said that to Louie only this afternoon. It was, in its way, a radical statement for Paul Janssen, whose great uncle Owen had chastised him for being a playboy.

Maybe Britt is unique after all, he mused. He got me involved.

He ordered another scotch. Or maybe it had nothing to do with Farley, but with Paul Janssen growing up. He smiled to himself. That's what Allison would say. He'd grown up, at least enough to feel responsible for protecting a guy who'd done some dumb things, because the guy deserved at least one more chance, and there was something bigger at stake that was worth saving.

He felt uncomfortable and drank his scotch. Responsible. Protecting. Saving.

Which was a lot more than he had done for Laura. We had something big at stake, too, he thought, but I let it go. I didn't try to understand her or protect her or work things out so we could try to go on from there.

He sat back and let himself think of Laura. He had been holding back since Farley talked about her, but he no longer could: her image came to him; he pictured her sitting in a restaurant, having brunch with Farley, saying something to make him feel good about himself. *You are a kind and lovely lady.*

Laura. He said her name slowly, as he had not allowed himself to do for years, feeling her presence through the softness of her name, remembering the scent of her hair, the lilt of her voice, the laughter in her eyes. Laura.

I'm throwing a party when the tour is over and I'm inviting Laura. So you'll meet her.

"Mr. Paul Janssen?" He looked up. One of the hotel desk clerks stood beside his booth, plugging in a telephone. "There is a call for you from Boston, and since I saw you come in here, I took the liberty. . ."

"Thank you." He picked it up. "Paul Janssen."

"Paul, it's Allison. Am I interrupting something? I couldn't wait to talk to you. I had to tell someone and you're the only one . . . Listen, Ben just told me: Laura's bought all of Grandpa's hotels! All four of them! Can you believe it? It makes me feel so strange, I don't really know how to feel. We were all so angry at her, but you have to admire her anyway, don't you? She *bought* them! Isn't it incredible? Of course Daddy won't talk about it, he's furious, but there was nothing he could do to stop it. . . ."

Paul half listened. Laura, he said to himself, and found himself smiling broadly. Good for you.

I'm inviting Laura. So you'll meet her.

CHAPTER 22

JUDD Gardner. Felix stood beside the crib, the name burning into him as if it were a branding iron. The baby slept, blond hair curled damply at his forehead, his mouth a small pink flower. "Daddy's mesmerized," Allison said wonderingly to Ben. "He's never liked babies before." Ben nodded, watching Felix intently.

After a long moment, Felix turned and met Ben's eyes with a savagery that made Ben take an instinctive step back. *Judd's son.* How could he not have known? What weakness, what insane blind spot had kept him from recognizing Ben Gardner the instant he saw him? He was not the image of Judd, at least as well as Felix could remember Judd when he was young, before he came back wounded from the war, with haunted eyes and a twisted smile that grew worse when he found his company gone. But there were resemblances, and Felix told himself he should have caught them: he prided himself on knowing what was going on when others were still stumbling. Yet this time all he had known was that those blond good looks were the kind he most hated, and that he hated Ben Gardner.

Leni had wept when she heard the baby's name. "Did you know?" Felix had demanded. They were leaving the Beacon Hill house after their first visit to see the baby; he was two days old and Allison and Ben had just brought him home. "Did you recognize him?"

"Yes." She looked out the window on her side of the car. "But I don't want to talk about it. No one is going to talk about it. Allison is happy, she has a good marriage and a lovely family, and we're going to leave them alone."

"You can do what you want; I'm getting him out of the company. And out of our family, no matter how long it takes. He's out to destroy me, that smirking bastard. There's no other reason for him to be here."

"He's in love with Allison and you're not going to—"

"Bullshit. He's using her to get at me. Are you still such an infantile romantic that you can't see that?"

"You're not going to touch them, Felix. What will you say? That I was sleeping with his father and you don't like to remember that?" She paused, but Felix was silent. "Is that what you'll tell your board? That your son-in-law, a man you trusted as head of security and just a few months ago made vice president for development, suddenly deserves to be kicked out of the company? For what reason?" She waited. "That was a question," she said evenly.

"I don't know yet," he said furiously. "I'll think of something. But he's not staying—"

"He is part of our family," Leni said deliberately. "He is making Allison happy. He hasn't shown one sign of wanting to harm us, *and you are going to keep quiet and leave him alone.*"

He turned on her. "And if I don't? What are you threatening?"

She gave him a long look. "I don't threaten, Felix. If I decide to do something, I'll do it, with no warning."

That was the threat. That had always been the threat. And he had always known it, though he had not let himself acknowledge it, any more than he had let himself recognize Ben's resemblance to the man he had most hated in the world. "You cried," he flung at her. "When you heard what they'd named him, you cried. You still remember him."

"I'll always remember him," Leni said. She looked at him. "And so will you."

* * *

"I've never heard him so stubborn," the Philadelphia Realtor told Laura when he called her in Chicago to report that Felix had refused her offer for the Philadelphia Salinger. "I tried to change his mind, but he wouldn't budge."

"But why not? You told me he was pushing you to sell."

"Right, he was. I thought he'd jump at it. I haven't the vaguest why he turned it down. He did say he wants to look at the other offers we've had."

Laura lined up four pencils on her desk, pushed them so they seemed to fall to the side, then lined them up again. "You told me there weren't any others."

"Not that I'd take seriously. But it's hard for me to read him; he may grab one. I suggest you consider raising yours a quarter of a million; better yet, a half . . ."

"Not yet."

"But think about it."

"I'll let you know."

Furious, she slammed the pencils into the leather pencil holder Clay had given her the day the Chicago Beacon Hill opened. *He can't turn it down. We made a good offer, the only decent one he's had on that hotel. He sold the New York Salinger to us without any trouble; what's his problem now? Damn it, he can't do this. I had it all planned.*

On impulse, she picked up the telephone and called Currier in New York. "Wes, you said you knew someone on the Salinger Hotel board."

"Cole Hatton; I handled a merger for him."

"Can you talk to him and find out why Felix refused our offer on the Philadelphia Hotel?"

"He refused it? I thought he was ready to accept it."

"So did I."

"I'll talk to Cole." An hour later he called back. "It seems you're a powerful influence on Felix, even after all these years. He found out you're an officer of OWL Development and called a halt to everything; he won't sell to you. There was a battle royal at the board meeting; they even had a second one, a week later, to discuss the hotel, and Cole said Felix was even angrier then than he had been before, as if something else had happened that they didn't know about. He just dug in his heels. And he won, at least for now. You could wait him out."

"I can't take the chance. I want that hotel."

"My dear, you can't force him to sell to you. Why don't we talk about it next week, when you're here? My secretary found a couple of apartments for you to look at; we can do that and think about what to do with Felix."

"Fine." But she was already thinking about it. *Who does he think he is, refusing to sell to me? He's the one who cheated me; I didn't cheat him. I've never done anything to him. So what right does he have to stand in my way now?*

She needed a walk. She always thought more clearly when she was outside and moving. But in the lobby, she found Ginny Starrett. "I came to take you shopping," Ginny said. "There's a French designer doing a trunk show at Elizabeth Arden, and you've been working too hard."

"Not today, Ginny. I need to be outside for a while and I'm going for a walk. Why don't you come with me?"

"Because I don't go for walks, as you well know. If it isn't up and down the aisles of stores, I don't do it. How about lunch? Will you be back in time?"

"I'll make sure I am. I'll meet you here at one."

Ginny kissed her cheek and left the lobby as Laura watched: a trim, smart lady of indeterminate age who wore clothes designed only for her, who traveled from country to country as casually as city dwellers take cabs from one place to another, who took an interest in almost everything, and loved being motherly to Laura. But because she had never had a daughter, she was mostly a very good friend who gave a great deal of advice.

And I'm lucky to have her, Laura thought, walking the two short blocks to the lake. She and Kelly talked every week by telephone, and she went to dinner parties almost every night, but she was slow to make close friends, and the times Ginny was in Chicago were the times Laura felt most complete. Lunch with Ginny, she thought, and smiled to herself, looking forward to it.

The May morning was warm, and the beach and park were crowded with sunbathers, bicyclists, and joggers who followed the water's edge where fishermen sat on upended buckets, playing their rods and swapping stories. Sailboats were white crescents against the silvery lake that was whipped into small skittering waves by an offshore breeze, and Laura found a secluded spot to take off her shoes and stockings and suit jacket. She wanted to run on the fine-grained sand, but not in a business skirt, and so she walked, the wind in her face, the sun making it feel like summer.

By summer she had planned to have all four hotels and be living in New York. By summer she had planned to be running her own small empire.

She sat on one of the huge limestone blocks that lined the shore. Felix couldn't stop her, not when she was this far along; there had to be a way to make him change his mind. He was a businessman; he had to be convinced it was good business to sell quickly, even to OWL Development. He had to be handled. And the only way to do that was to use what she knew about him.

She knew a lot about him: he was stubborn, vindictive, acquisitive; a good businessman, but not as good as he could be, because he didn't trust anyone and he was always trying to prove he was better than his father. And he preened himself on his ability to make decisions quickly and decisively, often without even discussing them with anyone else.

Quickly and decisively, without discussions with anyone else.

All she had to do was find something to convince him he had to make a quick, decisive decision.

The sun blazed straight overhead; the breeze had died down. Nannies were taking small children home for lunch and naps; sailboat owners were stowing away lunches for an afternoon on the lake. It would soon be time to meet Ginny. Laura put on her shoes, grimacing as they crimped her feet, and walked back to the hotel.

"So did you solve your problem?" Ginny asked as they sat at a corner table in the Beacon Hill restaurant.

"Halfway solved," Laura said. "How did you know?"

"You get a dark look in your eyes, and when you look at people you don't quite connect with them. What's the problem?"

Laura told her. "What I need is something that will make him think he has to sell quickly to protect his investment in the hotel."

"Meaning he couldn't sell to anyone else?"

"Not at a price close to ours. And he has to think he might not even get that if he doesn't sell in a hurry."

Ginny sipped her soup. "If you knew something was wrong with the hotel, something dire, like that other one in Philadelphia where people were dying of Legionnaire's disease, he'd sell at any price."

Laura laughed. "Yes he would, but nobody's dying."

"What a shame. Well, what if he finds out it's falling apart? Defective plaster or something that can't be fixed. Ever. So who'd buy it?"

"No one, including me," Laura said with another laugh. "Wait a minute." She put down her soup spoon and gazed out the window, then slowly turned back to Ginny. "What if he thought no one would be allowed to tear it down or modernize it?"

"It wouldn't be worth a hell of a lot to anybody. Old buildings are only good investments if they can be spiffed up. But that doesn't do you any good; anybody can do anything to that building."

"They can't if it's a landmark."

Ginny frowned. "It isn't a landmark."

"But what if the Philadelphia city government decides it is? Then it can't be torn down and the facade can't be changed. The interior could be renovated, but not the exterior. What would that do to its selling price?"

"Drop it to the basement. Did anybody ever talk about making it a landmark?"

"It was on a list of buildings the Landmark Commission was considering. They decided it didn't qualify; the architecture is good but not historically significant. But that's not the point. What if Felix believes the commission is about to change its mind?"

"Why would he believe that if it's not true? Oh." They looked at each other, their eyes bright, like two young girls with a secret. "Somebody tells him it's true."

"Somebody very reliable tells him it *might* be true. And since Felix believes in fast decisions, without consulting anyone—"

Ginny was smiling broadly. "I love it. It's deliciously sly. Who gives him the news?"

"I don't know yet. Do you know anyone in government in Philadelphia?"

"Not a one. I know some Bucks County society, but they're no help. Architects? Contractors?"

Laura shook her head. "It has to be someone who'd know what goes on in the commission's meetings. Maybe someone who covers them . . ." Her voice trailed away. "Yank Bosworth," she murmured.

"I beg your pardon?"

"A newspaper reporter in Boston. I knew him a long time ago."

"You need someone in Philadelphia, not Boston."

"But he might know someone in Philadelphia. Ginny, excuse me. I want to call him; I can't wait. I'll be right back."

She had not seen or heard from Yank since the trial. But that last morning after the verdict was announced, his hands had held hers tightly and he had smiled to let her know she had a friend. *If you ever need me, you know where to find me.*

"Bosworth here," he said, answering his telephone when Laura called.

"Yank, it's Laura Fairchild," she said. "I know it's been a long—"

"Laura! My God, how the hell are you? Where are you? What're you up to?"

"I'm in Chicago, and I've got a small problem. Have you time to hear a quick story?"

"Stories are my business. Shoot." He listened, tapping a pencil on his teeth, his comments an undercurrent as Laura talked. Suddenly he sat straight. "Son of a bitch! He won't sell just because you're part of it? Why's he so uptight? After all this time . . ."

"I don't know, but—"

"But it doesn't matter. Right. The thing to do is get him to change his tune. You think a rumor will do it?"

"It might, but it can't sound like a rumor, Yank; it has to sound real."

"Right. So who do I know in Philly who might do the deed? No, wait a minute. Do we really need Philly? Hey, Laura, I want to do this myself. Okay with you?"

"You don't write about Philadelphia, and you don't write about architecture."

"I write about whatever's news as long as it's in cities. I'm a city reporter, remember? Listen, I can do this; it'll make me feel good all over; I never did like the bastard and I had a crush on you, so what could be better? Okay? No charge, either, though you might buy me a drink if you're ever in Boston."

"I'll buy you one in New York. I'm moving there next month."

"No shit! I might take you up on that. Listen, I'm going to call him. Okay? Then I'll call you back."

"I don't know, Yank; if you're not in Philadelphia . . ."

"I'm in Boston, which is better all around. Trust me; I won't let you down. I'll get back to you sometime today."

He rubbed his hands as he hung up. The only drawback to being a reporter was reporting dramas instead of acting them out. Now he'd act one out—an act of chivalry. He wondered how much she'd changed in the past four years. He remembered her stricken eyes, her cold fingers between his hands, her face like stone. He'd wanted to cuddle her and tell her everything would be okay. But a gentleman didn't take a lady in distress to bed. Besides, he had a wife and a little boy, and he was crazy about both of them. But this much he could do for Laura. And taking even a tiny gouge out of Felix Salinger was a noble act worth the doing.

Here we go, he thought, and picked up the telephone.

"Yank Bosworth of the Boston *Globe*," he said briskly to Felix's secretary, and then repeated it to Felix when he came on. "I'm gathering information for a possible series on architecture of the eighties, specifically on the struggle between classic buildings and more cost-effective use of urban land. In that connection, I wondered if you have a comment on landmark status for the Philadelphia Salinger."

"There is no such status. It was rejected."

"Yes sir, that's correct. But I understand there's talk of expanding landmark status in order to keep the scale of the cities; in other words, architectural excellence may not be the only—"

"Where did you hear that?"

"I spoke to a potential purchaser of an older building just a few minutes ago, a person very aware of the problems of landmark status, who told me the issue should be taken seriously." His voice picked up speed and he rattled along. "Of course I'm going to research this more fully, and if you like I'll get back to you in a few weeks, but I was hoping I could get a comment from you today; one never knows how quickly these designations may be voted, especially since there always will be resistance from owners, some of which, of course, is very rational, but not always treated so by landmark commissions, which have their own mandate, and of course you know Philadelphia is a very special city, keenly aware of its historic heritage, our founding fathers, the Declaration of Independence, the thirteen colonies—"

"I have nothing to say," Felix said and slammed down the telephone. He was breathing hard. Impossible. But just the kind of thing these half-assed city governments did when they wanted to look good for the media. Potential purchaser worried about landmark status. Resistance from owners. Philadelphia and its historic heritage.

He'd waited too long. He couldn't get a decent price for the place now; he'd have to come down to—

But he'd been offered nine million for it.

A smile came to Felix's lips. She'd pay him nine million and then find herself stuck with a hotel she couldn't do anything with. She'd pay him nine million for the privilege of owning a dump nobody wanted. Let her have it, he thought. I'd almost give it to her.

He called his Realtor in Philadelphia. "Did OWL withdraw their offer for nine million?"

"No," the Realtor said. His voice was startled. "But I told them you'd rejected it, and they won't go any higher."

"Do they know about a Landmark Commission ruling on the hotel?"

The Realtor opened his mouth, and then closed it. Somebody was spreading a rumor. Somebody was always spreading some rumor or other, but this one was a miracle. It had been a slow month for real estate; if he sold the Salinger, he and his wife could take the vacation in the Bahamas they'd been dreaming of for three slow years. "I don't know what they know," he said honestly.

"I want this settled today. Go to Chicago if you have to; get it done. I'll expect to hear from you tonight; call me at home. Is that clear?"

"Perfectly. May I congratulate you, Mr. Salinger; it's a very wise move."

"Yes," Felix said. He hung up, his face flushed with triumph. The Philadelphia Salinger was sold.

* * *

"It was an excellent dinner," Laura said to Gérard Lyon, the chef of the Washington Salinger restaurant. "And this is a pleasant room. It seems to be the only part of the hotel that's busy."

"Truly," Lyon agreed. "The hotel does poorly; my restaurant thrives."

"You would think," Laura said carefully, "that in a major city, a hotel so well situated would be very successful."

Lyon put out his hands, palms up, in Gallic resignation. "There is, shall we say, not the best management. Also, we hear for some time the owner is looking for a buyer, but the price is high. Meantime, it is like an orphan: it gets little attention. I, however, have nothing to do with it; my restaurant and some personal matters take up all my time."

"Personal matters," Laura repeated. "I'd like to hear about them. Can you join me for coffee?"

Lyon glanced swiftly around the restaurant. It was almost midnight, and the few customers who remained had been served dessert and coffee. "With pleasure," he said and took the armchair opposite Laura. Immediately the maitre d' appeared. "Coffee, and more for Madame Fairchild. And two apricot brandies. If you like," he said to Laura.

She nodded. "Thank you. Your English is perfect; have you been in this country long?"

"Seven years. But I learn English in school, when I am ten. It is essential that a world-class chef know English."

Laura smiled. "When you were ten you wanted to be a chef?"

"I did not want," he corrected gravely. "I knew it was my destiny to be one. So I prepared myself."

She glanced at the large room, too brightly decorated for her taste, but impeccably maintained. "And everything happened as you wished."

"Many things, madame. Life does not give us everything; if it did, we might become proud, and then the gods would punish us for being like them."

They smiled together. A waiter served coffee and liqueur. Lyon looked sharply at the small balloon glass. "This is not apricot," he snapped.

The waiter looked startled. "No, sir. It's peach."

"That I can see. And why is it peach?"

"Because the maitre d' gave it to me and said you ordered it."

"I ordered apricot! Is this a place of imbeciles? Take this back and bring what I ordered!" He turned to Laura. "My apologies. One should control one's temper. We were discussing—?"

"Whether life gives us everything. Which of your wishes did not come true?"

"Ah." He hesitated, but she asked again, leaning forward in her chair, and he found himself talking to her as he did not talk to many strangers, and almost never to women, whom he considered more interested in themselves than in others. But this woman seemed different. Besides being beautiful, she listened. She sat quietly, she did not wriggle or cross her legs, she did not suddenly pull out a mirror to put on lipstick. She kept her eyes on him, and her mouth did not twitch as if waiting for a chance to talk. And so he talked.

The waiter had brought the proper liqueurs, and he sipped coffee and brandy as he told Laura about his boyhood in the south of France, his training as a chef with the legendary Roger Verge, and his move to America. "It is, of course, not all that we hoped. I dreamed of my own restaurant, with my wife running it, instead of what you see: a room gaudy with these colors I do not like and a careless maitre d' who does not know apricots from peaches, and management I never see: they are off in Boston."

"Why do you stay?" Laura asked softly, and it struck Lyon that this was something she had been waiting to say. "You must have many offers to go elsewhere."

"Truly. But we have a son, you see, and he has some . . . what we call . . . learning problems. He is a good boy, a good son, but he has trouble in school. Here we have a good place for him; he is happy; he does well. My wife says we cannot jump him from place to place. And so we stay."

"But there must be other schools," Laura said. "There are special schools in every city."

He shrugged. "I think the same. My wife says why change when he is happy and doing well?"

They fell silent. The room was empty now except for the waiters quietly clearing the tables and resetting them for the next day. The maitre d' walked about, supervising, avoiding Lyon's glare. Laura held her brandy, breathing the fragrance of apricots before she sipped. It was heady; its warmth suffused her. Then she put down her glass and folded her hands on the table. "I've recently bought two hotels, one in Philadelphia and one in New York. They're both old and neglected, but I intend to make them as elegant as when they were young; I've already done that with a hotel in Chicago. The New York hotel has a coffee shop and a bar; that's all. I have plans for a dining room that will be one of the finest in the city, decorated in soft colors, with a piano or harp as background, a maitre d' who knows every fruit brandy that is available, and the most renowned chef, who will share in its profits and be given free rein to devise new dishes and menus. His wife would manage it if she desired." She paused. Lyon was gazing at her as if spellbound. "I would, of course, help the chef and his family in any way I could, to find a place to live and a school for their son. I would also pay their son's tuition for the first year." Again there was a brief pause. "The only condition is that the chef would have to begin working for me immediately, to help design the dining room, the kitchen, the new coffee shop, and so on. His salary would begin the day he arrives in New York even if the dining room won't open for a year and even if he takes a month off to move and get settled in his new home." She smiled at Lyon and let the smile linger. "I would like very much to have you join me in New York, monsieur."

"Madame," Lyon breathed. "I am overwhelmed. To *build* a dining room! And in New York City! It is the dream of every great chef. I will discuss it with my wife, but I see no impediments, especially if you help us find a school for our boy. I see only happiness. A month here to give notice, that is all, and then—"

"Perhaps I wasn't clear enough," said Laura. "I need you immediately."

"But madame, one cannot just vanish from a place of employment! One gives proper notice, perhaps helps a new chef begin—"

Laura was shaking her head. "We must be clear on this." Her voice, Lyon noted, had hardened; everything about her was more businesslike. She was just as beautiful, but now it was as if she sat behind a desk. "I want you in New York next week. I'll pay your hotel expenses while you find a place to live, and I'll pay for your traveling back here to help your wife close up your house. We'll find a school for your son as quickly as possible, so all of you can be together, but you must agree to begin working for me on Monday."

"Four days from now," Lyon murmured. He looked at his hands; he gazed about the room; he repeated her words to himself: share in the profits, free hand, wife to manage the room. He met Laura's eyes; she was watching him steadily. I hope I am always on her side, he thought. She would make a formidable opponent. And then he nodded. "I will be at the hotel in New York on Monday morning."

Laura smiled and held out her hand. "I'm very glad. We're going to work well together, you and I."

Lyon took her hand and smiled back. "Truly," he said.

* * *

Three weeks later, with the Washington Salinger's occupancy rate hovering at thirty-five percent and a dining room that had been closed since its chef's abrupt departure, Felix put up barely a struggle. His board made the decision, and the Washington Salinger was sold to OWL Development for ten million dollars.

The next night, Laura sat at dinner with Ginny and Currier at Windows on the World, looking out over Manhattan, New Jersey, Brooklyn, and Queens. "The last time we celebrated a purchase," Currier said, "you were worrying about money."

"I still am," Laura said dreamily. "But not this minute. I don't want to talk about money or worries or even work." Holding a glass of champagne, she looked out the window. A hundred stories below, the green sward of Central Park looked like a green brush stroke in the center of the tightly-woven tapestry of buildings that was Manhattan, crammed into an impossibly small bit of land bounded by two rivers. A place of mysteries, of hidden treasures and entanglements and snares, a place Currier once said she would make her own.

Owen's four hotels, she thought. My hotels. Ginny, Clay, Kelly—and Wes, waiting for me. Almost a family. My family.

Sparks of champagne danced against her lip as she drank; it was as heady as the brandy she had breathed when she was seducing Gérard Lyon into coming to New York. Everything she did these days was as heady as brandy and champagne, as if she were running toward a dream city through fields thick with flowers, a little dizzy from the perfumed brilliance around her and from the dream, first so close, then reachable, now hers.

It was a headiness intoxicating enough to make her believe she had all she needed. She didn't need the kind of family she had once longed for; she didn't need children. She didn't need anything more than what she had now: work, friendships, and the realization, when she woke each morning, that she could do what she wanted, overcome any obstacle, reach any goal.

As the sky darkened beyond the window, the lights in the restaurant gradually dimmed, making more brilliant the lights below, on the streets and in the windows of Manhattan. Laura knew she had already gone beyond her desire for Owen's hotels, even beyond the drive to settle her score with Felix. This is what I need, she repeated to herself with a silent toast to the glittering tapestry far below, and all I'll ever need: to know I can take on any opponent, and win.

* * *

Ben had checked the story on landmark status for the Philadelphia Salinger and reported to the board that he could find nothing in it. "I also talked to the reporter at the *Globe*," he said at the board meeting. "He claims he only wanted a statement on landmark status in general and its possible effect on the Philadelphia hotel if the commission changed its mind. I have no idea why he thought the commission might do that, but if he had any reason to think so, it was a logical question to ask the owner of the hotel. He insists he never said that the status had been changed."

"What the hell," Cole Hatton said. "Whether he did or not, Felix thought he did. I have no problem with Felix thinking this or that or any damn thing he wants to. Where I have a problem is Felix riding off in all directions without looking around to see if we're with him. You see my problem, Felix?"

A month later, when the board met again, the sale of the Washington Salinger was approved in fifteen minutes. "I don't give a damn what you think of her," Hatton said to Felix just before the vote. "Her money's good and she always pops up with it at just the right time. I'd like to meet her. She sounds like one tough, smart lady. And ten million is a decent price for a hotel that's got nothing going for it. Anybody know what happened to the chef?"

No one knew. Felix had an idea, from the description the maitre d' had given of the woman who had dined alone and then talked to Lyon until well after midnight, but he said nothing. He cast his vote with everyone else for the sale of the Washington Salinger, his face frozen. But within, he seethed with frustrated fury. She hadn't been stopped. Somehow she had arranged events to go her way. And the culmination of it had come within a month of his discovery of Ben Gardner's identity. It was no wonder he felt frustrated and over-fatigued. Anyone would be, surrounded as he was by enemies.

He would have to do something about both of them. Think about what to do, then arrange it. No matter how long it took, he would think of something to make him once more victorious.

Ben had been watching Felix, noting how Felix never met his eyes or addressed him directly anymore, but when Asa introduced the new budget and the board began to discuss it, he let his thoughts wander. That tough, smart lady Hatton had talked about was his sister. He tried to match the image of a savvy, hard-nosed businesswoman with the young girl he'd last heard sobbing on the telephone because she thought he'd betrayed her. How could it be the same person? He couldn't even imagine how she would look now; all he could see in his mind was his pretty little sister, one of the most talented little thieves he'd known, who looked at him with her big eyes and thought he was wonderful. They'd had good times together, he thought, turning to the next page of the budget so the others would think he was with them. Good, loving times. Until it all blew apart.

And he didn't see how he could get it together again. Now less than ever before. Because even if he could think of a way to reach out to Laura, how the hell could he introduce her to his new family as his sister and expect to have the welcome mat put out, after she'd just shown them all up by getting most of her inheritance back, even though Felix had done his damnedest to stop her? And what would it do to his position in the family, to be connected to her? He knew how they'd reacted when they found out Laura had lied to them about herself; he could imagine how they'd feel about him. Introduce Laura as his sister? He might as well throw a bomb in the family's midst and watch the pieces fly.

He might be able to tell Allison, he thought that evening as he unlocked the front door of the house on Beacon Hill. He'd thought about it so many times, but every time he did, it seemed so complicated and unlikely that he gave it up. Laura was happy and getting what she wanted, and so was he. It was probably better that they stayed as they were.

"Mrs. Gardner is in the garden," the housekeeper said when he asked where Allison was, and he walked through the house to the back door. When he opened it, he stood still for a moment, watching Allison before she saw him. She sat on a low chair between beds of roses, nursing Judd. Her red skirt was spread around her like the petals of a rose, her breast was whiter than the white blouse she had opened, and Judd's blond head nestled against it with a burst of light. The sun's rays slanted low over the stone wall, bathing the two of them in a deep golden light, and, high above, a cardinal sang a long trill that floated with pure sweetness into the garden.

Ben held his breath, afraid to move. The scene was so perfect, like a painting of paradise, he wanted to fix it in his mind. But just then Allison looked up, her face bright. "I'm so glad you're here. Do you know you have a very greedy son?"

"He's only greedy because he appreciates his wonderful mother." He bent over her and kissed her, making himself part of paradise. He sat on the grass beside Allison, and together they watched their son, whose small mouth made little sucking motions even though he had fallen asleep. "He's getting big," Ben said. "He'll be walking in a couple of months."

Allison laughed. "When he's six months old? Your inexperience is showing."

"You and Judd have a lot to teach me," he agreed with a smile. He felt relaxed and content. "What did you do today?"

"Wandered around with Molly, looking for galleries."

A small frown cut into his contentment. "You're going ahead with that?"

"I think so. Yes, I am. I really want something to do outside the house, something useful and challenging. I know art, at least I know twentieth-century, and Molly knows nineteenth-, so we're a good team. . . ." When he was silent, she said defensively, "I have the time and the money, and I'd still be with you and Judd as much as I am now. . . . You don't really mind, do you?"

"Of course not. You shouldn't even ask. As you say, you have the money."

"Ben, don't do that."

"Do what?"

"Talk that way. In that tone of voice. We haven't worried about money for a long time."

"You never worry about money."

"I think about it; I don't worry about it. Why can't you do the same? What difference does it make if everything isn't equal? We're living on your salary, isn't that enough? If I want to do something extra—"

"We have a lot of extras around here. Vacations, redecorating the house, giving parties on your father's boat, the car you gave me for my birthday. . ."

"Oh, all right," she said, nervous and angry. "If it's going to be such an *issue*, I won't open the gallery. Just, please, don't ruin things; they're so wonderful. . . ."

"I'm sorry." Ben put his arm around her. "I don't want to ruin anything; you're right, everything is wonderful. And you'll have your gallery. I think it's a great idea. I'll help you all I can. Maybe I'll even buy something from you."

"I'll save you the best. If you let me give you a discount."

"I expect a discount. Won't I be a preferred customer?"

She smiled. "You're always preferred. It's so good having you back; I don't like it when you travel. The house seems twice as big and five times as empty. Why can't someone else go?"

"Your father wants me to go. It was one of the prices for moving up to vice president for development." He wants me to slip up somewhere, Ben thought, and the European hotel market is confusing enough for an American that the chances are better there than here. "But it won't last long," he said to Allison. "One of these days I'll arrange it so I don't have to go."

"If you don't, I'll go with you," she murmured comfortably. "Judd and nanny and all."

He chuckled. "There's nothing that will impress the Europeans more than a hotel man with his entourage." He bent his head and kissed her, his arm around her, his hand cupped over the baby's head, and they sat together, talking quietly, until shadows filled the garden and the nanny came to get Judd. As they walked into the house, Ben lingered in the doorway, gazing at the lush roses beneath the pale sky tinged with pink and gray, hearing the echo of Allison's voice.

My home, he thought. My wife. My son. Allison was right. It was perfect.

Though it would be even more perfect when he could also say: My company.

* * *

Clay sat cross-legged on the water bed, surveying his new home. Beyond the high windows were the renovated warehouses of SoHo and the skyscrapers of Manhattan; in the open expanse of the uncarpeted loft, strange furniture huddled in clusters, looking tiny and lost; a window air conditioner hummed and spat; and beside him a young girl slept, her bare bottom smooth and cool beneath his hand.

It was early morning. He had just awakened, and in that unfamiliar room, at a time when he was usually still asleep, he had a moment of dizziness and fright: he didn't know where he was. He didn't even know the name of the girl beside him. It wasn't Myrna, he knew that; Myrna was still in Chicago, giving him time to miss her so much he'd call her and tell her he wanted to marry her. And he did miss her. He might even call her. Everybody he knew in Chicago had been getting married the last few months he'd been there: it was a rash, an epidemic, a kind of mass hypnosis. So he might call Myrna eventually: she'd been faithful for a long time. But first he had to figure out where he was.

He sat very still; the girl slept. It was very simple, really; he was in a loft he'd sublet from a musician who was on the road. He had a place to live for a few months while he looked for something more permanent; he had furniture, even if it sagged and bulged like a has-been heavyweight; he had company, the little girl next to him, who modeled brassieres for Bloomingdale's catalogues and had a weakness for blond men with mustaches; and he had a new job.

Clay Fairchild, he announced with silent grandeur. Vice president for quality control of OWL Development. Citizen of New York City. World traveler, for business and pleasure. Fabulous poker player. Lover of women.

He grinned. Not bad for a kid who'd been picking pockets less than ten years before. Of course it was mainly because he'd been smart enough to stick with Laura, but that was all right: he gave his sister full credit. Terrific lady. Brains and looks and a hell of a cook when she had him over for dinner. He wouldn't be anywhere without Laura. Ginny Starrett kept telling him that, but he knew it anyway. Without Laura, he'd have spent a few years tagging along with Ben on penny-ante break-ins until Ben hooked up with Allison Salinger, and then that would have been it; no way would that conniving bastard have brought his little brother into that set-up; he'd want it all for himself.

So Clay owed everything he had to Laura. Well, almost everything. He had his own talents, too, and he was doing fine with them: he was driving a new Corvette, he had a stereo system that could knock over the Empire State Building, and on his last trip to Europe to check out some new ideas in hotels for Laura, he'd bought two Rodolfo suits that made him look like the high-powered executive he'd always known he was.

He put his legs over the edge of the water bed and heaved himself out. The young girl made protesting noises as the waves he'd made tossed her back and forth, but she slept on, and she was still asleep when Clay had showered and dressed and left for his new office on the top floor of the New York Beacon Hill.

The minute he walked in the door, it was a real high. Everything was happening at once; walls were knocked down, floors were stripped to the bare concrete, old toilets and bathtubs lay in corners like porcelain corpses, light bulbs dangled, and a haze of dust hung over everything. Within half an hour, the luster of his Rodolfo suit had faded, his hands were grimy, his nose itched, and his eyes watered. But he was grinning because he loved it: things were changing before his very eyes, he couldn't predict today exactly what everything would be like tomorrow, and there were mysteries—what's behind the wall that's being torn down, or under the carpet that's being pulled up, or inside the closets being ripped out?

It was wonderful, and he hated to leave it to go to his office on the top floor, a dump if he ever saw one. He knew it was temporary and some-day they'd have a decent place, but still it was a drag to go there and leave the bustling activity below.

He could hear them all day. While he and Laura and the small staff planned the redesign of the Philadelphia and Washington hotels and the opening of the New York Beacon Hill by the end of the year, they could hear the workmen moving closer, one floor at a time. Now and then Clay couldn't stand it any longer, and he'd drag Laura with him for an inspection. They would check on the two- and three-room suites being put together from individual rooms; the double baths in each, of sea green marble with white fixtures; the sculptured pattern in the lobby ceiling that was newly traced in gold leaf, with a chandelier that had been rescued from some crumbling castle in England; the Victorian sconces found in a jumbled pile in the basement that had been polished and installed in the corridors where they'd been when Owen built the hotel sixty years before. And they would end their inspection back on the top floor, half of which was being transformed into the dining room, a secluded pastel aerie, a French garden in the middle of the city.

By now the ideas were Laura's, going far beyond the ones she and Owen had worked on when they sat opposite each other at his Chippendale desk. Everything he had planned was being done, but it was not enough for her. She had been traveling about on weekends, staying in other hotels, studying them; she read hotel industry magazines; she dreamed of new fantasies that could become reality in her own hotels. As the weeks went by, the luxuries multiplied; so did the costs. And she was in a hurry; that sent costs up even more.

But it didn't matter. The stunning success of the Chicago Beacon Hill and her vision for her other hotels outweighed everything else. So far, when she'd needed money, she'd gotten it. She'd used it with great success in Chicago, and she would everywhere else, too. And when she needed more, she would find it.

It had become easy to believe the tap would never run dry.

"Reporting for duty," Clay said, walking into her office at exactly nine o'clock. He knew she'd been there since seven, sometimes even earlier, but she'd never asked him to show up at the crack of dawn, and so he didn't. He figured if he couldn't get his work done in a regular day, he had too much work and ought to have an assistant. "You look beautiful and deep in thought."

She smiled at him as he kissed her. "How was the movie last night?"

"Good. You should see it."

"I will sometime."

"You don't get out enough." He sat on a corner of her desk. "It isn't good for you to sit home and brood."

"I don't brood," she said with a laugh. "I work."

"You work too much. Where's Wes these days?"

"On one of his consulting trips. I'll see him when he gets back."

"Is that still on?"

"What do you mean?"

"Well, you don't date anybody else—"

"Yes, I do; I just don't talk about it."

"I know what you do; you have dates for dinner parties and those fancy benefit parties you go to. I meant real dates—dinner and a nightclub and then bed. How many of those do you have?"

"Dinner and a nightclub once in a while."

"That's all?"

"That's all."

"Well, that's what I meant. You don't date, you still go out with Wes when he's in town, and the two of you are sort of . . . *close* when he's in the office. So are you going to marry him one of these days after all?"

"No. But we are close—we've been together for a long time—and it's nice to have someone to go out with." *And sleep with now and then— even though I once said I didn't want to anymore—and talk to and share my worries with.* "What about you and Myrna?"

"I haven't decided. But if you're lonesome and want my scintillating company more than once a week, you can call me up, you know. I don't like the idea of you alone all the time."

"I'm not alone all the time, but thank you, Clay. You have your own life; once a week with your sister is enough, I think."

"Just let me know; I'm yours if you want me." He stood up. "I need some coffee. Is there anything to eat in that refrigerator of yours?"

"Sweet rolls and fruit. Help yourself. And then would you check these purchasing reports? They just came in from Chicago, and it looks as if Henry's using some new suppliers; you may have to go out there and talk to him." She pulled her desk calendar to her. "I want you at a meeting with the lighting people at three; there's a problem with the fixtures we chose for the conference room. And at five we're meeting with Gérard about the dining room tables and chairs—did you say something?"

"I was about to comment on the idea of having a meeting at five o'clock, but I guess you don't want to hear that."

She smiled. "I guess I don't. And I'd like you to go to Philadelphia on Thursday to talk to our suppliers—here's the list—and make sure we're getting everything we ordered. It shouldn't take more than a couple of days."

"Great idea. I was thinking of it anyway; the architect's been calling with a lot of changes—not big ones, but they ought to be looked at. Then I may go on to Chicago for the weekend; see how Myrna's doing. And then there's that quality control convention Monday and Tuesday in Denver. I could go there from Chicago."

"That sounds all right."

"Good." He grinned. "You won't see me for a whole week. But I'll call in."

"Just a minute, Clay, there's one other thing. Did you fire a security man yesterday?"

"Oh, shit, did I forget to tell you about that? Right. I didn't like the way he worked, he didn't know how to take orders, so I let him go. I thought, when I'm in Chicago this weekend I'd talk to some of the guys on the security staff and bring one of them here next week. If that's okay with you."

"I thought we agreed you wouldn't fire anyone without checking with me."

"Right, we did. I should have. He really got to me. I'm sorry, Laura; it won't happen again, I promise. I do know who I'm working for: a wonderful lady who's understanding and tolerant and very loving to her brother. You should meet her sometime; you'd like her."

Laura smiled. "I don't want it happening again, Clay."

"Right. Is it okay if I have my breakfast now?"

"Clay, for heaven's sake—! You don't have to ask permission; go get your breakfast. Here, don't forget these reports."

He gave her a small salute, took some food from the refrigerator and left. Laura rested her head on her hand and gazed out the window. She shouldn't have reacted that way to his joke about breakfast. But he made her feel frustrated and impatient just when she wanted to rely on him. One minute he was a man, handling a job that was already complicated and would get more so as they opened the three hotels that were all being renovated at the same time; the next he was a little boy looking gleeful over the chance to get away from the office for a week. He was smart but lazy, and he resisted growing up. It was one of the reasons she still did not confide in him. When they had dinner together, Clay told her about his girls, his loft, even his card games, since she no longer criticized him for them, but he asked few questions about her and none about the finances of the business that she ran and he worked for.

Laura knew he didn't want details; he didn't want to worry or know that she had worries. In many ways, he liked being her little brother. Or a son, she thought; children don't want to know if their parents have worries, either.

But maybe that was partly her fault. If Clay liked being a little brother or a son, she liked being an older sister or even a mother; it made her feel as if she had a real family. And even if he did ask about her finances, she probably wouldn't tell him very much since she really confided only in Currier about money. Not even in Ginny, though she knew she could.

Ginny asked no questions about money. She and Laura talked about almost everything else, and she figured when Laura wanted to talk to her about money, she'd do it on her own. She could even ask me to invest in OWL Development, Ginny thought as she stopped at Laura's office to pick her up. It's probably a good investment. But there aren't many times when friendship and money make a good mix, so we'll let that go, too.

"I just had an idea," Laura said as she sat beside her in her limousine. "Tell me what you think of it."

It was one of the hottest days of August, but air conditioning kept the gray velvet luxury of the limousine cool and quiet as they drove from Laura's hotel to Greenwich Village. A foldout silver tray with iced Perrier and lime was in front of them, and Ginny was filling their glasses. She handed one to Laura, noting the brightness of her eyes. "You always have an idea," she said. "Or a dozen. What's this one?"

"Well, I do have a few. Shall I save the best for last?" Her smile was mischievous, secretive, pleased with herself and the world. Ginny smiled back. No one could help but smile back when Laura looked like that. In fact, Ginny had never met anyone whose excitement was as contagious as hers. As Laura talked about the design of the suites in the hotel and the antique wardrobes in the corridors that would hold linen and cleaning supplies so maids would not have to push unwieldy, unlovely carts around, she was so involved in what she was saying that her face lost its cool reticence and glowed with pleasure. Shoot, Ginny thought, a man ought to make her look like that, not a hotel. But of course it was more than a hotel: it was Laura's work, her dream, almost her whole life.

"Now—are you ready for this?—the best idea of all," Laura said, her smile wide and happy. "I really want your opinion of it."

"You already told me it's the best of all," Ginny murmured.

Laura laughed. "I want to make the New York Beacon Hill so exclusive that no one can stay in it without a recommendation from a former guest."

There was a silence. Ginny contemplated her. "Very bold. Very risky. Very clever. There's a little place in London that does that, and I must say, it's comforting, even for a tough Texan who can take anything, to know you're sleeping in a bed that's only been slept in by somebody you know or have heard of."

"I'm counting on others feeling that way, too," Laura said. She leaned forward, filled with nervous energy, as if she could push the limousine faster down Seventh Avenue, through the crowded garment district where men pushing racks of clothing made better time than they did. The chauffeur calmly swung the wheel, slipping between a car and a delivery truck, weaving around a taxi picking up a fare and another letting one off, and in a few minutes passed Madison Square Garden and then was in Chelsea, where the traffic eased and he could speed up.

Watching Laura's nervous energy, Ginny shook her head. "What're you going to do with yourself when you finish your hotels?"

"Oh, buy another one, maybe. Or, better yet . . ." She hesitated, as if she were still unsure of herself. "I've been thinking the past few weeks—and I haven't told anyone yet, not even Wes—what I'd really like to do when I've got the hotels running smoothly . . . what I really want is to buy into the Salinger Corporation."

Ginny stared at her. Still wanting to even scores, she thought, and be as big as Owen told her she could be. When the blue-eyed devil would Laura start to live just for herself? She'd told Ginny the story about the Salingers soon after the Chicago Beacon Hill opened, when Ginny was spending a lot of time in Chicago, trying to mother her. She hadn't made it a long story, and she hadn't told it with a lot of emotion, but Ginny had gotten the picture: there was plenty of emotion there, even after all this time, especially about Paul. Laura had talked about him even more briefly than about his family, which made Ginny sure she was still in love with him, since stories tend to get longer the more removed we are from the subject. But to try to buy into the family company . . . that seemed to be going a mite too far.

"What for?" she asked bluntly. "You'd be damned uncomfortable sitting on that board with your few little votes against the rest of them."

"I'd be part of the company, the way I was supposed to be. I'd be voting the way I think Owen would."

"And if you don't know how he'd vote?"

"I'd vote the way I want."

"Well, that part is sensible." Ginny thought for a minute. "Flying pretty high, honey."

"I didn't say I could do it. I only said I want to."

"So far, what you've wanted you've managed to get. But even if you found somebody to sell you some shares, my guess is you'd need a heap of money."

"It's a long way off, Ginny. I'm just thinking about it."

"A lot, sounds like. Well, keep me informed about your thinking."

"I will." She sat forward again, picking out familiar landmarks as they drove. "Almost there. I hope you like it; it's the only place I've seen that I'd really like to live in."

"Then what do you care whether I like it or not?" Ginny asked.

"I need your sharp eye. The rent is too low, so there may be something wrong with the house that I'm not seeing."

"But hasn't Wes seen it?"

Laura nodded. "He says I should take it. But I want to know what you think."

In the Village, the chauffeur parked on Grove Street, and Ginny and Laura walked through a narrow passage between two houses to a small cobblestone court lined with a solid row of narrow, three-story brick houses, white-shuttered, looking out on gnarled trees where birds sang. "My God," Ginny breathed. "Who would have thought—?"

"Wes found it," Laura said. She opened one of the doors with a key. "It's empty; the owner is in Europe for two years. If I don't rent it by tonight, I have to return the key."

"Or it turns back into a pumpkin," Ginny murmured. She followed Laura, who flew up and down the stairs, pointing out details preserved from the 1830 construction, her face bright with excitement. Ginny's heels clicked smartly on the pine plank floors as her shrewd glance appraised the new kitchen, the four fireplaces, the large bedroom on the third floor, and the roof garden, bare from neglect but bordered with planters ready for flowers, and tubs where small trees could grow. "One in a million," she pronounced when they returned to the living room on the second floor. "And that's about what it would cost to buy. What's the rent?"

"Two thousand a month," Laura said.

"Impossible. They could get three times that."

"That's what I said. It's too low."

Ginny perched on a windowsill. The house was very small: living room, dining room, library, kitchen, bedroom. But the kitchen and baths were new, there was a finished basement, plus those four fireplaces and the roof garden. And the privacy of Grove Court.

It also had Currier's approval. And that was the answer, Ginny suddenly thought. It seemed likely that Wes Currier's check made up the difference between what the owner was asking and the rent Laura would be charged.

Of course I don't know that for sure, Ginny thought. And neither does Laura, even though she may wonder about it. So I surely won't be the one to bring it up.

She had known the minute she stepped into Grove Court that this was the place where Laura should live. It reminded her of Laura's description of the compound on Cape Cod; it was reminiscent of the narrow, shaded streets of Beacon Hill, and also the DePaul neighborhood in Chicago where Laura had lived. She was making it big in a tough business, Ginny thought, and she'd come to one of the toughest cities in the world, but she was happiest in small, enclosed places: small towns, family enclaves, close-knit neighborhoods. That was what she needed, a place to belong. She needed Grove Court.

"It might not be all that strange," she said to Laura. "There are owners who'll take a lower rent if they know they're getting a tenant with top credentials, somebody who'll take care of the place like their very own."

Laura nodded slowly. "But it may be that Wes is—"

"I very much doubt it," Ginny said briskly. "I think this is the place for you and you ought to grab it."

Laura walked the length of the living room to the front windows and looked up as the brilliant red of a cardinal flashed across the courtyard, from one tree to another. A nanny walked by, shepherding a small child pedaling a wooden car; behind them a spaniel bounded into view, followed by an elderly woman, reading as she walked, a leash looped over her arm. *Home. For as long as I can stay.*

"Thank you," she said, turning from the window. Her face bright again, she put her arms around Ginny and kissed her. "I love it when you give good advice. And I love you. Will you be my first dinner guest? As soon as I buy some furniture, that is."

"I'd be privileged. And let me help pick out your furniture. Next to spending my own money, there's nothing I like better than spending somebody else's. You'll want a long sofa here, with an oversize coffee table—oh, shoot." She looked sheepishly at Laura. "I'm sounding like Wes, aren't I? Trying to take over what's really your project. I'll stop; I won't say another word."

"Not quite like Wes," Laura laughed. "He doesn't stop so easily. But I'd like to have you help me. Can you do it this week? I want to move in as soon as possible."

"I can do it tomorrow. Ten o'clock? I'll pick you up at your office."

But there was a brief delay the next morning at ten, because, just as Ginny arrived, Laura's telephone rang.

"I'll just be a minute," she told Ginny and picked it up.

"Hi, there, sweetheart, how are you, it's Britt." His voice was loud and excited. "I'm calling to invite you to my party."

CHAPTER 23

THE third theft was in Palm Springs on the first day of September. Clay had told Laura he would be in Los Angeles for the Labor Day weekend, visiting friends. It was an easy drive from the city to Palm Springs, and to the sprawling house screened by tall trees and manicured shrubs where he made his surefooted way, first to the living room and then to the master bedroom. It was nine-thirty at night: the hour always full on the datebook he had found in Amelia Laughton's purse; the hour when the residents of Palm Springs were busy entertaining or being entertained; the hour when darkness hid Clay's passage through the house and his gloved hands as they gently lifted paintings from the Laughtons' walls. He worked swiftly, whistling softly as he stacked the paintings beside the door. Then, because he felt so terrific, he added a pair of Dürer prints he decided he wanted just for himself. And when he was through, he drove sedately through the hushed streets, amiably saluting a chauffeur in a black Mercedes who was gazing in boredom at the sky.

Three weeks later, Sid and Amelia Laughton told everyone about the robbery at Britt Farley's celebration party in a Manhattan mansion Louie had rented for the occasion.

"One Picasso," Amelia said to Emily Janssen and anyone else who cared to listen. "A Miró, three late Braques and a pair of Dürer prints. It is too revolting; the only week all summer our couple took a vacation and left the house empty—"

"No sign of a break-in," Sid replied to a question. "They had a key. *And* the code for the alarm system—"

"*And* knew our couple would be gone that week," said Amelia, plucking a shrimp from a tray as a waiter passed within reach.

"Or were watching the house," said Sid. "Hard to tell; we don't have any clues. Anyway, they knew what they wanted: they went straight to the paintings; didn't touch another thing."

"The only bright side," said Amelia, "is that the police aren't the only ones investigating it; the insurance company brought their top man in: very experienced, very dedicated, very determined. We've talked to him twice and I was impressed: if anyone can track down the thieves, he can."

There was a stir at the door as Britt Farley arrived. "Late for his own party," Amelia murmured. "But it is a grand entrance, isn't it?"

He wore a white tuxedo with a red tie and cummerbund, and over it a white cape lined in red, and as he stood in the doorway, surveying his guests, he looked like the ruler of a mythical kingdom waiting for his subjects to bow. "Well, why not?" Amelia said, and swept him a deep, flourishing curtsy.

Laughter filled the room. Britt threw Amelia a kiss as his guests crowded around him, congratulating him on the tour, telling him how wonderful he looked, asking about his plans. The Laughtons' robbery was forgotten, as well as a good deal of other gossip; everything revolved around Britt. Among themselves, the guests said he didn't look good: he'd lost weight, his face was gaunt and pouchy, and his eyes were too shiny and fixedly staring: he was on something. But none of them said it very loudly, and no one said it in his vicinity. Instead they touched him and stroked him and made him feel like a star.

At the other end of the silk-hung reception room, Paul stood alone beside the bar, watching. The tour had ended four weeks before with a record amount raised for the hungry, more than half of it from the hugely successful concert in Washington. The publicity had been heavy and favorable, but no call had come inviting Farley to star in a new television series, and little by little he had sunk from high expectations to brooding indifference. It was Louie who made all the arrangements for the party. "I wanted to cancel it," he told Paul, "but he wouldn't let me. He's up one minute and down the next, and when he's up, he wants to star in something and this party is it, and he isn't giving it up."

It was a good thing the film was almost finished, Paul thought. The few interviews he still needed, and the editing, did not involve Britt at all.

But despite Farley's mood swings, his party would be a success because that was what everyone wanted, and New Yorkers were wonderfully adept at turning parties to their own purposes. Everyone would stroke and praise Britt Farley, hold his attention, stay close to him, and be seen as his intimate friend so that whatever followed—a comeback as a world star or the end of his career—they could talk about it as insiders. That was why they were there.

And why am I here? Paul wondered. Because Britt and Louie both had asked him, because Emily wanted to come, because he had two cameramen filming the party in case there was something they could use, but mainly because—

And then he saw her.

She was in white, her shoulders and arms bare, her chestnut hair gleaming red-bronze in the bright light. It was cut short—Paul had never imagined her with short hair—and skillfully shaped to frame her beauty, emphasizing her wide-spaced eyes and warm mouth, making her look older and more sophisticated. But she is older and more sophisticated, he told himself; it's been six years . . .

He gazed at her, catching quick glimpses as the crowd between them shifted, trying to match her image to his memories. He felt the past blur and slip away, and the stunning woman in the doorway seemed more and more a stranger.

He saw someone greet her and introduce a friend. Laura smiled at them. And with that smile, the past swept over Paul in a torrent of remembered feelings, and he found himself moving toward her, making his way through the crowd of guests. They surrounded him, chattering, drinking, laughing. Brilliant gowns and summer tuxedos were crammed together in tight clusters; now and then long fingers darted out to snatch the hors d'oeuvres that seemed to float past, held high by waiters struggling to move. Everyone shifted, parting and coming together, blocking Paul's way.

When he reached the doorway she was gone. It took him a minute to find her, enveloped in Farley's arms. "God, Laura, am I glad you're here!" Farley boomed. "You're late!"

"I couldn't get away from the office any earlier. Britt, what's wrong?"

He looked down at her, his arms still around her. "Meaning?"

"You look tired, and you've lost weight. And why are you so glad to see me?"

"Because you're a smart, beautiful lady who likes me even when I'm a bad boy." He closed his eyes for a moment. "'A-course you're right, sweetheart: I've lost weight and I'm tired. But there's nothing wrong! Everything's fine! I've been working like a drone; you wouldn't believe it: the tour and the movie... Did you know I've been making a movie? Not me, you know, I'm not making it, but I'm *it*—I'm the movie—how about that?"

"It's wonderful, Britt."

"And I want you to meet the genius who thought of it; he's here somewhere—" His bright, fixed eyes scanned the crowd and found Paul. "Hey, friend, here's my sweetheart Laura, the lady I told you about." He turned, bringing Laura with him. "Laura, this is the genius who got me in my own movie."

Laura's eyes widened in shock. The crowded room wavered before her, like a picture seen through a rainy window, and she swayed against Farley's arm.

He never noticed. "You two are the only ones who don't bullshit me, you know that? Means a lot to me. A lot of people act like I'm dumb, but you don't and I like that. So you oughta be friends. Paul, you want to get this lady a drink?"

Paul had already moved to her, his hand outstretched. "I'd be very pleased to get Miss Fairchild a drink."

Laura took his hand.

"Great," said Farley; he was already distracted by someone who was beckoning to him, and he drifted away.

The noise level rose higher. Paul and Laura stood still, their hands clasped. He looked so much older, she thought: the lines in his face had subtly deepened, making it look narrower and harder. But he was more handsome than she remembered, and taller; his hair more unruly, his skin darker. His hands—the long tense fingers holding hers—were as familiar as her own.

"Do you want a drink?" he asked.

She shook her head.

"Then let's find a quiet place."

She took her hand from his. "I'm not sure that's a good idea."

"I am." He put his hand on her arm. "Laura, please."

At the sound of his voice saying her name, she began to tremble. *It isn't fair; everything was fine. I'd forgotten him.* Involuntarily, she smiled.

"What is it?" Paul asked. And she remembered he'd always done that: wanted to share whatever it was that made her smile.

"I was thinking I'd forgotten you. And that was absurd."

His hand tightened on her arm. "We can go upstairs. They won't serve dinner for another hour."

He looked for Emily; she was happily surrounded by her own crowd, and he knew he would not be missed. His hand still on Laura's arm, he led the way, and together, they moved through the crowd, prying guests apart so they could squeeze through.

Laura was almost unaware of the party. Her arm burned where Paul's hand held it; their bodies pressed together in the crush of people. And then they were on the stairs, free of the crowd. But when they reached the dining room that took up almost the entire third floor of the mansion, everything was confusion as tables were still being readied for the four hundred guests. "Upstairs," Paul said again, and they climbed another wide, carpeted stairway to the ballroom. It was eerily quiet, the bandstand chairs and music stands awaiting the orchestra, the flowering trees shadowed in the half-light. Paul led Laura to one of the couches along the wall, and she sat in the corner, curled up with her legs under her, like a young girl.

He sat in the other corner, and they were silent. "I'm sorry," he said at last. "I've thought of so many things to say to you over the years, and now none of them seems right. Except... I'm sorry. I behaved badly toward you, we all did, and I've wanted to tell you how sorry I am, for all of it."

"Thank you."

They were silent again. "I've wanted to congratulate you, too," he said. "It's wonderful that you've bought those hotels. And I understand the one in Chicago is very fine; Ben told Allison it's—"

Laura's head snapped around. "Ben," she said flatly.

"Oh, of course, you don't know him. Ben Gardner, Allison's husband. So much has happened... my God, so many years... Ben's a good man. I like him, though for some reason we're not as close as I hoped we'd be. He's a vice president of the company, and Allison gives me his news when she thinks I'd be interested. He says your Chicago hotel is one of the best in the country."

"He's right," she said coldly. She was trembling again. Ben and that family, together, talking about her. She took a deep breath and looked around the room, away from Paul. "And you're married," she said at last.

"Yes. I didn't know you knew."

"Ginny Starrett is a friend of mine."

"I don't know her," said Paul.

"She knows Leni."

All the names, all the events: unshared. They were strangers.

"You're very beautiful," Paul said, trying to find a way back. "You were always lovely, but now you're more..." He wanted to say she looked more polished, more distant, colder, but he could not. Instead, almost helplessly, he said, "You cut your hair."

She smiled faintly at the obviousness of his comment. "A long time ago. I wanted to look different."

"You are. You're—"

"I wanted to *be* different."

"Time does that."

She nodded. "I didn't know that when I cut it. I was leaving Boston and everybody I loved had turned away from me, and I didn't want to be me. It hurt too much."

"My God." Paul leaned toward her, his hand reaching out; he wanted to take her in his arms and hold her to him. It was not a sexual desire, not yet: he wanted to comfort her for the pain behind her level voice. He could almost feel her body in his—the idea of holding her was so real —but she ignored his reaching out.

"Britt says you've made a movie about him. I never knew you were interested in—" She bit off her words; she would not refer to their years together. "Is that what you're doing now? No more photography?"

"I may go back to photography sometime, but right now filmmaking fascinates me. It has a freedom and an aliveness I've never known before, a way of creating whole worlds in such a brief space, and creating lives. . . ." She was looking at him, and he remembered how good it had been, long ago, to tell her his thoughts and know he would be understood. "Creating lives, Laura, that's the extraordinary thing. Movement and stillness, dialogue and silence. It's not obvious—at least it wasn't to me until I learned it—the use of opposites to show different sides of a person or a scene, the wonderful, crazy logic that people create as they go along, the irrational way they act when they think something that touches them deeply is true or false. . . ."

A long silence fell. Laura was looking at him in wonder, at the fervor in his voice, the passion for creating that she had never seen in him in all the time she had known him. Owen would have loved it, she thought; he would have said, 'I was right about that boy; he just needed time.' But then she heard the echo of Paul's last words; they hung in the air between them. It seemed they could not get away from the past: it kept curving back to them, no matter what they talked about.

"Tell me about your hotels," he said. "How did you buy them?"

"With other people's money."

"One of Owen's first lessons," he smiled. "Do you like it?"

"Being in debt?"

He chuckled. "Owning hotels; running them."

Laura's smile had met his. Quickly, she looked away, then, her face calm, turned back to him. "I love it. It's as if I owned four wonderful homes—well, they're not all wonderful yet, but pretty soon they will be."

"You're renovating all of them?"

"I couldn't do anything else. There isn't much to save except the exterior and the magnificent lobbies. And the corridors: they're much grander than anything built today. All the rest . . . Owen had plans, you know; we worked on them for years . . ."

"I know," he said quietly.

"And they're wonderful. I've expanded them a little"—she gave a small laugh—"a lot, sometimes, but I get carried away by the excitement of it."

"Expanded how?"

She told him about the hotels, about making them as much like private homes as she could, and then she talked about the people she hired and how they worked together. It did not matter that he was a member of the Salinger family and the staffs she was talking about ran hotels that had been partly his: she found herself talking easily, even about Gérard Lyon and the special school she had found for his son in New York. And then, in answer to another question, she told him about the small house she had rented in Grove Court.

"Do you like New York?" he asked then.

"I think I will. It's already changed me." She smiled at him and he had a glimpse of the mischievous smile he remembered. "I walk faster, I talk faster, I even breathe faster; I walk sideways down the street to get past people, especially at noon when everybody's out for lunch; and every once in a while I find myself thinking if something didn't happen in New York it didn't happen. Period. That's when I look for a reason to go to Chicago for a couple of days."

Their laughter rang out in the huge, empty room, and for a moment they were joined.

But then Laura looked away again until, as before, her face was calm. "I haven't had a chance to find out if I'll like it or not; I haven't had time to get to know it. I grew up here, you know"—there was a note of challenge and defiance in her voice, but he seemed not to notice it—"and now everything is so different for me that it's as if I've never been here. Someday I'll take the time to explore it. Right now, I spend most of my time at my work."

"And it's what you hoped it would be? When Owen was teaching you about hotels, and you wanted one of your own, is it everything you hoped?"

"Much better. There's something so special about it, Paul: feeling that they're my houses, where the door is always open, and watching people enjoy them, knowing I can make them comfortable and happy and give them what they like and what they'll remember, and then seeing them come back because they did remember me and want to come..." Embarrassed, she put a hand to her face. "I think we should go back downstairs."

"Is someone waiting for you?"

"No." Then, not wanting him to know how much she was alone, she added, "Not tonight. There is someone I see a great deal; he's out of town this week... But your wife will wonder where you are."

"She probably won't miss me until it's time to sit down for dinner."

Laura gazed at him, her face impassive. "What does she do?"

"She's a model. Magazines, mostly. She's very good."

"I've probably seen her, then, without knowing who she is. How odd that seems. Do you have children?"

"No, Emily doesn't want..." He paused, reluctant to sound as if he were complaining. "She's concentrating on her career for a few years. I thought it was a good idea. Laura, there are some things I'd like to say—"

"Tell me more about your films," she said. "Is there someone you work with?"

He made a gesture of impatience. "I have a partner, Larry Gould—"

"Gould? Didn't you know him in college?"

"Yes, you're amazing to remember that."

She shook her head. She hadn't meant to let him know that she remembered anything of their past. "Tell me about him."

"He makes television commercials, but we formed a separate company for documentaries..." He told her all of it, from the time he had first talked to Larry about getting out of society photography in New York, to the failure of their first film, and then to the idea for a film on Britt Farley. "He's perfect for what I want to do; show the secret face we all have behind our public one, or the hidden scene behind the one everybody sees..." He talked on, easily, as Laura asked questions, and they leaned toward each other on the couch, absorbed in each other.

"And Los Angeles?" she asked. "Do you like it?"

"I don't know. I feel the way you do about New York: I haven't taken the time to make sense of it. It's beautiful and ugly and everything in between. It's fascinating and deserves exploring, but I haven't done it because I've been too busy and Emily isn't interested. I've thought a lot about the way you and I used to explore the Cape; I'd like to do that in Los Angeles."

There was a pause the length of a heartbeat as Laura saw the surprise in his dark eyes; he hadn't meant to say that. But he had, and she drew back. "That's hardly fair, is it? Or is it all right to fool around with a thief and a fortune hunter now that you're safely married?"

"God damn it—!" he exclaimed. "I told you when we sat down—I said I was sorry—"

"You didn't say you'd been wrong."

"I don't know if I was wrong. You told me—"

"Then what were you apologizing for? Damn it, if you and your whole family can't admit you were wrong—"

"You told me Felix was right! Or don't you remember that? I asked you if he was telling the truth, and you said yes. I've never forgotten that; it's very convenient if you have—"

"I haven't forgotten." Her voice was like ice. "But you didn't wait to find out what that meant. Just now you told me you want to find the secret face behind the public one, and the hidden scene... Doesn't that mean the hidden story, too? Or isn't that important with people you know? You couldn't have thought it was very important with me; you took Felix's story at face value and helped your family force me out. Force me away from my home."

Silenced, Paul gazed across the ghostly expanse of the ballroom. "You're right, I didn't try." He gave a bitter laugh. "My ego was hurt. I thought I'd been loved for my fortune instead of myself."

"You couldn't have believed that. Not after what we had."

"I didn't want to believe it. You didn't give me any reason to believe anything else."

"Why wasn't it enough that I'd loved you, and been yours, for two years? How many times did I have to prove that?"

"Only once," he said coldly. "But you were too arrogant. You'd come there to rob us and God knows what else, but we were supposed to say that wasn't important, nothing was important but Laura Fairchild's saying she loved us. Does it occur to you that you might have told us your story instead of waiting for us to beg you to tell it? We'd made you one of us for a long time; my family had loved you and sheltered you, given you an education, a home, friendship... and I'd given you my love. But you didn't trust me—"

"And I was right! I couldn't trust any of you!"

"You didn't know that. You walked out; you couldn't be bothered to try to straighten things out, help us when we were confused and feeling betrayed."

"I was the one who was accused," Laura said angrily. "You can't make your family sound like victims!"

"In a way we were, as much as you. You were accused of something;

so what? A lot of people are accused of one thing or another, and most of them fight back, but not Laura Fairchild! What was it? You were too good for that? We were supposed to take you at your word, and never doubt you, because you were you? No other reason? I loved you! Didn't I deserve some explanation?"

"You mean that was your right?"

"All of us, including you, had the right to understand what was happening to us."

"And that was more important than trust? If you couldn't trust me, what good would an explanation have been? You still don't trust me; you still don't believe your family was wrong and unfair—"

"They're my family, Laura; I can't call them liars—"

"I was going to be your wife, and you called me one."

He paused. "I would have believed you if you'd told me I was wrong."

"Trust," Laura said furiously. "Trust. Remember? I didn't expect my future husband to—" She stopped abruptly. "It doesn't matter. It was so long ago; what difference does it make? We've each found our own lives; why can't we let the past go?" She stood. "I'm going downstairs—"

"No, wait a minute. Laura, I'm sorry; I didn't mean any of that. We should have trusted each other, you as much as I. Maybe we were too young—God knows we were young, both of us—but it shouldn't matter now, it shouldn't prevent us talking, and knowing how we feel about each other—"

"I don't want to know! What good would it do? We'll never be free of the past, and, anyway, you have a wife, and I'm very busy—I've made my own life—I have friends, I have a brother, and a man who wants to marry me: I have a family, too!"

She bit her lip. She was shaking and her voice was unsteady. Paul had stood, too, and was facing her, and she could feel herself swaying toward him, wanting him, feeling his arms around her, his lips on hers, remembering that dark look in his eyes that embraced her and made her feel safe forever. False! Foolish! She was never safe with one person, only with her own achievements. Her feelings weren't important; she could learn to master them. She was ashamed of her weakness with Paul; she should be in complete control of herself and her life; that was the only way to get rid of the past. She'd made such a good start; it would just take a little longer than she'd thought.

She put out her hand. "Good-bye," she said, and heard only the smallest waver in her voice. "Good luck with the film on Britt and . . . everything else you do."

Paul took her hand and held it. He wasn't sure he wanted to be free of the past. It was as if someone had played a huge joke on him: the past stood between them, yet that was their time together and he didn't want to forget it. "My dear..." he began, and then stopped. He wanted to say they owed it to each other to find out what they still had together, but the words did not come. He did not understand her, neither the girl she had been nor the woman she was now, and he saw no way back to her. He would not ask her, while he was married to Emily, to have a trial friendship to discover if they could trust each other; he was sure she wouldn't do it even if he had the bad taste to ask her. And whatever he felt for Laura, he could not walk away from Emily. He'd married her, he'd taken her into his life, and he wouldn't drop her because he thought he might be in love with someone from his past—or just caught up in memories and guilt and a longing for a simpler, more youthful time.

Laura was watching him with a small, wistful smile. "Nothing is as simple as we thought it was."

For a moment Paul let himself enjoy the harmony of their thoughts, remembering the joy it had always given him. His smile met hers. "It might be, if we knew what we wanted, and then stuck with it."

"It doesn't matter anymore," she said softly. "It's too late." Impulsively, before she could stop herself, she moved closer to him, and without thinking he enfolded her in his arms, knowing at least that he wanted her. But Laura kept a space between them. She lay her hand along his face, aching inside with all the tears she could not shed, and the emptiness of knowing they had lost each other all over again. She felt the familiar lines of his face, the prominent cheekbones, the texture of his skin, its warmth warming her fingers, and his thick hair with touches of gray she had not noticed before. She memorized it all once again—*my love, my love*—as if she could make him a part of her, held within her wherever she was, like a secret self. For a long moment they stood together at the side of the empty dance floor, like a couple about to begin a waltz. And then they separated. "Good-bye, Paul," she said. "I won't see you downstairs; I'm going home. I don't want to see you again."

He felt the pull of his body to go to her, to kiss her and hold her close and tell her nothing else mattered: they were together. The sadness in her eyes filled his vision; he wanted to bring lightness to them, and laughter, but too much stood in the way. He forced himself to keep his hands at his side. "I'm sorry," he said, then gestured with helplessness. "Such a dull word, for all the things I'd like to say. I wish I had a better one. But there seems to be more to apologize for than to celebrate. Good luck with your hotels."

"Thank you. I'll watch for the film on Britt."

As she turned away, Paul said simply, "You know, I love you very much. I've never stopped. That doesn't seem to have anything to do with all the other things that stand between us."

Laura stood still for a long moment, then shook her head, as if shaking it free of his words. "Good-bye," she said, her back to him, and walked to the door.

"I would like to know if you still feel the same," he said. "I have no right to ask, but I'd like to hear you say you don't. Or you do."

Slowly, she turned and looked at him across the empty room that echoed with voices and laughter long since gone. Her hand made a small movement toward him. "I love you with all my heart," she said, and then, swiftly, she went through the door, and was gone.

CHAPTER 24

INVITATIONS arrived in each day's mail. Ever since she had moved to New York, Laura had been included in dinners and benefit parties, but with Farley's party and the fall season, she suddenly became a catch. Manhattan society is constantly on the lookout for fresh faces attached to people who are making their mark, whether legally or illegally; it makes no real difference as long as they are getting media attention. And since stories on Laura and her hotels had appeared in *The Wall Street Journal*, *The New York Times*, *Newsweek*, and *Vogue*, and several television talk shows had invited her to appear, doors all over the city were opened to her. It was a definite plus that she was young and beautiful and unattached, even better that she had connections to Wes Currier and Ginny Starrett, and best of all that she had an air of mystery and refused to discuss her past. So the invitations poured in.

Laura accepted as many as she could squeeze into her evenings. She worked in her office from seven in the morning until seven at night, went to Grove Court to bathe and change, and then left for a dinner party or benefit ball or two or three parties in one night. By the time she returned home, she had barely enough energy to strip off her clothes and slide into bed, to awaken five hours later and begin another day.

"You don't have any time to think," said Ginny as they sat in Laura's roof garden on a Saturday afternoon halfway through October, watching gardeners plant trees. "I thought I had a crazy social life, but yours is crazier."

"I think at work," Laura said.

"But that's thinking about work."

"That's all I want to think about."

"Well, everybody goes through that," Ginny said ruminatively. "I did every time Wylie let slip accidentally on purpose that he was sleeping with somebody new. But then one day, for some reason, probably because women are like rubber and keep bouncing back, you start to feel better, and you can think about anything you want, because it doesn't hurt anymore. And when that happens, you are going to be one worn-out lady in need of a vacation."

Laura smiled. "When that happens, I'll take one."

"How about next March?" Ginny asked promptly. "I'm going to Paris for a couple of weeks, and I want you to come along. The way you're painting the town these days, and working too hard to shop, by March you'll be in tatters and in need of a whole new wardrobe, not to mention some fun."

"Thank you, Ginny. I'll think about it."

"No, you won't. You'll forget about it because you're so all-fired wound up in those hotels you can't even seriously imagine what Paris might be like. Chilly in March, sometimes downright cold and rainy, but also quiet. No tourists, the stores are full, the museums are empty, and you're treated almost like a native. The perfect place to unwind. I would love an answer now. Like yes."

"Yes," said Laura unexpectedly. "It sounds wonderful."

Taken aback, Ginny said, "Well. By golly. Can I have it in writing?"

Laura laughed and reached for a pad of paper. She scribbled a note and handed it to Ginny.

Ginny skimmed it. "Why does it say 'no more than two weeks'?"

"Because that's all I can manage. The Philadelphia hotel opens in May, and once I've got it running smoothly I want to start thinking about ways to get some of the Salinger stock."

"You haven't forgotten that."

"I don't forget much about the Salingers," Laura said lightly, but Ginny knew how much she meant it. "Anyway, there's so much going on now I shouldn't go away at all, but—"

"But I'm so persuasive, and you don't like to have spare time to think. Of course, by then you'll be over this blip in your life and raring to—" She saw Laura's face tighten. "Shoot, I'm sorry, honey, that was crude. I know you're having a hard time; I don't mean to make light of it. What kind of tree is that, the one he's just planting?"

"Flowering plum. And the others are flowering crab and cherry and mock orange. I love them: next April every branch and twig will be covered with pink and purple and white flowers. Everything spring ought to be."

"Pity they won't be flowering for your housewarming party."

"Maybe we should cancel it then."

Ginny grinned. "You can't get out of it that easily. I know you don't want to give a party; I even understand it; but you have to believe me: it's a good idea to have one. A new house isn't really yours until you greet people at your door and feed them and make them welcome to set their backsides down on your furniture. Anyway, we've got it all planned, so we have to have it. And your house is ready."

"And beautiful. The most beautiful house in New York. Thanks to you."

"You chose everything; I just got good prices. Good teamwork, I'd say."

Laura put her hand on Ginny's and they sat quietly, watching one gardener hold the tree while the other heaped fresh dark soil around it. The rooftop had been transformed from the bare dusty space Laura had first seen to a cedar deck with white wrought-iron chairs as lacy as a New Orleans balcony, a matching round table with an umbrella, an old fashioned wooden swing. Against the brick wall were green- and purple-leaved trees and stepped planters luxuriant with chrysanthemums, asters, and dahlias, with space left for rose bushes and annuals in the spring.

It was a tiny oasis, green and fragrant, and in creating it Laura had put herself in the company of the few thousand New Yorkers lucky enough to have the space and money to claim a little nature for themselves. In a concrete city of shadowed canyons, hurtling traffic, the rattle of jack-hammers, and graffiti and mountains of bagged garbage alongside elegant buildings, the terraces and flat roofs of apartment buildings sprouted trees and bloomed with flowers, each jewel-like garden a haven floating above the everyday world.

Or it will be a haven, Laura thought, when I spend more than an hour a week here.

The entire house was a haven, even now, when she used it mostly as a bedroom and a dressing room. Someday, she thought, when I can face quiet hours again, I'll use it the way it's meant to be used. The rooms were sparely furnished, but with such glowing colors, warm with the patina of age, that they were like an embrace. Nothing was sleekly new; everything was as mellow as if it had been there for years, putting families at their ease. The furniture was country French, in hand-rubbed golden fruitwood, the windows were hung with pale muslin, the chairs and loveseats were upholstered in small flowered prints. Scattered on the pine plank floors were rugs in rich wines and blues, and brass fire tools stood beside the fireplaces in the living room, library, dining room, and bedroom. There was also the newly decorated kitchen, but Laura rarely went in it. She ate out, even when she and Clay had their weekly dinners; she was too busy to be domestic, and not much interested in it anyway.

But the kitchen was crowded on a Saturday night at the end of October when it was taken over by the caterer and his staff for Laura's housewarming party. They had arrived while she was still at work and had immediately made the house their own, setting up a bar in the living room and another in the roof garden, and dinner tables for four or six throughout the house; finding Laura's trays in the pantry and arranging hors d'oeuvres on them; and building fires in the fireplaces, even though the night was warm, with an autumn haze that made the full moon seem faintly blurred as it shone on the arriving guests.

"You look gorgeous," Flavia Guarneri said to Laura, sweeping her with a critical eye as she stood in the small foyer. "You, too, Wes," she added briefly to Currier, who stood at Laura's side, then turned again to Laura. "Every time I see you you're better dressed; either you're learning fast or the hotels are very successful."

"Both," Laura said easily, smiling at Flavia's lack of subtlety. She was wearing blue silk, the same color as her eyes, strapless, with a filmy stole of the same blue. The dress outlined her slender curves and made more vivid her white skin and chestnut curls. She stood straight, her head high and proud, and whatever she felt was masked by her quiet face and cool smile; no one knew what she was thinking.

Currier stopped to talk to someone as she went upstairs to the living room to talk to her guests. She was relieved to have him no longer at her side. Ginny had been right: having a party made the house truly hers, and it bothered her that Currier had assumed the role of host the minute he walked in, even though they hadn't seen each other for a month. He keeps changing the definition of friendship, she thought, marveling again at his tenacity. I'll have to talk to him about it. "Can I get you anything, Rosa?" she asked, bending over the armchair where Rosa sat. "Something to eat or drink? Someone to talk to?"

"I'm very happy," Rosa said, patting Laura's cheek. "I'm glad to be here. It always makes me feel good when I know people I care about haven't forgotten me even though I'm too old and feeble to be much use." Laura was laughing at her and she smiled widely. "Well, it's true I don't feel all that old, but these days I'm spending more time thinking about the past than the future, and that's a sign of advanced age if there ever was one. Just now I was thinking back to your other house-warming, in Mr. Owen's house, the one you gave when Allison was engaged to that Thad person. Of course I was mostly in the kitchen, but even so I remember what a strange crowd you put together that night: Allison's friends from college, and those workmen—carpenters and such—and of course Mr. Owen stopped by, didn't he? And so did Leni. And Paul."

Laura nodded.

"It's another strange crowd tonight, isn't it?" Rosa asked shrewdly. "There's that young couple who own a restaurant down the street, and the landscaper who did your roof garden, and a countess, and Flavia Guarneri, who has half the world's jewels around her neck, and that handsome Carlos Something who looks like he's imagining gyrations in bed with every woman he talks to—"

"Rosa!"

"I know, I know, I'm not normally into talking that way, but that's another sign of age: the older I get, the more I say why not. I talked to your friend Ginny; she was kind enough to remember that dinner Kelly and I made in your hotel in Chicago. Have you talked to Kelly lately?"

"No, I've been so busy, and she hasn't called in a couple of months. I invited her tonight; she should be here."

"Over there," Rosa said, gesturing. "Behind the crowd coming upstairs."

Kelly was moving toward them, and in a minute she and Laura hugged each other. "Fabulous house; not like I ever thought a New York house would be."

"Where's John?" Laura asked, looking around.

"Not here. I'll tell you about it sometime when you're not busy being a hostess."

Laura heard the different note in her voice. She lifted Kelly's left hand and looked at the ringless fingers. "When did that happen?"

"One month ago today. I'll tell you all about it; maybe tomorrow we'll have lunch or something?"

"Of course. Who's running Darnton's?"

"We sold it. You really want to hear this?"

"Of course I do."

"Well, in a nutshell, somebody made an offer we couldn't refuse—you know how long John's been wanting to sell—so we got a heap of money and traveled around the world and then split. It just didn't work.

John wants to play for the rest of his life; I need to do something. I thought I'd come to your office on Monday and ask if you happened to have a job for me."

They exchanged a look, remembering the day, six years earlier, when Laura had arrived at Darnton's needing a job. "Of course I do. I'm not sure what, but we'll find something that's perfect for you." She turned as she felt a hand on her arm, and met Carlos Serrano's carelessly seductive black eyes.

"Beautiful one, you will have dinner with me while I am in the city? I will call to arrange it; I have only two weeks. And I must tell you I came this morning from your hotel in Chicago, and it was perfection; I salute you."

Laura smiled. It was impossible to resist Carlos's charm, though almost everyone knew it was as automatic with him as breathing. "I'm glad you were comfortable; we were lucky to find a wonderful manager—" She stopped, her head tilted as if listening to her own words. "Please excuse me . . ." She turned back to find Kelly, who was talking to Rosa. "How would you like to live in Washington?" she asked Kelly.

"I have no idea. Why?"

"I own a hotel there, and it needs everything: manager, assistant manager, even a chef for the dining room."

"A manager and a chef," Kelly repeated. Her face had brightened. "I have a chef. Or I will have. The one we had at Darnton's doesn't like the new owners, and he told me if I ever went back to a hotel he'd love to work with me. And Washington sounds interesting."

They smiled at each other with the excitement of new beginnings and everything falling into place. "Lunch tomorrow," Laura said. "We'll talk about it. I'd need you right away."

"I'm ready right away."

Laura kissed her cheek. "We'll see each other more often. We'll almost be neighbors."

"And working together again. I like that."

Clay came up and gave Kelly a hug. "Great to see you. Where's John?"

"He couldn't make it. You look very successful: tall, blond, and handsome; pretty girl clinging to your arm; distinguished mustache; classy suit. Is this the wide-eyed boy who wanted to spend his days driving vintage cars around our island?"

Clay winked. "Same kid; he just grew up and learned to use his own motor instead of somebody else's. Kelly, would you mind if I took Laura away for a minute?"

"Be my guest. But you wouldn't be talking business at a party, would you?"

"Never." He gave her a kiss and then took Laura's arm. "I'm sorry; I just thought I'd tell you . . ." They took a few steps, finding a clear spot in a corner. "I found out this afternoon that the security guy I fired a couple of months ago is working for the Salingers."

"Well?"

"Well, it doesn't sound good, does it? I mean, he knows all about the kind of card locks we use on our doors, the television monitors in the corridors, the safes in the rooms—"

"I don't understand. You think he'll break into our hotels?"

"Who knows? He knows an awful lot about us."

"Clay, this isn't a war. We don't have armies and spies; we're not out to destroy each other."

"Felix might be. Or Ben. What about Ben?"

"*Ben?* He's got his own family and his own life. I'm sure he's very happy, and I don't believe he'd do anything to hurt us. Anyway, I'm sure he's not doing robberies anymore; he's part of a wealthy family; why would he risk it?"

"Maybe he needs money."

"I'm sure he has all the money he needs. Anyway, even if he was still stealing, he wouldn't choose us out of the whole world—"

"He would if he had information that made it easier."

"That's enough! I don't want to talk about it! Ben isn't stealing, I just know he's not, and we haven't had a single reported theft, and that's all! What a crazy thing for you to worry about. Who's the girl you brought tonight?"

"Rosemary. She thinks I need taking care of."

"Well, maybe you do."

"That's what Myrna always said. I liked it for a while but then it was sort of smothering, like a prison. No freedom, no risks, no excitement—"

"Just love and belonging and somebody to care what the hell happens to you. Awful."

He gave her a sharp look. "How come you don't marry Wes, if you think it's such a good deal?"

"Because I don't love Wes. If I did, I would. I do think marriage is a good deal. It might help you—" She stopped.

"Grow up. Right? You think I need to grow up."

"Sometimes."

Currier was beside her, his hand on her arm. "You're ignoring your guests."

She felt a moment of resentment, then squelched it. "You're right. I'll see you later, Clay; have a good time."

"I will." He gave her a wide smile. "You give a hell of a party and I love you, and if you think I should call Myrna, I will."

Laura kissed his cheek. "I love you, too, and I think you should do what makes you happy."

On the stairway to the roof garden, Currier said, "You spoil him."

She frowned. "How?"

"You don't tell him what to do. You could make him toe the line, work harder, settle down."

"You mean treat him even more like a child?" They stood at the top of the stairs. "You don't understand Clay, Wes. He's been looking for someone to take care of him ever since our parents died. He turned to Ben and Ben let him down, so he turned to me. Of course I could tell him what to do. He might do it. But that wouldn't help him grow up and take responsibility for his own life. Anyway, I don't want to run his life. I have my hands full with my own."

"I've offered to help you with that."

Without replying, she pushed open the door to the roof garden and immediately was surrounded by her guests, and it was five hours before the last guest had gone and they were alone again. The caterer and his staff were still in the kitchen, washing the liqueur glasses and dessert plates they had retrieved from unlikely corners throughout the house, but Laura and Currier were alone, sitting in the two armchairs in the bay window of her living room. All the lamps had been turned off but one. "Wonderful party," he said. "You have a way of making everyone feel special."

"Thank you." Her voice was almost inaudible.

After a moment, he said, "Something's been bothering you ever since I got back this afternoon. Are you going to tell me what it is?"

She sat back, her face in the shadows. "I don't want us to be together anymore, Wes."

He watched her steadily, his body controlled and very still. "I thought we agreed to be friends as long as we lived apart."

Laura made a gesture of frustration. "Friends. That's a code word. It means we go out together and sometimes we sleep together, and now all of a sudden it means you act the host at my parties. It means you don't expect to marry me, but in every other way you'd still be my husband. We'd share everything except an address." She gave a small laugh. "I can understand why you're so successful in business, Wes. You don't give up; you keep the pressure on until others bend just enough to fit most of what you originally wanted."

He smiled. "But you've known that for a long time, and all that time you've enjoyed sharing your life with me. If you've met someone else, I can understand that, but it doesn't mean everything has to be broken off completely."

"I haven't met anyone. Not anyone new." She hesitated. "I saw Paul a few weeks ago, while you were gone."

At that, Currier's face underwent a subtle change. He was supremely confident of his ability to contend with opponents he could see and evaluate, but his skills were weak, and perhaps useless, with a shadowy figure from Laura's past whom he had never met. "You're going back to him?"

"No. Of course not. For one thing, he's married—"

"Married? You never told me that."

She smiled faintly. "There are probably thousands of things I've never told you, Wes." They were silent; the only sounds were the rattling of dishes and muffled conversation from the kitchen. "All that matters is that I'm in love with him, and it isn't fair to you, it's not honest, for me to live as if someday I might love you. Because I won't, Wes. If I haven't by now, I'm not going to. I can't believe you haven't accepted that for a long time; it's just that you've been comfortable with me, so you ignored what you knew. I like you, I like being with you and working with you, but that's all. And you shouldn't be spending your time with me when you could be finding someone else who will give you what you want."

"It's more than being comfortable," he said, his voice rough. "Damn it, I've never stopped wanting you. I do a lot of running around in my life, and I like stability and affection at home, and you give me that, even if you don't love me. Is that irrational? Then I'm irrational. And now that you have your own home—"

"Are you paying part of the rent on this place?" she asked abruptly.

"No." One of Wes Currier's greatest skills was the ability to move from one thought to another without effort. "Of course not. I would have asked you first."

Laura bowed her head slightly. "Thank you. Then what part *did* you play in setting my rent?"

He gave a short laugh. "I hoped you'd just chalk it up to good fortune. I convinced the owner to reduce it. It was a very small favor. But that's all I did; I made no promises on your behalf. Yes, I did; I made one. I promised him you wouldn't get emotional and wreck the place the night you chose to break off with your lover."

She heard the pain in his voice. "It was more than a small favor, Wes, and I thank you. Isn't it amazing that I'm still thanking you after all these years? You'd think I would have learned to stand on my own feet by now."

"You're running a corporation that owns four hotels; you're standing very tall, my dear."

Laura winced, wishing she could love him; it would have made everything so much simpler. "I wouldn't be here if it weren't for you. And you're still propping me up. That can't go on forever."

"Why not?" He leaned forward. "Laura, I love you. I've loved you for so many years I've come to count on it." He stopped for a moment, and Laura knew it was difficult for him to admit that. "When I come back from a trip I want to know I'll be coming back to you. I've counted on having you there, waiting for me, for so long that . . . damn it, I'm afraid to lose you! Can't you understand that?"

"Wes, don't, please don't. You don't mean that—"

"Goddam it, of course I mean it. How many people do you think have ever heard me say that? You've got to understand this: I've come to rely on you."

"No," Laura said quietly. "You've come to rely on having me."

"It's the same thing. Don't shake your head; I'm telling you it's the same thing: I've had you for five years. You've been there when I wanted you, you've given me what I needed, you've taken from me when I wanted to give to you. I counted on that, and you could count on me. You still can." He leaned forward and took her hand and held it, though it was unresponsive. "Listen to me. What you feel for me is love of a kind; you couldn't have been to me what you have been if you didn't feel something very real. You know it; you can't deny it." There was a silence. "Can you? You've felt something!"

"Of course," she said quietly. "But it's not what you or I would call—"

"Don't tell me what I'd call it! If I want to call it love, that's what I'll call it! But whatever it is, you still feel it; those things don't die so quickly." He saw her face change. "As you well know. And if you feel it and I still want to take care of you, we could go on together just as we have. We could—"

"Don't say that!" She pulled her hand away, her eyes blazing. "You demean yourself. Why would you settle for that? You deserve better than me; you deserve a woman who'll love you and appreciate your taking care of her, even if that means making decisions for her . . . someone who'll give you her attention when you want it. Why do you stay with me? Because I'm an unfinished story? The woman who didn't bend to fit your scenario?"

"Because I love you," he said harshly. "And because even if you didn't love me and didn't always fit my scenario, as you call it, you gave me more than any woman I've loved."

"What did I give you, Wes? What was so special—?"

"My God, you don't know, even now. You gave me the companionship of an independent woman who has her own goals and thinks for herself but still allows a man to help her. You even asked for my help; you weren't too arrogant to admit you could use it. And you acted lovingly, whatever you thought you felt. We were partners in every sense of the word. I still want that, and I think you do, too. I know you do; you don't want to make every major decision alone—"

"Why should I? I have a partner."

Caught short, he laughed reluctantly. "I deserved that. Of course we're still partners."

"I hope we always will be," she said. "But for the rest—I meant what I said. All of it. This is the only way I can be honest." She stood and walked to the door. "I want you to leave, Wes. Please."

He stayed where he was. "You'll live with memories. With a ghost. You call that honest?"

"I'll live with myself, and I won't be pretending. That's honest enough for me. And when I see you at the office and we work together and like each other and respect each other, that will be honest, too. I'm offering you a loving friendship. I wish you could be satisfied with that, Wes; it's more than a lot of people have."

For a moment he felt ashamed. He had thought of himself as wiser and more persistent than Laura for so long that it embarrassed him to think that, somewhere along the way, she had overtaken and passed him. He stood and went to her. "I'll call you in a few days; we haven't gone over the quarterly statements yet."

"Oh." She was taken aback by his abrupt acceptance. Maybe I wanted him to try a little harder, she thought wryly. But she knew she didn't. She was satisfied—at least for tonight. In a week, two weeks, two months, in an empty bed or sitting alone in a restaurant, she might long for him. But she'd face that when the time came. For now, she was relieved. "Good night, dear Wes. And thank you for . . . so much. For everything."

He kissed her lightly on the lips. "I'll talk to you soon." And he went down the stairs to the front door and into the courtyard, then disappeared through the passageway into the street.

Laura listened to his receding footsteps. Then she turned: the caterer's staff was loading the last of the dishes and extra chairs onto a trolley, to roll it down the same passageway through which Currier had gone. She said goodnight to them, spoke briefly to the caterer, and then closed and locked the door behind them.

Her house was clean. And silent. Not a sound came from the great city beyond the court. She walked through her neat, shadowy rooms; she stood in the roof garden where the sounds of traffic reached her and reminded her she was in New York, with work to do and her own empire to build. Then she went downstairs again and into her bedroom. The last flames were lazily dancing in the fireplace, and she sat on the crewel-worked chaise, watching them.

Starting again; alone and beginning a new time in my life. Isn't it amazing, she mused, though no one was there to answer, how many times in a lifetime a person starts again?

Part V

CHAPTER 25

T HE fourth theft was in Carlos Serrano's apartment high above the pounding surf of Acapulco's beach. It was widely known that he had amassed one of the world's great collections of Mexican impressionists, and six of those paintings, neatly cut from their frames, were gone when he returned in November from visiting friends in New York, Miami, and Palm Beach. The police found no sign of forced entry, nor were there any clues. They interviewed Carlos Serrano's personal staff, everyone who worked in the building, and vendors who delivered goods to its wealthy residents, and got nowhere. But by then they were not alone in the investigation: a special insurance investigator had been brought in months earlier, after the robbery of Britt Farley's apartment.

Sam Colby had retired four years earlier, at sixty-five. Long-since divorced, his children grown, he had moved to a retirement community in Phoenix, looking for sunshine and companionship. But he was bored and with every month that passed he felt a year older; he'd even begun talking to himself. He was tired of seeing nobody but his own generation, and he boiled with pent-up energy, envying everyone who was still running around the world doing things. And since the insurance business still talked about his legendary career in tracking down stolen art, saving companies from paying millions of dollars in claims, he called a former assistant of his, now an executive, and said he'd like an assignment now and then, to keep from shriveling up and blowing away like a dried mushroom. It wasn't long before he got a telephone call from the director of a consortium of insurance companies, asking him to come to New York.

Once there, he was given two files: one on the theft of three Toulouse-Lautrec paintings from Flavia Guarneri's New York apartment and the other on the theft, more than a year later, of Remington sculptures from Britt Farley's apartment in Paris. "You gotta be kidding," Colby said, thumbing through them. "A year and then some apart, an ocean apart, paintings in one, sculptures in the other—what the hell have I got to go on?"

"Nothing but the method," the director said.

"Method? You mean no clues? That's a method? That's a couple smart cookies who know their business."

"Could be. But if we're dumb enough to pay you to look into it, are you going to thumb your nose at us?"

Colby grinned and gave a small salute. "You'll be hearing from me."

He was small and hunched, his fingers gnarled from arthritis, his face a map of fine lines from which his sharp black eyes looked out at a world he was sure was filled with potential lawbreakers kept honest only through fear of people like him. Each night he prayed that this case wouldn't fade away to nothing, that it would be big enough to keep him busy, and that he would solve it with the brilliance of his most glorious years and thus get more cases, and be busy until the day he died.

He interviewed Flavia Guarneri, and the maid and butler she had fired, and then he tried to interview Britt Farley. But Farley was distracted by a concert tour he was giving and a film being made about him, so Colby waited until both were finished. While he was waiting, he received another call from New York. A major theft of early twentieth-century paintings had occurred in the Palm Springs home of Sid and Amelia Laughton. And the method was the same.

For the first time, Sam Colby felt the familiar thrill of the hunt. There might be something here after all. Paris, New York, Palm Springs: that wouldn't be a problem for real professionals. What was even more interesting were the dates: the Farley theft had been in June, and the Laughton theft in September. Four months' elapsed time instead of a year and a half. Whoever it was—a ring or a couple of guys or even a solo—either they were getting cocky or desperate for money. And for an investigator, that was a major break.

Two months later, in November, Carlos Serrano's Acapulco apartment was robbed. Then Sam Colby knew for sure that he was blessed in the eyes of the Lord. He'd thought he was going to waste away in that damned desert, and instead he'd been given what could be one of the major stories of the art world, and one of the biggest jobs of his life.

* * *

It was supposed to be a holiday for just the two of them, but at the last minute Judd caught a cold and Allison wanted to stay with him, so Ben went to New York alone. He traveled so much for Salinger Hotels that it wasn't a novelty, but this time he was almost glad to be alone: he could shop at leisure for Allison's Christmas present, and he wanted to visit the studios of some young artists he'd been hearing about.

Art had become a passion with Ben. He had begun buying paintings soon after he and Allison were married, when he watched her buy for pleasure and as an investment. When she decided to open an art gallery in Boston, his buying speeded up, partly so he could share her interests but also because he wanted possessions that he bought simply because they pleased him. All his life Ben had taken care of his needs, but he had never bought something just because it gave him a good feeling to look at it.

And he was a good buyer. He found that he had an instinct about which artists would last; he bought carefully and unemotionally; and already some of the painters whose works he had bought only a year or two earlier for modest sums were being "discovered" by gallery owners and art critics. Already Ben was worth considerably more than when he'd started collecting—which was what had to happen if he ever hoped to pull his own weight in his wife's family.

Shopping for Christmas presents on his trip to New York, he went to Fortunoff and bought a slender diamond necklace for Allison, with a sapphire heart suspended from it. Then, at Ruth Blumka's, he found a rock crystal teapot for Leni. As he filled out the mailing form for it to be shipped to his house on Beacon Hill, he felt a strange melancholy. He wanted Leni's love, or at least her approval, and as far as he could tell he'd never gotten either one. In all the time he had been part of that family, Leni had been friendly, carefully proper in remembering Christmas and his birthday, interested in his work and his opinions when the family was at dinner... but Ben never stopped feeling that she was wary of him. He told himself it was ridiculous, but still it seemed to him she was watching for him to say something or do something, as if she were waiting to find out why he was there. He didn't worry about it as much as he had the first year, when he kept expecting some kind of bombshell, but it still bothered him.

His work and his shopping done for the day, he strolled through the city. It was mild for December, and the sun was shining, and with a wry pleasure he walked the streets he had once scouted for burglaries or places to hide from possible pursuit. He walked them now with an easy stride. He knew what he was doing, he had most of what he wanted, and New York held no threats for him. It was still his favorite city, and he felt at home there.

It was almost five when he turned down Fifty-eighth Street and saw a white canopy he didn't remember seeing before. Then he saw the brass plate beside the entrance that said 'Beacon Hill'. The New York Beacon Hill, he thought. He remembered it, when it was the New York Salinger, as a sooty, narrow building indistinguishable from thousands of others in the city. Now the brick exterior glowed a soft red, the street level was faced with glass and white marble polished to a satin finish, and the white canopy stretched to the curb from a lofty entrance bordered in brass.

On impulse, Ben walked into the small lobby and stood in the center of it, beneath a crystal chandelier, amid groups of people returning from shopping and sightseeing, stopping at the concierge's antique desk for their messages or to pick up theater and concert tickets. The lobby was hushed and serene in pale gray, violet, and green, with a fleur-de-lis pattern in the carpet and an iris print in the draperies; the few pieces of furniture were baroque and heavily carved. To the side was the lounge, its tables all filled, with a small string orchestra in a far corner, playing Viennese waltzes. Just outside the door to the lounge a young woman stood behind a long table, wrapping Christmas presents for the guests.

I'd like to stay here, Ben thought. And he knew, as the words came to him, that he had paid Laura the highest compliment of all.

He wondered if she was there. It would be easy for him to find out, even to see her. But he couldn't do it. He wasn't ready to tell the Salingers about the two of them, and if Laura didn't already despise him, she certainly would when he told her he couldn't bring her into his family, at least not yet. I just can't take the chance of upsetting everything, he thought; maybe of losing everything. I don't feel secure enough to unload all my secrets, especially Laura. I trust Allison, but . . .

But he didn't know how much he could trust her. Or whether she trusted him enough to have it withstand a barrage of secrets.

I'll think about it, he said to himself; I'll figure it out. There had to be a way to bridge the gap of years of silence. Was it ever too late to patch a family together again? He didn't know. He didn't even know if Laura wanted it.

He turned to leave the lobby, pausing to take a last look into the lounge. He recognized a number of the guests: a senator who frequently stayed at the Boston Salinger, the owner of a famous ski resort, and the wealthiest developer in Hawaii, Albert Inouti, whom Ben had talked to about building a Salinger hotel on Honolulu. Inouti always stayed at the Carlyle; if he had changed hotels, it was a major coup for Laura.

Inouti saw him and waved, and Ben returned the greeting, but he did not want to talk to any of them, and so he went on. Outside, the street seemed even noisier and more frenetic after the serenity of the Beacon Hill. *Beacon Hill.* For the first time he understood the name. A great hotel becomes a home to the person who creates it, and Laura had named her hotels after the home she most loved and probably still thought of as hers. If that was true, he had taken her home away. And that would make it harder than ever, or impossible, for them to patch up anything.

He strode away, putting distance between himself and that lovely hotel. At the Plaza, a block from the Beacon Hill, he turned to go inside. He had two hours before his dinner with the architect on the new Salinger hotel; time for a leisurely drink and then a walk back to Leni's and Felix's townhouse, where he was staying, to shower and change. But as he crossed the lobby, he came to an abrupt halt. Leni Salinger was standing at the bank of elevators, waiting to go upstairs.

What the hell, Ben thought. Felix said she was visiting friends in Virginia. And what's she doing in the Plaza Hotel when she has her own house on Fifty-first Street? He started toward her and then stopped again. She was not alone.

It might not have been clear to everyone, but it was obvious to Ben that the tall young man standing slightly behind her was in fact with her. He never took his eyes off her, his hand hovered near her elbow, he stayed close to her as someone jostled him. Leni looked straight ahead, but something in her stance suggested a slight leaning back. She wore a dark dress with a mink coat over her shoulders, and she carried a Coach Musette bag: a purse large enough to double as an overnight bag.

The elevator doors opened, and Leni and the young man stepped aside, waiting for it to empty. Without thinking, Ben strode forward and put his hand on her arm.

She spun around, ready to cut down this stranger who dared touch her, and then saw who it was. Her eyes closed for a brief, agonizing second. "Ben," she said without inflection. "I didn't know you were in town."

"Felix said I could use your house; he said you were in Virginia."

She nodded. "I changed my plans."

Ben looked pointedly at the young man who was staying at the side while others pushed past to fill the elevator. For a long moment the three of them stood there, until Leni made a gesture of resignation. "Will Baker, Ben Gardner," she said.

Ben did not take the young man's outstretched hand. "If you'll excuse us, I'd like to take my mother-in-law to tea."

"Oh." He tried to decide where to look. "Sure. I, uh, I have an appointment, so . . . sure. Have a nice time." Confused, a little scared, he disappeared into the crowded lobby.

Leni moved her arm from Ben's grasp. "I'd rather have a drink."

"Good. So would I."

They walked without speaking into the Oak Room, and when they were seated in the bar Leni studied the room as if she had never seen it before. Ben admired her sleek, angular elegance, the perfect bow of her silk blouse, the way she contained her emotions—embarrassment or anger? he wondered—the only sign of them the flush across her high, prominent cheekbones. "Vodka and tonic?" he asked.

She smiled faintly at his remembering. "Thank you."

They were silent again until their drinks were before them. "I suppose you think you've done a good deed," Leni said.

"I don't know," he said frankly. "I didn't think about it."

"Then think about it now."

"All right." He contemplated her. "I don't suppose this was a first. You want me to think about it? That won't take long. I think it's a goddam shame that a very classy lady makes her body a playground for—"

Her drink splashed onto the table. "How dare you talk to me like that! Who do you think you are? You don't know anything about—"

"I know you're Allison's mother, she loves you and thinks you're perfect and—"

"Don't. Don't say that. I'm not perfect." She gave him a small smile. "I don't want to be; it would be such a burden."

"Well, you don't have to worry about it," he said coldly. "It's a burden you don't have."

She looked at him wonderingly. He was furious, and in his anger he seemed very young. "There are so many things you don't understand," she said.

"How can I? You don't talk to me; I hardly know you, after all this time. Why the hell are you doing this to yourself? My God, the thought of you . . . how many hotel rooms . . . how many beds . . . how many studs pawing you like a cheap—"

"Stop it!" she exclaimed. "You sound like—" She laughed nervously. "Like a lover."

"How about a son-in-law?" he flung at her. "Or anybody in your family who cares about you. How often do you do it?"

"Whenever I feel like it," she snapped. "Whenever it pleases me."

"Why? Why the hell do you—?"

"I don't know," she said, surprising herself. "But it shouldn't make any difference to you. If I'm satisfied—"

"Are you? Satisfied, happy, proud? Everything wonderful in your life?"

"I told you it's none of your business!"

"The hell it isn't; I care about you, and that's enough to make it my business." He turned sharply as the waiter appeared. "The same for both of us." He gazed at Leni. "Ever since I met you, something about you reminded me of something—I don't even know what—but you're important to me. And you're important to my wife. And if you think I'm going to let you go around like a goddam call girl—"

"Oh, Ben, for heaven's sake, stop it." Leni shook her head. "This is embarrassing, but it's not a Greek tragedy. I'm the same person you've known since you married Allison, and if I've disappointed you I'm sorry, but you'll get over it. We're not a family of saints or gods, you know; don't ask so much of us."

Ben stared into his drink. Once he had hated them all: the name Salinger was enough to set him shaking with fury. Now they were his family, and he wanted them to be everything a family should be. Felix was different; Felix didn't fit; but the rest of them had to be perfect.

"Besides," Leni was saying, "are you so above reproach you can demand perfection of us? Are you always honest? Do you do nothing that can be criticized?"

He looked up and met her eyes, then looked away. "I want you to make me part of your family. But you don't, not really; you watch me as if you think I'm about to attack you or take something from you. Isn't it good enough that I'm in love with Allison? Doesn't that make me good enough to be close to you, too? I want a whole family, not part of one, but you don't like me. I think I understand why Felix doesn't accept me, but why the hell don't you?"

"Why are you here?" Leni asked.

"Here?"

"Married to Allison."

"Because I love her. She's my wife; we have a son. What the hell kind of question is that?"

"Why did you meet Allison?"

Ben's voice grew cautious. "She told you how we met."

"You didn't arrange to meet her?"

"Arrange—? What the hell does that mean? As if I knew who she was? How would I know who she was?" He stopped, hearing himself protest too much. "Did you wonder that with her first husband?"

"No. But it turned out her first husband married her for her money."

"And you think I did."

"I don't know. I don't know what you want from us."

"Love. A family. People I care about who care about me."

"That's all? From the beginning?"

"From the beginning," he said evenly. He didn't care anymore about lying to Leni. He had fallen in love with Allison—he hadn't expected to, but he had—and that was all that was important. He wouldn't lie about his two years with Allison, but he'd lie all he had to about the years before that.

Leni shook her head. "I'm sorry, Ben, but I don't believe it. There was something about you, that first day at the airport. You didn't look as if you were in love with Allison; you were a lot more interested in the rest of us. You looked . . . careful. And cautious. As if you were trying to memorize us and figure out who'd be on your side. As if you were putting on an act."

"That's not true! Oh, what the hell, I don't know what I looked like but I was meeting all of you for the first time and I was nervous— anybody would have been—and anyway, who are you to accuse me of putting on an act when you're the one who's been pretending: the loving wife, the loving mother, the *lady*—dodging in and out of hotel rooms—"

"You're so much like your father," Leni said clearly. "So full of fire."

"*My father?*"

"And you look so much like him. I tried to think you didn't, but of course you do."

"*My father?* What the hell do you know about my father?"

"We were lovers. I was nineteen and he was—"

"What? Wait a minute. You and my father were . . . Is this some crazy kind of joke?"

"I know it sounds like—"

"You knew my father and you were lovers? Bullshit. What about my mother? And me? Where was I?"

"Your mother had left Judd because he was drinking. You were living with her; you were only eight, almost nine. I met Judd and fell in love with him, and we lived together for a year. I loved him"—her voice caught and she stopped and then went on—"more than anyone I've ever known."

Ben could not take it in. "You knew my father? And you never told me?"

"I was waiting. I thought you'd found us because of Judd. I didn't know why, but I couldn't think of any other reason for such an incredible coincidence. And I didn't know how to talk to you about him. I've never talked about him to anyone; I didn't know anyone who might have understood what it was like, being with him and loving him even when so many things were wrong." She looked at Ben. "Your hair grows the way his did, and you have almost the same profile, and that little line between your eyes, and your smile... He was terribly unhappy, but for a while what we had was lovely; for a while we did have love... and hope...."

Ben looked at his hands, remembering his father's haunted eyes the last months of his life. "'However long we were loved,'" he murmured. "'It was not long enough.'"

"What? What did you say?"

"It was a poem my father liked. He said it was about a dream he had once of a girl with soft..." His voice faded away and he stared at Leni with stunned eyes. "With soft hands and a love that wouldn't die. That was you. *That was you.* I can't believe... You were with him, in that hole in the Village, with the broken chairs—"

"And the mattress on the floor." She smiled wistfully. "It was my one attempt at rebellion. Judd said I couldn't keep it up, and he may have been right; I wish I could know for sure whether I was a real rebel or only playing at one. But he sent me away, and I went back to my parents and sleeping in ordinary beds and eating ordinary meals at ordinary times, and then I made a proper marriage. I've never been a very brave person, Ben."

He made a quick gesture with his hand; he would have liked to talk about that, but not now. "What was he like? He didn't talk about himself much, and I've forgotten a lot."

Leni told him everything she knew about Judd. She re-created that small dilapidated apartment, the moments of sweetness that had brightened it, and the unhappy ones that had made it seem darker and more cramped, a prison for Judd, with Leni trying to be the angel who could free him. She made Judd seem as real as if he were sitting at the table with them: his classic golden looks, ravaged by alcohol and rage; his tenderness and her adoration; their laughter in the days and even weeks when he could overcome the corrosive anger inside him; the poetry he quoted that she still remembered; their dreams of a trip to Europe and a new life that both of them knew would never take place; the books they read together and the jokes they shared; their quarrels when he drank too much; the passion he taught her on that mattress on the floor; the way he frightened her, and himself as well, when his anger swelled and seemed to consume him from within.

"He told me about that," Ben mused aloud. He had forgotten where he was as he listened to Leni's soft reverie; he had been recalling his father, feeling envious of Leni for knowing Judd better than he ever had, and gripped again by the helpless anger and terrible loss he had felt when Judd moved out of the house and they saw each other only once or twice a week—and then even that was snatched from him when he was thirteen and Judd died.

He remembered that day. He'd gone to see him with a book he'd stolen from a sidewalk book stand outside the Argosy because it was his father's birthday. He found him on the mattress, lying on his stomach, very cold. He tried to close his eyes, but they wouldn't stay closed. He could still feel the softness of his father's eyelids as he tried to close them; he could still taste the salt of the tears he had sobbed, alone with his father's body. Reliving it all, he dropped his guard over the present. "He told me all about his anger and how it was eating him up inside. He knew he was sick. He said he'd probably never have a chance to get back what he'd lost, and I'd have to do it for him, get revenge on the man who stole—" He sucked in his breath with a sharp hiss, and the mood was broken.

"What is it?" Leni asked.

Ben looked at her through narrowed eyes. "You don't know."

"I know someone stole Judd's company; it was what started his drinking. He lost his company and all the money he'd put into it and then his family: he lost them all. He and Felix were talking about it the day—" This time she was the one who stopped.

"Felix was there?" Ben asked. "But they didn't see each other after . . . You didn't tell me Felix was there."

Leni gestured to the waiter and waited until he replaced their drinks. "That's another story."

"I want to hear it." He looked at his watch. "I'm going to cancel my dinner plans; do you have anyone to call?"

She shook her head. "You've already changed my dinner plans."

He smiled faintly and asked the waiter to bring a telephone. Leni watched him as he made his call. He had Judd's blond hair and blue eyes, his high, straight cheekbones, his wide mouth. But behind his horn-rimmed glasses, his eyes were clearer than Judd's, and he had a kind of hard self-awareness and self-confidence that Leni had never seen in Judd. Perhaps Judd had had them before she met him; perhaps that was where Ben got them. Or Ben created them in himself when he lost his father and had to make his own way in a tough world. She wondered how he was with Allison: if he had Judd's tenderness and quick anger and the elusiveness that had kept Leni on edge, never knowing how much he loved her or could ever share with her.

Not much, she thought sadly. He sent me away, after all.

"I want to hear it," Ben said again as he hung up the telephone. "How did you meet Felix?"

Leni told him. She did not spare herself, or Judd, or Felix. "They made some kind of a bargain. I never understood what it was; I wasn't really paying attention. All I knew was that Judd was sending me away, and I thought I'd die because of it. They said they'd been roommates in college, and Judd said he didn't remember much about the past. That wasn't true; I knew he did; but nothing was making sense that night. All I really cared about was that Judd wouldn't let me stay with him. He told me"—her voice grew very soft—"'I have nothing to give you, and you deserve a kingdom.' I kept hearing him say that for years. He meant it, I know he did, and I'm sure that's why he took the money from Felix. I don't know why Felix offered it, but I know why Judd took it: so that I couldn't tell him he needed me to support him. He took what Felix offered, and then he sent me away."

Ben shook his head; there was too much to think about. "He never told you who stole his company from him?"

"He said he would if he needed to. And he said he'd told his son, and his son would get revenge—" Once again the words stopped in her throat. Her eyes met Ben's for a long moment. She was very pale. "It was Felix, wasn't it? Of course it was Felix. If I'd been paying more attention . . . if I'd been thinking . . . That's why Felix paid him. So he'd go away without telling me. My God. All these years I've lived with Felix, and he was the one who destroyed Judd." She leaned her head on her hand. And then in a moment, sharply, she drew back in her chair. "And that's why you married Allison. To get Judd's revenge."

Ben sat very still. The chatter and bustle of the room had faded away; there was just the two of them. And my whole future, he thought. He started to shake his head, to tell Leni it wasn't true, he had never thought of revenge. But he didn't do it. If he lied now, Leni would never accept him. Her suspicions would grow and fester and eventually sway Allison; she was too close to her mother not to be affected by them. It was better to take a chance with the truth, at least part of it.

"I thought about it," he said cautiously. Leni stiffened and pushed back her chair. "Wait, please listen. It wasn't planned, my meeting Allison. In fact, I'd forgotten about revenge. There was a time"—he shook his head, remembering—"when I thought of putting spiders in your car; that was the most damaging thing I could think of to make Felix sorry for what he'd done. But then I got older and it all seemed so far away; I was in Europe, I was doing work I liked. . . . But then I met Allison and of course I remembered; I remembered everything. The people she talked about—Owen and Felix and Asa—were names my father had taught me. And you were right: when we flew back to Boston for the wedding, I wasn't in love with Allison; I just wanted to get into your family. But now I am. I am in love with her."

He stopped, as if that explained everything. Leni looked at him icily. "How convenient. Now that you're part of the family and the company, you've decided you love your wife."

"That's not true." He glared at her, angry that his simple explanation wasn't enough. "I would have gone on living with Allison without loving her, and I would have made her as happy as I could, because I needed her, to be part of Felix's company. But I fell in love with her. I don't know when it happened; all I know is, the day I sat with her in the hospital, when Judd was being born, I knew I loved her. I knew she was my whole life."

"Very pretty," Leni said. Her chair was still pushed back from the table. "But I don't know why any of us should ever believe you again."

"Because it's true," he lashed out, and once again Leni thought he sounded very young. "And because I'm faithful to her. I'm not screwing in hotel rooms—"

"Oh, my God," she said wearily.

"You don't like my talking about it? Well, I don't like you telling me I don't love my wife. Look, I can't force you to believe that I love Allison, but you know damn well *she* believes it. She doesn't know about the past, but she knows about today; she knows that she and Judd are the center of my world. I wish you'd believe that and let me be part of your family; I want that more than anything."

"I'm sure you do." Leni brought her chair closer to the table. She watched the waiter bring fresh drinks in response to Ben's signal. "I'm drinking far too much."

"I'll escort you home," Ben said formally. "And if you don't want me to stay in the guest room tonight, I'll go to a hotel."

She broke into laughter, and suddenly the tension was broken. "Of course you'll stay there; we bought that house so everyone could use it." She fell silent. "We," she murmured. "Felix and I. Do you know, we've been married for twenty-eight years. I married him five months after Judd sent me away. I didn't know what else to do, and my parents thought it would help me redeem myself and that seemed so important at the time . . ." She turned her glass within her fingers. "I have to think about Felix. About what I'll do."

"You don't have much with him," Ben said. "Isn't that why you"—he paused—"needed others?"

She smiled faintly at his new carefulness. "I needed others because I don't sleep with Felix and I miss it, and young men give me pleasure and make me feel young. That's what you've been wanting to know, isn't it?"

"I'm sorry," Ben murmured. "They make you feel like you're nineteen again? And with my father?"

Leni gazed at him. "I don't now. That's either very clever or very true. I don't know."

"But maybe that was it. And maybe I felt the same way: that it was like being with my father again if I could get back at Felix. We both got caught in the past." He stared at his hands. "Maybe, if we believe each other, we can get beyond it."

They sat quietly. "I'm glad you loved my father," Ben said suddenly. "I'm sure he loved you. I'm sure he did from things he said."

Leni smiled. "Thank you." She felt tired and old, and Ben seemed very young. "Thank you, my dear. And thank you for stopping me today. It had gone on much too long. It was becoming absurd. And hard to live with."

"So is loneliness," Ben said.

She studied him: so hard one minute, so tender the next. "I'd rather live with the loneliness," she said.

Ben reached across the table and took her hand. "We'll help you, if you'll let us."

Leni put her other hand over his. He was very strong, she thought. "Of course I'll let you. I'm so glad you're part of us."

They sat for a moment. The bar was almost empty, and for the first time silence enclosed them. Then Ben smiled broadly. "Since we're both free for the evening, will you have dinner with me? Suddenly I feel very hungry."

* * *

Louie answered when Sam Colby called. "You can't talk to Mr. Farley for a couple of weeks," he said. "We're negotiating a new television series, and he gets upset if he's interrupted when things are iffy. I'm sure you understand."

"I've got a few iffy things on my plate, too," Colby muttered, but he didn't push it; he had other people to talk to. "I'll call again in two weeks and we'll set up a time. He'll be in this country, I assume."

"Until March. Then Paris for a week; a documentary film on his life is entered in a film festival there."

"Ah, I've heard about that film. The director followed him around and such?"

"Paul Janssen. Works out of L.A. You've heard of him, of course."

Colby hadn't, but he wouldn't admit it. He wasn't much for documentaries; he preferred James Bond movies and westerns, and once in a while something about space travel. "So he's going to Paris to see himself on the screen."

"Partly."

"He hasn't seen it?"

"No, the agreement with Janssen was that we wouldn't ask to see it before it was released. Is all this relevant to the theft from Mr. Farley's apartment?"

"Everything is relevant." Colby tilted back his chair, prepared to explain. "In an investigation, every bit of information is like a seed. Some of them sprout, some are duds, but a good investigator never ignores any of them or tosses any out, since he never knows which might be a live one that—"

"Good, that's fine," Louie said. "You call in a couple, three weeks; we'll cooperate all we can."

Colby hung up slowly. He should have known better: managers were busy people; they didn't have time to learn the fine points of investigating a crime. They probably didn't care, either; most people weren't nearly curious enough. The trouble was, he had no one to talk to. All the men he used to work with had retired or died; the young men in the insurance offices around town wanted to get home to their wives and kids, not sit in a bar with Sam Colby and chew the fat to get through the hours until it was time to go to sleep. The worst time had been three weeks ago, when he had to get through Christmas and New Year's alone, but even now it seemed the evenings were longer than a year ago; they got longer the older he got. He could always go to his hotel room and watch television, but the shows were either about families, which made him even more lonely, or about detectives, which made him snort, because he knew more than all those macho actors put together.

I'll interview somebody, he thought. After all, that's what I'm here for, and I don't mind working at night: long hours don't scare a good investigator. But he soon found that Flavia Guarneri was in Italy until February; Sid and Amelia Laughton were in Palm Springs for a week; Carlos Serrano was in Mexico—and, of course, Britt Farley was upset because things were iffy.

"Well, then, this Paul Janssen," Colby said aloud. "He probably can tell me more about Farley than Farley can." But Paul was in Los Angeles. "How about I come out, then," Colby said on the telephone when

Paul said he wouldn't be in New York for several weeks. "I'll leave tonight, and I can see you in the morning."

"I don't know how I can help you," Paul said. "Or how much time I can give you; I'm editing a film on a tight deadline. I'll tell you what: if you're flying all night, come for breakfast." He gave his Bel Air address, and Sam Colby ended the conversation humming a happy tune. He had a lot to do; it was going to be a busy time.

He was at Paul's house at seven the next morning and found him dressed and sitting on the deck. At that hour, the air was sparkling, and Colby stood admiring the view. "Makes a man glad to be a man and not a bird; they see all this but don't appreciate it the way we do."

Paul smiled. "Coffee? And help yourself to the rest."

There were cinnamon rolls and almond croissants, a basket of raisin muffins and a bowl heaped high with fruit. Everything but a Mrs. Janssen, Colby thought, and wondered, as he filled his plate, if there was one.

"How can I help you?" Paul asked.

"Ah." Colby settled back, ready for a long chat. "I'm interested in Britt Farley. I'm told you've been following him around, talking to him, observing him, that sort of thing, and it occurred to me you'd be able to tell me, for one thing, if he's as broke as they say he is."

"I can't answer that," Paul said shortly. "I'd think you'd want to ask him directly."

"Directly doesn't always work. I'm an insurance investigator, Mr. Janssen, and what I'm wondering is, what do you think are the chances that Farley faked the theft of his Remingtons?"

"For the insurance," Paul said. Colby nodded, beaming at being so quickly understood. "I don't know. I hadn't thought of it. He seemed furious that they were gone, and even angrier, if that's possible, that a stranger invaded his apartment, especially without having to break in. He'd thought the place was secure."

Colby nodded. "But that doesn't really rule out a bit of play acting, does it? You see—" He finished his cinnamon roll, surreptitiously licked his fingers, and picked up a muffin. "We always have to treat that possibility very seriously. I don't like being cynical about people—the good Lord knows I'd like to love my fellowman and be charitable to each and every one of his failings, but that's not so easy for somebody in my business. Now, I am charitable, don't misunderstand me; it's just that I'm also cynical because otherwise I would have been out of work a long time ago instead of being the best in the business."

"Are you?" asked Paul, amused.

"The best," Colby declared. "Ask around; they'll tell you. I've got awards and letters of appreciation, and somebody even put me in a book once, about art forgeries. That was glorious, to read my name in a book. It's immortality—if you don't think I'm blaspheming."

"I don't at all," Paul said and refilled Colby's cup.

"So I'm asking, you see, could he have faked it. Did he need to. Was he smart enough. Did he act like it. That sort of thing."

"I don't think Britt faked that theft."

"My other questions," Colby prompted.

"You should ask him."

"If he's smart enough?"

"If I said yes, you'd think I was suggesting something."

"Smart fella." Colby grinned. "Good muffins. Your wife make them?"

Paul chuckled at the idea of Emily in the kitchen. "No. In any event, she's out of town." He looked at his watch. "Is there anything else you want to ask?"

Colby saw the morning loom ahead, with nothing to do. "Well, now, there are a number of things. Could you tell me . . ." He pulled out all the questions he thought Paul might be able and willing to answer. He asked about Farley's schedule when he was at home in Paris and when he was on the road, the people who came to see him most frequently and those who were hangers-on, Louie's access to his apartment and his hotel rooms when they were traveling, the kinds of parties Farley had given during the tour, how much money was raised for the hungry and how much payment Farley had taken for his time.

"None," said Paul to the last question. He stood. "I've enjoyed talking to you, but I should have been at my studio an hour ago."

"Might I come along?" Colby asked. "I've never seen a film edited."

Paul shook his head. "No, I'm sorry. My partner and the PBS executives who are funding it are the only ones who see it before it's released."

"And it's going to be in a film festival? Louie Glass mentioned it. Like the Academy Awards?"

"Not quite; the Cinéma du Réel is just for documentaries." He held out his hand. "It was a pleasure to meet you."

"How about dinner? I'm taking the red-eye back, so I have plenty of time, and I'd appreciate the opportunity to buy you a dinner and hear about the film business. And since your wife is away, you might like some company."

Involuntarily, Paul smiled. But when Colby reddened, he felt sorry for him. "I'd like that. Why don't you come to the studio about seven? We'll go from there." He wrote on a pad of paper. "Here's the address. I'll see you then. And you can tell me what it's like, being an insurance investigator."

"I'll do that. It always helps to talk things out; you might have some ideas for me."

"I've told you all I can about Britt."

"Understood, understood. But I'm talking about something else. You see, I'm not only looking into Mr. Farley's robbery; I've got four on my mind. His and three others. Very similar. Very, very similar. And what I'm looking for is a thread. Now there might not be one; we can't assume..." Paul was walking away and he was following. "Well, can't fritter away the morning; we've both got a lot of work to do. We'll talk tonight. Maybe you can help me find my thread. Because, by God, there's some connection between all these robberies, even though they're scattered all the hell over the world—I didn't mention that—but there's a connection. Fifty years of experience tells me there is, and, by God, I'll find it."

Paul led the way through the living room and down the stairs to the garage while Colby followed, still talking. "People tend to underestimate Sam Colby when they first meet him, but after a while they find they're wrong. That's part of my success. I'll tell you about that tonight, too."

Paul opened his car door, and Colby was forced to turn to his rented car. "But the main thing is, I stick with things. I don't let go. If there's a connection here, I'll find it, and then I'll find who's behind it. You can be sure of that."

Paul waved as he drove away, smiling to himself. He will find it, he reflected; he probably can find anything he sets his mind to. He thought about him as he merged with the morning traffic on the freeway. An impressive man. Because beneath the talkativeness and the desperate reaching out for companionship, there had been glimpses of the professional tracker—dogged, shrewd, and implacable—and also a man stuck in retirement who would bring every skill he had to this case, because solving cases was the only way he felt alive.

I wouldn't want him hunting me, Paul thought with another smile. He found himself looking forward to dinner. He wanted to know more about Sam Colby and the whole shadowy business of art theft: who does it and how, where stolen works end up, how often they're recovered, how often the thieves are caught....

Excitement began to build inside him. A colorful, garrulous old man with a lifelong, fascinating career; the whole world of art and money and international connections; a complicated case of four robberies just unfolding...

He had his next film.

CHAPTER 26

THE plaza in front of the Centre Pompidou slopes gently downward, forming a kind of amphitheater in front of the art museum where jugglers, jazz bands, clowns, and street theater groups perform beneath the Parisian sun. Ginny and Laura stopped to watch a group of circus performers in a tumbling act, then strolled over to a fire-eater who had attracted a crowd of children. "In Texas we'd ask him to do it with a branding iron," Ginny murmured as they moved on. "What would you like next? I made reservations for lunch, but we can skip it and do the museum instead. Or something else you haven't seen."

"Is there anything I haven't seen?" Laura asked with a laugh. "We've been on the move ever since we got here."

"And we're leaving tomorrow, so we ought to be moving faster. The more you walk in Paris, the bigger it gets, have you noticed? But we'll come back another time. Now that I've talked you into one vacation, you'll take others: I predict it."

"You're very good to me, Ginny. Have I told you how grateful I am?"

"You have. And here we are at l'Escargot, so I guess we're about to have lunch. Is that all right?"

"Fine. I'm hungry and I need to sit for a while."

"That makes two of us."

The restaurant was built in 1832, and Laura tilted back her head to admire the elaborately painted ceiling while Ginny chattered in Texas-accented French with the waitress. In one of the huge mirrors spaced about the room she saw Ginny and herself as if they were in a painting: two American women, similarly dressed in beautifully-cut wool suits and silk blouses, fine leather walking shoes, and shoulder bags. They looked prosperous, well-groomed, and poised, but what Laura saw most of all was the affection between them. Ginny had given up trying to be motherly, which made them even better friends, and the two of them were close and comfortable together.

And I'm very lucky, she thought, as Ginny finished ordering and turned back to her, switching to Texas-accented English. "Now, where were we?"

"I was telling you how grateful I am for all the things you do for me."

"So you were. Well, I'll tell you, I'm grateful, too. I love taking people around Paris because it makes me feel like it's my city, but mostly I love doing things for you because you're grateful without overdoing it. I've always had more money than I know what to do with, even before I took Wylie to the cleaners—a poor form of revenge for all that humiliation, but we use whatever weapons we have—and I've noticed that when people have a lot of money, other people tend to be ridiculously grateful for simple things. They can't stop saying thank you, or you've made their life worthwhile, or you're the next thing to a saint; and you don't have to be brilliant to figure out that what they really mean is they want more of your money and your attention, and so they're laying it on you to keep giving. It's all bullshit, and I can't abide it. But you're never anything like that; you mean what you say and you don't say it too often. Which is why I'm having a good time. Also, I might add, I'm getting an education. How many times have I come to Paris and checked out hotels, even poking into linen closets? How many times have I cut down my shopping to look at drapery fabrics? Never. And eating three-star dinners and thinking of new menus for back home . . . You haven't stopped working all week."

"Yes, I have. This has been fun, not work. The work starts when I get home and try to use everything I've learned."

"Well, then, our last day has to be extra fun. Dinner tonight at Ledoyen; it's quite luscious: all velvet and lace and candelabras, and the food is sublime. Then jazz at New Morning; it's quite the place to be these days. And after lunch, the Pompidou, since we're in the neighborhood. Unless you've had too much art."

"No. It all sounds wonderful."

Ginny nodded with satisfaction. "I do appreciate traveling with someone who approves of my plans. It gets so difficult when one has to make endless compromises."

Laura laughed and did not say that the next time she came to Paris she would have her own schedule. This week was Ginny's, and it had been like an enormous platter of hors d'oeuvres, giving her a taste of everything in that glorious city that she would want to savor on her own terms, in her own time. Paris seemed very special to her; it had its jumbled neighborhoods, like any other city, its jarring architecture, its slums and litter and graffiti, but, unlike many other cities, there was a sense of design: streets planned for the vistas they provided, neighborhoods and vast structures like the Place des Vosges built with an eye to harmony and scale, open space designed with gardens, not just urban greenery. And since Laura spent so much time trying to keep her emotions in check and her life in order, she felt at home in Paris after only a week; she knew she would come back, most likely alone. She had discovered, in traveling for her hotels, that she didn't mind being alone on a trip. Often she missed having someone to nudge and say, 'Oh, look, look how beautiful that is,' but the rest of the time she was satisfied to be on her own, learning about the world on her own terms.

But this trip to Paris was Ginny's, and after lunch she let her lead her through the vastness of the Pompidou, at some displays elbow to elbow with people, but even more crowded with its own collections. "It's a tossed salad of a museum," Ginny pronounced. "I love it 'cause it's as chaotic as the world out there. Paintings and sculptures and television and films and radio all mixed into one—"

"Laura!" a familiar baritone boomed. "Goddam if it isn't my sweetheart in the middle of Paris!" Dozens of people turned to look as Britt Farley swept Laura into an embrace and then put out an arm to include Ginny. "Two lovely ladies in Par-ee! What are you doing here? Small world, right? Hey, this is the damnedest piece of luck, you're just in time! Would you believe it, there's a film contest downstairs—documentaries—*Cinéma du Réel*," he brought out in mangled French. "It's a big deal here, and we've won first place! How about that! Well, truth to tell, Paul won; I haven't even seen it yet, but what the hell, I'll love it, right, since it won? You will, too; you're just in time; they're showing it this afternoon. Isn't that the damnedest piece of luck? You can sit with me and hold my hand if I'm nervous. Come on, you wouldn't say no, would you?"

"I can't say anything," Laura laughed, pulling out of his clutching arms. *Paul is here. He must be; it's his film. Of course he's here.* "I don't think so, Britt . . ."

She hadn't let herself think about Paul for more than fleeting moments since that evening in the ballroom. Now, as Farley asked her again, she was torn. *I can't see him; it would be crazy; what good would it do?*

"Ginny has other plans," she said. "I'm sorry, but we really can't."

"A-course you can! It's only an hour—one little hour out of your vacation—Ginny, tell her you'll come."

"It's up to Laura," Ginny said.

"Shit, Laura, how many times am I gonna have a movie about me? This is it, and I want you to sit with me. Come on."

He was holding her hand, and Laura let him pull her toward him. *I could just stay long enough to see the film,* she told herself. It would be interesting to see what kind of work he's doing.

Watching her face, Ginny made the decision. Laura had told her about Paul, not a great deal, but enough to give Ginny clues to what she was feeling now. Scared to go, Ginny thought, and dying to go. "Well, why not?" she said briskly. "As long as we're out of here by six; we do have plans for dinner."

"No, no, you'll eat with us. I'll take care of it. Come on, come on. Goddam, if this isn't the damnedest luck . . ."

Us. Paul and . . . who else?

"Coked to his cowlick," Ginny was murmuring as they followed Britt to a doorway that led to the exterior escalators, enclosed in glass tubes that allowed a panoramic view of the Marais. "But he seems more or less under control." She glanced at Laura. "How about you? We won't stay if you'd rather not."

I want to stay. I want to go. Damn it, it's such a big world; I go for years without seeing people I've known in the past; why can't Paul and I just disappear from each other's lives?

Paul and I. Her heart sank at the sweetness of the phrase.

One more time won't matter.

"It's fine," she said to Ginny as they came to the bottom of the escalator. "It should be interesting."

"Interesting," Ginny repeated. "What a word." They reached the entrance to the auditorium, and Britt grandly led them past the guard and down the aisle to the seats reserved for his party. "Paul!" he boomed past the row of people sitting there. "Look who I found! How about this for fantastic?"

Paul stood, his eyes meeting Laura's in surprise. But then, reflexively, he looked down to the woman beside him, and Laura followed his look. She was blonde and lovely, with a slightly petulant sophistication and perfect skin: a woman Laura had seen dozens of times on magazine covers and in stories on haute couture. Emily. Staring at Laura in puzzlement, wondering who it was who'd gotten Britt so excited.

Beside Emily were Tom and Barbara Janssen and then Leni, looking at her with astonishment.

Behind Laura, the aisle was filled with people finding their seats. There was no place to run. She wasn't even sure she wanted to. She shivered at the challenge. She wasn't the same person; she was their equal now. If they didn't want her, let them say so.

But Leni was perfect. "Laura, my dear, how delightful. I almost wouldn't have known you; you're so very lovely. Please sit down; we can have a chat before the film begins."

Britt had put up his hand, ready to make introductions; now, as Thomas and Barbara also greeted Laura, he looked confused. "You already know each other. Goddam, small world. Ginny, do you know everybody?" Without waiting, he introduced them. "Now if you'll excuse me," he said. "I have a little friend waiting for me outside. Be right back."

He strode up the aisle, parting the crowds as if they were the Red Sea. Paul leaned forward. "Laura, I'm glad Britt found you. Are you on vacation? I'm glad you're here." He cleared his throat, wondering why he was acting like an adolescent.

"Congratulations on your film," Laura said, her eyes meeting his. "Britt told me about the award."

"Thank you." He paused briefly. "I'd like you to meet my wife. Emily Janssen, Laura Fairchild."

"How do you do," Emily murmured; a small frown was between her eyes.

"I'm pleased to meet you," Laura said and reached forward, holding out her hand.

Emily, eyebrows raised, stood up, awkwardly reaching across Leni and Thomas and Barbara, and the two women shook hands.

"I've admired you for years," Laura said. "You have wonderful style."

Emily smiled. She didn't understand how everyone seemed to know Laura, or what her sudden appearance meant to them, but she recognized genuine praise when she heard it, and that was always enough for Emily. "So very kind . . ." she said and sat down again, and after a moment Paul sat beside her, separated from Laura by all the others. Thomas and Barbara Janssen leaned forward and greeted Laura. "You're looking marvelous," Thomas said. "Marvelous," Barbara echoed.

"Thank you," Laura said gravely, and then there was a silence and Thomas and Barbara sat back in their seats, concentrating on reading the festival program.

Leni and Laura looked at each other. "You're the one who has style, my dear," Leni said quietly. When Laura did not respond, she said, "How long has it been?"

"Seven years," Laura replied evenly. "Or six, since we did see each other at the trial."

Leni gazed at her. She looked older, certainly older than her twenty-eight years. She was the same age as Allison, but her face had more experience in it, more pain, more control. But who would have guessed she would turn out to be so stunning, with such poise, wearing a suit whose designer Leni recognized and wearing it as it was meant to be worn, with a straight back and a proud head? "You've done well," she said quietly. "We hear about you, of course, quite frequently. I do congratulate you on your hotels."

"Thank you." Laura turned to look straight ahead, at the large screen on the stage. Nothing had changed: she still loved Leni, still wanted her to love her, still wanted to be like her: cool, serene, unmarked by passions or even passing fancies. *Why can't I just think of these people as part of my past?*

"Tell me about the hotels," Leni said. "It does seem strange that they're yours, though I want you to know I'm glad they are. That was a terrible time we went through, my dear, and none of us acted well, especially those of us who were silent. It always amazes me how easily we forget that being silent is as much an action as doing something. I've wanted to apologize to you and tell you that perhaps we were too hasty in judging you . . ." She made a small gesture with her slender, manicured hand. "This is hardly the time or the place, but—"

"How is Allison?"

"Oh, very well. Very happy. She's married, you know, or did you? To a fine young man named Ben Gardner. I wasn't sure of him at first, but he's very fine, very direct and honest, and very much in love with Allison. You'd like him; the two of you are rather alike. There's something about the way you hold your head and look at everyone as if you're studying them . . ." She gave a small laugh. "Isn't it strange, I hadn't thought of it before, but you and Ben are really quite alike in that way. He and Allison have a baby boy, a lovely child, he'll be a year old in May, and she's running an art gallery with a friend. She wanted to be here today, but she just couldn't get away. She'll be so sorry when I tell her you were here. She still misses you, I think; I know she'd agree that we ought to put those bad times behind us."

"Felix, too?" Laura asked evenly. "Felix wants to forget the past?"

"No," Leni said. "But Felix and I—" She stopped. "Please tell me about you. I can hardly believe all the things I've heard about your hotels, and your corporation. It's quite amazing; it sounds as if you've done the most astonishing things in an incredibly short time."

Laura looked at her in silence. *Amazing. Astonishing. Incredible.* Poor Leni, what a lot of trouble she was having with the idea that a thief and kitchen maid could do what Laura Fairchild was doing. And she had the nerve to apologize for *perhaps* acting too hastily in the past! She still thought they'd probably been right about Laura Fairchild: a thief, a liar, a fortune hunter who got Paul to propose and then manipulated and terrorized a dying man into naming her in his will.

"Why don't you see for yourself?" she asked icily. "Isn't that the best way to find out how amazing they are? Tell me when you'd like to come, and I'll make a reservation for you at the New York Beacon Hill. Stay as long as you'd like; we'd be so pleased to welcome you there. As our guest."

Leni winced at her anger, but she admired her, too. The invitation was bold and clever; it showed a woman who could control herself and take the offensive. No wonder she was talked about as a superb executive. And the invitation was intriguing. Why shouldn't I stay in her hotel? Leni thought. It would enrage Felix, of course, if he heard about it, but that was no longer a consideration. "I think—" she began, when the lights in the auditorium faded out and a spotlight picked out a man on the stage.

As he welcomed the audience and spoke briefly about Paul Janssen's film, the first-place winner in its category, Farley and a young girl slipped into the end seats. The stage went dark, and the film began.

It was titled *An American Hero*, and Laura heard Farley's jubilant sigh as the words appeared over a wide view of the jammed Washington mall, with Britt Farley on stage. But as the film unfolded, she forgot he was there; she forgot her anger at Leni and the closeness of Paul and his wife and parents. She was caught up in the story.

It unfolded like a novel, the camera and the unseen narrator following Farley from his early days in television to the Tour for the Hungry that had ended only eight months ago. Gasps were heard from the audience when his early days were shown, and everyone was reminded of the charm of his rugged good looks and boyish smile, and the easy strength of the baritone that swung between singing and talking, to tell a tale. Those who had known him along the way reminisced; photos were shown from old albums, pages from *People* and *Esquire*, and scenes from late-night talk shows. In the background was the music Farley had sung in his teens and college years, imperceptibly shifting to the harder beat and lyrics of his television series, when he combined acting and singing, and then shifting again to a still harder beat, with a dark tone, while the lighting grew harsh and starkly shadowed.

It was the fall of the hero: first a scene from the tape of the disastrous rehearsal that had led to his series being abruptly halted, then his displays of temper and erratic mood changes in press conferences, and finally the long struggle of the Tour for the Hungry, with his effort to keep going and climb out of the depths to which he had fallen. In the final scene, on the Washington mall, Farley stood on a raised platform surrounded by hundreds of thousands of fans who had not forgotten what they had loved. He clung to the microphone, looking at the horizon beyond the mass of faces, and sang the songs they remembered, his voice strong one moment, slipping to a gravelly whisper the next. Suddenly, another Britt Farley stood beside him: in a double exposure, the young, vigorous, handsome singer of less than a dozen years before stood and sang in unison with the singer of today. And then the young Farley vanished, and all that was left to fill the screen was the haggard face of Britt Farley today, and his haunted eyes. And the silent question, which no one could answer, of what his future would be.

The image froze, the credits rolled across it, and the audience burst into applause; many of them had tears in their eyes. "My God," Ginny said to Laura, "that man is a genius." The applause continued as the lights came up, and the man on the stage beckoned to Paul, who joined him there. Leni and Laura turned to each other, applauding and smiling. For one perfect moment they loved each other, and they both loved Paul and rejoiced for him. And then the moment was gone. Laura stopped applauding and clasped her hands in her lap.

The audience was standing, giving Paul an ovation, and it was when she stood with them that Laura saw Britt's empty seat. The young girl was still there, smiling at anyone who looked her way, but Britt was nowhere to be seen, and so he did not hear Paul's brief speech thanking everyone who had worked on the film, but most of all Britt Farley, for his courageous and generous cooperation.

Thomas was talking about dinner, a celebration; Emily had joined Paul on the stage, taking his arm and accepting the congratulations of those who were surrounding him. Leni was answering a question from Barbara. And Laura knew she had to get out of there. She'd been sitting with the family, but she was completely separate from them, sharing nothing, certainly not Paul's triumph. It's their night, not mine, she thought; Ginny and I are going to our own dinner.

"Please congratulate Paul for me," she said to Leni, beneath the noise of the audience. "It's a brilliant film. We can't stay; will you tell him I think he's a superb filmmaker?"

"Of course," Leni said. She and Ginny talked briefly while Laura said good-bye to the Janssens, then she turned to Laura. "Perhaps we'll see each other again."

Laura gave her a long look. "Soon, I hope. I did invite you to my hotel."

"So you did." Leni hadn't forgotten; she'd simply not made up her mind. Now she did. With a smile, she held out her hand, and automatically Laura took it, their cool hands clasped together. "I accept with pleasure. I'm greatly looking forward to being a guest in your Beacon Hill hotel."

*   *   *

In May, the Philadelphia Hospital Women's Board held its annual benefit fashion show and luncheon as the first event in the new Beacon Hill dining room, one day before the hotel officially opened. The three hundred women who, alone or with husbands, could be said to run the city's institutions were given a tour of the hotel by Laura Fairchild, and their names were inscribed in the guest book so they could get a reservation at any Beacon Hill hotel, thus eliminating the necessity of being recommended by a former guest. The lunch was sublimely French, the wine a mellow Montrachet, and the blush pink roses at each place perfectly matched the tablecloth and napkins. The ramp for the fashion show was placed so that everyone had an unobstructed view without moving from her table, and the music was not deafening, as at too many fashion shows. The event was remembered as an afternoon of utter perfection in which a million dollars was raised for the hospital, and ball gowns, sportswear, and lingerie worth close to two million were sold by the designers who had mounted the show, and who had agreed, in response to Laura's suggestion, to donate to the hospital a percentage of the profit.

Laura stayed in Philadelphia the first week the hotel was open, helping with the myriad small details she could anticipate from openings in Chicago and New York. Clay was away that week, too, talking to manufacturers in the South about a problem with the linens they had been receiving. So it was the manager of the New York Beacon Hill who greeted Leni Salinger when she arrived on a warm Wednesday afternoon and was seated at the antique desk in the small lobby where the concierge arranged her registration for the penthouse suite. "If there is anything I can do, madame," he said, handing her the plastic card that took the place of keys in all Beacon Hill hotels, "please call me. I am always here, or one of my assistants. And one of them will now escort you upstairs."

As Leni turned to go, a dark man with a brilliant smile came to the desk. He turned his concentrated smile and intense look on her, and she knew he was the kind who never missed an attractive woman. She was the one who turned away, pausing to view the lobby.

"Ah, Mr. Serrano," she heard the concierge say. "Here are your messages, and there was a call just a moment ago. Mr. Sam Colby would like to see you this evening. He would like you to call him. His number . . . one moment. . ." He wrote on a piece of paper and held it out.

"Not tonight; impossible. You will please call him for me; tell him sometime next week I will try to . . ."

Leni heard no more as she was led to one of the elevators at the back of the lobby. There were four of them, paneled in the same mahogany that alternated with French tapestries on the walls. Leni remembered that wood: Owen told her once it had been his favorite extravagance when he built the hotel. The tapestries were new—a splendid idea— but Leni saw that Laura had kept all the best things. Approvingly, she saw it again in the upstairs corridors: broad, brightly lit by antique wall sconces, the fleur-de-lis carpet new but retaining the air of a bygone time, the picture moldings intact and framing large landscapes from the last century.

She followed the assistant concierge to the end of the corridor, where he led her into her suite: two rooms in mint green and ivory, her favorite colors, with an arrangement of thaleonopsis orchids, the flowers she loved best, on the French coffee table. Beside the flowers was a tea service, the teapot steaming beneath its cozy, and a silver tray with a porcelain plate of finger sandwiches and petits fours. Propped against the flowers was a handwritten note on a card embossed with an iris. "I hope you enjoy your stay. Laura."

There was a discreet knock at the door. "Your maid, madame," said the assistant concierge as he went to open the door. "If you need other assistance, please call us." He was gone before Leni could tip him. But of course it would not be done at this time; she knew that. All of them would expect something when she left, and it would be much larger than the small amounts dribbled out in most hotels.

She stood at the window overlooking Fifty-eighth Street while the maid unpacked her bags, hung her dresses and blouses in the closet, and put her lingerie and sweaters in the antique bureau. One dress and two blouses she kept out. "I will have these ironed and returned within a few moments, madame," she said and quietly left.

Leni wandered through the rooms, picking up books that would provide her poetry or short stories, even crossword puzzles, if she wished. In an armoire she found a television set, videocassette recorder, and stereo; a compartment in the lower part concealed a refrigerator stocked with food and wine, including her favorite duck and cognac pâté. Opening the antique desk, she discovered that one side held a small computer and printer. In each of the two marble bathrooms were men's and women's velour robes monogrammed with the same iris that was on Laura's card, and a polished rosewood box containing shampoos, shaving materials, and a variety of soaps. A booklet on the desk told her she could have a dinner party in her suite or in the private dining room on her floor, prepared by chef Gérard Lyon of the Beacon Hill Dining Room; if a larger dinner party was required, the hotel had made arrangements with several three-star restaurants which would give preference to Beacon Hill guests and their parties; the Beacon Hill stenographers, hairdressers, seamstresses, tailors, and maids would come to her suite when called; the newspapers of her choice would be at her door each morning; the hotel limousine was available for service to and from the airports, and arrangements could be made to use them at night for dining and the theater . . . The list went on and on, and Leni read it several times.

Where did she learn all this? We couldn't have taught her because we don't do these things in our own hotels. We do them in our homes, but we've never—And that was the answer. Laura had bought Owen's hotels and made each of them—Leni assumed they were all the same—into the home she remembered.

And it was wonderfully effective. As she stood in the luxurious living room, glimpsing through the doorway the wide bed with its satin comforter, she felt as pampered as she did in her own home, with her own belongings and staff. Leni Salinger, world traveler, had never felt that in any hotel before, not even in the ones that bore her name.

She had allowed herself three days to find out what kind of a hotel Laura ran. As she bathed and changed, using the Hermès bath oil she found in the rosewood box, she thought she could stay a month, getting away from everything she had to worry about at home, simply being a tourist in Manhattan and a cosseted guest of the Beacon Hill.

We ought to have her working for us, she thought.

She was due at a fund-raising meeting in Rockefeller Center at four, and at three-thirty she left her room and rode the elevator to the lobby. She stopped at the concierge's desk to arrange for theater tickets for the evening; she would call one of her friends to join her.

The concierge was answering questions asked by a short, powerfully built man with a large head and a deep, almost gruff voice. Leni waited, glancing around the lobby. She recognized Daniel Inouti, a Hawaiian developer Felix had once thought of working with, one of San Francisco's most successful winery owners, a Colombian billionaire who often stayed at the Boston Salinger, a European king and queen temporarily out of a throne. But why not, she thought with amusement. Who else can afford Laura's prices?

"I'm so sorry," the man in front of her said, turning to her and stepping aside. "I didn't see you."

"I don't object to waiting," Leni said calmly. "There's no reason you shouldn't finish your business."

He smiled. "Hotel business: I only needed information. Please, go ahead."

He was at least three inches shorter than Leni, but his air of authority made him seem taller. His suit was skillfully cut to minimize the disproportion between his short stature and broad shoulders; his gray hair was thick and his nose large, adding to his leonine look. And his smile had worldliness and charm. Leni returned the smile, liking him, wondering what part he played in Laura's hotel that led him to ask the concierge for information.

But he had stepped aside for her, so she turned and requested the tickets she wanted. "Of course, Madame Salinger," the concierge said, and from the corner of her eye Leni saw the sudden alertness of the man beside her.

"Excuse me," he said. "You're Leni Salinger?"

"Yes?"

"Wes Currier." He extended his hand. "I'm glad to see you at the Beacon Hill. I hope you find everything satisfactory."

She put her hand in his. "Do you have some interest in this hotel?"

"As an investor. I like to ask questions and greet some of the guests when I'm in town." He smiled again. "Fortunately, I'm indulged."

His name was vaguely familiar. Felix would probably recognize it, Leni thought, but she didn't keep up with the money men unless they were on her list to be contacted for fund-raising campaigns. "It's a lovely hotel," she said. "Now I'll leave you to your questions; I'm due at a meeting."

"We might share a cab," he said. "I have to be downtown in half an hour."

"No, I'm walking. It was pleasant talking to you—"

"Then I'll walk with you. If I may."

Leni met his eyes: serious, interested, determined. A man older than I, she thought with brief humor; what a novelty. "I'd like that," she said, and they left the hotel together.

Currier took her arm as they crossed the street, making their way between cars that were backed up through the intersection. "Are you staying in New York long?"

"I'll be at the hotel for three days," she replied.

He led her around a blanket spread on the sidewalk with scarves and wallets displayed for sale. "And how long will you be in New York?"

She laughed, liking his quickness. "I live in New York."

"I thought the Salingers lived in Boston."

"I spend most of my time here now."

"But not in hotels."

"No, I have a house on the East Side. And you live here?"

"I have an apartment I rarely see. Why are you staying at the Beacon Hill?"

"I come from a hotel family; I wanted to see what it was like. What better way than to stay there?"

The noise of jackhammers drowned out their voices, and they waited until they had walked some distance away. "And what is it like?" Currier asked.

"A home. My home, yours, any home built by people who care about beauty and comfort and have excellent taste. I'm very impressed with Laura. I'm told her Chicago hotel is just as fine."

"It is. She's got a special touch."

"And that's why you invested in her corporation? I wondered how she got the money for all that she's done. Have you known her long?"

"A number of us are investors; we all have confidence in her. Do you like living in Manhattan?"

"Yes, but it's not really new for me. I've been staying here for a number of years. Why do you rarely see your apartment?"

"I spend most of my time traveling."

They edged their way through a crowd watching a man play a shell game on a small folding table, keeping up a steady patter as his hands moved three cups in a blur of action; then they walked around a hot dog wagon and a young boy with his head back as he ate. "He looks like a sword swallower," Leni laughed. "I imagine the hot dog is considerably more fun."

"And better tasting."

"Do you travel for your work or for pleasure?" she asked.

"Work. I'd trade it for pleasure but it hasn't happened yet. It's surprising how difficult it is to arrange events as we'd like, even when we're old enough to identify the options and wealthy enough to buy them."

Leni stopped. "I like that. It's what I've been thinking, but not quite as clearly." She looked up; they were standing before one of the buildings in Rockefeller Center. "This is where my meeting is. I've enjoyed our walk."

"What time will you be finished?" Currier asked.

"Probably about six."

"Will you meet me upstairs, in the Rainbow Room? We'll have a drink and then decide where to go for dinner."

"Yes," she said without hesitation. "At six."

Currier watched her walk into the building, then hailed a taxi to drive downtown. He was so struck by her that it took him a moment to sort out his feelings. He didn't know what he had expected, from the things Laura had told him, but he had not anticipated her air of cool serenity, her soft, measured speech, and, in such striking contrast, the uncertain look in her eyes, as if she were starting something new, something uncharted, and had no idea what to expect from it or just how she should behave.

I spend most of my time in New York now.

That could be the uncharted territory: being single. Currier knew he could find out; he had people in Boston who knew all the gossip and would tell him what was happening, but he didn't want to do that. He wanted Leni Salinger to tell him herself.

Staring unseeing out of the taxi window, he remembered her smile and felt the attraction that had drawn him to her even before he knew her name. He warned himself not to act like a teenager, to go slowly and to calculate what he wanted. But he'd been going slowly with women since he and Laura had separated seven months earlier. He'd taken them out and slept with a few of them, but he'd made no effort to know or even like them. He'd gone through similar periods following his divorces, but after his years with Laura, he wanted much more, and he didn't want to wait. He was lonely and bereft, angry that with all his strengths and resources he couldn't have the simplest of relationships—though he knew there was nothing simple about marriage—at a time when he was wealthy and energetic enough to enjoy everything he'd been putting off for later.

So why should he go slowly with Leni Salinger? He was attracted to her, and she was to him; he wanted to spend time with her and know all about her; he wanted to sleep with her. And she had that uncertainty in her eyes that told him she was as ripe for a new man as he was for a woman, as ready to start again, as willing to take risks once again. It didn't even matter what her status was with Felix. If they were still married, it didn't seem to be much of a marriage, and Currier had never let loose ends bother him; they could always be tied up quickly and efficiently when someone wanted it badly enough.

The taxi passed Bleecker Street, and he thought of Laura, whose house on Grove Court was only a few blocks away. He'd meant to call her today to talk about expenses: the costs of renovating the hotels were running higher than they had anticipated. But it could wait. He allowed himself a moment of reverie about the times they had spent together and his persistent hopes, kept artificially high by his refusal to accept failure. Artificial, he thought. As artificial as her idea that she could build a life free of the baggage of the past.

The reverie faded, as dreams do upon waking. Laura was a business partner and a friend, and he had other things to think about. He reached Wall Street and had his meeting with his clients, and less than two hours later he was in the Rainbow Room at Rockefeller Center, seated beside a window where he could watch the entrance. In a few moments Leni Salinger was walking toward him, and he stood, holding a chair for her. And when she saw him, she smiled.

CHAPTER 27

THE fifth theft was just before dawn. It was July, in the midst of a heat wave, and one of the neighbors was preparing for an early-morning run. She saw Clay from the back but thought nothing of it, since he was using a key to unlock the front door, and Felix and Leni were known to let family members and friends use the house when they were not in town.

No one else saw or heard anything as Clay quietly let himself in. Beside the door was the alarm panel; with his gloved finger he punched in the code that turned off the system, and then took a quick look around in the faint light from a street lamp. He was in a tiny foyer, with a guest room and bath to his right. Straight ahead was a stairway going up: beside it was a short, narrow hall leading to the dining room and, beyond it, the kitchen and a walled garden. He took the steep stairs two at a time and in a moment stood in the living room, pitch-dark except for a sliver of light coming from the street through fringed velvet drapes. With a small flashlight he made a swift survey of the curved velvet couches, the carved round table in the center of the room, the paintings hung against small-figured wallpaper. Posh, he thought; too good for old Felix. But what he was looking for wasn't there, and he went through an archway into the library.

He flashed the light swiftly around the paneled room and sighed with relief. The three Rouaults hung in a niche above a velvet love seat.

Propping the flashlight on a table, he took them down and slipped them into an artist's leather case he had folded inside his dark jacket. Then he turned in place, using the flashlight again to study the room. There was only one other painting, and behind it he found the wall safe. Taking a piece of paper from his pocket and following the combination written on it, copied from the one he had found tucked in Leni's purse right beside the code for the alarm at the front door, he opened the safe and rummaged within. It was empty except for the documents dealing with the purchase of the house. What the fuck, he thought angrily; why does he have a safe if he doesn't have anything to keep in it? Not a damn thing for me. Disgusted, he closed and locked it, automatically straightening the picture covering it. Then he froze as a sharp noise broke the silence.

It came from outside—the backyard of this house, or maybe next door—and it sounded like something slammed shut. A screen door. Maybe. He waited. Absolute silence, as silent as the moment he entered. He stayed, not moving, barely breathing, for five minutes. A window, he thought. That's what it sounded like. Someone in a nearby house had opened a window, flung it up, so that it made that sharp sound.

It isn't in this house; I'm all right. Stupid to panic, but Ben always taught me never to take anything for granted. *You never know when the danger may be real.* That's what he taught me. And look how far it's gotten me.

Time to get out. He picked up the artist's case, then paused to consider the desk. Why not? It was still dark outside; he had time for a quick look; he might find some cash.

The desk was enormous, finished on both sides so two people could work at it at the same time, facing each other. Each side had cabinet doors and drawers flanking a kneehole opening, and he opened them, rifled and closed them with an efficiency born of confidence and experience. But once again he found no money; only papers and letters, most of them Leni's.

The top drawer on the other side was fuller than the others. An eelskin wallet lay beneath some of the papers and envelopes; it held credit cards with Leni's name, and ninety-five dollars. With a snort, he threw it on the desk and began flipping through the envelopes, taking a swift look inside each. Nothing, nothing, goddam it . . .

Something was stuck at the back, and he tugged at it; it would not come free. Shit, what's wrong with it? He pulled again at the paper his fingers had found. And then he thought of a hidden compartment. That's it, he thought with rising excitement. What else could it be? It's an old desk; it looks just like the one in Owen's office; and in the old days they used to make those little hidden places all the time.

He yanked out the drawer and set it on the floor. There was a crack at the back; the envelope he had been tugging had been stuck there. He pulled it free and pondered a way to find a hidden compartment. He opened the doors flanking the kneehole opening and peered inside with his flashlight. At the back of one of them was a removable panel, held with four brass screws.

Beyond the window he saw the first pale light of dawn. His heart pounding, he used a small screwdriver he kept in his pocket to remove the screws and lift out the panel. But there was no hidden compartment: the panel was simply an access for repairing the desk. One envelope lay at the bottom of the narrow opening, nothing else. Goddam it, I wasted all this time, he thought, and was about to put back the panel when he saw the name written on the envelope. *Laura Fairchild.*

He snatched it up. It was thick, a long document of some kind, and Laura's name was written in a bold, sloping handwriting he recognized as Owen's. This must be Owen's desk after all, he thought—*and this is the letter he wrote her, the one she couldn't find.* It must have slipped through the crack in the drawer. And it's been hidden since he died.

The room was growing brighter, and Clay's heart was pounding in his ears. He hated the daylight. He was taking too long. He tucked the letter into the inside pocket of his jacket, replaced the four brass screws, returned the papers and envelopes and the eelskin wallet to the drawer, and slid it into place. He made a quick survey of the room. Everything neat; everything in order. Carrying his artist's case, he sped down the stairs to the entrance, carefully reset the alarm, and slipped through the front door, locking it behind him.

A car passed; he flattened himself against the door until it was out of sight. He checked the street to right and left, then strode the long block to Lexington, past still-sleeping houses. At the corner, a taxi was approaching. He casually hailed it and was driven away.

* * *

When the family left for the summer compound at the Cape at the beginning of July, Leni agreed to come, too. Felix had insisted, angry with her and alarmed, and Allison had made wistful comments about how little any of them saw her now that she spent most of her time in New York. And so she agreed. She knew she had to talk to Felix sometime; she had been avoiding him ever since her talk with Ben at the Plaza six months earlier.

Six months of seeing as little of him as possible, after more than a year of refusing to share his bedroom. It had been a long time since she bothered with excuses; she simply told him she wasn't interested. She wondered how long he would contain whatever rage he felt. He was consumed with the company. There were problems with the board, especially pressures on him to sell some of the hotels to increase their working capital; they'd been overextended for some time. More important, he had been forced to contain his fury at Ben since Judd's birth— his certainty that Ben had tricked him and would destroy him if he did not destroy Ben first—while, at the same time, the two of them worked together every day, with as few words as possible, on the building of two new Salinger hotels.

Of course, Felix told Leni none of this; she learned it from Ben and Thomas. Felix told her almost nothing; she told him even less. And if he could see a difference in her since she had begun spending as much time in Wes Currier's apartment as at her own Manhattan town house, he did not say so. She doubted he saw it: it had been a long time since he really saw her. Leni thought he probably still thought of her as she was when he took her away from Judd.

"I'd forgotten how beautiful it is here," she said to Allison at breakfast. It was the weekend of the Fourth of July, and the upper Cape was so crowded that the residents of Osterville stayed home, entertaining each other. Wearing shorts and polo shirts, Allison and Leni had brought coffee and croissants to the lawn outside the big kitchen of Leni's house, and they sat there, watching Judd take his first tottering steps, between a wrought-iron bench and Allison's lap. "I've missed the Cape and didn't know I was missing it."

"You've been very busy in New York."

Leni sighed. "A sarcastic daughter makes a mother feel like a failure."

Allison laughed. "You don't at all; you think I've turned out very well. I'm sorry I was sarcastic, it's just that I've missed you. Have you been loving New York or wanting to stay out of Boston?"

"Both."

Allison looked at her keenly. "You're having a good time."

"Yes. I did in Paris, too. I didn't tell you very much about Paris."

"You told us all about it. What did you leave out?"

"What Laura and I talked about."

Instinctively, Allison looked behind her, to the kitchen where Laura had worked, memories flooding her, mixing love and loss and anger. She turned back and then Judd was there, crowing in triumph as he fell into her arms. She caught him and kissed him, nuzzling his soft cheek and neck before setting him on his feet again. She picked up her mug of coffee. "You said you talked about her hotels and you told her you thought we might have been too hasty. You said she's very beautiful and still angry at us."

"And she challenged me to stay in one of her hotels and see what it was like. And I accepted."

Allison stared at her. "Why didn't you tell me? Are you going to? Maybe I'll come with you."

"I already have. I stayed there a couple of months ago. And I didn't tell you, because I didn't want it to look like an invasion of the Salingers; I wanted to go alone."

"And what did you find?" Ben asked. They looked up sharply, shading their eyes against the sun.

"My light-footed husband," Allison said gaily. "We didn't hear you."

"Tennis shoes," he said, leaning down to kiss her, then kissing Leni's cheek. "I had an early game with Thomas. I'm leaving for the city as soon as I dress, but first I want to hear the end of Leni's story."

"Did you hear she stayed in one of Laura's hotels?"

"Yes. Which one?"

"New York," Leni replied. "Ben, it's an extraordinary place."

"Tell me." He sat down and poured coffee from the thermos Allison had beside her, then held out his hand as Judd came up to them. "By God, look at this! Next he'll be jogging around the yard." He held Judd to him, resting his cheek on his son's soft blond hair. "How's my boy?" he asked softly. "Good on his feet, I see. That's what you'll need all your life, Judd, to be quick on your feet. Remember that." He set him to walking again, then turned to Leni. "Tell me," he repeated.

She described the rooms, the services, the personal attention. She had given a dinner party one night, for ten—Currier had been there, but she did not mention him—and she had made various requests for services over the three days that had been unfailingly satisfied. "Either they have better training than any other hotel I've ever stayed in or the whole staff has been hypnotized. But it's more than the staff; it's the atmosphere—though I suppose the staff plays the biggest part in that, too."

Ben nodded. He felt proud of Laura, and envious. Leni had never raved about any of the Salinger hotels she had stayed in, even after he'd started working for the company and, he thought, improving them. It occurred to him that this was the perfect time to tell them the truth about him and Laura: while they were admiring her and Leni was re-membering talking to her in Paris.

"I wish she could work for us," Leni was saying. "With us, I mean; how foolish to think she'd ever work for us again. Or for anyone. I wrote to her after I left, thanking her and telling her what a lovely time it had been, and I suggested that we might think about working together some day, but she never answered. I'm sure she still hates us, and of course we still don't know what to think of her, do we? Felix won't even let anyone mention her name. I find it all very confusing, even after all these years. Such a pity that it's so hard to forget the past . . ."

Ben stood. This was not the time for the truth. He wasn't sure the time ever would come. He'd waited too long; now he would have to explain his silence as well as everything else. "I'm going to shower," he said, reaching down and scooping up his son. "I'll see you soon, young man. Take care of your mother; she's very special. I love you." He leaned down once again to Allison. "And I love you." He sat Judd in Allison's lap and crossed the terrace to the house.

Leni and Allison looked at each other. "Protect it," Leni said softly. "What you and Ben have is so wonderful . . . I wish I had better advice to give you, but I haven't. Just, understand how wonderful it is so you can protect it and keep it strong."

"I wish you had something like it," Allison said boldly. She had never asked her mother about her marriage.

"So do I." The sun was hot and the air barely stirred; Leni looked through the trees at the ocean, an expanse of deep blue speckled with white sails and small, colorful windsurfers. She felt relaxed and comfortable, less like a mother, more like a friend. Perhaps it was because she and Allison were both mothers now, perhaps because Allison was more sure of herself than before, and more serene: happy enough to enjoy a friend she had known all her life. Whatever it was, Leni found herself able to talk to Allison without the fear she had had in the past that, if her daughter knew she was unhappy, she might be scarred for life and never able to make a happy marriage of her own. "I married for the wrong reasons," she said. "And stayed married for the wrong reasons: because it was the thing to do, because I couldn't think of good alternatives, because I was afraid. And then Felix wanted it so much."

"Wanted what?"

"Marriage. Marriage to me."

"Not just . . . you? He didn't want you for yourself?"

Leni smiled faintly. "I doubt that he would understand the question. He wanted me because I stood for something, some idea of style he thought was essential. He wanted me because it was important to him to have possessions that other men admired, and I was frequently admired. He wanted me because I was in love with someone he despised and, I think, in an odd way, feared."

"Were you? You never told me any of this. Who was it?"

"Oh, it was so long ago. We all love when we're young and then marry others. Allison, would it bother you if I divorced Felix?"

"It doesn't seem that it would make much difference, does it? You've really left him already; you're hardly ever with him. You haven't talked to him about it?"

"No. I keep putting it off. I just don't want to have anything to do with him, even getting a divorce. I want to *be* divorced but not go through the process, and I can almost pretend, as long as I'm not with him . . . Well, that's shameful, I know; I'm not proud of it, but besides having to deal with it, there are his rages. . . ."

"But you've lived with him so long. How come all of a sudden you don't want to have anything to do with him? He hasn't changed, has he? He seems the same to me, more wrapped up in business maybe, but that's about all."

Leni struggled with the words that were waiting to be said. But she couldn't say them. There was no reason for Allison ever to know about Judd and what Felix had done to him. "Maybe I feel I finally know him in a way I never did before. Or maybe I'm angry at myself for letting so many years go by without doing anything. You know, my dear—" Judd lurched to her this time, and she held him in her arms, close, warm, smelling of fresh grass and summer. Feeling his silken skin beneath her lips, she wanted to weep for what was lost.

"What?" Allison asked.

Leni set Judd on the grass again, but he shook his head; he was through walking. He sat in front of her and picked up a wooden toy, solemnly trying to chew it to bits. "Something happens in a marriage," she said slowly. "Not to everyone, of course, but to so many women . . . after a while they start to look beyond their marriage, or around it, for whatever happiness they can make. It's as if their marriage becomes a fact of life, like nearsightedness or deafness, that has to be endured and adapted to. It's not crippling, but it prevents some things from ever happening. And they accept that. They know what they have isn't the best—it may not even be very good—but it's become part of them; they've gotten used to skirting it and looking past it, and they've never been taught to think of a life that doesn't include marriage. And the years go by. That's not something to be proud of, but it explains a lot of my generation. I think it's less true of yours."

"But what would change that?" Allison asked softly, feeling closer to her mother than she ever had before.

"Sometimes nothing. But sometimes some kind of spark starts a conflagration, and then marriage—*this* marriage, this fact of life—becomes intolerable."

"And she leaves."

"Usually."

"But if there's been a spark, or if something's been building between the two of you, then he must know, don't you think? Do you . . . when you're together . . . do you—"

"Sleep together? No. I can't. Of course he knows something is terribly wrong, worse than it's ever been between us, but I think he's avoiding it, too. To keep it from being final."

"Poor Daddy," Allison mused, and Leni winced, feeling the first stab of jealousy that parents feel when a child shows love or sympathy for the one they're divorcing. "I think he tried, don't you? He just never knew how to love us the way we wanted to be loved."

"Probably." They sat in silence, watching Judd, breathing the fresh sea-scented air so rich it was like wine after the acrid air of Boston and New York.

"Leni," Ben said from the doorway. The two women turned. His voice was tight, and he was very pale.

"What is it?" Allison cried. "What's wrong?"

"The police just called. Your house was robbed last night. They—"

"No!" Allison exclaimed. "I don't believe it!"

"Oh, God." Leni closed her eyes. "I hate this. I hate it, I hate it. . . ." She looked at Ben. "Do they know what was taken?"

"The Rouaults in the library. They want you to check and see if anything else is missing. Thank God you weren't there; that's the main thing. It doesn't matter what was taken, but you might have been hurt."

Leni frowned. "Whoever they are, they know something about art: those were the most valuable things in the house. But how did they get in? What about the alarm?"

"No one knows. The housekeeper was the one who called the police; the alarm was set when she arrived this morning, and they checked it and found it working."

"Impossible," Leni said. "Anyone going near the stairs would have set it off."

"I know. Are you going to New York?"

"It seems I have to." She stood, looking ruefully at Allison. "We've been through this before, haven't we?"

"It's not fair," Allison exclaimed. "Thieves ought to keep records and pass them around so they all know who's been robbed and they can pick somebody new after that. It's so awful!" she burst out, looking at Judd, thinking of him asleep and vulnerable. "Breaking into someone's home—"

"How did they break in?" Leni asked Ben.

"The police don't think they did. There's no sign of it."

"You mean they had a key?"

"Something like it."

"I don't believe it. None of us has ever lost one." She sighed. "Allison, I'm so sorry; we were having such a lovely talk. I'll try to be back tomorrow."

But it was a week before Leni was back at the Cape. She went through the rooms of her house and dozens of drawers and closets; she watched the police dust for fingerprints and look in the garden for footprints; she called a stop to their questioning of her housekeeper before she became hysterical, and then questioned her herself, more gently, and, she thought, equally thoroughly, and had no reason to suspect her. And when it was all done, she found nothing missing but the three Rouaults. Owen's old desk looked as if it had been searched, but it didn't seem that anything had been taken; her wallet and the money inside were still there. And the safe looked untouched; of course, there was nothing in it, but still it was good to know it had not been forced open.

Nothing had been forced. The house looked serene and protected. Still, Leni talked to her neighbors, and jointly they hired a watchman to patrol the stretch of houses along that side of the street, from eight at night to six the next morning. Currier was in Europe, and she called him to tell him what had happened and what she was doing.

"Locking the barn door," she said wryly. "But I do feel better having a watchman here."

"So do I. Did the agency give you his references?"

"Yes, he seems fine."

"If you need help checking them, call my assistant. He can do the telephoning for you. And make sure the agency notifies the police; sometimes they don't get around to it for a week or two. And of course the neighbors across the street should be told."

"Yes, they should. Thank you. I hadn't thought of that." She smiled. He almost always found a way to make himself central to the things she did and then dominate them by making decisions or suggestions she couldn't ignore. But she didn't resent it; in fact, she was beginning to count on it. For more than half her life she had been accustomed to a man who didn't care what she did or what she thought, as long as she was available when he wanted her. What a novelty, she thought, as she had thought once before about Currier, to find a man who wants to take care of me. At my age, I deserve it.

She wondered if at some point she might find him overbearing. Possibly, she thought. But after more than twenty-eight years with Felix, it could be a long time before I feel that way about Wes.

They saw each other that summer in a house he had rented in Maine, but most of the time Leni was at the Cape. It was made easier for her by

Felix's spending the summer in Boston, except for a few weekends, and those were the ones Leni spent with Currier. Wherever they were, the New York police kept in touch with them, but only to say they had no leads. Felix was bitter. "Someone has it in for us; nobody gets robbed twice."

"The other one was ten years ago, Daddy," Allison said. "If it's the same person, he's awfully patient."

"Or she is."

Allison spun on him. "We don't know *anything*," she said vehemently. "It's just a coincidence and we all hate it, but there isn't anything we can do except hire a watchman, and Mother's already done that."

Felix did more: he had all the locks changed and spotlights installed at the front and back of the house. However, the neighbors objected to the blinding lights, so they were removed. In the end, the new locks and a private watchman had to satisfy him, and soon the robbery faded into the background. No one had been hurt, as Owen had been in the first robbery, and the paintings were insured. Besides, an insurance investigator had called to tell them he was working on the case and would be coming to the Cape to interview them; perhaps the paintings would be recovered. Although, as Leni said, none of her jewelry, except one bracelet, had ever been found; her necklace, the piece she had most loved and longed to have back, had not turned up even though she had advertised a reward for its return. They couldn't count on anything being found, ever.

"That's correct," Sam Colby said when he talked to them a week later. They were sitting on the broad veranda of Leni's house and Colby sat back, stretching out his legs, admiring the view. "You can't count on anything. A lot of these thefts are commissioned by—"

"Commissioned!" Ben exclaimed.

"Right. By private collectors who know where the art is. They go to auctions, they have friends in art galleries who tip them off when a major painting is sold, and so on, and they hire thieves to steal what they want. Sometimes they use a broker to find the thieves; it keeps them one step removed from the theft. Whichever, the art ends up in private collections all over the world, and it's never seen again, except by a few friends of the collector. And nobody talks. Why should they? Maybe someday they'll want some art that somebody else owns, and they're not about to make it harder for themselves by blowing the whistle on a friend who's done it."

"I've heard of that," Allison said. "Some of our customers in the gallery know people who've had paintings stolen, and they never show up at auctions or estate sales so everyone assumes they're locked up in someone's home."

"Exactly." Colby beamed. "Well, now, Mrs. Salinger, these Rouaults that were taken from your home, let's talk about them. Where did you buy them?"

He led Leni through a history of the paintings, the security system in the town house, the testimony of the housekeeper, and then her own schedule. "How often are you there?"

"Quite a bit. Less this summer, of course, but usually I spend several days a week there."

"But your home is in Boston?"

"Beverly—it's a suburb of Boston," she corrected him gently. "But actually I have two homes. I'm on a number of boards in New York— hospitals and museums and so on—and I enjoy the theater and the concerts, so it's convenient for me to be there."

"So you have a schedule that other people would know?"

"Some of the time. I often make up my mind at the last minute. Sometimes I travel from New York without coming back to Boston, or I travel from Boston; it varies."

"Trips to other countries?"

"Sometimes."

"And you stay with friends or in hotels?"

"Both."

"You stay in your family hotels when you travel?"

"Always."

"Except once," Allison murmured.

"Well, yes," Leni said. "Once I stayed in a Beacon Hill hotel. But that was unusual."

"Why did you stay in a Beacon Hill hotel?"

"To find out what it was like. It's new; we're always looking for new ideas for our hotels."

"And where was that?"

"In New York."

Colby nodded. "Now then, your board meetings. Your trips may be on the spur of the moment, but your meetings are regular, is that right? Second Tuesday of every month; that sort of thing?"

"Yes, except for special ones."

"And you have a calendar where you write them down? Hanging on the refrigerator in the kitchen? Or in the hall next to the phone?"

Leni smiled. "I'm afraid I'm not in the kitchen often enough to keep a calendar there. I have a desk calendar in Boston and one in New York."

"Nothing else?"

"No. Well, of course, my own date book."

"Date book. All your meetings and luncheons and so on?"

"Yes."

"Anything else?"

"No."

"Not, for example, the code for the alarm in your house?"

"Oh. Yes, I think it is. I don't know why I write it down every year when I get a new book—I know it by heart—but I do."

"Most people do; you'd be surprised. Anything else? Money machine code?"

"I'm afraid I keep that, too, but it's in my checkbook."

"So there's nothing else in your date book."

"No. Yes. The combination for the wall safe in the study. But none of this helps, you know; the date book and my checkbook are always in my purse."

"And always with you?"

"Always."

"Even when you change purses?"

"Of course."

"You change outfits; you take everything out of one purse—lipstick, comb, mirror, wallet, keys, date book, everything—and transfer them to a purse that matches the new outfit?"

"Exactly."

"But when you go out at night, you only take a small purse? No room for keys and date book and so on?"

"Yes."

"So everybody on the staff of your Boston house and your New York house has access to the date book. Not to mention your keys."

"I have absolute confidence in my staff."

"I understand. But someone knew you wouldn't be in your town house at four-thirty in the morning of July second."

"What's that?" Ben asked. "How do you know the time? No one's mentioned it."

"A neighbor saw somebody at the door at four-thirty. She was getting ready to go running as soon as it got light, and she saw him."

"Him," Ben repeated. "Everyone's always said 'they.'"

"Well, there might have been more than one. The neighbor only saw one man. He could have had accomplices waiting somewhere."

The questioning went on: around and around Colby went, and the longer he pursued every angle, the more uncomfortable Allison became. They'd been through this and it was hateful—all this suspicion—and she didn't want to have anything to do with it. When Colby began to ask about repairmen who came to the New York and Beverly houses, caterers Leni used regularly, friends who visited frequently, she excused herself and went to see if the nanny had gotten Judd up from his nap. She didn't believe anybody on the staff was involved; nobody they knew was involved. We should just leave it alone, she thought, walking upstairs to the nursery. We have so many more important things to think about. As soon as Colby leaves, we'll put it behind us, we'll forget it. We'll just leave it alone.

*　*　*

The fourth Beacon Hill hotel opened in early October, in Washington, D.C., when the city had awakened to the fall. Laura and Currier were both there, greeting regular guests and new ones who had heard of the Beacon Hill and booked months in advance when they knew it would be open when Congress was back in session. It was the smoothest opening of the four; Laura knew most of the pitfalls, and Kelly had worked harder than anyone to avoid them—"so you'll keep me around," she told Laura as they had a drink together at the end of the day. "I didn't know how much I wanted to get off that island until I got off that island. Or maybe it was getting away from John and not having to feel guilty about liking hard work." She raised her glass. "Thanks. I'm having the time of my life."

Laura touched her glass to Kelly's. "You've done a wonderful job; I can't find anything to worry about."

"You will when we talk about some of the cost overruns. But we're booked solid until Thanksgiving, so maybe we shouldn't be worrying about money."

"I always worry about money. I didn't hear about overruns."

"None of them was big enough to call you about, and they all piled up in the last three weeks when we were pushing to get open on time. We'll go over the books tomorrow morning; I don't think you'll find anything too surprising."

"I'm never surprised when things cost more than I thought they would," Laura said dryly. "Let's do the books day after tomorrow. We'll have enough tomorrow with the benefit."

The gala that officially opened the Washington Beacon Hill was a benefit for the symphony orchestra, held the first weekend the hotel was open. Five hundred people in politics, business, and the arts dined and danced in the penthouse ballroom, launching the city's social season and bringing the hotel a year's worth of publicity in one evening. Laura took time out to dance the first dance with Currier. "You're looking especially lovely," he said. "I've always liked you best in white."

She smiled. "Thank you." She wore a white organza blouse with a demure collar, and an amber taffeta skirt that swirled behind her as they waltzed. "And you look sleek and satisfied," she said. "A new business triumph? Or a new woman?"

"Would you mind if it were a new woman?"

She was silent as they made a full turn about the floor. "A little, because I'd be a little envious. But that's all. I'm happy for you, Wes; I hope she's very good to you. Do I know her?"

"Yes, but I'd rather not tell you who it is until I know what will come of it. She's married, for one thing, though it hasn't been much of a marriage for a long time." He held her closer for a moment. "You're a lovely lady, my dear."

Laura flushed and kissed his cheek. "What a nice thing for a partner to say."

They finished the dance in silence. "Speaking of partners," Currier said as they left the dance floor, "I'd like to go over the books here before I leave. Is tomorrow morning all right for you?"

"Fine. I've already talked to Kelly about it. I'll be in her office at ten." She stopped. "Wes, Britt Farley just came in."

"Where?" He followed her look. "I'll be damned. I'll go talk to him; we may have to ask him to leave if he's going to make trouble."

"He doesn't look as if he would. He looks different. Better than I've ever seen him. I'll talk to him. Will you dance with Senator Brook-stone's wife? She's sitting by herself, and she doesn't look happy about it."

"Then I'll try to make her happy. Thank you for the dance."

"It was lovely, Wes."

She skirted the dance floor and reached Farley at his table as he was ordering from a waiter. "Two vodkas with tonic, easy on the vodka, and one white wine for the lady." He saw Laura and his face brightened. "I was watching you dance. You look gorgeous. Laura, this is my good friend Laura. Took me a while to realize that was my favorite name for a lady."

Laura and the young girl shook hands. "Sit with us," Farley said. "I know you're busy, but sit for five minutes."

She took the chair he held for her. "I looked for you after Paul's film. Where did you go?"

"Back to the hotel and cried like a baby. Blubbered and threw up and thought about killing myself. You believe that?"

"Yes."

"I knew you would. Louie says I'm exaggerating. But, shit, he wasn't there. What the hell, you saw that movie: my handsome self fifteen feet high, looking like some fucking god, and then my rotten self at the end, a lousy wreck... Paul's good, you know; he's a goddam genius. He did something that made me look even better in the beginning—you know? I mean, I'm not the smartest guy in the world, but I think he did something with the lighting or contrast or something and made me look sensational. And that made me look even worse at the end. And all I could think was I'd been shitting on myself for years, and I'll tell you, that did something to me. Paul did that: showed me things nobody else did. Jesus, Laura, why didn't anybody tell me I looked like that?"

"You had a mirror."

"I didn't look. Or I didn't see what was there. That's what my shrink says. He says I saw my idealized image wherever I went. Do you know what that means?"

"I think so. You aren't on anything now?"

"Vodka and tonic," he said as the drinks were placed before him. "Two a day, max. And my shrink, once a day, five days a week. Workouts on Nautilus every morning. Tennis lessons every afternoon. Talking to Louie once or twice a day to convince him I'm ready for work, even though he says he can't sell me yet. Playing with Laura—my new Laura—at night. And these guys, a support group. A bunch of weirdos like myself trying to clean up their act. I call them whenever I need to talk to somebody. Does it sound dull?"

"It sounds like hard work."

"That's it; I knew you'd get it. It's a goddam tough job, and I hate it. But every time I think it's not worth it, I look at that fucking film. Paul gave me a videotape. It's my bedtime story, to scare me into being a good boy."

Laura put her hand on his. "You really are scared."

"Scared to death, sweetheart. Because what if I can't do it? I don't want to die, you know... shit, why am I talking like this at your party? Hey, dance with me." He turned to the young girl. "Laura, you don't mind, do you? She's an old friend."

The girl shook her head, and Farley led Laura to the dance floor. They made a striking couple, and others turned to watch. "Don't feel sorry for me," he said. "Everybody's scared of something. My shrink told me that. We're all scared and running from something or other—the past, the present, the future, whatever—and I'm just the same. It's just that I'm scared of never *not* being scared. What do you think? You think I'll make it?"

"I think you have a good chance," she said softly. "Some things stay with us and you'll have to keep on fighting, but it gets easier after a while."

"I'm in love with you, did you know that?" he asked.

"Yes." She smiled gently. "But you've got your Laura, Britt, and it looks to me like she's crazy about you, and I think you could love her if you let yourself."

"Christ, you sound like my shrink. I could do this or that if I let myself. Why do I stop myself? Tell me that. If I know something is good for me, why don't I just go ahead and do the goddam thing, whatever it is?"

She shook her head. "I don't know."

Why can't I forget Paul and my anger at the Salingers and this feeling that I have to get more from them? I know it would be good for me to forget, so why can't I do it?

The dance was over. "I'm supposed to be working, helping Kelly run everything. Call me, Britt; let me know how you are."

"Say a prayer for me," he said mockingly.

"I will." She kissed his cheek and left him at his table with his Laura and his two drinks, max, and the private war he was waging with himself.

Couples stopped her as she crossed the dance floor; she was invited to balls and dinner parties in Chicago and Philadelphia and New York. "After all, you do have hotels there; you must be there a lot." "I am, but I'm never sure when," she replied. "I'll call you; we'll be in touch; thanks so much..." Sometimes the world seemed glued together by parties, she thought. If they all stopped, would everyone fly off into space and disappear? Or sink into lonely little wells because they had nothing to do that night?

She was smiling to herself as she came upon Clay, dancing with Myrna. "My goodness," she blurted, then apologized. "I'm sorry, you took me by surprise. Clay, I thought you were in New York. And I didn't know you and Myrna were together."

"We're deciding that now," Myrna said. "Clay says he wants it."

"It?" Laura asked.

"Myrna wants it," Clay said. "I just want her to move to New York and live in my loft and see how we like it."

"We lived together in Chicago and liked it fine," Myrna said.

He shrugged. "I just want to try it for a while. Things are kind of getting out of hand, and I thought it might be nice to have you back."

"What does that mean?" Laura asked. "Out of hand."

"There's a lot going on," he said, gesturing. "Like the job. It's bigger than I expected—more responsibility, more money riding on my decisions. That's not easy to live with. And I thought it might be a good idea to relax a little bit. Not cut out the excitement—you know me, Laura, I have to have action or I go crazy—but kind of balance it with something a little more—"

"Quiet," Myrna said. "And stable. Men need that," she told Laura. "Without us they just go off in all directions. I love Clay and I want to take care of him, and if you don't mind—"

"Hey, you don't have to ask Laura's permission to woo me!" Clay said with a short laugh. "She's not my guardian. Beloved sister and employer, but not guardian."

He was acting very oddly, Laura thought. Just having been with Farley, she wondered if he was on drugs. But he didn't seem to be; he seemed mostly the way he always was: sweet and charming, with more energy than he could contain, too many plans at once, a dependence on women. It occurred to her that he was only a little younger than Paul had been when they had been planning their wedding. But Paul had been a man, and Clay was still a boy, afraid of being forced to grow up, probably afraid of marriage. But he'd called Myrna, and he knew she wanted marriage. *Getting out of hand.* His gambling, she thought. Well, he'll have to get over it, the same as Britt with his drugs. And if Myrna can help him, good for her.

"Whatever you two decide is fine with me," she said. "If there's anything I can do, let me know. Just answer one question, Clay. How come you're here? I thought it was Philadelphia this week and Washington the week after."

"It was. But I promised Myrna she could come to the party, and we drove over from Philly. I'm not missing much work; we'll be back there before noon tomorrow. Hey, Laura, don't frown at me; I can't stand it when you do. What's so terrible about coming to a party if you're practically in the neighborhood?"

Laura hesitated. "Nothing; it's all right. I guess I just like to know where you are. Have a good time. Call me in the morning before you leave, will you? I'll be in Kelly's office."

"Sure thing."

"Thanks, Laura," Myrna said.

Laura wasn't sure what she was being thanked for, but Ginny was waving to her from the bar at the end of the room, so she nodded, kissed Clay, and left them. When she turned to look back, they were dancing again, so slowly and sinuously it was almost as if they were making love.

Ginny was in slinky black covered in paillettes that reflected every beam of light. "What do you think?" she asked Laura. "Do I look like a sex symbol or the wicked witch of the night?"

"Sex wins," Laura laughed. "Have you been here long?"

"Long enough to see you dancing with Britt. The word is that you'll marry him."

Laura sighed. "I wish 'the word' was that the Beacon Hill is the best hotel in Washington. Or that all the Beacon Hills are the best, wherever they are. Or even that Laura Fairchild is the best hotel executive in America. Why does the word always have to be about somebody sleeping with somebody, or marrying somebody, or not sleeping or not getting married?"

"People like sex better than business, you know that. They like business, too, especially if it's ruthless, but sex comes first. The best combination was you and Wes. Sleeping together, working together, making money together."

"We weren't ruthless."

"Well, three out of four isn't bad." They laughed, and Ginny said, "Can we have a drink together? I want to talk to you about something."

"Sex or business?"

"Business."

"Then I'd love it."

They sat on high-backed stools at the Victorian bar that Laura had rescued from a mansion being torn down at the time the Beacon Hill was being renovated. "Two Armagnacs," Ginny said to the bartender, then bent close to Laura to be heard beneath the orchestra and the high pitch of conversation without raising her voice. "A party isn't your usual place to talk business, but once I make up my mind about doing something nice, I have to spit it out or I feel like I'll choke to death on it. So listen. Whatever the word is for anybody else, for me it's that this hotel is sensational. And you're absolutely right: every Beacon Hill is the best. No hotel can ever be the same as home—you know that, I know that— but you've come closer than anybody I know. You are an impressive lady and I love you."

She paused to wave to Daniel Inouti, who was waving to her from across the room. "He's building two hotels for the Salingers; I think he's here as a spy."

"He was invited," Laura said with a laugh. "And why would he be spying? Everything I've done has been written about in hotel magazines. Anyway, Felix doesn't like small hotels; he likes them big and anonymous, with small rooms and high prices. Sort of like a one-night stand."

Ginny's eyes gleamed. "I like that. And you don't like him."

"That's hardly a secret."

"But you want to buy into his company."

"You know why; I've told you that story."

"So you have." Their drinks arrived, and she sipped at hers. "Good. You always stock your bars with the best."

"Ginny, you're being coy. What did you want to talk about?"

"You. And the Salingers. Do you still want to buy shares in that company?"

"Of course. But I haven't found a way to get the money, and I don't know if any of them would be willing to sell even if I did have it."

"That's what I want to talk about. You've never asked me to invest in OWL Development; you've never asked for a loan. I like that: friendship and business don't mix. Usually. However, I have now seen you open four hotels, and I've watched them take off. What's your occupancy rate?"

"Overall? Between seventy-five and eighty-eight percent."

"Unheard of in the industry. Right?"

Laura nodded. She was tense with excitement because she knew now what Ginny was going to say.

"Right," Ginny repeated. "So you're good. We all know that. So I want to be in this with you. I've talked to my accountants and so on, and I'm planning on loaning you the money to buy into Salinger Hotels."

Laura put her arm around Ginny and lay her cheek against hers. They sat that way for a moment, without saying anything, without needing to say anything. Then she straightened. "So many people have helped me," she said quietly; Ginny had to strain to hear her words. "I've been so lucky to find so many wonderful people . . ."

"It's not luck," Ginny said flatly. "Don't you know how much you give to people? You listen to their problems, you don't judge them, you invite them to your parties, whoever they are, you don't talk about yourself as much as you pay attention to them. Remember Chicago? I thought you were a fool to sit with Britt at brunch the day after he barked up that damned ruckus, but I was wrong; now he's your friend for life. Not that he can do much for you—"

"I didn't do it so he'd do something for me."

"That's the point! You do those things because you care about people. I know, I know, you do care; you've had your own bad times. But not everybody who has them remembers them. Well, anyway"—she sat back and drank her sherry—"you shouldn't be surprised that people do things for you. However, I am loaning you money because you are a terrific businesswoman and a good bet. I have been known to get sentimental, but not—at least I sincerely hope not—when I'm handing over ten million dollars."

Stunned, Laura stared at her. The talk and laughter in the room and the pulsing beat of the orchestra seemed to swell, washing over her. "How much?"

"Ten million. Give or take a few."

"How do you know? You mean someone *is* selling shares?"

Ginny nodded. "A friend of a friend. They're in some trouble over there—Felix expanded too fast, and they've got some hard work ahead to get back to as solid as they'd like, and one of the board members wants to bail out while the price is good. He owns two percent of the company; ten million dollars' worth, which is what I'm offering you so you can buy in. We'll talk about interest and other terms tomorrow; I can promise they'll be very favorable. If this sounds agreeable to you."

Of my thirty percent holdings in Salinger Hotels Incorporated, I leave twenty-eight percent, divided equally, to my sons Felix and Asa Salinger. And to my most beloved Laura Fairchild, who has brought joy and love to the last years of my life, I leave the remaining two percent of my shares...

Two percent.

Owen, we've done it.

Laura took Ginny's hand between hers and once again leaned forward to kiss her cheek. "Dearest Ginny," she said. "It sounds wonderfully agreeable."

CHAPTER 28

THE sixth theft was of four Matisse line drawings from the Hawaiian estate of Daniel Inouti, stolen while he was in London for an Easter gathering of his far-flung family. Nothing else was taken, no clues were left, and the caretakers in their adjoining apartment slept through the night undisturbed.

Sam Colby was in a rage. Six! Six different locations on two continents, with no clues, except they all had the same pattern. What the hell did he have to hang an investigation on? He took it as a personal insult, and as soon as he could arrange it, he flew to Hawaii to talk to Inouti, who arrived from London the same day.

"Tell me everything!" he said to Inouti.

"About what?" Inouti asked.

"Everything, damn it! How do I know what's going to be useful until I hear it?" They sat on a veranda overlooking the ocean. Around them were brilliant displays of orchids and hibiscus; above, the sky was cloudless and birds soared. Colby noticed none of it. He might as well have been in a windowless office. "Start with the staff; at least half the time they're the guilty ones. How many houses do you own?"

"Four."

Colby sighed and launched into his questions. From there they turned to Inouti's four offices and the staffs in each, his close business associates, the sixty-four members of his family, and the people with whom he socialized. "Okay, now your travel schedule."

"Almost no one knows that but my secretary."

"But people can call her and find out where you are."

"Of course. It would be impossible to do business if I couldn't be reached. I have no reason to hide myself."

"Right. So I want to know where you've been in the past year."

"Why is that?"

"Because there's a thief who knew when you'd be away from Hawaii, and I don't want him or them to be the only ones with information around here. Okay?"

Inouti reached into his pocket and brought out a thick leather-covered appointment book. "I can read to you everywhere I have been."

"Fine." As Inouti read, Colby wrote, and for the first time noticed that the sun was almost down. Someone once told him he should be sure to see a Hawaiian sunset if he ever had a chance. Well, I blew it, he thought. Maybe tomorrow. "Can we turn on a light?" he asked.

Inouti pulled a bell cord, and a servant appeared and lit an overhead light and then a row of oil-filled lamps along the edge of the veranda. After an hour, they had gotten through only five months of Inouti's busy year, and at that point he invited Colby to have dinner with him. "I have no plans, and you must be hungry."

"I'd appreciate it," Colby replied.

The meal was lavish and the conversation good, and Colby let himself relax and enjoy it. But when it was over, and Inouti had finished his cigar, he pushed back his chair. "Back to work." He had to have a breakthrough. He had to solve these damn thefts or he'd go back to retirement and die of boredom.

They took their cognacs into the living room, and Colby opened his notebook. "We stopped with Madrid. Where were you after that?"

"In San Francisco with my married daughter for a month, then in Hong Kong with my son and his family. From there, in August, I went to Bangkok."

"And stayed where?"

"At the Bangkok Regency."

"And you had meetings there."

"Oh, yes, many."

"And after that?"

"To Amsterdam. And I stayed at the Amsterdam Salinger. And, yes, I had meetings in my suite, and I suppose most of the men there knew I was then going to New York."

"And in New York?"

"The Beacon Hill. And of course I had meetings there, too, and I am sure I mentioned I was then going to Washington, D.C. And in Washington—this was in October—I stayed at another Beacon Hill; it had just opened."

Colby was writing, trying to keep up with Inouti's rapid speech. But his hand suddenly stopped. "The Beacon Hill," he murmured.

"Yes. They are by far the most civilized hotels I know. Have you been to any of them?"

"Not yet. Let's go on: October to now."

"I was here until February, when I was in Geneva, at the Geneva Marquis, and then I went to Rome and stayed with friends until I went to London for Easter with my family. And that is a whole year of my life."

"Who'd you travel with?" Colby asked.

"Ah, Mr. Colby, that is private." Colby tried to insist, for the sake of a complete investigation, but he was not pushing as hard as he might have been. Because behind his businesslike frown and matter-of-fact voice, Sam Colby was churning with excitement. He had the breakthrough he'd been looking for. He'd bet his bottom dollar he'd found the thread that connected six different robberies in six different cities on two continents and the island of Hawaii.

* * *

He was wrong. When he returned to New York and reread his notes he realized only five of the six had something in common. Serrano didn't fit the pattern. So he had to talk to him again. This time Paul wanted to go along.

"No, no, no," Colby told him. "I've told you before, I'll tell you again, that's no way to run an interview. Who's gonna give me straight answers with a camera pointed at his head, grinding away?"

"They don't grind," Paul said patiently. "And Britt Farley talked straight; most of the time he forgot the cameraman was there. When he wanted him gone, we sent him away. Sam, I can't make a film about you if I can't film you at work."

"You've been doing that. In my office, talking to insurance people and forgery experts and investigators in Europe, going through apartments that were robbed—and we never would have gotten permission for that if you hadn't known a couple of the victims. Anyway, you've got all that on film. And a million hours of me talking about my life and how I work—"

"Only thirty or forty hours so far," Paul said. "And it's good, all of it, but it would be a lot better if there were some tension. What can make this film unique is an investigation in progress. Not a reenactment; audiences respond to the drama of the real thing. Sam, let me try it. If it doesn't work, I won't ask again; I'll find other ways to do it."

Colby wavered. He knew he was an expert interviewer, and the thought of preserving that on film for generations to come was irresistible. "Two conditions," he said. "You leave if Serrano wants you gone. And you don't tell a living soul what you hear in the interview. Not your wife, not your mother, not even your barber. I want your solemn promise."

"You have it. You can trust me, Sam; you know that."

"I think it. I never know anything until I have a stack of proof. Okay. Acapulco, tomorrow morning. The flight's at eight-thirty."

Carlos Serrano's apartment seemed to float above the bustling streets and crowded beaches of Acapulco: the walls were glass, and from a deep couch all Paul could see was the ocean merging with the cloudless sky of a clear April morning. Soaring gulls and white sails broke the blue vista beyond the windows; inside, the walls were a riot of color from oil paintings and shelves of ancient Peruvian pottery. One wall was conspicuously bare. "I keep it that way," Serrano said, "to remind me that I have been robbed once and therefore I must be more vigilant."

"Good," Colby nodded. "Well, now, I appreciate your seeing me again; you've been very patient, but I have a few more questions, and I'd like to review some of the answers you gave me before. I'm sorry if that inconveniences you."

"No, no. It is for my paintings, after all. Anything you wish."

Flipping through his notebook, Colby wrote the April date at the top of a fresh page. "I want to go over your schedule again for the year preceding the theft: the places you went, the people you saw, your houseguests here."

"You know the people I saw; we talked about them."

"I've already apologized for some repetition; I think it's necessary."

"In that case." Serrano opened a folder on a nearby table—"You see, inspector, I am prepared for you"—and took from it a stack of handwritten notes. "In fact, I remembered some things I had forgotten. You wish to start—when?"

"You were robbed a year ago last November. Start at the beginning of that year."

The cameraman already had filmed the huge room, the view, the art collection in the other twelve rooms of the apartment; now, standing discreetly in a far corner, he focused on Serrano. Paul made occasional notes on lighting, sound level, questions that showed Colby's expertise, and movements of his body and hands, even his head, that indicated he was especially interested in something. He was especially interested in meetings in hotels; Paul made a note to ask him about it later.

"And in Aspen, where did you stay?" Colby asked.

"I rented a home on Red Mountain, but that is not significant; I had no meetings there. Aspen was relaxation."

"For two months."

"The skiing in Aspen is very good. I also bought two paintings, at Joanne Lyon's excellent gallery, so there was a bit of business, too. But no meetings."

"All right; what about the summer?"

Serrano listed his travels for the summer: they were all with friends. "In September I was in Chicago to meet with cattle and feed brokers. That was—"

"You didn't mention Chicago last time we talked."

"That was one of the things I forgot. I stayed there at the Beacon Hill and had two meetings in a conference room in the hotel."

"How long were you there?"

"About five days."

"And then?"

Serrano went on talking, but Paul was studying Colby's face. It had changed somehow; he was no longer as interested as he had been. Something had given him what he wanted. Paul thought back. Aspen. Joanne Lyon's gallery. Friends' houses in Switzerland and Italy. Chicago. A meeting of cattle and feed brokers at the Beacon Hill.

"What was it?" he asked on the plane returning to New York.

Colby shook his head. "Can't tell you yet." And he opened his notebook, for once discouraging further conversation.

Because he had to think, he had to plan. He had to figure out how to weave a net with the beautiful fact that six robbery victims had one thing in common: they all had stayed at a Beacon Hill hotel within a few months of the time their houses were robbed.

*　*　*

It was almost summer before Ginny got her financing organized and completed the purchase of two percent of the shares of Salinger Hotels Incorporated. It was all done in her name. Later she would sell the shares to Laura for the money she was loaning her, but first she wanted everything in order. So she was the one who appeared at the June board eeting of the corporation to have her purchase approved. There was not even a debate; the Starrett name was known, and the vote was unanimous.

"Good to have you," Cole Hatton said. They had known each other casually for a long time.

"You'll be a strong addition to our board," Felix said formally. He had known Wylie Starrett years before, and Wylie always believed in big business getting bigger, so Felix assumed Ginny would be the same, since women got whatever business sense they had from their husbands, even if they later divorced them. Ginny would be his ally in his struggle to keep his empire intact, rather than selling off parts of it during brief periods of difficulty.

"It's only a few difficulties," he told Ginny when they had coffee after the meeting. "Hardly a crisis. Occupancy is down, but we all go through cycles in this business. Of course we'd like to have a larger cushion of cash, but that also goes through cycles. We're building two new hotels, after all, so costs are up, but that's nothing new, either."

"But I gather some of the board wants to sell off a few hotels," Ginny said, as if Hatton and the man who had sold her his shares had not told her all there was to know.

"A few of them," Felix said shortly, dismissing it. "It won't happen."

He changed the subject. There was no reason to tell her about his other difficulties: the sly bastard who'd wormed his way into the family; and Leni, in New York most of the time now, and barely civil to him when she was home: almost a stranger. She was as serene and coolly elegant as ever, but he felt he had hold of her by the thinnest of threads. Her sense of duty, her need for security, her admiration for him as a powerful businessman all seemed to have eroded; it was as if the two of them had no connection at all anymore.

But he did not press her, because he was afraid of breaking that thin thread. Even a stranger was better than no one, and she seemed willing to stay on as his wife. He could always find a woman when he needed one; that wasn't the issue. Sleeping with Leni was far less important than knowing she was his wife, and knowing the world knew.

"I've bought tickets to the Tanglewood Ball next month," he told her at dinner in June. They were in Allison's and Ben's Beacon Hill house, with Asa and Carol, and Thomas and Barbara Janssen; they never ate alone anymore. "We'll drive up that morning and see some of the country. I haven't had a day off in a long time."

"I don't think I'll be free," Leni said quietly. "And we've done it so many times . . . Allison, you and Ben should go; it's a lovely affair."

"Maybe we will," Allison said. "It will be good for Judd's sister or brother to get some culture right from the beginning."

"Allison!" Leni exclaimed, and Allison and Ben exchanged a smile the length of the table. "When did you find out?"

"This morning."

"When are you due? Oh, how wonderful for you both. And for Judd, though he probably won't think so at first. I'm so happy for you; isn't it lovely, so many good things happening..."

Felix said nothing, letting the others talk, covertly watching Ben with a seething rage. Judd Gardner's son, sitting in Owen's place, filling Owen's house with children, planning—Felix was sure of it—to take over the company and grab Owen's place there, too. The smug bastard, the conniving son of a bitch—he'd even made friends with Thomas Janssen and Cole Hatton—even Asa! And there was nothing Felix could do about it... nothing, nothing, nothing. At least not now. He hadn't given up; he never gave up when the stakes were high enough; he'd get rid of the fucking bastard. In spite of himself, even knowing how much control he would need in the next months with his board, getting rid of Ben Gardner was becoming the goal that pushed others aside.

He brooded about it even in the car going home. Asa drove, talking now and then to Carol, beside him, while Felix and Leni sat in the back seat, not touching.

"I want you at that ball in Tanglewood," he said when they stood at their front door in the warm night. "A number of people have asked about your absences; I can't ignore them, and I care what they think."

"And what do they think?" Leni asked.

"That we're separating. Some such nonsense."

"But we're never together, Felix. How can it be nonsense?"

"You're my wife. I've always given you great freedom because it suited you—"

"—and you."

"It suited both of us," he said.

"It suited you to ignore me until you needed me, because you don't want intimacy. You only want the form of things. It's so much easier than dealing with real people and real emotions."

"Bullshit. I knew what I wanted: I wanted you. You were the one who turned away, standoffish all your life, like your whole family."

Leni put her key in the door, but he put his hand over hers, stopping her. He felt her cringe from his touch, and then the rage that was just below the surface exploded. "You're not walking away from me! You'll do what I say! I ask damn little of you, but I want you at that affair in Tanglewood and you'll tell me, now, that you'll be there."

Panic swept through Leni. She could not bear his touch; she could not bear having him this close. But I'm married to him, she thought incoherently; as long as I am... why shouldn't he think...?

Why am I still here? I have a home in New York, and good friends there; I have Allison and her family, and Thomas and Barbara, and Wes...

But those were all known; they were part of her life. Everything else was unknown and frightening: divorce, being single, no longer being a wife. Losing a place and status that society recognized, losing the boundaries that kept life from being formless and open-ended.

I'm too old for that, she thought.

But other women do it; I'm not alone. Thousands, hundreds of thousands of them take the risks rather than live a half-life.... She remembered the wise words she had spoken to Allison about marriage that morning at the Cape. Why couldn't she use her own words to make a different kind of life for herself?

"I'm talking to you!" Felix raged through clenched teeth. Leni had not heard whatever he had said, but his hand was gripping her arm and they were standing very close in the white circle of the porch light, almost as if they were lovers.

"Let go of me, Felix. *Let go of me.*" Hearing herself say the words freed something inside her: she could talk, she could act, she could break out of her cowardice. "We started this way; let's not end the same way."

"What the hell are you talking about?"

"We started with you grabbing my arm and pulling me out of Judd's building. You even struck me. I don't want to end the same way." She jerked her arm from his and, caught by surprise, he let her go. Swiftly she unlocked the door and slipped into the house.

He followed her into the living room. A lamp had been left on, and its soft glow made the flowered chintz furniture homey and inviting: it was a room where there should have been love. Instead, they stood at opposite ends of it, like combatants, Felix standing ramrod straight, as he remembered Owen standing when he was being stern.

"No one said anything about ending," he said harshly. "We have a marriage as good as most people's—where the hell do you get these sentimental ideas that people are happy and loving? You'll stay where you are; you're better off than most. You've got your lover in New York—"

"What?"

"You've been seen together, more than once. But it doesn't matter. As long as you're discreet and live properly when you're here with me, we'll stay as we are. There's no reason to change; I *won't* change—"

"But I will." Her voice was low, and that was more ominous to Felix than if she had screamed at him. "I want a divorce, Felix. I've let this go on, and I shouldn't have. We don't have a marriage—we don't have any kind of marriage at all—and I can't imagine why you think so, why you tolerate whatever happens, even an unfaithful wife. Let it go, Felix, let it end; don't make me fight you; there's nothing left worth fighting for."

"You are not going to walk out on me. You're mine and you'll stay—"

"No. No, no, no. I bought into that once; I really believed I belonged to you. But not anymore. I'm forty-eight years old, and I'm not going to live half a life any longer."

"It's more of a life than you ever had before! I took you out of the gutter and gave you everything—"

"You took me from the bed of a man you'd robbed and destroyed!"

There was a sudden silence. "Ben," Felix rasped. "He told you. The bastard. To turn you against me. That's what he came here for. But he's a liar; whatever he told you—"

"He didn't lie," Leni flung at him. "He didn't tell me anything about you I didn't already know."

"When? How long?" He waited, but she was silent. "Then it was Judd. You saw him after we were married, and he told you. Weak-livered son of a bitch . . . took my money and broke his word."

"He kept his word," Leni said softly. "I never saw him again."

"You're lying. How else would you know? It was one of them. . . ."

"What difference does it make? If I'd really listened to the two of you that day, I would have known what was happening, and everything would have been different. But it doesn't matter anymore. All that matters is that I won't live with you anymore." She clasped her hands in front of her, wondering why it was so frightening to say these things. "There's nothing left for me to like about you, Felix, or even to be impressed by. I was impressed for a long time, and I thought that meant I loved you, or admired you, or respected you. Now none of that is true. I don't even like you anymore."

"Then goddam you for a whore and a liar!" he roared. "Fucking in New York and coming back here as if you belong here—!"

"You said I belonged! To you!" Her hand flew to her mouth, as if to stop her anger. Leni Salinger was supposed to be cool and controlled; she never shouted. "You're right. I shouldn't have come back. But why did you let me? Why do you want me now? What kind of man are you who wants a woman who doesn't want him?"

He looked at her, his face turning sallow as he remembered a time he had stopped kissing her because she was struggling against him. But then he had been so sure of himself: he had defeated Judd and somehow he knew, absolutely, that he would get Leni for himself. Now nothing was sure and for the first time Felix began to believe he would lose his wife, and he was terrified. "I need you," he said, almost inaudibly. "Too many things are happening that I didn't expect. I need someone to count on. Damn it, I haven't anyone to count on!"

Leni gazed at him. He was sixty-one years old, and in all those years he had not made one friend or kept one relative close enough to count on. He stood there, slouching now, his hair gray and grown long in back, his mustache still dark, trying to be Owen Salinger, who was loved by everyone.

"I need you! Do you hear me? I need you!"

"It's too late," she said quietly. "If you'd said that twenty years ago—or ten—my God, even five . . . but then if you'd been able to say it, or even think it, you'd have been a different person, and none of this would be happening. But now it's too late."

"It's not too late." He drew himself up again and walked the length of the room to her. "That fool isn't worth a single memory, much less a lifetime, and his son is no better. If you think I'll let you choose them over what we have together—"

"Don't touch me!" She dodged his outstretched hand and ran to the foyer. "We have nothing together, can't you understand that? Haven't you heard anything I've said?" She took the first step of the stairway to the second floor. "I'll say it again. I'm divorcing you, Felix. I apologize for not doing it years ago—I apologize for being a coward—but I'm doing it now, and there's nothing you can do to stop me. You wouldn't anyway; you don't want a scandal. You want the world to envy you."

"Just a minute!" His face was dark; he felt as if he were about to burst. "Where the hell do you think you're going?"

"To my bedroom. We've said everything there is to say; I'll talk to my lawyer in the morning—"

"You will not spend the night in this house."

"What?"

"It's my house. Get out!"

"What are you talking about? It's our house."

"I bought it; you live here on my sufferance. Get out!"

Leni stood indecisively on the stairway, looking at him, framed by the archway into the living room. She had been the one to make the house what it was: she had chosen the furniture, bought the paintings, organized the dinner parties. But it was all on Felix's money. "If that's what you want," she said at last. "I can stay with Allison and Ben. And tomorrow I'll go to New York—"

"You can go to hell, but you won't stay in that house either."

"That is my house! I chose it and furnished it—"

"It's mine, bought with my money, maintained by my money, and you will not set foot in it again."

"Felix, you can't do this."

"Can't? *Can't?* You have no idea what I can or can't do. You're a romantic fool; you always were. I'm putting new watchmen on the New York house; their instructions will be to keep you out. You can stay with your lover."

"I'll stay in the Beacon Hill hotel!" she flung at him.

"You fucking bitch, get the hell out of here!" His face was contorted with rage, but he was holding his mouth tight. He looked like a child trying not to weep, Leni thought suddenly.

But she was ashamed of herself; she was the one who had acted like a child, taunting him with Laura's hotel. "I'm sorry; I shouldn't have said that. Felix—please—it would be so much easier for both of us, and the family, if we could do this together, if we could cooperate—"

"Cooperate!" He spat the word. "With an ungrateful whore? I took you from a mattress on the floor and made you a woman who could go anywhere, and you never thanked me, never told me you knew what I saved you from. You never thanked me for the company I built for you! Cooperate? When did you cooperate with me? I didn't ask you to be here all the time, I didn't ask you to tell me your problems, I didn't ask you what you did all day. All I asked was that you make me feel proud. What have you done to make me feel proud? Not a goddam thing. I had to do it all myself, everything myself—" He took a harsh breath. "Get out of my house," he said, his voice dull. "Get out. I don't want you here."

Leni watched him as he sank into a chair and sat with his back to her. For the first time in their marriage she felt sorry for him, she pitied him, but she had no desire to comfort him. "Good-bye, Felix," she said quietly, and taking her shoulder bag from the table in the foyer she left the house. She hesitated before getting in her car—*bought with my money, maintained by my money, and you'll stay out of it*—but she had no other way to get to Boston. Felix had not followed her to stop her, so she got inside and started the engine, and then drove back to town on the same highway they had driven barely an hour earlier. But this time she was alone.

*   *   *

"The fact is, I'm on to something," Sam Colby told Paul over coffee and dessert. Emily had gone to bed. All through dinner in Paul's Sutton Place apartment Colby had talked about old friends, most of them dead now or off somewhere in retirement, and about his parents, whom he recalled with a misty memory that made them more lovable than he could have imagined when they were alive. But when Emily left, Paul steered the conversation to the art thefts. "Yep, I'm on to something," Colby repeated, absently watching the housemaid bring a fresh pot of coffee. "It's a good feeling, let me tell you, after all these months of nothing. I hate nothing. Some smart-ass crook out there making a fool of me: bad way to feel."

"That must mean more interviews," Paul said casually. "I'll make sure I have a cameraman ready."

"Nope. Sorry, but nope. I have to do this alone for a while. I'll tell you when I'm ready."

"Now look, we've been through this. I'm trying to make a film, and you told me I'd have all the help I need. You also told me everything was all right at the Serrano interview, so there's no reason I can't go along on others. You know damn well I won't violate any secrets; I'll hold everything until your investigation's done, but I've got to film it."

"I want you to, Paul, honest to God, but . . . well, shit, let me think about it."

"I had a new idea the other day," Paul said. "Tell me what you think of it. What I'd really like to do in this film is trace two lives: yours and the life of a painting. I'd follow the painting from the artist who creates it to the collector who buys it to the thief who steals it—"

"You left out the guy who commissions the theft."

"There may not be one."

"More and more there is. No other way to get rid of the really valuable pieces. I mean, you're not going to take a Van Gogh to your friendly Brooklyn pawnshop. The big money is from collectors who'll pay anywhere from fifty thousand up to a million for a painting they'd have to pay three, four, ten times as much for if they bought it direct. Or that they couldn't get, period, because it wasn't for sale. Pledged to a museum after the owner's death, something like that."

Paul nodded. He had his pencil out and was making notes. "Well, then, sometime after it's bought at auction or through a gallery, someone commissions its theft. I want to talk to him. Or her. And after that, the thief who steals it. And then you."

"How you gonna find the guy who commissions it? And the thief?"

"I thought you'd give me some names from those impressive cases you've solved. Or the case you're working on now. Let me in on your investigation, step by step, not just an interview here and there, and when you've got it solved, let me talk to everyone you've talked to, but by myself."

"Can't promise that. But I'll do the best I can. This is a big deal, believe me; what I'm on to is very big. And when I'm ready, you'll get it before anybody else. In time for your film, if you're willing to wait a little bit."

"How long?"

"How the devil do I know? Investigations are like lovemaking; you never know how long they'll take until you know what you've got in hand and how good it is. What do you care, if you get a good film?"

"This one's been optioned, Sam. One of the television networks wants it. They're helping fund it, and they've given me a deadline."

Colby stared at him. "TV? Network TV?"

"I won an award in Paris," Paul said dryly, "which made me an instant celebrity of sorts. The network's been wanting something on art ever since auction prices went through the ceiling, and true-to-life detective stories always get an audience. They want it in January."

"January? Six months? That's plenty of time."

"I have to finish filming, and I can't always schedule interviews when I want them, some I have to repeat for one reason or another, and then I have to edit the whole thing. Six months isn't that long."

"I'll have it wrapped up before then."

Paul was silent.

"You can't rush an old man, Paul. I have my own ways of doing things; that's how I got my reputation. And I promise it'll be worth your wait."

"All right. I'll work around your investigation. But you'll tell me as soon as you can. And let me film it."

"Word of honor. You won't be sorry. Tell you what. You want to talk to a thief? There's a guy in Seattle who's a whiz at repairing cars; that's what he does now that he's out of the slammer. I put him away for ripping off a couple art galleries out there. Here's his name; tell him I sent you. Call me when you get back, and I'll tell you if there's anything new to report."

The next morning Colby was back at work, finding out all he could about the Beacon Hill hotels without setting foot in them. There was time for that; no need to alarm anybody before he was sure of himself. He'd already found, through an employment agency, that a security man from the Chicago Beacon Hill had been fired by Clay Fairchild and had later gone to work for the Boston Salinger, and he'd interviewed him, but the guy didn't have much to say.

He mulled it over in his office. Chicago, New York, Philadelphia, Washington. How would it work? Somebody could have lined up a maid in each hotel and paid her to get into specific rooms when the guests were out and steal the keys to their houses or apartments or yachts or whatever. No, obviously not steal them; nobody reported any stolen keys. Make copies of them, then. Also security codes for alarms and combinations for safes.

Colby played with the idea of a maid in every hotel, then discarded it. Too risky. He was willing to bet the guy was looking for specific guests known to have specific art that somebody was willing to pay for, which meant he'd need a maid on each floor, since he wouldn't know which room the guest would get. Too many people for a safe operation.

Who else, if not maids? Who could get into a room and have time to make copies of keys, go through date books, and find security codes? Security people? Could be. They had entree to all the rooms. But to line up four security people in four hotels and not worry about one of them blowing the whistle . . . very, very chancy.

The same with the desk clerks, concierges, bellhops, restaurant people in each of the hotels. If it had to be four people, one in each hotel, it was just too damned unreliable.

Which left the executives. The president of the hotels, vice presidents for quality control, security, and maintenance, and maybe some secretaries. But secretaries would be missed if they went off somewhere for a few days. This had to be someone who routinely traveled to all the hotels, so if he—or she—were gone, everybody would think he or she was at one of the other hotels.

And that left, by simple elimination, Laura Fairchild, Clay Fairchild, and the other two vice presidents.

That meant more digging. He did a background check on all of them. And struck gold.

He couldn't believe his luck. He read through the record of Laura's and Clay's arrest and conviction for theft in New York, and the transcripts of the trial on Owen Salinger's will; he read them over and over, chuckling to himself—was ever anybody so blessed as Sam Colby?— and then he went to Boston and dug into the Salingers' background, reading old newspapers and society magazines. And there they were again: Laura and Clay Fairchild, listed among those questioned in connection with a jewelry theft almost eleven years ago from the family summer home in Cape Cod.

In the silence of the newspaper file room, Colby sat back with a deep sigh. Goddam if he wasn't a lucky man. A lot of it was genius, but part of it was luck: the luck of the Irish. He'd always had it. He shouldn't forget it and despair when things were bad. He gathered his notes together and left. He had an appointment with Felix Salinger.

"You didn't tell my secretary what this was about," Felix said as Colby took the chair across from his desk. "There's nothing I can tell you about the robbery in New York; I rarely used that house at the time it occurred."

"I understand. What I want to talk about is a little different, though it's a crucial part of my investigation." He leaned forward and lowered his voice. "What I have to talk about is very sensitive, Mr. Salinger, and I can't proceed until I have your word that our conversation will be kept absolutely confidential. Strictly, completely confidential."

"I do not gossip," Felix said coldly. He considered the robbery Leni's fault and Leni's problem: she was the one who had used the house; she was the one who had had her privacy violated. Now that the house was entirely his, and he had changed the locks and hired new watchmen, he didn't give a damn about the investigation.

He wouldn't even have agreed to see Colby, except that July was a slow month and he was bored and angry. He blamed it on Leni: a man abandoned by his wife had too many empty hours. He didn't even have board meetings to keep him busy preparing progress reports, because he'd canceled them for the summer; he was sick and tired of having to defend his way of running the company. He'd work things out, and by the time the board met in September he'd be in control again, as he should be. But, meanwhile, he was bored, and Colby was a diversion. "I do not gossip," he said again. "I keep my thoughts to myself."

Colby nodded. Ice in his veins, he thought. "Well, then. I'm investigating six robberies, five besides your own, all of which bear such strikingly similar features that I am working on the assumption that they were perpetrated by the same person or persons."

"Yes?"

"Now, as part of my investigation, I need information on certain people. Two of those people once worked for you, in fact lived with you, and I'd like to ask—"

Felix sprang forward in his chair, knocking over a pencil holder and sending pencils, letter openers, and felt-tip pens rolling in all directions. "*Lived with us?*"

"For approximately four years, in . . ." Colby checked his notebook and read the dates. "I'm speaking, of course, of Laura Fairchild and her brother, Clay Fairchild. If you don't mind answering some questions about them . . ."

"No." Felix sat back. "Not at all. Anything I can do."

Well, aren't we warm and jolly, Colby marveled silently. "We have no proof of anything," he began. "You understand how important that is. I'm only, as we say, fishing for information, which is why I had to insist on confidentiality." Felix nodded; he was tense, waiting. "Well, without proof, we seem to have a link between the six robbery victims. . . ." He described his theories to Felix, who listened with unwavering attention. "Now I could, of course, have these people tailed, but the robberies have been about six months apart, and what am I going to do while I wait for the next one? Sit on my hands? And even then we might miss it—tails aren't perfect—and then we might have to wait around for another six months, or more. And if I'm wrong about the Fairchilds or their vice presidents, I'm missing a chance to catch someone else. So you see my dilemma. I need to find all the information I can in the shortest possible time. So whatever you tell me . . ."

Felix talked. Unemotionally, he described Laura's appearance at the Cape Cod compound with her brother, how she wormed her way into Owen's affairs, the robbery of Leni's jewels—never recovered—that obviously was an inside job, obviously planned and carried out by Laura and Clay. He reviewed the family's return to Boston, with Laura and Clay still attached, like leeches. "She even got herself engaged to my nephew; made sure she'd be in the family for good."

"And who is that?" Colby asked, his pencil poised.

"Paul Janssen. He's a filmmaker in California."

Mother of God, Colby thought, automatically writing Paul's name in his notebook. What the devil have I got here?

"Are they still engaged?" he asked.

"Good God, no. Of course not. He kicked her out when the rest of us did. He's married to a Boston girl from a fine family. No, that didn't last long."

"How long?" Colby asked.

"A year. Perhaps two."

"They were engaged for two years? And never married?"

"No. My father died, and we discovered her duplicity and sent her packing. Both of them. We haven't seen them since."

"You saw them at the trial."

"Of course. I forgot that."

Colby sighed. He'd have to figure out what to do about Paul. Damn it, he liked him; he liked confiding in him. And he wanted to be in his movie. Network TV! The gods are fickle, he thought sadly.

He turned to a new page in his notebook. "It's a long way from a kitchen maid in your house to the owner of four hotels," he said to Felix. "What I'm wondering is, could you help me with what all this might have cost her."

"I am not privy to her finances."

Colby nodded. "But she bought those hotels from you. The same ones that were part of Owen Salinger's will." Felix looked at him in rigid silence and hastily Colby said, "So you know what she paid for them. And you must know what it costs, approximately, to renovate an old building. Plus labor costs to staff a hotel of a hundred or so rooms."

"Suites," Felix said coldly. "Three of the hotels are all suites. Only Chicago has both rooms and suites."

Keeps up with her, Colby noted. "Well, but you see what I'm getting at. It would be important if she's in debt up to her ears, that kind of thing. If you could help me out there . . ."

"Ah. Yes. Of course." He leaned back and began to reel off numbers. "She paid approximately ten million for three of the hotels; twenty for the New York Salinger. Renovation could have run twenty to thirty million each, maybe more; I haven't been in them but I've had reports. I would estimate, roughly, that she'd need ten million cash for each of three hotels—down payment on the mortgage, renovating costs, and start-up costs—and maybe fourteen million for the New York hotel. Then, of course, there are operating costs: depending on the ratio of staff to guests, they could run anywhere from fifty thousand to a hundred fifty thousand a room—"

"Per year?" Colby asked.

"Of course."

Colby was adding numbers. "Forty-four million just to open the doors on her hotels. Right? Three at ten million, one at fourteen. Before she gets her first customer."

"That's close."

"Where would she get money like that? She worked in your kitchen, right? And left your house with nothing? And at the trial she stated she was working as assistant manager at a resort in the Adirondacks. And then—boom—she shows up with forty-four million dollars in cash, buying hotels right and left. Where'd she get it?"

For the first time in the six weeks since Leni had left him, Felix felt a surge of pure joy. "She'd have to borrow it," he said.

"Okay. How do you go about borrowing forty-four million dollars when all you are is an assistant manager at a resort?"

"You con somebody into backing you," Felix said blandly. "She was good at that: she'd already gotten around two old men; somehow she found another one. More likely, more than one."

"Sounds like I'd like her on my side if I needed money," Colby said, making it a joke, but Felix did not smile. "Well, then, how would it work?"

Felix sat back and stared at the ceiling, and when he began to talk his whole manner changed: he became crisply professional, his thinking logical and almost abstract. "You need ten million dollars for the Chicago hotel. You form a corporation and sell shares: half to your backer for five million, the other half to yourself for five million, which you've borrowed from your backer."

"Then he's in for ten million."

"Yes, but your collateral is your half interest in the corporation. If you can't pay the loan to your backer, or the interest on it, he gets the whole corporation."

Colby nodded. "And the other three hotels?"

"You keep borrowing. Bring in other investors, sell them some of your shares. Which means you no longer own half the corporation. You may even need so much money you give up control: you may only own twenty or thirty percent of the corporation by the time you've sold enough shares to get the money you need. If your original backer is still on your side, the two of you probably have enough shares to outvote the new investors. Or not. I have no idea. But the main problem is your debt. At a guess"—he paused, then decided to make it twice as high as it probably was, to make her sound desperate—"you could owe half a million dollars a year in interest alone on what you've borrowed."

Colby whistled softly. "Paid out of the salary she takes from her hotels?"

"I don't know where else she'd get it."

"So she has to earn over half a million dollars a year to live on and pay her debt."

"I would assume so."

"Could she make that kind of salary from four hotels?"

Felix hesitated. "Possibly," he said reluctantly. "Salary and bonus based on how well the hotels do. But it would be very difficult. It would mean an unusually high occupancy rate in all four hotels, and extraordinarily high rates for rooms and suites."

"What's she charging for a suite in New York?" Colby asked.

Again Felix hesitated. "A thousand dollars to twenty-five hundred a night."

Colby whistled again. "And she's getting it?"

"I don't know what her occupancy rate is. I'm sure some people are paying it."

"So she could do it, but it wouldn't be easy."

"Exactly."

Colby fell into deep thought. Half a million a year in interest. She could probably pay that off with the commission from stolen paintings. The thefts had been running six to ten paintings a year; if she kept it up, she could be out of debt in no time. Or buy another hotel or two. Hell, he thought fancifully, she could even become an investor herself and buy into other corporations. Like the Salinger Hotels, for example.

Stop, he told himself. Don't jump to conclusions. It still could be her brother or the other VP's. But he didn't have a motive for those other characters. He sighed. Time to check into all their private lives. Also, he'd have to figure out a way, without alerting anybody, to get the travel patterns of all four of them: find out if they were in the vicinity of the thefts when they occurred.

Of course, he thought, as he put away his notebook and shook hands with Felix, it could be somebody entirely different, somebody who had a grudge against Laura Fairchild and wanted to set her up, or somebody who just needed a lot of money and had found some way—some connection, some friend who knew the workings of the Beacon Hill—to get into the hotels long enough to get keys made and find security codes. Or there might be another connection among the six robberies that he hadn't found, and the Beacon Hill hotels had nothing to do with them.

You never know, he mused as he rode the elevator from the top floor of the Boston Salinger. The case is a long way from being closed. But if he had to bet right now, today, he'd put his money on the very resourceful, very aggressive, and—evidently—supremely successful Laura Fairchild.

CHAPTER 29

A FTER dark, when the August sun had set and a cool breeze came up, Laura and Ginny went to the roof garden, taking with them the legal forms Ginny's lawyer had given her. "It seems extraordinarily simple," she said.

"The higher the numbers, the simpler it gets," Laura murmured wryly as she reread the documents. "It always amazes me how much easier it is to spend ten million dollars than ten ninety-five."

A bird sang three pure notes in descending order, repeating them again and again; children threw Frisbees in the courtyard, the traffic sounds of Manhattan were a steady chorus in the background, and amid flowering shrubs and the perfume of roses, Laura signed a promissory note for ten million dollars. And then she and Ginny put their signatures to a purchase agreement for Laura Fairchild to buy Virginia Starrett's shares in Salinger Hotels Incorporated.

"Done," Ginny said with satisfaction. "But you're going to have a hell of a row when you go up there next week for the September meeting and ask them to approve it."

"It won't be the first time I've had a row with the Salingers."

"I'd come along for moral support, but I guess I can't."

"No, we can't both legally be there."

"So you'll just show up at the meeting?"

"Yes."

"With no warning?"

"With no warning."

"You're a brave lady. Or you're all fired up for revenge."

Laura was silent, and they sat quietly, holding tall glasses of iced tea and nibbling almond tuiles that Laura had made for dessert.

"Wonderful dinner," Ginny said. "You are one terrific cook."

"Rosa was one terrific teacher," Laura replied with a smile. "She still sends me recipes every week. She'll be here over Labor Day; come for dinner then. She won't let me in the kitchen when she's in the house, and she's still the best chef I've ever known."

"And a reminder of happy times."

"Yes, but it doesn't hurt as much as it used to. I have a lot of other good times to remember: with you, and Kelly, and Clay, and so many of my times with Wes." She smiled ruefully. "Do you know, all I'm remembering these days are the good times we had together."

"So you miss him."

"Now and then. Well, a lot, really, but mostly because I haven't met anyone else I like half as well."

"With all the men you go out with?"

"How many have you met that you want to see more than once?"

Ginny sighed. "There is a significant shortage of desirable males. Which doesn't mean some of them aren't okay in bed."

"I suppose. I haven't found any I want to sleep with. Most of them have such anxious eyes. And the ones who don't are so sure every single woman in Manhattan is desperate for a man that they think they don't even have to be interesting to get all the women they want. I'd rather stay in my wonderful house and read and listen to music."

"Not true."

"Well, not every night. I'd love to find someone who's just fun and not demanding. But it really is all right, most of the time. Sometimes I come home from a party and wonder why I bothered to go."

"Because you're looking for a man, and you can't find one sitting at home listening to music."

"I hate what that sounds like: a hunter stalking Manhattan, trying to snare a man."

Ginny laughed. "I know plenty of women like that. But you're too cool and quiet to be anything like them."

Cool and quiet, Laura mused, thinking of the angers and longings and ambitions that churned so violently inside her she wondered others could not see them.

"But you'll find someone before they will," Ginny said. "I have no doubt."

"I do. I'm almost thirty—"

"Ancient," Ginny said mockingly.

"Getting on," Laura said with a smile. "But what if I don't find one? What happens then? Do I dry up and blow away? Or dissolve into a puddle and evaporate? I'd still be here, and I'd figure out some kind of life. I'd make more friends, men and women, especially women: sometimes I like spending an evening with them more than with men. I'd run my hotels, and buy some more as soon as I could swing it, and do a lot of traveling and go to concerts and the theater and play tennis, and have a good life. Would that be so awful?"

"It's not awful; it's the way I live, and I'm having a hell of a good time. But I've had a husband and a couple of kids; I did the whole happy-family scene, before it fell apart. I've done the things most of us want. Don't you want that? Don't you want a family?"

Laura looked beyond the roof garden at the lighted windows of Manhattan's towers. Some of the windows were offices, but many were homes, with single people or with families, all of them with their own stories: love and loss and pain and joy. Voices carried to her from the courtyard below: the shouts and laughter of children, one of her neighbors asking his wife if she wanted to go with him when he walked the dog, another neighbor calling one of the younger children to come to bed. "Yes, of course I'd like a family." She paused. "But I have one, in a way. You and Rosa mother me, and Clay acts like a brother or sort of a son, I'm never sure which, and Kelly is like a sister. That's more family than a lot of people have. And I'm making new friends; I'd make more if I could find the time. I've got more than most people."

"Except there's a big space that's still empty."

She looked again at the lighted towers. "I don't think about that very much. I have too many other things to think about. Look where I was eleven years ago. And now everything is going so well, and it all happened so fast, I get a little scared sometimes, as if it can't possibly last, and everything will come tumbling down around me."

"Avoid superstition," Ginny said. "It's disruptive in a well-ordered world. What's that? Is somebody here?"

There were footsteps on the stairs and then Clay stood in the doorway. "The door was open so we came in. If I'd been a thief I could have walked off with the whole place, and you wouldn't even have known I was here. Hi, Ginny." He bent over and kissed Laura on both cheeks. "You look beautiful. Your hair's getting longer; I like it."

"Just a little. Hello, Myrna, come and have some iced tea."

"I'd love some. We walked and it's awfully hot. It feels cooler up here."

Clay sprawled in a chair, drained one glass and poured another. "That saved my life. I was gasping for the last three blocks. I kept wanting to stop in a bar, but Myrna wouldn't let me, even though my life was at stake. She's a tough lady."

"And—" Myrna prompted.

"And we're getting married," Clay said, his words running together. "The lady keeps telling me I need her, and I finally decided she's probably right."

Laura was smiling. "That's wonderful; I'm so glad." She rose and kissed Clay and then Myrna. "When will it be?"

"As soon as possible," Myrna said. "Clay likes to change his mind at the last minute. He thinks it's a sign of flexibility."

"And she thinks it's a sign of immaturity," Clay said with a sigh. "Is there hope for this marriage?"

Myrna smiled calmly. "There's hope for *you*; you're shaping up already."

Laura shot her a quick look. She didn't like Myrna any better than she ever had, but she'd thought for a long time that she probably was good for Clay. Now she began to feel uneasy. She wanted Clay to have a wife, not a director.

But Clay was jaunty and unperturbed. "Shaping up is right. I've made more vows than a monastery full of monks. You have no idea how much I'm giving up for marriage—except that I'm hanging onto a couple bad habits so I don't totally lose my touch. See, it's like this." He leaned forward and touched Laura's hand. "You've done a lot for me; I owe you a lot. I don't know where I'd be without you—probably on the run somewhere. I sure wouldn't be where I am, or have as much money, if I didn't have my job with the hotels. Your hotels. And I know you worry about me. So I thought it was about time I settled down."

Myrna looked satisfied, but Laura wasn't. "Isn't it better to get married for love than to please your sister?" she asked lightly.

"You're absolutely right," he said promptly. He reached out and took Myrna's hand. "And Myrna and I are in love."

"I'm glad," Laura said. It still didn't satisfy her, but she let it drop. How many times had she told herself she couldn't run Clay's life, and didn't want to even if she could? It was enough that they were friends, and family, and could turn to each other if they needed to. "Now let me tell you *my* news," she said. "I've just become a shareholder in Salinger Hotels."

"What?" Clay looked confused. "Salinger Hotels? *You* own—? But you can't. The family owns it. They don't let anybody else in."

"There are three outsiders—I mean three others. A long time ago, when Owen was building two or three hotels a year, he needed extra cash, and he sold part of his holdings to some friends. The only condition—"

Clay let out a whoop. "You own shares in the Salinger Hotels? *You* own shares? How about that! You've got it all—the hotels and a piece of the company that son of a bitch took away from you. . . . You're going to sit at a board meeting with old Felix, and he can't kick you out! Hot damn! Hey, we've got to celebrate!" He stopped, a scowl between his eyes. "Condition? What condition?"

"The bylaws say that none of the board members can sell their shares without the approval of the whole board, unless they're selling to a relative of the Salinger family."

Clay's scowl deepened. "So how can you own anything? Shit, Laura, Felix wouldn't approve it; his dumb brother wouldn't either. None of them would." He saw Laura and Ginny exchange a smile. "What's that about?"

"I said they needed approval unless they were selling to a relative of the Salinger family," Laura said.

"But you're not a relative! You would be if you'd married Paul, but you didn't."

"I know that," she said evenly. "But I'm Allison Salinger's sister-in-law."

Clay stared at her. Then his face lit up. "Ho-ly shit! Ben!"

"Who's Ben?" Myrna asked.

And Laura and Clay told her.

*   *   *

By the end of September, Sam Colby had a stack of reports on Clay Fairchild and the other two vice presidents of OWL Development, who were also vice presidents of the Beacon Hill hotels. The two vice presidents were the kind of guys he might have liked to go bowling with, but to an investigator they were dull and quickly forgotten. But Clay Fairchild—ah, he was a different matter.

Gambling, Colby read from his reports. Very heavy stakes with very high-powered groups. And high living: fancy car, good clothes, expensive loft in SoHo, a string of girlfriends—a couple of them fairly well-known models who'd picked out jewelry that Clay paid for—and he had an account at Tiffany's where he bought jewelry for his sister; the clerk knew them both. He couldn't do all that on the salary Felix had said he probably made in his position. So either he won big at cards or he had another source of income.

Quite a pair, the Fairchilds, Colby mused. A pair. Well, maybe they were; maybe they worked the whole thing together. A brother and sister team! Wouldn't that make a film for Paul! Might even be made into a TV miniseries! And the star would be Sam Colby, who everybody thought was rocking and rotting away in a retirement village!

Except that . . . how the hell could he tell Paul?

Maybe he hates her, Colby thought; then there's no problem. But maybe he has a lingering soft spot for an old flame. Then I'd be the messenger with the bad news.

I won't tell him; I'll wait until I have something more definite, he told himself, and went off to meet him; they were having a drink at Paul's club. Colby had tried to stretch it to dinner, but Paul had said firmly that he and Emily had other plans. Colby thought it was mostly that Emily didn't care about Paul's filmmaking and didn't want it to interfere with their dinner, but whatever it was, the best he could do was drinks.

"How was Seattle?" he asked as soon as they sat down.

"I enjoyed your thief; he gave me a lot of background, and he did it on camera. He also sent you his regards."

"He's a good man." Colby was breathing deeply, absorbing through every pore the atmosphere of the Metropolitan Club: subdued, wealthy, and male. He eyed the leathers and gilt and intricate decor of windows and ceilings that recalled a grander age; he reveled in the pungent aroma of cigars; he sank deeper into his chair. He could have stayed forever. "What else did you do out there?"

"Looked up an old friend from college and did some sailing. Tell me about your investigation. How close are you to solving it? How much can I worm out of you?"

Colby laughed. "You can't worm things out of Sam Colby. But I guess it's okay to give you a rough idea. No more than that, though; don't push me for more. This is it: I've got a hypothesis, right? No proof, but strong assumptions based on intelligent analysis of information gathered over a period of time—"

"Sam, cut out the bullshit. I'm already impressed by you. Tell me what you've got."

"I am telling you. What would you think if you found something that all six robbery victims did, or experienced, within a few months of being robbed?"

"I'd think it was worth looking into."

"Right. That's what I've been doing." Colby stretched out his legs. It felt so good to talk to somebody who was intelligent and impressed by him. "This is what I found. The people involved in what those six victims had in common are in a perfect position to commit the robberies; they travel often enough to get to the locations where the robberies occurred and back again without attracting suspicion; they live in a way that requires a lot of money; and they have a history of theft and chicanery."

When he did not go on, Paul frowned in thought. "How many people, and how are they involved with the victims?"

"Two people, and they're executives in a corporation that all six deal with on occasion."

Still frowning, Paul repeated it to himself. He wasn't sure why Colby seemed so afraid of giving away his hypothesis, circling around it like a wary cat, but it was pretty clear that, given time and camaraderie and enough scotch, the whole story would come out. He signaled for another round of drinks. "It's not a crime to be an executive in a corporation or do a lot of traveling or need a lot of money or have a history of theft."

"True," said Colby sadly.

"But it's an interesting set of circumstances."

"Exactly what I said to myself."

"And you've questioned these executives?"

"No, no. I thought about it, but I don't want to alert them."

"Have them followed."

"I thought of that, too. But it could take months."

"Search their homes. Maybe they kept some of the stolen art."

"Could be. But if they didn't, and I don't find anything, they'd know I'm after them and lie low, and I'd be nowhere."

"Or on the wrong track."

"That could be, too. But I trust my instincts."

There was a silence. A new drink had appeared at Colby's elbow, and he picked it up, feeling mellow but suddenly gloomy about his case. "Sam," Paul said, "who are the two executives?"

He looked up. "Why?"

"Why not? What's the big secret? I'm not going to advertise your hypothesis. I'm not a spy from an enemy camp. I'm your friend, and maybe I can help you decide what to do next."

"You *are* a friend," Colby said, nodding. "A good friend. But I can't tell you. It's too . . . tricky."

Paul scrutinized his worried face. "I know them," he hazarded. "Is that it? It's someone I know, and you think I wouldn't be happy to hear it."

Colby took a long drink. What a pleasure to talk to a smart guy. He probably could tell Paul anything; smart guys understand how complicated life can be. "That's close."

"What the hell, Sam, if they're innocent there's no problem—we'll wait until you find the guilty ones—but if they really are pulling off these robberies I'd like to know it. It's always nice to know if one's friends are moonlighting as thieves."

"That's true, but it's a little more complicated than that. Life always is, isn't it? You aren't close to them anymore—I doubt you cared about both of them, anyway; it was just one of them, and her I guess you don't see anymore . . ." He paused, wondering if he should have gotten into this discussion.

But it was too late. "My God," Paul said. He was very pale. "You're talking about Laura Fairchild."

"And her brother," Colby added. He was feeling less mellow.

"You're out of your mind. She wouldn't—my God, do you know what you're saying? She's one of the most respected businesswomen in America, she owns an important group of hotels. . . ." He stopped. "They all stayed at a Beacon Hill hotel, is that it? That's your hypothesis? For Christ's sake, Sam, those people stay at every damned hotel in the world; they spend more time in hotels than in their own homes; that's not anything to connect them!"

Colby wavered, but then he sat up and looked at Paul. "The only thing I've found that those people have in common is that they all stayed at a Beacon Hill hotel within six months of being robbed. All six of them stayed in lots of other hotels in that time but not the same ones. Whoever robbed them had keys and security codes. How would they get them? They'd go into a hotel room and make wax molds of keys and find security codes in notebooks or checkbooks or whatever crazy places people write them. That's all they'd have to do. They'd leave the room; nothing would be gone; nobody would be suspicious. And a few weeks or months later there's a robbery thousands of miles away. You think that's such a crazy hypothesis?"

Paul was silent. "It's a good hypothesis," he said at last. "But it doesn't point to Laura. She's not a thief. But even if she were, she wouldn't rob her own guests; she wouldn't jeopardize everything she's got—for what? For a few dollars?"

"For hundreds of thousands, and you know it. You know what's been stolen. And she's in debt up to her ears from her hotels. Her brother likes to gamble, too, big-time, not penny-ante stuff, and he's been spending like he wins all the time. And he's in charge of quality control, which means he's all over those hotels. Listen." He hesitated. "You just said she's not a thief. How do you know? She was once, wasn't she? And there was a time when you weren't so sure of her, right? I mean, how come you're so positive now—"

Paul was out of his chair. "You've been talking to Felix."

"Sure I have. What the hell, Paul, I knew this would happen; you don't like the evidence so you blame me for it. I was only doing my job!" Heads turned in the hushed room and frowns were aimed at Colby. Embarrassed, he lowered his voice. "Could you sit down so we can talk like friends?" When Paul was again in his chair, he said, "She lived with them, she worked for them, why wouldn't I talk to Felix?"

"Because he doesn't know a damn thing about Laura. Why didn't you ask me? I know her better than he does."

"Then why aren't you married to her?"

Paul was silent.

"Because you thought she was a thief—right?—and conned Owen Salinger out of his money and went after yours. So why are you getting mad at me if I think the same thing?"

"Because I was wrong." It was the first time Paul had ever said it, and as he did, he knew it was the truth. It was as if a window had opened, letting in a blast of fresh air: he felt a sense of freedom, a lifting of an enormous weight. Whatever Laura had said that day, and for whatever reason, she wasn't a thief or a fortune hunter. She loved Owen and he loved her, and even though he was a sick man, he knew exactly what he was doing when he added that codicil to his will.

And she loved me, Paul thought.

"I was wrong," he said again. "We all were. And so are you, damn it. You're wasting your time."

Colby shook his head. "I don't know that. I can't just drop the whole idea because you say so. I would if I could, honest to God, I like working with you and talking to you, and we're going to have a terrific movie—we are going to have a movie, aren't we?"

It hit Paul then. He'd forgotten the film. "I don't know. I'll have to think about it." But he already knew the answer. "Whatever we do, we won't use this investigation unless you come up with another solution."

"*I haven't got one.* Don't you understand? Everything points to her, or her brother, or the two of them working together, and I can't just make up something else out of my head! Shit, I knew this would happen, I knew it, I knew it. You wouldn't drop the movie; we've got months in it. And the TV! The network! They want it, right? They've paid for part of it! You have to make it! You can't just drop it and let everybody down!"

"Don't tell me what I can or can't do, Sam." Paul's voice was like steel. Colby had never heard him talk like that. "You have no proof, you said yourself it was only a hypothesis, and I'm not filming you while you hound Laura or put together circumstantial evidence to trap her. If you come up with another solution, call me. If you're given another case to work on, call me. I like you, and I think we'd have one hell of a good film, but it won't be this one, not the way it's going."

"Television . . ." Colby said feebly.

"That's my problem, not yours." He looked at his watch. "My wife is waiting for me." He turned and strode out of the room.

Colby felt exposed and clumsy. He'd done everything wrong; he'd even forgotten that he had a job to do. Paul had said he should have asked him about Laura; why hadn't he done that? He needed all the information he could get; why the hell hadn't he asked Paul to give him some?

He looked at his watch. Shit, there was almost an hour before Paul had to meet his wife; maybe he could catch him and calm him down, and then they could talk like civilized men. He ran down the marble stairs to the entrance and saw Paul just going out the door. "Paul! We have time to talk!" But Paul did not pause; Colby watched as he turned toward Fifth Avenue and was swallowed up by the crowds. He didn't hear me, he thought, didn't even slow down.

In fact, Paul had heard his shout, but nothing would have made him turn back. He was going to see Laura.

Her hotel was less than three blocks away. If she was in the city, if she was in her office, if she would see him . . .

He had not been in the Beacon Hill, and he was aware of the feeling of warmth and luxury that surrounded him the moment he entered the lobby, but he did not stop to look around; he walked to the antique desk in the corner and told the concierge he wanted to see Miss Fairchild. "It's urgent," he said. He took one of his cards from his wallet and wrote on the back, *Please.* "If you'd take this to her. . ."

"One moment," the concierge said, and a few moments later was holding a nearby door open for Paul. "Miss Fairchild's office is the last on the right."

It was a large room in light colors, with a sofa along one wall, a round table with four chairs, and an oval rosewood table piled with papers and books. There was no desk. Laura stood behind the oval table. She wore a blue business suit and a silk blouse, her head was high, and her face showed no emotion at all. Paul paused in the doorway. She was stunningly beautiful and almost formidable: he had never seen her in a setting where the power was hers.

"Please come in," she said, and it was her low voice that broke the spell; everything else about her was different, but not that voice that had once told him she loved him.

She gestured toward the couch, and they sat on it together. "You told the concierge it was urgent."

"Yes." He paused, and Laura wondered what it could be that made him so reluctant to begin. Waiting for him, she sat on the edge of the couch, her back straight, her hands folded in her lap, trying to adjust to the sight of Paul Janssen in her office. This was a part of her life so separate from him that it was the only place she could go for long periods without thinking of him; she had never even tried to imagine him here. Now she looked at him—this tall, lean man in dark trousers and a gray sport jacket of raw silk—and she wished him gone. He seemed to fill her office, taking more space than he deserved; he filled her vision and her thoughts, bringing back memories. "What is it that is so urgent?"

He leaned toward her. "I'm working on a film about an investigator for insurance companies; his specialty is stolen art and he's working on a case. . . ." He paused briefly. "There have been six major art thefts in the past three years, identical in the way they were carried out, so it seems one person or persons did them. The people who were robbed were Flavia Guarneri, Britt Farley, Sid and Amelia Laughton, Carlos Serrano, Leni and Felix Salinger, and Daniel Inouti."

Laura looked stunned. "I know them all. They've all been guests in my hotels. Not Felix, of course, but Leni . . . They've all been robbed? But that's incredible."

"That's why I'm here." Rapidly, bluntly, he told her about Colby's investigation. "He has no proof, but I don't know what he's going to do next, and I had to tell you—you had to know that he suspects you or Clay, or both of you."

She was sitting very still, her eyes far away. The color had drained from her face. "No," she said. It was almost a whisper. "No, no, no."

Paul moved toward her, to take her in his arms, to shield her from pain—I'm always causing her pain, he thought with something like despair—but then he pulled back. He knew he couldn't, not yet. "I'd like to help if I can," he said quietly.

She looked at him, her face like stone. "Why? You thought I was guilty once; why should you help me this time? Maybe your investigator is right: once a thief always a thief. Why wouldn't he be right? I masterminded the whole thing—"

"No, you didn't. You didn't mastermind anything. Not now and not before. I know that—"

"*Know* it? Now that someone says I committed another crime, you suddenly know I didn't do the first?"

Involuntarily, he smiled. "It doesn't sound logical, and I can't explain it, but, yes, I know it. I should have trusted you then, I should have believed in you enough to know you wouldn't lie to me, and now I do believe it. I'm seven years older; is that reason enough? I think I've changed in those years. I've thought a lot about us, and about myself: what kind of person I am, what's really important to me, what I've done wrong in the past . . . Damn it, I can't put it all in one neat package; do I have to?"

She was staring at him. "I don't know. It might help me understand. You think I should just believe you—"

"It goes two ways," he shot back. "You didn't trust me or believe me either, when we were together. You didn't tell me anything about your past or why you and Clay chose our family to work for, and you didn't stand up to Felix when he made that row over Owen's will. If you'd told me the truth, told all of us the truth, and believed in us, we might have gotten past that; we might not have lost all these years. . . ."

Laura was silent, thinking of Ben. She still hadn't told all the truth.

"You can't believe that?" Paul asked, his voice bleak.

"Yes." Her voice was low. "I should have told you. I didn't know how. I was so afraid of losing you, losing all of you—I couldn't do it." She lifted her hands and let them fall. "There always seemed to be good reasons for secrecy. I'm sorry. I should have told you. I wish I had." The last words were barely audible. "But the rest of it," she said more clearly. "Your believing in *me* . . . I don't know. I don't even know how to think about it. How can I, when you've just told me about this man, this investigation? If you're right and he's going to accuse me—"

"I'm not sure he is. I don't know what Sam will do next; he did admit he might be on the wrong track. I just wanted you to be on your guard—"

"I don't know what that means!" It was a cry for help, and this time Paul could not hold back; he took her in his arms and cradled her to him. She clung for a moment, then tried to break away. "No, this doesn't help . . . it just makes things worse—"

"It makes things right," he said and kissed her. His arms tightened around her as if he would bring her inside him if he could, his mouth opened hers, his tongue entwined with hers as he had dreamed of more times than he ever had let himself acknowledge.

Laura let herself go. She held him to her and her body opened to his, fitting itself to his, close, closer, bringing him into the empty space that had been there, the dry patch in her heart, since she had walked out of Owen's house. She had missed him, and longed for him, and now she held him with all her strength and let herself admit that whatever she did with her life, Paul was part of her and always would be. Owen had given her pride and confidence and helped her grow up and turn away from her past; Paul had given her the love that made her feel complete, and a woman. She knew it now; she did not shrink from it or try to deny it. She let herself want him and admit that she wanted him, even if it was just for this brief moment when nothing else could intrude.

"I love you," he said, his lips against hers. "Dearest Laura, I love you. I've missed you and wanted you and never stopped loving you—"

With a gasp, Laura tore herself away. "But you married. And made another life." Her voice shook. "And for years you thought I was—"

"I was wrong! I told you; I'm trying to make you understand—"

"I can't!" She began to walk around the office with agitated steps. "What do you want me to do? Think of you as a lover again? As a husband? Even if you didn't have a wife, how could I do that? Just... switch all my thinking? Just like that? One minute I have a life I understand and can plan for—a life I made and can count on *and enjoy*—and the next I'm supposed to change it all because you show up and tell me you want to be a part of it? How can you be part of it?" She stood beside the window, looking at him. Her voice was firm now, and her gaze level; her other thoughts were pushed back and she was in control of herself again. "I can't even take the time to think about you. You've brought me something else to think about. Theft... and accusations... I've tried to get away from this for eleven years! And you want me to think about love?"

His eyes held hers. "I could be a friend, if not a lover, and I might be able to help you, if you'd let me."

She took a long breath. "What did you mean when you said I should be on my guard?"

"I meant it looks like somebody's setting you up, or using you. And Sam has two suspects, not one."

There was a pause, then Laura's eyes darkened. "You mean Clay. You're telling me to be on my guard against Clay!"

"Right. That's what I'm telling you. He could have done it; anyone in his job would have access to every part of every one of your hotels, and he could use the money. He gambles—did you know that?—and for big stakes. Laura, too many things point to him for any reasonable person to ignore—"

"Reasonable! Who are you to talk about being reasonable? You want me to believe you've changed and you trust me even though it's not logical and I shouldn't expect it to be! Well, I'll tell you—*logically* and *reasonably* and *trustingly*—that Clay is not a thief. He hasn't stolen any art; he wouldn't do that to me even if he wanted to! He loves me and he cares about what I'm trying to build here! He's a part of it—part of my company—he'd be hurting himself to hurt the hotels—he's getting married—he's grown up—*he's* the one who's changed, not you!"

She knew that wasn't true even as she said it, but the words were tumbling out, mixed up with the love and longing she'd cut off while they burned inside her, her anger at herself for letting down her defenses, and the cold fury that had returned—almost exactly as she remembered it—from the time Paul and his family first accused her and Clay of thefts and lies and deception. "You don't know anything about Clay!" she cried. "Or me! You don't know—"

"You're right, I don't. But I want to." He strode across the office to stand close to her. "Damn it, Laura, I love you and I want to make up for the years we lost. I want to know you again; I want to know the woman you've become. You're right, I don't know anything about Clay, but what if Sam is right about him? Should I turn away and pretend Sam never talked to me when I know he might be hurting you? You've *been* hurt—I know it, because I caused it—and I'm damned if I want you hurt again. I love you; I want to help you, protect you if I can, from anyone who's doing you harm—"

"Stop. Please stop." Laura's voice was so low he had to bend closer to hear her; she had turned away to look through the narrow window blinds at the street outside. "I know you think you're trying to help me, but you can't help me by attacking Clay. He's my family; he's stayed with me all these years, and I won't let you or anyone try to make me stop trusting him. You wanted me to trust in you and your family; you want me to trust in you now. Then you can't ask me not to trust in Clay."

There was a long silence. The sound of car horns came faintly through the window; in the corridor beyond the closed door of Laura's office, a man's voice said good night and a woman's voice responded. Paul glanced at the small clock on Laura's rosewood table. He was very late. "I'm sorry," he said, his voice as low as hers. "You're right, of course. You should believe in him and trust him." He hesitated. "I think blind trust may be as bad as no trust at all, but you know him, and Sam and I don't, and you may be right. Laura . . ." He took her hand and she turned to him. Her eyes were shadowed; he could not tell what she was thinking. "I have to leave; I wish I didn't, but I'm already late . . ."

She nodded. "Good-bye, Paul. Thank you for wanting to help. I'm sorry we quarreled again; we seem to do that more easily than anything else."

"No. We love more easily than anything else. Or we would, if we'd let ourselves. We did once; I haven't forgotten it. And neither have you."

"I'll never forget it," she said simply. "But we can't regain the past; too many things have happened since." Suddenly she smiled. "I've spent all these years trying to wipe out the past, and now I'm talking about regaining it. Nothing makes much sense, does it?"

His smile met hers. "If we find a way to regain it, that will make sense. *We* make sense, together."

Laura reached up and lay her hand along his face. "I wish we did." Then she walked to the door and opened it. "Good-bye, Paul."

When he reached her, he stopped. "I want to see you again."

"I have to think about it. I have so many things to think about. I'll call you."

He searched her face. "If I don't hear from you, I'll be on the phone, or camping outside your office."

"I'll call—when I have something to say."

Paul bent his head and kissed her. Their lips clung for a moment, and then he said, "Soon," and was gone.

Laura shut the door behind him and walked back to the table she used as her desk. So much work to do, she thought, looking at the reports she had meant to read in the last hour of the day, and another stack of literature she had to read to prepare for the Salinger Hotels board meeting. Tomorrow. The meeting was tomorrow, and she still had to give her secretary instructions for the day, while she was in Boston. She sat down and picked up a memo from Gérard Lyon requesting new equipment for the kitchen and another sous chef because business was so good. But after reading a few lines she put it aside and swiveled her chair to stare again out the window.

I think blind trust may be as bad as no trust at all.

She thought about Clay, back through the years. His adoration of Ben, how he had followed him around and wanted to drop out of school, as Ben had done, and live by stealing and whatever jobs he could get, as Ben did.

His restlessness at work. *What the hell, Laura, you've got to admit it's just a job—even if it is your hotel—and everybody needs something more than that, something risky or free or whatever. . . .* His love of fancy cars and expensive clothes. The loft he rented and the way he'd furnished it. The gifts he bought her. His gambling.

He gambles—did you know that?—and for big stakes. How did Paul know that? From the investigator, probably. Colby. But how did Colby know?

"What difference does it make?" She heard the words wrenched out of her in the quiet office, and she dropped the memo she was holding and leaned her head on her hands. *I don't believe a word of what Paul said; someone else is stealing that art, and there are simple explanations for everything Clay does.*

She turned back to her table and looked again at Lyon's memo. But it was no use. She swept the reports aside. I can't think about them; I can't think about work.

I have to know what the simple explanations are.

She looked at her gold clock. Clay had bought it for her at Tiffany's. Seven forty-five. He'd be home by now. She reached for the telephone. Just to make sure.

* * *

Emily was sitting with a group of people in the Atlantis bar when Paul arrived. He kissed her cheek. "I'm sorry I'm late; the time got away from me."

She introduced him to the others. "They've been keeping me company," she said lightly. "It's a good thing I found them; otherwise I would have sat here for over half an hour alone."

Paul glanced around, recognizing three television actors, a fashion model, and a Broadway star. "You're never alone in this place; that's why you always ask me to meet you here. Shall we go to dinner?"

"My, aren't we short-tempered?" she murmured as they walked down First Avenue. "Is it me, or was it a trying day?"

"It was a trying day, but I didn't think I was being short-tempered." Emily was silent. "Did you talk to Barry?"

"No. He had people in from Rome. His secretary said he'd be free Monday. He'll have to see me then or I'll make a terrible fuss. He knows I'm unhappy; he can't keep putting me off."

"I'm sure he'll see you; you're his favorite model."

"He isn't acting like it."

There was a pause. "And what did you do today?" Paul asked.

"Shopped for cruise clothes."

He glanced at her. "Are you going on a cruise?"

"There's a whole group going to St. Thomas in December. I thought we'd go with them; you'll be finished with the film by then."

"I'm not sure of that."

"You told me you'd be finished by then! I'd love to go to St. Thomas, Paul. Or is it your family? Couldn't we skip Christmas with them just once?"

"Of course we could. I wasn't thinking of them."

"What, then?"

They reached Il Nido, and Paul held the door for Emily. Instantly, the maitre d' appeared in the small, jammed entryway. Emily's beauty always got attention, even in Manhattan, where women are expected to be beautiful, and almost immediately they were led to a table in the middle of the restaurant, where they could be seen by everyone. Paul took in the room: it was one of his favorites, with rough plaster walls crosshatched with dark timbers, suggesting an Italian nobleman's house. Dusky mirrors of beveled glass reflected the diners, and he recognized a number of directors and designers, and an actor from a movie that had won an Oscar that spring. Emily always chose places where she would not be the only celebrity. Marriage to her had taught Paul that there was even greater celebrity in numbers, when the famous could feel themselves part of an exclusive club instead of adrift in a fickle world.

Paul ordered a bottle of wine, and Emily said again, "What, then? If you're not thinking about your family, what are you thinking about?"

"The film. I'm changing the focus, and that's going to set it back quite a bit. If I even do it at all."

She stared at him. "It's more than half finished. And the network has it scheduled for ratings month. You can't just tell them you're not going to deliver it; they might never help fund another one!"

"That's a chance I'll have to take," he said. "I don't like the way the film is shaping up, and I'm not going to make it the way it now stands."

"What about Sam Colby?"

"I haven't decided what I'm going to do, Emily. I want to think about it."

The head waiter brought the wine, and Emily waited until their glasses were filled. "I think you're right. You should drop it."

"That isn't what I said."

"But you're leaning toward dropping it; you're even willing to risk having the network drop *you*. Aren't I right? You'd really rather drop it and do something else."

"I'd rather drop it than do it the way it is now. But I like the idea of a film about Sam. If I could get him to lead us through some earlier cases, I could still use a lot of what I have. It's not the best way, but it might work."

"Or it might not. Why take the chance?"

"Because I have nothing else I'm excited about right now."

"But what about something really different? A different kind of film."

"I don't want to do a different kind of film. Why would I? I'm just getting to the point where I feel comfortable with documentaries; I know what I want to do and, most of the time, how to do it."

"But you could learn another kind, too." She leaned forward, putting her hand on his. "Paul, someone suggested that I do a television miniseries. Models are doing that now, moving into films and television, and I think I'd love it. And I know I'd be good at it. There's a book I read when we were on the coast; it's wonderful, and a friend of mine wants to do a script with me as the heroine. He's sure he can get somebody at NBC or HBO interested if he can get a name director."

Paul was frowning as he watched her animated face. "You're not suggesting that I direct it."

"Yes, I am. It would be wonderful for you."

"It would not. Emily, what the hell are you thinking of?"

The headwaiter appeared at their table. "If I may... the specialties..." he said and, without pausing, reeled off his list. By the time they had ordered and he was gone, Emily's face was set. "You needn't make it sound as if I'm crazy. When I told you once I didn't think a photographer could make films, you said you could learn anything you set your mind to. That's all I'm asking you to do. And this is the best time, when you're already dissatisfied and ready for something new."

"I didn't say I was dissatisfied, or that I was ready for something new."

"Well, you should be! What do you get from all the work you do? An obscure award from a festival in France!"

"I'm very proud of that award," Paul said quietly.

Emily bit her lip. "I'm sorry, of course you are. I am, too. But this is a new opportunity, Paul, and it's incredible... these don't come along very often!"

"What opportunity?"

"For me to star in a miniseries!"

Paul drained his wine glass and sat back as a waiter immediately materialized and refilled it. He contemplated Emily. "You want me to transform myself into a director of television films so you can star in one."

"I hear people talk about you a lot in Los Angeles," she said. "You have a real name out there, and so do I, and so does my friend who writes scripts. The three of us couldn't miss, Paul. And it's something I need."

There was a pause. Then Paul nodded. "That's the real reason, isn't it? You're not getting as much work as you were last year."

"Well, there are always fads," she said, brushing it aside. "Right now they want tall, rangy girls, sort of all-American. But it will pass; I'm not really worried, not at all. It's just that I'm ready for something new; I'm sure you agree with that. You were the one always looking for something new, remember? All I'm asking is that you be what you say you are."

"I'm a documentary filmmaker." His eyes were somber as he gazed at her. "But you want me to be something else, something I have no interest in being."

"How do you know? You've never tried it!"

"You need a director with a name. More important, you need one you can get to. And you think you've got one, across the table from you, and in your bed."

"What does that mean?"

Their appetizers arrived but they ignored them. "You wanted to be a model and you asked me to photograph you, and you used my portfolio to impress Marken. And now you want me to use my name to help you get a miniseries because your modeling career seems to be fading."

Her head was high. "What's wrong with a wife asking a husband to help her?"

"I wasn't your husband when you asked me to photograph you." He smiled wryly. "Do you know, Emily, a little more than seven years ago, I believed a woman I loved was a fortune hunter. It was one of the reasons I turned my back on her. But I ended up marrying one anyway, didn't I?"

"What are you talking about?"

"You had plenty of your own money, so it never occurred to me that you might be one, but you wanted other things: to be married, to be a model, and now you want to be an actress on television. And I'm the means for getting what you want."

"That's what a husband does. I can't believe you're saying these things to me. I'm a good wife; I read books about filmmaking so you have someone to talk to, I read newspapers so we can talk about politics if you want, I'm home more than most women in my profession—I work very hard to be home as often as possible. I do things properly, Paul, and I've done everything I know to be a good wife."

"You have been. But that's not enough to make me drop something I care deeply about just because you have a fantasy—"

"I know it's not enough. I know you want children. We could think about a family now, if it's really important to you; we've been married long enough. . . ."

"Emily," Paul said, and his voice was so gentle she became terrified. She wanted him to shout, so she'd know he cared about what they were saying.

"And all those dinner parties," she rushed on. "I gave them for you as much as me, so you'd meet people who could help you. I've done so much to help you! In fact, if you want to talk about your photographs of me, they helped you as much as me, they *made* you in New York, they got you all those commissions! I knew they would, but you make it sound as if I wasn't thinking about you at all. *You're* the one who wasn't thinking about *me*; you only think about yourself and your damned films. It isn't important what I want, what I need—all that's important to you is doing exactly what you want, when you want it. You are a selfish man, Paul Janssen; I had no idea how selfish and self-centered and stubborn you are—"

"Emily, stop it." Surrounded by hearty voices and loud laughter, Paul heard the strain of hysteria in Emily's cultivated voice, and he pushed back his chair and walked around the table to her side. "We're going home." He beckoned to the maitre d'. "I'm sorry. It has nothing to do with your staff; everything was perfect, as always. Put the dinner on my account."

The maitre d' bowed. "I hope the illness passes quickly."

He knew it was not an illness, Paul thought; he knew it was a quarrel. He probably saw more than his share of them. "Thank you," he said, and in a moment he and Emily were walking the few blocks to Sutton Place. "I didn't mean to get so excited," Emily said. "We can talk sensibly, can't we? But you shouldn't call me a fortune hunter when I just want help. Everybody does, you know, especially women; we don't go grabbing and pushing and *doing* the way men do. That's probably why we live longer; we let others smooth the road for us. All women do that, Paul, and you know it."

"Not all women," he said quietly. He nodded to the doorman who held the door for them and they rode the elevator in silence, and were silent until they stood in the darkened living room. Manhattan glittered below them like a fairyland of jeweled spires, and Paul felt a sense of longing and then, unexpectedly, a leap of joy. *I'll call you—when I have something to say.* She might not, and she might not want to see him again if he called her, but it was more than he'd had for years; it was enough to make him feel that moment of joy. "Emily, I want us to separate; I want a divorce."

"No!" She spun around to look at him. "I don't think you mean that, Paul. I know you don't. We've had some problems, and things aren't perfect, but it just doesn't make sense for us to get divorced. We don't have to live together if you'd rather not—you can live here and I'll live in the house in Bel Air—but we still can be friends and do things for each other. You're not in love with anyone else, and neither am I, so there's no reason why that wouldn't work perfectly well."

"And if one of us does fall in love with someone else?"

"Then we can talk about a divorce if it seems really important. But there's no rush."

Paul gazed through the huge windows at the shining city below. It stretched to the horizon, and if it had dangers, they were not visible from where he stood. "I think we'd better talk about it now," he said.

* * *

There was no answer at Clay's apartment, and after an hour of calling, and trying to do some of her work between calls, Laura left for home. But outside the hotel, she changed her mind and took a taxi to his building. She'd wait for him there. The telephone wasn't any good, anyway: she wanted to see his face when she asked him—whatever she decided to ask him; she hadn't figured it out yet. Of course Paul was wrong, but still, she wanted to talk to Clay as soon as possible. Just to make sure.

"They're out, Miss Fairchild," the doorman said in the lobby of the large building that had been converted from an old printing factory to high-priced lofts.

"I know," Laura said. "I'll wait for them upstairs." The doorman touched his hat as she went past him to the elevator. He knew she had her own key; Clay had given her one when she was helping him furnish the loft soon after he moved in.

All the lamps were on, and in the bright light Laura was struck by the neatness of the apartment. Myrna's influence, she thought. She wandered restlessly through the huge room divided into areas by clusters of furniture and tall plants. She sat down and looked at the magazines on the coffee table, leafing through them, listening to the sounds of traffic on Greene Street and occasional footsteps from the apartment above. Then she began to wander again; she couldn't sit still.

At the end of the room, a wall of bookshelves screened the bedroom. One closet along the far wall stood open and she saw Myrna's clothes and shoes, neatly arranged. The other closet was open only a crack, as if it had been given a hasty shove and had not quite closed. Laura glimpsed one of Clay's elegant suits, and his shoes piled on the floor. That's odd, she thought; Clay is so particular about his shoes. Idly, she opened the closet door. The shoes were crammed into a small space left beside a metal file cabinet. Laura shook her head. What a crazy place for a file cabinet; he has a whole loft to use, and he squeezes it into his closet instead. Maybe that's where he keeps his love letters, and he doesn't want Myrna to see them.

She closed the closet door and skirted the bed to look at the books on the other wall. She took some down, leafed through them, then put them back. Finally she kept one and carried it into the living room where she sat in an armchair, trying again to read. At midnight, she gave up. She was tired and worried, and felt foolish for being worried.

I'm getting myself worked up over absolutely nothing, she thought. I'll see Clay at the office tomorrow—

But tomorrow was the Salinger board meeting. She was catching an eight o'clock plane to Boston. Well, then, she'd come here first, for breakfast, and talk to Clay privately then.

But as she left, something nagged at her, and she turned back. Why was that filing cabinet in his closet? It didn't make sense. He was so finicky about his shoes, polishing them and keeping them stuffed with paper so they wouldn't lose their shape; why would he jam a file cabinet next to them when he had other closets all over the apartment?

Because the bedroom closet was the only one with a lock.

She'd noticed that when she furnished the apartment. There was only one closet with a lock. And now that he wasn't living alone anymore, he'd put the file cabinet in that closet. *That's a lot of trouble to go through just to keep old love letters hidden.*

Standing in the middle of the room, she wavered. It was Clay's closet; she had no right to look inside it. She should go home. But Paul's words echoed in her memory, and the silence of the apartment made them seem even louder. *Just to make sure. That's why I'm here.*

In the bedroom, she opened the closet again and tugged at the top drawer of the filing cabinet. It opened easily, and she burst out with a little laugh. All this agonizing over nothing... She looked at the upright folders and recognized her own writing: the letters she had written to Clay when he lived in Philadelphia and, later, when he stayed in Chicago before coming to New York. He saved them all, she thought; I never knew that. There were photographs of her, too, and of Kelly and John Darnton, and all the girls he had gone with since high school. It's all so innocent, Laura thought with relief. I should have known. I *did* know; I told Paul he was wrong.

She reached down casually and pulled at the bottom drawer. And found it locked.

She knelt before the cabinet. *I wish I was home.* She sat on her heels and looked at the locked drawer. The metal shone in the lamplight. *Just to make sure; just to make sure; just to make sure.* And then, using a credit card and a nail file, she picked the lock.

Damn it, I shouldn't be this good at it; I should have forgotten how.

She pulled open the drawer. It was empty except for a thick envelope, turned over so she couldn't see the name and address on it, and a box of polished mahogany. She lifted the box; the wood was silky in her hands. She raised the lid. The box was lined in blue velvet, and, lying upon it, dazzling in its ruby and diamond brilliance, was Leni Salinger's necklace.

CHAPTER 30

C LAY parked in the garage a block from his loft, and all the way home he and Myrna continued the argument they'd started at the party. They had a lot of these lately: quarrels that started from nowhere and blew up like a balloon and then exploded with shouting and a broken cup or two, and then the two of them would fall into bed, and Myrna would get on top, or suck him for a long time, until they were friendly again.

"I don't want to, that's why," Clay said as they passed the doorman. "I'm not giving you—"

"Mr. Fairchild," the doorman said. "Miss Fairchild was here earlier to see you. She left about an hour ago."

"She came here? Did she say what it was about?"

"No, sir. She waited upstairs for a while and then left."

"She probably left a note," Clay muttered. "Something to do in the morning." In the elevator, he picked up where he had left off. "I don't want to go to any more of these damned benefits because I hate putting on a fucking tuxedo, I hate the food they serve, and I hate being looked up and down by the people who go to them."

"They're looking you up and down because they like what they see. Clay, those are the people you read about in the paper! One of these days we'll have our picture in the paper, too."

"I don't want my picture in the paper. And I don't read about them—

you do. I don't give a damn about them. Stuffed shirts who have too
much money and think they run the world . . ."

He unlocked the door. "I mean it, Myrna, you can yell your head off
but you're not going to haul me to any more of them. Christ, all I need
is a nagging, pushy, social-climbing wife."

"You don't deserve any wife at all," she shot back. "I'm trying to make
you better, get you in the right circles—"

"Fuck it, lady, don't make me better; just leave me the hell alone!"

"Maybe I should! Maybe we ought to call the whole thing off!"

"Sounds like a damn good idea to me!"

She strode away and disappeared around a wall of cabinets into the
kitchen. Clay paced the room, looking for a note from Laura. Nothing.
Maybe I should call her, he thought; it might be important; why else
would she come over here? But it was two-thirty in the morning; he
couldn't call now; he'd see her at work. Pulling off his cummerbund and
black tie, he went into the bedroom and flung them on the bed. "Like a
jail suit," he muttered, unbuttoning his shirt. "Worse, all that starch—"
He stopped, his hands stilled on one of his buttons. Hadn't he closed his
closet door? It was open a crack; he was sure he'd closed it.

He shut his eyes and thought back. Maybe not. He'd been in a hurry;
Myrna was calling him from the front door, saying they'd be late. He'd
given it a shove; it may not have closed all the way. And even if he'd left
it open, nobody was around.

Laura was. And if something had made her curious . . .

He opened the door and looked inside. Everything was where it
should be, even a pair of cufflinks he'd left on top of the file cabinet.
Leaning down, he pulled on the bottom drawer. Locked. Nothing to
worry about.

Still . . .

He took out his key ring and used a small brass key to open the
drawer. The envelope was there. The box was there. He reached inside
and lifted the lid of the box.

Empty.

He staggered and went down on one knee. His head felt as if somebody had cracked him one. He knelt there and started to shake. She'd
found it. And taken it. After all these years of trusting him and believing
him, she knew—

What? What did she know? That he'd done the job eleven years ago,
on the Cape. That he was the one who'd fought with Owen in the
hallway when the old fool reached for the light switch. But that was all
she knew. She didn't know about any other robberies; she probably
didn't even know there'd been any. How could she? They were all the

hell over the place—Paris, Acapulco, Palm Springs—there was no way she could know about them.

But she wouldn't trust him anymore. She wouldn't love him anymore. And if she did find out about the others...

His head was throbbing and he was shaking all over. He was scared to death. He had to get out of there. She'd call him in the morning, or wait for him in his office, and confront him with those big eyes, looking at him as if he'd let her down and he couldn't stand it.

She wouldn't help him anymore, or worry about him, or try to take care of him. She wouldn't give a damn about him ever again because now she knew he'd lied to her all these years. He'd even made her think it was Ben, and she'd loved Ben so much.

She'd fire him.

He started to cry. She was the only person in the world he loved, and the only person whose love he cared about, and now he'd lost it.

He should have sold the fucking necklace. But he'd never been able to let go of it. At first he'd thought he'd sell it, like the rest of Leni's jewels, but it was too valuable and too well known. And then he knew he didn't really want to sell it, because those bastards had kicked him and Laura out, and the necklace was like a badge of honor: he'd fucked the Salingers. He would pick it up and run it through his fingers and think, They want it back but they'll never get it. They took Laura's inheritance and kicked us out. They stole from us; I stole from them.

But after a while he almost forgot the necklace. The past few years he'd barely looked at it. He had so many other things going for him: bigger stakes, bigger risks, the greatest time of his life.

"Clay?" Myrna was calling from the kitchen, as if they'd never had a fight. "I've got cheese and crackers; do you want some?"

He tried to answer, but he was crying and only a strangled sound came out.

"Clay?"

"Yeah. Wait."

"I was thinking of hot spiced wine. Unless you want brandy."

"Brandy."

"Then bring some from the buffet, okay?"

"Okay. Few minutes."

"Take your time. I know what I'll do. I'll make hot wine and spike it with brandy. That ought to get my man in a good mood before I take him off to bed."

Got to get out of here. The words were a drumbeat inside him. Out of here, out of here, out... He couldn't face Laura; he couldn't bear to see that she hated him. Out, out, out. Shaking, tears streaming down his face, he pulled a duffel bag from under the bed and threw pants and sweaters into it, shirts, underpants, socks, an extra pair of shoes. Yanking off his dress shirt and tuxedo pants, he pulled on Levi's and a fisherman's sweater, socks and loafers, and a dark cap.

He yanked open the top drawer of the file cabinet and took from the back, hidden behind Laura's letters, two manila envelopes. He slipped them into his duffel bag. From another folder, he took three of his favorite pictures of Laura and put them between the envelopes to keep them from getting crushed.

All that had taken barely five minutes. From the bottom drawer he grabbed the thick envelope with Laura's name on it in Owen's handwriting. She must not have noticed it, he thought; she must have been so blown away at finding the necklace she didn't look at anything else. The envelope went into the duffel bag, too. He didn't know what he'd do with it—he knew she didn't need it anymore, now that she'd bought the shares in Salinger Hotels—but maybe someday it would help him find a way to make her love him again.

"Clay? Just about ready."

"Wait."

He zipped shut the duffel. He was still crying but he moved instinctively, slithering around the bookshelves and along the wall of the huge room with a speed and silence he'd perfected in years of practice. At the front door he grabbed his leather bomber jacket from the coat closet. And then, without a backward glance, he opened the door in absolute silence and closed it behind him, and was gone.

* * *

The flight to Boston was storm-tossed as the plane flew through rain and turbulent winds, and Laura gave up trying to concentrate on the meeting to come. *Clay, not Ben. Clay, not Ben.* All night the refrain had kept her awake. *And the other thefts—everything Paul said—probably true, probably true, probably true.* Her thoughts were as turbulent as the storm that had started about three in the morning and which still raged. She had wanted her own family. She had wanted it so badly she never looked beyond it to see the signs that were there. *The clues were all there for me to see, but I wanted to believe in him.*

Very early, Myrna had called, her voice angry. "He's gone. Snuck out while I was making him spiced wine. I thought he'd come back, but I think some of his clothes are gone, too. It was just a silly quarrel; everybody has them; but this time he took off. I suppose he's with you; he always runs to you as if you're his mommy. Please let me talk to him."

"I haven't seen him," Laura had said. She knew why Clay had left, but she would never tell Myrna; it would only make everything worse. She'd have to think about how to find him—or maybe leave him alone until he worked things out for himself and came back—but she couldn't think about it now; she had no time. She had to think about the Salinger board meeting.

She hadn't decided what she would do there. Until last night, she'd planned on walking in and exposing Ben for what he was, identifying herself as his sister. Why should she care if that hurt him with the Salingers? Look what he'd done to her.

But now she knew he hadn't done anything to her. He hadn't robbed the Salingers, he hadn't fought with Owen, he hadn't betrayed her. He'd told the truth, and she hadn't believed him; she'd told him she never wanted to see him again. She'd sent him away just as cruelly as the Salingers had sent her away.

Now that she knew that, how could she jeopardize everything he had? She had no right to invade the life he'd made and reveal his secrets.

But if she didn't tell them who she was, she couldn't get her stock purchase approved.

She didn't know what she would do. There was no reason to go to Boston if she was not going to claim her right to the shares as Ben's sister. But she had dreamed of confronting Felix for so long—so he would know she had gotten back what he had stolen from her—that the thought of giving it up forever made her feel empty inside. *I know I shouldn't want it; I've already got so much, and I have to think of Ben. . . .* But she did want it. It was inextricably entwined with the drive that had fueled her ever since Felix sent her away.

I can't decide now, she told herself. *I'll think of something on the plane. There's still time. I can't miss this meeting, I can't just give it up and forget about it, there must be a way. . . .*

By the time the plane had landed in Boston and she was in a taxi, riding through the familiar tunnel to the city, she was feeling queasy and light-headed, and it didn't seem to matter whether it was from the flight, or the long sleepless hours in bed after she had left Clay's apartment, or her apprehension about what lay ahead. Felix. And Ben.

At the Boston Salinger, everything was the same, yet everything was different. The hotel stood in haughty grandeur overlooking the Public Gardens: the lobby was crowded with businesspeople in gray and brown suits, all carrying identical briefcases; in the corner, Jules LeClair, impeccable and not a day older, sat at his desk handing out keys and advice. But the lobby was not as big as Laura remembered, and Jules was not as daunting, and the overhead chandelier was certainly smaller and less brilliant than in her memory. And some of the ashtrays needed cleaning; she remembered the lobby as always spotless and shining. Amidst the turmoil of her thoughts, she smiled. What had changed was Laura Fairchild.

She was late because of the storm, and she walked quickly to the elevators, before Jules could see her. She rode to the top floor, so swept by memories she was thinking of nothing else as she walked past the receptionist to the conference room door and opened it. She stood just inside, waiting for the men at the long table to notice her.

Ben saw her first. Looking up from the papers he was scanning, he frowned at the interruption, then looked puzzled because he saw someone he thought he knew . . . and then, his eyes wide with astonishment, he shoved back his chair. But before he could say anything, Felix was on his feet. "What the hell are you doing here? Get out!"

"Good morning, Felix," Laura said. Turmoil churned within her, but outwardly she was as cool as her severely cut ice blue suit. "Good morning, gentlemen." She came to the table and held out her hand to the man seated nearest to her. "Laura Fairchild."

His eyebrows rose. "Cole Hatton." He stood and shook her hand.

Across the table from Hatton sat Thomas Janssen, and Laura turned to him, holding out her hand. "I'm glad to see you again."

"My goodness, Laura," he said simply, and held her hand in his.

"This is a board meeting," Felix snapped. "If you don't leave, I'll have you removed."

Laura moved on and held out her hand to Asa. He looked at it, but he could not take it. Confused, his eyes darting about the room, all he could do was nod and turn away.

Laura hesitated; then, her face flushed, she introduced herself to the next two men, whom she did not know. They both stood and shook her hand. And then she was beside Ben, her hand out. "Good morning."

Their eyes met for a long moment: it seemed to Laura to last forever. Then Ben took her hand. "Good morning. I'm glad to see you." He moved aside so that his chair was free. "Will you sit down?"

"She will not." Felix's lips were a thin line. "This is a closed meeting!"

Cole Hatton interrupted. "I'd like to know why Miss Fairchild is here."

Laura sat in Ben's chair and took from her briefcase the purchase agreement she and Ginny had signed. "Virginia Starrett has sold me her shares in Salinger Hotels Incorporated. Since the purchase must be approved by the board, I thought it would be expedient for me to come in person—"

"Expedient!" Felix's face was dark; veins bulged at the sides of his forehead. "Bullshit! You came to make trouble! You know this board will not approve that purchase—"

"Felix," Cole Hatton said, "we haven't discussed this. I have no idea how I would vote on Miss Fairchild's purchase."

"Irrelevant," Felix snapped. "It will not be approved. This woman has—"

"I dislike being called irrelevant," Hatton said, his color rising.

"This woman has no moral character—no moral fiber—she is not fit to own a portion of this company—"

"Yes, you said that before," Thomas Janssen said mildly. He looked at Laura. She sat straight, with Ben beside her; he was watching her with that odd look of surprise, almost wonder, he'd had when she first appeared. They hold their heads the same way, Thomas thought; they even look a little alike: something about the eyes . . . "But I think we should listen to Laura. It's been a long time, you know, and things change, and perhaps we could benefit from her expertise."

"This matter is not on today's agenda," Felix snapped. "It will have to—"

"What's been a long time?" one of the other board members asked.

"What does moral fiber have to do with business?" the man beside him asked.

"This woman's hotels are under investigation for criminal activities," Felix said, his voice rising.

"'Criminal'?" Thomas asked.

"Thefts of fine art, massive thefts—"

"The hotels are stealing art?" Hatton demanded. "Pretty lively for a hotel, if you ask me. Well, Miss Fairchild, you tell us. Are you in trouble with the law?"

"No," she said.

"Police questioning you about your hotels running around stealing art?"

"No."

"Police questioning you about anything?"

"No."

"Police *talking* to you about anything?"

"No."

"Well, I don't need more than that. Miss Fairchild's name is one of the best in the business. I don't know what investigation you're talking about, Felix, but it strikes me as *irrelevant*. If Miss Fairchild has a purchase agreement from Virginia Starrett, I say we vote on it and get on with the meeting. It's a simple up or down vote. And I so move."

"You may if you insist," Felix said furiously. "In fact, I'll second it. And I vote no. Asa?"

Asa looked at the table. "No," he mumbled.

"So that settles it," Felix said. "Approval requires three-fourths of the board, and Asa and I, together, have almost a third. We'll go on with the meeting as soon as"—he gestured toward Laura, unable to say her name—"leaves." There was a pause. Laura stared at her hands clasped on the edge of the table. "I'm waiting."

"Of course the two of you can block it," Thomas said, "but I would like to discuss it further. I can make a motion to do that, if you'd like; I don't want to think we might be acting too hastily for a second time with Laura. If this is a bona fide sale, it seems to me she has a right to her shares. She paid a great deal of money for them. I for one am quite amazed—"

"Yes, we are all amazed," Felix said sarcastically. "The vote has been taken, and no new motion is on the floor. But since you bring it up, if the money was stolen, as it probably was, then the sale would be invalid on that ground alone."

"It was not stolen," Laura said clearly. She stood and walked to the windows, where she turned to look at them. Her voice was steady. "I thought most members of this board would be willing to vote on my ownership without prejudice. I especially hoped that Asa . . . Well, I did hope that Asa might. This *is* a bona fide sale," she said to Thomas. "If you want to ask Ginny Starrett about it, I'll give you her telephone number. And you were right about needing my hotel expertise: someone isn't cleaning the ashtrays in the lobby."

With a strangled oath, Felix shoved back his chair and almost ran around the table to the door. "This meeting is adjourned! *Adjourned!*" He opened the door. "Until you can behave—" He stopped and pulled himself up with stiff formality. "Until this board can behave in a businesslike manner."

"Just a minute!" Ben had moved around the corner of the table and now stood in Felix's place. "I didn't hear a motion for adjournment." He looked at each member of the board. "Is there one?"

"I moved adjournment!" Felix exploded. "You heard me."

"I didn't hear a second," Ben said evenly. His look fastened on Asa, pinning him down, and Asa, suddenly unsure of where the real power lay, this time kept silent. Everyone kept silent. "There is no second," Ben said. "It seems this meeting is still in session. Laura, you had the floor."

He waited for her to identify herself as his sister. He didn't know why she'd waited this long; she wouldn't get her shares approved any other way. He felt a strange kind of relief, and dread. He didn't know what would happen, but from the moment he had seen her—this wonderfully beautiful woman who was his sister—all his love for her had welled up, and he knew that, whatever happened, they would not deny each other again. She's my family, he thought with love and pride. And he waited for her to tell them who she was.

But she was silent. "Laura," he said again, "you were saying—?"

Her eyes met his. She knew she couldn't do it. She'd thought she would have everything she wanted as soon as she owned a piece of the Salinger empire, but now that she was on the verge of having it, she knew there was more. There was Ben. She loved him and she had done him a terrible wrong, and she was not going to do another. He'll tell the truth in his own time, she thought, or he won't; that's up to him. I'm not going to force him; I owe him at least my silence. Because it wasn't only Clay I was blind about; it was Ben, too. Paul, I'm sorry; you were more right than you knew.

She closed her eyes briefly. I'm getting pretty tired of apologizing, she thought, but it was my own fault.

"Laura," Ben said urgently. "We're waiting." She opened her eyes. They were all watching her. She looked at Ben and shook her head.

"What is this?" Cole Hatton demanded. "*What* are we waiting for?"

Ben took a long breath. What the hell, he thought; it had to happen sometime. I wish I'd had the guts to do it long ago. I wish I didn't feel as if I were on the edge of a cliff right now. "We're not going to wait any longer," he said quietly. "We're going to approve the sale of Virginia Starrett's shares to Laura Fairchild. I'd like to introduce her to you again, correctly this time." He glanced at Felix, who stood beside the door, frozen, knowing, somehow, that something terrible was going to happen. Ben reached out his hand, and Laura stepped forward to take it, her eyes wide, a smile trembling on her lips. "May I present my sister," Ben said clearly, and put his arm around her, and they stood together and faced the board of directors of Salinger Hotels Incorporated.

*　*　*

Her three rooms were exactly as she had left them, shining in the sunlight that had broken through when the storm passed. "They're too beautiful to change," Ben said as Laura walked through them. She was silent, trying to hold in the memories that battered her: all the love and laughter of the years she had lived there, the excitement of making a glorious new life, the exhilaration of discovering what Laura Fairchild could be, and do, and feel. "We used it for Judd for a while, but now we keep it as a guest apartment. Allison thought we might eventually put Judd's sister in it, when she gets old enough."

"Will it be a sister?" Laura asked. She was surprised at how normal her voice sounded.

"That's Allison's prediction."

Laura stood before the fireplace, looking at Paul's photograph of the three children building a sand castle. "I always thought of them as the three of us," she said softly. "You and Clay wanting to fly the pirate flag, and me thinking about ribbons and a room of my own."

"It's a brilliant photograph," said Ben. "Do you ever see him anymore?"

"Now and then."

He heard the change in her voice. "Are you still in love with him?"

"I've been so busy," she said vaguely. "I haven't had time to fall in love with anyone else."

Ben was about to say he'd asked a serious question, but he stopped himself. He couldn't expect her to trust him with confidences, not this soon; first they had to get used to being together. And that was so hard, so amazing. He wondered if he looked as stunned as he still felt; it all had happened so quickly and everything was changing, minute by minute, while he tried to keep up. "Are you able to keep up with all this?" he asked.

"Almost." She smiled. "I was prepared, you see: I knew I'd be at that meeting. But still, to see you, and be with you... Ben, we have so many things to talk about."

"Do you want to go through the rest of the house first?"

"Not now. I mostly wanted to see Owen's rooms and mine. I'll make some lunch, and we can talk in the living— Damn." Her face was burning. "I'm sorry; I'm behaving as if I live here."

Ben put his arms around her. "You should live here. I wish there was some way—"

"No. Of course not." She held him, then moved away. "I have a wonderful house in New York and that's where my work is; I couldn't live here even if you gave the house to me. I like the idea of you and Allison here, and Judd and Judd's sister. When will they get back?"

"I have no idea. Whenever Leni comes up from New York—did you know she's living there now? She's left Felix."

"I didn't know. How strange—I always thought of the family as staying the same. I knew I was changing, and years were going by, but whenever I thought of them, they were exactly the same."

"Nobody's the same; wait until you see Allison. They'll be here around five, I guess. Whenever the two of them go shopping, it seems to take most of the afternoon. I assume Judd is at the park now that the storm is over, and his nanny always has him back between four and five. It's the cook's day off; we'll make lunch together, is that all right?"

"I'd like that."

In Rosa's kitchen, the new cook had rearranged the utensils and dishes, and Laura felt resentful: what was wrong with the way she and Rosa had kept it? "Smoked chicken," Ben said, taking packages from the refrigerator. "Chèvre. Sliced tomatoes." He rummaged in the pantry. "Baguettes. Coffee or tea?"

"Tea, please."

In silence, they arranged the food on trays; there was so much to say they didn't know where to begin. But for Laura it was the first quiet time she had had since talking to Paul in her office the day before—impossible that it was only yesterday, she thought—and she let the silence surround her and ease the turmoil that had raged beneath her cool surface. It felt, eerily, like it might be the calm between two halves of a hurricane, but it was all right: whatever she had to face when she returned to New York and Colby's investigation, for now she was safe on Beacon Hill, in this loved house, and with Ben.

They carried the trays to the living room and sat on a velvet sofa Allison had moved to the bay window overlooking the cobblestones and tall trees of Mount Vernon Street. The storm had driven some of the red and bronze leaves from the trees, and they lay like fragments of stained glass on the brick sidewalks, glowing in the afternoon sun.

"Why didn't you tell them who you were?" Ben asked as he poured their tea. "I expected you to."

"I didn't want to hurt you with your family. If you'd wanted them to know about me, you would have told them, and obviously you hadn't. I know what it's like to be afraid of having a secret exposed, and I couldn't do it to you."

"I still don't understand." He handed her a cup. "I thought you hated me, ever since the robbery at the Cape."

"I did. I was wrong, Ben. I found out last night . . . Clay did it. He stole Leni's jewels."

Ben's hand froze. Then, carefully, he broke apart a baguette and buttered it. "I thought so. I even told you to ask him, didn't I? Clay was never one to resist temptation. How did you find out?"

"He still has the necklace. Had it. I found it and took it." She told him about her search in Clay's bedroom.

Ben sighed. "Idiot. Why the hell he didn't get rid of it . . ."

"I can't ask him; he's gone. But I'm glad he didn't; now I can give it back to Leni. I brought it with me. I thought I'd give it to you to return to her."

"Now you can do it yourself. What do you mean, he's gone?"

"Myrna—the girl he lives with—called this morning and said he was gone and it looked like he'd taken some clothes. I suppose the doorman told him I was there, and then he looked for the necklace and knew I had it. And he ran away. He always hated it when I scolded him; he—" Her throat tightened and she stopped. "I worried about him," she said, her voice low. "He was like a little boy trying to be a big man, but he was so sweet to me, and I wanted him to succeed and be happy. And grow up. But there's more, Ben; at least it looks like there's something more . . ."

Quickly she told him about Paul's film and Sam Colby. "I don't know if Clay has anything to do with it—I can't believe he'd endanger the hotels that way—"

"He probably thought no one would make the connection. And he had all that temptation laid out in front of him, every day, every month. Can you think of anybody else in the hotels who might have done it?"

"No. Well, me. That's what Sam Colby thinks."

"He's an ass if he does. No one who's done what you have with those hotels would jeopardize them. Clay would, because he never could look ahead to the consequences of things. But you do; if you didn't, you wouldn't be where you are now."

"How would Sam Colby know that?"

"We'll tell him."

"And accuse Clay?"

"If that's the choice. My God, Laura, Clay hasn't worried about you; he's put you in the most damnable position—"

"We don't know that."

"We know it, because we know Clay."

Laura clasped and unclasped her hands. "I didn't do a very good job with him, did I?"

"You sound like a parent. You can't take the responsibility for Clay; I should do that. I gave him a bad start."

Laura turned to him. "What did you do after the robbery?"

"You mean did I go on with my old ways?" He shook his head. "I never robbed anyone again. I thought about it—it was my only skill, you might say—but everything about it was wrong. It only took me twenty-six years to decide that. How's that for moral fiber? We should have brought it up at the board meeting when Felix looked like he was about to have a stroke."

"He wouldn't have understood it."

"No; he didn't even understand that we'd voted to adjourn. He wasn't functioning well."

"We gave him a bad time."

"Couldn't have happened to a nicer guy." They smiled together, then fell silent. "I can't believe it," Ben said. "I don't know how to feel. You're here and we're talking as if it's the most normal thing in the world, but it's not: it's a spectacular miracle. God, I've missed you; you have no idea how much I've missed you and wanted to see you—and been furious at you because you didn't believe me. Did you get my last letter?"

"Yes. I hated you for living in this house."

"I knew you would. After I mailed it I knew it was the most asinine thing I'd ever done. I should have called you. I couldn't do it; isn't that crazy?"

"Neither could I," Laura said. "I thought about it a lot, but I didn't know what to say; I was still so angry and hurt. What a waste anger is. . . . And then after a while I thought we'd gotten so far apart it didn't matter, we didn't care about each other anymore. But we never get that far apart, do we?"

"I hope not. At least not when we really love someone. Are you thinking about Paul?"

She smiled. "I think about Paul a great deal."

"You're very different, you know. I'd never have guessed you could be so cool and sure of yourself."

She laughed. "That's what the world is supposed to see. Inside, there's something like a cauldron, boiling away. You're different, too: gentler, calmer, much more confident. . . . You look very handsome and distinguished in those glasses. Like a diplomat about to bring nations together."

He smiled. "Right now I just want to bring us together."

"We are, aren't we? I mean, we're getting there. I feel strange with you, but then not strange, as if we've only been away for a little while. I want to hear all about you, all the things you didn't tell me in your letters. But . . ." She picked at her food. "Rosa would say the most important thing is to eat; then we can handle anything."

"Wise lady."

"A wonderful lady. Ben, I'm sorry for what I said." She put down her fork and leaned toward him. "All those terrible things I said to you at the Cape. I know I was young, but I should have believed you, I should have trusted you, at least I should have *thought* a little bit instead of just striking out. I'm so sorry for all of it, for hurting you and sending you away, and for not seeing what I should have seen . . ."

"Laura, it's all right, I know all that. I knew it then."

"No, you sounded so hurt—angry, but hurt, too—my God, more

anger and more hurt—and I loved you, but I thought you didn't love me."

"That's usually the problem," Ben said dryly. He put his arm around Laura, and she rested her head on his shoulder. "The evidence was against me. And you loved Owen and needed him more than you needed me."

"But that was all I thought of. Myself and what I wanted, not you, not even Clay. I didn't even try to think about how he might have done the robbery if you hadn't; I was too worried about myself and losing what I wanted—"

"Hey," Ben said softly. "You're overdoing the hair shirt. I accept all your apologies now and in the future, and if you'll give me a chance I'll make a few of my own."

Laura broke into laughter. "Dear Ben, it's so wonderful to have you back—" She turned up her face to kiss his cheek, and that was when Allison and Leni walked into the living room.

"My God," Allison gasped. "Ben? What the hell is going on?"

Laura and Ben turned sharply, but before either of them could speak, they looked at each other and burst out laughing, and could not stop.

Allison, six months pregnant, flushed with fatigue, stood in the center of the room, looking toward the bay window. All she could see were silhouettes as the laughter rang out. "Is it funny?" she asked furiously. "Will somebody please let me in on the—"

"Allison," said Leni, her voice strained, "it's Laura."

"What? Laura? *Laura?* Oh, for God's sake, how did you do that?" She burst into tears. "God damn it, can't you leave the men of this family alone?"

The laughter died. Ben leaped from the couch and went to Allison, enfolding her in his arms. "It isn't what you think. Allison, darling Allison, listen. Please."

"You *laughed,*" she said accusingly.

"Yes, but only because—oh, Christ, it's so complicated—"

"No, it's not; it's very simple. *I'm* very simple. I never suspected—never even *thought*—"

"Allison, I'm Ben's sister," said Laura. Her low clear voice rode over Allison's, cutting it off.

There was silence for the length of a heartbeat, and then Allison tore away from Ben's embrace. "Sister! My God, the oldest line in the world! Sister! Couldn't you think of something original? You were always so clever—how stupid do you think I am?"

"You're not," Laura said quickly, before Ben could speak. She went to stand beside him. "You helped make me what I am, you taught me a lot about the world, and you made me much too clever to use a tired old line that no one would believe. I'm telling you the truth; I *am* Ben's sister."

"I don't want to hear that!"

"Damn it, Allison, listen to me; I'm trying to tell you—"

"Don't you swear at me! You're here with my husband, lying to me—!"

"She's not lying!" Ben exclaimed. "If you'd listen—"

"Why should I?"

"Because I'm asking you to! Laura's telling the truth, and if you'd just be quiet for a minute, maybe we could get past this crazy scene. . . ." He waited, as if to see if what he'd set in motion would collapse.

But this time Allison was silent, and Laura said quietly. "The time I did lie to you was long ago, when I lived here. I wish I hadn't. I can't tell you how much I wish I hadn't. We all did each other harm, and I wish we could undo it, but couldn't we start, now, to tell the truth? Ben is my brother—half brother, really; Clay and I were born after our mother remarried, but we never thought of ourselves as anything but brother and sister when we were growing up. We kept it from you because"—she took a long breath—"Clay and I thought he'd done the robbery at the Cape, the first summer we were there, and I wouldn't see him anymore after that. I chose you over him, and we hadn't seen each other since that day. Eleven years . . . We were both wrong to keep it a secret, and I'm sorry we did—I'm sorry we did so many things—but you have to believe me . . ." Involuntarily she smiled. "This isn't a love affair; it's a reunion."

This time the silence was longer.

"It's crazy," said Allison.

"Indeed it is," agreed Leni. "But after all . . ." She looked from Laura to Ben and back again, and there was doubt in her voice.

"I did want to tell you," Ben said to Allison. "But the longer I put it off the harder it got."

"You lied to me. The whole time we've known each other."

Ben looked at Leni. "Please help us."

And Laura echoed it. "Please. If you'd let me . . . let us . . . We want to end the lying. We want to tell you everything."

Leni came to Laura and stood close to her, studying her face. Laura met her eyes, and for a long moment the two women stood that way, as if searching for a time that was gone. Then Leni nodded, without smiling. "I'd like to hear it," she said. She went to the sofa, took off her hat and jacket, and sat down. She lifted the cozy off the teapot and looked inside. "How nice. There's enough for all of us. Allison, come sit beside me. Ben, bring chairs for you and Laura. We'll have tea." She waited while Ben brought two armchairs to the tea table, and he and Laura sat down, facing the bay window. Leni poured tea. "Now," she said, "Allison and I would like very much to hear everything."

Laura could not remember her ever being so formidable. She wondered briefly if it was leaving Felix that had helped her achieve that confident authority, but then Ben began to talk and she listened to him, her tea growing cold.

"It was my fault: I thought up the robbery of your house on the Cape. A child's revenge," he said to Leni, "for Judd. I didn't tell you that when we talked before."

Leni stared at him. "You used Laura and Clay?"

"Yes," he said roughly. "I used them. And I've never forgiven myself for it."

"Judd?" Allison said in bewilderment.

"Not our Judd," Ben replied. "My father." And then he told it all, beginning with the day his mother told his father she wouldn't live with him anymore because of the spiral of despair and drinking that followed the theft of his company. His words were measured as he told Allison—and Laura, too, because she had never heard it—the story of Felix and Judd, and the vow of revenge that had sparked everything the young Ben Gardner had done in the years after his father's death.

When his story reached the time that Laura and Clay arrived at the house in Osterville, Laura picked it up, her low voice following his with barely a pause.

Taking turns, they told everything, up to the board meeting that morning. They did not mention Colby's investigation. That was another story, for another day. The afternoon light faded, the nanny brought Judd home and took him to the kitchen for his dinner, Allison turned on the lamp beside her, and Ben and Laura told their story.

When they finished, Allison was crying. "If you'd told me, if you'd just told me," she said to Laura. "I loved you so much, and I wanted to believe you . . . but then Daddy said you'd done all those things, and you didn't deny it—my God, your face was so cold!—and you looked at us as if you didn't know us."

"She didn't," Leni said. "We'd become strangers." She leaned forward and took Laura's hand. "I'm so sorry, my dear. So terribly sorry. We gave you love and a home and then took them from you; I can't think of anything worse that people can do to each other."

"They can lie," Laura said. "And that's what we did." A wistful smile touched her lips. "I've wanted to tell you I was sorry for that for a long time. But when we lived with you I was too afraid, and afterward, I was too hurt. And angry."

They sat in silence for a moment. Leni had struggled with herself briefly, wondering if she should tell Laura and Allison her part in the story. But she kept silent. It had nothing to do with what was happening in this room—a recapturing of loves that had been lost—and it would not add to anyone's understanding of the past eleven years. It was better to keep it between her and Ben. There will always be secrets, she thought; that's why we need trust, and understanding, and love.

"But once you get past all the anger," Allison said wonderingly, "we feel the same way about each other. Don't we?"

"Yes," Laura said. Her heart was pounding; it seemed impossible that she and Allison could be friends again.

"If feelings are enough," Allison said, suddenly doubtful. She looked at her mother. "Can we really just forget everything? All of us? Or will we always wonder if there are more secrets and more lies, so we can't ever be sure . . . ?"

Leni knew she was talking about her husband, not Laura. "I don't imagine we'll ever forget," she said. "In fact, I hope we don't. If we forget the past we'll never know how far we've come. But feelings . . . No, I don't think feelings are enough. We have to understand what happened and truly believe we can overcome it to protect the feelings we have. Love and friendship and a good marriage are worth protecting."

Allison nodded. "You said that this summer at the Cape." The others watched her as she frowned to herself. Laura sat very still. If Allison could accept everything she had heard and love Ben and Laura . . . Then all of us will have moved past that time, she thought, forgiven each other, and become a family again. Except for Clay. I still have to think of what to do about Clay. But so much would be changed, so much would be wonderful . . .

"I always wanted a sister," said Allison. "Remember, Laura, how we used to pretend we were sisters? Now we really are. Isn't that amazing?"

Laura let out her breath. "Yes," she said softly. She held out her hand and Allison took it. "Amazing," she repeated, and they smiled together.

Ben loudly cleared his throat. "Does that include a husband?"

Allison laughed. "Probably." She looked up at him as he came to sit on the arm of the love seat, beside her. "I love you. I can't imagine a life without you."

Leaning over, Ben kissed her. Laura turned away, trying to hide her envy. But her eyes met Leni's, and Leni knew.

"Oh," Laura said. "I almost forgot. . . ." She reached down and opened her purse and took out Leni's necklace. "I brought this for you; I was going to give it to Ben, but it's much better this way. I'm so sorry we ever planned it . . ."

Leni held the necklace in the palm of her hand. "But if you hadn't, you wouldn't be part of our family today." She gave Laura a smile so open and loving that Laura caught her breath; it was as if the years had disappeared. "Welcome back, dearest Laura. We've missed you. You'll stay with us tonight, won't you? Can you wait until tomorrow to go back? I'll be leaving then; we could go together. We have so much to talk about, much more than we can fit into one evening." She stood and held out her arms.

Laura went to her, dazed by the strangeness of what was happening. "I'd like very much to stay," she said.

Leni held her as if she were a little girl, and smiled. "It's such a relief," she murmured. "Such a wonderful relief to know we weren't wrong in our love. It's quite worth waiting for, to discover that."

* * *

How did she get the money?

It was the second time she'd made a fool of him: first with his father, and now with his board of directors, and this time he wasn't going to let it go, the way he had before; this time he'd find a way to destroy her. And it would be through the money; everything came down to money in the end. Whatever anyone did was done because of money. Whatever anyone thought was the result of thinking first about money. He'd get her through the money.

So think. How does a conniving witch who hasn't a penny to her name get the money to buy four hotels and, on top of that, two percent of one of the top corporations in America? She steals it, she forges checks, she prints money in her basement—for Christ's sake, this is no time for jokes—she cons some poor old sucker on his deathbed, somebody who prefers her to his own family . . .

But that's not a crime. You can't get her for that.

Unless it's fraud. And there has to be fraud. There's no way she could have gotten that money legally.

But it could be theft. Jewels. Or art. Colby thought she was doing it; he didn't try to hide what he thought. But it wasn't big enough. She couldn't get the kind of money she'd need . . . Could she? He hadn't asked Colby which paintings were stolen. The Rouaults he'd been robbed of were worth a fortune at auction, but how much could someone get fencing them? A fraction of their worth.

Unless they were stolen for someone who was willing to pay for them.

Then she might have gotten half a million for the three of them. But to buy the hotels and the shares, she needed at least twenty million, cash.

Maybe it was a little of everything. Fraud, theft, and wheedling it out of men. Fraud, theft, and trickery. A stew of money.

He had to see what her finances were. And he had ways of doing that. It was expensive, but the few times he'd done it with other people who were in his way, it had been well worth it.

It took three days. His informants had to find out which banks she used for mortgages, construction loans, and corporate and personal banking, and then find the people from whom they could buy the information. But it was done quietly and simply, and then he had it all. She was up to her neck in debt.

A smile twisted his mouth. He'd been exaggerating when he told Colby her interest payments could be half a million dollars a year, but he was a lot closer than he'd known; it was probably about three hundred fifty thousand. And it had to come out of those four hotels, plus a salary high enough to support her in New York. Unless it all disintegrated.

She had to have an impossibly high occupancy rate to make that kind of money. That meant creating and keeping the unshakable trust and good will of her clientele.

And what would her clientele think when they heard she was being investigated for a string of art thefts?

All it took was a hint of trouble to worry the kind of people who paid a thousand dollars a night for a suite.

She was as vulnerable as a rabbit in a field of foxes. All he had to figure out was how to make it public and still protect himself.

And so it was that the next afternoon, the last day of September and one of the hottest afternoons in Boston's history, Felix Salinger held a news conference in his air-conditioned office on the top floor of the Boston Salinger Hotel. He wore a dark suit; he looked somber and respectable; he looked like the essence of old Boston as he spoke to business reporters from *Advertising Age* and *Business Week*, stringers from *The Wall Street Journal*, *The New York Times*, and *The Chicago Tribune*, and a reporter from the Associated Press. They weren't the top people in town; he didn't expect that. But they were good enough.

And they did what he expected them to do with the story he gave them. In the next day's newspapers, and sitting like time bombs in the offices of the two weekly magazines, were stories quoting him as he defended Laura Fairchild.

Felix Salinger, owner of Salinger Hotels Incorporated and a vice president of the International Hotel Association, said yesterday there was no truth to rumors that Laura Fairchild, principal owner of the prestigious Beacon Hill hotels, is using her hotels to mastermind thefts of irreplaceable art.

"We have looked into the rumors, and there is absolutely no truth to them," he said from his office in the Boston Salinger Hotel. "Such irresponsible talk damages the entire industry by causing customers to lose faith in our ability to ensure their safety, when the truth is we are better equipped to ensure it than ever before."

Mr. Salinger was referring to several thefts of notable artworks from well-known collectors, all of whom had been guests at one of the four Beacon Hill hotels shortly before having their homes burglarized. It had not been publicly revealed, prior to this time, that six major thefts on two continents over the past three years may be related. Mr. Salinger said that no one knew who was responsible for the thefts. "But we do know," he said, "that members of the International Hotel Association police themselves, and I can assure the public that our hotels are safe and will remain so. If there is a common element to these thefts, I am confident it will be found to be something other than the fact that the victims were guests at one of the Beacon Hill hotels."

The art thefts are under investigation at the present time.

*　*　*

The next day, the telephone in Laura's office rang constantly. And in her four hotels, cancellations poured in.

CHAPTER 31

T HE story became known in newspaper and television newsrooms as "Felix's Bullshit": his "defense" that was in fact a knife in Laura Fairchild's back. The smart ones knew it as soon as they saw the story tucked away in the business section. They talked about Felix with contempt, but also with a kind of grudging admiration—"The son of a bitch can't even be sued for libel; he said she *didn't* do it"—and they knew he'd done them a favor by handing them a great story with everything in it: big money, international society, art thefts, a beautiful young woman, and posh hotels. And so with enthusiastic persistence they began telephoning Laura, and before the morning was half gone her secretary had memorized the standard response: "I'm sorry, but Miss Fairchild is in a meeting and can't be disturbed; she hasn't seen the newspaper story, but as soon as she does she'll probably have a statement for you. We'll let you know."

Laura had seen it and read it a hundred times; that was another open secret. But none of the reporters accused the secretary of lying; they simply showed up at the New York Beacon Hill and camped in the lobby.

"Laura," her secretary said on the intercom, "Sam Colby is on the telephone. I thought this one you'd want to take."

Laura nodded. "Thanks." She exchanged a quick look with Ginny, who was sitting on the couch, and picked up the telephone. "Yes, Mr. Colby."

"I'd like to see you, Miss Fairchild. I'm sorry I haven't called earlier."

"So am I. You might have had the courtesy to talk to me first."

"I said I was sorry!" Sam Colby was in a rage, and his words burst out like a blast from a shotgun. "I was conducting a serious investigation— quietly, to protect everyone involved—and never in all my experience has someone done this, gone sneaking to the press with *my* story, twisting it for his own—" He bit back his words. "Please excuse me; I've had a difficult morning."

"Have you," Laura said dryly. "I can't see you today, Mr. Colby; perhaps tomorrow or the next day. I'll put my secretary on; she'll make an appointment for you."

"I'd prefer today, Miss Fairchild."

"But I wouldn't. I've had a difficult morning, too." She rang her secretary, then hung up the telephone. "I should have seen him today, shouldn't I?" she asked Ginny.

"Oh, I don't know that it makes much difference." Ginny reached for the coffeepot. "More?"

"Yes, thanks." She shivered. "It's only the beginning of October; why is it so cold? I should have worn a sweater."

"You should have poisoned Felix when you were cooking for his family. You're cold because you're nervous and worried, honey; it hasn't a fig to do with the weather. You'll feel better when you find that brother of yours and he confesses and gets you off the hook."

"I don't know when we'll find him. And he may not be the thief."

"I'll be glad to watch his face while he tells us he isn't. And I imagine you'll find him soon, now that Ben's hired a detective to look for him."

Laura shivered again. "I hate that. Sending a detective to hunt down Clay. . ."

"Honey, he has not been kind to you."

Laura looked at her hands. "I know." She stared at them, longing for Paul. Leni and Allison had told her he was in London, and she had called him from the house on Beacon Hill the night she had stayed there. She had said good night to Ben and Allison and Leni and gone upstairs, to curl up in her familiar window seat in her old sitting room, and think back over the long day that had begun with the Salinger board meeting. And then she had known there was one more momentous step she had to take, and she had reached for the telephone and called him at the London Salinger. But he was not there. "He asked us to take his messages," the desk clerk said. "He's traveling on the continent for a few days." After girding herself to call him and tell him about Ben, she had been so disappointed she couldn't think of anything to do next. She did the only thing she could: she left a message, asking him to call her in New York. That had been five days ago, and she had not heard from him.

The secretary called on the intercom. "It's Ben Gardner, Laura; he says he's a relative and you'll definitely talk to him."

A laugh escaped Laura. "He's right."

"I just want you to know I'll be there this afternoon," Ben said. "The detective called. Nothing yet, but he's working on it. And Allison sends her love."

They were reaching out to her, Laura thought; a family, enfolding her when she was in trouble. Her family. "Ben, I love to hear from you, but you don't have to come down. There's nothing for you to do here. I'll tell the reporters something or other, and talk to Myrna again about where Clay might have gone, and then Ginny and I are going to try to stop the cancellations. If we can convince people they're safe here, we'll be all right."

Ben did not tell her how hard that would be without a solution to the thefts; she knew it already. "You'll call me if you need me?"

"Of course; it's wonderful to know I can. I'll call you even if I don't need you."

He chuckled. "I'll talk to you this afternoon."

When Laura hung up, she began to pace around her office. "What am I going to say to the reporters?"

"That you're as clean as a Girl Scout in a convent, and as soon as you locate Clay you'll have a story for them, and until then they can get their asses out of here and leave you alone."

Laura shook her head. "I can't tell them about Clay until I'm sure. I have no proof; neither has Colby. But I could say we've found out who the thief is and he's not with the hotels anymore. That's the truth, and it ought to help people feel confident about staying here."

"If they believe it."

Laura glanced at the list of cancellations that lay on her desk. "Some of them may."

The intercom rang again; Currier was on the phone. Laura picked it up. "I tried to call you, Wes. Your secretary said you were out of town."

"I'm in Dallas; I'll be in New York by two. And at three we have a meeting with the investors."

"We have a meeting—?"

"They've called it. Ordered it. They're worried about their money, Laura; you can't blame them."

"Wes, that story only appeared yesterday. They could give me a little time to straighten things out."

"That's what I'm going to recommend; I think you can weather this. Other hotels have survived crises, and they weren't as good as the Beacon Hill. But just because I believe that doesn't mean the others do; they want to know your plans. They've bought the right to know what they are."

There was a pause. "Of course. Where is the meeting?"

"In my office. I thought you'd feel better in familiar territory."

"Thank you, Wes. I'll be there."

Ginny was watching her thoughtfully. "Your money men?"

Laura nodded. "Worried about their money."

"You look mighty cool for a lady who's just been ordered into a lions' den."

Laura smiled faintly. "I have to be cool; they don't want to think they've invested in an emotional woman. But I know them pretty well; they're reasonable men and they've had a lot of confidence in me from the start. I'm not really worried."

"Sweetie, you're saying that for my benefit. You don't want me to worry about *my* millions. Well, you listen to me. I'd be a damn fool if I wasn't worried, but it's not a very big worry right now, and I can live with it. I'm not about to call my note; in fact, I'm doing the opposite. You can stop paying me for... oh, say six months. That'll cut down your monthly expenses and give you some breathing space until we get your hotels filled up again. I'll write you a letter on that; my accountant likes things to be in writing."

"Thank you, Ginny," Laura said. Her voice was husky. "I hope it won't take six months."

"I hope so, too, but I won't starve if it does. What are you going to tell the money men?"

"Probably the same thing I'll tell the press. As much of the truth as I can. I want to keep it as simple as possible."

But when she faced them in Currier's office, it was the investors who used that word. "We'll keep it simple, Laura," said Tim Alcott. He had made himself the spokesman for the three whom Currier had brought in when Laura wanted to buy the New York Salinger. Currier had argued against it at the time, since the new investors, voting together, would be able to outvote him and Laura, and control OWL Development, but she had been so determined to buy while she had the chance that he had given in. It had never been a problem until Laura sat with them at a round granite-topped table in Currier's office and Tim Alcott said, "We'll keep it simple." He owned Alcott Foods, the largest frozen-food company in the world, and he liked to say that he'd gotten where he was by being as hard and cold as his products. "We need to be sure we have a handle on OWL Development. We've got a substantial investment in it, and we want to have a substantial feeling of security, and right now we don't have that. You're getting cancellations right and left. If that isn't reversed *soon* we're going to be stuck with four very pretty, very empty buildings. So we're interested in how you plan to reverse it."

There always had been smiles when the five of them met; Laura hadn't realized how much she had taken those smiles for granted until now, when she saw around the table only the hard scrutiny of men appraising a piece of merchandise to see whether or not it was a good bargain. She wished she'd worn a suit instead of a silk dress. She wished she hadn't let her hair grow. She wished she looked more like a man.

Folding her hands on the table, she sat straight and took her time. "There was in fact a thief in the Beacon Hill hotels. We think we've identified him: someone who was part of the company and evidently used his position to gain access to the homes of our guests. He no longer works for us. In addition, we're expanding our security staff. All that information will be in a letter I'm sending to everyone who has ever stayed in a Beacon Hill hotel. I'm also meeting in a day or two with Sam Colby, the insurance investigator who is working on the thefts, and we hope to announce very soon that the matter is resolved."

"How soon?"

"Who's the thief?"

"Where is he?"

"You *think* you know?"

The three of them were all talking at once.

"I think we might let Laura speak," Currier said.

"I can't tell you who he is," she said quietly, "until we have proof, and until he's charged—"

"You don't have proof?"

"Not yet. We're working on that."

"So what is it you *think* you know? Is he talking? Who's questioning him?"

"The important thing," Laura said, "is that we're making contact with our guests. Besides the letter I'm writing, Virginia Starrett and I are going to be calling all those who have cancelled, and almost a hundred others, to reassure them about the hotels, to tell them we're satisfied that only one person was responsible for the thefts and he no longer works for us, and to ask them to stay with us again. I'm sure many of them will renew their reservations, and once they come back and find everything perfectly normal—"

"For God's sake!" Alcott exploded. "Everything is not *perfectly normal!* These hotels are tainted by scandal! You're nattering away about all this standard operating crap, but that's not what we need. We need action! And facts! And *good* publicity, for a change! Who is this thief you've got hidden away? I am asking you, young lady: *who is he?*"

"I can't tell you that. I won't accuse anyone publicly until I know for sure he's guilty."

"This isn't public, damn it, this is a closed meeting!"

"You'd talk, Tim. You want good publicity. I'm not going to take that chance."

"Goddam it to hell!" His face was beet-colored. "Who are you to tell me what I'd do? Huh? Where do you get off being so goddam cocky here? Now you listen to me: you sure as hell are going to tell us who this is you're talking about! We each paid nine million dollars for the right to know what the fuck is going on around here, and to change it if we don't like it, and I'm telling you now, there is no way you can clear the name of these hotels until you produce a thief, and I want to know who—it—is."

"No. I'm sorry, Tim."

"Okay, you want to play rough, we'll play rough. You won't tell us who it is because it's you. You've been burglaring your way around the world; everybody knows it—"

"Ridiculous," Currier snapped. "Are you out of your mind, Tim? Laura wouldn't—"

"Oh, wouldn't she. She owes a pile of money—*you* know how much she owes, Wes—and she had all these turkeys sleeping under her roof, ripe for plucking, and she worked it! She worked it for three years! Right? Am I right?"

"No! Of course not!" Laura's eyes were dark with anger. "You have absolutely no reason to believe that. You've been involved with these hotels almost from the beginning; you've seen what I've done with them. I've made them what they are, and I wouldn't risk them for anything. I certainly wouldn't steal—"

"Is that so! Well let me tell you something, young lady. I've got a friend over at the *Daily News*, and he told me there's going to be stories in tomorrow morning's papers that say you were convicted of theft once already, and that there was some fight over an inheritance you weaseled out of somebody—I don't know the details and I don't give a shit right now—but this is not a sterling reputation we're talking about! Here's three of us came in with nine mill each because Wes told us it was a good deal, and now we find out we backed a convicted crook!"

Laura had met Currier's eyes, seeing the shock in them and knowing it reflected her own, and then she looked away, past all the investors, at a large painting behind Currier's desk: an abstract in shades of blue, gray, and black. I never noticed how gloomy it is, she thought. Like a collection of shadows.

There were shadows everywhere. Again and again they crossed her sunlit path; no matter how fast she ran, she could never outrun them.

Currier looked at Laura, giving her a chance to speak, but she couldn't; she felt as if she were smothered by shadows; and after a moment he spoke for her. "You don't believe Laura is the thief, Tim; I know damn well you don't. You're using it as a ploy to get rid of her."

"You got it, Wes." Alcott nodded. "We're getting rid of her. I don't know if she stole anything or not—I don't give a damn. The only thing I know for sure is that she's got to go. These hotels aren't going to wait around until a mythical thief is produced, or this young lady decides to fess up and bow out on her own. The only way we can make people think we've got safe places for them to lay their precious heads is to make a clean sweep and put in a new boss."

Currier looked at Laura again, his eyes urging her to defend herself, but she sat frozen, barely breathing, her eyes on Alcott's small mouth.

"The three of us got twenty-seven million bucks in this outfit, Wes; you think we're gonna sit on our duffs while Laura tries to sweet-ass people into spending their money in places they don't trust? Shit, you know better than that. So what I'm doing, I'm calling this meeting to order, and I'm making a motion that we remove Laura Fairchild from the position of president of OWL Development."

They can't do this.

"Do I hear a second?"

This is my company. They can't steal it from me.

"Second," the investor on his right said firmly.

I'm not going to let that happen again—at least not without a fight.

"All those in favor—"

"According to the rules, we have discussion before a vote!" Laura's voice whipped across the table. She pushed back her chair and stood up. "If no one else has anything to say, I have." She looked down at Alcott and the two men on either side of him. "You've had your millions in this company for two years, and you were perfectly satisfied as long as the value of your investment was increasing and you were getting my loan payments on time. You didn't give a damn about anything else. I could have been running whorehouses or bookie joints or heroin distribution centers for all you cared; you never even came around to look. And you weren't concerned about who I was, either: from the first day you met me you never ran a character check on me. All you cared about when Wes introduced us was the return on investment in the Chicago Beacon Hill; you did look at our books there."

"You're wasting our time," the investor on Alcott's right said, and looked at his watch.

"This is *my* time," Laura said furiously. But then she swallowed hard. *Don't blow it. Don't yell at them. They'll call you a hysterical woman.* She clasped her hands loosely in front of her. "I'd appreciate it if you would listen. It's not a small matter, and all I ask is a few minutes."

The investor on Alcott's left gave her a long look. "Fair enough. Go ahead."

From then on, Laura spoke directly to him. "When I was fifteen, I was caught leaving a house I'd robbed. I was convicted and put on probation for a year. Since the day that happened, I haven't stolen or committed any other crime. I finished high school and college, and I've worked for everything I have. We all have things in our past that we want to put away. Tim, you've had one divorce, and your second wife committed suicide—"

"Goddam it! Who the fuck do you think you—"

"It's public knowledge," Currier said mildly, trying not to smile. "Sit back and listen, Tim; Laura has the floor."

Laura gave him a quick, grateful look, then went on as if no one had interrupted. "That's not a sterling reputation to offer a woman who might be thinking of marrying you. But I imagine you'd tell her she shouldn't judge you by your past, or punish you for the actions of those who marry you—or work for your company."

Her voice was low and even. The room was quiet. She looked at the three investors. "Ten years from now, are you still going to be punishing your teenagers for trying marijuana or drinking too much beer or shoplifting from a store? Or will you judge them as the adults they've become? That's all I'm asking you to do now—judge me the same way you invested in me; by what I'm accomplishing now. You were satisfied to let me make money for you; you never lost money or had any reason to think you would. I don't think you're going to lose any now. I can run these hotels better than anyone you could bring in—"

"Christ," Alcott snorted. "The CEO of Hilton or Marriott, or Coca-Cola, for Christ's sake, could run this corporation; it's a *business*, you know, or have you forgotten that with all your dribble about teenagers?"

"I haven't forgotten. You're right: another CEO could run OWL Development, but the Beacon Hill hotels wouldn't be the same. You don't have any idea what I do to make them different from all the other luxury hotels in the world; no one knows, because I don't publicize it. The CEO of Coca-Cola wouldn't have the relationship I've built up with our guests over the past years; he wouldn't know about the letters I write to them before they arrive and after they leave, or the way I train my staffs to give the kind of service no one else does, or how many of the personal touches that make the hotels special are mine and no one else's. These aren't a bunch of buildings that just happened: they're Laura Fairchild's hotels, and no one else could step in and keep them that way; they would be different within a week."

"Different is what we want," said the investor to Alcott's right. "Why the fuck would we want them the same when everybody thinks they're happy hunting grounds for thieves?"

"You mean people are going to change their minds because you bring in a new CEO?" Laura demanded. "What will have changed? The person at the top. Will that convince them there's no longer a thief running around the corridors? I'll tell you what they'll be convinced of: that you don't have confidence in the management of the hotels they've enjoyed and recommended to their friends. They'll be convinced that they've been wrong every time they said a good thing about a Beacon Hill hotel, and they're right to be afraid to come back. And if they do come back, they'll find the Beacon Hill is no longer what they remembered. You will have made everything even worse than it is now. But if I stay, we—all of us, together—will be telling our guests that even though the Beacon Hill has had a serious problem—*and tell me one company or institution that hasn't, at some time in its history*—their judgment was excellent: the hotels are as solid and well-managed as they always thought."

She took a long breath. "I am not going to walk quietly away from this company. We've had a setback—a terrible one, I know, but not irreversible. Not if we work together to keep the reputation of the Beacon Hill hotels exactly what it has been from the beginning. Our guests want to trust me. If we give them reasons to do it, they will, as they always have. They're sophisticated enough to know that it usually takes a lot more than one problem to bring down a solid company, especially when that problem is being resolved—will be resolved. You have my word on that."

She looked at each of them again: wealthy, powerful men who wanted to be sure they were backing a winner. "Damn it, you trusted me once; we built a major hotel group in a few years! And I'm giving you my word that I'll do everything I can to—"

"Stay in power," Alcott said flatly. "Have you finished?"

Laura gazed at him. "To keep the hotels, and OWL Development, as strong and profitable as we all assumed they would be in the beginning. Now I've finished, Tim."

"Then I'd like a vote on my motion, which is to remove Laura Fairchild from her position as president of OWL Development. I vote yes." Ostentatiously, to show he was going by the rules, he wrote his vote on a pad in front of him, then turned to the man on his right, waiting for his vote.

"Yes."

Alcott nodded with satisfaction and recorded the vote. "Laura?"

"No." Her mouth was dry. Years of dreams and hard work, and it came down to this: a group of people saying one word.

Alcott wrote down her vote. "Wes?"

"No."

"Of course." He wrote, then, smiling, he turned to the man on his left.

"No."

There was a moment of stunned silence. A wave of exultation swept through Laura, and her eyes were bright as she met those of the man whose vote had allowed her to stay on as president of OWL Development.

"You're right: the hotels are a reflection of you," he said. "I think that's the best thing we have going for us."

With a grunt, the investor on Alcott's right pushed back his chair. "One minute," Alcott said quickly. "I think before we leave we should take care of one more piece of business. I think we'd all agree that we need some reassurance here. We have damn little information, and that always makes me nervous. So I'm making another motion: that Laura has thirty days to clean up this mess. If we're in no better shape in thirty days, then she leaves and we get somebody in to salvage things. Even thirty days may be too long; who knows? I sure as hell wouldn't want it to be more than that. But we have to know what's going on! Agreed?" He looked around the table.

The man on his right nodded. "I'll second that motion."

"Discussion?" Alcott asked, looking at Laura.

But Currier spoke first. "I think thirty days is fair, but automatic dismissal isn't. If Tim allows, I'll amend the motion to say that in thirty days we look at the situation and take another vote on whether Laura stays."

Alcott glanced at the man on his left and understood he would vote against him again. He shrugged. "Amend it, then."

When they voted, all were in favor. "Thirty days," Alcott said to Laura as they all stood. "It would be best for all of us if you didn't take that long."

"I agree," she said, and held out her hand.

"Keep us informed," he said, and shook her hand.

She stood beside the table, watching them leave, suddenly feeling drained and exhausted. *Thirty days. One month. When I was a little girl that seemed like such a long, long time.*

* * *

The next day's edition of the *Daily News* carried a report of the meeting in Currier's office in a story that included Laura's background, brief descriptions of the victims of the six robberies, and the only words the reporter had been able to squeeze out of Sam Colby: "We're making progress; we expect an arrest soon."

It was that story that made an executive of a television network wonder why Paul Janssen was in Europe when he was supposed to be making a film for them about Sam Colby, who was in New York. "I'm flying back in a few days," Paul said when the executive called. He was impatient. He had just returned to his hotel and found the message from Laura; he held the slip of paper with her name on it and was driven by urgency: he had to call her. "I have someone to call; I'll get back to you in a few minutes."

"Hold on. Why are you over there when you've got a start on a hell of a story in your own backyard?"

Paul took a breath. "I told you I'm using a different investigation to show how Colby operates; we've got good footage on police and some of the victims—"

"Different investigation? We've got a hot story that's popping off the pages; everybody wants it and you've got a head start on the whole world. Why the hell would you use a different one?"

"Hot story? What are you talking about?"

"Oh, shit, you don't even know. . . . Hold on, I'll read you the stories." He pulled them from his folder on Colby and read Felix's statement and parts of two later stories from the *Daily News*. "I'll ask Colby if I can send a cameraman to film his next interview with the Fairchild gal so you won't miss out on it. Then if you get cracking, as soon as Colby wraps it up we've got a film. We'll air it as soon as we can, while it's still hot. We can always use it again during ratings month. Forget any ideas you had about another story; this is the one we want."

"I'm not doing this one," Paul said. *That's what she called me about.* "I wrote you a note on this two weeks ago; I told you I was using a different story and I'd tell you about it as soon as I knew what it was."

"A note? I never got it. Oh, wait, maybe I did. I don't know; it didn't matter then. It only matters now. This thing has broken in the last five days, and that's what matters. Listen, this is the film we want: Colby's investigation of six thefts that came from the Beacon Hill hotels. God, the ratings! Who could of guessed, when you started—?"

"I am not doing a film on the Beacon Hill hotels," Paul said. "Sam and I talked about this some time ago; it may not even be the hotels. He isn't sure; nobody is. I want to use an investigation that's complete—he'll take us through the whole thing—so I don't have to worry about finding out at the last minute that all my footage is on a dead-end investigation. I'll get this to you as soon as I can—"

"I don't want whatever 'this' is. I want the film I want. I don't know what your real reason is for not doing it, but we're paying for a good part of this film and, damn it, we have a right to tell you how to do it."

"No one has that right. Is that clear? Do you think funding this film made you its producer or censor? This was my film from the first, and I make it the way I decide or I don't make it at all. At least not for you."

"Then goddam it, you don't make it for us. I don't like your attitude, Paul. The trouble with you rich playboys is you aren't hungry enough: you don't lose enough if you fail. This is just a hobby for you so you think you don't have to take orders. Well, this is one order you'll take. If you don't deliver this film, on time, the way we want it, we'll never show any of your stuff on this network again, much less give you any money, for Christ's sake. Will that make you think a little bit?"

"I don't have to. I don't give in to blackmail."

"That's a mean word; don't use it, Paul. This is a negotiation. You just shoot the film the way you've been doing, then you add footage on the hotels and the Fairchild gal, and her gang, if she's got one, that's pulling off the thefts—"

"No," said Paul in disgust. "And that's final."

He hung up, then immediately picked up the telephone to call Laura. But she was not in her office; her secretary would say only that she was in a meeting and would not be back that day. "Tell her Paul Janssen called," he said. "Tell her I'm coming home."

*   *   *

At the same moment that Paul hung up, Clay stopped at a newsstand on Perea Street, in the center of Mexico City, and bought a copy of the *New York Daily News*, to read about home. He sat in a cafe, ordered coffee, and opened the paper. And on the second page he found himself staring at a large picture of Laura. Rapidly, he read the story beneath it. She was suspected of being a thief. And her hotels, and her position with them, were in jeopardy.

He stared at it, rereading it all that day and evening. He didn't believe it. But it was there, in front of him: son of a bitch, it was true.

He brooded over it. Something else dumped on him. He was miserable enough at having to leave New York; he'd been gone less than two weeks, and already he couldn't stand it; he was going crazy, knowing that Laura didn't love him anymore and that he'd probably never see her again. Christ, he thought, how did they put it all together? He'd been so sure they wouldn't: he'd never gone to the same city twice; he'd never left a fingerprint or anything that would connect one job to the others; he'd always sold the stuff to one broker who sold them to his clients, and the broker didn't even know his name or anything about the Beacon Hill hotels, so he couldn't give it away. He'd had it all figured out; it was absolutely brilliant. So how the fuck had they gotten to the hotels?

And Laura. Blaming it on Laura. Clay sat in the library at the University of Mexico City, reading back issues of the *New York Daily News*. He was barely mentioned. Goddam it, didn't they think he was clever enough to think it up? Why did they think it was Laura? Nobody ever gave him credit; first it was Ben who was the smart one, and then it was Laura. Shit, I was the one who worked out the robbery at the Cape; I'm the one who's been lifting high-priced art for three years, with nobody being the wiser; everything was perfect until Laura found that fucking necklace, and now this other thing—Christ, it couldn't have come at a worse time. . . .

Oh, Clay, you're always thinking of yourself. Laura's voice was so clear in his head he panicked and looked around the hushed room to see where she was. *Just once couldn't you think about somebody else? We all have problems, you know; you're not the only one . . .*

She'd said that when he was complaining about having to share a secretary with the part-time accountant Laura had hired. He hadn't wanted to share anything; he was vice president for maintenance and quality control, and he deserved his own private secretary. *I'll get you one when I can; I'm trying to keep the payroll down. I'm sure you can understand that.*

Sure, he'd said, and kissed her, because he didn't want her mad at him. And that night he'd brought her flowers and a bottle of wine and they'd cooked dinner together at her place, and everything was fine; she still loved him.

But now she wouldn't. He'd gotten her in a hell of a mess, and she'd never love him again. She'd think he never thought of anybody but himself.

He left the library and went to a bar on Madero Street. The streets were even more crowded than in New York, but it didn't make him feel at home; everybody talked in Spanish, and he was an outsider. He brooded over a scotch and thought about himself. He had to: if he didn't, who would? Nobody cared about him.

Laura cared about him. For a long time. But no more.

He couldn't ever go back. There was no place for him anymore; no job, no sister, nobody who cared about him.

Well, shit, if he couldn't go back, why not tell them he'd done those jobs, and then they wouldn't blame Laura? What difference did it make to him? He was safe here; nobody knew where he was; he could call them up and tell them, and that would be the end of it. It wouldn't even stop him from doing more jobs when he needed money and excitement.

He finished his drink. The trouble with that was, he'd need some proof or they might think he was lying to protect his sister. Well, he had proof; he could send it to them. He wouldn't phone them; he'd write to this guy, Sam Colby, and tell him the whole story, and send one of the manila envelopes he'd taken from his file cabinet when he fled his apartment. There were the two original Dürer prints inside that he'd taken from the Laughtons because he liked them, not because his broker had wanted them for somebody. And there were also six keys, copies made from wax impressions he'd taken in the rooms of Beacon Hill guests while they were out for the evening. Each was labeled: Guarneri, Laughton, Farley, Serrano. . . . How was that for proof? Perfect, that's how it was. He'd send them to Colby. He could do that.

He could do that for Laura. Then she couldn't say he was only thinking about himself.

"The same," he said to the bartender, and in a minute another scotch appeared in front of him. What if it wasn't enough, though? What if all that nifty proof didn't bring people back to her hotels? Or what if it took a few months, maybe even a year, to get everybody back? She wouldn't have any money coming in. His confession wouldn't do a damn thing to help her there. She needed money to make the payments on her loans, and to keep the staffs of the hotels paid, and maintenance and all the rest. Thousands of dollars a month.

Well, she had those shares of Salinger Hotels stock. She could sell them, and then she wouldn't have so much to pay off every month. But that wouldn't solve anything. Anyway, she shouldn't have to sell her stock; she just bought it, and she was so excited about it, finally getting what she should have had in the beginning, after Owen left it to her in his—

"Goddam son of a bitch! I can take care of that, too!"

People stared. He'd been hunched over on his bar stool for over an hour, a solitary figure scowling as he downed his drinks. Now he sat up, his small mustache stretched above a wide grin. "It's perfect! It's beautiful!"

He'd send Owen's letter to Colby, along with the Dürer prints and the keys. He'd read the letter a dozen times: it proved Owen was totally in his right mind when he decided to leave Laura the hotels and his house and two percent of his shares in the company. Well, she'd bought the hotels and the shares, and she might not want the Beacon Hill house anymore, but how about another two percent of the company? Another ten million bucks' worth. She sure as hell could use that.

Unless the letter was too old to do any good after all these years. I need a lawyer, Clay thought. He started to laugh. That seemed very funny to him.

But the next morning he got very serious and went to see a law professor at the university. "I'm a law student at UCLA," he said earnestly. "I'm on a vacation and I brought some of my work and I need some information, and if you could help me..."

"I do not know the laws of all your states," the professor said.

"Well, this is general. Do you know if a jury's verdict can be cancelled years later if new evidence is found that shows it was wrong?"

"Ah, this I know. It cannot. Once a verdict is given, unless it is immediately appealed, it is final and cannot be changed."

"But if it was wrong—"

"Even then. Except in cases of life or death, new evidence by itself can accomplish nothing."

"Shit," Clay muttered.

"Of course, if you find the new evidence was willfully withheld from the jury, then that would be fraud. If you can prove the deception, you might successfully prosecute someone for fraud. If that is what you wish to do."

Slowly, Clay looked up. "Fraud."

"If that is what you wish to prove. I gather this is not something you are doing for law school; this is a personal matter?"

"No! Well, sort of. I'm getting information for a friend."

"Of course. Is there anything else you wish to know?"

He shook his head. "You've been great. Thanks."

Felix in jail for fraud. The idea was so delicious Clay could almost taste it. He walked across the campus and took a bus into the center of the city. Felix in jail for fraud. They'd get back at him for what he did to Laura. And if he asked them to keep Owen's letter a secret so he could stay out of jail, they might do that—in exchange for ten million dollars' worth of shares in Salinger Hotels, made out to Laura. Maybe more than that.

Absolutely beautiful. They had the bastard coming and going.

Except—he didn't know how to do it. If he sent the letter to Laura, who'd believe her if she said Felix had hidden it? Even if he wrote to Colby or somebody, telling them he'd taken it from Felix's desk, who'd believe him? The only way would be if Felix still had the letter and other people saw him with it.

He wandered into the Cafe Cordova for lunch and ordered *huevos* and a beer. When the beer came, he poured it slowly into his glass. And as he did so, an image came to him: a safe, nearly empty, in a New York town house on Fifty-first Street. If the letter was in Felix's safe, and he didn't know it, and he opened it in front of witnesses, there wasn't one single fucking thing he could say that would convince anybody that he hadn't hidden it to keep Laura from getting her inheritance.

Goddam, Clay thought, staring at his beer. That would do it. That would do it for Laura. And it would take care of Felix, too.

He grinned, feeling excitement build inside him. Of course he'd be doing it for Laura, only for her, but still, it was fantastic: really different, really dangerous. For the first time in his life, he was going to break into a house not to take something out, but to put it in.

CHAPTER 32

LAURA was speaking with the concierge when Paul arrived. At first she did not see him. "Everything must be the same," she was saying. "Just because we have empty rooms doesn't mean the service will change."

"I agree, Madame Fairchild. I told my assistant to take his vacation now because this week I can spare him but in a short time, when all is resolved and our guests return, I will need him once again."

Laura smiled. "Very good," she murmured.

"I have also told . . . ah, excuse me." He looked behind Laura. "Yes, sir, may I help you?"

"When Miss Fairchild is free," Paul said.

Laura spun about and found herself almost in his arms. Their eyes held, and her hand came up and met his. Their fingers twined. "Welcome home," she said softly. Her face was flushed.

He smiled at her, and she felt the years drop away. "When you're finished here . . ."

"Yes." She turned, her hand still clasped in Paul's, and swiftly concluded her conversation with the concierge. "Anything else we'll take care of tomorrow. Unless you have any questions?"

"No, madame. Everything is under control."

"Yes," Laura murmured. "Perhaps now it is." She looked at Paul. "Where would you like to go?"

"I'd like to see your house."

She smiled at him. "I'd like you to be there." They walked through the lobby, hand in hand, not speaking. They barely spoke in the taxi; there was too much to say. It was enough to sit together, their hands still entwined, their bodies touching, their eyes meeting in a smile while the driver wove through traffic and talked back to a radio talk show.

Inside the house, Laura closed the door. "I would very much like to kiss you."

Paul chuckled. "My love . . ." He took her in his arms, and they kissed in a long embrace. "I picked a terrible time to be away," he said at last.

"But a wonderful time to come back. I did want you so, the last few days. . . ."

He kissed her again, holding her, rediscovering how her body fit to his. "Do you know how often I've dreamed of this? I've had so many conversations with you in my head you'll be hearing them for the next fifty years. Do you know how many things I want to do for you? Do you have any idea how much I love you?"

"Paul, what are you talking about?" She drew back and looked at him. "What about Emily? I can't pretend she doesn't exist."

"My God, you don't know. No, of course not, how could you? Emily is in California. We're getting a divorce. I can't be sure when it will happen, but soon. I'll tell you about it later. Not now."

"No, not now." Her eyes shone. She was warm, so warm; her blood sang and her mouth opened beneath his. "I want to make love to you," she said. She smiled with a hint of the liveliness he remembered. "It's very hard when a woman has to think of everything, Paul; you haven't even mentioned it. Does that mean you can't be sure when it will happen?"

He laughed. "I'm sure of love. And pleasure." He held out his hand, and she took it as they walked upstairs. "Your house gives pleasure. It's like the rooms you did at Owen's house: filled with the most wonderful light and warmth."

"A labor of love," Laura said. "I needed a place that was comforting."

In the bedroom, in the pale amber light from the lamps in the courtyard, Paul took her in his arms. "Wherever we are, whatever we're doing, if you need comfort, my darling, this is where you'll find it. I promise you that. No questions, no doubts, ever again. This is where we belong."

Laura put back her head and held his look. "And I promise you love and trust and sharing, and to protect you, if I can, from pain . . ."

"My God," he exclaimed. "How much I wanted to hear that, for so long, and didn't know it." His lips met hers, and when they kissed it was as if it were the first time, and as if they had never been apart. "Do you remember that room?" he asked. "Everything was white: the curtains and the moonlight—and you were wearing white. And I loved you."

"And took over a year to tell me," she said with a soft laugh.

"Not the first time I was a fool." He slipped her jacket off her shoulders and slid his hands under her cashmere sweater, spanning her waist, then moving along her warm skin to her breasts, full and straining toward him. "So much to make up for," he said.

"No, not make up for," she murmured. "We're starting again." Her body was drawn to his, she felt she was melting against him, opening to him with an abandon she had forgotten. But something held her back. *Ben*.

She had not told it all. And she could not make love to Paul, she could not start again, until no more secrets lay between them.

"Paul." Her voice was husky; she had to pull herself from him.

He held her still, his hands on her waist, and searched her eyes. "Tell me," he said.

They sat on the chaise beside the window; a sliver of a moon shone through the tree branches just beyond, flickering as the breeze stirred the few remaining leaves. "There's something I have to tell you, and it can't wait. I want you to know now, because I love you and whatever happens I want you to know the truth; there can't be any more lies."

He waited, watching her.

"I've never told you that I have a brother, another brother besides Clay. A half brother, so our names are different, but we were very close once. We quarreled and he went to Europe to live, and we hadn't seen each other for years. But now we've found each other again and I want you to understand why I didn't tell you about him, why I didn't tell anyone about him and he didn't tell anyone about me...." She hesitated, then looked straight at him. "It's Ben."

The room was silent. "I assume you mean Ben Gardner."

She tightened at the flatness of his voice. "Yes. I was with him last week, in Boston. If you'll listen for a few minutes—" In a rush, barely stopping for breath, she told him as briefly as she could the story she and Ben had told Allison and Leni. And then, still without a pause, she said, "There's one thing more. I think you were right about Clay. I'm not sure—I have to talk to him, and I don't know where he is right now—but I found out, after you left my office, that he was the one who stole Leni's jewels at the Cape years ago. That doesn't mean he's the thief Sam Colby is looking for... I still can't believe... well, I just don't know. But I owe you an apology about that, too."

It was easier now. She had told it all, and her voice was steady. "I seem to have been wrong about a lot of very important things. I always liked to think I was so grown-up, but I've behaved like a scared little kid, and that makes it hard to—"

"You aren't the only one," Paul said quietly. "My poor darling, worrying about all your apologies . . . do you think you're the only one?"

At the love in his voice, Laura's breath came out in a ragged sigh. She hadn't realized how tightly she had been holding herself until now, when every muscle in her body loosened and she found her palms were wet in her clenched hands.

"We were all scared kids," Paul said. He put his arm around her and held her, and Laura rested her head on his shoulder. "Scared we'd been fooled, or taken advantage of, or done out of something. Scared we'd been wrong, and scared to admit it. But I was the worst; when I got scared I forgot everything I knew and loved about you; I turned away when you needed me most, and made you wretched—"

"I think this is what Ben calls a hair shirt," Laura murmured. Laughter bubbled inside her; *it's all right; it's all right; I've told it all, and everything is all right*.

"Hair shirt," Paul repeated. He chuckled. "I'm overdoing it? I'm enjoying it?"

"A little, I think. Ben and I did, too. As if the more we apologize and the better we do it, the faster we erase the past."

"I don't want to erase it. I want to learn from it." His voice roughened. "And make you part of me." He turned her toward him and kissed her again, with a fierceness that was also a promise, and at last Laura let herself go: the barriers were gone.

They pulled off their clothes, helping each other, until once again they stood in each other's arms, their bodies curving together as they remembered, softness and hardness fitting together, already one. "I missed you; I wanted you . . ." Paul said, his hands moving over Laura's body, shaping it, molding it, as if he were drawing it from memory. She slipped her hand between their bodies and slid her curved fingers and palm along his hardness, listening to the sigh that broke from his throat, remembering it, loving the feeling of knowing she could do that to him. But then Paul's fingers were between her legs, wet with her, and everything in Laura was open to him, and longing. "I dreamed of you, dreamed of this, dreamed of us . . ." she said, moving against him. Their tongues found each other; Laura felt she had been starving, and could not eat or drink enough.

"Laura," Paul said, and the passionate sound of her name on his lips swept them up, held them, at last shutting everything out. Arms around each other, they went to the bed and lay on their sides, facing each other, smiling at each other, and as they kissed, Laura opened her legs and Paul thrust deep inside her. "Better," she sighed. "Oh... much better... than a dream." Her voice was as soft as the afternoon breeze that came through the open window; it seemed to taste of wine. And as they moved together in a rhythm their bodies had never forgotten, they were so closely entwined they made one shadow on the wall beside the bed.

* * *

Laura slept, and when she woke, the moon had moved past the window. She opened her eyes and saw Paul watching her. She smiled drowsily. "I dreamed of that, too: waking up and finding you here. Did I sleep long?"

He slipped an arm beneath her and cradled her to his chest. "About an hour. Long enough for me to begin to believe this is real."

"It felt so good. I haven't slept much the past week." She closed her eyes again and placed small kisses on his chest, his nipples, the hollow of his throat. Making love to Paul was being strong and whole and loved, not battered by the actions of others; it was a tie to a past when she was with Owen. And it was a new beginning.

Paul raised himself on one elbow and leaned over her to kiss her eyes and her lips and then move down to take her breasts into his mouth, first one and then the other, playing his tongue over the nipples, slowly, teasingly, while his hand just as slowly and lightly moved along the soft skin inside her thighs. Laura lay against the pillows, letting the waves of sensation build within her, lifting her as if she were weightless; she floated through a dream, and the dream was Paul and all the longings she had held in the secret places of her heart, even when she thought she had put them away forever.

They made love slowly, tasting each other, drinking each other, relearning the tiny sounds and movements, gestures and expressions that only a loved one knows and treasures and remembers, laughing softly as the past and the present merged and the emptiness inside them was filled with joy, and they were complete. They made love and talked through a long night that was theirs alone. The sounds of the city's traffic, punctuated with horns, came to them through the open window as if from a distant place. The air had turned cool, and they pulled the comforter over them, and the closeness of being wrapped together aroused them again and, almost without moving, Paul was inside Laura and they moved in a harmony that was as new and as familiar as their love.

Laura reached up to turn on a lamp beside the bed, and shadows danced on the wall. "Friendly shadows," she murmured. "There were so many I was afraid of."

"No more," Paul said quietly. "We have only those we make for ourselves." He kissed her smiling lips. "Don't go away; I'll be right back." He slid from the bed and walked across the room, and Laura watched him, tall and lean, as graceful as an athlete or a dancer, his muscles taut with coiled energy. We're both like that, she thought: impatient and aggressive, wanting to create and achieve and win. But at one time Paul had been different. She remembered how they had talked at dinner in Owen's kitchen about work and what it meant to them. Paul had been flippant and careless—he couldn't imagine caring about work—and she had been serious and determined, and worried about the differences between them. How much he's changed, she thought. And yet the young man she had fallen in love with was still there. As she stretched in bed, remembering the weight of his body on hers, the embrace in his eyes, the laughter in his voice, she loved him with a passion that astonished her with its intensity. *It was as if a lantern lit our way through the years, and it was always bright.* Owen had said that about Iris. And now we've found it, too, Laura thought, watching him come back to her. We'll light each other's way. My love, who seems so right in my bedroom, so natural a part of the home I thought I was making only for myself. My first love. And I never got over him. She smiled.

"Yes?" he asked, sliding in beside her.

"I love you."

He put an arm beneath her shoulders. "I love you, my darling. Although I must admit that I'm also thinking a great deal right now about food."

Laura laughed. "Poor darling, you haven't eaten since you got off the plane."

"And not much on the plane, either. Shall I prepare you a feast and serve you in bed?"

"No, I'm beginning to feel like I'm rooted here. Let's make something together and eat in the breakfast room, as if we live here and aren't just camping out."

"We could live here, if you'd like to. But I'd have to build a darkroom. Have you a guest room I could use?"

"Yes, but I don't think I want to give it up; I like to have a place for Rosa when she visits. We may have to find something bigger—" She stopped. "We did this once before. At the Cape. Started talking about what kind of home we'd have before we even talked about getting married. Paul, you and Emily are still married."

"We're going to change that as soon as possible. She's not fighting a divorce, and we're still friends. Especially if I can find someone to help her in films. I haven't told you about that; I will. There are so many things we haven't talked about. Would you have a bathrobe for me to wear?"

"Nothing that would fit you."

"No men here? Or only small ones."

She smiled. "No men." She slipped an ivory satin caftan over her head and waited for him.

With a sigh, Paul pulled on his pants and shirt. "Do you require shoes at the dinner table?"

"Not if it's a casual evening," she laughed, and they went downstairs barefoot.

It was nearly midnight. The courtyard was quiet, and the kitchen was bright and warm, with oak cabinets and Pennsylvania Dutch tiles on the walls. Laura took eggs and salad ingredients from the refrigerator. "If you'll make the salad, I'll do the omelets. And there's French bread; we can warm it up. And wine."

They worked together for a moment. "Tell me about Ben," Paul said. "Why were you in Boston?"

Stunned, Laura looked at him. So much had happened, and he knew none of it. "There was a Salinger board meeting," she said, and she went over the past week, from the time Paul had come to her office to the meeting with the OWL investors. "So many changes," she said, "and I don't know what other ones are ahead."

"Whatever they are, we'll be together. We'll share them instead of reporting back to each other later, and we'll make up for all that went wrong."

Laura shook her head. "I told you, I don't want to make up for anything; I want to start again. I've been angry for so long, and trying to make up for things that happened—I don't even want to think that way anymore. The past is over, Paul. I want to love you and be loved and share my life with you, not have some kind of contest, keeping score or measuring what we owe each other or whether we've done enough..." She looked at him, a little frown between her eyes. "Is there anything wrong with that?"

"Nothing. It's what I want, too. But I want you to understand that I'm not trying to deny the past. There's so much I regret—"

"Oh, regrets." Laura sighed and put her fingers on his lips. "We both have more than enough of those. But let's not have any now. We'll sort it all out later. I want to tell you about Ben and Clay, how we grew up and loved each other, all the good times we had, and the ones that were bad. . . . There were so many things I wanted to tell you when we were together; I always thought it was unfair that you could tell me anything you wanted but I had to be so careful. And now I don't. It's like being free for the first time, not having to guard myself when I talk to you." Her eyes grew shadowed. "Clay doesn't have that. He's never been able to be himself with anyone, not even me."

"Tell me about him," Paul said, and for a few minutes Laura talked about their childhood, how close they had been when they thought they had nothing. Paul began to understand the charm and sweetness in Clay that had helped blind Laura, and others, to what he really was. And he learned much about Laura herself that he had never known. "We kept trying to prove how brave and grown up and invulnerable we were, but we weren't; we were all looking for love and a home. Ben found it, and I tried to make Clay believe he had one with me, but he never believed it. Or it was never enough. And so he never outran his past." She was silent a moment. "I think he was happiest with Kelly and John's vintage cars. They were wonderful toys, they didn't make demands on him, they were luxurious enough to make him feel rich, and they made him the center of attention when he drove them. They gave him everything he wanted. If we'd stayed at Darnton's, he might never have started stealing again."

"But he'd already been gambling, hadn't he?" She nodded, and Paul said, "It was nothing you did, you must believe that. It wasn't because you left Darnton's, or because you were busy with your hotels, or even because he wasn't as happy as he thought he should be. If it was anything, I'd bet it was because he never got over feeling smart and invulnerable, like a kid on Halloween with a terrific mask that fools or scares the hell out of everybody. There was nothing you could have done about that, my love. Do you believe that?"

She smiled slightly. "Sometimes."

There was a pause. "By the way," Paul said, to deflect her thoughts, "I talked to my parents yesterday, before I left London. Did you know that Leni is marrying again, as soon as her divorce is final?"

"No, how wonderful for her. She didn't mention it when we were together last week." She poured eggs into the omelet pan. "Is it someone you know?"

"I haven't met him, but you have. Wes Currier. My mother says he—what is it?"

Laura had looked stunned for an instant, then she burst out laughing. "Are you serious?"

"About what? Currier? Of course; why wouldn't I be? My mother says they're very happy together; he's very solicitous of Leni, and he looks like he wants to give her the world and make her happy. I think it's fine. Why is it funny?"

"You know that Wes was the first investor in my company?"

"Yes, my father told me. I thought it showed he has good sense."

"But that's all you know." She was swirling the pan and did not look at him.

"Yes. Is there something else?"

She hesitated barely an instant. *No more secrets; no more lies.* "We were lovers for a long time. He wanted to marry me, and I thought about it a lot, but I never could. It wasn't Wes so much; it was me. I couldn't get over the idea that there was supposed to be someone else at the end of the rainbow." She slipped the omelet onto a plate. "You should eat this right away, while I make the other one."

Paul took the pan from her and put it down. Holding her face in both hands, he kissed her. "We're going to drink a toast first." He handed her a glass of wine and took her other hand in his. "To the rainbow, my love, and the gold we've found at its end."

They drank to each other, and then, dreamily, Laura made her own omelet. They sat at the small table in the kitchen alcove, eating slowly, warm and loved and loving, talking of their different lives, beginning the long rediscovery that would bring them into each other's separate worlds and make them fully one with each other once again. Very late at night, as they stood to return to the bedroom, Paul put his arm around Laura and held her close. "One more thing," he said. "I'm going to find Clay. I'll work with Ben and hire anyone I have to, but whatever it takes, my love, I'm going to find him and bring him back, and clear up this mess he's made for you, once and for all."

CHAPTER 33

THE key no longer worked. Clay had expected that—everybody changed locks after a robbery—but it had been worth a quick try. The alarm code probably had been changed, too. Anyway, there was a guard, which meant the front door couldn't be used. From across the street, he'd watched one guard leave and another take his place at midnight, and then everything was quiet. He settled back to watch the house.

At one-thirty, the guard came out and walked down the street. Asshole, Clay thought contemptuously. That's no way to do a job. But he wasn't complaining; it made everything easier for him. It was after the guard had disappeared around the corner that Clay had tried the key, the only one he hadn't sent to Colby when he'd mailed the Dürer and the other five keys that afternoon, as soon as he had arrived in New York. At one-forty-five the guard came back, carrying a package from the delicatessen and another from the liquor store next door. Fifteen minutes, Clay thought. Not a lot, but probably enough.

He walked away from the house, to the third house from the corner. He'd chosen it because it was completely screened from the sidewalk and street by the overhanging branches of a ginkgo tree. At a few minutes before two, he grasped the drainpipe and scaled the wall.

He looked at his watch. Three and a half minutes. Not bad for four stories.

He tipped his hat to himself before adjusting the rope coiled at an angle across his chest, retying his shoes, and then turning to make his way, smoothly, silently, across the four roofs to Felix and Leni's house. A cool breeze blew; orange and red-brown leaves drifted to the rooftops and the street below; sodium lights turned the sidewalks a garish orange but left the rooftops in darkness, exactly the way Clay liked them.

He reached the place he sought, and leaned over the edge to look at the attic window in the center of the rear wall. Nothing was close to it—no drainpipe, no ivy, no decorative plaster work; it was alone in an expanse of Hudson River graystone. And therefore, the expert in Clay reasoned, probably not wired as part of the alarm system.

He slipped the coiled rope over his head and tied one end to a chimney a few feet from the edge. Carefully, he laid the rope beside the chimney, crossed to the front of the roof, where he could watch the street, and sat down to wait. He'd give the guard an hour to take another stroll over to Lexington. It would be so much easier if the guy made a habit of it.

He stretched out his legs, leaning back comfortably against the parapet, and thought about Laura. She wouldn't like what he was doing. It wouldn't matter to her that he was putting something back, not stealing; she'd say it was wrong. Probably wouldn't even love him for doing it for her, because she'd think he should have found another way to do it. He shrugged in the darkness. Even if there was another way, it wouldn't be fun or exciting. But she wouldn't understand that. Probably wouldn't appreciate his getting her involved, either; it would be like she was an accessory, if she knew what he'd done.

I better not tell her, he thought with a sigh. I'll just tell her the letter was there all the time. Then she won't scold me for breaking in, and she won't be a part of it. She'll just thank me for my help.

He nodded, pleased with himself. There was always a solution; he always found one. He hummed to himself, very softly, and waited. At a few minutes before three, he heard the front door open and close. Peering over the parapet, he saw the guard walking up the street with long, easy steps. Ass, Clay thought again, and grinned to himself. Swiftly, he moved to the back of the roof. He took the free end of the rope in his gloved hands, played it out, and went over the side.

He felt so great he could have let out a whoop of joy. This was it. He'd committed himself, he was into the real danger, everything *counted*. He was as alive as he ever would be. His heartbeat was up, his breathing quick and shallow, and he was grinning in the darkness as he rappeled down the rough stone to the attic window. Hanging there, feet against the stone, he looked through the glass with a tiny flashlight held in the protection of his curved hand and studied the inside window frame. No visible wires; better than a fifty-fifty chance that it was all right. He pried it open and eased it up, holding his breath, waiting for the piercing cry of the alarm. There was none. For a few seconds, he listened to the beautiful, perfect silence, then pushed the window higher and slipped inside.

From there it was only a minute before he stood once again in Felix's study. New paintings over the sofa, he noted briefly; too bad I don't have anything to carry them in. He pushed the other painting aside to get to the safe, and twirled the combination he had used before. How about that, he marveled; old Felix didn't think about changing it. The safe was still empty except for the small pile of documents on the purchase of the house. Clay took Owen's letter, in its envelope, from the shirt pocket beneath his sweater and slid it beneath the house documents, as far back as it would go. Then he closed and locked the safe, adjusted the painting over it, and took the stairs back to the attic. How about that. Couldn't be easier.

But there was still danger; his heart still pounded. Holding the end of the rope, he climbed through the window, closed it with one hand, and went up the stone wall, pulling on the rope with his hands while his feet walked up the rough surface. On the roof, he untied the rope from the chimney and carried it with him back across the four roofs. In the shadow of the ginkgo tree, using the same drainpipe he had used before, he began to climb down the wall.

Too late, he heard the guard. The same tree that helped screen his descent from the roof also partially screened the guard, who was just returning. "Hey! What the fuck . . . !" the guard shouted, and Clay froze.

But only for a second. He dropped the rest of the way to the ground and began to run. The guard saw him in the orange glow of the streetlight. "Hey!" he yelled again, but Clay kept running, a dark shape dashing down the sidewalk. But the guard was just as fast; he was trained to react, and he did, pulling out his gun and firing. And then it was over, as quickly as it had begun. The dark form turned the corner onto Lexington and was gone.

Lights came on; a door opened. "What's going on?" someone demanded.

"Some goon trying to break in," the guard said. "He's gone, but we gotta call the police. I'll take care of it. Go back to bed. Everything's fine. Under control."

He'd have to figure out a story about why he'd been outside, the guard thought as he walked down the street and let himself into Felix's house. Probably say he'd heard a noise and went to check and saw this bozo climbing the wall and fired over his head and scared him off. I did fire over his head, he thought. Except that last shot, when he wouldn't stop. That might have got him. He shrugged. Nothing in this house, he thought, picking up the telephone to call the police. That's all that matters; nothing happened here.

* * *

Laura heard the sound first; a scraping somewhere downstairs. Ben was in the guest room—he had come for the weekend while Paul was in Los Angeles, talking to Emily—but Laura didn't wait to see if he would investigate. Putting on a robe, she walked down the stairs to the foyer and looked into the court. It was empty; no one was about at four in the morning. But the scraping was there again; it came from the front door. "What is it?" Ben asked. He was coming up from the guest room in the basement, tying his robe. "It sounds like a dog."

"I don't know," Laura said. "I can't see anything." Then they both heard, faintly, Laura's name, once, then twice. "That sounds like Clay!" she exclaimed, and ran to the door.

When she opened it, a dark form fell at her feet. She gave a sharp scream. "Ben!"

Ben was just behind her; he switched on a light and dropped to his knees. "My God, it is Clay. And there's blood . . . Clay! Where are you hurt?"

"Is that *Ben?*" Clay asked. He lay on the floor, scowling at Ben. "Son of a bitch . . . What the fuck are you doing in New York? I want Laura. Son of a—"

"Clay, I'm here," Laura said. "Ben, should we move him? Can we get him to the couch in the library?"

"Lots of blood," said Clay. His breathing was short and ragged. "One little bullet. Tried to stop it with my shirt, but the fucking thing kept bleeding and bleeding . . . Oh, God, it hurts, it *hurts* . . ."

"We have to call an ambulance," Laura said.

"I will; you stay with him." Ben went to the desk in the library and dialed 911. Laura could hear his low voice beneath Clay's ragged breathing.

"What's Ben *doing* here?" Clay asked. "Didn't know you even talked to him . . ."

She was taking off his dark cap and his shoes. He was dressed all in black; she tried not to think of that. "It just happened; so much has happened. . . . Clay, you shouldn't have run off—"

Ben was kneeling beside them again. "Where did it happen?" he asked Clay brusquely.

"Uptown."

He looked at Laura. "If he's come this far, it probably won't hurt to move him to the couch. Can you take his feet?"

"I can walk." Clay struggled to sit up.

"Shut up and lie still." They carried him into the library and lay him on the couch. "I need a scissors," Ben said.

Laura brought it to him from the desk, and he cut open Clay's sweater from bottom to top. A blood-soaked shirt was wadded against his back near his side. Laura brought a pile of clean towels from the guest bathroom, and Ben folded one of them and pressed it against the wound. "I don't know a damn thing about bullet wounds. I don't know whether any organs were hit or if he's just losing too much blood. Or both."

"Are they sending an ambulance? When will it be here?"

"They said a few minutes."

"Ambulance!" Clay cried. "No, damn it, no ambulance . . . the police will know . . . don't call—"

"I already did," Ben said shortly. "You think we're going to sit here and watch you bleed to death?"

"Fuck you! Oh, shit, Laura, it hurts, it hurts so much. . . ."

"Ben, help me," she said. "I want to hold him." Ben raised Clay's upper body so Laura could sit at the end of the couch and take him into her arms. She cradled him, his weight heavy against her breasts. "Clay, we have to get you to a hospital."

He shook his head. "Stay right here." He closed his eyes. "So sleepy. Feels so good here. Maybe . . . take a nap. How 'bout a kiss? Please?"

She bent her head and kissed his forehead and his closed eyes, smoothing back his hair with her hand. "Where were you, Clay?"

She meant where had he gone when he fled nearly two weeks earlier, but he misunderstood her. He opened his eyes and started to tell her about his great excursion to Felix's house, but then he remembered he'd decided something else when he was waiting on the roof. He frowned. It was hard to remember everything, but he knew he shouldn't tell her; for some reason, he'd decided not to. "Coming to say good-bye," he said. "Kiss you good-bye. Going somewhere. Mexico, Europe, somewhere. Haven't decided."

Ben had pulled a hassock close to the couch. "At four in the morning you weren't coming to see Laura. You were doing a job."

"No! Not stealing a goddam fucking thing. *Wasn't*. Walking around, uh, thinking."

"Then how did you get shot?"

"Oh. Mugged. Somebody robbed *me*. How 'bout that? And I fought him and . . . he shot."

"In the back," Ben said flatly.

"Saw the gun and ran." Clay grinned crookedly. "You'd do the same, right, old buddy? Couple smart brothers, good team, know when to run?"

"Right," Ben said, feeling himself respond to Clay's charm. Even now he had it. "But I don't believe you."

"Christ's sake!" Clay yelled, then grimaced in pain.

"Ben, let it go," Laura said. "What difference does it make?"

"Good," said Clay. He took a few short breaths. "Listen, I have to tell you . . . God, Laura, I'm sleepy. You know? Can't stay awake. Funny. Never bothered me before. Staying up late. Listen, I wanted to tell you . . . Could I have something to drink? Awful thirsty."

"I'll get it," said Ben. He went through the doorway to the dining room and on to the kitchen.

Clay's eyes were closed again. "Sorry. That's what I came to say. Sorry for what I did. Really fucked up . . . Got you in trouble. Didn't mean to. Sorry . . ." The word came out in a sigh. "Tried to quit. You know? But I . . . couldn't."

"Clay," Laura said, taking the glass Ben handed her. "Can you drink this?"

She held the glass to his lips and he drank avidly. "God, that's good." He opened his eyes for a moment but, heavy-lidded, they fell closed again. "Good old Ben. How are you, buddy? Been a long time, hasn't it? Go away now . . . I'm talking to my sister. Laura? You know I love you? Don't want you to think . . ." The word faded away. "Tried to quit. Poker, stealing, all of it. But it was like dying. Can you understand? Oh, shit, you can't, you can't—"

He was trying to sit up, and Laura held him more tightly. "Hush, Clay, I understand. Don't get up, I'm right here."

"Listen! You listening? *Never meant to hurt you!*" He opened his eyes; they were bright with excitement, and his words came faster. "Have to understand that. Never thought anybody'd figure it out. Thought you were out of it. Wouldn't have done it if I thought . . . you'd get stuck. Worst part—" He began to laugh, grimacing as he did. "Worst part. I wanted to tell you about it. How great it was. Too good to pass up. But you wouldn't love me if you knew, would you? Poor little Laura. Wanted a family so bad she put her money on Clay. Bad choice. But, goddam, I loved you for it. Sticking by me, thinking nice things about me. Must have been hard sometimes." He smiled wistfully and his hand came up, making vague motions until Laura took it in hers. "I wanted a family, too. But I guess . . . not enough. See—listen, Laura, you've gotta get this—*I tried to quit!* But I couldn't do it. I'd go all empty, you know? Like I'd dried up. Empty, dead, hollow. No more Clay. And then I'd plan a new job, and everything'd light up. Danger, excitement, and I'd be alive. Fantastic! Up there on his roof... King of the—"

"Whose roof?" Ben asked sharply.

"Just... roof. Anybody's. King of the world. Remember when we were kids we'd climb high up and feel—" He started to laugh again. "Backfired, didn't it? Wanted to feel alive. But maybe I'll die instead. Laura? You think I'm going to die?"

"No, you can't, you'll start again..." Laura was crying. For the first time since Felix had told her to leave Owen's house, she let the tears come. Ben was sitting on the arm of the couch, and she lay her head on his lap and cried because Clay wanted so much to be alive.

"Hey, don't. Don't cry," Clay said. "Can't stand it. You've got to be happy, not crying. Can't stand it if I thought I made you cry. Probably won't die. Too lucky. Just going to sleep awhile... so sleepy..."

He lay still. Laura's weeping was the only sound. "Wait," Clay said suddenly. "Shit, almost forgot. Listen, get Felix. Get him to open his safe. People there. Okay?"

"What are you talking about?"

"Owen's letter. In there."

"*Owen's letter*? In Felix's safe? But that's impossible. Clay, how do you know? How did it get there? Did you... my God, did you have something to do with it?"

"No, no, no, no. Wrong." His breathing was coming faster, and his hands made clutching motions at the air. "Saw it in the safe. When I stole Rouaults." He felt her stiffen. "Sorry, sorry, sorry. Doesn't matter now. The safe! Damn it, listen! Trying to tell you. *Important*. Get Felix to open it. In front of people. Okay?"

Laura looked at Ben. "I don't see what good it will do. He wrote it years ago."

"Lawyer," Clay said desperately. "Get one. Can't tell you why... too sleepy. Fucking lucky shot. Almost made it, but not quite... Felix! Promise about Felix! *Promise!*"

"I promise," Laura said. "Don't worry, Clay. I promise."

He sighed. "Good. That's good." A smile flickered on his pale lips beneath the brave mustache. "I was going to write. Tell you all this. Never thought I'd be... in your lap. Crazy, right? Love you, Laura. Wanted you to love me and... be proud of me..." The word trailed off in a long breath that grew thinner and thinner and then was gone.

"Clay!" Laura cried through the tears that had started again. They filled her eyes and spilled over, and when she held her face close to Clay's they wet a dirt smudge along the side of his face. "Clay, you'll be all right! We're going to take care of you, you'll get well and start again. You will, you will, everybody can start again! There's so much good in you, I know there is! Clay, you'll start again and this time..."

The words were lost in her tears. She cried for all their hopes and dreams, and the wrong turnings they had made, and the beauty all around them that was so fragile it would break if they did not cherish and protect it. She cried for Clay, whom she had loved and tried to take care of, and had never really known. Her body shook with the force of her tears, because it was too late for so much, and there would not be enough time for so much more.

"Laura," Ben said. His voice was very gentle. "Let me help you up."

She shook her head. "I don't want to. I want to hold him." But then she raised her head and looked at Clay, and she knew what Ben meant. "Oh, no! No, no..." The words were a shuddering cry. She kissed Clay's cheeks and forehead, wet with her tears, and lay her fingers on his lips. "Poor Clay," she whispered. "Poor, sweet Clay. Always so proud of yourself, so happy and excited when... when you thought you were a big man.... Oh, God, I'm so sorry," she wept. "I thought you'd be all right, I thought you had plenty of time to grow up, and now you won't, ever.... He can't be dead!" she cried to Ben. "He can't be! He's so young!"

There were tears in Ben's eyes. He caressed Laura's head. "He was very young," he said softly. Laura put her head on his lap, and they wept for Clay. And that was how the ambulance driver found them when he arrived: the three of them, together for the first time since they had had dinner together on a wharf on Cape Cod, eleven years before.

CHAPTER 34

C OLBY was waiting in front of Laura's house when they returned from the cemetery. The first one he saw was Paul, with his arm around Laura. What the hell, Colby thought. So that's why he changed his film. He saw Laura's eyes widen in surprise as she saw him. "I'm sorry to intrude, Miss Fairchild—"

"God damn it, Sam," Paul said furiously, "couldn't you wait a day or two? Laura isn't the one you're looking for. We'll tell you the whole story later; just believe me: it wasn't Laura."

"I know it wasn't," Colby said calmly. "Just hold your horses. I wouldn't intrude if it wasn't important. I'd like to talk to Miss Fairchild, if we could go inside."

"Not now, damn it! We're expected at a friend's house for lunch, and you can damn well wait until tomorrow or the next day."

Laura put her hand on his. "It's all right, Paul. Ginny won't mind if we're a little late." She turned and unlocked her door, and the three of them went into the library. "What is it, Mr. Colby?"

Still standing, since no one had invited him to sit, Colby said, "First, may I extend my condolences, Miss Fairchild. I know you and your brother were close and worked together. It's a real loss for you, and I'm sorry. Terrible shock, too, the way it happened; it isn't too often that someone is shot during a mugging, but when it does happen, it's a real tragedy."

Laura was silent, and if Colby expected her to revise the story she had given the police of how Clay was shot, he was disappointed.

"But what I mainly came for," he went on, "is to tell you that your brother wrote to me."

Laura stared at him. "What?"

"I received a letter from him late yesterday; it was mailed in Manhattan, but it was sent to me in care of the *Daily News*, so it took a while to get to me. I'd like to talk to you about it and then ask you a favor."

Involuntarily Laura glanced at the couch draped with an afghan to hide the bloodstains. She shivered and turned back to Colby. "I'm sorry; please sit down."

He sat on the edge of an armchair. Laura and Paul were on the couch, close together, his arm around her shoulders. "Your brother sent me the keys to five homes. I don't know where the sixth is, the one to the Salinger house on Fifty-first Street, but the others are labeled with the names of the five people whose robberies I've been investigating; you know who they are." Laura was watching him intently. She had frowned at the mention of the Salingers, but that was all; Colby was willing to swear she didn't know where the key was or whether her brother had used it more than once. "He told me in his letter how he'd made copies of keys, security codes, travel schedules, and so on when guests were in your hotels, and how he broke into their homes when he knew they'd be away. And he sent me two fifteenth-century prints that he had kept for himself because, he said, he liked them. He said everything else he stole was for a broker who had clients willing to commission the theft of the art they wanted."

Laura shook her head. "A broker? How did he meet him? It sounds so organized, so professional—Clay always seemed so young and casual about things."

"He wasn't casual about these jobs. He was clever and careful. And smart."

A small laugh that was almost a sob broke from her. "He would have loved to hear you say that."

Colby shrugged, then caught himself; he shouldn't act casual when somebody'd just died. Not that she seemed prostrate with grief, but her eyes were red and she had a kind of dazed look, like she was holding herself tight together, walking around and talking and doing everything normal, but not really connecting with any of it. She hasn't taken it all in yet, Colby thought; lots of things she hasn't really grasped. Involuntarily, he lowered his voice and spoke in a gentle way quite unlike him. "Based on the keys and the prints, and your brother's letter, I'm completely satisfied that he was behind these robberies I've been working on.

I have no proof that the two of you weren't working together, but I trust my instincts, and they tell me you didn't know a thing about it. You're in the clear, and I apologize for any inconvenience I've caused you. Of course I had nothing to do with the story getting to the press, and the problems in your hotels, which I sincerely hope are resolved very soon. In fact I hope I can be of some assistance there."

Paul looked at him sharply. "How? You're not ready to go to the press with this story."

"Right. I'm not ready. But if you remember, I said I had a favor to ask. The reason I'm not ready to go to the press is that my investigation isn't over. The thief wasn't my real target, you know. I work for insurance companies, and the sad truth is, they're less concerned with thieves than with recovering what was stolen. That's my real job, because if I don't get back those artworks, my bosses pay out hefty sums, which of course they'd rather not do. So I'm still working on this case. I'll be searching your brother's apartment in SoHo, but first I wonder if you'd allow me to go through what he had on him when he came here."

Laura frowned. "You're looking for the name of his broker."

"Right." Colby beamed; it was wonderful when someone understood him. "He told me he'd been dealing with one, but he didn't tell me the name. I assume he wanted to continue working with him in the future. . . ." He saw Laura's face freeze. "Well, we won't go into that. But I do need that name. It might mean I could wrap up the whole affair in a few days; I can't be sure, but it's a possibility. In that case, of course, I'd go to the press with the information, and it might be of great interest to people who stay in your hotels."

"The press," Laura said numbly, thinking of Clay's name spread in all the newspapers and television news reports.

"It's going to happen eventually," Colby said as gently as he could. "One way or another, it's going to come out. From what I understand, you might have to do it yourself, to convince people your hotels are okay. If I announce the name of the broker, that might be what people remember. Now, I'm sure your brother had the name and telephone number memorized, but even so, he most likely wrote it down at some point and maybe tucked it away. That's my hope, my best lead. So it's very important, and I'd be very grateful—"

"I'll be right back," Laura said, and left the room.

Colby gave Paul a sidelong look. "She's lucky to have such a good friend at such a trying time."

Paul smiled. "Sam, you're fishing. This has nothing to do with your investigation."

"True. But it might affect my film. If you're too busy with her, when do you get me on television?"

"I don't know yet. It won't be the network; that fell through. But I'm going to finish the film and either sell it to cable or try to get it distributed to theaters. One way or another, we'll make you famous, Sam."

"It's not for me, you know," Colby said earnestly. "It's for my grandchildren. They'd get such a kick out of it."

Paul chuckled. "Of course they would."

They heard Laura's footsteps on the stairs. "Clay had nothing with him but his wallet," she said, coming into the room. "The police went through it and didn't find anything except a key to a locker at the airport. There was an overnight bag there, and a return ticket to Mexico City. We didn't even know he'd been there. . . ." She shook her head slightly. "They have the overnight bag; I'll have it tomorrow, if you need it."

"I won't know until I see the wallet." He held out his hand.

"As long as you look at it here. You can't take it away."

"That's fine. By the way, if I find something, could I ask you to keep it quiet until I've made my move? In other words, no press conferences or answering questions from reporters until you hear from me. Can you do that?"

"How long will it be?"

"I don't know. I hope no more than a few days."

She nodded. "I can wait a few days."

"Thanks," he said, and, from habit, turned his back as he went through the wallet. Amid lists and notes, a picture of Laura, and five hundred dollars in cash, he found a folded paper with a list of ten- and thirteen-digit telephone numbers. New York, Colby noted; Geneva, Paris, Rome, London. He sent up a prayer. Stick with me, God. We've hung in this long; if I can hit it with one of these numbers, we're home free.

He returned everything but the folded paper to the wallet and handed it to Laura. "Thank you, Miss Fairchild."

"You kept a piece of paper. May I see it?"

Colby gave it to her.

"You'll let me know when you've called all of them?" she asked.

"As soon as I know something," he said, taking back the paper. "You can count on me. I'll let myself out now. I appreciate your help. Paul, we'll be talking soon, right?"

"I'm sure we will," Paul said with a smile. The last thing Colby saw before he closed the door behind him was Laura Fairchild's face as she turned to Paul. Lucky guy, he thought enviously. Lucky guy.

But he didn't dwell on it. The list of numbers burned in his pocket, and he pulled it out to study it in the taxi taking him to his office. He had to wait until the next morning to begin calling, and then, for four hours, he called one after another. Five had been disconnected, three rang steadily without an answer, four had been changed and belonged to shops in Geneva and Rome. Two responded with tape recordings giving forwarding numbers in Rome and Milan. When Colby punched the buttons on his telephone with the forwarding numbers, both resulted in error messages. Fucking Italian phone companies, he swore silently, and punched the numbers again. And again heard recorded error messages. Not possible, he thought. He might have written one incorrectly, but not two. He studied the numbers. Both began with thirty-nine and ended with ninety-three. Ah, Colby sighed. Cute. The dialing code for Italy was thirty-nine. He punched the numbers in backward, and within five minutes was speaking to the houseman for a man whose name Colby recognized: a high-living playboy who collected rare coins and beautiful women. He also was a known gambler—horse races, roulette, and poker—which was probably how he met Fairchild, Colby thought.

He sent up another prayer, then called Interpol in Rome.

He sat back. It would take a while for them to get back to him. He thought again of Laura Fairchild's face as she turned to Paul. Well, Paul is indeed a lucky guy, he ruminated, but isn't the luckiest fella of all Sam Colby, who's got a hell of a lot of good years ahead? Thanks to Clay Fairchild. He tipped an imaginary hat to Clay. Somehow, that kid, who'd made a habit of letting people down because he only cared about himself, had managed in the end to do one truly good deed: mail a confession, and plenty of proof, to the one person who could make the best use of it. He'd saved his sister a bunch of trouble, and he'd also given Sam Colby a ticket out of that retirement town, back to where the action was.

Probably the only good deed he'd ever done in his selfish life, but it was a doozy. He really did deserve a tip of the hat.

*   *   *

In the week before Clay's death, Laura had sent a letter, with her own signature, to everyone who had ever stayed in a Beacon Hill hotel, assuring them of the hotels' safety. She was beginning another when she began to receive answers to the first. Flavia Guarneri called. "I'd like to come back, my dear, but there's that little feeling of danger that just stops me dead in my tracks. Not about you, of course, I'm sure I can have confidence in you. But your staff does cause me a teeny bit of worry. I do sympathize; isn't it a tragedy how hard it is to get good help? The minute you can tell us you've solved it, everything will be different."

Carlos Serrano called. "Next time I am in New York, I pledge to you I will stay in your charming hotel. The hell with it. Live dangerously I say. I will tell the press, anyone, that Carlos is not afraid of a little danger!"

Don't do me any favors, Laura said to herself. But aloud, she thanked him. "We'll look forward to seeing you, Carlos."

The Laughtons did not call; they simply appeared at the Washington Beacon Hill, stayed for three days, and then left. They wrote Laura a note, telling her the hotel was as splendid as ever, and Kelly Darnton the best manager ever, but none of their friends was willing to stay in a Beacon Hill hotel until they were sure it was absolutely safe.

Nothing is absolutely safe, Laura thought, and filed the letter with the others.

Britt Farley was in Europe; he cabled Laura that he would not be in the States for a long time.

Daniel Inouti did not respond. Neither did anyone else among the hundreds to whom letters had been sent.

And then Clay's death revived the interest of the newspaper reporters, who had left Laura alone for several days: almost instantly, they were telephoning again, and a few took up their old positions outside her office. Laura refused to speak to them; her secretary would only repeat the story about how Clay had been shot. One *Daily News* reporter knew there had been a packet for Sam Colby from Clay Fairchild, but he kept it quiet: Colby had promised him first crack at the story, and he wasn't going to let anyone else get an inkling that anything was up. The rest of the reporters wrote stories that speculated and recapped the story about Laura and the Beacon Hill hotels, but, with no new information, they finally turned to other news.

The lobby was empty of reporters the night Laura left her office to join Paul's family for dinner. At one of the widely spaced tables in the discreet elegance of Chanterelle, the two of them told Thomas and Barbara the story that everyone would soon know. "We're not sure," Paul concluded, "why it's important to have witnesses when Felix opens the safe and takes out the letter, but the likeliest reason is that it would make it impossible for Felix to deny that he had it."

Thomas Janssen frowned slightly. "Does it matter after all these years? Laura has almost everything Owen left her."

"Clay thought it was important," Laura said. "And I promised him I'd do it. I would anyway; I want the letter. Just for myself. So I have to find a way to get it out."

"We'll find a way," Paul corrected gently. He turned to his father. "Couldn't we think up a reason to hold a shareholders' meeting in New York, at Felix's house? Most of us either live here now or spend a lot of time here; if we can make it sound plausible, we could have as many as twenty people there. There's always something we could discuss, isn't there? So if it turns out it's not important to have had Felix open the safe in front of us, there's been no harm done, except we've had a meeting." He smiled at Thomas. "I thought you'd take care of talking to Felix."

Thomas met his son's smile. "Dumping it in my lap." But then, gazing thoughtfully at his coffee cup, he said, "Cole and I have been talking about easing Felix out as president. It's been a while since any of us has had a good feeling about what's happening to the company. We hadn't planned to move so soon, but perhaps . . ."

And so it was that Thomas Janssen called Felix and told him the family wanted a special shareholders' meeting. "We'd like it to be in New York," he said. "I know you're going to be there for a couple of weeks, and so are we, and a number of the others live there. Far more convenient for everyone."

"It is not convenient," Felix said flatly. "Our annual meeting is in March; we'll wait until then."

"A number of us would rather do it now," Thomas said, his voice as unemotional as Felix's. "We're worried about the direction of the company, Felix. The New York hotel is six months behind schedule, and expenses are far greater than we were led to anticipate; business is down in some of the other hotels; and there's been some extremely unfortunate publicity. We're not satisfied, and we don't want to wait until spring to talk about it. If I didn't think it was important, I wouldn't have brought it up."

There was a long silence. "You said a number of you want a meeting. Who are they?"

"I can't speak for them. We'll all have a chance to speak at the meeting."

"I'll think about calling one. But it won't be in New York; we have no meeting place in New York."

"We would if that hotel was finished, as it was supposed to be. I'm suggesting that we have the meeting at your house. There are only twenty-two of us; we can easily meet in your library."

"In my home? Don't be an ass." Felix let out his breath in anger. Leni was a shareholder. So was the Fairchild woman. They would not set foot in his home. "There will be no shareholders' meetings in my home. Ever."

"Then we can rent a conference room in a hotel. Of course there are more chances of reporters hearing about it, and I don't think we want that."

"Reporters? What are you talking about?"

"You've made the Salinger name rather prominent lately, Felix. They might think you're still news."

Again, Felix was silent. No one in his family, not even Asa, had mentioned his press conference and the stories that had sprung from it. In his mind, he'd called them all fools. Only fools are afraid to do what has to be done, or are embarrassed by publicity. But now he felt a ripple of alarm. He hadn't bothered to find out how they felt, and now, suddenly, he got the first inkling that things might be getting out of hand. How had Thomas gotten him to talk about a meeting in New York when he'd just said he wouldn't have one there?

"I'll think about calling a meeting in Boston," he said sharply. "In a month or so, if enough shareholders wish it. Until then, there is nothing more to discuss."

"I think there is," Thomas corrected. He was beginning to enjoy himself. He was so used to being the mild-mannered Salinger in-law that the chance to become actively involved in the company, against Felix's opposition, was refreshing. If Felix were more pleasant, he thought, I wouldn't be feeling so good. "We're going to have the meeting in New York, a week from tomorrow, at three o'clock in the afternoon. I hope you'll be there. If you're not, we'll be forced to go ahead without you."

"You can't do that."

"You know we can, Felix. Asa is out of town, but he'll be back in time for the meeting and, as vice president, he can chair it."

This time Felix barely paused; he could not miss that meeting, and he knew it. "I'll be there. But not at my home. That's final. Find another place."

"I'll do my best. But if the newspapers find out we're going to talk about the possibility of changing the leadership of the company—"

"*What?*"

"Surely you understood what I meant when I said we were worried about the direction of the company."

Felix did not reply. Of course he had understood it, but why would he say so?

"If the press finds out about it," Thomas said, "then it becomes quite a story, at least for business editors. And since the features editors already know you give them juicy material—"

"All right." He'd been right: things were getting out of hand. He had to talk to Asa. *Asa is out of town.* But he could be found, and he could be managed. He always could. And as long as Asa voted with him, the two of them could beat any motion with their controlling ownership of the company. He'd talk to Asa. That would take care of it. "We'll meet at my home. Once. Only once."

"We'll see you next week, then," Thomas said. The minute he hung up, he called Paul. "We'll have to make our plans. Can you have lunch with me tomorrow? I'll have Cole join us. And then I'll call Asa. He's in hiding, afraid Felix can talk him out of whatever he decides to do. We have to keep his courage up for the next week."

"We ought to be able to do that," Paul said, and turning from the telephone, he told Laura what had been done.

She smiled and nodded, but she was distracted. Half of the thirty days she had been given were already gone. She had called Currier and Leni to congratulate them, and Currier had brought up the money she owed. He already had allowed her to stop her payments to him until she knew what she would do. "And that's about all I can do, Laura. I can't loan you more—"

"I'm not asking for more, Wes."

"You may not be, but I've thought about it."

"Thank you, but that's not a solution, and we both know it."

"Have you heard anything from that investigator?"

"No. Not yet."

Ginny talked about money, too. "I'd love to come up with another ten million, Laura, but it's like pulling the guts out of a chicken; once you've done it you can't do it again."

Laura laughed and kissed her. "I wouldn't take it if you could. Thank you, Ginny; I love you."

"What are you going to do?"

"Meet this month's payroll; I can still do that. And then, I guess, start making telephone calls. Nothing will change until I convince some people to come back. Somebody has to be the first, and I guess the Laughtons weren't enough."

"Will you tell them about Clay?"

"Sam Colby asked me to keep it quiet, so I will, at least for a while. If I have to, I will."

But two days later, Colby called. He reached Laura at home, before she left for work. Paul was pouring coffee, the windows were open in the sunlight, and she was skimming the newspaper when the telephone rang. She answered it absently, then sat up quickly. "What?" she asked.

"I said, I'm holding a news conference. I'd invite you, but it's me they're going to want to talk to. And it might be a little painful for you."

"No, I don't want to be there. But can you tell me about it?" Laura held the telephone away from her ear, and Paul leaned forward so they could listen to Colby together.

"It's neat and straightforward. We got the broker. He still had the paintings from Clay's last job, and he gave us the names of his clients who had the rest. We worked with Interpol, and we had simultaneous raids in five cities in the homes of some respectable millionaires you wouldn't believe if I told you, and we got everything back. You might call it a bonanza. That's what I call it, anyway. So I'm giving it all to the press: names, dates, places. I'll also tell them you're absolutely out of it. That should help, don't you think?"

"Yes." *Yes, yes, yes, that will help.* But she was crying, for Clay. If there was any other way . . . But there wasn't. Clay had gotten her into this mess, and Clay would have to get her out.

"Sam, one more thing," Paul said, taking the phone. "Can you mention that Laura dismissed Clay from the hotels as soon as she discovered what he was doing?"

"No problem. That should help even more. Anything else?"

"Laura?" Paul asked.

She shook her head.

"Let us know how it goes," Paul said. "We'll be in Laura's office."

"You'll hear how it goes," Colby said ruefully. "You'll be bombarded. You better make notes on what you had for breakfast; they're going to want that and everything else about you. I make the news, but Miss Fairchild is a lot prettier than I am, so she'll get more space. But, then, I'm going to be in a movie. Right?"

"Probably," Paul said with a laugh. He talked to Colby for a few more minutes, then hung up. "Shall I stay with you today?" he asked Laura. "There are a few of the cousins I haven't reached for the shareholders' meeting; I can call them from your office."

"Yes, I'd like you there."

He stayed in the office all that day and the next, standing near Laura while she repeated to the reporters what Colby had already told them and fended off their questions about how she felt about her brother. "I'm unhappy about him and I miss him," she said briefly and would say no more. "They're not going to put my grief on their evening news," she said angrily to Paul after an afternoon of having microphones thrust in her face; and the reporters on television were much more perfunctory than they would have been if Laura had been willing to weep for the cameras.

On the third day after Colby's announcement, Paul was with Laura again in her office when other telephone calls began coming in. Kelly called at noon; reservations were beginning to pick up. The managers in Chicago and Philadelphia called at five with the same message. And at five-thirty, Flavia Guarneri called.

"Laura, my dear," she said, her voice like syrup, "it's almost like being allowed to come home again."

CHAPTER 35

FELIX positioned himself at Owen's desk and waited, silent and stone-faced, while twenty shareholders gathered in his library. He looked to the opposite side of the room when Laura arrived with Paul—what the hell was she doing with Paul?—and again a few minutes later, when Leni walked in, wearing a fur jacket he did not recognize. Last of all came Asa's wife, Carol, and then Asa, avoiding Felix's eyes. Felix stood. "Asa, I'd like to see you for a few minutes before we begin."

"I d-d-d-don't think. . . ." Asa's eyes darted about the room and came to rest in urgent appeal on Thomas Janssen.

"There's no need to wait," Thomas said. "We're all here and everyone is ready."

"In a minute," Felix snapped. "Asa." He gestured toward the door. Asa, looking hunted, went to it, with Felix at his heels.

An uncomfortable silence fell when they were gone. Ben and Paul talked quietly; they sat on two chairs against the wall, and beside them, Allison and Leni sat with Laura on the love seat beneath the new paintings that had replaced the stolen Rouaults. The others in the room watched, but did not join them. They had greeted Laura cautiously, then held back, waiting for more clues. It was true that she was sitting with Leni and Allison, but it was impossible to forget the last time the family had been gathered in a library, when Owen's will had been read and Laura had been exposed, shamed, and forced to leave.

There were just too many upheavals in the family these days: all the meetings and discussions about forcing Felix to resign, Leni divorcing Felix, Laura reappearing—and she and Ben were brother and sister!—and something between her and Paul again. Emily was in California and, from what everyone heard, staying there; and Leni and Allison were sitting with Laura, which meant they'd forgiven her. But nobody could be sure. Nobody knew what to think. So they waited, hoping for some kind of signal that would tell them the right thing to do.

"I wanted Wes to be here," Leni said to Laura. Allison was talking to one of her cousins, and Laura almost felt she and Leni were alone, their heads close together, their shoulders touching. "But we knew it would inflame Felix, so he stayed away."

"You look so happy," Laura said.

"I am," Leni replied simply. "Isn't it strange, how easy it is for me to talk to you about him? It's as if nothing any of us did before I left Felix has anything to do with what's happening now, almost as if we're all different people."

Laura nodded without comment. If Leni wanted to think the past vanished so easily and completely, why should she contradict her? "Wes is very different from Felix," she said.

"Not as much as you think." Leni smiled with tenderness and amusement. "In fact, he's very much like Felix. He's what Felix would have been if he had been a good man. Wes wants to dominate and control; he needs to know he's in the center of events; he doesn't suffer fools gladly or have patience with people who are slower than he. But Wes believes in love and intimacy, and Felix doesn't. Wes is willing to bend with someone he loves, and even learn. Felix can't; he has too much anger inside him. He needs to control people or, if he can't do that, defeat them. But when he can't win, or it's harder than he expected, his anger spills over, and he has to fight to control himself, to keep from exploding in public. Felix's life is one long balancing act, and that takes so much of his energy he doesn't have any left over for love and a family."

Laura was nodding. It was all true. Leni, who had lived with both men, saw them more clearly than anyone. "In the most important ways, they're very different."

Leni smiled. "That's why I'm marrying Wes. I don't mind being taken care of—in fact, I'm used to it and I prefer it—but I want to be loved, not owned." She paused reflectively. "A long time ago, before I met Felix, I was in love with someone. And when he sent me away, he said, 'Find someone strong and powerful, someone who can use your strength. You'll be happy then.' It took more than twenty-eight years, but I think

I've finally done it." There was another pause. "Will you and Paul come to visit us?"

"Of course. I'd like it if we're all friends."

They talked quietly, and Allison turned to join in, and it was the three of them, close together, that Felix saw when he returned, before he quickly jerked his head in another direction. He crossed the room, with Asa a few steps behind. Paul tried to read Asa's face but could not; his deep frown could be from anger or from shame at being cowed. He met his father's eyes, and Cole Hatton's. They couldn't count on Asa after all; he was too fearful.

This family is fueled by fear, Paul thought. Everyone is afraid someone will take something from us. If we had less money, we probably wouldn't be so worried. He wondered what the cutoff point was: with one sum of money people were happy, but if they had a dollar more, they pulled their wagons in a circle and lived in fear that the rest of the world might get too close. We'll have to teach our children to be generous, he reflected, and to believe in themselves so they aren't afraid of taking risks, and to understand that the real tragedy is not losing money, but losing trust and love.

He reached out and took Laura's hand. She had been listening to Allison, and she returned his clasp before she turned to him, her eyes soft and warm on his, her smile as open as he remembered from the time they had first loved. The careful, closed look on her face was gone. And then Felix cleared his throat.

Standing behind Owen's desk, his gaze skidding around the room just above everyone's head, he called the meeting to order. "Thomas, you requested this meeting. You said you had questions about Salinger Hotels."

"I do. But first"—Paul felt Laura's hand tighten on his—"there are some documents that might be helpful to us. If you would get them for us, Felix . . . I believe they're in your safe."

Felix stared at him. "My safe? What are you talking about? There's nothing there of the slightest interest to anyone here."

"I believe there is," Thomas said easily.

Felix's eyes narrowed. He saw Paul and Ben watching him closely, and also Cole Hatton, while the others simply looked curious. They've put something together, he thought, and once again alarm cut through him. He'd gotten Asa in line, but, still, there seemed to be a conspiracy here. What the fuck were they up to? He shook his head once, sharply. "If you have something to say, Thomas, you have the floor. If you want to try diversionary tactics to cover the fact that you haven't enough votes to accomplish anything, we can adjourn this meeting now."

Cole Hatton said lazily, "If there's something we ought to see in that safe, I for one want to see it."

"So do I," said Barbara Janssen.

"There doesn't seem to be much harm in opening it," said Paul.

Felix felt besieged. This wasn't random; they had orchestrated it.

"Well, why not?" one of the cousins asked. "At least then we could get on with the meeting."

"He knows what he has in his own safe," another cousin protested.

Another shrugged. "So? We could still open it; we're not getting anywhere this way." "Right," some of the others said. "Why not, Felix?" "If they're wrong, it won't take any time to find out." "I don't get it, but what the hell?"

Surrounded by a rising chorus, Felix said angrily, "There is nothing in that safe. But if you insist on this charade..." He went to the corner behind him and pushed aside a large painting. He dialed the combination and swung the door open without bothering to glance inside. "As you see. Except for one or two documents relating to the purchase of this house—"

"What's that envelope?" Thomas asked. He was standing, and looking straight into the safe.

"What?" Felix asked.

"There's a rather sizable envelope in there. At the back, under some papers. I'd say it's more than one or two documents."

Unthinkingly, Felix yanked the door wide open and, reaching to the back of the safe, pulled out a thick envelope. Those sitting close to him could see, across the front of it, in a bold, black handwriting, Laura's name.

Felix recognized it. He stared at it as if it were alive. "It wasn't in there; it was thrown out with the trash, years ago—" Abruptly, he stopped.

"Obviously not," Thomas said.

"That's Grandpa's handwriting!" Allison exclaimed. "And it's addressed to Laura!" Bewildered, she looked at it in Felix's hand. "How did you get a letter addressed to Laura?"

Leni was watching Felix, frowning as she thought back. "Laura told us about a letter from Owen, a long time ago. She went to get it, to show it to us, but she couldn't find it." Still frowning, she looked around the room.

"Is that the letter?" Barbara Janssen asked.

Laura held out her hand. "May I see it, please?"

Felix's head felt as if something were being screwed tighter and tighter around it; he was having trouble breathing. In his own house: things happening he didn't know about. The envelope dropped from his hand. There was no way he could fathom its journey from Owen's study to his locked safe.

"Please," Laura repeated.

Felix looked at her with a dullness so unusual in him that everyone stared in shock and dismay. In the silence, Thomas reached to the floor and picked up the envelope. He walked across the room and gave it to Laura.

She closed her eyes and ran her fingers over the heavily textured envelope, remembering how Owen always hated flimsy stationery. One corner was slightly torn. It was a thing of wonder to her that she held it in her hands again, as she had seven years earlier, when she had asked Owen to keep it for her. Beneath her closed lids, tears filled her eyes. She opened them to see Paul holding out a handkerchief. She smiled at him as she took it. To the others, she said, "If you'll excuse me . . ."

It had been opened, she saw; someone had read it. Everyone was watching, except for Felix, who stared at the floor, the safe, the desk, and then back again. Laura took out the letter, many pages, closely written in Owen's bold, slanting strokes, and ran her trembling fingers over it; she could almost believe he was there, sitting at his desk, looking up now and then to smile at her as he filled pages and graph sheets with his notes.

"Perhaps you'll read it to us," said Paul.

"It's very long," Laura said. "And I think most of it is about renovating the hotels."

"Read us some of it," said Allison. She was crying. "I'm so ashamed. So *ashamed*. I didn't believe in it; I thought you were making it up. I don't know how you can ever forgive us. We were so incredibly cruel; I don't think we're usually like that; how could we do that to you?"

"I'd lied to you," Laura said softly.

"Well, we can all apologize to each other later," said Leni. "Right now, I'd like to hear Laura read that letter, at least some of it. Unless you feel it is too personal, my dear."

"I don't know; I've never read it." Laura looked at the salutation. "But I don't mind."

"Please," Paul said, and she began to read.

"Beloved Laura, it is a fine day outside, as fine as I feel. But at my age a prudent man contemplates his mortality, and the things he may never have a chance to finish, and so today, while my mind is clear and my hand still strong, and my heart perhaps steadier than ever, I am writing to put in concise form the plans you and I have made together, for my hotels, because you know better than anyone what they mean to me. But first I want you to know that I am planning to change my will, leaving to you a small part of the family company—"

Voices were raised. "Felix, when did you read this?" Barbara Janssen demanded.

Felix said nothing; his gaze was fixed hypnotically on Owen's letter.

"Go on," Paul said to Laura.

"—a small part of the family company, and this house, and all of my own corporation. This means the hotels will be yours when I die, and therefore you will be the one to oversee their rebirth if I cannot."

"And you've done just that," Leni said. "So wonderfully. He was right to trust you."

Laura was skimming the letter, going through the pages. "These are the plans we made; I'd remembered most of them. Oh, he wanted to change those outside lights; I'd forgotten that." The room was silent; no one wanted to interrupt. Then she drew in a sharp breath.

"What is it?" Paul asked.

Laura looked at him. "He knew. . . ."

She bent her head and read from the last page, her voice low.

"I have respected your privacy, dearest Laura, but I must tell you I found it trying at times. I have known about your youthful peccadilloes for quite a while, including your conviction and probation for burglary. I thought you knew me well enough, my dear, to know that I am not happy with mysteries; I like a world where I know the answers. I did some checking with the New York Police Department, which is many years behind in cleaning out old files, and I found your secret. It seems very sad to me that you cannot trust me with it, even now, after all our years together. It tells me the depth of your fears that you cannot tell the truth and get the past over with. I hope, when you find your own triumphs as a wise, strong, very lovely woman, you will be able to deal with your past and make it part of your future. I'm afraid the chances are I won't be around to see that, but I feel sure it will happen. I'm so proud of you, dearest Laura; for a long time I have thought of you as the daughter Iris and I never had. And so I leave you something else in addition to those legacies I am adding to my will: my great pride in you, and my love, to carry with you after I am gone."

The last words were muffled. Laura was crying. Paul put his arm around her. "There was a greatness to Owen," he said softly. "Someday, if I work at it, I may be almost the man he was."

There was a silence in the room. It wasn't only revenge I wanted, Laura thought through her tears. It wasn't to take on any opponent and win. It was to be worthy of Owen's love and trust and faith in me. I knew I wanted to fulfill his dream, but I didn't know how much I wanted to be worthy of him.

"I don't understand," Asa's wife, Carol, said. "If Felix had the letter when Laura was looking for it, why didn't he show it to us? Why didn't you, Felix?"

"He didn't want to," one of the cousins said impatiently.

"Is that true, Felix?" asked another cousin. "You didn't want Laura to inherit?"

"That's an awful thing to say," objected a third cousin. "That would be... what would that be?"

"Fraud," said Thomas Janssen quietly.

Felix's head shot up. As if he were just awakening, he shook himself and focused his look on Thomas. "What was that?"

"Fraud," Thomas repeated. "It is fraud to withhold a document pertinent to a court case. The jury never would have found for you had they known about this letter."

"I didn't withhold it," Felix said shortly. "I never saw it."

"But you said it had been thrown out with the trash," Cole Hatton recalled. "How did you know that?"

There was a pause, then Felix shrugged. "I did see it, earlier. It was on my father's desk."

"On it?" Thomas asked.

Once more he shrugged. "What difference does it make? It was in the drawer. I was looking for something and I found it. When I went back later, it was gone. I assumed, when"—he gestured toward Laura—"didn't show it to the family, it had been thrown out. Evidently someone else had taken it. And planted it in my safe. That's a criminal act, planting evidence that incriminates someone."

"It would be if you could prove it," said Hatton. "Can you?"

"Is this an inquisition? That letter was planted! Someone wanted it to look as if I've had it all these years. I did not have it! And that's all there is to it!"

"Tell me one thing," Thomas said. "If you saw it in Owen's desk, why didn't you tell us that when Laura said there had been a letter? I remember we all waited in Owen's library while she went to look for it. Why didn't you say anything then? And later, why didn't you tell the court? As a matter of fact, why did you even *go* to court? You knew, from the letter, that Owen was perfectly healthy when he decided to change his will, but you didn't say anything at the will reading, and you brought that suit to invalidate Laura's inheritance when you knew Owen wanted her to have it. I think we deserve an explanation of this; you took us into a painful lawsuit, with considerable publicity, and made us believe we'd been cheated by someone we cared for. We've been influenced by what you've done, Felix, and we deserve an explanation."

"Daddy?" Allison demanded. Her eyes blazed. "You *hid* it? You *lied* to us?"

"Shit," one of the cousins said and another said, "I wouldn't have believed it, you know?" and another called out, "What the hell for, Felix? I mean, she wasn't taking all that much from you."

"*Daddy,*" Allison repeated furiously, "you *stole!* You blamed Laura for stealing, but you were the one who stole her inheritance! And you ruined what we had. We were all so happy! *Why did you do it?*"

Felix glared at all of them. "I am not required to explain anything. That document was placed in my safe illegally. She did it!" he roared, pointing at Laura. "She snuck in here—she's always been a thief— snuck in and planted it, and now she sits there, smirking, trying to make a fool of me. I can't believe you're taking her seriously!"

"I'm quite sure Laura did nothing of the kind," Thomas said. "But the fact is, it doesn't matter how it got there. It might have flown by itself into your safe, for all I care. What's really important is that you've admitted you saw it and concealed your knowledge of it. At the least, that's withholding evidence. At the worst, it's fraud, and Laura could sue you, with all of us as witnesses. That would be bad for the hotels and therefore bad for all of us. Are you going to sue him, Laura?"

She shook her head. "I don't know. Can I? After all these years?"

"Absolutely. There is no statute of limitations on fraud."

Felix's face was contorted. "There will be no lawsuit. This company has enough problems without—" He took a sharp breath. "No one is going to sue anyone. We can all—work together—" The words were wrenched out of him.

"Laura?" Hatton said.

"I don't know yet. I have to think about it." *That's what Clay knew. It was his joke on Felix. Maybe that's why he came back, to tell me he knew it was in the safe.*

"But even if Laura doesn't do anything," Carol said hesitantly, looking at Asa, beside her, and then at Thomas, "what happened was wrong, wasn't it? Shouldn't something happen when something is wrong?"

"You mean, should someone be punished?" Thomas asked. Slowly, trying to understand, she nodded. "It's not for us to punish Felix," he said. "But the whole business certainly makes me wonder if I want him to continue to lead the company."

"I agree," Hatton said. "It doesn't suggest wise leadership. Which is what we've been worried about for a long time, even before this affair of withholding evidence."

"That's why this meeting was called," Thomas went on. "Felix, for some time the consensus has been that you should step down as president and chairman of the board—"

"I will not," Felix said instantly. "You're using this illegal maneuver, this sham—"

"Perhaps I didn't make myself clear. *For some time* the consensus has been that you should step down. There are a number of significant problems in the company—you said so yourself, just now—and we don't think you can solve them."

"I will not have this discussed today. It was not on the agenda—we had no agenda. You gave me no warning—"

"You're wrong. I told you we'd be discussing your position in the company when I called you about the meeting."

"I don't remember. It's irrelevant, in any case. You can't push this through; you don't have the votes."

"I could make a motion," Hatton said. "But first, I think we might just go around the room and find out how the shareholders feel. We all know about the problems in the company; we've been talking about them for the past few weeks—months, in fact—and now, since Owen's letter was found, we have additional information. So I'd like to get everyone's opinion on the motion I intend to make to elect Thomas Janssen chairman of the board and Ben Gardner president—"

"You son of a bitch! You'll never do it! You and your gang are a minority, goddam it! You don't have the votes!"

"Oh, yes, we do," Asa said, very clearly, and for the first time anyone could remember, he did not stutter.

There was a dead silence in the room. The color had drained from Felix's face. "Before we ask everyone for an opinion," Hatton said, "I want to add that we are also discussing a merger of two hotel chains. If—and only if—Ben is elected president, and Thomas chairman of the board, Laura has agreed to discuss a merger of the Salinger and Beacon Hill hotels." Questions and comments rose in a flurry throughout the room and he went on, above them. "Each would retain its individuality, and the Beacon Hill name would remain, but we would be one company."

"Judd's son and Owen's daughter," Leni murmured. "Getting back what was stolen from them."

Felix heard her. Slowly, he turned to face Ben. Their eyes held in a long look and Felix was the first to look away. His glance passed over the twenty men and women who were strangers to him. They were all against him. So was his father. He'd been so sure, when Owen died, that he was finally free of his long shadow. But Owen had dominated the afternoon.

And so had Judd, Felix thought involuntarily. After all this time, it was as if Judd had come back, to eclipse Felix Salinger.

Hatton was asking the people in the room if they would support Thomas Janssen and Ben Gardner at the head of the company, but Felix paid no attention. His thoughts were a whirlpool, sucking him down. If I hadn't fought his will, none of this would have happened. No, it wasn't the will; it was before that. If I'd told them about the letter... No, it was even before that. If I'd let Judd keep his puny little company ... But it was there for the taking; I couldn't ignore it. And it wasn't puny; it was growing. It's still making money for us. He had no right to it anyway; he wasn't strong or smart.

It doesn't matter; none of it matters; it's done. I don't believe in looking back; the past is irrelevant. I have to get clear and think of what to do next.

But in the wild churning of his thoughts, no ideas came to him. He heard the sounds of voices, but what he saw was Judd's son with his arm around Felix's daughter, pregnant with their second child. Ben Gardner, president of Salinger Hotels, father of Salingers, someday head of the Salinger family ... The thought filled his throat like bile.

His glance moved past Ben and Allison and then, before he could stop himself, he was looking at Laura, meeting her eyes. He saw the look in them, and his color rose in rage. Pity. This bitch, who came from nothing, who stole and connived and lied and fucked her way into this room, was *pitying* him!

He had to get away. He couldn't think straight. He had to get away from all of them, not have to look at them. Then he could think of what he'd do next.

Without a backward glance, without a word, he walked out of his library, down the stairs, and out of the house. He'd go back to Boston, to his own office, where he belonged. And then he'd think of what to do next.

In the library, the conversation had stopped when Felix walked out the door. The family was subdued, and most of them were not sure how to feel: they were used to Felix, he'd been running the company for as long as they could remember, but it really was time for a change, and it would be better for everyone if he made it easy for them, instead of starting a bruising family fight.

After a moment, Paul said musingly, "The last time we all got together to hear a document read, Laura left the house. This time it was Felix. There's a nice symmetry in that."

"But I think we ought to leave," Laura said. "He should have the privacy of his own house to come back to. Can we go on with the meeting somewhere else?"

"We can adjourn to my apartment," Paul said. "If it's all right with Ben."

Ben grinned at him. "I haven't been elected yet. We should ask Thomas."

Thomas shook his head. "No one has elected me, either. Asa? As vice president, would you agree to adjourn to Sutton Place?"

"I think you should make the decision on your own." Asa's voice was hoarse, and he cleared his throat. "I don't think I should hang around. I'm sort of the past, you know? I went along with Felix all these years; he scared the shit out of me—of course, you all knew that—and I never quite knew why. It's not good to dislike a brother; it poisons a family. It poisoned all these years for me when I felt like a nothing. I think I'd like to retire. Maybe Carol and I can get to know you all in new ways if we're out of the company. I think that's what I'd like to do. So I can't decide about adjourning the meeting."

"Yes, you can," Paul said gently. None of them had ever heard Asa say so much without stuttering, and they all were smiling at him for his triumph. "We need you. And the board hasn't accepted your resignation yet."

So Asa made the decision, adjourning the meeting for half an hour, to continue at Paul's Sutton Place apartment. Everyone stood up, gathering jackets and purses and briefcases, and, one at a time, they came up to Laura and apologized. As they passed by, on their way out the door, it was almost as if she and Paul were in a reception line, greeting the Salingers, and being welcomed back.

Ben and Allison kissed Laura and left the room. Leni put her arms around Paul and Laura. "It's a good family, isn't it? Even with its problems. I'm so glad we're all a part of it."

Then Laura and Paul were alone in the library. Paul held her, and she lay her head against his chest. A sense of rightness filled her, wiping away the last vestige of the fear she had had since childhood of being an outsider. No longer, she thought. Now I belong.

Beside her, Owen's desk gleamed in the light of a small desk lamp; his letter rustled in her hand. *I hope, when you find your own triumphs as a wise, strong, very lovely woman, you will be able to deal with your past and make it part of your future.*

In her memory, she saw the love in his eyes when he looked at her; she could feel his hand upon her hair. And then she saw his broad smile.

I knew you could do it, he said.

ABOUT THE AUTHOR

Judith Barnard and Michael Fain—the two halves of "Judith Michael" —are husband-and-wife writing partners. Each of their novels—*Deceptions, Possessions,* and *Private Affairs*—has been a national best-seller. The couple divide their time between Chicago and Aspen.